WESTWARD HO! OR, THE V(
ADVENTURES OF SIR AMYAS LEIGH, KNIGHT, OF BURROUGH, IN THE COUNTY OF DEVON, IN THE REIGN OF HER MOST GLORIOUS MAJESTY QUEEN ELIZABETH
BY
Charles Kingsley

WESTWARD HO! OR, THE VOYAGES AND ADVENTURES OF SIR AMYAS LEIGH, KNIGHT, OF BURROUGH, IN THE COUNTY OF DEVON, IN THE REIGN OF HER MOST GLORIOUS MAJESTY QUEEN ELIZABETH

Published by Silver Scroll Publishing

New York City, NY

First published circa 1875

Copyright © Silver Scroll Publishing, 2015

All rights reserved

Except in the United States of America, this book is sold subject to the condition that it shall not, by way of trade or otherwise, be lent, re-sold, hired out, or otherwise circulated without the publisher's prior consent in any form of binding or cover other than that in which it is published and without a similar condition including this condition being imposed on the subsequent purchaser.

ABOUT SILVER SCROLL PUBLISHING

Silver Scroll Publishing is a digital publisher that brings the best historical fiction ever written to modern readers. Our comprehensive catalogue contains everything from historical novels about Rome to works about World War I.

TO THE RAJAH SIR JAMES BROOKE, K.C.B. AND GEORGE AUGUSTUS SELWYN, D.D. BISHOP OF NEW ZEALAND THIS BOOK IS DEDICATED

By one who (unknown to them) has no other method of expressing his admiration and reverence for their characters.

That type of English virtue, at once manful and godly, practical and enthusiastic, prudent and self-sacrificing, which he has tried to depict in these pages, they have exhibited in a form even purer and more heroic than that in which he has drest it, and than that in which it was exhibited by the worthies whom Elizabeth, without distinction of rank or age, gathered round her in the ever glorious wars of her great reign.

C. K. FEBRUARY, 1855.

WESTWARD HO!: CHAPTER I

HOW MR. OXENHAM SAW THE WHITE BIRD

All who have travelled through the delicious scenery of North Devon must needs know the little white town of Bideford, which slopes upwards from its broad tide-river paved with yellow sands, and many-arched old bridge where salmon wait for autumn floods, toward the pleasant upland on the west. Above the town the hills close in, cushioned with deep oak woods, through which juts here and there a crag of fern-fringed slate; below they lower, and open more and more in softly rounded knolls, and fertile squares of red and green, till they sink into the wide expanse of hazy flats, rich salt-marshes, and rolling sand-hills, where Torridge joins her sister Taw, and both together flow quietly toward the broad surges of the bar, and the everlasting thunder of the long Atlantic swell. Pleasantly the old town stands there, beneath its soft Italian sky, fanned day and night by the fresh ocean breeze, which forbids alike the keen winter frosts, and the fierce thunder heats of the midland; and pleasantly it has stood there for now, perhaps, eight hundred years since the first Grenville, cousin of the Conqueror, returning from the conquest of South Wales, drew round him trusty Saxon serfs, and free Norse rovers with their golden curls, and dark Silurian Britons from the Swansea shore, and all the mingled blood which still gives to the seaward folk of the next county their strength and intellect, and, even in these levelling days, their peculiar beauty of face and form.

But at the time whereof I write, Bideford was not merely a pleasant country town, whose quay was haunted by a few coasting craft. It was one of the chief ports of England; it furnished seven ships to fight the Armada: even more than a century afterwards, say the chroniclers, "it sent more vessels to the northern trade than any port in England, saving (strange juxtaposition!) London and Topsham," and was the centre of a local civilization and enterprise, small perhaps compared with the vast efforts of the present day: but who dare despise the day of small things, if it has proved to be the dawn of mighty ones? And it is to the sea-life and labor of Bideford, and Dartmouth, and Topsham, and Plymouth (then a petty place), and many another little western town, that England owes the foundation of her naval and commercial glory. It was the men of Devon, the Drakes and Hawkins', Gilberts and Raleighs, Grenvilles and Oxenhams, and a host more of "forgotten worthies," whom we shall learn one day to honor as they deserve, to whom she owes her commerce, her colonies, her very existence. For had they not first crippled, by their West Indian raids, the ill-gotten resources of the Spaniard, and then crushed his last huge effort in Britain's Salamis, the glorious fight of 1588, what had we been by now but a popish appanage of a world-tyranny as cruel as heathen Rome itself, and far more devilish?

It is in memory of these men, their voyages and their battles, their faith and their valor, their heroic lives and no less heroic deaths, that I write this book; and if now and then I shall seem to warm into a style somewhat too stilted and pompous, let me be excused for my subject's sake, fit rather to have been sung than said, and to have proclaimed to all true English hearts, not as a novel but as an epic (which some man may yet gird himself to write), the same great message which the songs of Troy, and the Persian wars, and the trophies of Marathon and Salamis, spoke to the hearts of all true Greeks of old.

One bright summer's afternoon, in the year of grace 1575, a tall and fair boy came lingering along Bideford quay, in his scholar's gown, with satchel and slate in hand, watching wistfully the shipping and the sailors, till, just after he had passed the bottom of the High Street, he came opposite to one of the many taverns which looked out upon the river. In the open bay window sat merchants and gentlemen, discoursing over their afternoon's draught of sack; and outside the door was gathered a group of sailors, listening earnestly to some one who stood in the midst. The boy, all alive for any sea-news, must needs go up to them, and take his place among the sailor-lads who were peeping and whispering under the elbows of the men; and so came in for the following speech, delivered in a loud bold voice, with a strong Devonshire accent, and a fair sprinkling of oaths.

"If you don't believe me, go and see, or stay here and grow all over blue mould. I tell you, as I am a gentleman, I saw it with these eyes, and so did Salvation Yeo there, through a window in the lower room; and we measured the heap, as I am a christened man, seventy foot long, ten foot broad, and twelve foot high, of silver bars, and each bar between a thirty and forty pound weight. And says Captain Drake: 'There, my lads of Devon, I've brought you to the mouth of the world's treasure-house, and it's your own fault now if you don't sweep it out as empty as a stock-fish.'"

"Why didn't you bring some of they home, then, Mr. Oxenham?"

"Why weren't you there to help to carry them? We would have brought 'em away, safe enough, and young Drake and I had broke the door abroad already, but Captain Drake goes off in a dead faint; and when we came to look, he had a wound in his leg you might have laid three fingers in, and his boots were full of blood, and had been for an hour or more; but the heart of him was that, that he never knew it till he dropped, and then his brother and I got him away to the boats, he kicking and struggling, and bidding us let him go on with the fight, though every step he took in the sand was in a pool of blood; and so we got off. And tell me, ye sons of shotten herrings, wasn't it worth more to save him than the dirty silver? for silver we can get again, brave boys: there's more fish in the sea than ever came out of it, and more silver in Nombre de Dios than would pave all the streets in the west country: but of such captains as Franky Drake, Heaven never makes but one at a time; and if we lose him, good-bye to England's luck, say I, and who don't agree, let him choose his weapons, and I'm his man."

He who delivered this harangue was a tall and sturdy personage, with a florid black-bearded face, and bold restless dark eyes, who leaned, with crossed legs and arms akimbo, against the wall of the house; and seemed in the eyes of the schoolboy a very magnifico, some prince or duke at least. He was dressed (contrary to all sumptuary laws of the time) in a suit of crimson velvet, a little the worse, perhaps, for wear; by his side were a long Spanish rapier and a brace of daggers, gaudy enough about the hilts; his fingers sparkled with rings; he had two or three gold chains about his neck, and large earrings in his ears, behind one of which a red rose was stuck jauntily enough among the glossy black curls; on his head was a broad velvet Spanish hat, in which instead of a feather was fastened with a great gold clasp a whole Quezal bird, whose gorgeous plumage of fretted golden green shone like one entire precious stone. As he finished his speech, he took off the said hat, and looking at the bird in it—

"Look ye, my lads, did you ever see such a fowl as that before? That's the bird which the old Indian kings of Mexico let no one wear but their own selves; and therefore I wear it,—I, John Oxenham of South Tawton, for a sign to all brave lads of Devon, that as the Spaniards are the masters of the Indians, we're the masters of the Spaniards:" and he replaced his hat.

A murmur of applause followed: but one hinted that he "doubted the Spaniards were too many for them."

"Too many? How many men did we take Nombre de Dios with? Seventy-three were we, and no more when we sailed out of Plymouth Sound; and before we saw the Spanish Main, half were gastados, used up, as the Dons say, with the scurvy; and in Port Pheasant Captain Rawse of Cowes fell in with us, and that gave us some thirty hands more; and with that handful, my lads, only fifty-three in all, we picked the lock of the new world! And whom did we lose but our trumpeter, who stood braying like an ass in the middle of the square, instead of taking care of his neck like a Christian? I tell you, those Spaniards are rank cowards, as all bullies are. They pray to a woman, the idolatrous rascals! and no wonder they fight like women."

"You'm right, captain," sang out a tall gaunt fellow who stood close to him; "one westcountry-man can fight two easterlings, and an easterling can beat three Dons any day. Eh! my lads of Devon?

"Come," said Oxenham, "come along! Who lists? who lists? who'll make his fortune?

"Who'll list?" cried the gaunt man again; "now's your time! We've got forty men to Plymouth now, ready to sail the minute we get back, and we want a dozen out of you Bideford men, and just a boy or two, and then we'm off and away, and make our fortunes, or go to heaven.

"Now," said Oxenham, "you won't let the Plymouth men say that the Bideford men daren't follow them? North Devon against South, it is. Who'll join? who'll join? It is but a step of a way, after all, and sailing as smooth as a duck-pond as soon as you're past Cape Finisterre. I'll run a Clovelly herring-boat there and back for a wager of twenty pound, and never ship a bucketful all the way. Who'll join? Don't think you're buying a pig in a poke. I know the road, and Salvation Yeo, here, too, who was the gunner's mate, as well as I do the narrow seas, and better. You ask him to show you the chart of it, now, and see if he don't tell you over the ruttier as well as Drake himself."

On which the gaunt man pulled from under his arm a great white buffalo horn covered with rough etchings of land and sea, and held it up to the admiring ring.

"See here, boys all, and behold the pictur of the place, dra'ed out so natural as ever was life. I got mun from a Portingal, down to the Azores; and he'd pricked mun out, and pricked mun out, wheresoever he'd sailed, and whatsoever he'd seen. Take mun in your hands now, Simon Evans, take mun in your hands; look mun over, and I'll warrant you'll know the way in five minutes so well as ever a shark in the seas."

And the horn was passed from hand to hand; while Oxenham, who saw that his hearers were becoming moved, called through the open window for a great tankard of sack, and passed that from hand to hand, after the horn.

The school-boy, who had been devouring with eyes and ears all which passed, and had contrived by this time to edge himself into the inner ring, now stood face to face with the hero of the emerald crest, and got as many peeps as he could at the wonder. But when he saw the sailors, one after another, having turned it over a while, come forward and offer to join Mr. Oxenham, his soul burned within him for a nearer view of that wondrous horn, as magical in its effects as that of Tristrem, or the enchanter's in Ariosto; and when the group had somewhat broken up, and Oxenham was going into the tavern with his recruits, he asked boldly for a nearer sight of the marvel, which was granted at once.

And now to his astonished gaze displayed themselves cities and harbors, dragons and elephants, whales which fought with sharks, plate ships of Spain, islands with apes and palm-trees, each with its name over-written, and here and there, "Here is gold;" and again, "Much gold and silver;" inserted most probably, as the words were in English, by the hands of Mr. Oxenham himself. Lingeringly and longingly the boy turned it round and round, and thought the owner of it more fortunate than Khan or Kaiser. Oh, if he could but possess that horn, what needed he on earth beside to make him blest!

"I say, will you sell this?"

"Yea, marry, or my own soul, if I can get the worth of it."

"I want the horn,—I don't want your soul; it's somewhat of a stale sole, for aught I know; and there are plenty of fresh ones in the bay."

And therewith, after much fumbling, he pulled out a tester (the only one he had), and asked if that would buy it?

"That! no, nor twenty of them."

The boy thought over what a good knight-errant would do in such case, and then answered, "Tell you what: I'll fight you for it."

"Thank 'ee, sir!

"Break the jackanapes's head for him, Yeo," said Oxenham.

"Call me jackanapes again, and I break yours, sir." And the boy lifted his fist fiercely.

Oxenham looked at him a minute smilingly. "Tut! tut! my man, hit one of your own size, if you will, and spare little folk like me!"

"If I have a boy's age, sir, I have a man's fist. I shall be fifteen years old this month, and know how to answer any one who insults me."

"Fifteen, my young cockerel? you look liker twenty," said Oxenham, with an admiring glance at the lad's broad limbs, keen blue eyes, curling golden locks, and round honest face. "Fifteen? If I had half-a-dozen such lads as you, I would make knights of them before I died. Eh, Yeo?"

"He'll do," said Yeo; "he will make a brave gamecock in a year or two, if he dares ruffle up so early at a tough old hen-master like the captain."

At which there was a general laugh, in which Oxenham joined as loudly as any, and then bade the lad tell him why he was so keen after the horn.

"Because," said he, looking up boldly, "I want to go to sea. I want to see the Indies. I want to fight the Spaniards. Though I am a gentleman's son, I'd a deal liever be a cabin-boy on board your ship." And the lad, having hurried out his say fiercely enough, dropped his head again.

"And you shall," cried Oxenham, with a great oath; "and take a galloon, and dine off carbonadoed Dons. Whose son are you, my gallant fellow?"

"Mr. Leigh's, of Burrough Court."

"Bless his soul! I know him as well as I do the Eddystone, and his kitchen too. Who sups with him to-night?"

"Sir Richard Grenville."

"Dick Grenville? I did not know he was in town. Go home and tell your father John Oxenham will come and keep him company. There, off with you! I'll make all straight with the good gentleman, and you shall have your venture with me; and as for the horn, let him have the horn, Yeo, and I'll give you a noble for it."

"Not a penny, noble captain. If young master will take a poor mariner's gift, there it is, for the sake of his love to the calling, and Heaven send him luck therein." And the good fellow, with the impulsive generosity of a true sailor, thrust the horn into the boy's hands, and walked away to escape thanks.

"And now," quoth Oxenham, "my merry men all, make up your minds what mannered men you be minded to be before you take your bounties. I want none of your rascally lurching longshore vermin, who get five pounds out of this captain, and ten out of that, and let him sail without them after all, while they are stowed away under women's mufflers, and in tavern cellars. If any man is of that humor, he had better to cut himself up, and salt himself down in a barrel for pork, before he meets me again; for by this light, let me catch him, be it seven years hence, and if I do not cut his throat upon the streets, it's a pity! But if any man will be true brother to me, true brother to him I'll be, come wreck or prize, storm or calm, salt water or fresh, victuals or none, share and fare alike; and here's my hand upon it, for every man and all! and so—

After which oration Mr. Oxenham swaggered into the tavern, followed by his new men; and the boy took his way homewards, nursing his precious horn, trembling between hope and fear, and blushing with maidenly shame, and a half-sense of wrong-doing at having revealed suddenly to a stranger the darling wish which he had hidden from his father and mother ever since he was ten years old.

Now this young gentleman, Amyas Leigh, though come of as good blood as any in Devon, and having lived all his life in what we should even now call the very best society, and being (on account of the valor, courtesy, and truly noble qualities which he showed forth in his most eventful life) chosen by me as the hero and centre of this story, was not, saving for his good looks, by any means what would be called now-a-days an "interesting" youth, still less a "highly educated" one; for, with the exception of a little Latin, which had been driven into him by repeated blows, as if it had been a nail, he knew no books whatsoever, save his Bible, his Prayer-book, the old "Mort d'Arthur" of Caxton's edition, which lay in the great bay window in the hall, and the translation of "Las Casas' History of the West Indies," which lay beside it, lately done into English under the title of "The Cruelties of the Spaniards." He devoutly believed in fairies, whom he called pixies; and held that they changed babies, and made the mushroom rings on the downs to dance in. When he had warts or burns, he went to the white witch at Northam to charm them away; he thought that the sun moved round the earth, and that the moon had some kindred with a Cheshire cheese. He held that the swallows slept all the winter at the bottom of the horsepond; talked, like Raleigh, Grenville, and other low persons, with a broad Devonshire accent; and was in many other respects so very ignorant a youth, that any pert monitor in a national school might have had a hearty laugh at him. Nevertheless, this ignorant young savage, vacant of the glorious gains of the nineteenth century, children's literature and science made easy, and, worst of all, of those improved views of English history now current among our railway essayists, which consist in believing all persons, male and female, before the year 1688, and nearly all after it, to have been either hypocrites or fools, had learnt certain things which he would hardly have been taught just now in any school in England; for his training had been that of the old Persians, "to speak the truth and to draw the bow," both of which savage virtues he had acquired to perfection, as well as the equally savage ones of enduring pain cheerfully, and of believing it to be the finest thing in the world to be a gentleman; by which word he had been taught to understand the careful habit of causing needless pain to no human being, poor or rich, and of taking pride in giving up his own pleasure for the sake of those who were weaker than himself. Moreover, having been entrusted for the last year with the breaking of a colt, and the care of a cast of young hawks which his father had received from Lundy Isle, he had been profiting much, by the means of those coarse and frivolous amusements, in perseverance, thoughtfulness, and the habit of keeping his temper; and though he had never had a single "object lesson," or been taught to "use his intellectual powers," he knew the names and ways of every bird, and fish, and fly, and could read, as cunningly as the oldest sailor, the meaning of every drift of cloud which crossed the heavens. Lastly, he had been for some time past, on account of his extraordinary size and strength, undisputed cock of the school, and the most terrible fighter among all Bideford boys; in which brutal habit he took much delight, and contrived, strange as it may seem, to extract from it good, not only for himself but for others, doing justice among his school-fellows with a heavy hand, and succoring the oppressed and afflicted; so that he was the terror of all the sailor-lads, and the pride and stay of all the town's boys and girls, and hardly considered that he had done his duty in his calling if he went home without beating a big lad for bullying a little one. For the rest, he never thought about thinking, or felt about feeling; and had no ambition whatsoever beyond pleasing his father and mother, getting by honest means the maximum of "red quarrenders" and mazard cherries, and going to sea when he was big enough. Neither was he what would be now-a-days called by many a pious child; for though he said his Creed and Lord's Prayer night and morning, and went to the service at the church every forenoon, and read the day's Psalms with his mother every evening, and had learnt from her and from his father (as he proved well in after life) that it was infinitely noble to do right and infinitely base to do wrong, yet (the age of children's religious books not having yet dawned on the world) he knew nothing more of theology, or of his own soul, than is contained in the Church Catechism. It is a question, however, on the whole, whether, though grossly ignorant (according to our modern notions) in science and religion, he was altogether untrained in manhood, virtue, and godliness; and whether the barbaric narrowness of his information was not somewhat counterbalanced both in him and in the rest of his generation by the depth, and breadth, and healthiness of his education.

So let us watch him up the hill as he goes hugging his horn, to tell all that has passed to his mother, from whom he had never hidden anything in his life, save only that sea-fever; and that only because he foreknew that it would give her pain; and because, moreover, being a prudent and sensible lad, he knew that he was not yet old enough to go, and that, as he expressed it to her that afternoon, "there was no use hollaing till he was out of the wood."

So he goes up between the rich lane-banks, heavy with drooping ferns and honeysuckle; out upon the windy down toward the old Court, nestled amid its ring of wind-clipt oaks; through the gray gateway into the homeclose; and then he pauses a moment to look around; first at the wide bay to the westward, with its southern wall of purple cliffs; then at the dim Isle of Lundy far away at sea; then at the cliffs and downs of Morte and Braunton, right in front of him; then at the vast yellow sheet of rolling sand-hill, and green alluvial plain dotted with red cattle, at his feet, through which the silver estuary winds onward toward the sea. Beneath him, on his right, the Torridge, like a land-locked lake, sleeps broad and bright between the old park of Tapeley and the charmed rock of the Hubbastone, where, seven hundred years ago, the Norse rovers landed to lay siege to Kenwith Castle, a mile away on his left hand; and not three fields away, are the old stones of "The Bloody Corner," where the retreating Danes, cut off from their ships, made their last fruitless stand against the Saxon sheriff and the valiant men of Devon. Within that charmed rock, so Torridge boatmen tell, sleeps now the old Norse Viking in his leaden coffin, with all his fairy treasure and his crown of gold; and as the boy looks at the spot, he fancies, and almost hopes, that the day may come when he shall have to do his duty against the invader as boldly as the men of Devon did then. And past him, far below, upon the soft southeastern breeze, the stately ships go sliding out to sea. When shall he sail in them, and see the wonders of the deep? And as he stands there with beating heart and kindling eye, the cool breeze whistling through his long fair curls, he is a symbol, though he knows it not, of brave young England longing to wing its way out of its island prison, to discover and to traffic, to colonize and to civilize, until no wind can sweep the earth which does not bear the echoes of an English voice. Patience, young Amyas! Thou too shalt forth, and westward ho, beyond thy wildest dreams; and see brave sights, and do brave deeds, which no man has since the foundation of the world. Thou too shalt face invaders stronger and more cruel far than Dane or Norman, and bear thy part in that great Titan strife before the renown of which the name of Salamis shall fade away!

Mr. Oxenham came that evening to supper as he had promised: but as people supped in those days in much the same manner as they do now, we may drop the thread of the story for a few hours, and take it up again after supper is over.

"Come now, Dick Grenville, do thou talk the good man round, and I'll warrant myself to talk round the good wife."

The personage whom Oxenham addressed thus familiarly answered by a somewhat sarcastic smile, and, "Mr. Oxenham gives Dick Grenville" (with just enough emphasis on the "Mr." and the "Dick," to hint that a liberty had been taken with him) "overmuch credit with the men. Mr. Oxenham's credit with fair ladies, none can doubt. Friend Leigh, is Heard's great ship home yet from the Straits?"

The speaker, known well in those days as Sir Richard Grenville, Granville, Greenvil, Greenfield, with two or three other variations, was one of those truly heroical personages whom Providence, fitting always the men to their age and their work, had sent upon the earth whereof it takes right good care, not in England only, but in Spain and Italy, in Germany and the Netherlands, and wherever, in short, great men and great deeds were needed to lift the mediaeval world into the modern.

And, among all the heroic faces which the painters of that age have preserved, none, perhaps, hardly excepting Shakespeare's or Spenser's, Alva's or Farina's, is more heroic than that of Richard Grenville, as it stands in Prince's "Worthies of Devon;" of a Spanish type, perhaps (or more truly speaking, a Cornish), rather than an English, with just enough of the British element in it to give delicacy to its massiveness. The forehead and whole brain are of extraordinary loftiness, and perfectly upright; the nose long, aquiline, and delicately pointed; the mouth fringed with a short silky beard, small and ripe, yet firm as granite, with just pout enough of the lower lip to give hint of that capacity of noble indignation which lay hid under its usual courtly calm and sweetness; if there be a defect in the face, it is that the eyes are somewhat small, and close together, and the eyebrows, though delicately arched, and, without a trace of peevishness, too closely pressed down upon them, the complexion is dark, the figure tall and graceful; altogether the likeness of a wise and gallant gentleman, lovely to all good men, awful to all bad men; in whose presence none dare say or do a mean or a ribald thing; whom brave men left, feeling themselves nerved to do their duty better, while cowards slipped away, as bats and owls before the sun. So he lived and moved, whether in the Court of Elizabeth, giving his counsel among the wisest; or in the streets of Bideford, capped alike by squire and merchant, shopkeeper and sailor; or riding along the moorland roads between his houses of Stow and Bideford, while every woman ran out to her door to look at the great Sir Richard, the pride of North Devon; or, sitting there in the low mullioned window at Burrough, with his cup of malmsey before him, and the lute to which he had just been singing laid across his knees, while the red western sun streamed in upon his high, bland forehead, and soft curling locks; ever the same steadfast, God-fearing, chivalrous man, conscious (as far as a soul so healthy could be conscious) of the pride of beauty, and strength, and valor, and wisdom, and a race and name which claimed direct descent from the grandfather of the Conqueror, and was tracked down the centuries by valiant deeds and noble benefits to his native shire, himself the noblest of his race. Men said that he was proud; but he could not look round him without having something to be proud of; that he was stern and harsh to his sailors: but it was only when he saw in them any taint of cowardice or falsehood; that he was subject, at moments, to such fearful fits of rage, that he had been seen to snatch the glasses from the table, grind them to pieces in his teeth, and swallow them: but that was only when his indignation had been aroused by some tale of cruelty or oppression, and, above all, by those

West Indian devilries of the Spaniards, whom he regarded (and in those days rightly enough) as the enemies of God and man. Of this last fact Oxenham was well aware, and therefore felt somewhat puzzled and nettled, when, after having asked Mr. Leigh's leave to take young Amyas with him and set forth in glowing colors the purpose of his voyage, he found Sir Richard utterly unwilling to help him with his suit.

"Heyday, Sir Richard! You are not surely gone over to the side of those canting fellows (Spanish Jesuits in disguise, every one of them, they are), who pretended to turn up their noses at Franky Drake, as a pirate, and be hanged to them?"

"My friend Oxenham," answered he, in the sententious and measured style of the day, "I have always held, as you should know by this, that Mr. Drake's booty, as well as my good friend Captain Hawkins's, is lawful prize, as being taken from the Spaniard, who is not only hostis humani generis, but has no right to the same, having robbed it violently, by torture and extreme iniquity, from the poor Indian, whom God avenge, as He surely will."

"Amen," said Mrs. Leigh.

"I say Amen, too," quoth Oxenham, "especially if it please Him to avenge them by English hands."

"And I also," went on Sir Richard; "for the rightful owners of the said goods being either miserably dead, or incapable, by reason of their servitude, of ever recovering any share thereof, the treasure, falsely called Spanish, cannot be better bestowed than in building up the state of England against them, our natural enemies; and thereby, in building up the weal of the Reformed Churches throughout the world, and the liberties of all nations, against a tyranny more foul and rapacious than that of Nero or Caligula; which, if it be not the cause of God, I, for one, know not what God's cause is!" And, as he warmed in his speech, his eyes flashed very fire.

"Hark now!" said Oxenham, "who can speak more boldly than he? and yet he will not help this lad to so noble an adventure."

"You have asked his father and mother; what is their answer?"

"Mine is this," said Mr. Leigh; "if it be God's will that my boy should become, hereafter, such a mariner as Sir Richard Grenville, let him go, and God be with him; but let him first bide here at home and be trained, if God give me grace, to become such a gentleman as Sir Richard Grenville."

Sir Richard bowed low, and Mrs. Leigh catching up the last word—

"There, Mr. Oxenham, you cannot gainsay that, unless you will be discourteous to his worship. And for me—though it be a weak woman's reason, yet it is a mother's: he is my only child. His elder brother is far away. God only knows whether I shall see him again; and what are all reports of his virtues and his learning to me, compared to that sweet presence which I daily miss? Ah! Mr. Oxenham, my beautiful Joseph is gone; and though he be lord of Pharaoh's household, yet he is far away in Egypt; and you will take Benjamm also! Ah! Mr. Oxenham, you have no child, or you would not ask for mine!"

"And how do you know that, my sweet madam!" said the adventurer, turning first deadly pale, and then glowing red. Her last words had touched him to the quick in some unexpected place;

and rising, he courteously laid her hand to his lips, and said—"I say no more. Farewell, sweet madam, and God send all men such wives as you."

"And all wives," said she, smiling, "such husbands as mine."

"Nay, I will not say that," answered he, with a half sneer—and then, "Farewell, friend Leigh—farewell, gallant Dick Grenville. God send I see thee Lord High Admiral when I come home. And yet, why should I come home? Will you pray for poor Jack, gentles?"

"Tut, tut, man! good words," said Leigh; "let us drink to our merry meeting before you go." And rising, and putting the tankard of malmsey to his lips, he passed it to Sir Richard, who rose, and saying, "To the fortune of a bold mariner and a gallant gentleman," drank, and put the cup into Oxenham's hand.

The adventurer's face was flushed, and his eye wild. Whether from the liquor he had drunk during the day, or whether from Mrs. Leigh's last speech, he had not been himself for a few minutes. He lifted the cup, and was in act to pledge them, when he suddenly dropped it on the table, and pointed, staring and trembling, up and down, and round the room, as if following some fluttering object.

"There! Do you see it? The bird!—the bird with the white breast!"

Each looked at the other; but Leigh, who was a quick-witted man and an old courtier, forced a laugh instantly, and cried—"Nonsense, brave Jack Oxenham! Leave white birds for men who will show the white feather. Mrs. Leigh waits to pledge you."

Oxenham recovered himself in a moment, pledged them all round, drinking deep and fiercely; and after hearty farewells, departed, never hinting again at his strange exclamation.

After he was gone, and while Leigh was attending him to the door, Mrs. Leigh and Grenville kept a few minutes' dead silence. At last—"God help him!" said she.

"Amen!" said Grenville, "for he never needed it more. But, indeed, madam, I put no faith in such omens."

"But, Sir Richard, that bird has been seen for generations before the death of any of his family. I know those who were at South Tawton when his mother died, and his brother also; and they both saw it. God help him! for, after all, he is a proper man."

"So many a lady has thought before now, Mrs. Leigh, and well for him if they had not. But, indeed, I make no account of omens. When God is ready for each man, then he must go; and when can he go better?"

"But," said Mr. Leigh, who entered, "I have seen, and especially when I was in Italy, omens and prophecies before now beget their own fulfilment, by driving men into recklessness, and making them run headlong upon that very ruin which, as they fancied, was running upon them."

"And which," said Sir Richard, "they might have avoided, if, instead of trusting in I know not what dumb and dark destiny, they had trusted in the living God, by faith in whom men may remove mountains, and quench the fire, and put to flight the armies of the alien. I too know, and know not how I know, that I shall never die in my bed."

"God forfend!" cried Mrs. Leigh.

"And why, fair madam, if I die doing my duty to my God and my queen? The thought never moves me: nay, to tell the truth, I pray often enough that I may be spared the miseries of imbecile old age, and that end which the old Northmen rightly called 'a cow's death' rather than a man's. But enough of this. Mr. Leigh, you have done wisely to-night. Poor Oxenham does not go on his voyage with a single eye. I have talked about him with Drake and Hawkins; and I guess why Mrs. Leigh touched him so home when she told him that he had no child."

"Has he one, then, in the West Indies?" cried the good lady.

"God knows; and God grant we may not hear of shame and sorrow fallen upon an ancient and honorable house of Devon. My brother Stukely is woe enough to North Devon for this generation."

"Poor braggadocio!" said Mr. Leigh; "and yet not altogether that too, for he can fight at least."

"So can every mastiff and boar, much more an Englishman. And now come hither to me, my adventurous godson, and don't look in such doleful dumps. I hear you have broken all the sailor-boys' heads already."

"Nearly all," said young Amyas, with due modesty.. "But am I not to go to sea?"

"All things in their time, my boy, and God forbid that either I or your worthy parents should keep you from that noble calling which is the safeguard of this England and her queen. But you do not wish to live and die the master of a trawler?"

"I should like to be a brave adventurer, like Mr. Oxenham."

"God grant you become a braver man than he! for, as I think, to be bold against the enemy is common to the brutes; but the prerogative of a man is to be bold against himself."

"How, sir?"

"To conquer our own fancies, Amyas, and our own lusts, and our ambition, in the sacred name of duty; this it is to be truly brave, and truly strong; for he who cannot rule himself, how can he rule his crew or his fortunes? Come, now, I will make you a promise. If you will bide quietly at home, and learn from your father and mother all which befits a gentleman and a Christian, as well as a seaman, the day shall come when you shall sail with Richard Grenville himself, or with better men than he, on a nobler errand than gold-hunting on the Spanish Main."

"O my boy, my boy!" said Mrs. Leigh, "hear what the good Sir Richard promises you. Many an earl's son would be glad to be in your place."

"And many an earl's son will be glad to be in his place a score years hence, if he will but learn what I know you two can teach him. And now, Amyas, my lad, I will tell you for a warning the history of that Sir Thomas Stukely of whom I spoke just now, and who was, as all men know, a gallant and courtly knight, of an ancient and worshipful family in Ilfracombe, well practised in the wars, and well beloved at first by our incomparable queen, the friend of all true virtue, as I trust she will be of yours some day; who wanted but one step to greatness, and that was this, that in his hurry to rule all the world, he forgot to rule himself. At first, he wasted his estate in show and luxury, always intending to be famous, and destroying his own fame all the while by his vainglory and haste. Then, to retrieve his losses, he hit upon the peopling of Florida, which thou and I will see done some day, by God's blessing; for I and some good friends of mine have an errand there as well as he. But he did not go about it as a loyal man, to advance the honor of his queen, but his own honor only, dreaming that he too should be a king; and was not ashamed to tell her majesty that he had rather be sovereign of a molehill than the highest subject of an emperor."

"They say," said Mr. Leigh, "that he told her plainly he should be a prince before he died, and that she gave him one of her pretty quips in return."

"I don't know that her majesty had the best of it. A fool is many times too strong for a wise man, by virtue of his thick hide. For when she said that she hoped she should hear from him in his new principality, 'Yes, sooth,' says he, graciously enough. 'And in what style?' asks she. 'To our dear sister,' says Stukely: to which her clemency had nothing to reply, but turned away, as Mr. Burleigh told me, laughing."

"Alas for him!" said gentle Mrs. Leigh. "Such self-conceit—and Heaven knows we have the root of it in ourselves also—is the very daughter of self-will, and of that loud crying out about I, and me, and mine, which is the very bird-call for all devils, and the broad road which leads to death."

"It will lead him to his," said Sir Richard; "God grant it be not upon Tower-hill! for since that Florida plot, and after that his hopes of Irish preferment came to naught, he who could not help himself by fair means has taken to foul ones, and gone over to Italy to the Pope, whose infallibility has not been proof against Stukely's wit; for he was soon his Holiness's closet counsellor, and, they say, his bosom friend; and made him give credit to his boasts that, with three thousand soldiers he would beat the English out of Ireland, and make the Pope's son king of it."

"Ay, but," said Mr. Leigh, "I suppose the Italians have the same fetch now as they had when I was there, to explain such ugly cases; namely, that the Pope is infallible only in doctrine, and quoad Pope; while quoad hominem, he is even as others, or indeed, in general, a deal worse, so that the office, and not the man, may be glorified thereby. But where is Stukely now?"

"At Rome when last I heard of him, ruffling it up and down the Vatican as Baron Ross, Viscount Murrough, Earl Wexford, Marquis Leinster, and a title or two more, which have cost the Pope little, seeing that they never were his to give; and plotting, they say, some hare-brained expedition against Ireland by the help of the Spanish king, which must end in nothing but his shame and ruin. And now, my sweet hosts, I must call for serving-boy and lantern, and home to my bed in Bideford."

And so Amyas Leigh went back to school, and Mr. Oxenham went his way to Plymouth again, and sailed for the Spanish Main.

CHAPTER II: HOW AMYAS CAME HOME THE FIRST TIME

Five years are past and gone. It is nine of the clock on a still, bright November morning; but the bells of Bideford church are still ringing for the daily service two hours after the usual time; and instead of going soberly according to wont, cannot help breaking forth every five minutes into a jocund peal, and tumbling head over heels in ecstasies of joy. Bideford streets are a very flower-garden of all the colors, swarming with seamen and burghers, and burghers' wives and daughters, all in their holiday attire. Garlands are hung across the streets, and tapestries from every window. The ships in the pool are dressed in all their flags, and give tumultuous vent to their feelings by peals of ordnance of every size. Every stable is crammed with horses; and Sir Richard Grenville's house is like a very tavern, with eating and drinking, and unsaddling, and running to and fro of grooms and serving-men. Along the little churchyard, packed full with women, streams all the gentle blood of North Devon,—tall and stately men, and fair ladies, worthy of the days when the gentry of England were by due right the leaders of the people, by personal prowess and beauty, as well as by intellect and education. And first, there is my lady Countess of Bath, whom Sir Richard Grenville is escorting, cap in hand (for her good Earl Bourchier is in London with the queen); and there are Bassets from beautiful Umberleigh, and Carys from more beautiful Clovelly, and Fortescues of Wear, and Fortescues of Buckland, and Fortescues from all quarters, and Coles from Slade, and Stukelys from Affton, and St. Legers from Annery, and Coffins from Portledge, and even Coplestones from Eggesford, thirty miles away: and last, but not least (for almost all stop to give them place), Sir John Chichester of Ralegh, followed in single file, after the good old patriarchal fashion, by his eight daughters, and three of his five famous sons (one, to avenge his murdered brother, is fighting valiantly in Ireland, hereafter to rule there wisely also, as Lord Deputy and Baron of Belfast); and he meets at the gate his cousin of Arlington, and behind him a train of four daughters and nineteen sons, the last of whom has not yet passed the town-hall, while the first is at the Lychgate, who, laughing, make way for the elder though shorter branch of that most fruitful tree; and so on into the church, where all are placed according to their degrees, or at least as near as may be, not without a few sour looks, and shovings, and whisperings, from one high-born matron and another; till the churchwardens and sidesmen, who never had before so goodly a company to arrange, have bustled themselves hot, and red, and frantic, and end by imploring abjectly the help of the great Sir Richard himself to tell them who everybody is, and which is the elder branch, and which is the younger, and who carries eight quarterings in their arms, and who only four, and so prevent their setting at deadly feud half the fine ladies of North Devon; for the old men are all safe packed away in the corporation pews, and the young ones care only to get a place whence they may eye the ladies. And at last there is a silence, and a looking toward the door, and then distant music, flutes and hautboys, drums and trumpets, which come braying, and screaming, and thundering merrily up to the very church doors, and then cease; and the churchwardens and sidesmen bustle down to the entrance, rods in hand, and there is a general whisper and rustle, not without glad tears and blessings from many a woman, and from some men also, as the wonder of the day enters, and the rector begins, not the morning service, but the good old thanksgiving after a victory at sea.

And what is it which has thus sent old Bideford wild with that "goodly joy and pious mirth," of which we now only retain traditions in our translation of the Psalms? Why are all eyes fixed, with greedy admiration, on those four weather-beaten mariners, decked out with knots and ribbons by loving hands; and yet more on that gigantic figure who walks before them, a beardless boy, and yet with the frame and stature of a Hercules, towering, like Saul of old, a head and shoulders above all the congregation, with his golden locks flowing down over his shoulders? And why, as the five go instinctively up to the altar, and there fall on their knees before the rails, are all eyes turned to the pew where Mrs. Leigh of Burrough has hid her face between her hands, and her hood rustles and shakes to her joyful sobs? Because there was fellow-feeling of old in merry England, in county and in town; and these are Devon men, and men of Bideford, whose names are Amyas Leigh of Burrough, John Staveley, Michael Heard, and Jonas Marshall of Bideford, and Thomas Braund of Clovelly: and they, the first of all English mariners, have sailed round the world with Francis Drake, and are come hither to give God thanks.

It is a long story. To explain how it happened we must go back for a page or two, almost to the point from whence we started in the last chapter.

For somewhat more than a twelvemonth after Mr. Oxenham's departure, young Amyas had gone on quietly enough, according to promise, with the exception of certain occasional outbursts of fierceness common to all young male animals, and especially to boys of any strength of character. His scholarship, indeed, progressed no better than before; but his home education went on healthily enough; and he was fast becoming, young as he was, a right good archer, and rider, and swordsman (after the old school of buckler practice), when his father, having gone down on business to the Exeter Assizes, caught (as was too common in those days) the gaol-fever from the prisoners; sickened in the very court; and died within a week.

And now Mrs. Leigh was left to God and her own soul, with this young lion-cub in leash, to tame and train for this life and the life to come. She had loved her husband fervently and holily. He had been often peevish, often melancholy; for he was a disappointed man, with an estate impoverished by his father's folly, and his own youthful ambition, which had led him up to Court, and made him waste his heart and his purse in following a vain shadow. He was one of those men, moreover, who possess almost every gift except the gift of the power to use them; and though a scholar, a courtier, and a soldier, he had found himself, when he was past forty, without settled employment or aim in life, by reason of a certain shyness, pride, or delicate honor (call it which you will), which had always kept him from playing a winning game in that very world after whose prizes he hankered to the last, and on which he revenged himself by continual grumbling. At last, by his good luck, he met with a fair young Miss Foljambe, of Derbyshire, then about Queen Elizabeth's Court, who was as tired as he of the sins of the world, though she had seen less of them; and the two contrived to please each other so well, that though the queen grumbled a little, as usual, at the lady for marrying, and at the gentleman for adoring any one but her royal self, they got leave to vanish from the little Babylon at Whitehall, and settle in peace at Burrough. In her he found a treasure, and he knew what he had found.

Mrs. Leigh was, and had been from her youth, one of those noble old English churchwomen, without superstition, and without severity, who are among the fairest features of that heroic time. There was a certain melancholy about her, nevertheless; for the recollections of her childhood carried her back to times when it was an awful thing to be a Protestant. She could remember among them, five-and-twenty years ago, the burning of poor blind Joan Waste at Derby, and of Mistress Joyce Lewis, too, like herself, a lady born; and sometimes even now, in her nightly dreams, rang in her ears her mother's bitter cries to God, either to spare her that fiery torment, or to give her strength to bear it, as she whom she loved had borne it before her. For her mother, who was of a good family in Yorkshire, had been one of Queen Catherine's bedchamber women, and the bosom friend and disciple of Anne Askew. And she had sat in Smithfield, with blood curdled by horror, to see the hapless Court beauty, a month before the paragon of Henry's Court, carried in a chair (so crippled was she by the rack) to her fiery doom at the stake, beside her fellow-courtier, Mr. Lascelles, while the very heavens seemed to the shuddering mob around to speak their wrath and grief in solemn thunder peals, and heavy drops which hissed upon the crackling pile.

Therefore a sadness hung upon her all her life, and deepened in the days of Queen Mary, when, as a notorious Protestant and heretic, she had had to hide for her life among the hills and caverns of the Peak, and was only saved, by the love which her husband's tenants bore her, and by his bold declaration that, good Catholic as he was, he would run through the body any constable, justice, or priest, yea, bishop or cardinal, who dared to serve the queen's warrant upon his wife.

So she escaped: but, as I said, a sadness hung upon her all her life; and the skirt of that dark mantle fell upon the young girl who had been the partner of her wanderings and hidings among the lonely hills; and who, after she was married, gave herself utterly up to God.

And yet in giving herself to God, Mrs. Leigh gave herself to her husband, her children, and the poor of Northam Town, and was none the less welcome to the Grenvilles, and Fortescues, and Chichesters, and all the gentle families round, who honored her husband's talents, and enjoyed his wit. She accustomed herself to austerities, which often called forth the kindly rebukes of her husband; and yet she did so without one superstitious thought of appeasing the fancied wrath of God, or of giving Him pleasure (base thought) by any pain of hers; for her spirit had been trained in the freest and loftiest doctrines of Luther's school; and that little mystic "Alt-Deutsch Theologie" (to which the great Reformer said that he owed more than to any book, save the Bible, and St. Augustine) was her counsellor and comforter by day and night.

And now, at little past forty, she was left a widow: lovely still in face and figure; and still more lovely from the divine calm which brooded, like the dove of peace and the Holy Spirit of God (which indeed it was), over every look, and word, and gesture; a sweetness which had been ripened by storm, as well as by sunshine; which this world had not given, and could not take away. No wonder that Sir Richard and Lady Grenville loved her; no wonder that her children worshipped her; no wonder that the young Amyas, when the first burst of grief was over, and he knew again where he stood, felt that a new life had begun for him; that his mother was no more to think and act for him only, but that he must think and act for his mother. And so it was, that on the very day after his father's funeral, when school-hours were over, instead of coming straight home, he walked boldly into Sir Richard Grenville's house, and asked to see his godfather.

"You must be my father now, sir," said he, firmly.

And Sir Richard looked at the boy's broad strong face, and swore a great and holy oath, like Glasgerion's, "by oak, and ash, and thorn," that he would be a father to him, and a brother to his mother, for Christ's sake. And Lady Grenville took the boy by the hand, and walked home with him to Burrough; and there the two fair women fell on each other's necks, and wept together; the one for the loss which had been, the other, as by a prophetic instinct, for the like loss which was to come to her also. For the sweet St. Leger knew well that her husband's fiery spirit would never leave his body on a peaceful bed; but that death (as he prayed almost nightly that it might) would find him sword in hand, upon the field of duty and of fame. And there those two vowed everlasting sisterhood, and kept their vow; and after that all things went on at Burrough as before; and Amyas rode, and shot, and boxed, and wandered on the quay at Sir Richard's side; for Mrs. Leigh was too wise a woman to alter one tittle of the training which her husband had thought best for his younger boy. It was enough that her elder son had of his own accord taken to that form of life in which she in her secret heart would fain have moulded both her children. For Frank, God's wedding gift to that pure love of hers, had won himself honor at home and abroad; first at the school at Bideford; then at Exeter College, where he had become a friend of Sir Philip Sidney's, and many another young man of rank and promise; and next, in the summer of 1572, on his way to the University of Heidelberg, he had gone to Paris, with (luckily for him) letters of recommendation to Walsingham, at the English Embassy: by which letters he not only fell in a second time with Philip Sidney, but saved his own life (as Sidney did his) in the Massacre of St. Bartholomew's Day. At Heidelberg he had stayed two years, winning fresh honor from all who knew him, and resisting all Sidney's entreaties to follow him into Italy. For, scorning to be a burden to his parents, he had become at Heidelberg tutor to two young German princes, whom, after living with them at their father's house for a year or more, he at last, to his own great delight, took with him down to Padua, "to perfect them," as he wrote home, "according to his insufficiency, in all princely studies." Sidney was now returned to England; but Frank found friends enough without him, such letters of recommendation and diplomas did he carry from I know not how many princes, magnificos, and learned doctors, who had fallen in love with the learning, modesty, and virtue of the fair young Englishman. And ere Frank returned to Germany he had satiated his soul with all the wonders of that wondrous land. He had talked over the art of sonneteering with Tasso, the art of history with Sarpi; he had listened, between awe and incredulity, to the daring theories of Galileo; he had taken his pupils to Venice, that their portraits might be painted by Paul Veronese; he had seen the palaces of Palladio, and the merchant princes on the Rialto, and the argosies of Ragusa, and all the wonders of that meeting-point of east and west; he had watched Tintoretto's mighty hand "hurling tempestuous glories o'er the scene;" and even, by dint of private intercession in high places, had been admitted to that sacred room where, with long silver beard and undimmed eye, amid a pantheon of his own creations, the ancient Titian, patriarch of art, still lingered upon earth, and told old tales of the Bellinis, and Raffaelle, and Michael Angelo, and the building of St. Peter's, and the fire at Venice, and the sack of Rome, and of kings and warriors, statesmen and poets, long since gone to their account, and showed the sacred brush which Francis the First had stooped to pick up for him. And (license forbidden to Sidney by his friend Languet) he had been to Rome, and seen (much to the scandal of good Protestants at home) that "right good fellow," as Sidney calls him, who had not yet eaten himself to death, the Pope for the time being. And he had seen the frescos of the Vatican, and heard Palestrina preside as chapel-master over the performance of his own music beneath the dome of St. Peter's, and fallen half in love with those luscious strains, till he was awakened from his dream by the recollection that beneath that same dome had gone up thanksgivings to the God of heaven for those blood-stained streets, and shrieking women, and heaps of insulted corpses, which he had beheld in Paris on the night of St. Bartholomew. At last, a few months before his father died, he had taken back his pupils to their home in Germany, from whence he was dismissed, as he wrote, with rich gifts; and then Mrs. Leigh's heart beat high, at the thought that the wanderer would return: but, alas! within a month after his father's death, came a long letter from Frank, describing the Alps, and the valleys of the Waldenses (with whose Barbes he had had much talk about the late horrible persecutions), and setting forth how at Padua he had made the acquaintance of that illustrious scholar and light of the age, Stephanus Parmenius (commonly called from his native place, Budaeus), who had visited Geneva with him, and heard the disputations of their most learned doctors, which both he and Budaeus disliked for their hard judgments both of God and man, as much as they admired them for their subtlety, being themselves, as became Italian students, Platonists of the school of Ficinus and Picus Mirandolensis. So wrote Master Frank, in a long sententious letter, full of Latin quotations: but the letter never reached the eyes of him for whose delight it had been penned: and the widow had to weep over it alone, and to weep more bitterly than ever at the conclusion, in which, with many excuses, Frank said that he had, at the special entreaty of the said Budaeus, set out with him down the Danube stream to Buda, that he might, before finishing his travels, make experience of that learning for which the Hungarians were famous throughout Europe. And after that, though he wrote again and again to the father whom he fancied living, no letter in return reached him from home for nearly two years; till, fearing some mishap, he hurried back to England, to find his mother a widow, and his brother Amyas gone to the South Seas with Captain Drake of Plymouth. And yet, even then, after years of absence, he was not allowed to remain at home. For Sir Richard, to whom idleness was a thing horrible and unrighteous, would have him up and doing again before six months were over, and sent him off to Court to Lord Hunsdon.

There, being as delicately beautiful as his brother was huge and strong, he had speedily, by Carew's interest and that of Sidney and his Uncle Leicester, found entrance into some office in the queen's household; and he was now basking in the full sunshine of Court favor, and fair ladies' eyes, and all the chivalries and euphuisms of Gloriana's fairyland, and the fast friendship of that bright meteor Sidney, who had returned with honor in 1577, from the delicate mission on behalf of the German and Belgian Protestants, on which he had been sent to the Court of Vienna, under color of condoling with the new Emperor Rodolph on his father's death. Frank found him when he himself came to Court in 1579 as lovely and loving as ever; and, at the early age of twenty-five, acknowledged as one of the most remarkable men of Europe, the patron of all men of letters, the counsellor of warriors and statesmen, and the confidant and advocate of William of Orange, Languet, Plessis du Mornay, and all the Protestant leaders on the Continent; and found, moreover, that the son of the poor Devon squire was as welcome as ever to the friendship of nature's and fortune's most favored, yet most unspoilt, minion.

Poor Mrs. Leigh, as one who had long since learned to have no self, and to live not only for her children but in them, submitted without a murmur, and only said, smiling, to her stern friend—"You took away my mastiff-pup, and now you must needs have my fair greyhound also."

"Would you have your fair greyhound, dear lady, grow up a tall and true Cotswold dog, that can pull down a stag of ten, or one of those smooth-skinned poppets which the Florence ladies lead about with a ring of bells round its neck, and a flannel farthingale over its loins?"

Mrs. Leigh submitted; and was rewarded after a few months by a letter, sent through Sir Richard, from none other than Gloriana herself, in which she thanked her for "the loan of that most delicate and flawless crystal, the soul of her excellent son," with more praises of him than I have room to insert, and finished by exalting the poor mother above the famed Cornelia; "for those sons, whom she called her jewels, she only showed, yet kept them to herself: but you, madam, having two as precious, I doubt not, as were ever that Roman dame's, have, beyond her courage, lent them both to your country and to your queen, who therein holds herself indebted to you for that which, if God give her grace, she will repay as becomes both her and you." Which epistle the sweet mother bedewed with holy tears, and laid by in the cedar-box which held her household gods, by the side of Frank's innumerable diplomas and letters of recommendation, the Latin whereof she was always spelling over (although she understood not a word of it), in hopes of finding, here and there, that precious excellentissimus Noster Franciscus Leighius Anglus, which was all in all to the mother's heart.

But why did Amyas go to the South Seas? Amyas went to the South Seas for two causes, each of which has, before now, sent many a lad to far worse places: first, because of an old schoolmaster; secondly, because of a young beauty. I will take them in order and explain.

Vindex Brimblecombe, whilom servitor of Exeter College, Oxford (commonly called Sir Vindex, after the fashion of the times), was, in those days, master of the grammar-school of Bideford. He was, at root, a godly and kind-hearted pedant enough; but, like most schoolmasters in the old flogging days, had his heart pretty well hardened by long, baneful license to inflict pain at will on those weaker than himself; a power healthful enough for the victim (for, doubtless, flogging is the best of all punishments, being not only the shortest, but also a mere bodily and animal, and not, like most of our new-fangled "humane" punishments, a spiritual and fiendish torture), but for the executioner pretty certain to eradicate, from all but the noblest spirits, every trace of chivalry and tenderness for the weak, as well, often, as all self-control and command of temper. Be that as it may, old Sir Vindex had heart enough to feel that it was now his duty to take especial care of the fatherless boy to whom he tried to teach his qui, quae, quod: but the only outcome of that new sense of responsibility was a rapid increase in the number of floggings, which rose from about two a week to one per diem, not without consequences to the pedagogue himself.

For all this while, Amyas had never for a moment lost sight of his darling desire for a sea-life; and when he could not wander on the quay and stare at the shipping, or go down to the pebble-ridge at Northam, and there sit, devouring, with hungry eyes, the great expanse of ocean, which seemed to woo him outward into boundless space, he used to console himself, in school-hours, by drawing ships and imaginary charts upon his slate, instead of minding his "humanities."

Now it befell, upon an afternoon, that he was very busy at a map, or bird's-eye view of an island, whereon was a great castle, and at the gate thereof a dragon, terrible to see; while in the foreground came that which was meant for a gallant ship, with a great flag aloft, but which, by reason of the forest of lances with which it was crowded, looked much more like a porcupine carrying a sign-post; and, at the roots of those lances, many little round o's, whereby was signified the heads of Amyas and his schoolfellows, who were about to slay that dragon, and rescue the beautiful princess who dwelt in that enchanted tower. To behold which marvel of art, all the other boys at the same desk must needs club their heads together, and with the more security, because Sir Vindex, as was his custom after dinner, was lying back in his chair, and slept the sleep of the just.

But when Amyas, by special instigation of the evil spirit who haunts successful artists, proceeded further to introduce, heedless of perspective, a rock, on which stood the lively portraiture of Sir Vindex—nose, spectacles, gown, and all; and in his hand a brandished rod, while out of his mouth a label shrieked after the runaways, "You come back!" while a similar label replied from the gallant bark, "Good-bye, master!" the shoving and tittering rose to such a pitch that Cerberus awoke, and demanded sternly what the noise was about. To which, of course, there was no answer.

"You, of course, Leigh! Come up, sir, and show me your exercitation."

Now of Amyas's exercitation not a word was written; and, moreover, he was in the very article of putting the last touches to Mr. Brimblecombe's portrait. Whereon, to the astonishment of all hearers, he made answer—

"All in good time, sir!" and went on drawing.

"In good time, sir! Insolent, veni et vapula!"

But Amyas went on drawing.

"Come hither, sirrah, or I'll flay you alive!"

"Wait a bit!" answered Amyas.

The old gentleman jumped up, ferula in hand, and darted across the school, and saw himself upon the fatal slate.

"Proh flagitium! what have we here, villain?" and clutching at his victim, he raised the cane. Whereupon, with a serene and cheerful countenance, up rose the mighty form of Amyas Leigh, a head and shoulders above his tormentor, and that slate descended on the bald coxcomb of Sir

Vindex Brimblecombe, with so shrewd a blow that slate and pate cracked at the same instant, and the poor pedagogue dropped to the floor, and lay for dead.

After which Amyas arose, and walked out of the school, and so quietly home; and having taken counsel with himself, went to his mother, and said, "Please, mother, I've broken schoolmaster's head."

"Broken his head, thou wicked boy!" shrieked the poor widow; "what didst do that for?"

"I can't tell," said Amyas, penitently; "I couldn't help it. It looked so smooth, and bald, and round, and—you know?"

"I know? Oh, wicked boy! thou hast given place to the devil; and now, perhaps, thou hast killed him."

"Killed the devil?" asked Amyas, hopefully but doubtfully.

"No, killed the schoolmaster, sirrah! Is he dead?"

"I don't think he's dead; his coxcomb sounded too hard for that. But had not I better go and tell Sir Richard?"

The poor mother could hardly help laughing, in spite of her terror, at Amyas's perfect coolness (which was not in the least meant for insolence), and being at her wits' end, sent him, as usual, to his godfather.

Amyas rehearsed his story again, with pretty nearly the same exclamations, to which he gave pretty nearly the same answers; and then—"What was he going to do to you, then, sirrah?"

"Flog me, because I could not write my exercise, and so drew a picture of him instead."

"What! art afraid of being flogged?"

"Not a bit; besides, I'm too much accustomed to it; but I was busy, and he was in such a desperate hurry; and, oh, sir, if you had but seen his bald head, you would have broken it yourself!"

Now Sir Richard had, twenty years ago, in like place, and very much in like manner, broken the head of Vindex Brimblecombe's father, schoolmaster in his day, and therefore had a precedent to direct him; and he answered—"Amyas, sirrah! those who cannot obey will never be fit to rule. If thou canst not keep discipline now, thou wilt never make a company or a crew keep it when thou art grown. Dost mind that, sirrah?"

"Yes," said Amyas.

"Then go back to school this moment, sir, and be flogged."

"Very well," said Amyas, considering that he had got off very cheaply; while Sir Richard, as soon as he was out of the room, lay back in his chair, and laughed till he cried again.

So Amyas went back, and said that he was come to be flogged; whereon the old schoolmaster, whose pate had been plastered meanwhile, wept tears of joy over the returning prodigal, and then gave him such a switching as he did not forget for eight-and-forty hours.

But that evening Sir Richard sent for old Vindex, who entered, trembling, cap in hand; and having primed him with a cup of sack, said—"Well, Mr. Schoolmaster! My godson has been somewhat too much for you to-day. There are a couple of nobles to pay the doctor."

"O Sir Richard, gratias tibi et Domino! but the boy hits shrewdly hard. Nevertheless I have repaid him in inverse kind, and set him an imposition, to learn me one of Phaedrus his fables, Sir Richard, if you do not think it too much."

"Which, then? The one about the man who brought up a lion's cub, and was eaten by him in play at last?"

"Ah, Sir Richard! you have always a merry wit. But, indeed, the boy is a brave boy, and a quick boy, Sir Richard, but more forgetful than Lethe; and—sapienti loquor—it were well if he were away, for I shall never see him again without my head aching. Moreover, he put my son Jack upon the fire last Wednesday, as you would put a football, though he is a year older, your worship, because, he said, he looked so like a roasting pig, Sir Richard."

"Alas, poor Jack!"

"And what's more, your worship, he is pugnax, bellicosus, gladiator, a fire-eater and swashbuckler, beyond all Christian measure; a very sucking Entellus, Sir Richard, and will do to death some of her majesty's lieges erelong, if he be not wisely curbed. It was but a month agone that he bemoaned himself, I hear, as Alexander did, because there were no more worlds to conquer, saying that it was a pity he was so strong; for, now he had thrashed all the Bideford lads, he had no sport left; and so, as my Jack tells me, last Tuesday week he fell upon a young man of Barnstaple, Sir Richard, a hosier's man, sir, and plebeius (which I consider unfit for one of his blood), and, moreover, a man full grown, and as big as either of us (Vindex stood five feet four in his high-heeled shoes), and smote him clean over the quay into the mud, because he said that there was a prettier maid in Barnstaple (your worship will forgive my speaking of such toys, to which my fidelity compels me) than ever Bideford could show; and then offered to do the same to any man who dare say that Mistress Rose Salterne, his worship the mayor's daughter, was not the fairest lass in all Devon."

"Eh? Say that over again, my good sir," quoth Sir Richard, who had thus arrived, as we have seen, at the second count of the indictment. "I say, good sir, whence dost thou hear all these pretty stories?"

"My son Jack, Sir Richard, my son Jack, ingenui vultus puer."

"But not, it seems, ingenui pudoris. Tell thee what, Mr. Schoolmaster, no wonder if thy son gets put on the fire, if thou employ him as a tale-bearer. But that is the way of all pedagogues and their sons, by which they train the lads up eavesdroppers and favor-curriers, and prepare them—sirrah, do you hear?—for a much more lasting and hotter fire than that which has scorched thy son Jack's nether-tackle. Do you mark me, sir?"

The poor pedagogue, thus cunningly caught in his own trap, stood trembling before his patron, who, as hereditary head of the Bridge Trust, which endowed the school and the rest of the Bideford charities, could, by a turn of his finger, sweep him forth with the besom of destruction; and he gasped with terror as Sir Richard went on—"Therefore, mind you, Sir Schoolmaster, unless you shall promise me never to hint word of what has passed between us two, and that neither you nor yours shall henceforth carry tales of my godson, or speak his name within a day's march of Mistress Salterne's, look to it, if I do not—"

What was to be done in default was not spoken; for down went poor old Vindex on his knees:—

"Oh, Sir Richard! Excellentissime, immo praecelsissime Domine et Senator, I promise! O sir, Miles et Eques of the Garter, Bath, and Golden Fleece, consider your dignities, and my old age—and my great family—nine children—oh, Sir Richard, and eight of them girls!—Do eagles war with mice? says the ancient!"

"Thy large family, eh? How old is that fat-witted son of thine?"

"Sixteen, Sir Richard; but that is not his fault, indeed!"

"Nay, I suppose he would be still sucking his thumb if he dared—get up, man—get up and seat yourself."

"Heaven forbid!" murmured poor Vindex, with deep humility.

"Why is not the rogue at Oxford, with a murrain on him, instead of lurching about here carrying tales and ogling the maidens?"

"I had hoped, Sir Richard—and therefore I said it was not his fault—but there was never a servitorship at Exeter open."

"Go to, man—go to! I will speak to my brethren of the Trust, and to Oxford he shall go this autumn, or else to Exeter gaol, for a strong rogue, and a masterless man. Do you hear?"

"Hear?—oh, sir, yes! and return thanks. Jack shall go, Sir Richard, doubt it not—I were mad else; and, Sir Richard, may I go too?"

And therewith Vindex vanished, and Sir Richard enjoyed a second mighty laugh, which brought in Lady Grenville, who possibly had overheard the whole; for the first words she said were—

"I think, my sweet life, we had better go up to Burrough."

So to Burrough they went; and after much talk, and many tears, matters were so concluded that Amyas Leigh found himself riding joyfully towards Plymouth, by the side of Sir Richard, and being handed over to Captain Drake, vanished for three years from the good town of Bideford.

And now he is returned in triumph, and the observed of all observers; and looks round and round, and sees all faces whom he expects, except one; and that the one which he had rather see than his mother's? He is not quite sure. Shame on himself!

And now the prayers being ended, the rector ascends the pulpit, and begins his sermon on the text:—

"The heaven and the heaven of heavens are the Lord's; the whole earth hath he given to the children of men;" deducing therefrom craftily, to the exceeding pleasure of his hearers, the iniquity of the Spaniards in dispossessing the Indians, and in arrogating to themselves the sovereignty of the tropic seas; the vanity of the Pope of Rome in pretending to bestow on them the new countries of America; and the justice, valor, and glory of Mr. Drake and his expedition, as testified by God's miraculous protection of him and his, both in the Straits of Magellan, and in his battle with the Galleon; and last, but not least, upon the rock by Celebes, when the Pelican lay for hours firmly fixed, and was floated off unhurt, as it were by miracle, by a sudden shift of wind.

Ay, smile, reader, if you will; and, perhaps, there was matter for a smile in that honest sermon, interlarded, as it was, with scraps of Greek and Hebrew, which no one understood, but every one expected as their right (for a preacher was nothing then who could not prove himself "a good Latiner"); and graced, moreover, by a somewhat pedantic and lengthy refutation from Scripture of Dan Horace's cockney horror of the sea—

and his infidel and ungodly slander against the impias rates, and their crews.

Smile, if you will: but those were days (and there were never less superstitious ones) in which Englishmen believed in the living God, and were not ashamed to acknowledge, as a matter of course, His help and providence, and calling, in the matters of daily life, which we now in our covert atheism term "secular and carnal;" and when, the sermon ended, the communion service had begun, and the bread and the wine were given to those five mariners, every gallant gentleman who stood near them (for the press would not allow of more) knelt and received the elements with them as a thing of course, and then rose to join with heart and voice not merely in the Gloria in Excelsis, but in the Te Deum, which was the closing act of all. And no sooner had the clerk given out the first verse of that great hymn, than it was taken up by five hundred voices within the church, in bass and tenor, treble and alto (for every one could sing in those days, and the west-country folk, as now, were fuller than any of music), the chant was caught up by the crowd outside, and rang away over roof and river, up to the woods of Annery, and down to the marshes of the Taw, in wave on wave of harmony. And as it died away, the shipping in the river made answer with their thunder, and the crowd streamed out again toward the Bridge Head, whither Sir Richard Grenville, and Sir John Chichester, and Mr. Salterne, the Mayor, led the five heroes of the day to await the pageant which had been prepared in honor of them. And as they went by, there were few in the crowd who did not press forward to shake them by the hand, and not only them, but their parents and kinsfolk who walked behind, till Mrs. Leigh, her stately joy quite broken down at last, could only answer between her sobs, "Go along, good people—God a mercy, go along—and God send you all such sons!"

"God give me back mine!" cried an old red-cloaked dame in the crowd; and then, struck by some hidden impulse, she sprang forward, and catching hold of young Amyas's sleeve—

"Kind sir! dear sir! For Christ his sake answer a poor old widow woman!"

"What is it, dame?" quoth Amyas, gently enough.

"Did you see my son to the Indies?—my son Salvation?"

"Salvation?" replied he, with the air of one who recollected the name.

"Yes, sure, Salvation Yeo, of Clovelly. A tall man and black, and sweareth awfully in his talk, the Lord forgive him!"

Amyas recollected now. It was the name of the sailor who had given him the wondrous horn five years ago.

"My good dame," said he, "the Indies are a very large place, and your son may be safe and sound enough there, without my having seen him. I knew one Salvation Yeo. But he must have come with—By the by, godfather, has Mr. Oxenham come home?"

There was a dead silence for a moment among the gentlemen round; and then Sir Richard said solemnly, and in a low voice, turning away from the old dame,—

"Amyas, Mr. Oxenham has not come home; and from the day he sailed, no word has been heard of him and all his crew."

"Oh, Sir Richard! and you kept me from sailing with him! Had I known this before I went into church, I had had one mercy more to thank God for."

"Thank Him all the more in thy life, my child!" whispered his mother.

"And no news of him whatsoever?"

"None; but that the year after he sailed, a ship belonging to Andrew Barker, of Bristol, took out of a Spanish caravel, somewhere off the Honduras, his two brass guns; but whence they came the Spaniard knew not, having bought them at Nombre de Dios."

"Yes!" cried the old woman; "they brought home the guns, and never brought home my boy!"

"They never saw your boy, mother," said Sir Richard.

"But I've seen him! I saw him in a dream four years last Whitsuntide, as plain as I see you now, gentles, a-lying upon a rock, calling for a drop of water to cool his tongue, like Dives to the torment! Oh! dear me!" and the old dame wept bitterly.

"There is a rose noble for you!" said Mrs. Leigh.

"And there another!" said Sir Richard. And in a few minutes four or five gold coins were in her hand. But the old dame did but look wonderingly at the gold a moment, and then—

"Ah! dear gentles, God's blessing on you, and Mr. Cary's mighty good to me already; but gold won't buy back childer! O! young gentleman! young gentleman! make me a promise; if you want God's blessing on you this day, bring me back my boy, if you find him sailing on the seas! Bring him back, and an old widow's blessing be on you!"

Amyas promised—what else could he do?—and the group hurried on; but the lad's heart was heavy in the midst of joy, with the thought of John Oxenham, as he walked through the churchyard, and down the short street which led between the ancient school and still more ancient town-house, to the head of the long bridge, across which the pageant, having arranged "east-the-water," was to defile, and then turn to the right along the quay.

However, he was bound in all courtesy to turn his attention now to the show which had been prepared in his honor, and which was really well enough worth seeing and hearing. The English were, in those days, an altogether dramatic people; ready and able, as in Bideford that day, to extemporize a pageant, a masque, or any effort of the Thespian art short of the regular drama. For they were, in the first place, even down to the very poorest, a well-fed people, with fewer luxuries than we, but more abundant necessaries; and while beef, ale, and good woollen clothes could be obtained in plenty, without overworking either body or soul, men had time to amuse themselves in something more intellectual than mere toping in pot-houses. Moreover, the half century after the Reformation in England was one not merely of new intellectual freedom, but of immense animal good spirits. After years of dumb confusion and cruel persecution, a breathing time had come: Mary and the fires of Smithfield had vanished together like a hideous dream, and the mighty shout of joy which greeted Elizabeth's entry into London, was the key-note of fifty glorious years; the expression of a new-found strength and freedom, which vented itself at home in drama and in song; abroad in mighty conquests, achieved with the laughing recklessness of boys at play.

So first, preceded by the waits, came along the bridge toward the town-hall a device prepared by the good rector, who, standing by, acted as showman, and explained anxiously to the bystanders the import of a certain "allegory" wherein on a great banner was depicted Queen Elizabeth herself, who, in ample ruff and farthingale, a Bible in one hand and a sword in the other, stood triumphant upon the necks of two sufficiently abject personages, whose triple tiara and imperial crown proclaimed them the Pope and the King of Spain; while a label, issuing from her royal mouth, informed the world that—

Which, having been received with due applause, a well-bedizened lad, having in his cap as a posy "Loyalty," stepped forward, and delivered himself of the following verses:—

With which sufficiently bad verses Loyalty passed on, while my Lady Bath hinted to Sir Richard, not without reason, that the poet, in trying to exalt both parties, had very sufficiently snubbed both, and intimated that it was "hardly safe for country wits to attempt that euphuistic, antithetical, and delicately conceited vein, whose proper fountain was in Whitehall." However, on went Loyalty, very well pleased with himself, and next, amid much cheering, two great tinsel fish, a salmon and a trout, symbolical of the wealth of Torridge, waddled along, by means of two human legs and a staff apiece, which protruded from the fishes' stomachs. They drew (or seemed to draw, for half the 'prentices in the town were shoving it behind, and cheering on the panting monarchs of the flood) a car wherein sate, amid reeds and river-flags, three or four pretty girls in robes of gray-blue spangled with gold, their heads wreathed one with a crown of the sweet bog-myrtle, another with hops and white convolvulus, the third with pale heather and golden fern. They stopped opposite Amyas; and she of the myrtle wreath, rising and bowing to him and the company, began with a pretty blush to say her say:—

And so ending, she took the wreath of fragrant gale from her own head, and stooping from the car, placed it on the head of Amyas Leigh, who made answer—

"There is no place like home, my fair mistress and no scent to my taste like this old home-scent in all the spice-islands that I ever sailed by!"

"Her song was not so bad," said Sir Richard to Lady Bath—"but how came she to hear Plymouth bells at Tamar-head, full fifty miles away? That's too much of a poet's license, is it not?"

"The river-nymphs, as daughters of Oceanus, and thus of immortal parentage, are bound to possess organs of more than mortal keenness; but, as you say, the song was not so bad—erudite, as well as prettily conceived—and, saving for a certain rustical simplicity and monosyllabic baldness, smacks rather of the forests of Castaly than those of Torridge."

So spake my Lady Bath; whom Sir Richard wisely answered not; for she was a terribly learned member of the college of critics, and disputed even with Sidney's sister the chieftaincy of the Euphuists; so Sir Richard answered not, but answer was made for him.

"Since the whole choir of Muses, madam, have migrated to the Court of Whitehall, no wonder if some dews of Parnassus should fertilize at times even our Devon moors."

The speaker was a tall and slim young man, some five-and-twenty years old, of so rare and delicate a beauty, that it seemed that some Greek statue, or rather one of those pensive and pious knights whom the old German artists took delight to paint, had condescended to tread awhile this work-day earth in living flesh and blood. The forehead was very lofty and smooth, the eyebrows thin and greatly arched (the envious gallants whispered that something at least of their curve was due to art, as was also the exceeding smoothness of those delicate cheeks). The face was somewhat long and thin; the nose aquiline; and the languid mouth showed, perhaps, too much of the ivory upper teeth; but the most striking point of the speaker's appearance was the extraordinary brilliancy of his complexion, which shamed with its whiteness that of all fair ladies round, save where open on each cheek a bright red spot gave warning, as did the long thin neck and the taper hands, of sad possibilities, perhaps not far off; possibilities which all saw with an inward sigh, except she whose doting glances, as well as her resemblance to the fair youth, proclaimed her at once his mother, Mrs. Leigh herself.

Master Frank, for he it was, was dressed in the very extravagance of the fashion,—not so much from vanity, as from that delicate instinct of self-respect which would keep some men spruce and spotless from one year's end to another upon a desert island; "for," as Frank used to say in his sententious way, "Mr. Frank Leigh at least beholds me, though none else be by; and why should I be more discourteous to him than I permit others to be? Be sure that he who is a Grobian in his own company, will, sooner or later, become a Grobian in that of his friends."

So Mr. Frank was arrayed spotlessly; but after the latest fashion of Milan, not in trunk hose and slashed sleeves, nor in "French standing collar, treble quadruple daedalian ruff, or stiff-necked rabato, that had more arches for pride, propped up with wire and timber, than five London Bridges;" but in a close-fitting and perfectly plain suit of dove-color, which set off cunningly the delicate proportions of his figure, and the delicate hue of his complexion, which was shaded from the sun by a broad dove-colored Spanish hat, with feather to match, looped up over the right ear with a pearl brooch, and therein a crowned E, supposed by the damsels of Bideford to stand for Elizabeth, which was whispered to be the gift of some most illustrious hand. This same looping up was not without good reason and purpose prepense; thereby all the world had full view of a beautiful little ear, which looked as if it had been cut of cameo, and made, as my Lady Rich once told him, "to hearken only to the music of the spheres, or to the chants of cherubim." Behind the said ear was stuck a fresh rose; and the golden hair was all drawn smoothly back and round to the left temple, whence, tied with a pink ribbon in a great true lover's knot, a mighty love-lock, "curled as it had been laid in press," rolled down low upon his bosom. Oh, Frank! Frank! have you come out on purpose to break the hearts of all Bideford burghers' daughters? And if so, did you expect to further that triumph by dyeing that pretty little pointed beard (with shame I report it) of a bright vermilion? But we know you better, Frank, and so does your mother; and you are but a masquerading angel after all, in spite of your knots and your perfumes, and the gold chain round your neck which a German princess gave you; and the emerald ring on your right fore-finger which Hatton gave you; and the pair of perfumed gloves in your left which Sidney's sister gave you; and the silver-hilted Toledo which an Italian marquis gave you on a certain occasion of which you never choose to talk, like a prudent and modest gentleman as you are; but of which the gossips talk, of course, all the more, and whisper that you saved his life from bravoes—a dozen, at the least; and had that sword for your reward, and might have had his beautiful sister's hand beside, and I know not what else; but that you had so many lady-loves already that you were loath to burden yourself with a fresh one. That, at least, we know to be a lie, fair Frank; for your heart is as pure this day as when you knelt in your little crib at Burrough, and said—

And who could doubt it (if being pure themselves, they have instinctive sympathy with what is pure), who ever looked into those great deep blue eyes of yours, "the black fringed curtains of whose azure lids," usually down-dropt as if in deepest thought, you raise slowly, almost wonderingly each time you speak, as if awakening from some fair dream whose home is rather in your platonical "eternal world of supra-sensible forms," than on that work-day earth wherein you nevertheless acquit yourself so well? There—I must stop describing you, or I shall catch the infection of your own euphuism, and talk of you as you would have talked of Sidney or of Spenser, or of that Swan of Avon, whose song had just begun when yours—but I will not anticipate; my Lady Bath is waiting to give you her rejoinder.

"Ah, my silver-tongued scholar! and are you, then, the poet? or have you been drawing on the inexhaustible bank of your friend Raleigh, or my cousin Sidney? or has our new Cygnet Immerito lent you a few unpublished leaves from some fresh Shepherd's Calendar?"

"Had either, madam, of that cynosural triad been within call of my most humble importunities, your ears had been delectate with far nobler melody."

"But not our eyes with fairer faces, eh? Well, you have chosen your nymphs, and had good store from whence to pick, I doubt not. Few young Dulcineas round but must have been glad to take service under so renowned a captain?"

"The only difficulty, gracious countess, has been to know where to fix the wandering choice of my bewildered eyes, where all alike are fair, and all alike facund."

"We understand," said she, smiling;—

The young scholar capped her distich forthwith, and bowing to her with a meaning look,

"'Then, Goddess, turn,' he cried, 'and veil thy light; Blinded by thine, what eyes can choose aright?'"

"Go, saucy sir," said my lady, in high glee: "the pageant stays your supreme pleasure."

And away went Mr. Frank as master of the revels, to bring up the 'prentices' pageant; while, for his sake, the nymph of Torridge was forgotten for awhile by all young dames, and most young gentlemen: and his mother heaved a deep sigh, which Lady Bath overhearing—

"What? in the dumps, good madam, while all are rejoicing in your joy? Are you afraid that we court-dames shall turn your Adonis's brain for him?"

"I do, indeed, fear lest your condescension should make him forget that he is only a poor squire's orphan."

"I will warrant him never to forget aught that he should recollect," said my Lady Bath.

And she spoke truly. But soon Frank's silver voice was heard calling out—

"Room there, good people, for the gallant 'prentice lads!"

And on they came, headed by a giant of buckram and pasteboard armor, forth of whose stomach looked, like a clock-face in a steeple, a human visage, to be greeted, as was the fashion then, by a volley of quips and puns from high and low.

Young Mr. William Cary, of Clovelly, who was the wit of those parts, opened the fire by asking him whether he were Goliath, Gogmagog, or Grantorto in the romance; for giants' names always began with a G. To which the giant's stomach answered pretty surlily—

"Mine don't; I begin with an O."

"Then thou criest out before thou art hurt, O cowardly giant!"

"Let me out, lads," quoth the irascible visage, struggling in his buckram prison, "and I soon show him whether I be a coward."

"Nay, if thou gettest out of thyself, thou wouldst be beside thyself, and so wert but a mad giant."

"And that were pity," said Lady Bath; "for by the romances, giants have never overmuch wit to spare."

"Mercy, dear lady!" said Frank, "and let the giant begin with an O."

"A ——"

"A false start, giant! you were to begin with an O."

"I'll make you end with an O, Mr. William Cary!" roared the testy tower of buckram.

"And so I do, for I end with 'Fico!'"

"Be mollified, sweet giant," said Frank, "and spare the rash youth of yon foolish knight. Shall elephants catch flies, or Hurlo-Thrumbo stain his club with brains of Dagonet the jester? Be mollified; leave thy caverned grumblings, like Etna when its windy wrath is past, and discourse eloquence from thy central omphalos, like Pythoness ventriloquizing."

"If you do begin laughing at me too, Mr. Leigh ——" said the giant's clock-face, in a piteous tone.

"I laugh not. Art thou not Ordulf the earl, and I thy humblest squire? Speak up, my lord; your cousin, my Lady Bath, commands you."

And at last the giant began:—

"Oh, bathos!" said Lady Bath, while the 'prentices shouted applause. "Is this hedge-bantling to be fathered on you, Mr. Frank?"

"It is necessary, by all laws of the drama, madam," said Frank, with a sly smile, "that the speech and the speaker shall fit each other. Pass on, Earl Ordulf; a more learned worthy waits."

Whereon, up came a fresh member of the procession; namely, no less a person than Vindex Brimblecombe, the ancient schoolmaster, with five-and-forty boys at his heels, who halting, pulled out his spectacles, and thus signified his forgiveness of his whilom broken head:—

"That the world should have been circumnavigated, ladies and gentles, were matter enough of jubilation to the student of Herodotus and Plato, Plinius and —— ahem! much more when the circumnavigators are Britons; more, again, when Damnonians."

"Don't swear, master," said young Will Cary.

"Gulielme Cary, Gulielme Cary, hast thou forgotten thy—"

"Whippings? Never, old lad! Go on; but let not the license of the scholar overtop the modesty of the Christian."

"More again, as I said, when, incolae, inhabitants of Devon; but, most of all, men of Bideford school. Oh renowned school! Oh schoolboys ennobled by fellowship with him! Oh most happy pedagogue, to whom it has befallen to have chastised a circumnavigator, and, like another Chiron, trained another Hercules: yet more than Hercules, for he placed his pillars on the ocean shore, and then returned; but my scholar's voyage—"

"Hark how the old fox is praising himself all along on the sly," said Cary.

"Mr. William, Mr. William, peace;—silentium, my graceless pupil. Urge the foaming steed, and strike terror into the rapid stag, but meddle not with matters too high for thee."

"He has given you the dor now, sir," said Lady Bath; "let the old man say his say."

"I bring, therefore, as my small contribution to this day's feast; first a Latin epigram, as thus—"

"Latin? Let us hear it forthwith," cried my lady.

And the old pedant mouthed out—

"Neat, i' faith, la!" Whereon all the rest, as in duty bound, approved also.

"This for the erudite: for vulgar ears the vernacular is more consonant, sympathetic, instructive; as thus:—

"Runs with a right fa-lal-la," observed Cary; "and would go nobly to a fiddle and a big drum."

"Hillo ho! schoolmaster!" shouted a voice from behind; "move on, and make way for Father Neptune!" Whereon a whole storm of raillery fell upon the hapless pedagogue.

"We waited for the parson's alligator, but we wain't for yourn."

"Allegory! my children, allegory!" shrieked the man of letters.

"What do ye call he an alligator for? He is but a poor little starved evat!"

"Out of the road, old Custis! March on, Don Palmado!"

These allusions to the usual instrument of torture in West-country schools made the old gentleman wince; especially when they were followed home by—

"Who stole Admiral Grenville's brooms, because birch rods were dear?"

But proudly he shook his bald head, as a bull shakes off the flies, and returned to the charge once more.

"Great Alexander, famed commander, wept and made a pother, At conquering only half the world, but Drake had conquer'd t'other; And Hercules to brink of seas!—"

"Oh—!"

And clapping both hands to the back of his neck, the schoolmaster began dancing frantically about, while his boys broke out tittering, "O! the ochidore! look to the blue ochidore! Who've put ochidore to maister's poll!"

It was too true: neatly inserted, as he stooped forward, between his neck and his collar, was a large live shore-crab, holding on tight with both hands.

"Gentles! good Christians! save me! I am mare-rode! Incubo, vel ab incubo, opprimor! Satanas has me by the poll! Help! he tears my jugular; he wrings my neck, as he does to Dr. Faustus in the play. Confiteor!—I confess! Satan, I defy thee! Good people, I confess! [Greek text]! The truth will out. Mr. Francis Leigh wrote the epigram!" And diving through the crowd, the pedagogue vanished howling, while Father Neptune, crowned with sea-weeds, a trident in one hand, and a live dog-fish in the other, swaggered up the street surrounded by a tall bodyguard of mariners, and followed by a great banner, on which was depicted a globe, with Drake's ship sailing thereon upside down, and overwritten—

"Now, lads!" cried Neptune; "hand me my parable that's writ for me, and here goeth!"

And at the top of his bull-voice, he began roaring—

"Holla, boys! holla! Blow up, Triton, and bring forward the freedom of the seas."

Triton, roaring through a conch, brought forward a cockle-shell full of salt-water, and delivered it solemnly to Amyas, who, of course, put a noble into it, and returned it after Grenville had done the same.

"Holla, Dick Admiral!" cried neptune, who was pretty far gone in liquor; "we knew thou hadst a right English heart in thee, for all thou standest there as taut as a Don who has swallowed his rapier."

"Grammercy, stop thy bellowing, fellow, and on; for thou smellest vilely of fish."

"Everything smells sweet in its right place. I'm going home."

"I thought thou wert there all along, being already half-seas over," said Cary.

"Ay, right Upsee-Dutch; and that's more than thou ever wilt be, thou 'long-shore stay-at-home. Why wast making sheep's eyes at Mistress Salterne here, while my pretty little chuck of Burrough there was playing at shove-groat with Spanish doubloons?"

"Go to the devil, sirrah!" said Cary. Neptune had touched on a sore subject; and more cheeks than Amyas Leigh's reddened at the hint.

"Amen, if Heaven so please!" and on rolled the monarch of the seas; and so the pageant ended.

The moment Amyas had an opportunity, he asked his brother Frank, somewhat peevishly, where Rose Salterne was.

"What! the mayor's daughter? With her uncle by Kilkhampton, I believe."

Now cunning Master Frank, whose daily wish was to "seek peace and ensue it," told Amyas this, because he must needs speak the truth: but he was purposed at the same time to speak as little truth as he could, for fear of accidents; and, therefore, omitted to tell his brother how that he, two days before, had entreated Rose Salterne herself to appear as the nymph of Torridge; which honor she, who had no objection either to exhibit her pretty face, to recite pretty poetry, or to be trained thereto by the cynosure of North Devon, would have assented willingly, but that her father stopped the pretty project by a peremptory countermove, and packed her off, in spite of her tears, to the said uncle on the Atlantic cliffs; after which he went up to Burrough, and laughed over the whole matter with Mrs. Leigh.

"I am but a burgher, Mrs. Leigh, and you a lady of blood; but I am too proud to let any man say that Simon Salterne threw his daughter at your son's head;—no; not if you were an empress!"

"And to speak truth, Mr. Salterne, there are young gallants enough in the country quarrelling about her pretty face every day, without making her a tourney-queen to tilt about."

Which was very true; for during the three years of Amyas's absence, Rose Salterne had grown into so beautiful a girl of eighteen, that half North Devon was mad about the "Rose of Torridge," as she was called; and there was not a young gallant for ten miles round (not to speak of her father's clerks and 'prentices, who moped about after her like so many Malvolios, and treasured up the very parings of her nails) who would not have gone to Jerusalem to win her. So that all along the vales of Torridge and of Taw, and even away to Clovelly (for young Mr. Cary was one of the sick), not a gay bachelor but was frowning on his fellows, and vying with them in the fashion of his clothes, the set of his ruffs, the harness of his horse, the carriage of his hawks, the pattern of his sword-hilt; and those were golden days for all tailors and armorers, from Exmoor to Okehampton town. But of all those foolish young lads not one would speak to the other, either out hunting, or at the archery butts, or in the tilt-yard; and my Lady Bath (who confessed that there was no use in bringing out her daughters where Rose Salterne was in the way) prophesied in her classical fashion that Rose's wedding bid fair to be a very bridal of Atalanta, and feast of the Lapithae; and poor Mr. Will Cary (who always blurted out the truth), when old Salterne once asked him angrily in Bideford Market, "What a plague business had he making sheep's eyes at his daughter?" broke out before all bystanders, "And what a plague business had you, old boy, to throw such an apple of discord into our merry meetings hereabouts? If you choose to have such a daughter, you must take the consequences, and be hanged to you." To which Mr. Salterne answered with some truth, "That she was none of his choosing, nor of Mr. Cary's neither." And so the dor being given, the belligerents parted laughing, but the war remained in statu quo; and not a week passed but, by mysterious hands, some nosegay, or languishing sonnet, was conveyed into The Rose's chamber, all which she stowed away, with the simplicity of a country girl, finding it mighty pleasant; and took all compliments quietly enough, probably because, on the authority of her mirror, she considered them no more than her due.

And now, to add to the general confusion, home was come young Amyas Leigh, more desperately in love with her than ever. For, as is the way with sailors (who after all are the truest lovers, as they are the finest fellows, God bless them, upon earth), his lonely ship-watches had been spent in imprinting on his imagination, month after month, year after year, every feature and gesture and tone of the fair lass whom he had left behind him; and that all the more intensely, because, beside his mother, he had no one else to think of, and was as pure as the day he was born, having been trained as many a brave young man was then, to look upon profligacy not as a proof of manhood, but as what the old Germans, and those Gortyneans who crowned the offender with wool, knew it to be, a cowardly and effeminate sin.

CHAPTER III

OF TWO GENTLEMEN OF WALES, AND HOW THEY HUNTED WITH THE HOUNDS, AND YET RAN WITH THE DEER

Amyas slept that night a tired and yet a troubled sleep; and his mother and Frank, as they bent over his pillow, could see that his brain was busy with many dreams.

And no wonder; for over and above all the excitement of the day, the recollection of John Oxenham had taken strange possession of his mind; and all that evening, as he sat in the bay-windowed room where he had seen him last, Amyas was recalling to himself every look and gesture of the lost adventurer, and wondering at himself for so doing, till he retired to sleep, only to renew the fancy in his dreams. At last he found himself, he knew not how, sailing westward ever, up the wake of the setting sun, in chase of a tiny sail which was John Oxenham's. Upon him was a painful sense that, unless he came up with her in time, something fearful would come to pass; but the ship would not sail. All around floated the sargasso beds, clogging her bows with their long snaky coils of weed; and still he tried to sail, and tried to fancy that he was sailing, till the sun went down and all was utter dark. And then the moon arose, and in a moment John Oxenham's ship was close aboard; her sails were torn and fluttering; the pitch was streaming from her sides; her bulwarks were rotting to decay. And what was that line of dark objects dangling along the mainyard?—A line of hanged men! And, horror of horrors, from the yard-arm close above him, John Oxenham's corpse looked down with grave-light eyes, and beckoned and pointed, as if to show him his way, and strove to speak, and could not, and pointed still, not forward, but back along their course. And when Amyas looked back, behold, behind him was the snow range of the Andes glittering in the moon, and he knew that he was in the South Seas once more, and that all America was between him and home. And still the corpse kept pointing back, and back, and looking at him with yearning eyes of agony, and lips which longed to tell some awful secret; till he sprang up, and woke with a shout of terror, and found himself lying in the little coved chamber in dear old Burrough, with the gray autumn morning already stealing in.

Feverish and excited, he tried in vain to sleep again; and after an hour's tossing, rose and dressed, and started for a bathe on his beloved old pebble ridge. As he passed his mother's door, he could not help looking in. The dim light of morning showed him the bed; but its pillow had not been pressed that night. His mother, in her long white night-dress, was kneeling at the other end of the chamber at her prie-dieu, absorbed in devotion. Gently he slipped in without a word, and knelt down at her side. She turned, smiled, passed her arm around him, and went on silently with her prayers. Why not? They were for him, and he knew it, and prayed also; and his prayers were for her, and for poor lost John Oxenham, and all his vanished crew.

At last she rose, and standing above him, parted the yellow locks from off his brow, and looked long and lovingly into his face. There was nothing to be spoken, for there was nothing to be concealed between these two souls as clear as glass. Each knew all which the other meant; each knew that its own thoughts were known. At last the mutual gaze was over; she stooped and kissed him on the brow, and was in the act to turn away, as a tear dropped on his forehead. Her little bare feet were peeping out from under her dress. He bent down and kissed them again and again; and then looking up, as if to excuse himself,—

"You have such pretty feet, mother!"

Instantly, with a woman's instinct, she had hidden them. She had been a beauty once, as I said; and though her hair was gray, and her roses had faded long ago, she was beautiful still, in all eyes which saw deeper than the mere outward red and white.

"Your dear father used to say so thirty years ago."

"And I say so still: you always were beautiful; you are beautiful now."

"What is that to you, silly boy? Will you play the lover with an old mother? Go and take your walk, and think of younger ladies, if you can find any worthy of you."

And so the son went forth, and the mother returned to her prayers.

He walked down to the pebble ridge, where the surges of the bay have defeated their own fury, by rolling up in the course of ages a rampart of gray boulder-stones, some two miles long, as cunningly curved, and smoothed, and fitted, as if the work had been done by human hands, which protects from the high tides of spring and autumn a fertile sheet of smooth, alluvial turf. Sniffing the keen salt air like a young sea-dog, he stripped and plunged into the breakers, and dived, and rolled, and tossed about the foam with stalwart arms, till he heard himself hailed from off the shore, and looking up, saw standing on the top of the rampart the tall figure of his cousin Eustace.

Amyas was half-disappointed at his coming; for, love-lorn rascal, he had been dreaming all the way thither of Rose Salterne, and had no wish for a companion who would prevent his dreaming of her all the way back. Nevertheless, not having seen Eustace for three years, it was but civil to scramble out and dress, while his cousin walked up and down upon the turf inside.

Eustace Leigh was the son of a younger brother of Leigh of Burrough, who had more or less cut himself off from his family, and indeed from his countrymen, by remaining a Papist. True, though born a Papist, he had not always been one; for, like many of the gentry, he had become a Protestant under Edward the Sixth, and then a Papist again under Mary. But, to his honor be it said, at that point he had stopped, having too much honesty to turn Protestant a second time, as hundreds did, at Elizabeth's accession. So a Papist he remained, living out of the way of the world in a great, rambling, dark house, still called "Chapel," on the Atlantic cliffs, in Moorwinstow parish, not far from Sir Richard Grenville's house of Stow. The penal laws never troubled him; for, in the first place, they never troubled any one who did not make conspiracy and rebellion an integral doctrine of his religious creed; and next, they seldom troubled even them, unless, fired with the glory of martyrdom, they bullied the long-suffering of Elizabeth and her council into giving them their deserts, and, like poor Father Southwell in after years, insisted on being hanged, whether Burleigh liked or not. Moreover, in such a no-man's-land and end-of-all-the-earth was that old house at Moorwinstow, that a dozen conspiracies might have been hatched there without any one hearing of it; and Jesuits and seminary priests skulked in and out all the year round, unquestioned though unblest; and found a sort of piquant pleasure, like naughty boys who have crept into the store-closet, in living in mysterious little dens in a lonely turret, and going up through a trap-door to celebrate mass in a secret chamber in the roof, where they were allowed by the powers that were to play as much as they chose at persecuted saints, and preach about hiding in dens and caves of the earth. For once, when the zealous parson of Moorwinstow, having discovered (what everybody knew already) the existence of "mass priests and their idolatry" at Chapel House, made formal complaint thereof to Sir Richard, and called on him, as the nearest justice of the peace, to put in force the act of the fourteenth of Elizabeth, that worthy knight only rated him soundly for a fantastical Puritan, and bade him mind his own business, if he wished not to make the place too hot for him; whereon (for the temporal authorities, happily for the peace of England, kept in those days a somewhat tight hand upon the spiritual ones) the worthy parson subsided,—for, after all, Mr. Thomas Leigh paid his tithes regularly enough,—and was content, as he expressed it, to bow his head in the house of Rimmon like Naaman of old, by eating Mr. Leigh's dinners as often as he was invited, and ignoring the vocation of old Father Francis, who sat opposite to him, dressed as a layman, and calling himself the young gentleman's pedagogue.

But the said birds of ill-omen had a very considerable lien on the conscience of poor Mr. Thomas Leigh, the father of Eustace, in the form of certain lands once belonging to the Abbey of Hartland. He more than half believed that he should be lost for holding those lands; but he did not believe it wholly, and, therefore, he did not give them up; which was the case, as poor Mary Tudor found to her sorrow, with most of her "Catholic" subjects, whose consciences, while they compelled them to return to the only safe fold of Mother Church (extra quam nulla salus), by no means compelled them to disgorge the wealth of which they had plundered that only hope of their salvation. Most of them, however, like poor Tom Leigh, felt the abbey rents burn in their purses; and, as John Bull generally does in a difficulty, compromised the matter by a second folly (as if two wrong things made one right one), and petted foreign priests, and listened, or pretended not to listen, to their plottings and their practisings; and gave up a son here, and a son there, as a sort of a sin-offering and scapegoat, to be carried off to Douay, or Rheims, or Rome, and trained as a seminary priest; in plain English, to be taught the science of villainy, on the motive of superstition. One of such hapless scapegoats, and children who had been cast into the fire to Moloch, was Eustace Leigh, whom his father had sent, giving the fruit of his body for the sin of his soul, to be made a liar of at Rheims.

And a very fair liar he had become. Not that the lad was a bad fellow at heart; but he had been chosen by the harpies at home, on account of his "peculiar vocation;" in plain English, because the wily priests had seen in him certain capacities of vague hysterical fear of the unseen (the religious sentiment, we call it now-a-days), and with them that tendency to be a rogue, which superstitious men always have. He was now a tall, handsome, light-complexioned man, with a huge upright forehead, a very small mouth, and a dry and set expression of face, which was always trying to get free, or rather to seem free, and indulge in smiles and dimples which were proper; for one ought to have Christian love, and if one had love one ought to be cheerful, and when people were cheerful they smiled; and therefore he would smile, and tried to do so; but his charity prepense looked no more alluring than malice prepense would have done; and, had he not been really a handsome fellow, many a woman who raved about his sweetness would have likened his frankness to that of a skeleton dancing in fetters, and his smiles to the grins thereof.

He had returned to England about a month before, in obedience to the proclamation which had been set forth for that purpose (and certainly not before it was needed), that, "whosoever had children, wards, etc., in the parts beyond the seas, should send in their names to the ordinary, and within four months call them home again." So Eustace was now staying with his father at Chapel, having, nevertheless, his private matters to transact on behalf of the virtuous society by whom he had been brought up; one of which private matters had brought him to Bideford the night before.

So he sat down beside Amyas on the pebbles, and looked at him all over out of the corners of his eyes very gently, as if he did not wish to hurt him, or even the flies on his back; and Amyas faced right round, and looked him full in the face with the heartiest of smiles, and held out a lion's paw, which Eustace took rapturously, and a great shaking of hands ensued; Amyas gripping with a great round fist, and a quiet quiver thereof, as much as to say, "I AM glad to see you;" and Eustace pinching hard with white, straight fingers, and sawing the air violently up and down, as much as to say, "DON'T YOU SEE how glad I am to see you?" A very different greeting from the former.

"Hold hard, old lad," said Amyas, "before you break my elbow. And where do you come from?"

"From going to and fro in the earth, and from walking up and down in it," said he, with a little smile and nod of mysterious self-importance.

"Like the devil, eh? Well, every man has his pattern. How is my uncle?"

Now, if there was one man on earth above another, of whom Eustace Leigh stood in dread, it was his cousin Amyas. In the first place, he knew Amyas could have killed him with a blow; and there are natures, who, instead of rejoicing in the strength of men of greater prowess than themselves, look at such with irritation, dread, at last, spite; expecting, perhaps, that the stronger will do to them what they feel they might have done in his place. Every one, perhaps, has the same envious, cowardly devil haunting about his heart; but the brave men, though they be very sparrows, kick him out; the cowards keep him, and foster him; and so did poor Eustace Leigh.

Next, he could not help feeling that Amyas despised him. They had not met for three years; but before Amyas went, Eustace never could argue with him, simply because Amyas treated him as beneath argument. No doubt he was often rude and unfair enough; but the whole mass of questions concerning the unseen world, which the priests had stimulated in his cousin's mind into an unhealthy fungus crop, were to Amyas simply, as he expressed it, "wind and moonshine;" and he treated his cousin as a sort of harmless lunatic, and, as they say in Devon, "half-baked." And Eustace knew it; and knew, too, that his cousin did him an injustice. "He used to undervalue me," said he to himself; "let us see whether he does not find me a match for him now." And then went off into an agony of secret contrition for his self-seeking and his forgetting that "the glory of God, and not his own exaltation," was the object of his existence.

There, dear readers, Ex pede Herculem; I cannot tire myself or you (especially in this book) with any wire-drawn soul-dissections. I have tried to hint to you two opposite sorts of men,—the one trying to be good with all his might and main, according to certain approved methods and rules, which he has got by heart, and like a weak oarsman, feeling and fingering his spiritual muscles over all day, to see if they are growing; the other not even knowing whether he is good or not, but just doing the right thing without thinking about it, as simply as a little child, because the Spirit of God is with him. If you cannot see the great gulf fixed between the two, I trust that you will discover it some day.

But in justice be it said, all this came upon Eustace, not because he was a Romanist, but because he was educated by the Jesuits. Had he been saved from them, he might have lived and died as simple and honest a gentleman as his brothers, who turned out like true Englishmen (as did all the Romish laity) to face the great Armada, and one of whom was fighting at that very minute under St. Leger in Ireland, and as brave and loyal a soldier as those Roman Catholics whose noble blood has stained every Crimean battlefield; but his fate was appointed otherwise; and the Upas-shadow which has blighted the whole Romish Church, blighted him also.

"Ah, my dearest cousin!" said Eustace, "how disappointed I was this morning at finding I had arrived just a day too late to witness your triumph! But I hastened to your home as soon as I could, and learning from your mother that I should find you here, hurried down to bid you welcome again to Devon."

"Well, old lad, it does look very natural to see you. I often used to think of you walking the deck o' nights. Uncle and the girls are all right, then? But is the old pony dead yet? And how's Dick the smith, and Nancy? Grown a fine maid by now, I warrant. 'Slid, it seems half a life that I've been away.

"And you really thought of your poor cousin? Be sure that he, too, thought of you, and offered up nightly his weak prayers for your safety (doubtless, not without avail) to those saints, to whom would that you—"

"Halt there, coz. If they are half as good fellows as you and I take them for, they'll help me without asking."

"They have helped you, Amyas."

"Maybe; I'd have done as much, I'm sure, for them, if I 'd been in their place."

"And do you not feel, then, that you owe a debt of gratitude to them; and, above all, to her, whose intercessions have, I doubt not, availed for your preservation? Her, the star of the sea, the all-compassionate guide of the mariner?"

"Humph!" said Amyas. "Here's Frank; let him answer."

And, as he spoke, up came Frank, and after due greetings, sat down beside them on the ridge.

"I say, brother, here's Eustace trying already to convert me; and telling me that I owe all my luck to the Blessed Virgin's prayers for me.

"It may be so," said Frank; "at least you owe it to the prayers of that most pure and peerless virgin by whose commands you sailed; the sweet incense of whose orisons has gone up for you daily, and for whose sake you were preserved from flood and foe, that you might spread the fame and advance the power of the spotless championess of truth, and right, and freedom,—Elizabeth, your queen."

Amyas answered this rhapsody, which would have been then both fashionable and sincere, by a loyal chuckle. Eustace smiled meekly, but answered somewhat venomously nevertheless—

"I, at least, am certain that I speak the truth, when I call my patroness a virgin undefiled."

Both the brothers' brows clouded at once. Amyas, as he lay on his back on the pebbles, said quietly to the gulls over his head—"I wonder what the Frenchman whose head I cut off at the Azores, thinks by now about all that."

"Cut off a Frenchman's head?" said Frank.

"Yes, faith; and so fleshed my maiden sword. I'll tell you. It was in some tavern; I and George Drake had gone in, and there sat this Frenchman, with his sword on the table, ready for a quarrel (I found afterwards he was a noted bully), and begins with us loudly enough about this and that; but, after awhile, by the instigation of the devil, what does he vent but a dozen slanders against her majesty's honor, one atop of the other? I was ashamed to hear them, and I should be more ashamed to repeat them."

"I have heard enough of such," said Frank. "They come mostly through lewd rascals about the French ambassador, who have been bred (God help them) among the filthy vices of that Medicean Court in which the Queen of Scots had her schooling; and can only perceive in a virtuous freedom a cloak for licentiousness like their own. Let the curs bark; Honi soit qui mal y pense is our motto, and shall be forever."

"But I didn't let the cur bark; for I took him by the ears, to show him out into the street. Whereon he got to his sword, and I to mine; and a very near chance I had of never bathing on the pebble ridge more; for the fellow did not fight with edge and buckler, like a Christian, but had some newfangled French devil's device of scryming and foining with his point, ha'ing and stamping, and tracing at me, that I expected to be full of eyelet holes ere I could close with him."

"Thank God that you are safe, then!" said Frank. "I know that play well enough, and dangerous enough it is."

"Of course you know it; but I didn't, more's the pity."

"Well, I'll teach it thee, lad, as well as Rowland Yorke himself,

"Rowland Yorke? Who's he, then?"

"A very roystering rascal, who is making good profit in London just now by teaching this very art of fence; and is as likely to have his mortal thread clipt in a tavern brawl, as thy Frenchman. But how did you escape his pinking iron?"

"How? Had it through my left arm before I could look round; and at that I got mad, and leapt upon him, and caught him by the wrist, and then had a fair side-blow; and, as fortune would have it, off tumbled his head on to the table, and there was an end of his slanders."

"So perish all her enemies!" said Frank; and Eustace, who had been trying not to listen, rose and said—

"I trust that you do not number me among them?"

"As you speak, I do, coz," said Frank. "But for your own sake, let me advise you to put faith in the true report of those who have daily experience of their mistress's excellent virtue, as they have of the sun's shining, and of the earth's bringing forth fruit, and not in the tattle of a few cowardly back-stair rogues, who wish to curry favor with the Guises. Come, we will say no more. Walk round with us by Appledore, and then home to breakfast."

But Eustace declined, having immediate business, he said, in Northam town, and then in Bideford; and so left them to lounge for another half-hour on the beach, and then walk across the smooth sheet of turf to the little white fishing village, which stands some two miles above the bar, at the meeting of the Torridge and the Taw.

Now it came to pass, that Eustace Leigh, as we have seen, told his cousins that he was going to Northam: but he did not tell them that his point was really the same as their own, namely, Appledore; and, therefore, after having satisfied his conscience by going as far as the very nearest house in Northam village, he struck away sharp to the left across the fields, repeating I know not what to the Blessed Virgin all the way; whereby he went several miles out of his road; and also, as is the wont of crooked spirits, Jesuits especially (as three centuries sufficiently testify), only outwitted himself. For his cousins going merrily, like honest men, along the straight road across the turf, arrived in Appledore, opposite the little "Mariner's Rest" Inn, just in time to see what Eustace had taken so much trouble to hide from them, namely, four of Mr. Thomas Leigh's horses standing at the door, held by his groom, saddles and mail-bags on back, and mounting three of them, Eustace Leigh and two strange gentlemen.

"There's one lie already this morning," growled Amyas; "he told us he was going to Northam."

"And we do not know that he has not been there," blandly suggested Frank.

"Why, you are as bad a Jesuit as he, to help him out with such a fetch."

"He may have changed his mind."

"Bless your pure imagination, my sweet boy," said Amyas, laying his great hand on Frank's head, and mimicking his mother's manner. "I say, dear Frank, let's step into this shop and buy a penny-worth of whipcord."

"What do you want with whipcord, man?"

"To spin my top, to be sure."

"Top? how long hast had a top?"

"I'll buy one, then, and save my conscience; but the upshot of this sport I must see. Why may not I have an excuse ready made as well as Master Eustace?"

So saying, he pulled Frank into the little shop, unobserved by the party at the inn-door.

"What strange cattle has he been importing now? Look at that three-legged fellow, trying to get aloft on the wrong side. How he claws at his horse's ribs, like a cat scratching an elder stem!"

The three-legged man was a tall, meek-looking person, who had bedizened himself with gorgeous garments, a great feather, and a sword so long and broad, that it differed little in size from the very thin and stiff shanks between which it wandered uncomfortably.

"Young David in Saul's weapons," said Frank. "He had better not go in them, for he certainly has not proved them."

"Look, if his third leg is not turned into a tail! Why does not some one in charity haul in half-a-yard of his belt for him?"

It was too true; the sword, after being kicked out three or four times from its uncomfortable post between his legs, had returned unconquered; and the hilt getting a little too far back by reason of the too great length of the belt, the weapon took up its post triumphantly behind, standing out point in air, a tail confest, amid the tittering of the ostlers, and the cheers of the sailors.

At last the poor man, by dint of a chair, was mounted safely, while his fellow-stranger, a burly, coarse-looking man, equally gay, and rather more handy, made so fierce a rush at his saddle, that, like "vaulting ambition who o'erleaps his selle," he "fell on t'other side:" or would have fallen, had he not been brought up short by the shoulders of the ostler at his off-stirrup. In which shock off came hat and feather.

"Pardie, the bulldog-faced one is a fighting man. Dost see, Frank? he has had his head broken."

"That scar came not, my son, but by a pair of most Catholic and apostolic scissors. My gentle buzzard, that is a priest's tonsure."

"Hang the dog! O, that the sailors may but see it, and put him over the quay head. I've a half mind to go and do it myself."

"My dear Amyas," said Frank, laying two fingers on his arm, "these men, whosoever they are, are the guests of our uncle, and therefore the guests of our family. Ham gained little by publishing Noah's shame; neither shall we, by publishing our uncle's."

"Murrain on you, old Franky, you never let a man speak his mind, and shame the devil."

"I have lived long enough in courts, old Amyas, without a murrain on you, to have found out, first, that it is not so easy to shame the devil; and secondly, that it is better to outwit him; and the only way to do that, sweet chuck, is very often not to speak your mind at all. We will go down and visit them at Chapel in a day or two, and see if we cannot serve these reynards as the badger did the fox, when he found him in his hole, and could not get him out by evil savors."

"How then?"

"Stuck a sweet nosegay in the door, which turned reynard's stomach at once; and so overcame evil with good."

"Well, thou art too good for this world, that's certain; so we will go home to breakfast. Those rogues are out of sight by now."

Nevertheless, Amyas was not proof against the temptation of going over to the inn-door, and asking who were the gentlemen who went with Mr. Leigh.

"Gentlemen of Wales," said the ostler, "who came last night in a pinnace from Milford-haven, and their names, Mr. Morgan Evans and Mr. Evan Morgans."

"Mr. Judas Iscariot and Mr. Iscariot Judas," said Amyas between his teeth, and then observed aloud, that the Welsh gentlemen seemed rather poor horsemen.

"So I said to Mr. Leigh's groom, your worship. But he says that those parts be so uncommon rough and mountainous, that the poor gentlemen, you see, being enforced to hunt on foot, have no such opportunities as young gentlemen hereabout, like your worship; whom God preserve, and send a virtuous lady, and one worthy of you."

"Thou hast a villainously glib tongue, fellow!" said Amyas, who was thoroughly out of humor;

"and a sneaking down visage too, when I come to look at you. I doubt but you are a Papist too, I do!"

"Well, sir! and what if I am! I trust I don't break the queen's laws by that. If I don't attend Northam church, I pay my month's shilling for the use of the poor, as the act directs; and beyond that, neither you nor any man dare demand of me."

"Dare! act directs! You rascally lawyer, you! and whence does an ostler like you get your shilling to pay withal? Answer me." The examinate found it so difficult to answer the question, that he suddenly became afflicted with deafness.

"Do you hear?" roared Amyas, catching at him with his lion's paw.

"Yes, missus; anon, anon, missus!" quoth he to an imaginary landlady inside, and twisting under Amyas's hand like an eel, vanished into the house, while Frank got the hot-headed youth away.

"What a plague is one to do, then? That fellow was a Papist spy!"

"Of course he was!" said Frank.

"Then, what is one to do, if the whole country is full of them?"

"Not to make fools of ourselves about them, and so leave them to make fools of themselves."

"That's all very fine: but—well, I shall remember the villain's face if I see him again."

"There is no harm in that," said Frank.

"Glad you think so."

"Don't quarrel with me, Amyas, the first day."

"Quarrel with thee, my darling old fellow! I had sooner kiss the dust off thy feet, if I were worthy of it. So now away home; my inside cries cupboard."

In the meanwhile Messrs. Evans and Morgans were riding away, as fast as the rough by-lanes would let them, along the fresh coast of the bay, steering carefully clear of Northam town on the one hand, and on the other, of Portledge, where dwelt that most Protestant justice of the peace, Mr. Coffin. And it was well for them that neither Amyas Leigh, nor indeed any other loyal Englishman, was by when they entered, as they shortly did, the lonely woods which stretch along the southern wall of the bay. For there Eustace Leigh pulled up short; and both he and his groom, leaping from their horses, knelt down humbly in the wet grass, and implored the blessing of the two valiant gentlemen of Wales, who, having graciously bestowed it with three fingers apiece, became thenceforth no longer Morgan Evans and Evan Morgans, Welshmen and gentlemen; but Father Parsons and Father Gampian, Jesuits, and gentlemen in no sense in which that word is applied in this book.

After a few minutes, the party were again in motion, ambling steadily and cautiously along the high table-land, towards Moorwinstow in the west; while beneath them on the right, at the mouth of rich-wooded glens, opened vistas of the bright blue bay, and beyond it the sandhills of Braunton, and the ragged rocks of Morte; while far away to the north and west the lonely isle of Lundy hung like a soft gray cloud.

But they were not destined to reach their point as peaceably as they could have wished. For just as they got opposite Clovelly dike, the huge old Roman encampment which stands about midway in their journey, they heard a halloo from the valley below, answered by a fainter one far ahead. At which, like a couple of rogues (as indeed they were), Father Campian and Father Parsons looked at each other, and then both stared round at the wild, desolate, open pasture (for the country was then all unenclosed), and the great dark furze-grown banks above their heads; and Campian remarked gently to Parsons, that this was a very dreary spot, and likely enough for robbers.

"A likelier spot for us, Father," said Eustace, punning. "The old Romans knew what they were about when they put their legions up aloft here to overlook land and sea for miles away; and we may thank them some day for their leavings. The banks are all sound; there is plenty of good water inside; and" (added he in Latin), "in case our Spanish friends—you understand?"

"Pauca verba, my son!" said Campian: but as he spoke, up from the ditch close beside him, as if rising out of the earth, burst through the furze-bushes an armed cavalier.

"Pardon, gentlemen!" shouted he, as the Jesuit and his horse recoiled against the groom. "Stand, for your lives!"

"Mater caelorum!" moaned Campian; while Parsons, who, as all the world knows, was a blustering bully enough (at least with his tongue), asked: What a murrain right had he to stop honest folks on the queen's highway? confirming the same with a mighty oath, which he set down as peccatum veniale, on account of the sudden necessity; nay, indeed fraus pia, as proper to support the character of that valiant gentleman of Wales, Mr. Evan Morgans. But the horseman, taking no notice of his hint, dashed across the nose of Eustace Leigh's horse, with a "Hillo, old lad! where ridest so early?" and peering down for a moment into the ruts of the narrow track-way, struck spurs into his horse, shouting, "A fresh slot! right away for Hartland! Forward, gentlemen all! follow, follow, follow!"

"Who is this roysterer?" asked Parsons, loftily.

"Will Cary, of Clovelly; an awful heretic: and here come more behind."

And as he spoke four or five more mounted gallants plunged in and out of the great dikes, and thundered on behind the party; whose horses, quite understanding what game was up, burst into full gallop, neighing and squealing; and in another minute the hapless Jesuits were hurling along over moor and moss after a "hart of grease."

Parsons, who, though a vulgar bully, was no coward, supported the character of Mr. Evan Morgans well enough; and he would have really enjoyed himself, had he not been in agonies of fear lest those precious saddle-bags in front of him should break from their lashings, and rolling to the earth, expose to the hoofs of heretic horses, perhaps to the gaze of heretic eyes, such a cargo of bulls, dispensations, secret correspondences, seditious tracts, and so forth, that at the very thought of their being seen, his head felt loose upon his shoulders. But the future martyr behind him, Mr. Morgan Evans, gave himself up at once to abject despair, and as he bumped and rolled along, sought vainly for comfort in professional ejaculations in the Latin tongue.

"Mater intemerata! Eripe me e—Ugh! I am down! Adhaesit pavimento venter!—No! I am not! El dilectum tuum e potestate canis—Ah! Audisti me inter cornua unicornium! Put this, too, down in—ugh!—thy account in favor of my poor—oh, sharpness of this saddle! Oh, whither, barbarous islanders!"

Now riding on his quarter, not in the rough track-way like a cockney, but through the soft heather like a sportsman, was a very gallant knight whom we all know well by this time, Richard Grenville by name; who had made Mr. Cary and the rest his guests the night before, and then ridden out with them at five o'clock that morning, after the wholesome early ways of the time, to rouse a well-known stag in the glens at Buckish, by help of Mr. Coffin's hounds from Portledge. Who being as good a Latiner as Campian's self, and overhearing both the scraps of psalm and the "barbarous islanders," pushed his horse alongside of Mr. Eustace Leigh, and at the first check said, with two low bows towards the two strangers—

"I hope Mr. Leigh will do me the honor of introducing me to his guests. I should be sorry, and Mr. Cary also, that any gentle strangers should become neighbors of ours, even for a day, without our knowing who they are who honor our western Thule with a visit; and showing them ourselves all due requital for the compliment of their presence."

After which, the only thing which poor Eustace could do (especially as it was spoken loud enough for all bystanders), was to introduce in due form Mr. Evan Morgans and Mr. Morgan Evans, who, hearing the name, and, what was worse, seeing the terrible face with its quiet searching eye, felt like a brace of partridge-poults cowering in the stubble, with a hawk hanging ten feet over their heads.

"Gentlemen," said Sir Richard blandly, cap in hand, "I fear that your mails must have been somewhat in your way in this unexpected gallop. If you will permit my groom, who is behind, to disencumber you of them and carry them to Chapel, you will both confer an honor on me, and be enabled yourselves to see the mort more pleasantly."

A twinkle of fun, in spite of all his efforts, played about good Sir Richard's eye as he gave this searching hint. The two Welsh gentlemen stammered out clumsy thanks; and pleading great haste and fatigue from a long journey, contrived to fall to the rear and vanish with their guides, as soon as the slot had been recovered.

"Will!" said Sir Richard, pushing alongside of young Cary.

"Your worship?"

"Jesuits, Will!"

"May the father of lies fly away with them over the nearest cliff!"

"He will not do that while this Irish trouble is about. Those fellows are come to practise here for Saunders and Desmond."

"Perhaps they have a consecrated banner in their bag, the scoundrels! Shall I and young Coffin on and stop them? Hard if the honest men may not rob the thieves once in a way."

"No; give the devil rope, and he will hang himself. Keep thy tongue at home, and thine eyes too, Will."

"How then?"

"Let Clovelly beach be watched night and day like any mousehole. No one can land round Harty Point with these south-westers. Stop every fellow who has the ghost of an Irish brogue, come he in or go he out, and send him over to me."

"Some one should guard Bude-haven, sir."

"Leave that to me. Now then, forward, gentlemen all, or the stag will take the sea at the Abbey."

And on they crashed down the Hartland glens, through the oak-scrub and the great crown-ferns; and the baying of the slow-hound and the tantaras of the horn died away farther and fainter toward the blue Atlantic, while the conspirators, with lightened hearts, pricked fast across Bursdon upon their evil errand. But Eustace Leigh had other thoughts and other cares than the safety of his father's two mysterious guests, important as that was in his eyes; for he was one of the many who had drunk in sweet poison (though in his case it could hardly be called sweet) from the magic glances of the Rose of Torridge. He had seen her in the town, and for the first time in his life fallen utterly in love; and now that she had come down close to his father's house, he looked on her as a lamb fallen unawares into the jaws of the greedy wolf, which he felt himself to be. For Eustace's love had little or nothing of chivalry, self-sacrifice, or purity in it; those were virtues which were not taught at Rheims. Careful as the Jesuits were over the practical morality of their pupils, this severe restraint had little effect in producing real habits of self-control. What little Eustace had learnt of women from them, was as base and vulgar as the rest of their teaching. What could it be else, if instilled by men educated in the schools of Italy and France, in the age which produced the foul novels of Cinthio and Bandello, and compelled Rabelais in order to escape the rack and stake, to hide the light of his great wisdom, not beneath a bushel, but beneath a dunghill; the age in which the Romish Church had made marriage a legalized tyranny, and the laity, by a natural and pardonable revulsion, had exalted adultery into a virtue and a science? That all love was lust; that all women had their price; that profligacy, though an ecclesiastical sin, was so pardonable, if not necessary, as to be hardly a moral sin, were notions which Eustace must needs have gathered from the hints of his preceptors; for their written works bear to this day fullest and foulest testimony that such was their opinion; and that their conception of the relation of the sexes was really not a whit higher than that of the profligate laity who confessed to them. He longed to marry Rose Salterne, with a wild selfish fury; but only that he might be able to claim her as his own property, and keep all others from her. Of her as a co-equal and ennobling helpmate; as one in whose honor, glory, growth of heart and soul, his own were inextricably wrapt up, he had never dreamed. Marriage would prevent God from being angry with that, with which otherwise He might be angry; and therefore the sanction of the Church was the more "probable and safe" course. But as yet his suit was in very embryo. He could not even tell whether Rose knew of his love; and he wasted miserable hours in maddening thoughts, and tost all night upon his sleepless bed, and rose next morning fierce and pale, to invent fresh excuses for going over to her uncle's house, and lingering about the fruit which he dared not snatch.

CHAPTER IV: THE TWO WAYS OF BEING CROST IN LOVE

And what all this while has become of the fair breaker of so many hearts, to whom I have not yet even introduced my readers?

She was sitting in the little farm-house beside the mill, buried in the green depths of the valley of Combe, half-way between Stow and Chapel, sulking as much as her sweet nature would let her, at being thus shut out from all the grand doings at Bideford, and forced to keep a Martinmas Lent in that far western glen. So lonely was she, in fact, that though she regarded Eustace Leigh with somewhat of aversion, and (being a good Protestant) with a great deal of suspicion, she could not find it in her heart to avoid a chat with him whenever he came down to the farm and to its mill, which he contrived to do, on I know not what would-be errand, almost every day. Her uncle and aunt at first looked stiff enough at these visits, and the latter took care always to make a third in every conversation; but still Mr. Leigh was a gentleman's son, and it would not do to be rude to a neighboring squire and a good customer; and Rose was the rich man's daughter and they poor cousins, so it would not do either to quarrel with her; and besides, the pretty maid, half by wilfulness, and half by her sweet winning tricks, generally contrived to get her own way wheresoever she went; and she herself had been wise enough to beg her aunt never to leave them alone,—for she "could not a-bear the sight of Mr. Eustace, only she must have some one to talk with down here." On which her aunt considered, that she herself was but a simple country-woman; and that townsfolks' ways of course must be very different from hers; and that people knew their own business best; and so forth, and let things go on their own way. Eustace, in the meanwhile, who knew well that the difference in creed between him and Rose was likely to be the very hardest obstacle in the way of his love, took care to keep his private opinions well in the background; and instead of trying to convert the folk at the mill, daily bought milk or flour from them, and gave it away to the old women in Moorwinstow (who agreed that after all, for a Papist, he was a godly young man enough); and at last, having taken counsel with Campian and Parsons on certain political plots then on foot, came with them to the conclusion that they would all three go to church the next Sunday. Where Messrs. Evan Morgans and Morgan Evans, having crammed up the rubrics beforehand, behaved themselves in a most orthodox and unexceptionable manner; as did also poor Eustace, to the great wonder of all good folks, and then went home flattering himself that he had taken in parson, clerk, and people; not knowing in his simple unsimplicity, and cunning foolishness, that each good wife in the parish was saying to the other, "He turned Protestant? The devil turned monk! He's only after Mistress Salterne, the young hypocrite."

But if the two Jesuits found it expedient, for the holy cause in which they were embarked, to reconcile themselves outwardly to the powers that were, they were none the less busy in private in plotting their overthrow.

Ever since April last they had been playing at hide-and-seek through the length and breadth of England, and now they were only lying quiet till expected news from Ireland should give them their cue, and a great "rising of the West" should sweep from her throne that stiff-necked, persecuting, excommunicate, reprobate, illegitimate, and profligate usurper, who falsely called herself the Queen of England.

For they had as stoutly persuaded themselves in those days, as they have in these (with a real Baconian contempt of the results of sensible experience), that the heart of England was really with them, and that the British nation was on the point of returning to the bosom of the Catholic Church, and giving up Elizabeth to be led in chains to the feet of the rightful Lord of Creation, the Old Man of the Seven Hills. And this fair hope, which has been skipping just in front of them for centuries, always a step farther off, like the place where the rainbow touches the ground, they used to announce at times, in language which terrified old Mr. Leigh. One day, indeed, as Eustace entered his father's private room, after his usual visit to the mill, he could hear voices high in dispute; Parsons as usual, blustering; Mr. Leigh peevishly deprecating, and Campian, who was really the sweetest-natured of men, trying to pour oil on the troubled waters. Whereat Eustace (for the good of the cause, of course) stopped outside and listened.

"My excellent sir," said Mr. Leigh, "does not your very presence here show how I am affected toward the holy cause of the Catholic faith? But I cannot in the meanwhile forget that I am an Englishman."

"And what is England?" said Parsons: "A heretic and schismatic Babylon, whereof it is written, 'Come out of her, my people, lest you be partaker of her plagues.' Yea, what is a country? An arbitrary division of territory by the princes of this world, who are naught, and come to naught. They are created by the people's will; their existence depends on the sanction of him to whom all power is given in heaven and earth—our Holy Father the Pope. Take away the latter, and what is a king?—the people who have made him may unmake him."

"My dear sir, recollect that I have sworn allegiance to Queen Elizabeth!"

"Yes, sir, you have, sir; and, as I have shown at large in my writings, you were absolved from that allegiance from the moment that the bull of Pius the Fifth declared her a heretic and excommunicate, and thereby to have forfeited all dominion whatsoever. I tell you, sir, what I thought you should have known already, that since the year 1569, England has had no queen, no magistrates, no laws, no lawful authority whatsoever; and that to own allegiance to any English magistrate, sir, or to plead in an English court of law, is to disobey the apostolic precept, 'How dare you go to law before the unbelievers?' I tell you, sir, rebellion is now not merely permitted, it is a duty."

"Take care, sir; for God's sake, take care!" said Mr. Leigh. "Right or wrong, I cannot have such language used in my house. For the sake of my wife and children, I cannot!"

"My dear brother Parsons, deal more gently with the flock," interposed Campian. "Your opinion, though probable, as I well know, in the eyes of most of our order, is hardly safe enough here; the opposite is at least so safe that Mr. Leigh may well excuse his conscience for accepting it. After all, are we not sent hither to proclaim this very thing, and to relieve the souls of good Catholics from a burden which has seemed to them too heavy?"

"Yes," said Parsons, half-sulkily, "to allow all Balaams who will to sacrifice to Baal, while they call themselves by the name of the Lord."

"My dear brother, have I not often reminded you that Naaman was allowed to bow himself in the house of Rimmon? And can we therefore complain of the office to which the Holy Father has appointed us, to declare to such as Mr. Leigh his especial grace, by which the bull of Pius the Fifth (on whose soul God have mercy!) shall henceforth bind the queen and the heretics only; but in no ways the Catholics, at least as long as the present tyranny prevents the pious purposes of the bull?"

"Be it so, sir; be it so. Only observe this, Mr. Leigh, that our brother Campian confesses this to be a tyranny. Observe, sir, that the bull does still bind the so-called queen, and that she and her magistrates are still none the less usurpers, nonentities, and shadows of a shade. And observe this, sir, that when that which is lawful is excused to the weak, it remains no less lawful to the strong. The seven thousand who had not bowed the knee to Baal did not slay his priests; but Elijah did, and won to himself a good reward. And if the rest of the children of Israel sinned not in not slaying Eglon, yet Ehud's deed was none the less justified by all laws human and divine."

"For Heaven's sake, do not talk so, sir! or I must leave the room. What have I to do with Ehud and Eglon, and slaughters, and tyrannies? Our queen is a very good queen, if Heaven would but grant her repentance, and turn her to the true faith. I have never been troubled about religion, nor any one else that I know of in the West country."

"You forget Mr. Trudgeon of Launceston, father, and poor Father Mayne," interposed Eustace, who had by this time slipped in; and Campian added softly—

"Yes, your West of England also has been honored by its martyrs, as well as my London by the precious blood of Story."

"What, young malapert?" cried poor Leigh, facing round upon his son, glad to find any one on whom he might vent his ill-humor; "are you too against me, with a murrain on you? And pray, what the devil brought Cuthbert Mayne to the gallows, and turned Mr. Trudgeon (he was always a foolish hot-head) out of house and home, but just such treasonable talk as Mr. Parsons must needs hold in my house, to make a beggar of me and my children, as he will before he has done."

"The Blessed Virgin forbid!" said Campian.

"The Blessed Virgin forbid? But you must help her to forbid it, Mr. Campian. We should never have had the law of 1571, against bulls, and Agnus Deis, and blessed grains, if the Pope's bull of 1569 had not made them matter of treason, by preventing a poor creature's saving his soul in the true Church without putting his neck into a halter by denying the queen's authority."

"What, sir?" almost roared Parsons, "do you dare to speak evil of the edicts of the Vicar of Christ?"

"I? No. I didn't. Who says I did? All I meant was, I am sure—Mr. Campian, you are a reasonable man, speak for me."

"Mr. Leigh only meant, I am sure, that the Holy Father's prudent intentions have been so far defeated by the perverseness and invincible misunderstanding of the heretics, that that which was in itself meant for the good of the oppressed English Catholics has been perverted to their harm."

"And thus, reverend sir," said Eustace, glad to get into his father's good graces again, "my father attaches blame, not to the Pope—Heaven forbid!—but to the pravity of his enemies."

"And it is for this very reason," said Campian, "that we have brought with us the present merciful explanation of the bull."

"I'll tell you what, gentlemen," said Mr. Leigh, who, like other weak men, grew in valor as his opponent seemed inclined to make peace, "I don't think the declaration was needed. After the new law of 1571 was made, it was never put in force till Mayne and Trudgeon made fools of themselves, and that was full six years. There were a few offenders, they say, who were brought up and admonished, and let go; but even that did not happen down here, and need not happen now, unless you put my son here (for you shall never put me, I warrant you) upon some deed which had better be left alone, and so bring us all to shame."

"Your son, sir, if not openly vowed to God, has, I hope, a due sense of that inward vocation which we have seen in him, and reverences his spiritual fathers too well to listen to the temptations of his earthly father."

"What, sir, will you teach my son to disobey me?"

"Your son is ours also, sir. This is strange language in one who owes a debt to the Church, which it was charitably fancied he meant to pay in the person of his child."

These last words touched poor Mr. Leigh in a sore point, and breaking all bounds, he swore roundly at Parsons, who stood foaming with rage.

"A plague upon you, sir, and a black assizes for you, for you will come to the gallows yet! Do you mean to taunt me in my own house with that Hartland land? You had better go back and ask those who sent you where the dispensation to hold the land is, which they promised to get me years ago, and have gone on putting me off, till they have got my money, and my son, and my conscience, and I vow before all the saints, seem now to want my head over and above. God help me!"—and the poor man's eyes fairly filled with tears.

Now was Eustace's turn to be roused; for, after all, he was an Englishman and a gentleman; and he said kindly enough, but firmly—

"Courage, my dearest father. Remember that I am still your son, and not a Jesuit yet; and whether I ever become one, I promise you, will depend mainly on the treatment which you meet with at the hands of these reverend gentlemen, for whom I, as having brought them hither, must consider myself as surety to you."

If a powder-barrel had exploded in the Jesuits' faces, they could not have been more amazed. Campian looked blank at Parsons, and Parsons at Campian; till the stouter-hearted of the two, recovering his breath at last—

"Sir! do you know, sir, the curse pronounced on those who, after putting their hand to the plough, look back?"

Eustace was one of those impulsive men, with a lack of moral courage, who dare raise the devil, but never dare fight him after he has been raised; and he now tried to pass off his speech by winking and making signs in the direction of his father, as much as to say that he was only trying to quiet the old man's fears. But Campian was too frightened, Parsons too angry, to take his hints: and he had to carry his part through.

"All I read is, Father Parsons, that such are not fit for the kingdom of God; of which high honor

I have for some time past felt myself unworthy. I have much doubt just now as to my vocation; and in the meanwhile have not forgotten that I am a citizen of a free country." And so saying, he took his father's arm, and walked out.

His last words had hit the Jesuits hard. They had put the poor cobweb-spinners in mind of the humiliating fact, which they have had thrust on them daily from that time till now, and yet have never learnt the lesson, that all their scholastic cunning, plotting, intriguing, bulls, pardons, indulgences, and the rest of it, are, on this side the Channel, a mere enchanter's cloud-castle and Fata Morgana, which vanishes into empty air by one touch of that magic wand, the constable's staff. "A citizen of a free country!"—there was the rub; and they looked at each other in more utter perplexity than ever. At last Parsons spoke.

"There's a woman in the wind. I'll lay my life on it. I saw him blush up crimson yesterday when his mother asked him whether some Rose Salterne or other was still in the neighborhood."

"A woman! Well, the spirit may be willing, though the flesh be weak. We will inquire into this. The youth may do us good service as a layman; and if anything should happen to his elder brother (whom the saints protect!) he is heir to some wealth. In the meanwhile, our dear brother Parsons will perhaps see the expediency of altering our tactics somewhat while we are here."

And thereupon a long conversation began between the two, who had been sent together, after the wise method of their order, in obedience to the precept, "Two are better than one," in order that Campian might restrain Parsons' vehemence, and Parsons spur on Campian's gentleness, and so each act as the supplement of the other, and each also, it must be confessed, gave advice pretty nearly contradictory to his fellow's if occasion should require, "without the danger," as their writers have it, "of seeming changeable and inconsistent."

The upshot of this conversation was, that in a day or two (during which time Mr. Leigh and Eustace also had made the amende honorable, and matters went smoothly enough) Father Campian asked Father Francis, the household chaplain, to allow him, as an especial favor, to hear Eustace's usual confession on the ensuing Friday.

Poor Father Francis dared not refuse so great a man; and assented with an inward groan, knowing well that the intent was to worm out some family secrets, whereby his power would be diminished, and the Jesuits' increased. For the regular priesthood and the Jesuits throughout England were toward each other in a state of armed neutrality, which wanted but little at any moment to become open war, as it did in James the First's time, when those meek missionaries, by their gentle moral tortures, literally hunted to death the poor Popish bishop of Hippopotamus (that is to say, London) for the time being.

However, Campian heard Eustace's confession; and by putting to him such questions as may be easily conceived by those who know anything about the confessional, discovered satisfactorily enough, that he was what Campian would have called "in love:" though I should question much the propriety of the term as applied to any facts which poor prurient Campian discovered, or indeed knew how to discover, seeing that a swine has no eye for pearls. But he had found out enough: he smiled, and set to work next vigorously to discover who the lady might be.

If he had frankly said to Eustace, "I feel for you; and if your desires are reasonable, or lawful, or possible, I will help you with all my heart and soul," he might have had the young man's secret heart, and saved himself an hour's trouble; but, of course, he took instinctively the crooked and suspicious method, expected to find the case the worst possible,—as a man was bound to do who had been trained to take the lowest possible view of human nature, and to consider the basest motives as the mainspring of all human action,—and began his moral torture accordingly by a series of delicate questions, which poor Eustace dodged in every possible way, though he knew that the good father was too cunning for him, and that he must give in at last. Nevertheless, like a rabbit who runs squealing round and round before the weasel, into whose jaws it knows that it must jump at last by force of fascination, he parried and parried, and pretended to be stupid, and surprised, and honorably scrupulous, and even angry; while every question as to her being married or single, Catholic or heretic, English or foreign, brought his tormentor a step nearer the goal. At last, when Campian, finding the business not such a very bad one, had asked something about her worldly wealth, Eustace saw a door of escape and sprang at it.

"Even if she be a heretic, she is heiress to one of the wealthiest merchants in Devon."

"Ah!" said Campian, thoughtfully. "And she is but eighteen, you say?"

"Only eighteen."

"Ah! well, my son, there is time. She may be reconciled to the Church: or you may change."

"I shall die first."

"Ah, poor lad! Well; she may be reconciled, and her wealth may be of use to the cause of Heaven."

"And it shall be of use. Only absolve me, and let me be at peace. Let me have but her," he cried piteously. "I do not want her wealth,—not I! Let me have but her, and that but for one year, one month, one day!—and all the rest—money, fame, talents, yea, my life itself, hers if it be needed—are at the service of Holy Church. Ay, I shall glory in showing my devotion by some special sacrifice,—some desperate deed. Prove me now, and see what there is I will not do!"

And so Eustace was absolved; after which Campian added,—

"This is indeed well, my son: for there is a thing to be done now, but it may be at the risk of life."

"Prove me!" cried Eustace, impatiently.

"Here is a letter which was brought me last night; no matter from whence; you can understand it better than I, and I longed to have shown it you, but that I feared my son had become—"

"You feared wrongly, then, my dear Father Campian."

So Campian translated to him the cipher of the letter.

"This to Evan Morgans, gentleman, at Mr. Leigh's house in Moorwinstow, Devonshire. News may be had by one who will go to the shore of Clovelly, any evening after the 25th of November, at dead low tide, and there watch for a boat, rowed by one with a red beard, and a Portugal by his speech. If he be asked, 'How many?' he will answer, 'Eight hundred and one.' Take his letters and read them. If the shore be watched, let him who comes show a light three times in a safe place under the cliff above the town; below is dangerous landing. Farewell, and expect great things!"

"I will go," said Eustace; "to-morrow is the 25th, and I know a sure and easy place. Your friend seems to know these shores well."

"Ah! what is it we do not know?" said Campian, with a mysterious smile. "And now?"

"And now, to prove to you how I trust to you, you shall come with me, and see this—the lady of whom I spoke, and judge for yourself whether my fault is not a venial one."

"Ah, my son, have I not absolved you already? What have I to do with fair faces? Nevertheless, I will come, both to show you that I trust you, and it may be to help towards reclaiming a heretic, and saving a lost soul: who knows?"

So the two set out together; and, as it was appointed, they had just got to the top of the hill between Chapel and Stow mill, when up the lane came none other than Mistress Rose Salterne herself, in all the glories of a new scarlet hood, from under which her large dark languid eyes gleamed soft lightnings through poor Eustace's heart and marrow. Up to them she tripped on delicate ankles and tiny feet, tall, lithe, and graceful, a true West-country lass; and as she passed them with a pretty blush and courtesy, even Campian looked back at the fair innocent creature, whose long dark curls, after the then country fashion, rolled down from beneath the hood below her waist, entangling the soul of Eustace Leigh within their glossy nets.

"There!" whispered he, trembling from head to foot. "Can you excuse me now?"

"I had excused you long ago;" said the kindhearted father. "Alas, that so much fair red and white should have been created only as a feast for worms!"

"A feast for gods, you mean!" cried Eustace, on whose common sense the naive absurdity of the last speech struck keenly; and then, as if to escape the scolding which he deserved for his heathenry—

"Will you let me return for a moment? I will follow you: let me go!"

Campian saw that it was of no use to say no, and nodded. Eustace darted from his side, and running across a field, met Rose full at the next turn of the road.

She started, and gave a pretty little shriek.

"Mr. Leigh! I thought you had gone forward."

"I came back to speak to you, Rose—Mistress Salterne, I mean."

"To me?"

"To you I must speak, tell you all, or die!" And he pressed up close to her. She shrank back, somewhat frightened.

"Do not stir; do not go, I implore you! Rose, only hear me!" And fiercely and passionately seizing her by the hand, he poured out the whole story of his love, heaping her with every fantastic epithet of admiration which he could devise.

There was little, perhaps, of all his words which Rose had not heard many a time before; but there was a quiver in his voice, and a fire in his eye, from which she shrank by instinct.

"Let me go!" she said; "you are too rough, sir!"

"Ay!" he said, seizing now both her hands, "rougher, perhaps, than the gay gallants of Bideford, who serenade you, and write sonnets to you, and send you posies. Rougher, but more loving, Rose! Do not turn away! I shall die if you take your eyes off me! Tell me,—tell me, now here—this moment—before we part—if I may love you!"

"Go away!" she answered, struggling, and bursting into tears. "This is too rude. If I am but a merchant's daughter. I am God's child. Remember that I am alone. Leave me; go! or I will call for help!"

Eustace had heard or read somewhere that such expressions in a woman's mouth were mere façons de parler, and on the whole signs that she had no objection to be alone, and did not intend to call for help; and he only grasped her hands the more fiercely, and looked into her face with keen and hungry eyes; but she was in earnest, nevertheless, and a loud shriek made him aware that, if he wished to save his own good name, he must go: but there was one question, for an answer to which he would risk his very life.

"Yes, proud woman! I thought so! Some one of those gay gallants has been beforehand with me. Tell me who—"

But she broke from him, and passed him, and fled down the lane.

"Mark it!" cried he, after her. "You shall rue the day when you despised Eustace Leigh! Mark it, proud beauty!" And he turned back to join Campian, who stood in some trepidation.

"You have not hurt the maiden, my son? I thought I heard a scream."

"Hurt her! No. Would God that she were dead, nevertheless, and I by her! Say no more to me, father. We will home." Even Campian knew enough of the world to guess what had happened, and they both hurried home in silence.

And so Eustace Leigh played his move, and lost it.

Poor little Rose, having run nearly to Chapel, stopped for very shame, and walked quietly by the cottages which stood opposite the gate, and then turned up the lane towards Moorwinstow village, whither she was bound. But on second thoughts, she felt herself so "red and flustered," that she was afraid of going into the village, for fear (as she said to herself) of making people talk, and so, turning into a by-path, struck away toward the cliffs, to cool her blushes in the sea-breeze. And there finding a quiet grassy nook beneath the crest of the rocks, she sat down on the turf, and fell into a great meditation.

Rose Salterne was a thorough specimen of a West-coast maiden, full of passionate impulsive affections, and wild dreamy imaginations, a fit subject, as the North-Devon women are still, for all romantic and gentle superstitions. Left early without mother's care, she had fed her fancy upon the legends and ballads of her native land, till she believed—what did she not believe?—of mermaids and pixies, charms and witches, dreams and omens, and all that world of magic in which most of the countrywomen, and countrymen too, believed firmly enough but twenty years ago. Then her father's house was seldom without some merchant, or sea-captain from foreign parts, who, like Othello, had his tales of—

And,—

All which tales, she, like Desdemona, devoured with greedy ears, whenever she could "the house affairs with haste despatch." And when these failed, there was still boundless store of wonders open to her in old romances which were then to be found in every English house of the better class. The Legend of King Arthur, Florice and Blancheflour, Sir Ysumbras, Sir Guy of

Warwick, Palamon and Arcite, and the Romaunt of the Rose, were with her text-books and canonical authorities. And lucky it was, perhaps, for her that Sidney's Arcadia was still in petto, or Mr. Frank (who had already seen the first book or two in manuscript, and extolled it above all books past, present, or to come) would have surely brought a copy down for Rose, and thereby have turned her poor little flighty brains upside down forever. And with her head full of these, it was no wonder if she had likened herself of late more than once to some of those peerless princesses of old, for whose fair hand paladins and kaisers thundered against each other in tilted field; and perhaps she would not have been sorry (provided, of course, no one was killed) if duels, and passages of arms in honor of her, as her father reasonably dreaded, had actually taken place.

For Rose was not only well aware that she was wooed, but found the said wooing (and little shame to her) a very pleasant process. Not that she had any wish to break hearts: she did not break her heart for any of her admirers, and why should they break theirs for her? They were all very charming, each in his way (the gentlemen, at least; for she had long since learnt to turn up her nose at merchants and burghers); but one of them was not so very much better than the other.

Of course, Mr. Frank Leigh was the most charming; but then, as a courtier and squire of dames, he had never given her a sign of real love, nothing but sonnets and compliments, and there was no trusting such things from a gallant, who was said (though, by the by, most scandalously) to have a lady love at Milan, and another at Vienna, and half-a-dozen in the Court, and half-a-dozen more in the city.

And very charming was Mr. William Cary, with his quips and his jests, and his galliards and lavoltas; over and above his rich inheritance; but then, charming also Mr. Coffin of Portledge, though he were a little proud and stately; but which of the two should she choose? It would be very pleasant to be mistress of Clovelly Court; but just as pleasant to find herself lady of Portledge, where the Coffins had lived ever since Noah's flood (if, indeed, they had not merely returned thither after that temporary displacement), and to bring her wealth into a family which was as proud of its antiquity as any nobleman in Devon, and might have made a fourth to that famous trio of Devonshire Cs, of which it is written,—

And Mr. Hugh Fortescue, too—people said that he was certain to become a great soldier—perhaps as great as his brother Arthur—and that would be pleasant enough, too, though he was but the younger son of an innumerable family: but then, so was Amyas Leigh. Ah, poor Amyas! Her girl's fancy for him had vanished, or rather, perhaps, it was very much what it always had been, only that four or five more girl's fancies beside it had entered in, and kept it in due subjection. But still, she could not help thinking a good deal about him, and his voyage, and the reports of his great strength, and beauty, and valor, which had already reached her in that out-of-the-way corner; and though she was not in the least in love with him, she could not help hoping that he had at least (to put her pretty little thought in the mildest shape) not altogether forgotten her; and was hungering, too, with all her fancy, to give him no peace till he had told her all the wonderful things which he had seen and done in this ever-memorable voyage. So that, altogether, it was no wonder, if in her last night's dream the figure of Amyas had been even more forward and troublesome than that of Frank or the rest.

But, moreover, another figure had been forward and troublesome enough in last night's sleep-world; and forward and troublesome enough, too, now in to-day's waking-world, namely, Eustace, the rejected. How strange that she should have dreamt of him the night before! and dreamt, too, of his fighting with Mr. Frank and Mr. Amyas! It must be a warning—see, she had met him the very next day in this strange way; so the first half of her dream had come true; and after what had past, she only had to breathe a whisper, and the second part of the dream would come true also. If she wished for a passage of arms in her own honor, she could easily enough compass one: not that she would do it for worlds! And after all, though Mr. Eustace had been very rude and naughty, yet still it was not his own fault; he could not help being in love with her. And—and, in short, the poor little maid felt herself one of the most important personages on earth, with all the cares (or hearts) of the country in her keeping, and as much perplexed with matters of weight as ever was any Cleophila, or Dianeme, Fiordispina or Flourdeluce, in verse run tame, or prose run mad.

Poor little Rose! Had she but had a mother! But she was to learn her lesson, such as it was, in another school. She was too shy (too proud perhaps) to tell her aunt her mighty troubles; but a counsellor she must have; and after sitting with her head in her hands, for half-an-hour or more, she arose suddenly, and started off along the cliffs towards Marsland. She would go and see Lucy Passmore, the white witch; Lucy knew everything; Lucy would tell her what to do; perhaps even whom to marry.

Lucy was a fat, jolly woman of fifty, with little pig-eyes, which twinkled like sparks of fire, and eyebrows which sloped upwards and outwards, like those of a satyr, as if she had been (as indeed she had) all her life looking out of the corners of her eyes. Her qualifications as white witch were boundless cunning, equally boundless good nature, considerable knowledge of human weaknesses, some mesmeric power, some skill in "yarbs," as she called her simples, a firm faith in the virtue of her own incantations, and the faculty of holding her tongue. By dint of these she contrived to gain a fair share of money, and also (which she liked even better) of power, among the simple folk for many miles round. If a child was scalded, a tooth ached, a piece of silver was stolen, a heifer shrew-struck, a pig bewitched, a young damsel crost in love, Lucy was called in, and Lucy found a remedy, especially for the latter complaint. Now and then she found herself on ticklish ground, for the kind-heartedness which compelled her to help all distressed damsels out of a scrape, sometimes compelled her also to help them into one; whereon enraged fathers called Lucy ugly names, and threatened to send her into Exeter gaol for a witch, and she smiled quietly, and hinted that if she were "like some that were ready to return evil for evil, such talk as that would bring no blessing on them that spoke it;" which being translated into plain English, meant, "If you trouble me, I will overlook (i. e. fascinate) you, and then your pigs will die, your horses stray, your cream turn sour, your barns be fired, your son have St. Vitus's dance, your daughter fits, and so on, woe on woe, till you are very probably starved to death in a ditch, by virtue of this terrible little eye of mine, at which, in spite of all your swearing and bullying, you know you are now shaking in your shoes for fear. So you had much better hold your tongue, give me a drink of cider, and leave ill alone, lest you make it worse."

Not that Lucy ever proceeded to any such fearful extremities. On the contrary, her boast, and her belief too, was, that she was sent into the world to make poor souls as happy as she could, by lawful means, of course, if possible, but if not—why, unlawful ones were better than none; for she "couldn't a-bear to see the poor creatures taking on; she was too, too tender-hearted." And so she was, to every one but her husband, a tall, simple-hearted rabbit-faced man, a good deal older than herself. Fully agreeing with Sir Richard Grenville's great axiom, that he who cannot obey cannot rule, Lucy had been for the last five-and-twenty years training him pretty smartly to obey her, with the intention, it is to be charitably hoped, of letting him rule her in turn when his lesson was perfected. He bore his honors, however, meekly enough, having a boundless respect for his wife's wisdom, and a firm belief in her supernatural powers, and let her go her own way and earn her own money, while he got a little more in a truly pastoral method (not extinct yet along those lonely cliffs), by feeding a herd of some dozen donkeys and twenty goats. The donkeys fetched, at each low-tide, white shell-sand which was to be sold for manure to the neighboring farmers; the goats furnished milk and "kiddy-pies;" and when there was neither milking nor sand-carrying to be done, old Will Passmore just sat under a sunny rock and watched the buck-goats rattle their horns together, thinking about nothing at all, and taking very good care all the while neither to inquire nor to see who came in and out of his little cottage in the glen.

The prophetess, when Rose approached her oracular cave, was seated on a tripod in front of the fire, distilling strong waters out of penny-royal. But no sooner did her distinguished visitor appear at the hatch, than the still was left to take care of itself, and a clean apron and mutch having been slipt on, Lucy welcomed Rose with endless courtesies, and—"Bless my dear soul alive, who ever would have thought to see the Rose of Torridge to my poor little place!"

Rose sat down: and then? How to begin was more than she knew, and she stayed silent a full five minutes, looking earnestly at the point of her shoe, till Lucy, who was an adept in such cases, thought it best to proceed to business at once, and save Rose the delicate operation of opening the ball herself; and so, in her own way, half fawning, half familiar—

"Well, my dear young lady, and what is it I can do for ye? For I guess you want a bit of old Lucy's help, eh? Though I'm most mazed to see ye here, surely. I should have supposed that pretty face could manage they sort of matters for itself. Eh?"

Rose, thus bluntly charged, confessed at once, and with many blushes and hesitations, made her soon understand that what she wanted was "To have her fortune told."

"Eh? Oh! I see. The pretty face has managed it a bit too well already, eh? Tu many o' mun, pure fellows? Well, 'tain't every mayden has her pick and choose, like some I know of, as be blest in love by stars above. So you hain't made up your mind, then?"

Rose shook her head.

"Ah—well," she went on, in a half-bantering tone. "Not so asy, is it, then? One's gude for one thing, and one for another, eh? One has the blood, and another the money."

And so the "cunning woman" (as she truly was), talking half to herself, ran over all the names which she thought likely, peering at Rose all the while out of the corners of her foxy bright eyes, while Rose stirred the peat ashes steadfastly with the point of her little shoe, half angry, half ashamed, half frightened, to find that "the cunning woman" had guessed so well both her suitors and her thoughts about them, and tried to look unconcerned at each name as it came out.

"Well, well," said Lucy, who took nothing by her move, simply because there was nothing to take; "think over it—think over it, my dear life; and if you did set your mind on any one—why, then—then maybe I might help you to a sight of him."

"A sight of him?"

"His sperrit, dear life, his sperrit only, I mane. I 'udn't have no keeping company in my house, no, not for gowld untowld, I 'udn't; but the sperrit of mun—to see whether mun would be true or not, you'd like to know that, now, 'udn't you, my darling?"

Rose sighed, and stirred the ashes about vehemently.

"I must first know who it is to be. If you could show me that—now—"

"Oh, I can show ye that, tu, I can. Ben there's a way to 't, a sure way; but 'tis mortal cold for the time o' year, you zee."

"But what is it, then?" said Rose, who had in her heart been longing for something of that very kind, and had half made up her mind to ask for a charm.

"Why, you'm not afraid to goo into the say by night for a minute, are you? And to-morrow night would serve, too; 't will be just low tide to midnight."

"If you would come with me perhaps—"

"I'll come, I'll come, and stand within call, to be sure. Only do ye mind this, dear soul alive, not to goo telling a crumb about mun, noo, not for the world, or yu'll see naught at all, indeed, now. And beside, there's a noxious business grow'd up against me up to Chapel there; and I hear tell how Mr. Leigh saith I shall to Exeter gaol for a witch—did ye ever hear the likes?—because his groom Jan saith I overlooked mun—the Papist dog! And now never he nor th' owld Father Francis goo by me without a spetting, and saying of their Ayes and Malificas—I do know what their Rooman Latin do mane, zo well as ever they, I du!—and a making o' their charms and incantations to their saints and idols! They be mortal feared of witches, they Papists, and mortal hard on 'em, even on a pure body like me, that doth a bit in the white way; 'case why you see, dear life," said she, with one of her humorous twinkles, "tu to a trade do never agree. Do ye try my bit of a charm, now; do ye!"

Rose could not resist the temptation; and between them both the charm was agreed on, and the next night was fixed for its trial, on the payment of certain current coins of the realm (for Lucy, of course, must live by her trade); and slipping a tester into the dame's hand as earnest, Rose went away home, and got there in safety.

But in the meanwhile, at the very hour that Eustace had been prosecuting his suit in the lane at Moorwinstow, a very different scene was being enacted in Mrs. Leigh's room at Burrough.

For the night before, Amyas, as he was going to bed, heard his brother Frank in the next room tune his lute, and then begin to sing. And both their windows being open, and only a thin partition between the chambers, Amyas's admiring ears came in for every word of the following canzonet, sung in that delicate and mellow tenor voice for which Frank was famed among all fair ladies:—

At which the simple sailor sighed, and longed that he could write such neat verses, and sing them so sweetly. How he would besiege the ear of Rose Salterne with amorous ditties! But still, he could not be everything; and if he had the bone and muscle of the family, it was but fair that Frank should have the brains and voice; and, after all, he was bone of his bone and flesh of his flesh, and it was just the same as if he himself could do all the fine things which Frank could do; for as long as one of the family won honor, what matter which of them it was? Whereon he shouted through the wall, "Good night, old song-thrush; I suppose I need not pay the musicians."

"What, awake?" answered Frank. "Come in here, and lull me to sleep with a sea-song."

So Amyas went in, and found Frank laid on the outside of his bed not yet undrest.

"I am a bad sleeper," said he; "I spend more time, I fear, in burning the midnight oil than prudent men should. Come and be my jongleur, my minnesinger, and tell me about Andes, and cannibals, and the ice-regions, and the fire-regions, and the paradises of the West."

So Amyas sat down, and told: but somehow, every story which he tried to tell came round, by crooked paths, yet sure, to none other point than Rose Salterne, and how he thought of her here and thought of her there, and how he wondered what she would say if she had seen him in this adventure, and how he longed to have had her with him to show her that glorious sight, till Frank let him have his own way, and then out came the whole story of the simple fellow's daily and hourly devotion to her, through those three long years of world-wide wanderings.

"And oh, Frank, I could hardly think of anything but her in the church the other day, God forgive me! and it did seem so hard for her to be the only face which I did not see—and have not seen her yet, either."

"So I thought, dear lad," said Frank, with one of his sweetest smiles; "and tried to get her father to let her impersonate the nymph of Torridge."

"Did you, you dear kind fellow? That would have been too delicious."

"Just so, too delicious; wherefore, I suppose, it was ordained not to be, that which was being delicious enough."

"And is she as pretty as ever?"

"Ten times as pretty, dear lad, as half the young fellows round have discovered. If you mean to win her and wear her (and God grant you may fare no worse!) you will have rivals enough to get rid of."

"Humph!" said Amyas, "I hope I shall not have to make short work with some of them."

"I hope not," said Frank, laughing. "Now go to bed, and to-morrow morning give your sword to mother to keep, lest you should be tempted to draw it on any of her majesty's lieges."

"No fear of that, Frank; I am no swash-buckler, thank God; but if any one gets in my way, I'll serve him as the mastiff did the terrier, and just drop him over the quay into the river, to cool himself, or my name's not Amyas."

And the giant swung himself laughing out of the room, and slept all night like a seal, not without dreams, of course, of Rose Salterne.

The next morning, according to his wont, he went into his mother's room, whom he was sure to find up and at her prayers; for he liked to say his prayers, too, by her side, as he used to do when he was a little boy. It seemed so homelike, he said, after three years' knocking up and down in no-man's land. But coming gently to the door, for fear of disturbing her, and entering unperceived, beheld a sight which stopped him short.

Mrs. Leigh was sitting in her chair, with her face bowed fondly down upon the head of his brother Frank, who knelt before her, his face buried in her lap. Amyas could see that his whole form was quivering with stifled emotion. Their mother was just finishing the last words of a well-known text,—"for my sake, and the Gospel's, shall receive a hundred-fold in this present life, fathers, and mothers, and brothers, and sisters."

"But not a wife!" interrupted Frank, with a voice stifled with sobs; "that was too precious a gift for even Him to promise to those who gave up a first love for His sake!"

"And yet," said he, after a moment's silence, "has He not heaped me with blessings enough already, that I must repine and rage at His refusing me one more, even though that one be—No, mother! I am your son, and God's; and you shall know it, even though Amyas never does!" And he looked up with his clear blue eyes and white forehead; and his face was as the face of an angel.

Both of them saw that Amyas was present, and started and blushed. His mother motioned him away with her eyes, and he went quietly out, as one stunned. Why had his name been mentioned?

Love, cunning love, told him all at once. This was the meaning of last night's canzonet! This was why its words had seemed to fit his own heart so well! His brother was his rival. And he had been telling him all his love last night. What a stupid brute he was! How it must have made poor Frank wince! And then Frank had listened so kindly; even bid him God speed in his suit. What a gentleman old Frank was, to be sure! No wonder the queen was so fond of him, and all the Court ladies!—Why, if it came to that, what wonder if Rose Salterne should be fond of him too? Hey-day! "That would be a pretty fish to find in my net when I come to haul it!" quoth Amyas to himself, as he paced the garden; and clutching desperately hold of his locks with both hands, as if to hold his poor confused head on its shoulders, he strode and tramped up and down the shell-paved garden walks for a full half hour, till Frank's voice (as cheerful as ever, though he more than suspected all) called him.

"Come in to breakfast, lad; and stop grinding and creaking upon those miserable limpets, before thou hast set every tooth in my head on edge!"

Amyas, whether by dint of holding his head straight, or by higher means, had got the thoughts of the said head straight enough by this time; and in he came, and fell to upon the broiled fish and strong ale, with a sort of fury, as determined to do his duty to the utmost in all matters that day, and therefore, of course, in that most important matter of bodily sustenance; while his mother and Frank looked at him, not without anxiety and even terror, doubting what turn his fancy might have taken in so new a case; at last—

"My dear Amyas, you will really heat your blood with all that strong ale! Remember, those who drink beer, think beer."

"Then they think right good thoughts, mother. And in the meanwhile, those who drink water, think water. Eh, old Frank? and here's your health."

"And clouds are water," said his mother, somewhat reassured by his genuine good humor; "and so are rainbows; and clouds are angels' thrones, and rainbows the sign of God's peace on earth."

Amyas understood the hint, and laughed. "Then I'll pledge Frank out of the next ditch, if it please you and him. But first—I say—he must hearken to a parable; a manner mystery, miracle play, I have got in my head, like what they have at Easter, to the town-hall. Now then, hearken, madam, and I and Frank will act." And up rose Amyas, and shoved back his chair, and put on a solemn face.

Mrs. Leigh looked up, trembling; and Frank, he scarce knew why, rose.

"No; you pitch again. You are King David, and sit still upon your throne. David was a great singer, you know, and a player on the viols; and ruddy, too, and of a fair countenance; so that will fit. Now, then, mother, don't look so frightened. I am not going to play Goliath, for all my cubits; I am to present Nathan the prophet. Now, David, hearken, for I have a message unto thee, O King!

"There were two men in one city, one rich, and the other poor: and the rich man had many flocks and herds, and all the fine ladies in Whitehall to court if he liked; and the poor man had nothing but—"

And in spite of his broad honest smile, Amyas's deep voice began to tremble and choke.

Frank sprang up, and burst into tears: "Oh! Amyas, my brother, my brother! stop! I cannot endure this. Oh, God! was it not enough to have entangled myself in this fatal fancy, but over and above, I must meet the shame of my brother's discovering it?"

"What shame, then, I'd like to know?" said Amyas, recovering himself. "Look here, brother Frank! I've thought it all over in the garden; and I was an ass and a braggart for talking to you as I did last night. Of course you love her! Everybody must; and I was a fool for not recollecting that; and if you love her, your taste and mine agree, and what can be better? I think you are a sensible fellow for loving her, and you think me one. And as for who has her, why, you're the eldest; and first come first served is the rule, and best to keep to it. Besides, brother Frank, though I'm no scholar, yet I'm not so blind but that I tell the difference between you and me; and of course your chance against mine, for a hundred to one; and I am not going to be fool enough to row against wind and tide too. I'm good enough for her, I hope; but if I am, you are better, and the good dog may run, but it's the best that takes the hare; and so I have nothing more to do with the matter at all; and if you marry her, why, it will set the old house on its legs again, and that's the first thing to be thought of, and you may just as well do it as I, and better too. Not but that it's a plague, a horrible plague!" went on Amyas, with a ludicrously doleful visage; "but so are other things too, by the dozen; it's all in the day's work, as the huntsman said when the lion ate him. One would never get through the furze-croft if one stopped to pull out the prickles. The pig didn't scramble out of the ditch by squeaking; and the less said the sooner mended; nobody was sent into the world only to suck honey-pots. What must be must, man is but dust; if you can't get crumb, you must fain eat crust. So I'll go and join the army in Ireland, and get it out of my head, for cannon balls fright away love as well as poverty does; and that's all I've got to say."

Wherewith Amyas sat down, and returned to the beer; while Mrs. Leigh wept tears of joy.

"Amyas! Amyas!" said Frank; "you must not throw away the hopes of years, and for me, too! Oh, how just was your parable! Ah! mother mine! to what use is all my scholarship and my philosophy, when this dear simple sailor-lad outdoes me at the first trial of courtesy!"

"My children, my children, which of you shall I love best? Which of you is the more noble? I thanked God this morning for having given me one such son; but to have found that I possess two!" And Mrs. Leigh laid her head on the table, and buried her face in her hands, while the generous battle went on.

"But, dearest Amyas!—"

"But, Frank! if you don't hold your tongue, I must go forth. It was quite trouble enough to make up one's mind, without having you afterwards trying to unmake it again."

"Amyas! if you give her up to me, God do so to me, and more also, if I do not hereby give her up to you!"

"He had done it already—this morning!" said Mrs. Leigh, looking up through her tears. "He renounced her forever on his knees before me! only he is too noble to tell you so."

"The more reason I should copy him," said Amyas, setting his lips, and trying to look desperately determined, and then suddenly jumping up, he leaped upon Frank, and throwing his arms round his neck, sobbed out, "There, there, now! For God's sake, let us forget all, and think about our mother, and the old house, and how we may win her honor before we die! and that will be enough to keep our hands full, without fretting about this woman and that.—What an ass I have been for years! instead of learning my calling, dreaming about her, and don't know at this minute whether she cares more for me than she does for her father's 'prentices!"

"Oh, Amyas! every word of yours puts me to fresh shame! Will you believe that I know as little of her likings as you do?"

"Don't tell me that, and play the devil's game by putting fresh hopes into me, when I am trying to kick them out. I won't believe it. If she is not a fool, she must love you; and if she don't, why, be hanged if she is worth loving!"

"My dearest Amyas! I must ask you too to make no more such speeches to me. All those thoughts I have forsworn."

"Only this morning; so there is time to catch them again before they are gone too far."

"Only this morning," said Frank, with a quiet smile: "but centuries have passed since then."

"Centuries? I don't see many gray hairs yet."

"I should not have been surprised if you had, though," answered Frank, in so sad and meaning a tone that Amyas could only answer—

"Well, you are an angel!"

"You, at least, are something even more to the purpose, for you are a man!"

And both spoke truth, and so the battle ended; and Frank went to his books, while Amyas, who must needs be doing, if he was not to dream, started off to the dockyard to potter about a new ship of Sir Richard's, and forget his woes, in the capacity of Sir Oracle among the sailors. And so he had played his move for Rose, even as Eustace had, and lost her: but not as Eustace had.

CHAPTER V: CLOVELLY COURT IN THE OLDEN TIME

The next morning Amyas Leigh was not to be found. Not that he had gone out to drown himself in despair, or even to bemoan himself "down by the Torridge side." He had simply ridden off, Frank found, to Sir Richard Grenville at Stow: his mother at once divined the truth, that he was gone to try for a post in the Irish army, and sent off Frank after him to bring him home again, and make him at least reconsider himself.

So Frank took horse and rode thereon ten miles or more: and then, as there were no inns on the road in those days, or indeed in these, and he had some ten miles more of hilly road before him, he turned down the hill towards Clovelly Court, to obtain, after the hospitable humane fashion of those days, good entertainment for man and horse from Mr. Cary the squire.

And when he walked self-invited, like the loud-shouting Menelaus, into the long dark wainscoted hall of the court, the first object he beheld was the mighty form of Amyas, who, seated at the long table, was alternately burying his face in a pasty, and the pasty in his face, his sorrows having, as it seemed, only sharpened his appetite, while young Will Cary, kneeling on the opposite bench, with his elbows on the table, was in that graceful attitude laying down the law fiercely to him in a low voice.

"Hillo! lad," cried Amyas; "come hither and deliver me out of the hands of this fire-eater, who I verily believe will kill me, if I do not let him kill some one else."

"Ah! Mr. Frank," said Will Cary, who, like all other young gentlemen of these parts, held Frank in high honor, and considered him a very oracle and cynosure of fashion and chivalry, "welcome here: I was just longing for you, too; I wanted your advice on half-a-dozen matters. Sit down, and eat. There is the ale."

"None so early, thank you."

"Ah no!" said Amyas, burying his head in the tankard, and then mimicking Frank, "avoid strong ale o' mornings. It heats the blood, thickens the animal spirits, and obfuscates the cerebrum with frenetical and lymphatic idols, which cloud the quintessential light of the pure reason. Eh? young Plato, young Daniel, come hither to judgment! And yet, though I cannot see through the bottom of the tankard already, I can see plain enough still to see this, that Will shall not fight."

"Shall I not, eh? who says that? Mr. Frank, I appeal to you, now; only hear."

"We are in the judgment-seat," said Frank, settling to the pasty. "Proceed, appellant."

"Well, I was telling Amyas, that Tom Coffin, of Portledge; I will stand him no longer."

"Let him be, then," said Amyas; "he could stand very well by himself, when I saw him last."

"Plague on you, hold your tongue. Has he any right to look at me as he does, whenever I pass him?"

"That depends on how he looks; a cat may look at a king, provided she don't take him for a mouse."

"Oh, I know how he looks, and what he means too, and he shall stop, or I will stop him. And the other day, when I spoke of Rose Salterne"—"Ah!" groaned Frank, "Ate's apple again!"—

"(never mind what I said) he burst out laughing in my face; and is not that a fair quarrel? And what is more, I know that he wrote a sonnet, and sent it to her to Stow by a market woman. What right has he to write sonnets when I can't? It's not fair play, Mr. Frank, or I am a Jew, and a Spaniard, and a Papist; it's not!" And Will smote the table till the plates danced again.

"My dear knight of the burning pestle, I have a plan, a device, a disentanglement, according to most approved rules of chivalry. Let us fix a day, and summon by tuck of drum all young gentlemen under the age of thirty, dwelling within fifteen miles of the habitation of that peerless Oriana."

"And all 'prentice-boys too," cried Amyas, out of the pasty.

"And all 'prentice-boys. The bold lads shall fight first, with good quarterstaves, in Bideford Market, till all heads are broken; and the head which is not broken, let the back belonging to it pay the penalty of the noble member's cowardice. After which grand tournament, to which that of Tottenham shall be but a flea-bite and a batrachomyomachy—"

"Confound you, and your long words, sir," said poor Will, "I know you are flouting me."

"Pazienza, Signor Cavaliere; that which is to come is no flouting, but bloody and warlike earnest. For afterwards all the young gentlemen shall adjourn into a convenient field, sand, or bog—which last will be better, as no man will be able to run away, if he be up to his knees in soft peat: and there stripping to our shirts, with rapiers of equal length and keenest temper, each shall slay his man, catch who catch can, and the conquerors fight again, like a most valiant main of gamecocks as we are, till all be dead, and out of their woes; after which the survivor, bewailing before heaven and earth the cruelty of our Fair Oriana, and the slaughter which her basiliscine eyes have caused, shall fall gracefully upon his sword, and so end the woes of this our lovelorn generation. Placetne Domini? as they used to ask in the Senate at Oxford."

"Really," said Cary, "this is too bad."

"So is, pardon me, your fighting Mr. Coffin with anything longer than a bodkin."

"Bodkins are too short for such fierce Bobadils," said Amyas; "they would close in so near, that we should have them falling to fisticuffs after the first bout."

"Then let them fight with squirts across the market-place; for by heaven and the queen's laws, they shall fight with nothing else."

"My dear Mr. Cary," went on Frank, suddenly changing his bantering tone to one of the most winning sweetness, "do not fancy that I cannot feel for you, or that I, as well as you, have not known the stings of love and the bitterer stings of jealousy. But oh, Mr. Cary, does it not seem to you an awful thing to waste selfishly upon your own quarrel that divine wrath which, as Plato says, is the very root of all virtues, and which has been given you, like all else which you have, that you may spend it in the service of her whom all bad souls fear, and all virtuous souls adore,—our peerless queen? Who dares, while she rules England, call his sword or his courage his own, or any one's but hers? Are there no Spaniards to conquer, no wild Irish to deliver from their oppressors, that two gentlemen of Devon can find no better place to flesh their blades than in each other's valiant and honorable hearts?"

"By heaven!" cried Amyas, "Frank speaks like a book; and for me, I do think that Christian gentlemen may leave love quarrels to bulls and rams."

"And that the heir of Clovelly," said Frank, smiling, "may find more noble examples to copy than the stags in his own deer-park."

"Well," said Will, penitently, "you are a great scholar, Mr. Frank, and you speak like one; but gentlemen must fight sometimes, or where would be their honor?"

"I speak," said Frank, a little proudly, "not merely as a scholar, but as a gentleman, and one who has fought ere now, and to whom it has happened, Mr. Cary, to kill his man (on whose soul may God have mercy); but it is my pride to remember that I have never yet fought in my own quarrel, and my trust in God that I never shall. For as there is nothing more noble and blessed than to fight in behalf of those whom we love, so to fight in our own private behalf is a thing not to be allowed to a Christian man, unless refusal imports utter loss of life or honor; and even then, it may be (though I would not lay a burden on any man's conscience), it is better not to resist evil, but to overcome it with good."

"And I can tell you, Will," said Amyas, "I am not troubled with fear of ghosts; but when I cut off the Frenchman's head, I said to myself, 'If that braggart had been slandering me instead of her gracious majesty, I should expect to see that head lying on my pillow every time I went to bed at night.'"

"God forbid!" said Will, with a shudder. "But what shall I do? for to the market tomorrow I will go, if it were choke-full of Coffins, and a ghost in each coffin of the lot."

"Leave the matter to me," said Amyas. "I have my device, as well as scholar Frank here; and if there be, as I suppose there must be, a quarrel in the market to-morrow, see if I do not—"

"Well, you are two good fellows," said Will. "Let us have another tankard in."

"And drink the health of Mr. Coffin, and all gallant lads of the North," said Frank; "and now to my business. I have to take this runaway youth here home to his mother; and if he will not go quietly, I have orders to carry him across my saddle."

"I hope your nag has a strong back, then," said Amyas; "but I must go on and see Sir Richard, Frank. It is all very well to jest as we have been doing, but my mind is made up."

"Stop," said Cary. "You must stay here tonight; first, for good fellowship's sake; and next, because I want the advice of our Phoenix here, our oracle, our paragon. There, Mr. Frank, can you construe that for me? Speak low, though, gentlemen both; there comes my father; you had better give me the letter again. Well, father, whence this morning?"

"Eh, company here? Young men, you are always welcome, and such as you. Would there were more of your sort in these dirty times! How is your good mother, Frank, eh? Where have I been, Will? Round the house-farm, to look at the beeves. That sheeted heifer of Prowse's is all wrong; her coat stares like a hedgepig's. Tell Jewell to go up and bring her in before night. And then up the forty acres; sprang two coveys, and picked a leash out of them. The Irish hawk flies as wild as any haggard still, and will never make a bird. I had to hand her to Tom, and take the little peregrine. Give me a Clovelly hawk against the world, after all; and—heigh ho, I am very hungry! Half-past twelve, and dinner not served? What, Master Amyas, spoiling your appetite with strong ale? Better have tried sack, lad; have some now with me."

And the worthy old gentleman, having finished his oration, settled himself on a great bench inside the chimney, and put his hawk on a perch over his head, while his cockers coiled themselves up close to the warm peat-ashes, and his son set to work to pull off his father's boots, amid sundry warnings to take care of his corns.

"Come, Master Amyas, a pint of white wine and sugar, and a bit of a shoeing-horn to it ere we dine. Some pickled prawns, now, or a rasher off the coals, to whet you?"

"Thank you," quoth Amyas; "but I have drunk a mort of outlandish liquors, better and worse, in the last three years, and yet never found aught to come up to good ale, which needs neither shoeing-horn before nor after, but takes care of itself, and of all honest stomachs too, I think."

"You speak like a book, boy," said old Cary; "and after all, what a plague comes of these newfangled hot wines, and aqua vitaes, which have come in since the wars, but maddening of the brains, and fever of the blood?"

"I fear we have not seen the end of that yet," said Frank. "My friends write me from the Netherlands that our men are falling into a swinish trick of swilling like the Hollanders. Heaven grant that they may not bring home the fashion with them."

"A man must drink, they say, or die of the ague, in those vile swamps," said Amyas. "When they get home here, they will not need it."

"Heaven grant it," said Frank; "I should be sorry to see Devonshire a drunken county; and there are many of our men out there with Mr. Champernoun."

"Ah," said Cary, "there, as in Ireland, we are proving her majesty's saying true, that Devonshire is her right hand, and the young children thereof like the arrows in the hand of the giant."

"They may well be," said his son, "when some of them are giants themselves, like my tall school-fellow opposite."

"He will be up and doing again presently, I'll warrant him," said old Cary.

"And that I shall," quoth Amyas. "I have been devising brave deeds; and see in the distance enchanters to be bound, dragons choked, empires conquered, though not in Holland."

"You do?" asked Will, a little sharply; for he had had a half suspicion that more was meant than met the ear.

"Yes," said Amyas, turning off his jest again, "I go to what Raleigh calls the Land of the Nymphs. Another month, I hope, will see me abroad in Ireland."

"Abroad? Call it rather at home," said old Cary; "for it is full of Devon men from end to end, and you will be among friends all day long. George Bourchier from Tawstock has the army now in Munster, and Warham St. Leger is marshal; George Carew is with Lord Grey of Wilton (Poor Peter Carew was killed at Glendalough); and after the defeat last year, when that villain Desmond cut off Herbert and Price, the companies were made up with six hundred Devon men, and Arthur Fortescue at their head; so that the old county holds her head as proudly in the Land of Ire as she does in the Low Countries and the Spanish Main."

"And where," asked Amyas, "is Davils of Marsland, who used to teach me how to catch trout, when I was staying down at Stow? He is in Ireland, too, is he not?"

"Ah, my lad," said Mr. Cary, "that is a sad story. I thought all England had known it."

"You forget, sir, I am a stranger. Surely he is not dead?"

"Murdered foully, lad! Murdered like a dog, and by the man whom he had treated as his son, and who pretended, the false knave! to call him father."

"His blood is avenged?" said Amyas, fiercely.

"No, by heaven, not yet! Stay, don't cry out again. I am getting old—I must tell my story my own way. It was last July,—was it not, Will?—Over comes to Ireland Saunders, one of those Jesuit foxes, as the Pope's legate, with money and bulls, and a banner hallowed by the Pope, and the devil knows what beside; and with him James Fitzmaurice, the same fellow who had sworn on his knees to Perrott, in the church at Kilmallock, to be a true liegeman to Queen Elizabeth, and confirmed it by all his saints, and such a world of his Irish howling, that Perrott told me he was fain to stop his own ears. Well, he had been practising with the King of France, but got nothing but laughter for his pains, and so went over to the Most Catholic King, and promises him to join Ireland to Spain, and set up Popery again, and what not. And he, I suppose, thinking it better that Ireland should belong to him than to the Pope's bastard, fits him out, and sends him off on such another errand as Stukely's,—though I will say, for the honor of Devon, if Stukely lived like a fool, he died like an honest man."

"Sir Thomas Stukely dead too?" said Amyas.

"Wait a while, lad, and you shall have that tragedy afterwards. Well, where was I? Oh, Fitzmaurice and the Jesuits land at Smerwick, with three ships, choose a place for a fort, bless it with their holy water, and their moppings and their scourings, and the rest of it, to purify it from the stain of heretic dominion; but in the meanwhile one of the Courtenays,—a Courtenay of Haccombe, was it?—or a Courtenay of Boconnock? Silence, Will, I shall have it in a minute—yes, a Courtenay of Haccombe it was, lying at anchor near by, in a ship of war of his, cuts out the three ships, and cuts off the Dons from the sea. John and James Desmond, with some small rabble, go over to the Spaniards. Earl Desmond will not join them, but will not fight them, and stands by to take the winning side; and then in comes poor Davils, sent down by the Lord Deputy to charge Desmond and his brothers, in the queen's name, to assault the Spaniards. Folks say it was rash of his lordship: but I say, what could be better done? Every one knows that there never was a stouter or shrewder soldier than Davils; and the young Desmonds, I have heard him say many a time, used to look on him as their father. But he found out what it was to trust Englishmen turned Irish. Well, the Desmonds found out on a sudden that the Dons were such desperate Paladins, that it was madness to meddle, though they were five to one; and poor Davils, seeing that there was no fight in them, goes back for help, and sleeps that night at some place called Tralee. Arthur Carter of Bideford, St. Leger's lieutenant, as stout an old soldier as Davils himself, sleeps in the same bed with him; the lacquey-boy, who is now with Sir Richard at Stow, on the floor at their feet. But in the dead of night, who should come in but James Desmond, sword in hand, with a dozen of his ruffians at his heels, each with his glib over his ugly face, and his skene in his hand. Davils springs up in bed, and asks but this, 'What is the matter, my son?' whereon the treacherous villain, without giving him time to say a prayer, strikes at him, naked as he was, crying, 'Thou shalt be my father no longer, nor I thy son! Thou shalt die!' and at that all the rest fall on him. The poor little lad (so he says) leaps up to cover his master with his naked body, gets three or four stabs of skenes, and so falls for dead; with his master and Captain Carter, who were dead indeed—God reward them! After that the ruffians ransacked the house, till they had murdered every Englishman in it, the lacquey-boy only excepted, who crawled out, wounded as he was, through a window; while Desmond, if you will believe it, went back, up to his elbows in blood, and vaunted his deeds to the Spaniards, and asked them—'There! Will you take that as a pledge that I am faithful to you?' And that, my lad, was the end of Henry Davils, and will be of all who trust to the faith of wild savages."

"I would go a hundred miles to see that Desmond hanged!" said Amyas, while great tears ran down his face. "Poor Mr. Davils! And now, what is the story of Sir Thomas?"

"Your brother must tell you that, lad; I am somewhat out of breath."

"And I have a right to tell it," said Frank, with a smile. "Do you know that I was very near being Earl of the bog of Allen, and one of the peers of the realm to King Buoncompagna, son and heir to his holiness Pope Gregory the Thirteenth?"

"No, surely!"

"As I am a gentleman. When I was at Rome I saw poor Stukely often; and this and more he offered me on the part (as he said) of the Pope, if I would just oblige him in the two little matters of being reconciled to the Catholic Church, and joining the invasion of Ireland."

"Poor deluded heretic," said Will Cary, "to have lost an earldom for your family by such silly scruples of loyalty!"

"It is not a matter for jesting, after all," said Frank; "but I saw Sir Thomas often, and I cannot believe he was in his senses, so frantic was his vanity and his ambition; and all the while, in private matters as honorable a gentleman as ever. However, he sailed at last for Ireland, with his eight hundred Spaniards and Italians; and what is more, I know that the King of Spain paid their charges. Marquis Vinola—James Buoncompagna, that is—stayed quietly at Rome, preferring that Stukely should conquer his paternal heritage of Ireland for him while he took care of the bona robas at home. I went down to Civita Vecchia to see him off; and though his younger by many years, I could not but take the liberty of entreating him, as a gentleman and a man of Devon, to consider his faith to his queen and the honor of his country. There were high words between us; God forgive me if I spoke too fiercely, for I never saw him again."

"Too fiercely to an open traitor, Frank? Why not have run him through?"

"Nay, I had no clean life for Sundays, Amyas; so I could not throw away my week-day one; and as for the weal of England, I knew that it was little he would damage it, and told him so. And at that he waxed utterly mad, for it touched his pride, and swore that if the wind had not been fair for sailing, he would have fought me there and then; to which I could only answer, that I was ready to meet him when he would; and he parted from me, saying, 'It is a pity, sir, I cannot fight you now; when next we meet, it will be beneath my dignity to measure swords with you.'

"I suppose he expected to come back a prince at least—Heaven knows; I owe him no ill-will, nor I hope does any man. He has paid all debts now in full, and got his receipt for them."

"How did he die, then, after all?"

"On his voyage he touched in Portugal. King Sebastian was just sailing for Africa with his new ally, Mohammed the Prince of Fez, to help King Abdallah, and conquer what he could. He persuaded Stukely to go with him. There were those who thought that he, as well as the Spaniards, had no stomach for seeing the Pope's son King of Ireland. Others used to say that he thought an island too small for his ambition, and must needs conquer a continent—I know not why it was, but he went. They had heavy weather in the passage; and when they landed, many of their soldiers were sea-sick. Stukely, reasonably enough, counselled that they should wait two or three days and recruit; but Don Sebastian was so mad for the assault that he must needs have his veni, vidi, vici; and so ended with a veni, vidi, perii; for he Abdallah, and his son Mohammed, all perished in the first battle at Alcasar; and Stukely, surrounded and overpowered, fought till he could fight no more, and then died like a hero with all his wounds in front; and may God have mercy on his soul!"

"Ah!" said Amyas, "we heard of that battle off Lima, but nothing about poor Stukely."

"That last was a Popish prayer, Master Frank," said old Mr. Cary.

"Most worshipful sir, you surely would not wish God not to have mercy on his soul?"

"No—eh? Of course not: but that's all settled by now, for he is dead, poor fellow."

"Certainly, my dear sir. And you cannot help being a little fond of him still."

"Eh? why, I should be a brute if I were not. He and I were schoolfellows, though he was somewhat the younger; and many a good thrashing have I given him, and one cannot help having a tenderness for a man after that. Beside, we used to hunt together in Exmoor, and have royal nights afterward into Ilfracombe, when we were a couple of mad young blades. Fond of him? Why, I would have sooner given my forefinger than that he should have gone to the dogs thus."

"Then, my dear sir, if you feel for him still, in spite of all his faults, how do you know that God may not feel for him still, in spite of all his faults? For my part," quoth Frank, in his fanciful way, "without believing in that Popish Purgatory, I cannot help holding with Plato, that such heroical souls, who have wanted but little of true greatness, are hereafter by some strait discipline brought to a better mind; perhaps, as many ancients have held with the Indian Gymnosophists, by transmigration into the bodies of those animals whom they have resembled in their passions; and indeed, if Sir Thomas Stukely's soul should now animate the body of a lion, all I can say is that he would be a very valiant and royal lion; and also doubtless become in due time heartily ashamed and penitent for having been nothing better than a lion."

"What now, Master Frank? I don't trouble my head with such matters—I say Stukely was a right good-hearted fellow at bottom; and if you plague my head with any of your dialectics, and propositions, and college quips and quiddities, you sha'n't have any more sack, sir. But here come the knaves, and I hear the cook knock to dinner."

After a madrigal or two, and an Italian song of Master Frank's, all which went sweetly enough, the ladies rose, and went. Whereon Will Cary, drawing his chair close to Frank's, put quietly into his hand a dirty letter.

"This was the letter left for me," whispered he, "by a country fellow this morning. Look at it and tell me what I am to do."

Whereon Frank opened, and read—

"I would have showed it my father," said Will, "but—"

"I verily believe it to be a blind. See now, this is the handwriting of a man who has been trying to write vilely, and yet cannot. Look at that B, and that G; their formae formativae never were begotten in a hedge-school. And what is more, this is no Devon man's handiwork. We say 'to' and not 'by,' Will, eh? in the West country?"

"Of course."

"And 'man,' instead of 'him'?"

"True, O Daniel! But am I to do nothing therefore?"

"On that matter I am no judge. Let us ask much-enduring Ulysses here; perhaps he has not sailed round the world without bringing home a device or two."

Whereon Amyas was called to counsel, as soon as Mr. Cary could be stopped in a long cross-examination of him as to Mr. Doughty's famous trial and execution.

Amyas pondered awhile, thrusting his hands into his long curls; and then—

"Will, my lad, have you been watching at the Deer Park End of late?"

"Never."

"Where, then?"

"At the town-beach."

"Where else?"

"At the town-head."

"Where else?"

"Why, the fellow is turned lawyer! Above Freshwater."

"Where is Freshwater?"

"Why, where the water-fall comes over the cliff, half-a-mile from the town. There is a path there up into the forest."

"I know. I'll watch there to-night. Do you keep all your old haunts safe, of course, and send a couple of stout knaves to the mill, to watch the beach at the Deer Park End, on the chance; for your poet may be a true man, after all. But my heart's faith is, that this comes just to draw you off from some old beat of yours, upon a wild-goose chase. If they shoot the miller by mistake, I suppose it don't much matter?"

"Marry, no."

"Or, again," chimed in old Mr. Cary, "as they say in the North—

"But why are you so ready to watch Freshwater to-night, Master Amyas?"

"Because, sir, those who come, if they come, will never land at Mouthmill; if they are strangers, they dare not; and if they are bay's-men, they are too wise, as long as the westerly swell sets in. As for landing at the town, that would be too great a risk; but Freshwater is as lonely as the Bermudas; and they can beach a boat up under the cliff at all tides, and in all weathers, except north and nor'west. I have done it many a time, when I was a boy."

"And give us the fruit of your experience now in your old age, eh? Well, you have a gray head on green shoulders, my lad; and I verily believe you are right. Who will you take with you to watch?"

"Sir," said Frank, "I will go with my brother; and that will be enough."

"Enough? He is big enough, and you brave enough, for ten; but still, the more the merrier."

"But the fewer, the better fare. If I might ask a first and last favor, worshipful sir," said Frank, very earnestly, "you would grant me two things: that you would let none go to Freshwater but me and my brother; and that whatsoever we shall bring you back shall be kept as secret as the commonweal and your loyalty shall permit. I trust that we are not so unknown to you, or to others, that you can doubt for a moment but that whatsoever we may do will satisfy at once your honor and our own."

"My dear young gentleman, there is no need of so many courtier's words. I am your father's friend, and yours. And God forbid that a Cary—for I guess your drift—should ever wish to make a head or a heart ache; that is, more than—"

"Those of whom it is written, 'Though thou bray a fool in a mortar, yet will not his folly depart from him,'" interposed Frank, in so sad a tone that no one at the table replied; and few more words were exchanged, till the two brothers were safe outside the house; and then—

"Amyas," said Frank, "that was a Devon man's handiwork, nevertheless; it was Eustace's handwriting."

"Impossible!"

"No, lad. I have been secretary to a prince, and learnt to interpret cipher, and to watch every pen-stroke; and, young as I am, I think that I am not easily deceived. Would God I were! Come on, lad; and strike no man hastily, lest thou cut off thine own flesh."

So forth the two went, along the park to the eastward, and past the head of the little wood-embosomed fishing-town, a steep stair of houses clinging to the cliff far below them, the bright slate roofs and white walls glittering in the moonlight; and on some half-mile farther, along the steep hill-side, fenced with oak wood down to the water's edge, by a narrow forest path, to a point where two glens meet and pour their streamlets over a cascade some hundred feet in height into the sea below. By the side of this waterfall a narrow path climbs upward from the beach; and here it was that the two brothers expected to meet the messenger.

Frank insisted on taking his station below Amyas. He said that he was certain that Eustace himself would make his appearance, and that he was more fit than Amyas to bring him to reason by parley; that if Amyas would keep watch some twenty yards above, the escape of the messenger would be impossible. Moreover, he was the elder brother, and the post of honor was his right. So Amyas obeyed him, after making him promise that if more than one man came up the path, he would let them pass him before he challenged, so that both might bring them to bay at the same time.

So Amyas took his station under a high marl bank, and, bedded in luxuriant crown-ferns, kept his eye steadily on Frank, who sat down on a little knoll of rock (where is now a garden on the cliff-edge) which parts the path and the dark chasm down which the stream rushes to its final leap over the cliff.

There Amyas sat a full half-hour, and glanced at whiles from Frank to look upon the scene around. Outside the southwest wind blew fresh and strong, and the moonlight danced upon a thousand crests of foam; but within the black jagged point which sheltered the town, the sea did but heave, in long oily swells of rolling silver, onward into the black shadow of the hills, within which the town and pier lay invisible, save where a twinkling light gave token of some lonely fisher's wife, watching the weary night through for the boat which would return with dawn. Here and there upon the sea, a black speck marked a herring-boat, drifting with its line of nets; and right off the mouth of the glen, Amyas saw, with a beating heart, a large two-masted vessel lying-to—that must be the "Portugal"! Eagerly he looked up the glen, and listened; but he heard nothing but the sweeping of the wind across the downs five hundred feet above, and the sough of the waterfall upon the rocks below; he saw nothing but the vast black sheets of oak-wood sloping up to the narrow blue sky above, and the broad bright hunter's moon, and the woodcocks, which, chuckling to each other, hawked to and fro, like swallows, between the tree-tops and the sky.

At last he heard a rustle of the fallen leaves; he shrank closer and closer into the darkness of the bank. Then swift light steps—not down the path, from above, but upward, from below; his heart beat quick and loud. And in another half-minute a man came in sight, within three yards of Frank's hiding-place.

Frank sprang out instantly. Amyas saw his bright blade glance in the clear October moonlight. "Stand in the queen's name!"

The man drew a pistol from under his cloak, and fired full in his face. Had it happened in these days of detonators, Frank's chance had been small; but to get a ponderous wheel-lock under weigh was a longer business, and before the fizzing of the flint had ceased, Frank had struck up the pistol with his rapier, and it exploded harmlessly over his head. The man instantly dashed the weapon in his face and closed.

The blow, luckily, did not take effect on that delicate forehead, but struck him on the shoulder: nevertheless, Frank, who with all his grace and agility was as fragile as a lily, and a very bubble of the earth, staggered, and lost his guard, and before he could recover himself, Amyas saw a dagger gleam, and one, two, three blows fiercely repeated.

Mad with fury, he was with them in an instant. They were scuffling together so closely in the shade that he was afraid to use his sword point; but with the hilt he dealt a single blow full on the ruffian's cheek. It was enough; with a hideous shriek, the fellow rolled over at his feet, and Amyas set his foot on him, in act to run him through.

"Stop! stay!" almost screamed Frank; "it is Eustace! our cousin Eustace!" and he leant against a tree.

Amyas sprang towards him: but Frank waved him off.

"It is nothing—a scratch. He has papers: I am sure of it. Take them; and for God's sake let him go!"

"Villain! give me your papers!" cried Amyas, setting his foot once more on the writhing Eustace, whose jaw was broken across.

"You struck me foully from behind," moaned he, his vanity and envy even then coming out, in that faint and foolish attempt to prove Amyas not so very much better a man.

"Hound, do you think that I dare not strike you in front? Give me your papers, letters, whatever Popish devilry you carry; or as I live, I will cut off your head, and take them myself, even if it cost me the shame of stripping your corpse. Give them up! Traitor, murderer! give them, I say!" And setting his foot on him afresh, he raised his sword.

Eustace was usually no craven: but he was cowed. Between agony and shame, he had no heart to resist. Martyrdom, which looked so splendid when consummated selon les regles on Tower Hill or Tyburn, before pitying, or (still better) scoffing multitudes, looked a confused, dirty, ugly business there in the dark forest; and as he lay, a stream of moonlight bathed his mighty cousin's broad clear forehead, and his long golden locks, and his white terrible blade, till he seemed, to Eustace's superstitious eye, like one of those fair young St. Michaels trampling on the fiend, which he had seen abroad in old German pictures. He shuddered; pulled a packet from his bosom, and threw it from him, murmuring, "I have not given it."

"Swear to me that these are all the papers which you have in cipher or out of cipher. Swear on your soul, or you die!"

Eustace swore.

"Tell me, who are your accomplices?"

"Never!" said Eustace. "Cruel! have you not degraded me enough already?" and the wretched young man burst into tears, and hid his bleeding face in his hands.

One hint of honor made Amyas as gentle as a lamb. He lifted Eustace up, and bade him run for his life.

"I am to owe my life, then, to you?"

"Not in the least; only to your being a Leigh. Go, or it will be worse for you!" And Eustace went; while Amyas, catching up the precious packet, hurried to Frank. He had fainted already, and his brother had to carry him as far as the park before he could find any of the other watchers. The blind, as far as they were concerned, was complete. They had heard and seen nothing. Whosoever had brought the packet had landed they knew not where; and so all returned to the court, carrying Frank, who recovered gradually, having rather bruises than wounds; for his foe had struck wildly, and with a trembling hand.

Half-an-hour after, Amyas, Mr. Cary, and his son Will were in deep consultation over the following epistle, the only paper in the packet which was not in cipher:—

"'DEAR BROTHER N. S. in Chto. et Ecclesia.

"This is to inform you and the friends of the cause, that S. Josephus has landed in Smerwick, with eight hundred valiant Crusaders, burning with holy zeal to imitate last year's martyrs of Carrigfolium, and to expiate their offences (which I fear may have been many) by the propagation of our most holy faith. I have purified the fort (which they are strenuously rebuilding) with prayer and holy water, from the stain of heretical footsteps, and consecrated it afresh to the service of Heaven, as the first-fruits of the isle of saints; and having displayed the consecrated banner to the adoration of the faithful, have returned to Earl Desmond, that I may establish his faith, weak as yet, by reason of the allurements of this world: though since, by the valor of his brother James, he that hindered was taken out of the way (I mean Davils the heretic, sacrifice well-pleasing in the eyes of Heaven!), the young man has lent a more obedient ear to my counsels. If you can do anything, do it quickly, for a great door and effectual is opened, and there are many adversaries. But be swift, for so do the poor lambs of the Church tremble at the fury of the heretics, that a hundred will flee before one Englishman. And, indeed, were it not for that divine charity toward the Church (which covers the multitude of sins) with which they are resplendent, neither they nor their country would be, by the carnal judgment, counted worthy of so great labor in their behalf. For they themselves are given much to lying, theft, and drunkenness, vain babbling, and profane dancing and singing; and are still, as S. Gildas reports of them, 'more careful to shroud their villainous faces in bushy hair, than decently to cover their bodies; while their land (by reason of the tyranny of their chieftains, and the continual wars and plunderings among their tribes, which leave them weak and divided, an easy prey to the myrmidons of the excommunicate and usurping Englishwoman) lies utterly waste with fire, and defaced with corpses of the starved and slain. But what are these things, while the holy virtue of Catholic obedience still flourishes in their hearts? The Church cares not for the conservation of body and goods, but of immortal souls.

"If any devout lady shall so will, you may obtain from her liberality a shirt for this worthless tabernacle, and also a pair of hose; for I am unsavory to myself and to others, and of such luxuries none here has superfluity; for all live in holy poverty, except the fleas, who have that consolation in this world for which this unhappy nation, and those who labor among them, must wait till the world to come.*

"Your loving brother,

"N. S."

"Sir Richard must know of this before daybreak," cried old Cary. "Eight hundred men landed! We must call out the Posse Comitatus, and sail with them bodily. I will go myself, old as I am. Spaniards in Ireland? not a dog of them must go home again."

"Not a dog of them," answered Will; "but where is Mr. Winter and his squadron?"

"Safe in Milford Haven; a messenger must be sent to him too."

"I'll go," said Amyas: "but Mr. Cary is right. Sir Richard must know all first."

"And we must have those Jesuits."

"What? Mr. Evans and Mr. Morgans? God help us—they are at my uncle's! Consider the honor of our family!"

"Judge for yourself, my dear boy," said old Mr. Cary, gently: "would it not be rank treason to let these foxes escape, while we have this damning proof against them?"

"I will go myself, then."

"Why not? You may keep all straight, and Will shall go with you. Call a groom, Will, and get your horse saddled, and my Yorkshire gray; he will make better play with this big fellow on his back, than the little pony astride of which Mr. Leigh came walking in (as I hear) this morning. As for Frank, the ladies will see to him well enough, and glad enough, too, to have so fine a bird in their cage for a week or two."

"And my mother?"

"We'll send to her to-morrow by daybreak. Come, a stirrup cup to start with, hot and hot. Now, boots, cloaks, swords, a deep pull and a warm one, and away!"

And the jolly old man bustled them out of the house and into their saddles, under the broad bright winter's moon.

"You must make your pace, lads, or the moon will be down before you are over the moors." And so away they went.

Neither of them spoke for many a mile. Amyas, because his mind was fixed firmly on the one object of saving the honor of his house; and Will, because he was hesitating between Ireland and the wars, and Rose Salterne and love-making. At last he spoke suddenly.

"I'll go, Amyas."

"Whither?"

"To Ireland with you, old man. I have dragged my anchor at last."

"What anchor, my lad of parables?"

"See, here am I, a tall and gallant ship."

"Modest even if not true."

"Inclination, like an anchor, holds me tight."

"To the mud."

"Nay, to a bed of roses—not without their thorns."

"Hillo! I have seen oysters grow on fruit-trees before now, but never an anchor in a rose-garden."

"Silence, or my allegory will go to noggin-staves."

"Against the rocks of my flinty discernment."

"Pooh—well. Up comes duty like a jolly breeze, blowing dead from the northeast, and as bitter and cross as a northeaster too, and tugs me away toward Ireland. I hold on by the rosebed—any ground in a storm—till every strand is parted, and off I go, westward ho! to get my throat cut in a bog-hole with Amyas Leigh."

"Earnest, Will?"

"As I am a sinful man."

"Well done, young hawk of the White Cliff!"

"I had rather have called it Gallantry Bower still, though," said Will, punning on the double name of the noble precipice which forms the highest point of the deer park.

"Well, as long as you are on land, you know it is Gallantry Bower still: but we always call it White Cliff when you see it from the sea-board, as you and I shall do, I hope, to-morrow evening."

"What, so soon?"

"Dare we lose a day?"

"I suppose not: heigh-ho!"

And they rode on again in silence, Amyas in the meanwhile being not a little content (in spite of his late self-renunciation) to find that one of his rivals at least was going to raise the siege of the Rose garden for a few months, and withdraw his forces to the coast of Kerry.

As they went over Bursdon, Amyas pulled up suddenly.

"Did you not hear a horse's step on our left?"

"On our left—coming up from Welsford moor? Impossible at this time of night. It must have been a stag, or a sownder of wild swine: or may be only an old cow."

"It was the ring of iron, friend. Let us stand and watch."

Bursdon and Welsford were then, as now, a rolling range of dreary moors, unbroken by tor or tree, or anything save few and far between a world-old furze-bank which marked the common rights of some distant cattle farm, and crossed then, not as now, by a decent road, but by a rough confused track-way, the remnant of an old Roman road from Clovelly dikes to Launceston. To the left it trended down towards a lower range of moors, which form the watershed of the heads of Torridge; and thither the two young men peered down over the expanse of bog and furze, which glittered for miles beneath the moon, one sheet of frosted silver, in the heavy autumn dew.

"If any of Eustace's party are trying to get home from Freshwater, they might save a couple of miles by coming across Welsford, instead of going by the main track, as we have done." So said Amyas, who though (luckily for him) no "genius," was cunning as a fox in all matters of tactic and practic, and would have in these days proved his right to be considered an intellectual person by being a thorough man of business.

"If any of his party are mad, they'll try it, and be stogged till the day of judgment. There are bogs in the bottom twenty feet deep. Plague on the fellow, whoever he is, he has dodged us! Look there!"

It was too true. The unknown horseman had evidently dismounted below, and led his horse up on the other side of a long furze-dike; till coming to the point where it turned away again from his intended course, he appeared against the sky, in the act of leading his nag over a gap.

"Ride like the wind!" and both youths galloped across furze and heather at him; but ere they were within a hundred yards of him, he had leapt again on his horse, and was away far ahead.

"There is the dor to us, with a vengeance," cried Cary, putting in the spurs.

"It is but a lad; we shall never catch him."

"I'll try, though; and do you lumber after as you can, old heavysides;" and Cary pushed forward.

Amyas lost sight of him for ten minutes, and then came up with him dismounted, and feeling disconsolately at his horse's knees.

"Look for my head. It lies somewhere about among the furze there; and oh! I am as full of needles as ever was a pin-cushion."

"Are his knees broken?"

"I daren't look. No, I believe not. Come along, and make the best of a bad matter. The fellow is a mile ahead, and to the right, too."

"He is going for Moorwinstow, then; but where is my cousin?"

"Behind us, I dare say. We shall nab him at least."

"Cary, promise me that if we do, you will keep out of sight, and let me manage him."

"My boy, I only want Evan Morgans and Morgan Evans. He is but the cat's paw, and we are after the cats themselves."

And so they went on another dreary six miles, till the land trended downwards, showing dark glens and masses of woodland far below.

"Now, then, straight to Chapel, and stop the foxes' earth? Or through the King's Park to Stow, and get out Sir Richard's hounds, hue and cry, and queen's warrant in proper form?"

"Let us see Sir Richard first; and whatsoever he decides about my uncle, I will endure as a loyal subject must."

So they rode through the King's Park, while Sir Richard's colts came whinnying and staring round the intruders, and down through a rich woodland lane five hundred feet into the valley, till they could hear the brawling of the little trout-stream, and beyond, the everlasting thunder of the ocean surf.

Down through warm woods, all fragrant with dying autumn flowers, leaving far above the keen Atlantic breeze, into one of those delicious Western combes, and so past the mill, and the little knot of flower-clad cottages. In the window of one of them a light was still burning. The two young men knew well whose window that was; and both hearts beat fast; for Rose Salterne slept, or rather seemed to wake, in that chamber.

"Folks are late in Combe to-night," said Amyas, as carelessly as he could.

Cary looked earnestly at the window, and then sharply enough at Amyas; but Amyas was busy settling his stirrup; and Cary rode on, unconscious that every fibre in his companion's huge frame was trembling like his own.

"Muggy and close down here," said Amyas, who, in reality, was quite faint with his own inward struggles.

"We shall be at Stow gate in five minutes," said Cary, looking back and down longingly as his horse climbed the opposite hill; but a turn of the zigzag road hid the cottage, and the next thought was, how to effect an entrance into Stow at three in the morning without being eaten by the bandogs, who were already howling and growling at the sound of the horse-hoofs.

However, they got safely in, after much knocking and calling, through the postern gate in the high west wall, into a mansion, the description whereof I must defer to the next chapter, seeing that the moon has already sunk into the Atlantic, and there is darkness over land and sea.

Sir Richard, in his long gown, was soon downstairs in the hall; the letter read, and the story told; but ere it was half finished—

"Anthony, call up a groom, and let him bring me a horse round. Gentlemen, if you will excuse me five minutes, I shall be at your service."

"You will not go alone, Richard?" asked Lady Grenville, putting her beautiful face in its nightcoif out of an adjoining door.

"Surely, sweet chuck, we three are enough to take two poor polecats of Jesuits. Go in, and help me to boot and gird."

In half an hour they were down and up across the valley again, under the few low ashes clipt flat by the sea-breeze which stood round the lonely gate of Chapel.

"Mr. Cary, there is a back path across the downs to Marsland; go and guard that." Cary rode off; and Sir Richard, as he knocked loudly at the gate—

"Mr. Leigh, you see that I have consulted your honor, and that of your poor uncle, by adventuring thus alone. What will you have me do now, which may not be unfit for me and you?"

"Oh, sir!" said Amyas, with tears in his honest eyes, "you have shown yourself once more what you always have been—my dear and beloved master on earth, not second even to my admiral Sir Francis Drake."

"Or the queen, I hope," said Grenville, smiling, "but pocas palabras. What will you do?"

"My wretched cousin, sir, may not have returned—and if I might watch for him on the main road—unless you want me with you."

"Richard Grenville can walk alone, lad. But what will you do with your cousin?"

"Send him out of the country, never to return; or if he refuses, run him through on the spot."

"Go, lad." And as he spoke, a sleepy voice asked inside the gate, "Who was there?"

"Sir Richard Grenville. Open, in the queen's name?"

"Sir Richard? He is in bed, and be hanged to you. No honest folk come at this hour of night."

"Amyas!" shouted Sir Richard. Amyas rode back.

"Burst that gate for me, while I hold your horse."

Amyas leaped down, took up a rock from the roadside, such as Homer's heroes used to send at each other's heads, and in an instant the door was flat on the ground, and the serving-man on his back inside, while Sir Richard quietly entering over it, like Una into the hut, told the fellow to get up and hold his horse for him (which the clod, who knew well enough that terrible voice, did without further murmurs), and then strode straight to the front door. It was already opened. The household had been up and about all along, or the noise at the entry had aroused them.

Sir Richard knocked, however, at the open door; and, to his astonishment, his knock was answered by Mr. Leigh himself, fully dressed, and candle in hand.

"Sir Richard Grenville! What, sir! is this neighborly, not to say gentle, to break into my house in the dead of night?"

"I broke your outer door, sir, because I was refused entrance when I asked in the queen's name. I knocked at your inner one, as I should have knocked at the poorest cottager's in the parish, because I found it open. You have two Jesuits here, sir! and here is the queen's warrant for apprehending them. I have signed it with my own hand, and, moreover, serve it now, with my own hand, in order to save you scandal—and it may be, worse. I must have these men, Mr. Leigh."

"My dear Sir Richard—!"

"I must have them, or I must search the house; and you would not put either yourself or me to so shameful a necessity?"

"My dear Sir Richard!—"

"Must I, then, ask you to stand back from your own doorway, my dear sir?" said Grenville. And then changing his voice to that fearful lion's roar, for which he was famous, and which it seemed impossible that lips so delicate could utter, he thundered, "Knaves, behind there! Back!"

This was spoken to half-a-dozen grooms and serving-men, who, well armed, were clustered in the passage.

"What? swords out, you sons of cliff rabbits?" And in a moment, Sir Richard's long blade flashed out also, and putting Mr. Leigh gently aside, as if he had been a child, he walked up to the party, who vanished right and left; having expected a cur dog, in the shape of a parish constable, and come upon a lion instead. They were stout fellows enough, no doubt, in a fair fight: but they had no stomach to be hanged in a row at Launceston Castle, after a preliminary running through the body by that redoubted admiral and most unpeaceful justice of the peace.

"And now, my dear Mr. Leigh," said Sir Richard, as blandly as ever, "where are my men? The night is cold; and you, as well as I, need to be in our beds."

"The men, Sir Richard—the Jesuits—they are not here, indeed."

"Not here, sir?"

"On the word of a gentleman, they left my house an hour ago. Believe me, sir, they did. I will swear to you if you need."

"I believe Mr. Leigh of Chapel's word without oaths. Whither are they gone?"

"Nay, sir—how can I tell? They are—they are, as I may say, fled, sir; escaped."

"With your connivance; at least with your son's. Where are they gone?"

"As I live, I do not know."

"Mr. Leigh—is this possible? Can you add untruth to that treason from the punishment of which I am trying to shield you?"

Poor Mr. Leigh burst into tears.

"Oh! my God! my God! is it come to this? Over and above having the fear and anxiety of keeping these black rascals in my house, and having to stop their villainous mouths every minute, for fear they should hang me and themselves, I am to be called a traitor and a liar in my old age, and that, too, by Richard Grenville! Would God I had never been born! Would God I had no soul to be saved, and I'd just go and drown care in drink, and let the queen and the Pope fight it out their own way!" And the poor old man sank into a chair, and covered his face with his hands, and then leaped up again.

"Bless my heart! Excuse me, Sir Richard—to sit down and leave you standing. 'S life, sir, sorrow is making a hawbuck of me. Sit down, my dear sir! my worshipful sir! or rather come with me into my room, and hear a poor wretched man's story, for I swear before God the men are fled; and my poor boy Eustace is not home either, and the groom tells me that his devil of a cousin has broken his jaw for him; and his mother is all but mad this hour past. Good lack! good lack!"

"He nearly murdered his angel of a cousin, sir!" said Sir Richard, severely.

"What, sir? They never told me."

"He had stabbed his cousin Frank three times, sir, before Amyas, who is as noble a lad as walks God's earth, struck him down. And in defence of what, forsooth, did he play the ruffian and the swashbuckler, but to bring home to your house this letter, sir, which you shall hear at your leisure, the moment I have taken order about your priests." And walking out of the house he went round and called to Cary to come to him.

"The birds are flown, Will," whispered he. "There is but one chance for us, and that is Marsland Mouth. If they are trying to take boat there, you may be yet in time. If they are gone inland we can do nothing till we raise the hue and cry to-morrow."

And Will galloped off over the downs toward Marsland, while Sir Richard ceremoniously walked in again, and professed himself ready and happy to have the honor of an audience in Mr. Leigh's private chamber. And as we know pretty well already what was to be discussed therein, we had better go over to Marsland Mouth, and, if possible, arrive there before Will Cary: seeing that he arrived hot and swearing, half an hour too late.

Note.—I have shrunk somewhat from giving these and other sketches (true and accurate as I believe them to be) of Ireland during Elizabeth's reign, when the tyranny and lawlessness of the feudal chiefs had reduced the island to such a state of weakness and barbarism, that it was absolutely necessary for England either to crush the Norman-Irish nobility, and organize some sort of law and order, or to leave Ireland an easy prey to the Spaniards, or any other nation which should go to war with us. The work was done—clumsily rather than cruelly; but wrongs were inflicted, and avenged by fresh wrongs, and those by fresh again. May the memory of them perish forever! It has been reserved for this age, and for the liberal policy of this age, to see the last ebullitions of Celtic excitability die out harmless and ashamed of itself, and to find that the Irishman, when he is brought as a soldier under the regenerative influence of law, discipline, self-respect, and loyalty, can prove himself a worthy rival of the more stern Norse-Saxon warrior. God grant that the military brotherhood between Irish and English, which is the special glory of the present war, may be the germ of a brotherhood industrial, political, and hereafter, perhaps, religious also; and that not merely the corpses of heroes, but the feuds and wrongs which have parted them for centuries, may lie buried, once and forever, in the noble graves of Alma and Inkerman.

CHAPTER VI: THE COMBES OF THE FAR WEST

And even such are those delightful glens, which cut the high table-land of the confines of Devon and Cornwall, and opening each through its gorge of down and rock, towards the boundless Western Ocean. Each is like the other, and each is like no other English scenery. Each has its upright walls, inland of rich oak-wood, nearer the sea of dark green furze, then of smooth turf, then of weird black cliffs which range out right and left far into the deep sea, in castles, spires, and wings of jagged iron-stone. Each has its narrow strip of fertile meadow, its crystal trout stream winding across and across from one hill-foot to the other; its gray stone mill, with the water sparkling and humming round the dripping wheel; its dark, rock pools above the tide mark, where the salmon-trout gather in from their Atlantic wanderings, after each autumn flood: its ridge of blown sand, bright with golden trefoil and crimson lady's finger; its gray bank of polished pebbles, down which the stream rattles toward the sea below. Each has its black field of jagged shark's-tooth rock which paves the cove from side to side, streaked with here and there a pink line of shell sand, and laced with white foam from the eternal surge, stretching in parallel lines out to the westward, in strata set upright on edge, or tilted towards each other at strange angles by primeval earthquakes;—such is the "mouth"—as those coves are called; and such the jaw of teeth which they display, one rasp of which would grind abroad the timbers of the stoutest ship. To landward, all richness, softness, and peace; to seaward, a waste and howling wilderness of rock and roller, barren to the fisherman, and hopeless to the shipwrecked mariner.

In only one of these "mouths" is a landing for boats, made possible by a long sea-wall of rock, which protects it from the rollers of the Atlantic; and that mouth is Marsland, the abode of the White Witch, Lucy Passmore; whither, as Sir Richard Grenville rightly judged, the Jesuits were gone. But before the Jesuits came, two other persons were standing on that lonely beach, under the bright October moon, namely, Rose Salterne and the White Witch herself; for Rose, fevered with curiosity and superstition, and allured by the very wildness and possible danger of the spell, had kept her appointment; and, a few minutes before midnight, stood on the gray shingle beach with her counsellor.

"You be safe enough here to-night, miss. My old man is snoring sound abed, and there's no other soul ever sets foot here o' nights, except it be the mermaids now and then. Goodness, Father, where's our boat? It ought to be up here on the pebbles."

Rose pointed to a strip of sand some forty yards nearer the sea, where the boat lay.

"Oh, the lazy old villain! he's been round the rocks after pollock this evening, and never taken the trouble to hale the boat up. I'll trounce him for it when I get home. I only hope he's made her fast where she is, that's all! He's more plague to me than ever my money will be. O deary me!"

And the goodwife bustled down toward the boat, with Rose behind her.

"Iss, 'tis fast, sure enough: and the oars aboard too! Well, I never! Oh, the lazy thief, to leave they here to be stole! I'll just sit in the boat, dear, and watch mun, while you go down to the say; for you must be all alone to yourself, you know, or you'll see nothing. There's the looking-glass; now go, and dip your head three times, and mind you don't look to land or sea before you've said the words, and looked upon the glass. Now, be quick, it's just upon midnight."

And she coiled herself up in the boat, while Rose went faltering down the strip of sand, some twenty yards farther, and there slipping off her clothes, stood shivering and trembling for a moment before she entered the sea.

She was between two walls of rock: that on her left hand, some twenty feet high, hid her in deepest shade; that on her right, though much lower, took the whole blaze of the midnight moon. Great festoons of live and purple sea-weed hung from it, shading dark cracks and crevices, fit haunts for all the goblins of the sea. On her left hand, the peaks of the rock frowned down ghastly black; on her right hand, far aloft, the downs slept bright and cold.

The breeze had died away; not even a roller broke the perfect stillness of the cove. The gulls were all asleep upon the ledges. Over all was a true autumn silence; a silence which may be heard. She stood awed, and listened in hope of a sound which might tell her that any living thing beside herself existed.

There was a faint bleat, as of a new-born lamb, high above her head; she started and looked up. Then a wail from the cliffs, as of a child in pain, answered by another from the opposite rocks. They were but the passing snipe, and the otter calling to her brood; but to her they were mysterious, supernatural goblins, come to answer to her call. Nevertheless, they only quickened her expectation; and the witch had told her not to fear them. If she performed the rite duly, nothing would harm her: but she could hear the beating of her own heart, as she stepped, mirror in hand, into the cold water, waded hastily, as far as she dare, and then stopped aghast.

A ring of flame was round her waist; every limb was bathed in lambent light; all the multitudinous life of the autumn sea, stirred by her approach, had flashed suddenly into glory;—

"And around her the lamps of the sea nymphs, Myriad fiery globes, swam heaving and panting, and rainbows, Crimson and azure and emerald, were broken in star-showers, lighting Far through the wine-dark depths of the crystal, the gardens of Nereus, Coral and sea-fan and tangle, the blooms and the palms of the ocean."

She could see every shell which crawled on the white sand at her feet, every rock-fish which played in and out of the crannies, and stared at her with its broad bright eyes; while the great palmate oarweeds which waved along the chasm, half-seen in the glimmering water, seemed to beckon her down with long brown hands to a grave amid their chilly bowers. She turned to flee; but she had gone too far now to retreat; hastily dipping her head three times, she hurried out to the sea-marge, and looking through her dripping locks at the magic mirror, pronounced the incantation—

The incantation was hardly finished, her eyes were straining into the mirror, where, as may be supposed, nothing appeared but the sparkle of the drops from her own tresses, when she heard rattling down the pebbles the hasty feet of men and horses.

She darted into a cavern of the high rock, and hastily dressed herself: the steps held on right to the boat. Peeping out, half-dead with terror, she saw there four men, two of whom had just leaped from their horses, and turning them adrift, began to help the other two in running the boat down.

Whereon, out of the stern sheets, arose, like an angry ghost, the portly figure of Lucy Passmore, and shrieked in shrillest treble—

"Eh! ye villains, ye roogs, what do ye want staling poor folks' boats by night like this?"

The whole party recoiled in terror, and one turned to run up the beach, shouting at the top of his voice, "'Tis a marmaiden—a marmaiden asleep in Willy Passmore's boat!"

"I wish it were any sich good luck," she could hear Will say; "'tis my wife, oh dear!" and he cowered down, expecting the hearty cuff which he received duly, as the White Witch, leaping out of the boat, dared any man to touch it, and thundered to her husband to go home to bed.

The wily dame, as Rose well guessed, was keeping up this delay chiefly to gain time for her pupil: but she had also more solid reasons for making the fight as hard as possible; for she, as well as Rose, had already discerned in the ungainly figure of one of the party the same suspicious Welsh gentleman, on whose calling she had divined long ago; and she was so loyal a subject as to hold in extreme horror her husband's meddling with such "Popish skulkers" (as she called the whole party roundly to their face)—unless on consideration of a very handsome sum of money. In vain Parsons thundered, Campian entreated, Mr. Leigh's groom swore, and her husband danced round in an agony of mingled fear and covetousness.

"No," she cried, "as I am an honest woman and loyal! This is why you left the boat down to the shoore, you old traitor, you, is it? To help off sich noxious trade as this out of the hands of her majesty's quorum and rotulorum? Eh? Stand back, cowards! Will you strike a woman?"

This last speech (as usual) was merely indicative of her intention to strike the men; for, getting out one of the oars, she swung it round and round fiercely, and at last caught Father Parsons such a crack across the shins, that he retreated with a howl.

"Lucy, Lucy!" shrieked her husband, in shrillest Devon falsetto, "be you mazed? Be you mazed, lass? They promised me two gold nobles before I'd lend them the boot!"

"Tu?" shrieked the matron, with a tone of ineffable scorn. "And do yu call yourself a man?"

"Tu nobles! tu nobles!" shrieked he again, hopping about at oar's length.

"Tu? And would you sell your soul under ten?"

"Oh, if that is it," cried poor Campian, "give her ten, give her ten, brother Pars—Morgans, I mean; and take care of your shins, Offa Cerbero, you know—Oh, virago! Furens quid faemina possit! Certainly she is some Lamia, some Gorgon, some—"

"Take that, for your Lamys and Gorgons to an honest woman!" and in a moment poor Campian's thin legs were cut from under him, while the virago, "mounting on his trunk astride," like that more famous one on Hudibras, cried, "Ten nobles, or I'll kep ye here till morning!" And the ten nobles were paid into her hand.

And now the boat, its dragon guardian being pacified, was run down to the sea, and close past the nook where poor little Rose was squeezing herself into the farthest and darkest corner, among wet sea-weed and rough barnacles, holding her breath as they approached.

They passed her, and the boat's keel was already in the water; Lucy had followed them close, for reasons of her own, and perceiving close to the water's edge a dark cavern, cunningly surmised that it contained Rose, and planted her ample person right across its mouth, while she grumbled at her husband, the strangers, and above all at Mr. Leigh's groom, to whom she prophesied pretty plainly Launceston gaol and the gallows; while the wretched serving-man, who would as soon have dared to leap off Welcombe Cliff as to return railing for railing to the White Witch, in vain entreated her mercy, and tried, by all possible dodging, to keep one of the party between himself and her, lest her redoubted eye should "overlook" him once more to his ruin.

But the night's adventures were not ended yet; for just as the boat was launched, a faint halloo was heard upon the beach, and a minute after, a horseman plunged down the pebbles, and along the sand, and pulling his horse up on its haunches close to the terrified group, dropped, rather than leaped, from the saddle.

The serving-man, though he dared not tackle a witch, knew well enough how to deal with a swordsman; and drawing, sprang upon the newcomer, and then recoiled—

"God forgive me, it's Mr. Eustace! Oh, dear sir, I took you for one of Sir Richard's men! Oh, sir, you're hurt!"

"A scratch, a scratch!" almost moaned Eustace. "Help me into the boat, Jack. Gentlemen, I must with you."

"Not with us, surely, my dear son, vagabonds upon the face of the earth?" said kind-hearted Campian.

"With you, forever. All is over here. Whither God and the cause lead"—and he staggered toward the boat.

As he passed Rose, she saw his ghastly bleeding face, half bound up with a handkerchief, which could not conceal the convulsions of rage, shame, and despair, which twisted it from all its usual beauty. His eyes glared wildly round—and once, right into the cavern. They met hers, so full, and keen, and dreadful, that forgetting she was utterly invisible, the terrified girl was on the point of shrieking aloud.

"He has overlooked me!" said she, shuddering to herself, as she recollected his threat of yesterday.

"Who has wounded you?" asked Campian.

"My cousin—Amyas—and taken the letter!"

"The devil take him, then!" cried Parsons, stamping up and down upon the sand in fury.

"Ay, curse him—you may! I dare not! He saved me—sent me here!"—and with a groan, he made an effort to enter the boat.

"Oh, my dear young gentleman," cried Lucy Passmore, her woman's heart bursting out at the sight of pain, "you must not goo forth with a grane wound like to that. Do ye let me just bind mun up—do ye now!" and she advanced.

Eustace thrust her back.

"No! better bear it, I deserve it—devils! I deserve it! On board, or we shall all be lost—William Cary is close behind me!"

And at that news the boat was thrust into the sea, faster than ever it went before, and only in time; for it was but just round the rocks, and out of sight, when the rattle of Cary's horsehoofs was heard above.

"That rascal of Mr. Leigh's will catch it now, the Popish villain!" said Lucy Passmore, aloud. "You lie still there, dear life, and settle your sperrits; you'm so safe as ever was rabbit to burrow. I'll see what happens, if I die for it!" And so saying, she squeezed herself up through a cleft to a higher ledge, from whence she could see what passed in the valley.

"There mun is! in the meadow, trying to catch the horses! There comes Mr. Cary! Goodness, Father, how a rid'th! he's over wall already! Ron, Jack! ron then! A'll get to the river! No, a wain't! Goodness, Father! There's Mr. Cary cotched mun! A's down, a's down!"

"Is he dead?" asked Rose, shuddering.

"Iss, fegs, dead as nits! and Mr. Cary off his horse, standing overthwart mun! No, a bain't! A's up now. Suspose he was hit wi' the flat. Whatever is Mr. Cary tu? Telling wi' mun, a bit. Oh dear, dear, dear!"

"Has he killed him?" cried poor Rose.

"No, fegs, no! kecking mun, kecking mun, so hard as ever was futeball! Goodness, Father, who did ever? If a haven't kecked mun right into river, and got on mun's horse and rod away!"

And so saying, down she came again.

"And now then, my dear life, us be better to goo hoom and get you sommat warm. You'm mortal cold, I rackon, by now. I was cruel fear'd for ye: but I kept mun off clever, didn't I, now?"

"I wish—I wish I had not seen Mr. Leigh's face!"

"Iss, dreadful, weren't it, poor young soul; a sad night for his poor mother!"

"Lucy, I can't get his face out of my mind. I'm sure he overlooked me."

"Oh then! who ever heard the like o' that? When young gentlemen do overlook young ladies, tain't thikketheor aways, I knoo. Never you think on it."

"But I can't help thinking of it," said Rose. "Stop. Shall we go home yet? Where's that servant?"

"Never mind, he wain't see us, here under the hill. I'd much sooner to know where my old man was. I've a sort of a forecasting in my inwards, like, as I always has when aught's gwain to happen, as though I shuldn't zee mun again, like, I have, miss. Well—he was a bedient old soul, after all, he was. Goodness, Father! and all this while us have forgot the very thing us come about! Who did you see?"

"Only that face!" said Rose, shuddering.

"Not in the glass, maid? Say then, not in the glass?"

"Would to heaven it had been! Lucy, what if he were the man I was fated to—"

"He? Why, he's a praste, a Popish praste, that can't marry if he would, poor wratch."

"He is none; and I have cause enough to know it!" And, for want of a better confidant, Rose poured into the willing ears of her companion the whole story of yesterday's meeting.

"He's a pretty wooer!" said Lucy at last, contemptuously. "Be a brave maid, then, be a brave maid, and never terrify yourself with his unlucky face. It's because there was none here worthy of ye, that ye seed none in glass. Maybe he's to be a foreigner, from over seas, and that's why his sperit was so long a coming. A duke, or a prince to the least, I'll warrant, he'll be, that carries off the Rose of Bideford."

But in spite of all the good dame's flattery, Rose could not wipe that fierce face away from her eyeballs. She reached home safely, and crept to bed undiscovered: and when the next morning, as was to be expected, found her laid up with something very like a fever, from excitement, terror, and cold, the phantom grew stronger and stronger before her, and it required all her woman's tact and self-restraint to avoid betraying by her exclamations what had happened on that fantastic night. After a fortnight's weakness, however, she recovered and went back to Bideford: but ere she arrived there, Amyas was far across the seas on his way to Milford Haven, as shall be told in the ensuing chapters.

CHAPTER VII: THE TRUE AND TRAGICAL HISTORY OF MR. JOHN OXENHAM OF PLYMOUTH

It was too late and too dark last night to see the old house at Stow. We will look round us, then, this bright October day, while Sir Richard and Amyas, about eleven o'clock in the forenoon, are pacing up and down the terraced garden to the south. Amyas has slept till luncheon, i. e. till an hour ago: but Sir Richard, in spite of the bustle of last night, was up and in the valley by six o'clock, recreating the valiant souls of himself and two terrier dogs by the chase of sundry badgers.

Old Stow House stands, or rather stood, some four miles beyond the Cornish border, on the northern slope of the largest and loveliest of those combes of which I spoke in the last chapter. Eighty years after Sir Richard's time there arose there a huge Palladian pile, bedizened with every monstrosity of bad taste, which was built, so the story runs, by Charles the Second, for Sir Richard's great-grandson, the heir of that famous Sir Bevil who defeated the Parliamentary troops at Stratton, and died soon after, fighting valiantly at Lansdowne over Bath. But, like most other things which owed their existence to the Stuarts, it rose only to fall again. An old man who had seen, as a boy, the foundation of the new house laid, lived to see it pulled down again, and the very bricks and timber sold upon the spot; and since then the stables have become a farm-house, the tennis-court a sheep-cote, the great quadrangle a rick-yard; and civilization, spreading wave on wave so fast elsewhere, has surged back from that lonely corner of the land—let us hope, only for a while.

But I am not writing of that great new Stow House, of the past glories whereof quaint pictures still hang in the neighboring houses; nor of that famed Sir Bevil, most beautiful and gallant of his generation, on whom, with his grandfather Sir Richard, old Prince has his pompous epigram—

I have to deal with a simpler age, and a sterner generation; and with the old house, which had stood there, in part at least, from gray and mythic ages, when the first Sir Richard, son of Hamon Dentatus, Lord of Carboyle, the grandson of Duke Robert, son of Rou, settled at Bideford, after slaying the Prince of South-Galis, and the Lord of Glamorgan, and gave to the Cistercian monks of Neath all his conquests in South Wales. It was a huge rambling building, half castle, half dwelling-house, such as may be seen still (almost an unique specimen) in Compton Castle near Torquay, the dwelling-place of Humphrey Gilbert, Walter Raleigh's half-brother, and Richard Grenville's bosom friend, of whom more hereafter. On three sides, to the north, west, and south, the lofty walls of the old ballium still stood, with their machicolated turrets, loopholes, and dark downward crannies for dropping stones and fire on the besiegers, the relics of a more unsettled age: but the southern court of the ballium had become a flower-garden, with quaint terraces, statues, knots of flowers, clipped yews and hollies, and all the pedantries of the topiarian art. And toward the east, where the vista of the valley opened, the old walls were gone, and the frowning Norman keep, ruined in the Wars of the Roses, had been replaced by the rich and stately architecture of the Tudors. Altogether, the house, like the time, was in a transitional state, and represented faithfully enough the passage of the old middle age into the new life which had just burst into blossom throughout Europe, never, let us pray, to see its autumn or its winter.

From the house on three sides, the hill sloped steeply down, and the garden where Sir Richard and Amyas were walking gave a truly English prospect. At one turn they could catch, over the western walls, a glimpse of the blue ocean flecked with passing sails; and at the next, spread far below them, range on range of fertile park, stately avenue, yellow autumn woodland, and purple heather moors, lapping over and over each other up the valley to the old British earthwork, which stood black and furze-grown on its conical peak; and standing out against the sky on the highest bank of hill which closed the valley to the east, the lofty tower of Kilkhampton church, rich with the monuments and offerings of five centuries of Grenvilles. A yellow eastern haze hung soft over park, and wood, and moor; the red cattle lowed to each other as they stood brushing away the flies in the rivulet far below; the colts in the horse-park close on their right whinnied as they played together, and their sires from the Queen's Park, on the opposite hill, answered them in fuller though fainter voices. A rutting stag made the still woodland rattle with his hoarse thunder, and a rival far up the valley gave back a trumpet note of defiance, and was himself defied from heathery brows which quivered far away above, half seen through the veil of eastern mist. And close at home, upon the terrace before the house, amid romping spaniels and golden-haired children, sat Lady Grenville herself, the beautiful St. Leger of Annery, the central jewel of all that glorious place, and looked down at her noble children, and then up at her more noble husband, and round at that broad paradise of the West, till life seemed too full of happiness, and heaven of light.

And all the while up and down paced Amyas and Sir Richard, talking long, earnestly, and slow; for they both knew that the turning point of the boy's life was come.

"Yes," said Sir Richard, after Amyas, in his blunt simple way, had told him the whole story about Rose Salterne and his brother,—"yes, sweet lad, thou hast chosen the better part, thou and thy brother also, and it shall not be taken from you. Only be strong, lad, and trust in God that He will make a man of you."

"I do trust," said Amyas.

"Thank God," said Sir Richard, "that you have yourself taken from my heart that which was my great anxiety for you, from the day that your good father, who sleeps in peace, committed you to my hands. For all best things, Amyas, become, when misused, the very worst; and the love of woman, because it is able to lift man's soul to the heavens, is also able to drag him down to hell. But you have learnt better, Amyas; and know, with our old German forefathers, that, as Tacitus saith, Sera juvenum Venus, ideoque inexhausta pubertas. And not only that, Amyas; but trust me, that silly fashion of the French and Italians, to be hanging ever at some woman's apron string, so that no boy shall count himself a man unless he can vagghezziare le donne, whether maids or wives, alas! matters little; that fashion, I say, is little less hurtful to the soul than open sin; for by it are bred vanity and expense, envy and heart-burning, yea hatred and murder often; and even if that be escaped, yet the rich treasure of a manly worship, which should be kept for one alone, is squandered and parted upon many, and the bride at last comes in for nothing but the very last leavings and caput mortuum of her bridegroom's heart, and becomes a mere ornament for his table, and a means whereby he may obtain a progeny. May God, who has saved me from that death in life, save you also!" And as he spoke, he looked down toward his wife upon the terrace below; and she, as if guessing instinctively that he was talking of her, looked up with so sweet a smile, that Sir Richard's stern face melted into a very glory of spiritual sunshine.

Amyas looked at them both and sighed; and then turning the conversation suddenly—

"And I may go to Ireland to-morrow?"

"You shall sail in the 'Mary' for Milford Haven, with these letters to Winter. If the wind serves, you may bid the master drop down the river tonight, and be off; for we must lose no time."

"Winter?" said Amyas. "He is no friend of mine, since he left Drake and us so cowardly at the Straits of Magellan."

"Duty must not wait for private quarrels, even though they be just ones, lad: but he will not be your general. When you come to the marshal, or the Lord Deputy, give either of them this letter, and they will set you work,—and hard work too, I warrant."

"I want nothing better."

"Right, lad; the best reward for having wrought well already, is to have more to do; and he that has been faithful over a few things, must find his account in being made ruler over many things. That is the true and heroical rest, which only is worthy of gentlemen and sons of God. As for those who, either in this world or the world to come, look for idleness, and hope that God shall feed them with pleasant things, as it were with a spoon, Amyas, I count them cowards and base, even though they call themselves saints and elect."

"I wish you could persuade my poor cousin of that."

"He has yet to learn what losing his life to save it means, Amyas. Bad men have taught him (and I fear these Anabaptists and Puritans at home teach little else), that it is the one great business of every one to save his own soul after he dies; every one for himself; and that that, and not divine self-sacrifice, is the one thing needful, and the better part which Mary chose."

"I think men are inclined enough already to be selfish, without being taught that."

"Right, lad. For me, if I could hang up such a teacher on high as an enemy of mankind, and a corrupter of youth, I would do it gladly. Is there not cowardice and self-seeking enough about the hearts of us fallen sons of Adam, that these false prophets, with their baits of heaven, and their terrors of hell, must exalt our dirtiest vices into heavenly virtues and the means of bliss? Farewell to chivalry and to desperate valor, farewell to patriotism and loyalty, farewell to England and to the manhood of England, if once it shall become the fashion of our preachers to bid every man, as the Jesuits do, take care first of what they call the safety of his soul. Every man will be afraid to die at his post, because he will be afraid that he is not fit to die. Amyas, do thou do thy duty like a man, to thy country, thy queen, and thy God; and count thy life a worthless thing, as did the holy men of old. Do thy work, lad; and leave thy soul to the care of Him who is just and merciful in this, that He rewards every man according to his work. Is there respect of persons with God? Now come in, and take the letters, and to horse. And if I hear of thee dead there at Smerwick fort, with all thy wounds in front, I shall weep for thy mother, lad; but I shall have never a sigh for thee."

If any one shall be startled at hearing a fine gentleman and a warrior like Sir Richard quote Scripture, and think Scripture also, they must be referred to the writings of the time; which they may read not without profit to themselves, if they discover therefrom how it was possible then for men of the world to be thoroughly ingrained with the Gospel, and yet to be free from any taint of superstitious fear, or false devoutness. The religion of those days was such as no soldier need have been ashamed of confessing. At least, Sir Richard died as he lived, without a shudder, and without a whine; and these were his last words, fifteen years after that, as he lay shot through and through, a captive among Popish Spaniards, priests, crucifixes, confession, extreme unction, and all other means and appliances for delivering men out of the hands of a God of love:—

"Here die I, Richard Grenville, with a joyful and quiet mind; for that I have ended my life as a true soldier ought, fighting for his country, queen, religion, and honor: my soul willingly departing from this body, leaving behind the lasting fame of having behaved as every valiant soldier is in his duty bound to do."

Those were the last words of Richard Grenville. The pulpits of those days had taught them to him.

But to return. That day's events were not over yet. For, when they went down into the house, the first person whom they met was the old steward, in search of his master.

"There is a manner of roog, Sir Richard, a masterless man, at the door; a very forward fellow, and must needs speak with you."

"A masterless man? He had better not to speak to me, unless he is in love with gaol and gallows."

"Well, your worship," said the steward, "I expect that is what he does want, for he swears he will not leave the gate till he has seen you."

"Seen me? Halidame! he shall see me, here and at Launceston too, if he likes. Bring him in."

"Fegs, Sir Richard, we are half afeard. With your good leave—"

"Hillo, Tony," cried Amyas, "who was ever afeard yet with Sir Richard's good leave?"

"What, has the fellow a tail or horns?"

"Massy no: but I be afeard of treason for your honor; for the fellow is pinked all over in heathen patterns, and as brown as a filbert; and a tall roog, a very strong roog, sir, and a foreigner too, and a mighty staff with him. I expect him to be a manner of Jesuit, or wild Irish, sir; and indeed the grooms have no stomach to handle him, nor the dogs neither, or he had been under the pump before now, for they that saw him coming up the hill swear that he had fire coming out of his mouth."

"Fire out of his mouth?" said Sir Richard. "The men are drunk."

"Pinked all over? He must be a sailor," said Amyas; "let me out and see the fellow, and if he needs putting forth—"

"Why, I dare say he is not so big but what he will go into thy pocket. So go, lad, while I finish my writing."

Amyas went out, and at the back door, leaning on his staff, stood a tall, raw-boned, ragged man, "pinked all over," as the steward had said.

"Hillo, lad!" quoth Amyas. "Before we come to talk, thou wilt please to lay down that Plymouth cloak of thine." And he pointed to the cudgel, which among West-country mariners usually bore that name.

"I'll warrant," said the old steward, "that where he found his cloak he found purse not far off."

"But not hose or doublet; so the magical virtue of his staff has not helped him much. But put down thy staff, man, and speak like a Christian, if thou be one."

"I am a Christian, though I look like a heathen; and no rogue, though a masterless man, alas! But I want nothing, deserving nothing, and only ask to speak with Sir Richard, before I go on my way."

There was something stately and yet humble about the man's tone and manner which attracted Amyas, and he asked more gently where he was going and whence he came.

"From Padstow Port, sir, to Clovelly town, to see my old mother, if indeed she be yet alive, which God knoweth."

"Clovally man! why didn't thee say thee was Clovally man?" asked all the grooms at once, to whom a West-countryman was of course a brother. The old steward asked—

"What's thy mother's name, then?"

"Susan Yeo."

"What, that lived under the archway?" asked a groom.

"Lived?" said the man.

"Iss, sure; her died three days since, so we heard, poor soul."

The man stood quite silent and unmoved for a minute or two; and then said quietly to himself, in Spanish, "That which is, is best."

"You speak Spanish?" asked Amyas, more and more interested.

"I had need to do so, young sir; I have been five years in the Spanish Main, and only set foot on shore two days ago; and if you will let me have speech of Sir Richard, I will tell him that at which both the ears of him that heareth it shall tingle; and if not, I can but go on to Mr. Cary of Clovelly, if he be yet alive, and there disburden my soul; but I would sooner have spoken with one that is a mariner like to myself."

"And you shall," said Amyas. "Steward, we will have this man in; for all his rags, he is a man of wit." And he led him in.

"I only hope he ben't one of those Popish murderers," said the old steward, keeping at a safe distance from him as they entered the hall.

"Popish, old master? There's little fear of my being that. Look here!" And drawing back his rags, he showed a ghastly scar, which encircled his wrist and wound round and up his fore-arm.

"I got that on the rack," said he, quietly, "in the Inquisition at Lima."

"O Father! Father! why didn't you tell us that you were a poor Christian?" asked the penitent steward.

"Because I have had naught but my deserts; and but a taste of them either, as the Lord knoweth who delivered me; and I wasn't going to make myself a beggar and a show on their account."

"By heaven, you are a brave fellow!" said Amyas. "Come along straight to Sir Richard's room."

So in they went, where Sir Richard sat in his library among books, despatches, state-papers, and warrants; for though he was not yet, as in after times (after the fashion of those days) admiral, general, member of parliament, privy councillor, justice of the peace, and so forth, all at once, yet there were few great men with whom he did not correspond, or great matters with which he was not cognizant.

"Hillo, Amyas, have you bound the wild man already, and brought him in to swear allegiance?"

But before Amyas could answer, the man looked earnestly on him—"Amyas?" said he; "is that your name, sir?"

"Amyas Leigh is my name, at your service, good fellow."

"Of Burrough by Bideford?"

"Why then? What do you know of me?"

"Oh sir, sir! young brains and happy ones have short memories; but old and sad brains too long ones often! Do you mind one that was with Mr. Oxenham, sir? A swearing reprobate he was, God forgive him, and hath forgiven him too, for His dear Son's sake—one, sir, that gave you a horn, a toy with a chart on it?"

"Soul alive!" cried Amyas, catching him by the hand; "and are you he? The horn? why, I have it still, and will keep it to my dying day, too. But where is Mr. Oxenham?"

"Yes, my good fellow, where is Mr. Oxenham?" asked Sir Richard, rising. "You are somewhat over-hasty in welcoming your old acquaintance, Amyas, before we have heard from him whether he can give honest account of himself and of his captain. For there is more than one way by which sailors may come home without their captains, as poor Mr. Barker of Bristol found to his cost. God grant that there may have been no such traitorous dealing here."

"Sir Richard Grenville, if I had been a guilty man to my noble captain, as I have to God, I had not come here this day to you, from whom villainy has never found favor, nor ever will; for I know your conditions well, sir; and trust in the Lord, that if you will be pleased to hear me, you shall know mine."

"Thou art a well-spoken knave. We shall see."

"My dear sir," said Amyas, in a whisper, "I will warrant this man guiltless."

"I verily believe him to be; but this is too serious a matter to be left on guess. If he will be sworn—"

Whereon the man, humbly enough, said, that if it would please Sir Richard, he would rather not be sworn.

"But it does not please me, rascal! Did I not warn thee, Amyas?"

"Sir," said the man, proudly, "God forbid that my word should not be as good as my oath: but it is against my conscience to be sworn."

"What have we here? some fantastical Anabaptist, who is wiser than his teachers."

"My conscience, sir—"

"The devil take it and thee! I never heard a man yet begin to prate of his conscience, but I knew that he was about to do something more than ordinarily cruel or false."

"Sir," said the man, coolly enough, "do you sit here to judge me according to law, and yet contrary to the law swear profane oaths, for which a fine is provided?"

Amyas expected an explosion: but Sir Richard pulled a shilling out and put it on the table. "There—my fine is paid, sirrah, to the poor of Kilkhampton: but hearken thou all the same. If thou wilt not speak an oath, thou shalt speak on compulsion; for to Launceston gaol thou goest, there to answer for Mr. Oxenham's death, on suspicion whereof, and of mutiny causing it, I will attach thee and every soul of his crew that comes home. We have lost too many gallant captains of late by treachery of their crews, and he that will not clear himself on oath, must be held for guilty, and self-condemned."

"My good fellow," said Amyas, who could not give up his belief in the man's honesty, "why, for such fantastical scruples, peril not only your life, but your honor, and Mr. Oxenham's also? For if you be examined by question, you may be forced by torment to say that which is not true."

"Little fear of that, young sir!" answered he, with a grim smile; "I have had too much of the rack already, and the strappado too, to care much what man can do unto me. I would heartily that I thought it lawful to be sworn: but not so thinking, I can but submit to the cruelty of man; though I did expect more merciful things, as a most miserable and wrecked mariner, at the hands of one who hath himself seen God's ways in the sea, and His wonders in the great deep. Sir Richard Grenville, if you will hear my story, may God avenge on my head all my sins from my youth up until now, and cut me off from the blood of Christ, and, if it were possible, from the number of His elect, if I tell you one whit more or less than truth; and if not, I commend myself into the hands of God."

Sir Richard smiled. "Well, thou art a brave ass, and valiant, though an ass manifest. Dost thou not see, fellow, how thou hast sworn a ten-times bigger oath than ever I should have asked of thee? But this is the way with your Anabaptists, who by their very hatred of forms and ceremonies, show of how much account they think them, and then bind themselves out of their own fantastical self-will with far heavier burdens than ever the lawful authorities have laid on them for the sake of the commonweal. But what do they care for the commonweal, as long as they can save, as they fancy, each man his own dirty soul for himself? However, thou art sworn now with a vengeance; go on with thy tale: and first, who art thou, and whence?"

"Well, sir," said the man, quite unmoved by this last explosion; "my name is Salvation Yeo, born in Clovelly Street, in the year 1526, where my father exercised the mystery of a barber surgeon, and a preacher of the people since called Anabaptists, for which I return humble thanks to God."

Sir Richard.—Fie! thou naughty knave; return thanks that thy father was an ass?

Yeo.—Nay, but because he was a barber surgeon; for I myself learnt a touch of that trade, and thereby saved my life, as I will tell presently. And I do think that a good mariner ought to have all knowledge of carnal and worldly cunning, even to tailoring and shoemaking, that he may be able to turn his hand to whatsoever may hap.

Sir Richard.—Well spoken, fellow: but let us have thy text without thy comments. Forwards!

Yeo.—Well, sir. I was bred to the sea from my youth, and was with Captain Hawkins in his three voyages, which he made to Guinea for negro slaves, and thence to the West Indies.

Sir Richard.—Then thrice thou wentest to a bad end, though Captain Hawkins be my good friend; and the last time to a bad end thou camest.

Yeo.—No denying that last, your worship: but as for the former, I doubt—about the unlawfulness, I mean; being the negroes are of the children of Ham, who are cursed and reprobate, as Scripture declares, and their blackness testifies, being Satan's own livery; among whom therefore there can be none of the elect, wherefore the elect are not required to treat them as brethren.

Sir Richard.—What a plague of a pragmatical sea-lawyer have we here? And I doubt not, thou hypocrite, that though thou wilt call the negroes' black skin Satan's livery, when it serves thy turn to steal them, thou wilt find out sables to be Heaven's livery every Sunday, and up with a godly howl unless a parson shall preach in a black gown, Geneva fashion. Out upon thee! Go on with thy tale, lest thou finish thy sermon at Launceston after all.

Yeo.—The Lord's people were always a reviled people and a persecuted people: but I will go forward, sir; for Heaven forbid but that I should declare what God has done for me. For till lately, from my youth up, I was given over to all wretchlessness and unclean living, and was by nature a child of the devil, and to every good work reprobate, even as others.

Sir Richard.—Hark to his "even as others"! Thou new-whelped Pharisee, canst not confess thine own villainies without making out others as bad as thyself, and so thyself no worse than others? I only hope that thou hast shown none of thy devil's doings to Mr. Oxenham.

Yeo.—On the word of a Christian man, sir, as I said before, I kept true faith with him, and would have been a better friend to him, sir, what is more, than ever he was to himself.

Sir Richard.—Alas! that might easily be.

Yeo.—I think, sir, and will make good against any man, that Mr. Oxenham was a noble and valiant gentleman; true of his word, stout of his sword, skilful by sea and land, and worthy to have been Lord High Admiral of England (saving your worship's presence), but that through two great sins, wrath and avarice, he was cast away miserably or ever his soul was brought to the knowledge of the truth. Ah, sir, he was a captain worth sailing under!

And Yeo heaved a deep sigh.

Sir Richard.—Steady, steady, good fellow! If thou wouldst quit preaching, thou art no fool after all. But tell us the story without more bush-beating.

So at last Yeo settled himself to his tale:—

"Well, sirs, I went, as Mr. Leigh knows, to Nombre de Dios, with Mr. Drake and Mr. Oxenham, in 1572, where what we saw and did, your worship, I suppose, knows as well as I; and there was, as you've heard maybe, a covenant between Mr. Oxenham and Mr. Drake to sail the South Seas together, which they made, your worship, in my hearing, under the tree over Panama. For when Mr. Drake came down from the tree, after seeing the sea afar off, Mr. Oxenham and I went up and saw it too; and when we came down, Drake says, 'John, I have made a vow to God that I will sail that water, if I live and God gives me grace;' which he had done, sir, upon his bended knees, like a godly man as he always was, and would I had taken after him! and Mr. O.

says, 'I am with you, Drake, to live or die, and I think I know some one there already, so we shall not be quite among strangers;' and laughed withal. Well, sirs, that voyage, as you know, never came off, because Captain Drake was fighting in Ireland; so Mr. Oxenham, who must be up and doing, sailed for himself, and I, who loved him, God knows, like a brother (saving the difference in our ranks), helped him to get the crew together, and went as his gunner. That was in 1575; as you know, he had a 140-ton ship, sir, and seventy men out of Plymouth and Fowey and Dartmouth, and many of them old hands of Drake's, beside a dozen or so from Bideford that I picked up when I saw young Master here."

"Thank God that you did not pick me up too."

"Amen, amen!" said Yeo, clasping his hands on his breast. "Those seventy men, sir,—seventy gallant men, sir, with every one of them an immortal soul within him,—where are they now? Gone, like the spray!" And he swept his hands abroad with a wild and solemn gesture. "And their blood is upon my head!"

Both Sir Richard and Amyas began to suspect that the man's brain was not altogether sound.

"God forbid, my man," said the knight, kindly.

"Thirteen men I persuaded to join in Bideford town, beside William Penberthy of Marazion, my good comrade. And what if it be said to me at the day of judgment, 'Salvation Yeo, where are those fourteen whom thou didst tempt to their deaths by covetousness and lust of gold?' Not that I was alone in my sin, if the truth must be told. For all the way out Mr. Oxenham was making loud speech, after his pleasant way, that he would make all their fortunes, and take them to such a Paradise, that they should have no lust to come home again. And I—God knows why—for every one boast of his would make two, even to lying and empty fables, and anything to keep up the men's hearts. For I had really persuaded myself that we should all find treasures beyond Solomon his temple, and Mr. Oxenham would surely show us how to conquer some golden city or discover some island all made of precious stones. And one day, as the captain and I were talking after our fashion, I said, 'And you shall be our king, captain.' To which he, 'If I be, I shall not be long without a queen, and that no Indian one either.' And after that he often jested about the Spanish ladies, saying that none could show us the way to their hearts better than he. Which speeches I took no count of then, sirs: but after I minded them, whether I would or not. Well, sirs, we came to the shore of New Spain, near to the old place—that's Nombre de Dios; and there Mr. Oxenham went ashore into the woods with a boat's crew, to find the negroes who helped us three years before. Those are the Cimaroons, gentles, negro slaves who have fled from those devils incarnate, their Spanish masters, and live wild, like the beasts that perish; men of great stature, sirs, and fierce as wolves in the onslaught, but poor jabbering mazed fellows if they be but a bit dismayed: and have many Indian women with them, who take to these negroes a deal better than to their own kin, which breeds war enough, as you may guess.

"Well, sirs, after three days the captain comes back, looking heavy enough, and says, 'We played our trick once too often, when we played it once. There is no chance of stopping another reco (that is, a mule-train, sirs) now. The Cimaroons say that since our last visit they never move without plenty of soldiers, two hundred shot at least. Therefore,' he said, 'my gallants, we must either return empty-handed from this, the very market and treasury of the whole Indies, or do such a deed as men never did before, which I shall like all the better for that very reason.' And we, asking his meaning, 'Why,' he said, 'if Drake will not sail the South Seas, we will;' adding profanely that Drake was like Moses, who beheld the promised land afar; but he was Joshua, who would enter into it, and smite the inhabitants thereof. And, for our confirmation, showed me and the rest the superscription of a letter: and said, 'How I came by this is none of your business: but I have had it in my bosom ever since I left Plymouth; and I tell you now, what I forbore to tell you at first, that the South Seas have been my mark all along! such news have I herein of plate-ships, and gold-ships, and what not, which will come up from Quito and Lima this very month, all which, with the pearls of the Gulf of Panama, and other wealth unspeakable, will be ours, if we have but true English hearts within us.'

"At which, gentles, we were like madmen for lust of that gold, and cheerfully undertook a toil incredible; for first we run our ship aground in a great wood which grew in the very sea itself, and then took out her masts, and covered her in boughs, with her four cast pieces of great ordnance (of which more hereafter), and leaving no man in her, started for the South Seas across the neck of Panama, with two small pieces of ordnance and our culverins, and good store of victuals, and with us six of those negroes for a guide, and so twelve leagues to a river which runs into the South Sea.

"And there, having cut wood, we made a pinnace (and work enough we had at it) of five-and-forty foot in the keel; and in her down the stream, and to the Isle of Pearls in the Gulf of Panama."

"Into the South Sea? Impossible!" said Sir Richard. "Have a care what you say, my man; for there is that about you which would make me sorry to find you out a liar."

"Impossible or not, liar or none, we went there, sir."

"Question him, Amyas, lest he turn out to have been beforehand with you."

The man looked inquiringly at Amyas, who said—

"Well, my man, of the Gulf of Panama I cannot ask you, for I never was inside it, but what other parts of the coast do you know?"

"Every inch, sir, from Cabo San Francisco to Lima; more is my sorrow, for I was a galley-slave there for two years and more."

"You know Lima?"

"I was there three times, worshipful gentlemen, and the last was February come two years; and there I helped lade a great plate-ship, the Cacafuogo,' they called her."

Amyas started. Sir Richard nodded to him gently to be silent, and then—

"And what became of her, my lad?"

"God knows, who knows all, and the devil who freighted her. I broke prison six weeks afterwards, and never heard but that she got safe into Panama."

"You never heard, then, that she was taken?"

"Taken, your worships? Who should take her?"

"Why should not a good English ship take her as well as another?" said Amyas.

"Lord love you, sir; yes, faith, if they had but been there. Many's the time that I thought to myself, as we went alongside, 'Oh, if Captain Drake was but here, well to windward, and our old crew of the "Dragon"!' Ask your pardon, gentles: but how is Captain Drake, if I may make so bold?"

Neither could hold out longer.

"Fellow, fellow!" cried Sir Richard, springing up, "either thou art the cunningest liar that ever earned a halter, or thou hast done a deed the like of which never man adventured. Dost thou not know that Captain Drake took that 'Cacafuogo' and all her freight, in February come two years?"

"Captain Drake! God forgive me, sir; but—Captain Drake in the South Seas? He saw them, sir, from the tree-top over Panama, when I was with him, and I too; but sailed them, sir?—sailed them?"

"Yes, and round the world too," said Amyas, "and I with him; and took that very 'Cacafuogo' off Cape San Francisco, as she came up to Panama."

One glance at the man's face was enough to prove his sincerity. The great stern Anabaptist, who had not winced at the news of his mother's death, dropt right on his knees on the floor, and burst into violent sobs.

"Glory to God! Glory to God! O Lord, I thank thee! Captain Drake in the South Seas! The blood of thy innocents avenged, O Lord! The spoiler spoiled, and the proud robbed; and all they whose hands were mighty have found nothing. Glory, glory! Oh, tell me, sir, did she fight?"

"We gave her three pieces of ordnance only, and struck down her mizzenmast, and then boarded sword in hand, but never had need to strike a blow; and before we left her, one of her own boys had changed her name, and rechristened her the 'Cacaplata.'"

"Glory, glory! Cowards they are, as I told them. I told them they never could stand the Devon mastiffs, and well they flogged me for saying it; but they could not stop my mouth. O sir, tell me, did you get the ship that came up after her?"

"What was that?"

"A long race-ship, sir, from Guayaquil, with an old gentleman on board,—Don Francisco de Xararte was his name, and by token, he had a gold falcon hanging to a chain round his neck, and a green stone in the breast of it. I saw it as we rowed him aboard. O tell me, sir, tell me for the love of God, did you take that ship?"

"We did take that ship, and the jewel too, and her majesty has it at this very hour."

"Then tell me, sir," said he slowly, as if he dreaded an answer; "tell me, sir, and oh, try and mind—was there a little maid aboard with the old gentleman?"

"A little maid? Let me think. No; I saw none."

The man settled his features again sadly.

"I thought not. I never saw her come aboard. Still I hoped, like; I hoped. Alackaday! God help me, Salvation Yeo!"

"What have you to do with this little maid, then, good fellow!" asked Grenville.

"Ah, sir, before I tell you that, I must go back and finish the story of Mr. Oxenham, if you will believe me enough to hear it."

"I do believe thee, good fellow, and honor thee too."

"Then, sir, I can speak with a free tongue. Where was I?"

"Where was he, Amyas?"

"At the Isle of Pearls."

"And yet, O gentles, tell me first, how Captain Drake came into the South Seas:—over the neck, as we did?"

"Through the Straits, good fellow, like any Spaniard: but go on with thy story, and thou shalt have Mr. Leigh's after."

"Through the Straits! O glory! But I'll tell my tale. Well, sirs both—To the Island of Pearls we came, we and some of the negroes. We found many huts, and Indians fishing for pearls, and also a fair house, with porches; but no Spaniard therein, save one man; at which Mr. Oxenham was like a man transported, and fell on that Spaniard, crying, 'Perro, where is your mistress? Where is the bark from Lima?' To which he boldly enough, 'What was his mistress to the Englishman?' But Mr. O. threatened to twine a cord round his head till his eyes burst out; and the Spaniard, being terrified, said that the ship from Lima was expected in a fortnight's time. So for ten days we lay quiet, letting neither negro nor Spaniard leave the island, and took good store of pearls, feeding sumptuously on wild cattle and hogs until the tenth day, when there came by a small bark; her we took, and found her from Quito, and on board 60,000 pezos of gold and other store. With which if we had been content, gentlemen, all had gone well. And some were willing to go back at once, having both treasure and pearls in plenty; but Mr. O., he waxed right mad, and swore to slay any one who made that motion again, assuring us that the Lima ship of which he had news was far greater and richer, and would make princes of us all; which bark came in sight on the sixteenth day, and was taken without shot or slaughter. The taking of which bark, I verily believe, was the ruin of every mother's son of us."

And being asked why, he answered, "First, because of the discontent which was bred thereby; for on board was found no gold, but only 100,000 pezos of silver."

Sir Richard Grenville.—Thou greedy fellow; and was not that enough to stay your stomachs?

Yeo answered that he would to God it had been; and that, moreover, the weight of that silver was afterwards a hindrance to them, and fresh cause of discontent, as he would afterwards declare. "So that it had been well for us, sirs, if we had left it behind, as Mr. Drake left his three years before, and carried away the gold only. In which I do see the evident hand of God, and His just punishment for our greediness of gain; who caused Mr. Oxenham, by whom we had hoped to attain great wealth, to be a snare to us, and a cause of utter ruin."

"Do you think, then," said Sir Richard, "that Mr. Oxenham deceived you wilfully?"

"I will never believe that, sir: Mr. Oxenham had his private reasons for waiting for that ship, for the sake of one on board, whose face would that he had never seen, though he saw it then, as I fear, not for the first time by many a one." And so was silent.

"Come," said both his hearers, "you have brought us thus far, and you must go on."

"Gentlemen, I have concealed this matter from all men, both on my voyage home and since; and I hope you will be secret in the matter, for the honor of my noble captain, and the comfort of his friends who are alive. For I think it shame to publish harm of a gallant gentleman, and of an ancient and worshipful family, and to me a true and kind captain, when what is done cannot be undone, and least said soonest mended. Neither now would I have spoken of it, but that I was inwardly moved to it for the sake of that young gentleman there" (looking at Amyas), "that he might be warned in time of God's wrath against the crying sin of adultery, and flee youthful lusts, which war against the soul."

"Thou hast done wisely enough, then," said Sir Richard; "and look to it if I do not reward thee: but the young gentleman here, thank God, needs no such warnings, having got them already both by precept and example, where thou and poor Oxenham might have had them also."

"You mean Captain Drake, your worship?"

"I do, sirrah. If all men were as clean livers as he, the world would be spared one half the tears that are shed in it."

"Amen, sir. At least there would have been many a tear spared to us and ours. For—as all must out—in that bark of Lima he took a young lady, as fair as the sunshine, sir, and seemingly about two or three-and-twenty years of age, having with her a tall young lad of sixteen, and a little girl, a marvellously pretty child, of about a six or seven. And the lady herself was of an excellent beauty, like a whale's tooth for whiteness, so that all the crew wondered at her, and could not be satisfied with looking upon her. And, gentlemen, this was strange, that the lady seemed in no wise afraid or mournful, and bid her little girl fear naught, as did also Mr. Oxenham: but the lad kept a very sour countenance, and the more when he saw the lady and Mr. Oxenham speaking together apart.

"Well, sir, after this good luck we were minded to have gone straight back to the river whence we came, and so home to England with all speed. But Mr. Oxenham persuaded us to return to the island, and get a few more pearls. To which foolishness (which after caused the mishap) I verily believe he was moved by the instigation of the devil and of that lady. For as we were about to go ashore, I, going down into the cabin of the prize, saw Mr. Oxenham and that lady making great cheer of each other with, 'My life,' and 'My king,' and 'Light of my eyes,' and such toys; and being bidden by Mr. Oxenham to fetch out the lady's mails, and take them ashore, heard how the two laughed together about the old ape of Panama (which ape, or devil rather, I saw afterwards to my cost), and also how she said that she had been dead for five years, and now that Mr. Oxenham was come, she was alive again, and so forth.

"Mr. Oxenham bade take the little maid ashore, kissing her and playing with her, and saying to the lady, 'What is yours is mine, and what is mine is yours.' And she asking whether the lad should come ashore, he answered, 'He is neither yours nor mine; let the spawn of Beelzebub stay on shore.' After which I, coming on deck again, stumbled over that very lad, upon the hatchway ladder, who bore so black and despiteful a face, that I verily believe he had overheard their speech, and so thrust him upon deck; and going below again, told Mr. Oxenham what I thought, and said that it were better to put a dagger into him at once, professing to be ready so to do. For which grievous sin, seeing that it was committed in my unregenerate days, I hope I have obtained the grace of forgiveness, as I have that of hearty repentance. But the lady cried out, 'Though he be none of mine, I have sin enough already on my soul;' and so laid her hand on Mr. Oxenham's mouth, entreating pitifully. And Mr. Oxenham answered laughing, when she would let him, 'What care we? let the young monkey go and howl to the old one;' and so went ashore with the lady to that house, whence for three days he never came forth, and would have remained longer, but that the men, finding but few pearls, and being wearied with the watching and warding so many Spaniards, and negroes came clamoring to him, and swore that they would return or leave him there with the lady. So all went on board the pinnace again, every one in ill humor with the captain, and he with them.

"Well, sirs, we came back to the mouth of the river, and there began our troubles; for the negroes, as soon as we were on shore, called on Mr. Oxenham to fulfil the bargain he had made with them. And now it came out (what few of us knew till then) that he had agreed with the Cimaroons that they should have all the prisoners which were taken, save the gold. And he, though loath, was about to give up the Spaniards to them, near forty in all, supposing that they intended to use them as slaves: but as we all stood talking, one of the Spaniards, understanding what was forward, threw himself on his knees before Mr. Oxenham, and shrieking like a madman, entreated not to be given up into the hands of 'those devils,' said he, 'who never take a Spanish prisoner, but they roast him alive, and then eat his heart among them.' We asked the negroes if this was possible? To which some answered, What was that to us? But others said boldly, that it was true enough, and that revenge made the best sauce, and nothing was so sweet as Spanish blood; and one, pointing to the lady, said such foul and devilish things as I should be ashamed either for me to speak, or you to hear. At this we were like men amazed for very horror; and Mr. Oxenham said, 'You incarnate fiends, if you had taken these fellows for slaves, it had been fair enough; for you were once slaves to them, and I doubt not cruelly used enough: but as for this abomination,' says he, 'God do so to me, and more also, if I let one of them come into your murderous hands.' So there was a great quarrel; but Mr. Oxenham stoutly bade put the prisoners on board the ships again, and so let the prizes go, taking with him only the treasure, and the lady and the little maid. And so the lad went on to Panama, God's wrath having gone out against us.

"Well, sirs, the Cimaroons after that went away from us, swearing revenge (for which we cared little enough), and we rowed up the river to a place where three streams met, and then up the least of the three, some four days' journey, till it grew all shoal and swift; and there we hauled the pinnace upon the sands, and Mr. Oxenham asked the men whether they were willing to carry the gold and silver over the mountains to the North Sea. Some of them at first were loath to do it, and I and others advised that we should leave the plate behind, and take the gold only, for it would have cost us three or four journeys at the least. But Mr. Oxenham promised every man 100 pezos of silver over and above his wages, which made them content enough, and we were all to start the morrow morning. But, sirs, that night, as God had ordained, came a mishap by some rash speeches of Mr. Oxenham's, which threw all abroad again; for when we had carried the treasure about half a league inland, and hidden it away in a house which we made of boughs, Mr. O. being always full of that his fair lady, spoke to me and William Penberthy of Marazion, my good comrade, and a few more, saying, 'That we had no need to return to England, seeing that we were already in the very garden of Eden, and wanted for nothing, but could live without labor or toil; and that it was better, when we got over to the North Sea, to go and seek out some fair island, and there dwell in joy and pleasure till our lives' end. And we two,' he said, 'will be king and queen, and you, whom I can trust, my officers; and for servants we will have the Indians, who, I warrant, will be more fain to serve honest and merry masters like us than those Spanish devils,' and much more of the like; which words I liked well,—my mind, alas! being given altogether to carnal pleasure and vanity,—as did William Penberthy, my good comrade, on whom I trust God has had mercy. But the rest, sirs, took the matter all across, and began murmuring against the captain, saying that poor honest mariners like them had always the labor and the pain, while he took his delight with his lady; and that they would have at least one merry night before they were slain by the Cimaroons, or eaten by panthers and lagartos; and so got out of the pinnace two great skins of Canary wine, which were taken in the Lima prize, and sat themselves down to drink. Moreover, there were in the pinnace a great sight of hens, which came from the same prize, by which Mr. O. set great store, keeping them for the lady and the little maid; and falling upon these, the men began to blaspheme, saying, 'What a plague had the captain to fill the boat with dirty live lumber for that giglet's sake? They had a better right to a good supper than ever she had, and might fast awhile to cool her hot blood;' and so cooked and ate those hens, plucking them on board the pinnace, and letting the feathers fall into the stream. But when William Penberthy, my good comrade, saw the feathers floating away down, he asked them if they were mad, to lay a trail by which the Spaniards would surely track them out, if they came after them, as without doubt they would. But they laughed him to scorn, and said that no Spanish cur dared follow on the heels of true English mastiffs as they were, and other boastful speeches; and at last, being heated with wine, began afresh to murmur at the captain. And one speaking of his counsel about the island, the rest altogether took it amiss and out of the way; and some sprang up crying treason, and others that he meant to defraud them of the plate which he had promised, and others that he meant to desert them in a strange land, and so forth, till Mr. O., hearing the hubbub, came out to them from the house, when they reviled him foully, swearing that he meant to cheat them; and one Edward Stiles, a Wapping man, mad with drink, dared to say that he was a fool for not giving up the prisoners to the negroes, and what was it to him if the lady roasted? the negroes should have her yet; and drawing his sword, ran upon the captain: for which I was about to strike him through the body; but the captain, not caring to waste steel on such a ribald, with his fist caught him such a buffet behind the ear, that he fell down stark dead, and all the rest stood amazed. Then Mr. Oxenham called out, 'All honest men who know me, and can trust me, stand by your lawful captain against these ruffians.' Whereon, sirs, I, and Penberthy my good comrade, and four Plymouth men, who had sailed with Mr. O. in Mr. Drake's ship, and knew his trusty and valiant conditions, came over to him, and swore before God to stand by him and the lady. Then said Mr. O. to the rest, 'Will you carry this treasure, knaves, or will you not? Give me an answer here.' And they refused, unless he would, before they started, give each man his share. So Mr. O. waxed very mad, and swore that he would never be served by men who did not trust him, and so went in again; and that night was spent in great disquiet, I and those five others keeping watch about the house of boughs till the rest fell asleep, in their drink. And next morning, when the wine was gone out of them, Mr. O. asked them whether they would go to the hills with him, and find those negroes, and persuade them after all to carry the treasure. To which they agreed after awhile, thinking that so they should save themselves labor; and went off with Mr. Oxenham, leaving us six who had stood by him to watch the lady and the treasure, after he had taken an oath of us that we would deal justly and obediently by him and by her, which God knows, gentlemen, we did. So he parted with much weeping and wailing of the lady, and was gone seven days; and all that time we kept that lady faithfully and honestly, bringing her the best we could find, and serving her upon our bended knees, both for her admirable beauty, and for her excellent conditions, for she was certainly of some noble kin, and courteous, and without fear, as if she had been a very princess. But she kept always within the house, which the little maid (God bless her!) did not, but soon learned to play with us and we with her, so that we made great cheer of her, gentlemen, sailor fashion—for you know we must always have our minions aboard to pet and amuse us—maybe a monkey, or a little dog, or a singing bird, ay, or mice and spiders, if we have nothing better to play withal. And she was wonderful sharp, sirs, was the little maid, and picked up her English from us fast, calling us jolly mariners, which I doubt but she has forgotten by now, but I hope in God it be not so;" and therewith the good fellow began wiping his eyes.

"Well, sir, on the seventh day we six were down by the pinnace clearing her out, and the little maid with us gathering of flowers, and William Penberthy fishing on the bank, about a hundred yards below, when on a sudden he leaps up and runs toward us, crying, 'Here come our hens' feathers back again with a vengeance!' and so bade catch up the little maid, and run for the house, for the Spaniards were upon us.

"Which was too true; for before we could win the house, there were full eighty shot at our heels, but could not overtake us; nevertheless, some of them stopping, fixed their calivers and let fly, killing one of the Plymouth men. The rest of us escaped to the house, and catching up the lady, fled forth, not knowing whither we went, while the Spaniards, finding the house and treasure, pursued us no farther.

"For all that day and the next we wandered in great misery, the lady weeping continually, and calling for Mr. Oxenham most piteously, and the little maid likewise, till with much ado we found the track of our comrades, and went up that as best we might: but at nightfall, by good hap, we met the whole crew coming back, and with them 200 negroes or more, with bows and arrows. At which sight was great joy and embracing, and it was a strange thing, sirs, to see the lady; for before that she was altogether desperate: and yet she was now a very lioness, as soon as she had got her love again; and prayed him earnestly not to care for that gold, but to go forward to the North Sea, vowing to him in my hearing that she cared no more for poverty than she had cared for her good name, and then—they being a little apart from the rest—pointed round to the green forest, and said in Spanish—which I suppose they knew not that I understood,—'See, all round us is Paradise. Were it not enough for you and me to stay here forever, and let them take the gold or leave it as they will?'

"To which Mr. Oxenham—'Those who lived in Paradise had not sinned as we have, and would never have grown old or sick, as we shall.'

"And she—'If we do that, there are poisons enough in these woods, by which we may die in each other's arms, as would to Heaven we had died seven years agone!'

"But he—'No, no, my life. It stands upon my honor both to fulfil my bond with these men, whom I have brought hither, and to take home to England at least something of my prize as a proof of my own valor.'

"Then she smiling—'Am I not prize enough, and proof enough?' But he would not be so tempted, and turning to us offered us the half of that treasure, if we would go back with him, and rescue it from the Spaniard. At which the lady wept and wailed much; but I took upon myself to comfort her, though I was but a simple mariner, telling her that it stood upon Mr. Oxenham's honor; and that in England nothing was esteemed so foul as cowardice, or breaking word and troth betwixt man and man; and that better was it for him to die seven times by the Spaniards, than to face at home the scorn of all who sailed the seas. So, after much ado, back they went again; I and Penberthy, and the three Plymouth men which escaped from the pinnace, keeping the lady as before.

"Well, sirs, we waited five days, having made houses of boughs as before, without hearing aught; and on the sixth we saw coming afar off Mr. Oxenham, and with him fifteen or twenty men, who seemed very weary and wounded; and when we looked for the rest to be behind them, behold there were no more; at which, sirs, as you may well think, our hearts sank within us.

"And Mr. O., coming nearer, cried out afar off, 'All is lost!' and so walked into the camp without a word, and sat himself down at the foot of a great tree with his head between his hands, speaking neither to the lady or to any one, till she very pitifully kneeling before him, cursing herself for the cause of all his mischief, and praying him to avenge himself upon that her tender body, won him hardly to look once upon her, after which (as is the way of vain and unstable man) all between them was as before.

"But the men were full of curses against the negroes, for their cowardice and treachery; yea, and against high Heaven itself, which had put the most part of their ammunition into the Spaniards' hands; and told me, and I believe truly, how they forced the enemy awaiting them in a little copse of great trees, well fortified with barricades of boughs, and having with them our two falcons, which they had taken out of the pinnace. And how Mr. Oxenham divided both the English and the negroes into two bands, that one might attack the enemy in front, and the other in the rear, and so set upon them with great fury, and would have utterly driven them out, but that the negroes, who had come on with much howling, like very wild beasts, being suddenly scared with the shot and noise of the ordnance, turned and fled, leaving the Englishmen alone; in which evil strait Mr. O. fought like a very Guy of Warwick, and I verily believe every man of them likewise; for there was none of them who had not his shrewd scratch to show. And indeed, Mr. Oxenham's party had once gotten within the barricades, but the Spaniards being sheltered by the tree trunks (and especially by one mighty tree, which stood as I remembered it, and remember it now, borne up two fathoms high upon its own roots, as it were upon arches and pillars), shot at them with such advantage, that they had several slain, and seven more taken alive, only among the roots of that tree. So seeing that they could prevail nothing, having little but their pikes and swords, they were fain to give back; though Mr. Oxenham swore he would not stir a foot, and making at the Spanish captain was borne down with pikes, and hardly pulled away by some, who at last reminding him of his lady, persuaded him to come away with the rest. Whereon the other party fled also; but what had become of them they knew not, for they took another way. And so they miserably drew off, having lost in men eleven killed and seven taken alive, besides five of the rascal negroes who were killed before they had time to run; and there was an end of the matter.*

"But the next day, gentlemen, in came some five-and-twenty more, being the wreck of the other party, and with them a few negroes; and these last proved themselves no honester men than they were brave, for there being great misery among us English, and every one of us straggling where he could to get food, every day one or more who went out never came back, and that caused a suspicion that the negroes had betrayed them to the Spaniards, or, maybe, slain and eaten them. So these fellows being upbraided, with that altogether left us, telling us boldly, that if they had eaten our fellows, we owed them a debt instead of the Spanish prisoners; and we, in great terror and hunger, went forward and over the mountains till we came to a little river which ran northward, which seemed to lead into the Northern Sea; and there Mr. O.—who, sirs, I will say, after his first rage was over, behaved himself all through like a valiant and skilful commander—bade us cut down trees and make canoes, to go down to the sea; which we began to do, with great labor and little profit, hewing down trees with our swords, and burning them out with fire, which, after much labor, we kindled; but as we were a-burning out of the first tree, and cutting down of another, a great party of negroes came upon us, and with much friendly show bade us flee for our lives, for the Spaniards were upon us in great force. And so we were up and away again, hardly able to drag our legs after us for hunger and weariness, and the broiling heat. And some were taken (God help them!) and some fled with the negroes, of whom what became God alone knoweth; but eight or ten held on with the captain, among whom was I, and fled downward toward the sea for one day; but afterwards finding, by the noise in the woods, that the Spaniards were on the track of us, we turned up again toward the inland, and coming to a cliff, climbed up over it, drawing up the lady and the little maid with cords of liana (which hang from those trees as honeysuckle does here, but exceeding stout and long, even to fifty fathoms); and so breaking the track, hoped to be out of the way of the enemy.

"By which, nevertheless, we only increased our misery. For two fell from that cliff, as men asleep for very weariness, and miserably broke their bones; and others, whether by the great toil, or sunstrokes, or eating of strange berries, fell sick of fluxes and fevers; where was no drop of water, but rock of pumice stone as bare as the back of my hand, and full, moreover, of great cracks, black and without bottom, over which we had not strength to lift the sick, but were fain to leave them there aloft, in the sunshine, like Dives in his torments, crying aloud for a drop of water to cool their tongues; and every man a great stinking vulture or two sitting by him, like an ugly black fiend out of the pit, waiting till the poor soul should depart out of the corpse: but nothing could avail, and for the dear life we must down again and into the woods, or be burned up alive upon those rocks.

"So getting down the slope on the farther side, we came into the woods once more, and there wandered for many days, I know not how many; our shoes being gone, and our clothes all rent off us with brakes and briars. And yet how the lady endured all was a marvel to see; for she went barefoot many days, and for clothes was fain to wrap herself in Mr. Oxenham's cloak; while the little maid went all but naked: but ever she looked still on Mr. Oxenham, and seemed to take no care as long as he was by, comforting and cheering us all with pleasant words; yea, and once sitting down under a great fig-tree, sang us all to sleep with very sweet music; yet, waking about midnight, I saw her sitting still upright, weeping very bitterly; on whom, sirs, God have mercy; for she was a fair and a brave jewel.

"And so, to make few words of a sad matter, at last there were none left but Mr. Oxenham and the lady and the little maid, together with me and William Penberthy of Marazion, my good comrade. And Mr. Oxenham always led the lady, and Penberthy and I carried the little maid. And for food we had fruits, such as we could find, and water we got from the leaves of certain lilies which grew on the bark of trees, which I found by seeing the monkeys drink at them; and the little maid called them monkey-cups, and asked for them continually, making me climb for them. And so we wandered on, and upward into very high mountains, always fearing lest the Spaniards should track us with dogs, which made the lady leap up often in her sleep, crying that the bloodhounds were upon her. And it befell upon a day, that we came into a great wood of ferns (which grew not on the ground like ours, but on stems as big as a pinnace's mast, and the bark of them was like a fine meshed net, very strange to see), where was very pleasant shade, cool and green; and there, gentlemen, we sat down on a bank of moss, like folk desperate and fordone, and every one looked the other in the face for a long while. After which I took off the bark of those ferns, for I must needs be doing something to drive away thought, and began to plait slippers for the little maid.

"And as I was plaiting, Mr. Oxenham said, 'What hinders us from dying like men, every man falling on his own sword?' To which I answered that I dare not; for a wise woman had prophesied of me, sirs, that I should die at sea, and yet neither by water or battle, wherefore I did not think right to meddle with the Lord's purposes. And William Penberthy said, 'That he would sell his life, and that dear, but never give it away.' But the lady said, 'Ah, how gladly would I die! but then la paouvre garse,' which is in French 'the poor maid,' meaning the little one. Then Mr. Oxenham fell into a very great weeping, a weakness I never saw him in before or since; and with many tears besought me never to desert that little maid, whatever might befall; which I promised, swearing to it like a heathen, but would, if I had been able, have kept it like a Christian. But on a sudden there was a great cry in the wood, and coming through the trees on all sides Spanish arquebusiers, a hundred strong at least, and negroes with them, who bade us stand or they would shoot. William Penberthy leapt up, crying 'Treason!' and running upon the nearest negro ran him through, and then another, and then falling on the Spaniards, fought manfully till he was borne down with pikes, and so died. But I, seeing no thing better to do, sate still and finished my plaiting. And so we were all taken, and I and Mr. Oxenham bound with cords; but the soldiers made a litter for the lady and child, by commandment of Senor Diego de Trees, their commander, a very courteous gentleman.

"Well, sirs, we were brought down to the place where the house of boughs had been by the river-side; there we went over in boats, and found waiting for us certain Spanish gentlemen, and among others one old and ill-favored man, gray-bearded and bent, in a suit of black velvet, who seemed to be a great man among them. And if you will believe me, Mr. Leigh, that was none other than the old man with the gold falcon at his breast, Don Francisco Xararte by name, whom you found aboard of the Lima ship. And had you known as much of him as I do, or as Mr. Oxenham did either, you had cut him up for shark's bait, or ever you let the cur ashore again.

"Well, sirs, as soon as the lady came to shore, that old man ran upon her sword in hand, and would have slain her, but some there held him back. On which he turned to, and reviled with every foul and spiteful word which he could think of, so that some there bade him be silent for shame; and Mr. Oxenham said, 'It is worthy of you, Don Francisco, thus to trumpet abroad your own disgrace. Did I not tell you years ago that you were a cur; and are you not proving my words for me?'

"He answered, 'English dog, would to Heaven I had never seen you!'

"And Mr. Oxenham, 'Spanish ape, would to Heaven that I had sent my dagger through your herring-ribs when you passed me behind St. Ildegonde's church, eight years last Easter-eve.' At which the old man turned pale, and then began again to upbraid the lady, vowing that he would have her burnt alive, and other devilish words, to which she answered at last—

"'Would that you had burnt me alive on my wedding morning, and spared me eight years of misery!' And he—

"'Misery? Hear the witch, senors! Oh, have I not pampered her, heaped with jewels, clothes, coaches, what not? The saints alone know what 'I have spent on her. What more would she have of me?'

"To which she answered only but this one word, 'Fool!' but in so terrible a voice, though low, that they who were about to laugh at the old pantaloon, were more minded to weep for her.

"'Fool!' she said again, after a while, 'I will waste no words upon you. I would have driven a dagger to your heart months ago, but that I was loath to set you free so soon from your gout and your rheumatism. Selfish and stupid, know when you bought my body from my parents, you did not buy my soul! Farewell, my love, my life! and farewell, senors! May you be more merciful to your daughters than my parents were to me!' And so, catching a dagger from the girdle of one of the soldiers, smote herself to the heart, and fell dead before them all.

"At which Mr. Oxenham smiled, and said, 'That was worthy of us both. If you will unbind my hands, senors, I shall be most happy to copy so fair a schoolmistress.'

"But Don Diego shook his head, and said—

"'It were well for you, valiant senor, were I at liberty to do so; but on questioning those of your sailors whom I have already taken, I cannot hear that you have any letters of license, either from the queen of England, or any other potentate. I am compelled, therefore, to ask you whether this is so; for it is a matter of life and death.'

"To which Mr. Oxenham answered merrily, that so it was: but that he was not aware that any potentate's license was required to permit a gentleman's meeting his lady love; and that as for the gold which they had taken, if they had never allowed that fresh and fair young May to be forced into marrying that old January, he should never have meddled with their gold; so that was rather their fault than his. And added, that if he was to be hanged, as he supposed, the only favor which he asked for was a long drop and no priests. And all the while, gentlemen, he still kept his eyes fixed on the lady's corpse, till he was led away with me, while all that stood by, God reward them for it, lamented openly the tragical end of those two sinful lovers.

"And now, sirs, what befell me after that matters little; for I never saw Captain Oxenham again, nor ever shall in this life."

"He was hanged, then?"

"So I heard for certain the next year, and with him the gunner and sundry more: but some were given away for slaves to the Spaniards, and may be alive now, unless, like me, they have fallen into the cruel clutches of the Inquisition. For the Inquisition now, gentlemen, claims the bodies and souls of all heretics all over the world (as the devils told me with their own lips, when I pleaded that I was no Spanish subject); and none that it catches, whether peaceable merchants or shipwrecked mariners, but must turn or burn."

"But how did you get into the Inquisition?"

"Why, sir, after we were taken, we set forth to go down the river again; and the old Don took the little maid with him in one boat (and bitterly she screeched at parting from us and from the poor dead corpse), and Mr. Oxenham with Don Diego de Trees in another, and I in a third. And from the Spaniards I learnt that we were to be taken down to Lima, to the Viceroy; but that the old man lived hard by Panama, and was going straight back to Panama forthwith with the little maid. But they said, 'It will be well for her if she ever gets there, for the old man swears she is none of his, and would have left her behind him in the woods, now, if Don Diego had not shamed him out of it.' And when I heard that, seeing that there was nothing but death before me, I made up my mind to escape; and the very first night, sirs, by God's help, I did it, and went southward away into the forest, avoiding the tracks of the Cimaroons, till I came to an Indian town. And there, gentlemen, I got more mercy from heathens than ever I had from Christians; for when they found that I was no Spaniard, they fed me and gave me a house, and a wife (and a good wife she was to me), and painted me all over in patterns, as you see; and because I had some knowledge of surgery and blood-letting, and my fleams in my pocket, which were worth to me a fortune, I rose to great honor among them, though they taught me more of simples than ever I taught them of surgery. So I lived with them merrily enough, being a very heathen like them, or indeed worse, for they worshipped their Xemes, but I nothing. And in time my wife bare me a child; in looking at whose sweet face, gentlemen, I forgot Mr. Oxenham and his little maid, and my oath, ay, and my native land also. Wherefore it was taken from me, else had I lived and died as the beasts which perish; for one night, after we were all lain down, came a noise outside the town, and I starting up saw armed men and calivers shining in the moonlight, and heard one read in Spanish, with a loud voice, some fool's sermon, after their custom when they hunt the poor Indians, how God had given to St. Peter the dominion of the whole earth, and St. Peter again the Indies to the Catholic king; wherefore, if they would all be baptized and serve the Spaniard, they should have some monkey's allowance or other of more kicks than pence; and if not, then have at them with fire and sword; but I dare say your worships know that devilish trick of theirs better than I."

"I know it, man. Go on."

"Well—no sooner were the words spoken than, without waiting to hear what the poor innocents within would answer (though that mattered little, for they understood not one word of it), what do the villains but let fly right into the town with their calivers, and then rush in, sword in hand, killing pell-mell all they met, one of which shots, gentlemen, passing through the doorway, and close by me, struck my poor wife to the heart, that she never spoke word more. I, catching up the babe from her breast, tried to run: but when I saw the town full of them, and their dogs with them in leashes, which was yet worse, I knew all was lost, and sat down again by the corpse with the babe on my knees, waiting the end, like one stunned and in a dream; for now I thought God from whom I had fled had surely found me out, as He did Jonah, and the punishment of all my sins was come. Well, gentlemen, they dragged me out, and all the young men and women, and chained us together by the neck; and one, catching the pretty babe out of my arms, calls for water and a priest (for they had their shavelings with them), and no sooner was it christened than, catching the babe by the heels, he dashed out its brains,—oh! gentlemen, gentlemen!—against the ground, as if it had been a kitten; and so did they to several more innocents that night, after they had christened them; saying it was best for them to go to heaven while they were still sure thereof; and so marched us all for slaves, leaving the old folk and the wounded to die at leisure. But when morning came, and they knew by my skin that I was no Indian, and by my speech that I was no Spaniard, they began threatening me with torments, till I confessed that I was an Englishman, and one of Oxenham's crew. At that says the leader, 'Then you shall to Lima, to hang by the side of your captain the pirate;' by which I first knew that my poor captain was certainly gone; but alas for me! the priest steps in and claims me for his booty, calling me Lutheran, heretic, and enemy of God; and so, to make short a sad story, to the Inquisition at Cartagena I went, where what I suffered, gentlemen, were as disgustful for you to hear, as unmanly for me to complain of; but so it was, that being twice racked, and having endured the water-torment as best I could, I was put to the scarpines, whereof I am, as you see, somewhat lame of one leg to this day. At which I could abide no more, and so, wretch that I am! denied my God, in hope to save my life; which indeed I did, but little it profited me; for though I had turned to their superstition, I must have two hundred stripes in the public place, and then go to the galleys for seven years. And there, gentlemen, ofttimes I thought that it had been better for me to have been burned at once and for all: but you know as well as I what a floating hell of heat and cold, hunger and thirst, stripes and toil, is every one of those accursed craft. In which hell, nevertheless, gentlemen, I found the road to heaven,—I had almost said heaven itself. For it fell out, by God's mercy, that my next comrade was an Englishman like myself, a young man of

Bristol, who, as he told me, had been some manner of factor on board poor Captain Barker's ship, and had been a preacher among the Anabaptists here in England. And, oh! Sir Richard Grenville, if that man had done for you what he did for me, you would never say a word against those who serve the same Lord, because they don't altogether hold with you. For from time to time, sir, seeing me altogether despairing and furious, like a wild beast in a pit, he set before me in secret earnestly the sweet promises of God in Christ,—who says, 'Come to me, all ye that are heavy laden, and I will refresh you; and though your sins be as scarlet, they shall be as white as snow,—till all that past sinful life of mine looked like a dream when one awaketh, and I forgot all my bodily miseries in the misery of my soul, so did I loathe and hate myself for my rebellion against that loving God who had chosen me before the foundation of the world, and come to seek and save me when I was lost; and falling into very despair at the burden of my heinous sins, knew no peace until I gained sweet assurance that my Lord had hanged my burden upon His cross, and washed my sinful soul in His most sinless blood, Amen!"

And Sir Richard Grenville said Amen also.

"But, gentlemen, if that sweet youth won a soul to Christ, he paid as dearly for it as ever did saint of God. For after a three or four months, when I had been all that while in sweet converse with him, and I may say in heaven in the midst of hell, there came one night to the barranco at Lima, where we were kept when on shore, three black devils of the Holy Office, and carried him off without a word, only saying to me, 'Look that your turn come not next, for we hear that you have had much talk with the villain.' And at these words I was so struck cold with terror that I swooned right away, and verily, if they had taken me there and then, I should have denied my God again, for my faith was but young and weak: but instead, they left me aboard the galley for a few months more (that was a whole voyage to Panama and back), in daily dread lest I should find myself in their cruel claws again—and then nothing for me, but to burn as a relapsed heretic. But when we came back to Lima, the officers came on board again, and said to me, 'That heretic has confessed naught against you, so we will leave you for this time: but because you have been seen talking with him so much, and the Holy Office suspects your conversion to be but a rotten one, you are adjudged to the galleys for the rest of your life in perpetual servitude.'"

"But what became of him?" asked Amyas.

"He was burned, sir, a day or two before we got to Lima, and five others with him at the same stake, of whom two were Englishmen; old comrades of mine, as I guess."

"Ah!" said Amyas, "we heard of that when we were off Lima; and they said, too, that there were six more lying still in prison, to be burnt in a few days. If we had had our fleet with us (as we should have had if it had not been for John Winter) we would have gone in and rescued them all, poor wretches, and sacked the town to boot: but what could we do with one ship?"

"Would to God you had, sir; for the story was true enough; and among them, I heard, were two young ladies of quality and their confessor, who came to their ends for reproving out of Scripture the filthy and loathsome living of those parts, which, as I saw well enough and too well, is liker to Sodom than to a Christian town; but God will avenge His saints, and their sins. Amen."

"Amen," said Sir Richard: "but on with thy tale, for it is as strange as ever man heard."

"Well, gentlemen, when I heard that I must end my days in that galley, I was for awhile like a madman: but in a day or two there came over me, I know not how, a full assurance of salvation, both for this life and the life to come, such as I had never had before; and it was revealed to me (I speak the truth, gentlemen, before Heaven) that now I had been tried to the uttermost, and that my deliverance was at hand.

"And all the way up to Panama (that was after we had laden the 'Cacafuogo') I cast in my mind how to escape, and found no way: but just as I was beginning to lose heart again, a door was opened by the Lord's own hand; for (I know not why) we were marched across from Panama to Nombre, which had never happened before, and there put all together into a great barranco close by the quay-side, shackled, as is the fashion, to one long bar that ran the whole length of the house. And the very first night that we were there, I, looking out of the window, spied, lying close aboard of the quay, a good-sized caravel well armed and just loading for sea; and the land breeze blew off very strong, so that the sailors were laying out a fresh warp to hold her to the shore. And it came into my mind, that if we were aboard of her, we should be at sea in five minutes; and looking at the quay, I saw all the soldiers who had guarded us scattered about drinking and gambling, and some going into taverns to refresh themselves after their journey. That was just at sundown; and half an hour after, in comes the gaoler to take a last look at us for the night, and his keys at his girdle. Whereon, sirs (whether by madness, or whether by the spirit which gave Samson strength to rend the lion), I rose against him as he passed me, without forethought or treachery of any kind, chained though I was, caught him by the head, and threw him there and then against the wall, that he never spoke word after; and then with his keys freed myself and every soul in that room, and bid them follow me, vowing to kill any man who disobeyed my commands. They followed, as men astounded and leaping out of night into day, and death into life, and so aboard that caravel and out of the harbor (the Lord only knows how, who blinded the eyes of the idolaters), 'with no more hurt than a few chance-shot from the soldiers on the quay. But my tale has been over-long already, gentlemen—"

"Go on till midnight, my good fellow, if you will."

"Well, sirs, they chose me for captain, and a certain Genoese for lieutenant, and away to go. I would fain have gone ashore after all, and back to Panama to hear news of the little maid: but that would have been but a fool's errand. Some wanted to turn pirates: but I, and the Genoese too, who was a prudent man, though an evil one, persuaded them to run for England and get employment in the Netherland wars, assuring them that there would be no safety in the Spanish Main, when once our escape got wind. And the more part being of one mind, for England we sailed, watering at the Barbadoes because it was desolate; and so eastward toward the Canaries. In which voyage what we endured (being taken by long calms), by scurvy, calentures, hunger, and thirst, no tongue can tell. Many a time were we glad to lay out sheets at night to catch the dew, and suck them in the morning; and he that had a noggin of rain-water out of the scuppers was as much sought to as if he had been Adelantado of all the Indies; till of a hundred and forty poor wretches a hundred and ten were dead, blaspheming God and man, and above all me and the Genoese, for taking the Europe voyage, as if I had not sins enough of my own already. And last of all, when we thought ourselves safe, we were wrecked by southwesters on the coast of Brittany, near to Cape Race, from which but nine souls of us came ashore with their lives; and so to Brest, where I found a Flushinger who carried me to Falmouth and so ends my tale, in which if I have said one word more or less than truth, I can wish myself no worse, than to have it all to undergo a second time."

And his voice, as he finished, sank from very weariness of soul; while Sir Richard sat opposite him in silence, his elbows on the table, his cheeks on his doubled fists, looking him through and through with kindling eyes. No one spoke for several minutes; and then—

"Amyas, you have heard this story. You believe it?"

"Every word, sir, or I should not have the heart of a Christian man."

"So do I. Anthony!"

The butler entered.

"Take this man to the buttery; clothe him comfortably, and feed him with the best; and bid the knaves treat him as if he were their own father."

But Yeo lingered.

"If I might be so bold as to ask your worship a favor?—"

"Anything in reason, my brave fellow."

"If your worship could put me in the way of another adventure to the Indies?"

"Another! Hast not had enough of the Spaniards already?"

"Never enough, sir, while one of the idolatrous tyrants is left unhanged," said he, with a right bitter smile. "But it's not for that only, sir: but my little maid—Oh, sir! my little maid, that I swore to Mr. Oxenham to look to, and never saw her from that day to this! I must find her, sir, or I shall go mad, I believe. Not a night but she comes and calls to me in my dreams, the poor darling; and not a morning but when I wake there is my oath lying on my soul, like a great black cloud, and I no nearer the keeping of it. I told that poor young minister of it when we were in the galleys together; and he said oaths were oaths, and keep it I must; and keep it I will, sir, if you'll but help me."

"Have patience, man. God will take as good care of thy little maid as ever thou wilt."

"I know it, sir. I know it: but faith's weak, sir! and oh! if she were bred up a Papist and an idolater; wouldn't her blood be on my head then, sir? Sooner than that, sooner than that, I'd be in the Inquisition again to-morrow, I would!"

"My good fellow, there are no adventures to the Indies forward now: but if you want to fight Spaniards, here is a gentleman will show you the way. Amyas, take him with you to Ireland. If he has learnt half the lessons God has set him to learn, he ought to stand you in good stead."

Yeo looked eagerly at the young giant.

"Will you have me, sir? There's few matters I can't turn my hand to: and maybe you'll be going to the Indies again, some day, eh? and take me with you? I'd serve your turn well, though I say it, either for gunner or for pilot. I know every stone and tree from Nombre to Panama, and all the ports of both the seas. You'll never be content, I'll warrant, till you've had another turn along the gold coasts, will you now?"

Amyas laughed, and nodded; and the bargain was concluded.

So out went Yeo to eat, and Amyas having received his despatches, got ready for his journey home.

"Go the short way over the moors, lad; and send back Cary's gray when you can. You must not lose an hour, but be ready to sail the moment the wind goes about."

So they started: but as Amyas was getting into the saddle, he saw that there was some stir among the servants, who seemed to keep carefully out of Yeo's way, whispering and nodding mysteriously; and just as his foot was in the stirrup, Anthony, the old butler, plucked him back.

"Dear father alive, Mr. Amyas!" whispered he: "and you ben't going by the moor road all alone with that chap?"

"Why not, then? I'm too big for him to eat, I reckon."

"Oh, Mr. Amyas! he's not right, I tell you; not company for a Christian—to go forth with creatures as has flames of fire in their inwards; 'tis temptation of Providence, indeed, then, it is."

"Tale of a tub."

"Tale of a Christian, sir. There was two boys pig-minding, seed him at it down the hill, beside a maiden that was taken mazed (and no wonder, poor soul!) and lying in screeching asterisks now down to the mill—you ask as you go by—and saw the flames come out of the mouth of mun, and the smoke out of mun's nose like a vire-drake, and the roaring of mun like the roaring of ten thousand bulls. Oh, sir! and to go with he after dark over moor! 'Tis the devil's devices, sir, against you, because you'm going against his sarvants the Pope of Room and the Spaniard; and you'll be Pixy-led, sure as life, and locked into a bog, you will, and see mun vanish away to fire and brimstone, like a jack-o'-lantern. Oh, have a care, then, have a care!"

And the old man wrung his hands, while Amyas, bursting with laughter, rode off down the park, with the unconscious Yeo at his stirrup, chatting away about the Indies, and delighting Amyas more and more by his shrewdness, high spirit, and rough eloquence.

They had gone ten miles or more; the day began to draw in, and the western wind to sweep more cold and cheerless every moment, when Amyas, knowing that there was not an inn hard by around for many a mile ahead, took a pull at a certain bottle which Lady Grenville had put into his holster, and then offered Yeo a pull also.

He declined; he had meat and drink too about him, Heaven be praised!

"Meat and drink? Fall to, then, man, and don't stand on manners."

Whereon Yeo, seeing an old decayed willow by a brook, went to it, and took therefrom some touchwood, to which he set a light with his knife and a stone, while Amyas watched, a little puzzled and startled, as Yeo's fiery reputation came into his mind. Was he really a salamander-sprite, and going to warm his inside by a meal of burning tinder? But now Yeo, in his solemn methodical way, pulled out of his bosom a brown leaf, and began rolling a piece of it up neatly to the size of his little finger; and then, putting the one end into his mouth and the other on the tinder, sucked at it till it was a-light; and drinking down the smoke, began puffing it out again at his nostrils with a grunt of deepest satisfaction, and resumed his dog-trot by Amyas's side, as if he had been a walking chimney.

On which Amyas burst into a loud laugh, and cried—

"Why, no wonder they said you breathed fire? Is not that the Indians' tobacco?"

"Yea, verily, Heaven be praised! but did you never see it before?"

"Never, though we heard talk of it along the coast; but we took it for one more Spanish lie. Humph—well, live and learn!"

"Ah, sir, no lie, but a blessed truth, as I can tell, who have ere now gone in the strength of this weed three days and nights without eating; and therefore, sir, the Indians always carry it with them on their war-parties: and no wonder; for when all things were made none was made better than this; to be a lone man's companion, a bachelor's friend, a hungry man's food, a sad man's cordial, a wakeful man's sleep, and a chilly man's fire, sir; while for stanching of wounds, purging of rheum, and settling of the stomach, there's no herb like unto it under the canopy of heaven."

The truth of which eulogium Amyas tested in after years, as shall be fully set forth in due place and time. But "Mark in the meanwhile," says one of the veracious chroniclers from whom I draw these facts, writing seemingly in the palmy days of good Queen Anne, and "not having" (as he says) "before his eyes the fear of that misocapnic Solomon James I. or of any other lying Stuart," "that not to South Devon, but to North; not to Sir Walter Raleigh, but to Sir Amyas Leigh; not to the banks of Dart, but to the banks of Torridge, does Europe owe the day-spring of the latter age, that age of smoke which shall endure and thrive, when the age of brass shall have vanished like those of iron and of gold; for whereas Mr. Lane is said to have brought home that divine weed (as Spenser well names it) from Virginia, in the year 1584, it is hereby indisputable that full four years earlier, by the bridge of Putford in the Torridge moors (which all true smokers shall hereafter visit as a hallowed spot and point of pilgrimage) first twinkled that fiery beacon and beneficent lodestar of Bidefordian commerce, to spread hereafter from port to port and peak to peak, like the watch-fires which proclaimed the coming of the Armada or the fall of Troy, even to the shores of the Bosphorus, the peaks of the Caucasus, and the farthest isles of the Malayan sea, while Bideford, metropolis of tobacco, saw her Pool choked with Virginian traders, and the pavement of her Bridgeland Street groaning beneath the savory bales of roll Trinadado, leaf, and pudding; and her grave burghers, bolstered and blocked out of their own houses by the scarce less savory stock-fish casks which filled cellar, parlor, and attic, were fain to sit outside the door, a silver pipe in every strong right hand, and each left hand chinking cheerfully the doubloons deep lodged in the auriferous caverns of their trunk-hose; while in those fairy-rings of fragrant mist, which circled round their contemplative brows, flitted most pleasant visions of Wiltshire farmers jogging into Sherborne fair, their heaviest shillings in their pockets, to buy (unless old Aubrey lies) the lotus-leaf of Torridge for its weight in silver, and draw from thence, after the example of the Caciques of Dariena, supplies of inspiration much needed, then as now, in those Gothamite regions. And yet did these improve, as Englishmen, upon the method of those heathen savages; for the latter (so Salvation Yeo reported as a truth, and Dampier's surgeon Mr. Wafer after him), when they will deliberate of war or policy, sit round in the hut of the chief; where being placed, enter to them a small boy with a cigarro of the bigness of a rolling-pin and puffs the smoke thereof into the face of each warrior, from the eldest to the youngest; while they, putting their hand funnel-wise round their mouths, draw into the sinuosities of the brain that more than Delphic vapor of prophecy; which boy presently falls down in a swoon, and being dragged out by the heels and laid by to sober, enter another to puff at the sacred cigarro, till he is dragged out likewise; and so on till the tobacco is finished, and the seed of wisdom has sprouted in every soul into the tree of meditation, bearing the flowers of eloquence, and in due time the fruit of valiant action." With which quaint fact (for fact it is, in spite of the bombast) I end the present chapter.

CHAPTER VIII: HOW THE NOBLE BROTHERHOOD OF THE ROSE WAS FOUNDED

It now falls to my lot to write of the foundation of that most chivalrous brotherhood of the Rose, which after a few years made itself not only famous in its native country of Devon, but formidable, as will be related hereafter, both in Ireland and in the Netherlands, in the Spanish Main and the heart of South America. And if this chapter shall seem to any Quixotic and fantastical, let them recollect that the generation who spoke and acted thus in matters of love and honor were, nevertheless, practised and valiant soldiers, and prudent and crafty politicians; that he who wrote the "Arcadia" was at the same time, in spite of his youth, one of the subtlest diplomatists of Europe; that the poet of the "Faerie Queene" was also the author of "The State of Ireland;" and if they shall quote against me with a sneer Lilly's "Euphues" itself, I shall only answer by asking—Have they ever read it? For if they have done so, I pity them if they have not found it, in spite of occasional tediousness and pedantry, as brave, righteous, and pious a book as man need look into: and wish for no better proof of the nobleness and virtue of the Elizabethan age, than the fact that "Euphues" and the "Arcadia" were the two popular romances of the day. It may have suited the purposes of Sir Walter Scott, in his cleverly drawn Sir Piercie Shafton, to ridicule the Euphuists, and that affectatam comitatem of the travelled English of which Languet complains; but over and above the anachronism of the whole character (for, to give but one instance, the Euphuist knight talks of Sidney's quarrel with Lord Oxford at least ten years before it happened), we do deny that Lilly's book could, if read by any man of common sense, produce such a coxcomb, whose spiritual ancestors would rather have been Gabriel Harvey and Lord Oxford,—if indeed the former has not maligned the latter, and ill-tempered Tom Nash maligned the maligner in his turn.

But, indeed, there is a double anachronism in Sir Piercie; for he does not even belong to the days of Sidney, but to those worse times which began in the latter years of Elizabeth, and after breaking her mighty heart, had full license to bear their crop of fools' heads in the profligate days of James. Of them, perhaps, hereafter. And in the meanwhile, let those who have not read "Euphues" believe that, if they could train a son after the fashion of his Ephoebus, to the great saving of their own money and his virtue, all fathers, even in these money-making days, would rise up and call them blessed. Let us rather open our eyes, and see in these old Elizabeth gallants our own ancestors, showing forth with the luxuriant wildness of youth all the virtues which still go to the making of a true Englishman. Let us not only see in their commercial and military daring, in their political astuteness, in their deep reverence for law, and in their solemn sense of the great calling of the English nation, the antitypes or rather the examples of our own: but let us confess that their chivalry is only another garb of that beautiful tenderness and mercy which is now, as it was then, the twin sister of English valor; and even in their extravagant fondness for Continental manners and literature, let us recognize that old Anglo-Norman teachableness and wide-heartedness, which has enabled us to profit by the wisdom and civilization of all ages and of all lands, without prejudice to our own distinctive national character.

And so I go to my story, which, if any one dislikes, he has but to turn the leaf till he finds pasturage which suits him better.

Amyas could not sail the next day, or the day after; for the southwester freshened, and blew three parts of a gale dead into the bay. So having got the "Mary Grenville" down the river into Appledore pool, ready to start with the first shift of wind, he went quietly home; and when his mother started on a pillion behind the old serving-man to ride to Clovelly, where Frank lay wounded, he went in with her as far as Bideford, and there met, coming down the High Street, a procession of horsemen headed by Will Cary, who, clad cap-a-pie in a shining armor, sword on thigh, and helmet at saddle-bow, looked as gallant a young gentleman as ever Bideford dames peeped at from door and window. Behind him, upon country ponies, came four or five stout serving-men, carrying his lances and baggage, and their own long-bows, swords, and bucklers; and behind all, in a horse-litter, to Mrs. Leigh's great joy, Master Frank himself. He deposed that his wounds were only flesh-wounds, the dagger having turned against his ribs; that he must see the last of his brother; and that with her good leave he would not come home to Burrough, but take up his abode with Cary in the Ship Tavern, close to the Bridge-foot. This he did forthwith, and settling himself on a couch, held his levee there in state, mobbed by all the gossips of the town, not without white fibs as to who had brought him into that sorry plight.

But in the meanwhile he and Amyas concocted a scheme, which was put into effect the next day (being market-day); first by the innkeeper, who began under Amyas's orders a bustle of roasting, boiling, and frying, unparalleled in the annals of the Ship Tavern; and next by Amyas himself, who, going out into the market, invited as many of his old schoolfellows, one by one apart, as Frank had pointed out to him, to a merry supper and a "rowse" thereon consequent; by which crafty scheme, in came each of Rose Salterne's gentle admirers, and found himself, to his considerable disgust, seated at the same table with six rivals, to none of whom had he spoken for the last six months. However, all were too well bred to let the Leighs discern as much; and they (though, of course, they knew all) settled their guests, Frank on his couch lying at the head of the table, and Amyas taking the bottom: and contrived, by filling all mouths with good things, to save them the pain of speaking to each other till the wine should have loosened their tongues and warmed their hearts. In the meanwhile both Amyas and Frank, ignoring the silence of their guests with the most provoking good-humor, chatted, and joked, and told stories, and made themselves such good company, that Will Cary, who always found merriment infectious, melted into a jest, and then into another, and finding good-humor far more pleasant than bad, tried to make Mr. Coffin laugh, and only made him bow, and to make Mr. Fortescue laugh, and only made him frown; and unabashed nevertheless, began playing his light artillery upon the waiters, till he drove them out of the room bursting with laughter.

So far so good. And when the cloth was drawn, and sack and sugar became the order of the day, and "Queen and Bible" had been duly drunk with all the honors, Frank tried a fresh move, and—

"I have a toast, gentlemen—here it is. 'The gentlemen of the Irish wars; and may Ireland never be without a St. Leger to stand by a Fortescue, a Fortescue to stand by a St. Leger, and a

Chichester to stand by both.'"

Which toast of course involved the drinking the healths of the three representatives of those families, and their returning thanks, and paying a compliment each to the other's house: and so the ice cracked a little further; and young Fortescue proposed the health of "Amyas Leigh and all bold mariners;" to which Amyas replied by a few blunt kindly words, "that he wished to know no better fortune than to sail round the world again with the present company as fellow-adventurers, and so give the Spaniards another taste of the men of Devon."

And by this time, the wine going down sweetly, caused the lips of them that were asleep to speak; till the ice broke up altogether, and every man began talking like a rational Englishman to the man who sat next him.

"And now, gentlemen," said Frank, who saw that it was the fit moment for the grand assault which he had planned all along; "let me give you a health which none of you, I dare say, will refuse to drink with heart and soul as well as with lips;—the health of one whom beauty and virtue have so ennobled, that in their light the shadow of lowly birth is unseen;—the health of one whom I would proclaim as peerless in loveliness, were it not that every gentleman here has sisters, who might well challenge from her the girdle of Venus: and yet what else dare I say, while those same lovely ladies who, if they but use their own mirrors, must needs be far better judges of beauty than I can be, have in my own hearing again and again assigned the palm to her? Surely, if the goddesses decide among themselves the question of the golden apple, Paris himself must vacate the judgment-seat. Gentlemen, your hearts, I doubt not, have already bid you, as my unworthy lips do now, to drink 'The Rose of Torridge.'"

If the Rose of Torridge herself had walked into the room, she could hardly have caused more blank astonishment than Frank's bold speech. Every guest turned red, and pale, and red again, and looked at the other as much as to say, "What right has any one but I to drink her? Lift your glass, and I will dash it out of your hand;" but Frank, with sweet effrontery, drank "The health of the Rose of Torridge, and a double health to that worthy gentleman, whosoever he may be, whom she is fated to honor with her love!"

"Well done, cunning Frank Leigh!" cried blunt Will Cary; "none of us dare quarrel with you now, however much we may sulk at each other. For there's none of us, I'll warrant, but thinks that she likes him the best of all; and so we are bound to believe that you have drunk our healths all round."

"And so I have: and what better thing can you do, gentlemen, than to drink each other's healths all round likewise: and so show yourselves true gentlemen, true Christians, ay, and true lovers? For what is love (let me speak freely to you, gentlemen and guests), what is love, but the very inspiration of that Deity whose name is Love? Be sure that not without reason did the ancients feign Eros to be the eldest of the gods, by whom the jarring elements of chaos were attuned into harmony and order. How, then, shall lovers make him the father of strife? Shall Psyche wed with Cupid, to bring forth a cockatrice's egg? or the soul be filled with love, the likeness of the immortals, to burn with envy and jealousy, division and distrust? True, the rose has its thorn: but it leaves poison and stings to the nettle. Cupid has his arrow: but he hurls no scorpions. Venus is awful when despised, as the daughters of Proetus found: but her handmaids are the Graces, not the Furies. Surely he who loves aright will not only find love lovely, but become himself lovely also. I speak not to reprehend you, gentlemen; for to you (as your piercing wits have already perceived, to judge by your honorable blushes) my discourse tends; but to point you, if you will but permit me, to that rock which I myself have, I know not by what Divine good hap, attained; if, indeed, I have attained it, and am not about to be washed off again by the next tide."

Frank's rapid and fantastic oratory, utterly unexpected as it was, had as yet left their wits no time to set their tempers on fire; but when, weak from his wounds, he paused for breath, there was a haughty murmur from more than one young gentleman, who took his speech as an impertinent interference with each man's right to make a fool of himself; and Mr. Coffin, who had sat quietly bolt upright, and looking at the opposite wall, now rose as quietly, and with a face which tried to look utterly unconcerned, was walking out of the room: another minute, and Lady Bath's prophecy about the feast of the Lapithae might have come true.

But Frank's heart and head never failed him.

"Mr. Coffin!" said he, in a tone which compelled that gentleman to turn round, and so brought him under the power of a face which none could have beheld for five minutes and borne malice, so imploring, tender, earnest was it. "My dear Mr. Coffin! If my earnestness has made me forget even for a moment the bounds of courtesy, let me entreat you to forgive me. Do not add to my heavy griefs, heavy enough already, the grief of losing a friend. Only hear me patiently to the end (generously, I know, you will hear me); and then, if you are still incensed, I can but again entreat your forgiveness a second time."

Mr. Coffin, to tell the truth, had at that time never been to Court; and he was therefore somewhat jealous of Frank, and his Court talk, and his Court clothes, and his Court company; and moreover, being the eldest of the guests, and only two years younger than Frank himself, he was a little nettled at being classed in the same category with some who were scarce eighteen. And if Frank had given the least hint which seemed to assume his own superiority, all had been lost: but when, instead thereof, he sued in forma pauperis, and threw himself upon Coffin's mercy, the latter, who was a true-hearted man enough, and after all had known Frank ever since either of them could walk, had nothing to do but to sit down again and submit, while Frank went on more earnestly than ever.

"Believe me; believe me, Mr. Coffin, and gentlemen all, I no more arrogate to myself a superiority over you than does the sailor hurled on shore by the surge fancy himself better than his comrade who is still battling with the foam. For I too, gentlemen,—let me confess it, that by confiding in you I may, perhaps, win you to confide in me,—have loved, ay and do love, where you love also. Do not start. Is it a matter of wonder that the sun which has dazzled you has dazzled me; that the lodestone which has drawn you has drawn me? Do not frown, either, gentlemen. I have learnt to love you for loving what I love, and to admire you for admiring that which I admire. Will you not try the same lesson: so easy, and, when learnt, so blissful? What breeds more close communion between subjects than allegiance to the same queen? between brothers, than duty to the same father? between the devout, than adoration for the same Deity?

And shall not worship for the same beauty be likewise a bond of love between the worshippers? and each lover see in his rival not an enemy, but a fellow-sufferer? You smile and say in your hearts, that though all may worship, but one can enjoy; and that one man's meat must be the poison of the rest. Be it so, though I deny it. Shall we anticipate our own doom, and slay ourselves for fear of dying? Shall we make ourselves unworthy of her from our very eagerness to win her, and show ourselves her faithful knights, by cherishing envy,—most unknightly of all sins? Shall we dream with the Italian or the Spaniard that we can become more amiable in a lady's eyes, by becoming hateful in the eyes of God and of each other? Will she love us the better, if we come to her with hands stained in the blood of him whom she loves better than us? Let us recollect ourselves rather, gentlemen; and be sure that our only chance of winning her, if she be worth winning, is to will what she wills, honor whom she honors, love whom she loves. If there is to be rivalry among us, let it be a rivalry in nobleness, an emulation in virtue. Let each try to outstrip the other in loyalty to his queen, in valor against her foes, in deeds of courtesy and mercy to the afflicted and oppressed; and thus our love will indeed prove its own divine origin, by raising us nearer to those gods whose gift it is. But yet I show you a more excellent way, and that is charity. Why should we not make this common love to her, whom I am unworthy to name, the sacrament of a common love to each other? Why should we not follow the heroical examples of those ancient knights, who having but one grief, one desire, one goddess, held that one heart was enough to contain that grief, to nourish that desire, to worship that divinity; and so uniting themselves in friendship till they became but one soul in two bodies, lived only for each other in living only for her, vowing as faithful worshippers to abide by her decision, to find their own bliss in hers, and whomsoever she esteemed most worthy of her love, to esteem most worthy also, and count themselves, by that her choice, the bounden servants of him whom their mistress had condescended to advance to the dignity of her master?—as I (not without hope that I shall be outdone in generous strife) do here promise to be the faithful friend, and, to my ability, the hearty servant, of him who shall be honored with the love of the Rose of Torridge."

He ceased, and there was a pause.

At last young Fortescue spoke.

"I may be paying you a left-handed compliment, sir: but it seems to me that you are so likely, in that case, to become your own faithful friend and hearty servant (even if you have not borne off the bell already while we have been asleep), that the bargain is hardly fair between such a gay Italianist and us country swains."

"You undervalue yourself and your country, my dear sir. But set your mind at rest. I know no more of that lady's mind than you do: nor shall I know. For the sake of my own peace, I have made a vow neither to see her, nor to hear, if possible, tidings of her, till three full years are past. Dixi?"

Mr. Coffin rose.

"Gentlemen, I may submit to be outdone by Mr. Leigh in eloquence, but not in generosity; if he leaves these parts for three years, I do so also."

"And go in charity with all mankind," said Cary. "Give us your hand, old fellow. If you are a

Coffin, you were sawn out of no wishy-washy elm-board, but right heart-of-oak. I am going, too, as Amyas here can tell, to Ireland away, to cool my hot liver in a bog, like a Jack-hare in March. Come, give us thy neif, and let us part in peace. I was minded to have fought thee this day—"

"I should have been most happy, sir," said Coffin.

—"But now I am all love and charity to mankind. Can I have the pleasure of begging pardon of the world in general, and thee in particular? Does any one wish to pull my nose; send me an errand; make me lend him five pounds; ay, make me buy a horse of him, which will be as good as giving him ten? Come along! Join hands all round, and swear eternal friendship, as brothers of the sacred order of the—of what. Frank Leigh? Open thy mouth, Daniel, and christen us!"

"The Rose!" said Frank quietly, seeing that his new love-philtre was working well, and determined to strike while the iron was hot, and carry the matter too far to carry it back again.

"The Rose!" cried Cary, catching hold of Coffin's hand with his right, and Fortescue's with his left. "Come, Mr. Coffin! Bend, sturdy oak! 'Woe to the stiffnecked and stout-hearted!' says Scripture."

And somehow or other, whether it was Frank's chivalrous speech, or Cary's fun, or Amyas's good wine, or the nobleness which lies in every young lad's heart, if their elders will take the trouble to call it out, the whole party came in to terms one by one, shook hands all round, and vowed on the hilt of Amyas's sword to make fools of themselves no more, at least by jealousy: but to stand by each other and by their lady-love, and neither grudge nor grumble, let her dance with, flirt with, or marry with whom she would; and in order that the honor of their peerless dame, and the brotherhood which was named after her, might be spread through all lands, and equal that of Angelica or Isonde of Brittany, they would each go home, and ask their fathers' leave (easy enough to obtain in those brave times) to go abroad wheresoever there were "good wars," to emulate there the courage and the courtesy of Walter Manny and Gonzalo Fernandes, Bayard and Gaston de Foix. Why not? Sidney was the hero of Europe at five-and-twenty; and why not they?

And Frank watched and listened with one of his quiet smiles (his eyes, as some folks' do, smiled even when his lips were still), and only said: "Gentlemen, be sure that you will never repent this day."

"Repent?" said Cary. "I feel already as angelical as thou lookest, Saint Silvertongue. What was it that sneezed?—the cat?"

"The lion, rather, by the roar of it," said Amyas, making a dash at the arras behind him. "Why, here is a doorway here! and—"

And rushing under the arras, through an open door behind, he returned, dragging out by the head Mr. John Brimblecombe.

Who was Mr. John Brimblecombe?

If you have forgotten him, you have done pretty nearly what every one else in the room had done. But you recollect a certain fat lad, son of the schoolmaster, whom Sir Richard punished for tale-bearing three years before, by sending him, not to Coventry, but to Oxford. That was the man. He was now one-and-twenty, and a bachelor of Oxford, where he had learnt such things as were taught in those days, with more or less success; and he was now hanging about Bideford once more, intending to return after Christmas and read divinity, that he might become a parson, and a shepherd of souls in his native land.

Jack was in person exceedingly like a pig: but not like every pig: not in the least like the Devon pigs of those days, which, I am sorry to say, were no more shapely than the true Irish greyhound who pays Pat's "rint" for him; or than the lanky monsters who wallow in German rivulets, while the village swineherd, beneath a shady lime, forgets his fleas in the melody of a Jew's harp—strange mud-colored creatures, four feet high and four inches thick, which look as if they had passed their lives, as a collar of Oxford brawn is said to do, between two tight boards. Such were then the pigs of Devon: not to be compared with the true wild descendant of Noah's stock, high-withered, furry, grizzled, game-flavored little rooklers, whereof many a sownder still grunted about Swinley down and Braunton woods, Clovelly glens and Bursdon moor. Not like these, nor like the tame abomination of those barbarous times, was Jack: but prophetic in face, figure, and complexion, of Fisher Hobbs and the triumphs of science. A Fisher Hobbs' pig of twelve stone, on his hind-legs—that was what he was, and nothing else; and if you do not know, reader, what a Fisher Hobbs is, you know nothing about pigs, and deserve no bacon for breakfast. But such was Jack. The same plump mulberry complexion, garnished with a few scattered black bristles; the same sleek skin, looking always as if it was upon the point of bursting; the same little toddling legs; the same dapper bend in the small of the back; the same cracked squeak; the same low upright forehead, and tiny eyes; the same round self-satisfied jowl; the same charming sensitive little cocked nose, always on the look-out for a savory smell,—and yet while watching for the best, contented with the worst; a pig of self-helpful and serene spirit, as Jack was, and therefore, like him, fatting fast while other pigs' ribs are staring through their skins.

Such was Jack; and lucky it was for him that such he was; for it was little that he got to fat him at Oxford, in days when a servitor meant really a servant-student; and wistfully that day did his eyes, led by his nose, survey at the end of the Ship Inn passage the preparations for Amyas's supper. The innkeeper was a friend of his; for, in the first place, they had lived within three doors of each other all their lives; and next, Jack was quite pleasant company enough, beside being a learned man and an Oxford scholar, to be asked in now and then to the innkeeper's private parlor, when there were no gentlemen there, to crack his little joke and tell his little story, sip the leavings of the guests' sack, and sometimes help the host to eat the leavings of their supper. And it was, perhaps, with some such hope that Jack trotted off round the corner to the Ship that very afternoon; for that faithful little nose of his, as it sniffed out of a back window of the school, had given him warning of Sabean gales, and scents of Paradise, from the inn kitchen below; so he went round, and asked for his pot of small ale (his only luxury), and stood at the bar to drink it; and looked inward with his little twinkling right eye, and sniffed inward with his little curling right nostril, and beheld, in the kitchen beyond, salad in stacks and fagots: salad of lettuce, salad of cress and endive, salad of boiled coleworts, salad of pickled coleworts, salad of angelica, salad of scurvy-wort, and seven salads more; for potatoes were not as yet, and salads were during eight months of the year the only vegetable. And on the dresser, and before the fire, whole hecatombs of fragrant victims, which needed neither frankincense nor myrrh; Clovelly herrings and Torridge salmon, Exmoor mutton and Stow venison, stubble geese and woodcocks, curlew and snipe, hams of Hampshire, chitterlings of Taunton, and botargos of Cadiz, such as Pantagruel himself might have devoured. And Jack eyed them, as a ragged boy eyes the cakes in a pastrycook's window; and thought of the scraps from the commoners' dinner, which were his wages for cleaning out the hall; and meditated deeply on the unequal distribution of human bliss.

"Ah, Mr. Brimblecombe!" said the host, bustling out with knife and apron to cool himself in the passage. "Here are doings! Nine gentlemen to supper!"

"Nine! Are they going to eat all that?"

"Well, I can't say—that Mr. Amyas is as good as three to his trencher: but still there's crumbs, Mr. Brimblecombe, crumbs; and waste not want not is my doctrine; so you and I may have a somewhat to stay our stomachs, about an eight o'clock."

"Eight?" said Jack, looking wistfully at the clock. "It's but four now. Well, it's kind of you, and perhaps I'll look in."

"Just you step in now, and look to this venison. There's a breast! you may lay your two fingers into the say there, and not get to the bottom of the fat. That's Sir Richard's sending. He's all for them Leighs, and no wonder, they'm brave lads, surely; and there's a saddle-o'-mutton! I rode twenty miles for mun yesterday, I did, over beyond Barnstaple; and five year old, Mr. John, it is, if ever five years was; and not a tooth to mun's head, for I looked to that; and smelt all the way home like any apple; and if it don't ate so soft as ever was scald cream, never you call me Thomas Burman."

"Humph!" said Jack. "And that's their dinner. Well, some are born with a silver spoon in their mouth."

"Some be born with roast beef in their mouths, and plum-pudding in their pocket to take away the taste o' mun; and that's better than empty spunes, eh?"

"For them that get it," said Jack. "But for them that don't—" And with a sigh he returned to his small ale, and then lingered in and out of the inn, watching the dinner as it went into the best room, where the guests were assembled.

And as he lounged there, Amyas went in, and saw him, and held out his hand, and said—

"Hillo, Jack! how goes the world? How you've grown!" and passed on;—what had Jack Brimblecombe to do with Rose Salterne?

So Jack lingered on, hovering around the fragrant smell like a fly round a honey-pot, till he found himself invisibly attracted, and as it were led by the nose out of the passage into the adjoining room, and to that side of the room where there was a door; and once there he could not help hearing what passed inside; till Rose Salterne's name fell on his ear. So, as it was ordained, he was taken in the fact. And now behold him brought in red-hand to judgment, not without a kick or two from the wrathful foot of Amyas Leigh. Whereat there fell on him a storm of abuse, which, for the honor of that gallant company, I shall not give in detail; but which abuse, strange to say, seemed to have no effect on the impenitent and unabashed Jack, who, as soon as he could get his breath, made answer fiercely, amid much puffing and blowing.

"What business have I here? As much as any of you. If you had asked me in, I would have come: but as you didn't, I came without asking."

"You shameless rascal!" said Cary. "Come if you were asked, where there was good wine? I'll warrant you for that!"

"Why," said Amyas, "no lad ever had a cake at school but he would dog him up one street and down another all day for the crumbs, the trencher-scraping spaniel!"

"Patience, masters!" said Frank. "That Jack's is somewhat of a gnathonic and parasitic soul, or stomach, all Bideford apple-women know; but I suspect more than Deus Venter has brought him hither."

"Deus eavesdropping, then. We shall have the whole story over the town by to-morrow," said another; beginning at that thought to feel somewhat ashamed of his late enthusiasm.

"Ah, Mr. Frank! You were always the only one that would stand up for me! Deus Venter, quotha? 'Twas Deus Cupid, it was!"

A roar of laughter followed this announcement.

"What?" asked Frank; "was it Cupid, then, who sneezed approval to our love, Jack, as he did to that of Dido and Aeneas?"

But Jack went on desperately.

"I was in the next room, drinking of my beer. I couldn't help that, could I? And then I heard her name; and I couldn't help listening then. Flesh and blood couldn't."

"Nor fat either!"

"No, nor fat, Mr. Cary. Do you suppose fat men haven't souls to be saved as well as thin ones, and hearts to burst, too, as well as stomachs? Fat! Fat can feel, I reckon, as well as lean. Do you suppose there's naught inside here but beer?"

And he laid his hand, as Drayton might have said, on that stout bastion, hornwork, ravelin, or demilune, which formed the outworks to the citadel of his purple isle of man.

"Naught but beer?—Cheese, I suppose?"

"Bread?"

"Beef?"

"Love!" cried Jack. "Yes, Love!—Ay, you laugh; but my eyes are not so grown up with fat but what I can see what's fair as well as you."

"Oh, Jack, naughty Jack, dost thou heap sin on sin, and luxury on gluttony?"

"Sin? If I sin, you sin: I tell you, and I don't care who knows it, I've loved her these three years as well as e'er a one of you, I have. I've thought o' nothing else, prayed for nothing else, God forgive me! And then you laugh at me, because I'm a poor parson's son, and you fine gentlemen: God made us both, I reckon. You?—you make a deal of giving her up to-day. Why, it's what I've done for three miserable years as ever poor sinner spent; ay, from the first day I said to myself, 'Jack, if you can't have that pearl, you'll have none; and that you can't have, for it's meat for your masters: so conquer or die.' And I couldn't conquer. I can't help loving her, worshipping her, no more than you; and I will die: but you needn't laugh meanwhile at me that have done as much as you, and will do again."

"It is the old tale," said Frank to himself; "whom will not love transform into a hero?"

And so it was. Jack's squeaking voice was firm and manly, his pig's eyes flashed very fire, his gestures were so free and earnest, that the ungainliness of his figure was forgotten; and when he finished with a violent burst of tears, Frank, forgetting his wounds, sprang up and caught him by the hand.

"John Brimblecombe, forgive me! Gentlemen, if we are gentlemen, we ought to ask his pardon. Has he not shown already more chivalry, more self-denial, and therefore more true love, than any of us? My friends, let the fierceness of affection, which we have used as an excuse for many a sin of our own, excuse his listening to a conversation in which he well deserved to bear a part."

"Ah," said Jack, "you make me one of your brotherhood; and see if I do not dare to suffer as much as any of you! You laugh? Do you fancy none can use a sword unless he has a baker's dozen of quarterings in his arms, or that Oxford scholars know only how to handle a pen?"

"Let us try his metal," said St. Leger. "Here's my sword, Jack; draw, Coffin! and have at him."

"Nonsense!" said Coffin, looking somewhat disgusted at the notion of fighting a man of Jack's rank; but Jack caught at the weapon offered to him.

"Give me a buckler, and have at any of you!"

"Here's a chair bottom," cried Cary; and Jack, seizing it in his left, flourished his sword so fiercely, and called so loudly to Coffin to come on, that all present found it necessary, unless they wished blood to be spilt, to turn the matter off with a laugh: but Jack would not hear of it.

"Nay: if you will let me be of your brotherhood, well and good: but if not, one or other I will fight: and that's flat."

"You see, gentlemen," said Amyas, "we must admit him or die the death; so we needs must go when Sir Urian drives. Come up, Jack, and take the oaths. You admit him, gentlemen?"

"Let me but be your chaplain," said Jack, "and pray for your luck when you're at the wars. If I do stay at home in a country curacy, 'tis not much that you need be jealous of me with her, I reckon," said Jack, with a pathetical glance at his own stomach.

"Sia!" said Cary: "but if he be admitted, it must be done according to the solemn forms and ceremonies in such cases provided. Take him into the next room, Amyas, and prepare him for his initiation."

"What's that?" asked Amyas, puzzled by the word. But judging from the corner of Will's eye that initiation was Latin for a practical joke, he led forth his victim behind the arras again, and waited five minutes while the room was being darkened, till Frank's voice called to him to bring in the neophyte.

"John Brimblecombe," said Frank, in a sepulchral tone, "you cannot be ignorant, as a scholar and bachelor of Oxford, of that dread sacrament by which Catiline bound the soul of his fellow-conspirators, in order that both by the daring of the deed he might have proof of their sincerity, and by the horror thereof astringe their souls by adamantine fetters, and Novem-Stygian oaths, to that wherefrom hereafter the weakness of the flesh might shrink. Wherefore, O Jack! we too have determined, following that ancient and classical example, to fill, as he did, a bowl with the lifeblood of our most heroic selves, and to pledge each other therein, with vows whereat the stars shall tremble in their spheres, and Luna, blushing, veil her silver cheeks. Your blood alone is wanted to fill up the goblet. Sit down, John Brimblecombe, and bare your arm!"

"But, Mr. Frank!—" said Jack, who was as superstitious as any old wife, and, what with the darkness and the discourse, already in a cold perspiration.

"But me no buts! or depart as recreant, not by the door like a man, but up the chimney like a flittermouse."

"But, Mr. Frank!"

"Thy vital juice, or the chimney! Choose!" roared Cary in his ear.

"Well, if I must," said Jack; "but it's desperate hard that because you can't keep faith without these barbarous oaths, I must take them too, that have kept faith these three years without any."

At this pathetic appeal Frank nearly melted: but Amyas and Cary had thrust the victim into a chair and all was prepared for the sacrifice.

"Bind his eyes, according to the classic fashion," said Will.

"Oh no, dear Mr. Cary; I'll shut them tight enough, I warrant: but not with your dagger, dear Mr. William—sure, not with your dagger? I can't afford to lose blood, though I do look lusty—I can't indeed; sure, a pin would do—I've got one here, to my sleeve, somewhere—Oh!"

"See the fount of generous juice! Flow on, fair stream. How he bleeds!—pints, quarts! Ah, this proves him to be in earnest!"

"A true lover's blood is always at his fingers' ends."

"He does not grudge it; of course not. Eh, Jack? What matters an odd gallon for her sake?"

"For her sake? Nothing, nothing! Take my life, if you will: but—oh, gentlemen, a surgeon, if you love me! I'm going off—I 'm fainting!"

"Drink, then, quick; drink and swear! Pat his back, Cary. Courage, man! it will be over in a minute. Now, Frank!—"

And Frank spoke—

"If plighted troth I fail, or secret speech reveal, May Cocytean ghosts around my pillow squeal; While Ate's brazen claws distringe my spleen in sunder, And drag me deep to Pluto's keep, 'mid brimstone, smoke, and thunder!"

"Placetne, domine?"

"Placet!" squeaked Jack, who thought himself at the last gasp, and gulped down full three-quarters of the goblet which Cary held to his lips.

"Ugh—Ah—Puh! Mercy on us! It tastes mighty like wine!"

"A proof, my virtuous brother," said Frank, "first, of thy abstemiousness, which has thus forgotten what wine tastes like; and next, of thy pure and heroical affection, by which thy carnal senses being exalted to a higher and supra-lunar sphere, like those Platonical daemonizomenoi and enthusiazomenoi (of whom Jamblichus says that they were insensible to wounds and flame, and much more, therefore, to evil savors), doth make even the most nauseous draught redolent of that celestial fragrance, which proceeding, O Jack! from thine own inward virtue, assimilates by sympathy even outward accidents unto its own harmony and melody; for fragrance is, as has been said well, the song of flowers, and sweetness, the music of apples—Ahem! Go in peace, thou hast conquered!"

"Put him out of the door, Will," said Amyas, "or he will swoon on our hands."

"Give him some sack," said Frank.

"Not a blessed drop of yours, sir," said Jack. "I like good wine as well as any man on earth, and see as little of it; but not a drop of yours, sirs, after your frumps and flouts about hanging-on and trencher-scraping. When I first began to love her, I bid good-bye to all dirty tricks; for I had some one then for whom to keep myself clean."

And so Jack was sent home, with a pint of good red Alicant wine in him (more, poor fellow, than he had tasted at once in his life before); while the rest, in high glee with themselves and the rest of the world, relighted the candles, had a right merry evening, and parted like good friends and sensible gentlemen of devon, thinking (all except Frank) Jack Brimblecombe and his vow the merriest jest they had heard for many a day. After which they all departed: Amyas and Cary to Winter's squadron; Frank (as soon as he could travel) to the Court again; and with him young Basset, whose father Sir Arthur, being in London, procured for him a page's place in Leicester's household. Fortescue and Chicester went to their brothers in Dublin; St. Leger to his uncle the Marshal of Munster; Coffin joined Champernoun and Norris in the Netherlands; and so the Brotherhood of the Rose was scattered far and wide, and Mistress Salterne was left alone with her looking-glass.

CHAPTER IX: HOW AMYAS KEPT HIS CHRISTMAS DAY

It was the blessed Christmas afternoon. The light was fading down; the even-song was done; and the good folks of Bideford were trooping home in merry groups, the father with his children, the lover with his sweetheart, to cakes and ale, and flapdragons and mummer's plays, and all the happy sports of Christmas night. One lady only, wrapped close in her black muffler and followed by her maid, walked swiftly, yet sadly, toward the long causeway and bridge which led to Northam town. Sir Richard Grenville and his wife caught her up and stopped her courteously.

"You will come home with us, Mrs. Leigh," said Lady Grenville, "and spend a pleasant Christmas night?"

Mrs. Leigh smiled sweetly, and laying one hand on Lady Grenville's arm, pointed with the other to the westward, and said:

"I cannot well spend a merry Christmas night while that sound is in my ears."

The whole party around looked in the direction in which she pointed. Above their heads the soft blue sky was fading into gray, and here and there a misty star peeped out: but to the westward, where the downs and woods of Raleigh closed in with those of Abbotsham, the blue was webbed and turfed with delicate white flakes; iridescent spots, marking the path by which the sun had sunk, showed all the colors of the dying dolphin; and low on the horizon lay a long band of grassy green. But what was the sound which troubled Mrs. Leigh? None of them, with their merry hearts, and ears dulled with the din and bustle of the town, had heard it till that moment: and yet now—listen! It was dead calm. There was not a breath to stir a blade of grass. And yet the air was full of sound, a low deep roar which hovered over down and wood, salt-marsh and river, like the roll of a thousand wheels, the tramp of endless armies, or—what it was—the thunder of a mighty surge upon the boulders of the pebble ridge.

"The ridge is noisy to-night," said Sir Richard. "There has been wind somewhere."

"There is wind now, where my boy is, God help him!" said Mrs. Leigh: and all knew that she spoke truly. The spirit of the Atlantic storm had sent forward the token of his coming, in the smooth ground-swell which was heard inland, two miles away. To-morrow the pebbles, which were now rattling down with each retreating wave, might be leaping to the ridge top, and hurled like round-shot far ashore upon the marsh by the force of the advancing wave, fleeing before the wrath of the western hurricane.

"God help my boy!" said Mrs. Leigh again.

"God is as near him by sea as by land," said good Sir Richard.

"True, but I am a lone mother; and one that has no heart just now but to go home and pray."

And so Mrs. Leigh went onward up the lane, and spent all that night in listening between her prayers to the thunder of the surge, till it was drowned, long ere the sun rose, in the thunder of the storm.

And where is Amyas on this same Christmas afternoon?

Amyas is sitting bareheaded in a boat's stern in Smerwick bay, with the spray whistling through his curls, as he shouts cheerfully—

"Pull, and with a will, my merry men all, and never mind shipping a sea. Cannon balls are a cargo that don't spoil by taking salt-water."

His mother's presage has been true enough. Christmas eve has been the last of the still, dark, steaming nights of the early winter; and the western gale has been roaring for the last twelve hours upon the Irish coast.

The short light of the winter day is fading fast. Behind him is a leaping line of billows lashed into mist by the tempest. Beside him green foam-fringed columns are rushing up the black rocks, and falling again in a thousand cataracts of snow. Before him is the deep and sheltered bay: but it is not far up the bay that he and his can see; for some four miles out at sea begins a sloping roof of thick gray cloud, which stretches over their heads, and up and far away inland, cutting the cliffs off at mid-height, hiding all the Kerry mountains, and darkening the hollows of the distant firths into the blackness of night. And underneath that awful roof of whirling mist the storm is howling inland ever, sweeping before it the great foam-sponges, and the gray salt spray, till all the land is hazy, dim, and dun. Let it howl on! for there is more mist than ever salt spray made, flying before that gale; more thunder than ever sea-surge wakened echoing among the cliffs of Smerwick bay; along those sand-hills flash in the evening gloom red sparks which never came from heaven; for that fort, now christened by the invaders the Fort Del Oro, where flaunts the hated golden flag of Spain, holds San Josepho and eight hundred of the foe; and but three nights ago, Amyas and Yeo, and the rest of Winter's shrewdest hands, slung four culverins out of the Admiral's main deck, and floated them ashore, and dragged them up to the battery among the sand-hills; and now it shall be seen whether Spanish and Italian condottieri can hold their own on British ground against the men of Devon.

Small blame to Amyas if he was thinking, not of his lonely mother at Burrough Court, but of those quick bright flashes on sand-hill and on fort, where Salvation Yeo was hurling the eighteen-pound shot with deadly aim, and watching with a cool and bitter smile of triumph the flying of the sand, and the crashing of the gabions. Amyas and his party had been on board, at the risk of their lives, for a fresh supply of shot; for Winter's battery was out of ball, and had been firing stones for the last four hours, in default of better missiles. They ran the boat on shore through the surf, where a cove in the shore made landing possible, and almost careless whether she stove or not, scrambled over the sand-hills with each man his brace of shot slung across his shoulder; and Amyas, leaping into the trenches, shouted cheerfully to Salvation Yeo—

"More food for the bull-dogs, Gunner, and plums for the Spaniards' Christmas pudding!"

"Don't speak to a man at his business, Master Amyas. Five mortal times have I missed; but I will have that accursed Popish rag down, as I'm a sinner."

"Down with it, then; nobody wants you to shoot crooked. Take good iron to it, and not footy paving-stones."

"I believe, sir, that the foul fiend is there, a turning of my shot aside, I do. I thought I saw him once: but, thank Heaven, here's ball again. Ah, sir, if one could but cast a silver one! Now, stand by, men!"

And once again Yeo's eighteen-pounder roared, and away. And, oh glory! the great yellow flag of Spain, which streamed in the gale, lifted clean into the air, flagstaff and all, and then pitched wildly down head-foremost, far to leeward.

A hurrah from the sailors, answered by the soldiers of the opposite camp, shook the very cloud above them: but ere its echoes had died away, a tall officer leapt upon the parapet of the fort, with the fallen flag in his hand, and rearing it as well as he could upon his lance point, held it firmly against the gale, while the fallen flagstaff was raised again within.

In a moment a dozen long bows were bent at the daring foeman: but Amyas behind shouted—
"Shame, lads! Stop and let the gallant gentleman have due courtesy!"

So they stopped, while Amyas, springing on the rampart of the battery, took off his hat, and bowed to the flag-holder, who, as soon as relieved of his charge, returned the bow courteously, and descended.

It was by this time all but dark, and the firing began to slacken on all sides; Salvation and his brother gunners, having covered up their slaughtering tackle with tarpaulings, retired for the night, leaving Amyas, who had volunteered to take the watch till midnight; and the rest of the force having got their scanty supper of biscuit (for provisions were running very short) lay down under arms among the sand-hills, and grumbled themselves to sleep.

He had paced up and down in the gusty darkness for some hour or more, exchanging a passing word now and then with the sentinel, when two men entered the battery, chatting busily together. One was in complete armor; the other wrapped in the plain short cloak of a man of pens and peace: but the talk of both was neither of sieges nor of sallies, catapult, bombard, nor culverin, but simply of English hexameters.

And fancy not, gentle reader, that the two were therein fiddling while Rome was burning; for the commonweal of poetry and letters, in that same critical year 1580, was in far greater danger from those same hexameters than the common woe of Ireland (as Raleigh called it) was from the Spaniards.

Imitating the classic metres, "versifying," as it was called in contradistinction to rhyming, was becoming fast the fashion among the more learned. Stonyhurst and others had tried their hands at hexameter translations from the Latin and Greek epics, which seem to have been doggerel enough; and ever and anon some youthful wit broke out in iambics, sapphics, elegiacs, and what not, to the great detriment of the queen's English and her subjects' ears.

I know not whether Mr. William Webbe had yet given to the world any fragments of his precious hints for the "Reformation of English poetry," to the tune of his own "Tityrus, happily thou liest tumbling under a beech-tree:" but the Cambridge Malvolio, Gabriel Harvey, had succeeded in arguing Spenser, Dyer, Sidney, and probably Sidney's sister, and the whole clique of beaux-esprits round them, into following his model of

after snubbing the first book of "that Elvish Queene," which was then in manuscript, as a base declension from the classical to the romantic school.

And now Spenser (perhaps in mere melancholy wilfulness and want of purpose, for he had just been jilted by a fair maid of Kent) was wasting his mighty genius upon doggerel which he fancied antique; and some piratical publisher (bitter Tom Nash swears, and with likelihood that

Harvey did it himself) had just given to the world,—"Three proper wittie and familiar Letters, lately past between two University men, touching the Earthquake in April last, and our English reformed Versifying," which had set all town wits a-buzzing like a swarm of flies, being none other than a correspondence between Spenser and Harvey, which was to prove to the world forever the correctness and melody of such lines as,

Let them pass—Alma Mater has seen as bad hexameters since. But then the matter was serious. There is a story (I know not how true) that Spenser was half bullied into re-writing the "Faerie Queene" in hexameters, had not Raleigh, a true romanticist, "whose vein for ditty or amorous ode was most lofty, insolent, and passionate," persuaded him to follow his better genius. The great dramatists had not yet arisen, to form completely that truly English school, of which Spenser, unconscious of his own vast powers, was laying the foundation. And, indeed, it was not till Daniel, twenty years after, in his admirable apology for rhyme, had smashed Mr. Campian and his "eight several kinds of classical numbers," that the matter was finally settled, and the English tongue left to go the road on which Heaven had started it. So that we may excuse Raleigh's answering somewhat waspish to some quotation of Spenser's from the three letters of "Immerito and G. H."

"Tut, tut, Colin Clout, much learning has made thee mad. A good old fishwives' ballad jingle is worth all your sapphics and trimeters, and 'riff-raff thurlery bouncing.' Hey? have I you there, old lad? Do you mind that precious verse?"

"But, dear Wat, Homer and Virgil—"

"But, dear Ned, Petrarch and Ovid—"

"But, Wat, what have we that we do not owe to the ancients?"

"Ancients, quotha? Why, the legend of King Arthur, and Chevy Chase too, of which even your fellow-sinner Sidney cannot deny that every time he hears it even from a blind fiddler it stirs his heart like a trumpet-blast. Speak well of the bridge that carries you over, man! Did you find your Redcross Knight in Virgil, or such a dame as Una in old Ovid? No more than you did your Pater and Credo, you renegado baptized heathen, you!"

"Yet, surely, our younger and more barbarous taste must bow before divine antiquity, and imitate afar—"

"As dottrels do fowlers. If Homer was blind, lad, why dost not poke out thine eye? Ay, this hexameter is of an ancient house, truly, Ned Spenser, and so is many a rogue: but he cannot make way on our rough English roads. He goes hopping and twitching in our language like a three-legged terrier over a pebble-bank, tumble and up again, rattle and crash."

"Nay, hear, now—

True, the accent gapes in places, as I have often confessed to Harvey, but—"

Harvey be hanged for a pedant, and the whole crew of versifiers, from Lord Dorset (but he, poor man, has been past hanging some time since) to yourself! Why delude you into playing Procrustes as he does with the queen's English, racking one word till its joints be pulled asunder, and squeezing the next all a-heap as the Inquisitors do heretics in their banca cava? Out upon him and you, and Sidney, and the whole kin. You have not made a verse among you, and never will, which is not as lame a gosling as Harvey's own—

"Hark, now! There is our young giant comforting his soul with a ballad. You will hear rhyme and reason together here, now. He will not miscall 'blind-folded,' 'blind-fold-ed, I warrant; or make an 'of' and a 'which' and a 'his' carry a whole verse on their wretched little backs."

And as he spoke, Amyas, who had been grumbling to himself some Christmas carol, broke out full-mouthed:—

"There, Edmunde Classicaster," said Raleigh, "does not that simple strain go nearer to the heart of him who wrote 'The Shepherd's Calendar,' than all artificial and outlandish

Why dost not answer, man?"

But Spenser was silent awhile, and then,—

"Because I was thinking rather of the rhymer than the rhyme. Good heaven! how that brave lad shames me, singing here the hymns which his mother taught him, before the very muzzles of Spanish guns; instead of bewailing unmanly, as I have done, the love which he held, I doubt not, as dear as I did even my Rosalind. This is his welcome to the winter's storm; while I, who dream, forsooth, of heavenly inspiration, can but see therein an image of mine own cowardly despair. Pah! away with frosts, icicles, and tears, and sighs—"

"And with hexameters and trimeters too, I hope," interrupted Raleigh: "and all the trickeries of self-pleasing sorrow."

"—I will set my heart to higher work than barking at the hand which chastens me."

"Wilt put the lad into the 'Faerie Queene,' then, by my side? He deserves as good a place there, believe me, as ever a Guyon, or even as Lord Grey your Arthegall. Let us hail him. Hallo! young chanticleer of Devon! Art not afraid of a chance shot, that thou crowest so lustily upon thine own mixen?"

"Cocks crow all night long at Christmas, Captain Raleigh, and so do I," said Amyas's cheerful voice; "but who's there with you?"

"A penitent pupil of yours—Mr. Secretary Spenser."

"Pupil of mine?" said Amyas. "I wish he'd teach me a little of his art; I could fill up my time here with making verses."

"And who would be your theme, fair sir?" said Spenser.

"No 'who' at all. I don't want to make sonnets to blue eyes, nor black either: but if I could put down some of the things I saw in the Spice Islands—"

"Ah," said Raleigh, "he would beat you out of Parnassus, Mr. Secretary. Remember, you may write about Fairyland, but he has seen it."

"And so have others," said Spenser; "it is not so far off from any one of us. Wherever is love and loyalty, great purposes, and lofty souls, even though in a hovel or a mine, there is Fairyland."

"Then Fairyland should be here, friend; for you represent love, and Leigh loyalty; while, as for great purposes and lofty souls, who so fit to stand for them as I, being (unless my enemies and my conscience are liars both) as ambitious and as proud as Lucifer's own self?"

"Ah, Walter, Walter, why wilt always slander thyself thus?"

"Slander? Tut.—I do but give the world a fair challenge, and tell it, 'There—you know the worst of me: come on and try a fall, for either you or I must down.' Slander? Ask Leigh here, who has but known me a fortnight, whether I am not as vain as a peacock, as selfish as a fox, as imperious as a bona roba, and ready to make a cat's paw of him or any man, if there be a chestnut in the fire: and yet the poor fool cannot help loving me, and running of my errands, and taking all my schemes and my dreams for gospel; and verily believes now, I think, that I shall be the man in the moon some day, and he my big dog."

"Well," said Amyas, half apologetically, "if you are the cleverest man in the world what harm in my thinking so?"

"Hearken to him, Edmund! He will know better when he has outgrown this same callow trick of honesty, and learnt of the great goddess Detraction how to show himself wiser than the wise, by pointing out to the world the fool's motley which peeps through the rents in the philosopher's cloak. Go to, lad! slander thy equals, envy thy betters, pray for an eye which sees spots in every sun, and for a vulture's nose to scent carrion in every rose-bed. If thy friend win a battle, show that he has needlessly thrown away his men; if he lose one, hint that he sold it; if he rise to a place, argue favor; if he fall from one, argue divine justice. Believe nothing, hope nothing, but endure all things, even to kicking, if aught may be got thereby; so shalt thou be clothed in purple and fine linen, and sit in kings' palaces, and fare sumptuously every day."

"And wake with Dives in the torment," said Amyas. "Thank you for nothing, captain."

"Go to, Misanthropos," said Spenser. "Thou hast not yet tasted the sweets of this world's comfits, and thou railest at them?"

"The grapes are sour, lad."

"And will be to the end," said Amyas, "if they come off such a devil's tree as that. I really think you are out of your mind, Captain Raleigh, at times."

"I wish I were; for it is a troublesome, hungry, windy mind as man ever was cursed withal. But come in, lad. We were sent from the lord deputy to bid thee to supper. There is a dainty lump of dead horse waiting for thee."

"Send me some out, then," said matter-of-fact Amyas. "And tell his lordship that, with his good leave, I don't stir from here till morning, if I can keep awake. There is a stir in the fort, and I expect them out on us."

"Tut, man! their hearts are broken. We know it by their deserters."

"Seeing's believing. I never trust runaway rogues. If they are false to their masters, they'll be false to us."

"Well, go thy ways, old honesty; and Mr. Secretary shall give you a book to yourself in the 'Faerie Queene'—'Sir Monoculus or the Legend of Common Sense,' eh, Edmund?"

"Monoculus?"

"Ay, Single-eye, my prince of word-coiners—won't that fit?—And give him the Cyclops head for a device. Heigh-ho! They may laugh that win. I am sick of this Irish work; were it not for the chance of advancement I'd sooner be driving a team of red Devons on Dartside; and now I am angry with the dear lad because he is not sick of it too. What a plague business has he to be paddling up and down, contentedly doing his duty, like any city watchman? It is an insult to the mighty aspirations of our nobler hearts,—eh, my would-be Ariosto?"

"Ah, Raleigh! you can afford to confess yourself less than some, for you are greater than all. Go on and conquer, noble heart! But as for me, I sow the wind, and I suppose I shall reap the whirlwind."

"Your harvest seems come already; what a blast that was! Hold on by me, Colin Clout, and I'll hold on by thee. So! Don't tread on that pikeman's stomach, lest he take thee for a marauding Don, and with sudden dagger slit Cohn's pipe, and Colin's weasand too."

And the two stumbled away into the darkness, leaving Amyas to stride up and down as before, puzzling his brains over Raleigh's wild words and Spenser's melancholy, till he came to the conclusion that there was some mysterious connection between cleverness and unhappiness, and thanking his stars that he was neither scholar, courtier, nor poet, said grace over his lump of horseflesh when it arrived, devoured it as if it had been venison, and then returned to his pacing up and down; but this time in silence, for the night was drawing on, and there was no need to tell the Spaniards that any one was awake and watching.

So he began to think about his mother, and how she might be spending her Christmas; and then about Frank, and wondered at what grand Court festival he was assisting, amid bright lights and sweet music and gay ladies, and how he was dressed, and whether he thought of his brother there far away on the dark Atlantic shore; and then he said his prayers and his creed; and then he tried not to think of Rose Salterne, and of course thought about her all the more. So on passed the dull hours, till it might be past eleven o'clock, and all lights were out in the battery and the shipping, and there was no sound of living thing but the monotonous tramp of the two sentinels beside him, and now and then a grunt from the party who slept under arms some twenty yards to the rear.

So he paced to and fro, looking carefully out now and then over the strip of sand-hill which lay between him and the fort; but all was blank and black, and moreover it began to rain furiously.

Suddenly he seemed to hear a rustle among the harsh sand-grass. True, the wind was whistling through it loudly enough, but that sound was not altogether like the wind. Then a soft sliding noise; something had slipped down a bank, and brought the sand down after it. Amyas stopped, crouched down beside a gun, and laid his ear to the rampart, whereby he heard clearly, as he thought, the noise of approaching feet; whether rabbits or Christians, he knew not, but he shrewdly guessed the latter.

Now Amyas was of a sober and business-like turn, at least when he was not in a passion; and thinking within himself that if he made any noise, the enemy (whether four or two-legged) would retire, and all the sport be lost, he did not call to the two sentries, who were at the opposite ends of the battery; neither did he think it worth while to rouse the sleeping company, lest his ears should have deceived him, and the whole camp turn out to repulse the attack of a buck rabbit.

So he crouched lower and lower beside the culverin, and was rewarded in a minute or two by hearing something gently deposited against the mouth of the embrasure, which, by the noise, should be a piece of timber.

"So far, so good," said he to himself; "when the scaling ladder is up, the soldier follows, I suppose. I can only humbly thank them for giving my embrasure the preference. There he comes! I hear his feet scuffling."

He could hear plainly enough some one working himself into the mouth of the embrasure: but the plague was, that it was so dark that he could not see his hand between him and the sky, much less his foe at two yards off. However, he made a pretty fair guess as to the whereabouts, and, rising softly, discharged such a blow downwards as would have split a yule log. A volley of sparks flew up from the hapless Spaniard's armor, and a grunt issued from within it, which proved that, whether he was killed or not, the blow had not improved his respiration.

Amyas felt for his head, seized it, dragged him in over the gun, sprang into the embrasure on his knees, felt for the top of the ladder, found it, hove it clean off and out, with four or five men on it, and then of course tumbled after it ten feet into the sand, roaring like a town bull to her majesty's liege subjects in general.

Sailor-fashion, he had no armor on but a light morion and a cuirass, so he was not too much encumbered to prevent his springing to his legs instantly, and setting to work, cutting and foining right and left at every sound, for sight there was none.

Battles (as soldiers know, and newspaper editors do not) are usually fought, not as they ought to be fought, but as they can be fought; and while the literary man is laying down the law at his desk as to how many troops should be moved here, and what rivers should be crossed there, and where the cavalry should have been brought up, and when the flank should have been turned, the wretched man who has to do the work finds the matter settled for him by pestilence, want of shoes, empty stomachs, bad roads, heavy rains, hot suns, and a thousand other stern warriors who never show on paper.

So with this skirmish; "according to Cocker," it ought to have been a very pretty one; for Hercules of Pisa, who planned the sortie, had arranged it all (being a very sans-appel in all military science) upon the best Italian precedents, and had brought against this very hapless battery a column of a hundred to attack directly in front, a company of fifty to turn the right flank, and a company of fifty to turn the left flank, with regulations, orders, passwords, countersigns, and what not; so that if every man had had his rights (as seldom happens), Don Guzman Maria Magdalena de Soto, who commanded the sortie, ought to have taken the work out of hand, and annihilated all therein. But alas! here stern fate interfered. They had chosen a dark night, as was politic; they had waited till the moon was up, lest it should be too dark, as was politic likewise: but, just as they had started, on came a heavy squall of rain, through which seven moons would have given no light, and which washed out the plans of Hercules of Pisa as if they had been written on a schoolboy's slate. The company who were to turn the left flank walked manfully down into the sea, and never found out where they were going till they were knee-deep in water. The company who were to turn the right flank, bewildered by the utter darkness, turned their own flank so often, that tired of falling into rabbit-burrows and filling their mouths with sand, they halted and prayed to all the saints for a compass and lantern; while the centre body, who held straight on by a trackway to within fifty yards of the battery, so miscalculated that short distance, that while they thought the ditch two pikes' length off, they fell into it one over the other, and of six scaling ladders, the only one which could be found was the very one which Amyas threw down again. After which the clouds broke, the wind shifted, and the moon shone out merrily. And so was the deep policy of Hercules of Pisa, on which hung the fate of Ireland and the Papacy, decided by a ten minutes' squall.

But where is Amyas?

In the ditch, aware that the enemy is tumbling into it, but unable to find them; while the company above, finding it much too dark to attempt a counter sortie, have opened a smart fire of musketry and arrows on things in general, whereat the Spaniards are swearing like Spaniards (I need say no more), and the Italians spitting like venomous cats; while Amyas, not wishing to be riddled by friendly balls, has got his back against the foot of the rampart, and waits on Providence.

Suddenly the moon clears; and with one more fierce volley, the English sailors, seeing the confusion, leap down from the embrasures, and to it pell-mell. Whether this also was "according to Cocker," I know not: but the sailor, then as now, is not susceptible of highly-finished drill.

Amyas is now in his element, and so are the brave fellows at his heels; and there are ten breathless, furious minutes among the sand-hills; and then the trumpets blow a recall, and the sailors drop back again by twos and threes, and are helped up into the embrasures over many a dead and dying foe; while the guns of Fort del Oro open on them, and blaze away for half an hour without reply; and then all is still once more. And in the meanwhile, the sortie against the deputy's camp has fared no better, and the victory of the night remains with the English.

Twenty minutes after, Winter and the captains who were on shore were drying themselves round a peat-fire on the beach, and talking over the skirmish, when Will Cary asked—

"Where is Leigh? who has seen him? I am sadly afraid he has gone too far, and been slain."

"Slain? Never less, gentlemen!" replied the voice of the very person in question, as he stalked out of the darkness into the glare of the fire, and shot down from his shoulders into the midst of the ring, as he might a sack of corn, a huge dark body, which was gradually seen to be a man in rich armor; who being so shot down, lay quietly where he was dropped, with his feet (luckily for him mailed) in the fire.

"I say," quoth Amyas, "some of you had better take him up, if he is to be of any use. Unlace his helm, Will Cary."

"Pull his feet out of the embers; I dare say he would have been glad enough to put us to the scarpines; but that's no reason we should put him to them."

As has been hinted, there was no love lost between Admiral Winter and Amyas; and Amyas might certainly have reported himself in a more ceremonious manner. So Winter, whom Amyas either had not seen, or had not chosen to see, asked him pretty sharply, "What the plague he had to do with bringing dead men into camp?"

"If he's dead, it's not my fault. He was alive enough when I started with him, and I kept him right end uppermost all the way; and what would you have more, sir?"

"Mr. Leigh!" said Winter, "it behoves you to speak with somewhat more courtesy, if not respect, to captains who are your elders and commanders."

"Ask your pardon, sir," said the giant, as he stood in front of the fire with the rain steaming and smoking off his armor; "but I was bred in a school where getting good service done was more esteemed than making fine speeches."

"Whatsoever school you were trained in, sir," said Winter, nettled at the hint about Drake; "it does not seem to have been one in which you learned to obey orders. Why did you not come in when the recall was sounded?"

"Because," said Amyas, very coolly, "in the first place I did not hear it; and in the next, in my school I was taught when I had once started not to come home empty-handed."

This was too pointed; and Winter sprang up with an oath—"Do you mean to insult me, sir?"

"I am sorry, sir, that you should take a compliment to Sir Francis Drake as an insult to yourself. I brought in this gentleman because I thought he might give you good information; if he dies meanwhile, the loss will be yours, or rather the queen's."

"Help me, then," said Cary, glad to create a diversion in Amyas's favor, "and we will bring him round;" while Raleigh rose, and catching Winter's arm, drew him aside, and began talking earnestly.

"What a murrain have you, Leigh, to quarrel with Winter?" asked two or three.

"I say, my reverend fathers and dear children, do get the Don's talking tackle free again, and leave me and the admiral to settle it our own way."

There was more than one captain sitting in the ring, but discipline, and the degrees of rank, were not so severely defined as now; and Amyas, as a "gentleman adventurer," was, on land, in a position very difficult to be settled, though at sea he was as liable to be hanged as any other person on board; and on the whole it was found expedient to patch the matter up. So Captain Raleigh returning, said that though Admiral Winter had doubtless taken umbrage at certain words of Mr. Leigh's, yet that he had no doubt that Mr. Leigh meant nothing thereby but what was consistent with the profession of a soldier and a gentleman, and worthy both of himself and of the admiral.

From which proposition Amyas found it impossible to dissent; whereon Raleigh went back, and informed Winter that Leigh had freely retracted his words, and fully wiped off any imputation which Mr. Winter might conceive to have been put upon him, and so forth. So Winter returned, and Amyas said frankly enough—

"Admiral Winter, I hope, as a loyal soldier, that you will understand thus far; that naught which has passed to-night shall in any way prevent you finding me a forward and obedient servant to all your commands, be they what they may, and a supporter of your authority among the men, and honor against the foe, even with my life. For I should be ashamed if private differences should ever prejudice by a grain the public weal."

This was a great effort of oratory for Amyas; and he therefore, in order to be safe by following precedent, tried to talk as much as he could like Sir Richard Grenville. Of course Winter could answer nothing to it, in spite of the plain hint of private differences, but that he should not fail to show himself a captain worthy of so valiant and trusty a gentleman; whereon the whole party turned their attention to the captive, who, thanks to Will Cary, was by this time sitting up, standing much in need of a handkerchief, and looking about him, having been unhelmed, in a confused and doleful manner.

"Take the gentleman to my tent," said Winter, "and let the surgeon see to him. Mr. Leigh, who is he?—"

"An enemy, but whether Spaniard or Italian I know not; but he seemed somebody among them, I thought the captain of a company. He and I cut at each other twice or thrice at first, and then lost each other; and after that I came on him among the sand-hills, trying to rally his men, and swearing like the mouth of the pit, whereby I guess him a Spaniard. But his men ran; so I brought him in."

"And how?" asked Raleigh. "Thou art giving us all the play but the murders and the marriages."

"Why, I bid him yield, and he would not. Then I bid him run, and he would not. And it was too pitch-dark for fighting; so I took him by the ears, and shook the wind out of him, and so brought him in."

"Shook the wind out of him?" cried Cary, amid the roar of laughter which followed. "Dost know thou hast nearly wrung his neck in two? His vizor was full of blood."

"He should have run or yielded, then," said Amyas; and getting up, slipped off to find some ale, and then to sleep comfortably in a dry burrow which he scratched out of a sandbank.

The next morning, as Amyas was discussing a scanty breakfast of biscuit (for provisions were running very short in camp), Raleigh came up to him.

"What, eating? That's more than I have done to-day."

"Sit down, and share, then."

"Nay, lad, I did not come a-begging. I have set some of my rogues to dig rabbits; but as I live, young Colbrand, you may thank your stars that you are alive to-day to eat. Poor young Cheek— Sir John Cheek, the grammarian's son—got his quittance last night by a Spanish pike, rushing headlong on, just as you did. But have you seen your prisoner?"

"No; nor shall, while he is in Winter's tent."

"Why not, then? What quarrel have you against the admiral, friend Bobadil? Cannot you let Francis Drake fight his own battles, without thrusting your head in between them?"

"Well, that is good! As if the quarrel was not just as much mine, and every man's in the ship. Why, when he left Drake, he left us all, did he not?"

"And what if he did? Let bygones be bygones is the rule of a Christian, and of a wise man too, Amyas. Here the man is, at least, safe home, in favor and in power; and a prudent youth will just hold his tongue, mumchance, and swim with the stream."

"But that's just what makes me mad; to see this fellow, after deserting us there in unknown seas, win credit and rank at home here for being the first man who ever sailed back through the Straits. What had he to do with sailing back at all! As well make the fox a knight for being the first that ever jumped down a jakes to escape the hounds. The fiercer the flight the fouler the fear, say I."

"Amyas! Amyas! thou art a hard hitter, but a soft politician."

"I am no politician, Captain Raleigh, nor ever wish to be. An honest man's my friend, and a rogue's my foe; and I'll tell both as much, as long as I breathe."

"And die a poor saint," said Raleigh, laughing. "But if Winter invites you to his tent himself, you won't refuse to come?"

"Why, no, considering his years and rank; but he knows too well to do that."

"He knows too well not to do it," said Raleigh, laughing as he walked away. And verily in half-an-hour came an invitation, extracted of course, from the admiral by Raleigh's silver tongue, which Amyas could not but obey.

"We all owe you thanks for last night's service, sir," said Winter, who had for some good reasons changed his tone. "Your prisoner is found to be a gentleman of birth and experience, and the leader of the assault last night. He has already told us more than we had hoped, for which also we are beholden to you; and, indeed, my Lord Grey has been asking for you already."

"I have, young sir," said a quiet and lofty voice; and Amyas saw limping from the inner tent the proud and stately figure of the stern deputy, Lord Grey of Wilton, a brave and wise man, but with a naturally harsh temper, which had been soured still more by the wound which had crippled him, while yet a boy, at the battle of Leith. He owed that limp to Mary Queen of Scots; and he did not forget the debt.

"I have been asking for you; having heard from many, both of your last night's prowess, and of your conduct and courage beyond the promise of your years, displayed in that ever-memorable voyage, which may well be ranked with the deeds of the ancient Argonauts."

Amyas bowed low; and the lord deputy went on, "You will needs wish to see your prisoner. You will find him such a one as you need not be ashamed to have taken, and as need not be ashamed to have been taken by you: but here he is, and will, I doubt not, answer as much for himself. Know each other better, gentlemen both: last night was an ill one for making acquaintances. Don Guzman Maria Magdalena Sotomayor de Soto, know the hidalgo, Amyas Leigh!"

As he spoke, the Spaniard came forward, still in his armor, all save his head, which was bound up in a handkerchief.

He was an exceedingly tall and graceful personage, of that sangre azul which marked high Visigothic descent; golden-haired and fair-skinned, with hands as small and white as a woman's; his lips were delicate but thin, and compressed closely at the corners of the mouth; and his pale blue eye had a glassy dulness. In spite of his beauty and his carriage, Amyas shrank from him instinctively; and yet he could not help holding out his hand in return, as the Spaniard, holding out his, said languidly, in most sweet and sonorous Spanish—

"I kiss his hands and feet. The senor speaks, I am told, my native tongue?"

"I have that honor."

"Then accept in it (for I can better express myself therein than in English, though I am not altogether ignorant of that witty and learned language) the expression of my pleasure at having fallen into the hands of one so renowned in war and travel; and of one also," he added, glancing at Amyas's giant bulk, "the vastness of whose strength, beyond that of common mortality, makes it no more shame for me to have been overpowered and carried away by him than if my captor had been a paladin of Charlemagne's."

Honest Amyas bowed and stammered, a little thrown off his balance by the unexpected assurance and cool flattery of his prisoner; but he said—

"If you are satisfied, illustrious senor, I am bound to be so. I only trust that in my hurry and the darkness I have not hurt you unnecessarily."

The Don laughed a pretty little hollow laugh: "No, kind senor, my head, I trust, will after a few days have become united to my shoulders; and, for the present, your company will make me forget any slight discomfort."

"Pardon me, senor; but by this daylight I should have seen that armor before."

"I doubt it not, senor, as having been yourself also in the forefront of the battle," said the Spaniard, with a proud smile.

"If I am right, senor, you are he who yesterday held up the standard after it was shot down."

"I do not deny that undeserved honor; and I have to thank the courtesy of you and your countrymen for having permitted me to do so with impunity."

"Ah, I heard of that brave feat," said the lord deputy. "You should consider yourself, Mr. Leigh, honored by being enabled to show courtesy to such a warrior."

How long this interchange of solemn compliments, of which Amyas was getting somewhat weary, would have gone on, I know not; but at that moment Raleigh entered hastily—

"My lord, they have hung out a white flag, and are calling for a parley!"

The Spaniard turned pale, and felt for his sword, which was gone; and then, with a bitter laugh, murmured to himself—"As I expected."

"I am very sorry to hear it. Would to Heaven they had simply fought it out!" said Lord Grey, half to himself; and then, "Go, Captain Raleigh, and answer them that (saving this gentleman's presence) the laws of war forbid a parley with any who are leagued with rebels against their lawful sovereign."

"But what if they wish to treat for this gentleman's ransom?"

"For their own, more likely," said the Spaniard; "but tell them, on my part, senor, that Don Guzman refuses to be ransomed; and will return to no camp where the commanding officer, unable to infect his captains with his own cowardice, dishonors them against their will."

"You speak sharply, senor," said Winter, after Raleigh had gone out.

"I have reason, Senor Admiral, as you will find, I fear, erelong."

"We shall have the honor of leaving you here, for the present, sir, as Admiral Winter's guest," said the lord deputy.

"But not my sword, it seems."

"Pardon me, senor; but no one has deprived you of your sword," said Winter.

"I don't wish to pain you, sir," said Amyas, "but I fear that we were both careless enough to leave it behind last night."

A flash passed over the Spaniard's face, which disclosed terrible depths of fury and hatred beneath that quiet mask, as the summer lightning displays the black abysses of the thunder-storm; but like the summer lightning it passed almost unseen; and blandly as ever, he answered:

"I can forgive you for such a neglect, most valiant sir, more easily than I can forgive myself. Farewell, sir! One who has lost his sword is no fit company for you." And as Amyas and the rest departed, he plunged into the inner tent, stamping and writhing, gnawing his hands with rage and shame.

As Amyas came out on the battery, Yeo hailed him:

"Master Amyas! Hillo, sir! For the love of Heaven, tell me!"

"What, then?"

"Is his lordship stanch? Will he do the Lord's work faithfully, root and branch: or will he spare the Amalekites?"

"The latter, I think, old hip-and-thigh," said Amyas, hurrying forward to hear the news from Raleigh, who appeared in sight once more.

"They ask to depart with bag and baggage," said he, when he came up.

"God do so to me, and more also, if they carry away a straw!" said Lord Grey. "Make short work of it, sir!"

"I do not know how that will be, my lord; as I came up a captain shouted to me off the walls that there were mutineers; and, denying that he surrendered, would have pulled down the flag of truce, but the soldiers beat him off."

"A house divided against itself will not stand long, gentlemen. Tell them that I give no conditions. Let them lay down their arms, and trust in the Bishop of Rome who sent them hither, and may come to save them if he wants them. Gunners, if you see the white flag go down, open your fire instantly. Captain Raleigh, we need your counsel here. Mr. Cary, will you be my herald this time?"

"A better Protestant never went on a pleasanter errand, my lord."

So Cary went, and then ensued an argument, as to what should be done with the prisoners in case of a surrender.

I cannot tell whether my Lord Grey meant, by offering conditions which the Spaniards would not accept, to force them into fighting the quarrel out, and so save himself the responsibility of deciding on their fate; or whether his mere natural stubbornness, as well as his just indignation, drove him on too far to retract: but the council of war which followed was both a sad and a stormy one, and one which he had reason to regret to his dying day. What was to be done with the enemy? They already outnumbered the English; and some fifteen hundred of Desmond's wild Irish hovered in the forests round, ready to side with the winning party, or even to attack the English at the least sign of vacillation or fear. They could not carry the Spaniards away with them, for they had neither shipping nor food, not even handcuffs enough for them; and as Mackworth told Winter when he proposed it, the only plan was for him to make San Josepho a present of his ships, and swim home himself as he could. To turn loose in Ireland, as Captain Touch urged, on the other hand, seven hundred such monsters of lawlessness, cruelty, and lust, as Spanish and Italian condottieri were in those days, was as fatal to their own safety as cruel to the wretched Irish. All the captains, without exception, followed on the same side. "What was to be done, then?" asked Lord Grey, impatiently. "Would they have him murder them all in cold blood?"

And for a while every man, knowing that it must come to that, and yet not daring to say it; till Sir Warham St. Leger, the marshal of Munster, spoke out stoutly: "Foreigners had been scoffing them too long and too truly with waging these Irish wars as if they meant to keep them alive, rather than end them. Mercy and faith to every Irishman who would show mercy and faith, was his motto; but to invaders, no mercy. Ireland was England's vulnerable point; it might be some day her ruin; a terrible example must be made of those who dare to touch the sore. Rather pardon the Spaniards for landing in the Thames than in Ireland!"—till Lord Grey became much excited, and turning as a last hope to Raleigh, asked his opinion: but Raleigh's silver tongue was that day not on the side of indulgence. He skilfully recapitulated the arguments of his fellow-captains, improving them as he went on, till each worthy soldier was surprised to find himself so much wiser a man than he had thought; and finished by one of his rapid and passionate perorations upon his favorite theme—the West Indian cruelties of the Spaniards, ". . . by which great tracts and fair countries are now utterly stripped of inhabitants by heavy bondage and torments unspeakable. Oh, witless Islanders!" said he, apostrophizing the Irish, "would to Heaven that you were here to listen to me! What other fate awaits you, if this viper, which you are so ready to take into your bosom, should be warmed to life, but to groan like the Indians, slaves to the Spaniard; but to perish like the Indians, by heavy burdens, cruel chains, plunder and ravishment; scourged, racked, roasted, stabbed, sawn in sunder, cast to feed the dogs, as simple and more righteous peoples have perished ere now by millions? And what else, I say, had been the fate of Ireland had this invasion prospered, which God has now, by our weak hands, confounded and brought to naught? Shall we then answer it, my lord, either to our conscience, our God, or our queen, if we shall set loose men (not one of whom, I warrant, but is stained with murder on murder) to go and fill up the cup of their iniquity among these silly sheep? Have not their native wolves, their barbarous chieftains, shorn, peeled, and slaughtered them enough already, but we must add this pack of foreign wolves to the number of their tormentors, and fit the Desmond with a body-guard of seven, yea, seven hundred devils worse than himself? Nay, rather let us do violence to our own human nature, and show ourselves in appearance rigorous, that we may be kind indeed; lest while we presume to be over-merciful to the guilty, we prove ourselves to be over-cruel to the innocent."

"Captain Raleigh, Captain Raleigh," said Lord Grey, "the blood of these men be on your head!"

"It ill befits your lordship," answered Raleigh, "to throw on your subordinates the blame of that which your reason approves as necessary."

"I should have thought, sir, that one so noted for ambition as Captain Raleigh would have been more careful of the favor of that queen for whose smiles he is said to be so longing a competitor. If you have not yet been of her counsels, sir, I can tell you you are not likely to be. She will be furious when she hears of this cruelty."

Lord Grey had lost his temper: but Raleigh kept his, and answered quietly—

"Her majesty shall at least not find me among the number of those who prefer her favor to her safety, and abuse to their own profit that over-tenderness and mercifulness of heart which is the only blemish (and yet, rather like a mole on a fair cheek, but a new beauty) in her manifold perfections."

At this juncture Cary returned.

"My lord," said he, in some confusion, "I have proposed your terms; but the captains still entreat for some mitigation; and, to tell you truth, one of them has insisted on accompanying me hither to plead his cause himself."

"I will not see him, sir. Who is he?"

"His name is Sebastian of Modena, my lord."

"Sebastian of Modena? What think you, gentlemen? May we make an exception in favor of so famous a soldier?"

"So villainous a cut-throat," said Zouch to Raleigh, under his breath.

All, however, were for speaking with so famous a man; and in came, in full armor, a short, bull-necked Italian, evidently of immense strength, of the true Caesar Borgia stamp.

"Will you please to be seated, sir?" said Lord Grey, coldly.

"I kiss your hands, most illustrious: but I do not sit in an enemy's camp. Ha, my friend Zouch! How has your signoria fared since we fought side by side at Lepanto? So you too are here, sitting in council on the hanging of me."

"What is your errand, sir? Time is short," said the lord deputy.

"Corpo di Bacco! It has been long enough all the morning, for my rascals have kept me and my friend the Colonel Hercules (whom you know, doubtless) prisoners in our tents at the pike's point. My lord deputy, I have but a few words. I shall thank you to take every soldier in the fort—Italian, Spaniard, and Irish—and hang them up as high as Haman, for a set of mutinous cowards, with the arch-traitor San Josepho at their head."

"I am obliged to you for your offer, sir, and shall deliberate presently as to whether I shall not accept it."

"But as for us captains, really your excellency must consider that we are gentlemen born, and give us either buena querra, as the Spaniards say, or a fair chance for life; and so to my business."

"Stay, sir. Answer this first. Have you or yours any commission to show either from the King of Spain or any other potentate?"

"Never a one but the cause of Heaven and our own swords. And with them, my lord, we are ready to meet any gentlemen of your camp, man to man, with our swords only, half-way between your leaguer and ours; and I doubt not that your lordship will see fair play. Will any gentleman accept so civil an offer? There sits a tall youth in that corner who would suit me very well. Will any fit my gallant comrades with half-an-hour's punto and stoccado?"

There was a silence, all looking at the lord deputy, whose eyes were kindling in a very ugly way.

"No answer? Then I must proceed to exhortation. So! Will that be sufficient?"

And walking composedly across the tent, the fearless ruffian quietly stooped down, and smote

Amyas Leigh full in the face.

Up sprang Amyas, heedless of all the august assembly, and with a single buffet felled him to the earth.

"Excellent!" said he, rising unabashed. "I can always trust my instinct. I knew the moment I saw him that he was a cavalier worth letting blood. Now, sir, your sword and harness, and I am at your service outside!"

The solemn and sententious Englishmen were altogether taken aback by the Italian's impudence; but Zouch settled the matter.

"Most noble captain, will you be pleased to recollect a certain little occurrence at Messina, in the year 1575? For if you do not, I do; and beg to inform this gentleman that you are unworthy of his sword, and had you, unluckily for you, been an Englishman, would have found the fashions of our country so different from your own that you would have been then hanged, sir, and probably may be so still."

The Italian's sword flashed out in a moment: but Lord Grey interfered.

"No fighting here, gentlemen. That may wait; and, what is more, shall wait till—Strike their swords down, Raleigh, Mackworth! Strike their swords down! Colonel Sebastian, you will be pleased to return as you came, in safety, having lost nothing, as (I frankly tell you) you have gained nothing, by your wild bearing here. We shall proceed to deliberate on your fate."

"I trust, my lord," said Amyas, "that you will spare this braggart's life, at least for a day or two. For in spite of Captain Zouch's warning, I must have to do with him yet, or my cheek will rise up in judgment against me at the last day."

"Well spoken, lad," said the colonel, as he swung out. "So! worth a reprieve, by this sword, to have one more rapier-rattle before the gallows! Then I take back no further answer, my lord deputy? Not even our swords, our virgin blades, signor, the soldier's cherished bride? Shall we go forth weeping widowers, and leave to strange embrace the lovely steel?"

"None, sir, by heaven!" said he, waxing wroth. "Do you come hither, pirates as you are, to dictate terms upon a foreign soil? Is it not enough to have set up here the Spanish flag, and claimed the land of Ireland as the Pope's gift to the Spaniard; violated the laws of nations, and the solemn treaties of princes, under color of a mad superstition?"

"Superstition, my lord? Nothing less. Believe a philosopher who has not said a pater or an ave for seven years past at least. Quod tango credo, is my motto; and though I am bound to say, under pain of the Inquisition, that the most holy Father the Pope has given this land of Ireland to his most Catholic Majesty the King of Spain, Queen Elizabeth having forfeited her title to it by heresy,—why, my lord, I believe it as little as you do. I believe that Ireland would have been mine, if I had won it; I believe religiously that it is not mine, now I have lost it. What is, is, and a fig for priests; to-day to thee, to-morrow to me. Addio!" And out he swung.

"There goes a most gallant rascal," said the lord deputy.

"And a most rascally gallant," said Zouch. "The murder of his own page, of which I gave him a remembrancer, is among the least of his sins."

"And now, Captain Raleigh," said Lord Grey, "as you have been so earnest in preaching this butchery, I have a right to ask none but you to practise it."

Raleigh bit his lip, and replied by the "quip courteous—"

"I am at least a man, my lord, who thinks it shame to allow others to do that which I dare not do myself."

Lord Grey might probably have returned "the countercheck quarrelsome," had not Mackworth risen—

"And I, my lord, being in that matter at least one of Captain Raleigh's kidney, will just go with him to see that he takes no harm by being bold enough to carry out an ugly business, and serving these rascals as their countrymen served Mr. Oxenham."

"I bid you good morning, then, gentlemen, though I cannot bid you God speed," said Lord Grey; and sitting down again, covered his face with his hands, and, to the astonishment of all bystanders, burst, say the chroniclers, into tears.

Amyas followed Raleigh out. The latter was pale, but determined, and very wroth against the deputy.

"Does the man take me for a hangman," said he, "that he speaks to me thus? But such is the way of the great. If you neglect your duty, they haul you over the coals; if you do it, you must do it on your own responsibility. Farewell, Amyas; you will not shrink from me as a butcher when I return?"

"God forbid! But how will you do it?"

"March one company in, and drive them forth, and let the other cut them down as they come out.—Pah!"

It was done. Right or wrong, it was done. The shrieks and curses had died away, and the Fort del Oro was a red shambles, which the soldiers were trying to cover from the sight of heaven and earth, by dragging the bodies into the ditch, and covering them with the ruins of the rampart; while the Irish, who had beheld from the woods that awful warning, fled trembling into the deepest recesses of the forest. It was done; and it never needed to be done again. The hint was severe, but it was sufficient. Many years passed before a Spaniard set foot again in Ireland.

The Spanish and Italian officers were spared, and Amyas had Don Guzman Maria Magdalena Sotomayor de Soto duly adjudged to him, as his prize by right of war. He was, of course, ready enough to fight Sebastian of Modena: but Lord Grey forbade the duel: blood enough had been shed already. The next question was, where to bestow Don Guzman till his ransom should arrive; and as Amyas could not well deliver the gallant Don into the safe custody of Mrs. Leigh at Burrough, and still less into that of Frank at Court, he was fain to write to Sir Richard Grenville, and ask his advice, and in the meanwhile keep the Spaniard with him upon parole, which he frankly gave,—saying that as for running away, he had nowhere to run to; and as for joining the Irish he had no mind to turn pig; and Amyas found him, as shall be hereafter told, pleasant company enough. But one morning Raleigh entered—

"I have done you a good turn, Leigh, if you think it one. I have talked St. Leger into making you my lieutenant, and giving you the custody of a right pleasant hermitage—some castle Shackatory or other in the midst of a big bog, where time will run swift and smooth with you, between hunting wild Irish, snaring snipes, and drinking yourself drunk with usquebaugh over a turf fire."

"I'll go," quoth Amyas; "anything for work." So he went and took possession of his lieutenancy and his black robber tower, and there passed the rest of the winter, fighting or hunting all day, and chatting and reading all the evening, with Senor Don Guzman, who, like a good soldier of fortune, made himself thoroughly at home, and a general favorite with the soldiers.

At first, indeed, his Spanish pride and stateliness, and Amyas's English taciturnity, kept the two apart somewhat; but they soon began, if not to trust, at least to like each other; and Don Guzman told Amyas, bit by bit, who he was, of what an ancient house, and of what a poor one; and laughed over the very small chance of his ransom being raised, and the certainty that, at least, it could not come for a couple of years, seeing that the only De Soto who had a penny to spare was a fat old dean at St. Yago de Leon, in the Caracas, at which place Don Guzman had been born. This of course led to much talk about the West Indies, and the Don was as much interested to find that Amyas had been one of Drake's world-famous crew, as Amyas was to find that his captive was the grandson of none other than that most terrible of man-hunters, Don Ferdinando de Soto, the conqueror of Florida, of whom Amyas had read many a time in Las Casas, "as the captain of tyrants, the notoriousest and most experimented amongst them that have done the most hurts, mischiefs, and destructions in many realms." And often enough his blood boiled, and he had much ado to recollect that the speaker was his guest, as Don Guzman chatted away about his grandfather's hunts of innocent women and children, murders of caciques and burnings alive of guides, "pour encourager les autres," without, seemingly, the least feeling that the victims were human beings or subjects for human pity; anything, in short, but heathen dogs, enemies of God, servants of the devil, to be used by the Christian when he needed, and when not needed killed down as cumberers of the ground. But Don Guzman was a most finished gentleman nevertheless; and told many a good story of the Indies, and told it well; and over and above his stories, he had among his baggage two books,—the one Antonio Galvano's "Discoveries of the World," a mine of winter evening amusement to Amyas; and the other, a manuscript book, which, perhaps, it had been well for Amyas had he never seen. For it was none other than a sort of rough journal which Don Guzman had kept as a lad, when he went down with the Adelantado Gonzales Ximenes de Casada, from Peru to the River of Amazons, to look for the golden country of El Dorado, and the city of Manoa, which stands in the midst of the White Lake, and equals or surpasses in glory even the palace of the Inca Huaynacapac; "all the vessels of whose house and kitchen are of gold and silver, and in his wardrobe statues of gold which seemed giants, and figures in proportion and bigness of all the beasts, birds, trees, and herbs of the earth, and the fishes of the water; and ropes, budgets, chests, and troughs of gold: yea, and a garden of pleasure in an Island near Puna, where they went to recreate themselves when they would take the air of the sea, which had all kind of garden herbs, flowers, and trees of gold and silver of an invention and magnificence till then never seen."

Now the greater part of this treasure (and be it remembered that these wonders were hardly exaggerated, and that there were many men alive then who had beheld them, as they had worse things, "with their corporal and mortal eyes") was hidden by the Indians when Pizarro conquered Peru and slew Atahuallpa, son of Huaynacapac; at whose death, it was said, one of the Inca's younger brothers fled out of Peru, and taking with him a great army, vanquished all that tract which lieth between the great Rivers of Amazons and Baraquan, otherwise called Maranon and Orenoque.

There he sits to this day, beside the golden lake, in the golden city, which is in breadth a three days' journey, covered, he and his court, with gold dust from head to foot, waiting for the fulfilment of the ancient prophecy which was written in the temple of Caxamarca, where his ancestors worshipped of old; that heroes shall come out of the West, and lead him back across the forests to the kingdom of Peru, and restore him to the glory of his forefathers.

Golden phantom! so possible, so probable, to imaginations which were yet reeling before the actual and veritable prodigies of Peru, Mexico, and the East Indies. Golden phantom! which has cost already the lives of thousands, and shall yet cost more; from Diego de Ordas, and Juan Corteso, and many another, who went forth on the quest by the Andes, and by the Orinoco, and by the Amazons; Antonio Sedenno, with his ghastly caravan of manacled Indians, "on whose dead carcasses the tigers being fleshed, assaulted the Spaniards;" Augustine Delgado, who "came to a cacique, who entertained him with all kindness, and gave him beside much gold and slaves, three nymphs very beautiful, which bare the names of three provinces, Guanba, Gotoguane, and Maiarare. To requite which manifold courtesies, he carried off, not only all the gold, but all the Indians he could seize, and took them in irons to Cubagua, and sold them for slaves; after which, Delgado was shot in the eye by an Indian, of which hurt he died;" Pedro d'Orsua, who found the cinnamon forests of Loxas, "whom his men murdered, and afterwards beheaded Lady Anes his wife, who forsook not her lord in all his travels unto death," and many another, who has vanished with valiant comrades at his back into the green gulfs of the primaeval forests, never to emerge again. Golden phantom! man-devouring, whose maw is never satiate with souls of heroes; fatal to Spain, more fatal still to England upon that shameful day, when the last of Elizabeth's heroes shall lay down his head upon the block, nominally for having believed what all around him believed likewise till they found it expedient to deny it in order to curry favor with the crowned cur who betrayed him, really because he alone dared to make one last protest in behalf of liberty and Protestantism against the incoming night of tyranny and superstition. Little thought Amyas, as he devoured the pages of that manuscript, that he was laying a snare for the life of the man whom, next to Drake and Grenville, he most admired on earth.

But Don Guzman, on the other hand, seemed to have an instinct that that book might be a fatal gift to his captor; for one day ere Amyas had looked into it, he began questioning the Don about El Dorado. Whereon Don Guzman replied with one of those smiles of his, which (as Amyas said afterwards) was so abominably like a sneer, that he had often hard work to keep his hands off the man—

"Ah! You have been eating of the fruit of the tree of knowledge, senor? Well; if you have any ambition to follow many another brave captain to the pit, I know no shorter or easier path than is contained in that little book."

"I have never opened your book," said Amyas; "your private manuscripts are no concern of mine: but my man who recovered your baggage read part of it, knowing no better; and now you are at liberty to tell me as little as you like."

The "man," it should be said, was none other than Salvation Yeo, who had attached himself by this time inseparably to Amyas, in quality of body-guard: and, as was common enough in those days, had turned soldier for the nonce, and taken under his patronage two or three rusty bases (swivels) and falconets (four-pounders), which grinned harmlessly enough from the tower top across the cheerful expanse of bog.

Amyas once asked him, how he reconciled this Irish sojourn with his vow to find his little maid? Yeo shook his head.

"I can't tell, sir, but there's something that makes me always to think of you when I think of her; and that's often enough, the Lord knows. Whether it is that I ben't to find the dear without your help; or whether it is your pleasant face puts me in mind of hers; or what, I can't tell; but don't you part me from you, sir, for I'm like Ruth, and where you lodge I lodge; and where you go I go; and where you die—though I shall die many a year first—there I'll die, I hope and trust; for I can't abear you out of my sight; and that's the truth thereof."

So Yeo remained with Amyas, while Cary went elsewhere with Sir Warham St. Leger, and the two friends met seldom for many months; so that Amyas's only companion was Don Guzman, who, as he grew more familiar, and more careless about what he said and did in his captor's presence, often puzzled and scandalized him by his waywardness. Fits of deep melancholy alternated with bursts of Spanish boastfulness, utterly astonishing to the modest and sober-minded Englishman, who would often have fancied him inspired by usquebaugh, had he not had ocular proof of his extreme abstemiousness.

"Miserable?" said he, one night in one of these fits. "And have I not a right to be miserable? Why should I not curse the virgin and all the saints, and die? I have not a friend, not a ducat on earth; not even a sword—hell and the furies! It was my all: the only bequest I ever had from my father, and I lived by it and earned by it. Two years ago I had as pretty a sum of gold as cavalier could wish—and now!"—

"What is become of it, then? I cannot hear that our men plundered you of any."

"Your men? No, senor! What fifty men dared not have done, one woman did! a painted, patched, fucused, periwigged, bolstered, Charybdis, cannibal, Megaera, Lamia! Why did I ever go near that cursed Naples, the common sewer of Europe? whose women, I believe, would be swallowed up by Vesuvius to-morrow, if it were not that Belphegor is afraid of their making the pit itself too hot to hold him. Well, sir, she had all of mine and more; and when all was gone in wine and dice, woodcocks' brains and ortolans' tongues, I met the witch walking with another man. I had a sword and a dagger; I gave him the first (though the dog fought well enough, to give him his due), and her the second; left them lying across each other, and fled for my life,—and here I am! after twenty years of fighting, from the Levant to the Orellana—for I began ere I had a hair on my chin—and this is the end!—No, it is not! I'll have that El Dorado yet! the Adelantado made Berreo, when he gave him his daughter, swear that he would hunt for it, through life and death.—We'll see who finds it first, he or I. He's a bungler; Orsua was a bungler—Pooh! Cortes and Pizarro? we'll see whether there are not as good Castilians as they left still. I can do it, senor. I know a track, a plan; over the Llanos is the road; and I'll be Emperor of Manoa yet—possess the jewels of all the Incas; and gold, gold! Pizarro was a beggar to what I will be!"

Conceive, sir, he broke forth during another of these peacock fits, as Amyas and he were riding along the hill-side; "conceive! with forty chosen cavaliers (what need of more?) I present myself before the golden king, trembling amid his myriad guards at the new miracle of the mailed centaurs of the West; and without dismounting, I approach his throne, lift the crucifix which hangs around my neck, and pressing it to my lips, present it for the adoration of the idolater, and give him his alternative; that which Gayferos and the Cid, my ancestors, offered the Soldan and the Moor—baptism or death! He hesitates; perhaps smiles scornfully upon my little band; I answer him by deeds, as Don Ferdinando, my illustrious grandfather, answered Atahuallpa at Peru, in sight of all his court and camp."

"With your lance-point, as Gayferos did the Soldan?" asked Amyas, amused.

"No, sir; persuasion first, for the salvation of a soul is at stake. Not with the lance-point, but the spur, sir, thus!"—

And striking his heels into his horse's flanks, he darted off at full speed.

"The Spanish traitor!" shouted Yeo. "He's going to escape! Shall we shoot, sir? Shall we shoot?"

"For Heaven's sake, no!" said Amyas, looking somewhat blank, nevertheless, for he much doubted whether the whole was not a ruse on the part of the Spaniard, and he knew how impossible it was for his fifteen stone of flesh to give chase to the Spaniard's twelve. But he was soon reassured; the Spaniard wheeled round towards him, and began to put the rough hackney through all the paces of the manege with a grace and skill which won applause from the beholders.

"Thus!" he shouted, waving his hand to Amyas, between his curvets and caracoles, "did my illustrious grandfather exhibit to the Paynim emperor the prowess of a Castilian cavalier! Thus!—and thus!—and thus, at last, he dashed up to his very feet, as I to yours, and bespattering that unbaptized visage with his Christian bridle foam, pulled up his charger on his haunches, thus!"

And (as was to be expected from a blown Irish garron on a peaty Irish hill-side) down went the hapless hackney on his tail, away went his heels a yard in front of him, and ere Don Guzman could "avoid his selle," horse and man rolled over into neighboring bog-hole.

"After pride comes a fall," quoth Yeo with unmoved visage, as he lugged him out.

"And what would you do with the emperor at last?" asked Amyas when the Don had been scrubbed somewhat clean with a bunch of rushes. "Kill him, as your grandfather did Atahuallpa?"

"My grandfather," answered the Spaniard, indignantly, "was one of those who, to their eternal honor, protested to the last against that most cruel and unknightly massacre. He could be terrible to the heathen; but he kept his plighted word, sir, and taught me to keep mine, as you have seen to-day."

"I have, senor," said Amyas. "You might have given us the slip easily enough just now, and did not. Pardon me, if I have offended you."

The Spaniard (who, after all, was cross principally with himself and the "unlucky mare's son," as the old romances have it, which had played him so scurvy a trick) was all smiles again forthwith; and Amyas, as they chatted on, could not help asking him next—

"I wonder why you are so frank about your own intentions to an enemy like me, who will surely forestall you if he can."

"Sir, a Spaniard needs no concealment, and fears no rivalry. He is the soldier of the Cross, and in it he conquers, like Constantine of old. Not that you English are not very heroes; but you have not, sir, and you cannot have, who have forsworn our Lady and the choir of saints, the same divine protection, the same celestial mission, which enables the Catholic cavalier single-handed to chase a thousand Paynims."

And Don Guzman crossed himself devoutly, and muttered half-a-dozen Ave Marias in succession, while Amyas rode silently by his side, utterly puzzled at this strange compound of shrewdness with fanaticism, of perfect high-breeding with a boastfulness which in an Englishman would have been the sure mark of vulgarity.

At last came a letter from Sir Richard Grenville, complimenting Amyas on his success and promotion, bearing a long and courtly message to Don Guzman (whom Grenville had known when he was in the Mediterranean, at the battle of Lepanto), and offering to receive him as his own guest at Bideford, till his ransom should arrive; a proposition which the Spaniard (who of course was getting sufficiently tired of the Irish bogs) could not but gladly accept; and one of Winter's ships, returning to England in the spring of 1581, delivered duly at the quay of Bideford the body of Don Guzman Maria Magdalena. Raleigh, after forming for that summer one of the triumvirate by which Munster was governed after Ormond's departure, at last got his wish and departed for England and the Court; and Amyas was left alone with the snipes and yellow mantles for two more weary years.

CHAPTER X: HOW THE MAYOR OF BIDEFORD BAITED HIS HOOK WITH HIS OWN FLESH

So it befell to Chaucer's knight in prison; and so it befell also to Don Guzman; and it befell on this wise.

He settled down quietly enough at Bideford on his parole, in better quarters than he had occupied for many a day, and took things as they came, like a true soldier of fortune; till, after he had been with Grenville hardly a month, old Salterne the Mayor came to supper.

Now Don Guzman, however much he might be puzzled at first at our strange English ways of asking burghers and such low-bred folk to eat and drink above the salt, in the company of noble persons, was quite gentleman enough to know that Richard Grenville was gentleman enough to do only what was correct, and according to the customs and proprieties. So after shrugging the shoulders of his spirit, he submitted to eat and drink at the same board with a tradesman who sat at a desk, and made up ledgers, and took apprentices; and hearing him talk with Grenville neither unwisely nor in a vulgar fashion, actually before the evening was out condescended to exchange words with him himself. Whereon he found him a very prudent and courteous person, quite aware of the Spaniard's superior rank, and making him feel in every sentence that he was aware thereof; and yet holding his own opinion, and asserting his own rights as a wise elder in a fashion which the Spaniard had only seen before among the merchant princes of Genoa and Venice.

At the end of supper, Salterne asked Grenville to do his humble roof the honor, etc. etc., of supping with him the next evening, and then turning to the Don, said quite frankly, that he knew how great a condescension it would be on the part of a nobleman of Spain to sit at the board of a simple merchant: but that if the Spaniard deigned to do him such a favor, he would find that the cheer was fit enough for any rank, whatsoever the company might be; which invitation Don Guzman, being on the whole glad enough of anything to amuse him, graciously condescended to accept, and gained thereby an excellent supper, and, if he had chosen to drink it, much good wine.

Now Mr. Salterne was, of course, as a wise merchant, as ready as any man for an adventure to foreign parts, as was afterwards proved by his great exertions in the settlement of Virginia; and he was, therefore, equally ready to rack the brains of any guest whom he suspected of knowing anything concerning strange lands; and so he thought no shame, first to try to loose his guest's tongue by much good sack, and next, to ask him prudent and well-concocted questions concerning the Spanish Main, Peru, the Moluccas, China, the Indies, and all parts.

The first of which schemes failed; for the Spaniard was as abstemious as any monk, and drank little but water; the second succeeded not over well, for the Spaniard was as cunning as any fox, and answered little but wind.

In the midst of which tongue-fence in came the Rose of Torridge, looking as beautiful as usual; and hearing what they were upon, added, artlessly enough, her questions to her father's: to her Don Guzman could not but answer; and without revealing any very important commercial secrets, gave his host and his host's daughter a very amusing evening.

Now little Eros, though spirits like Frank Leigh's may choose to call him (as, perhaps, he really is to them) the eldest of the gods, and the son of Jove and Venus, yet is reported by other equally good authorities, as Burton has set forth in his "Anatomy of Melancholy," to be after all only the child of idleness and fulness of bread. To which scandalous calumny the thoughts of Don Guzman's heart gave at least a certain color; for he being idle (as captives needs must be), and also full of bread (for Sir Richard kept a very good table), had already looked round for mere amusement's sake after some one with whom to fall in love. Lady Grenville, as nearest, was, I blush to say, thought of first; but the Spaniard was a man of honor, and Sir Richard his host; so he put away from his mind (with a self-denial on which he plumed himself much) the pleasure of a chase equally exciting to his pride and his love of danger. As for the sinfulness of the said chase, he of course thought no more of that than other Southern Europeans did then, or than (I blush again to have to say it) the English did afterwards in the days of the Stuarts. Nevertheless, he had put Lady Grenville out of his mind; and so left room to take Rose Salterne into it, not with any distinct purpose of wronging her: but, as I said before, half to amuse himself, and half, too, because he could not help it. For there was an innocent freshness about the Rose of Torridge, fond as she was of being admired, which was new to him and most attractive. "The train of the peacock," as he said to himself, "and yet the heart of the dove," made so charming a combination, that if he could have persuaded her to love no one but him, perhaps he might become fool enough to love no one but her. And at that thought he was seized with a very panic of prudence, and resolved to keep out of her way; and yet the days ran slowly, and Lady Grenville when at home was stupid enough to talk and think about nothing but her husband; and when she went to Stow, and left the Don alone in one corner of the great house at Bideford, what could he do but lounge down to the butt-gardens to show off his fine black cloak and fine black feather, see the shooting, have a game or two of rackets with the youngsters, a game or two of bowls with the elders, and get himself invited home to supper by Mr. Salterne?

And there, of course, he had it all his own way, and ruled the roast (which he was fond enough of doing) right royally, not only on account of his rank, but because he had something to say worth hearing, as a travelled man. For those times were the day-dawn of English commerce; and not a merchant in Bideford, or in all England, but had his imagination all on fire with projects of discoveries, companies, privileges, patents, and settlements; with gallant rivalry of the brave adventures of Sir Edward Osborne and his new London Company of Turkey Merchants; with the privileges just granted by the Sultan Murad Khan to the English; with the worthy Levant voyages of Roger Bodenham in the great bark Aucher, and of John Fox, and Lawrence Aldersey, and John Rule; and with hopes from the vast door for Mediterranean trade, which the crushing of the Venetian power at Famagusta in Cyprus, and the alliance made between Elizabeth and the Grand Turk, had just thrown open. So not a word could fall from the Spaniard about the Mediterranean but took root at once in right fertile soil. Besides, Master Edmund Hogan had been on a successful embassy to the Emperor of Morocco; John Hawkins and George Fenner had been to Guinea (and with the latter Mr. Walter Wren, a Bideford man), and had traded there for musk and civet, gold and grain; and African news was becoming almost as valuable as West Indian.

Moreover, but two months before had gone from London Captain Hare in the bark Minion, for Brazil, and a company of adventurers with him, with Sheffield hardware, and "Devonshire and Northern kersies," hollands and "Manchester cottons," for there was a great opening for English goods by the help of one John Whithall, who had married a Spanish heiress, and had an ingenio and slaves in Santos. (Don't smile, reader, or despise the day of small things, and those who sowed the seed whereof you reap the mighty harvest.) In the meanwhile, Drake had proved not merely the possibility of plundering the American coasts, but of establishing an East Indian trade; Frobisher and Davis, worthy forefathers of our Parrys and Franklins, had begun to bore their way upward through the Northern ice, in search of a passage to China which should avoid the dangers of the Spanish seas; and Anthony Jenkinson, not the least of English travellers, had, in six-and-twenty years of travel in behalf of the Muscovite Company, penetrated into not merely Russia and the Levant, but Persia and Armenia, Bokhara, Tartary, Siberia, and those waste Arctic shores where, thirty years before, the brave Sir Hugh Willoughby,

Everywhere English commerce, under the genial sunshine of Elizabeth's wise rule, was spreading and taking root; and as Don Guzman talked with his new friends, he soon saw (for he was shrewd enough) that they belonged to a race which must be exterminated if Spain intended to become (as she did intend) the mistress of the world; and that it was not enough for Spain to have seized in the Pope's name the whole new world, and claimed the exclusive right to sail the seas of America; not enough to have crushed the Hollanders; not enough to have degraded the Venetians into her bankers, and the Genoese into her mercenaries; not enough to have incorporated into herself, with the kingdom of Portugal, the whole East Indian trade of Portugal, while these fierce islanders remained to assert, with cunning policy and texts of Scripture, and, if they failed, with sharp shot and cold steel, free seas and free trade for all the nations upon earth. He saw it, and his countrymen saw it too: and therefore the Spanish Armada came: but of that hereafter. And Don Guzman knew also, by hard experience, that these same islanders, who sat in Salterne's parlor, talking broad Devon through their noses, were no mere counters of money and hucksters of goods: but men who, though they thoroughly hated fighting, and loved making money instead, could fight, upon occasion, after a very dogged and terrible fashion, as well as the bluest blood in Spain; and who sent out their merchant ships armed up to the teeth, and filled with men who had been trained from childhood to use those arms, and had orders to use them without mercy if either Spaniard, Portugal, or other created being dared to stop their money-making. And one evening he waxed quite mad, when, after having civilly enough hinted that if Englishmen came where they had no right to come, they might find themselves sent back again, he was answered by a volley of—

"We'll see that, sir."

"Depends on who says 'No right.'"

"You found might right," said another, "when you claimed the Indian seas; we may find right might when we try them."

"Try them, then, gentlemen, by all means, if it shall so please your worships; and find the sacred flag of Spain as invincible as ever was the Roman eagle."

"We have, sir. Did you ever hear of Francis Drake?"
"Or of George Fenner and the Portugals at the Azores, one against seven?"
"Or of John Hawkins, at St. Juan d'Ulloa?"
"You are insolent burghers," said Don Guzman, and rose to go.

"Sir," said old Salterne, "as you say, we are burghers and plain men, and some of us have forgotten ourselves a little, perhaps; we must beg you to forgive our want of manners, and to put it down to the strength of my wine; for insolent we never meant to be, especially to a noble gentleman and a foreigner."

But the Don would not be pacified; and walked out, calling himself an ass and a blinkard for having demeaned himself to such a company, forgetting that he had brought it on himself.

Salterne (prompted by the great devil Mammon) came up to him next day, and begged pardon again; promising, moreover, that none of those who had been so rude should be henceforth asked to meet him, if he would deign to honor his house once more. And the Don actually was appeased, and went there the very next evening, sneering at himself the whole time for going.

"Fool that I am! that girl has bewitched me, I believe. Go I must, and eat my share of dirt, for her sake."

So he went; and, cunningly enough, hinted to old Salterne that he had taken such a fancy to him, and felt so bound by his courtesy and hospitality, that he might not object to tell him things which he would not mention to every one; for that the Spaniards were not jealous of single traders, but of any general attempt to deprive them of their hard-earned wealth: that, however, in the meanwhile, there were plenty of opportunities for one man here and there to enrich himself, etc.

Old Salterne, shrewd as he was, had his weak point, and the Spaniard had touched it; and delighted at this opportunity of learning the mysteries of the Spanish monopoly, he often actually set Rose on to draw out the Don, without a fear (so blind does money make men) lest she might be herself drawn in. For, first, he held it as impossible that she would think of marrying a Popish Spaniard as of marrying the man in the moon; and, next, as impossible that he would think of marrying a burgher's daughter as of marrying a negress; and trusted that the religion of the one, and the family pride of the other, would keep them as separate as beings of two different species. And as for love without marriage, if such a possibility ever crossed him, the thought was rendered absurd; on Rose's part by her virtue, on which the old roan (and rightly) would have staked every farthing he had on earth; and on the Don's part, by a certain human fondness for the continuity of the carotid artery and the parts adjoining, for which (and that not altogether justly, seeing that Don Guzman cared as little for his own life as he did for his neighbor's) Mr. Salterne gave him credit. And so it came to pass, that for weeks and months the merchant's house was the Don's favorite haunt, and he saw the Rose of Torridge daily, and the Rose of Torridge heard him.

And as for her, poor child, she had never seen such a man. He had, or seemed to have, all the high-bred grace of Frank, and yet he was cast in a manlier mould; he had just enough of his nation's proud self-assertion to make a woman bow before him as before a superior, and yet tact enough to let it very seldom degenerate into that boastfulness of which the Spaniards were then so often and so justly accused. He had marvels to tell by flood and field as many and more than Amyas; and he told them with a grace and an eloquence of which modest, simple, old Amyas possessed nothing. Besides, he was on the spot, and the Leighs were not, nor indeed were any of her old lovers; and what could she do but amuse herself with the only person who came to hand?

So thought, in time, more ladies than she; for the country, the north of it at least, was all but bare just then of young gallants, what with the Netherland wars and the Irish wars; and the Spaniard became soon welcome at every house for many a mile round, and made use of his welcome so freely, and received so much unwonted attention from fair young dames, that his head might have been a little turned, and Rose Salterne have thereby escaped, had not Sir Richard delicately given him to understand that in spite of the free and easy manners of English ladies, brothers were just as jealous, and ladies' honors at least as inexpugnable, as in the land of demureness and duennas. Don Guzman took the hint well enough, and kept on good terms with the country gentlemen as with their daughters; and to tell the truth, the cunning soldier of fortune found his account in being intimate with all the ladies he could, in order to prevent old Salterne from fancying that he had any peculiar predilection for Mistress Rose.

Nevertheless, Mr. Salterne's parlor being nearest to him, still remained his most common haunt; where, while he discoursed for hours about

to the boundless satisfaction of poor Rose's fancy, he took care to season his discourse with scraps of mercantile information, which kept the old merchant always expectant and hankering for more, and made it worth his while to ask the Spaniard in again and again.

And his stories, certainly, were worth hearing. He seemed to have been everywhere, and to have seen everything: born in Peru, and sent home to Spain at ten years old; brought up in Italy; a soldier in the Levant; an adventurer to the East Indies; again in America, first in the islands, and then in Mexico. Then back again to Spain, and thence to Rome, and thence to Ireland. Shipwrecked; captive among savages; looking down the craters of volcanoes; hanging about all the courts of Europe; fighting Turks, Indians, lions, elephants, alligators, and what not? At five-and-thirty he had seen enough for three lives, and knew how to make the best of what he had seen.

He had shared, as a lad, in the horrors of the memorable siege of Famagusta, and had escaped, he hardly knew himself how, from the hands of the victorious Turks, and from the certainty (if he escaped being flayed alive or impaled, as most of the captive officers were) of ending his life as a Janissary at the Sultan's court. He had been at the Battle of the Three Kings; had seen Stukely borne down by a hundred lances, unconquered even in death; and had held upon his knee the head of the dying King of Portugal.

And now, as he said to Rose one evening, what had he left on earth, but a heart trampled as hard as the pavement? Whom had he to love? Who loved him? He had nothing for which to live but fame: and even that was denied to him, a prisoner in a foreign land.

Had he no kindred, then? asked pitying Rose.

"My two sisters are in a convent;—they had neither money nor beauty; so they are dead to me. My brother is a Jesuit, so he is dead to me. My father fell by the hands of Indians in Mexico; my mother, a penniless widow, is companion, duenna—whatsoever they may choose to call it—carrying fans and lapdogs for some princess or other there in Seville, of no better blood than herself; and I—devil! I have lost even my sword—and so fares the house of De Soto."

Don Guzman, of course, intended to be pitied, and pitied he was accordingly. And then he would turn the conversation, and begin telling Italian stories, after the Italian fashion, according to his auditory: the pathetic ones when Rose was present, the racy ones when she was absent; so that Rose had wept over the sorrows of Juliet and Desdemona, and over many another moving tale, long before they were ever enacted on an English stage, and the ribs of the Bideford worthies had shaken to many a jest which Cinthio and Bandello's ghosts must come and make for themselves over again if they wish them to be remembered, for I shall lend them no shove toward immortality.

And so on, and so on. What need of more words? Before a year was out, Rose Salterne was far more in love with Don Guzman than he with her; and both suspected each other's mind, though neither hinted at the truth; she from fear, and he, to tell the truth, from sheer Spanish pride of blood. For he soon began to find out that he must compromise that blood by marrying the heretic burgher's daughter, or all his labor would be thrown away.

He had seen with much astonishment, and then practised with much pleasure, that graceful old English fashion of saluting every lady on the cheek at meeting, which (like the old Dutch fashion of asking young ladies out to feasts without their mothers) used to give such cause of brutal calumny and scandal to the coarse minds of Romish visitors from the Continent; and he had seen, too, fuming with jealous rage, more than one Bideford burgher, redolent of onions, profane in that way the velvet cheek of Rose Salterne.

So, one day, he offered his salute in like wise; but he did it when she was alone; for something within (perhaps a guilty conscience) whispered that it might be hardly politic to make the proffer in her father's presence: however, to his astonishment, he received a prompt though quiet rebuff.

"No, sir; you should know that my cheek is not for you."

"Why," said he, stifling his anger, "it seems free enough to every counter-jumper in the town!"

Was it love, or simple innocence, which made her answer apologetically?

"True, Don Guzman; but they are my equals."

"And I?"

"You are a nobleman, sir; and should recollect that you are one."

"Well," said he, forcing a sneer, "it is a strange taste to prefer the shopkeeper!"

"Prefer?" said she, forcing a laugh in her turn; "it is a mere form among us. They are nothing to me, I can tell you."

"And I, then, less than nothing?"

Rose turned very red; but she had nerve to answer—

"And why should you be anything to me? You have condescended too much, sir, already to us, in giving us many a—many a pleasant evening. You must condescend no further. You wrong yourself, sir, and me too. No, sir; not a step nearer!—I will not! A salute between equals means nothing: but between you and me—I vow, sir, if you do not leave me this moment, I will complain to my father."

"Do so, madam! I care as little for your father's anger, as you for my misery."

"Cruel!" cried Rose, trembling from head to foot.

"I love you, madam!" cried he, throwing himself at her feet. "I adore you! Never mention differences of rank to me more; for I have forgotten them; forgotten all but love, all but you, madam! My light, my lodestar, my princess, my goddess! You see where my pride is gone; remember I plead as a suppliant, a beggar—though one who may be one day a prince, a king! ay, and a prince now, a very Lucifer of pride to all except to you; to you a wretch who grovels at your feet, and cries, 'Have mercy on me, on my loneliness, my homelessness, my friendlessness.' Ah, Rose (madam I should have said, forgive the madness of my passion), you know not the heart which you break. Cold Northerns, you little dream how a Spaniard can love. Love? Worship, rather; as I worship you, madam; as I bless the captivity which brought me the sight of you, and the ruin which first made me rich. Is it possible, saints and Virgin! do my own tears deceive my eyes, or are there tears, too, in those radiant orbs?"

"Go, sir!" cried poor Rose, recovering herself suddenly; "and let me never see you more." And, as a last chance for life, she darted out of the room.

"Your slave obeys you, madam, and kisses your hands and feet forever and a day," said the cunning Spaniard, and drawing himself up, walked serenely out of the house; while she, poor fool, peeped after him out of her window upstairs, and her heart sank within her as she watched his jaunty and careless air.

How much of that rhapsody of his was honest, how much premeditated, I cannot tell: though she, poor child, began to fancy that it was all a set speech, when she found that he had really taken her at her word, and set foot no more within her father's house. So she reproached herself for the cruelest of women; settled, that if he died, she should be his murderess; watched for him to pass at the window, in hopes that he might look up, and then hid herself in terror the moment he appeared round the corner; and so forth, and so forth:—one love-making is very like another, and has been so, I suppose, since that first blessed marriage in Paradise, when Adam and Eve made no love at all, but found it ready-made for them from heaven; and really it is fiddling while Rome is burning, to spend more pages over the sorrows of poor little Rose Salterne, while the destinies of Europe are hanging on the marriage between Elizabeth and Anjou: and Sir Humphrey Gilbert is stirring heaven and earth, and Devonshire, of course, as the most important portion of the said earth, to carry out his dormant patent, which will give to England in due time (we are not jesting now) Newfoundland, Nova Scotia, and Canada, and the Northern States; and to Humphrey Gilbert himself something better than a new world, namely another world, and a crown of glory therein which never fades away.

CHAPTER XI: HOW EUSTACE LEIGH MET THE POPE'S LEGATE

It is the spring of 1582-3. The gray March skies are curdling hard and high above black mountain peaks. The keen March wind is sweeping harsh and dry across a dreary sheet of bog, still red and yellow with the stains of winter frost. One brown knoll alone breaks the waste, and on it a few leafless wind-clipt oaks stretch their moss-grown arms, like giant hairy spiders, above a desolate pool which crisps and shivers in the biting breeze, while from beside its brink rises a mournful cry, and sweeps down, faint and fitful, amid the howling of the wind.

Along the brink of the bog, picking their road among crumbling rocks and green spongy springs, a company of English soldiers are pushing fast, clad cap-a-pie in helmet and quilted jerkin, with arquebus on shoulder, and pikes trailing behind them; stern steadfast men, who, two years since, were working the guns at Smerwick fort, and have since then seen many a bloody fray, and shall see more before they die. Two captains ride before them on shaggy ponies, the taller in armor, stained and rusted with many a storm and fray, the other in brilliant inlaid cuirass and helmet, gaudy sash and plume, and sword hilt glittering with gold, a quaint contrast enough to the meager garron which carries him and his finery. Beside them, secured by a cord which a pikeman has fastened to his own wrist, trots a bare-legged Irish kerne, whose only clothing is his ragged yellow mantle, and the unkempt "glib" of hair, through which his eyes peer out, right and left, in mingled fear and sullenness. He is the guide of the company, in their hunt after the rebel Baltinglas; and woe to him if he play them false.

"A pleasant country, truly, Captain Raleigh," says the dingy officer to the gay one. "I wonder how, having once escaped from it to Whitehall, you have the courage to come back and spoil that gay suit with bog-water and mud."

"A very pleasant country, my friend Amyas; what you say in jest, I say in earnest."

"Hillo! Our tastes have changed places. I am sick of it already, as you foretold. Would Heaven that I could hear of some adventure Westward-ho! and find these big bones swinging in a hammock once more. Pray what has made you so suddenly in love with bog and rock, that you come back to tramp them with us? I thought you had spied out the nakedness of the land long ago."

"Bog and rock? Nakedness of the land? What is needed here but prudence and skill, justice and law? This soil, see, is fat enough, if men were here to till it. These rocks—who knows what minerals they may hold? I hear of gold and jewels found already in divers parts; and Daniel, my brother Humphrey's German assayer, assures me that these rocks are of the very same kind as those which yield the silver in Peru. Tut, man! if her gracious majesty would but bestow on me some few square miles of this same wilderness, in seven years' time I would make it blossom like the rose, by God's good help."

"Humph! I should be more inclined to stay here, then."

"So you shall, and be my agent, if you will, to get in my mine-rents and my corn-rents, and my fishery-rents, eh? Could you keep accounts, old knight of the bear's-paw?"

"Well enough for such short reckonings as yours would be, on the profit side at least. No, no—

I'd sooner carry lime all my days from Cauldy to Bideford, than pass another twelve-month in the land of Ire, among the children of wrath. There is a curse upon the face of the earth, I believe."

"There is no curse upon it, save the old one of man's sin—'Thorns and thistles it shall bring forth to thee.' But if you root up the thorns and thistles, Amyas, I know no fiend who can prevent your growing wheat instead; and if you till the ground like a man, you plough and barrow away nature's curse, and other fables of the schoolmen beside," added he, in that daring fashion which afterwards obtained for him (and never did good Christian less deserve it) the imputation of atheism.

"It is sword and bullet, I think, that are needed here, before plough and harrow, to clear away some of the curse. Until a few more of these Irish lords are gone where the Desmonds are, there is no peace for Ireland."

"Humph! not so far wrong, I fear. And yet—Irish lords? These very traitors are better English blood than we who hunt them down. When Yeo here slew the Desmond the other day, he no more let out a drop of Irish blood, than if he had slain the lord deputy himself."

"His blood be on his own head," said Yeo, "He looked as wild a savage as the worst of them, more shame to him; and the ancient here had nigh cut off his arm before he told us who he was: and then, your worship, having a price upon his head, and like to bleed to death too—"

"Enough, enough, good fellow," said Raleigh. "Thou hast done what was given thee to do. Strange, Amyas, is it not? Noble Normans sunk into savages—Hibernis ipsis hiberniores! Is there some uncivilizing venom in the air?"

"Some venom, at least, which makes English men traitors. But the Irish themselves are well enough, if their tyrants would let them be. See now, what more faithful liegeman has her majesty than the Inchiquin, who, they say, is Prince of Themond, and should be king of all Ireland, if every man had his right?"

"Don't talk of rights in the land of wrongs, man. But the Inchiquin knows well that the true Irish Esau has no worse enemy than his supplanter, the Norman Jacob. And yet, Amyas are even these men worse than we might be, if we had been bred up masters over the bodies and souls of men, in some remote land where law and order had never come? Look at this Desmond, brought up a savage among savages, a Papist among Papists, a despot among slaves; a thousand easy maidens deeming it honor to serve his pleasure, a thousand wild ruffians deeming it piety to fulfil his revenge: and let him that is without sin among us cast the first stone."

"Ay," went on Raleigh to himself, as the conversation dropped. "What hadst thou been, Raleigh, hadst thou been that Desmond whose lands thou now desirest? What wilt thou be when thou hast them? Will thy children sink downwards, as these noble barons sank? Will the genius of tyranny and falsehood find soil within thy heart to grow and ripen fruit? What guarantee hast thou for doing better here than those who went before thee? And yet, cannot I do justice and love mercy? Can I not establish plantations, build and sow, and make the desert valleys laugh with corn? Shall I not have my Spenser with me, to fill me with all noble thoughts, and raise my soul to his heroic pitch? Is not this true knight-errantry, to redeem to peace and use, and to the glory of that glorious queen whom God has given to me, a generous soil and a more generous race? Trustful and tenderhearted they are—none more; and if they be fickle and passionate, will not that very softness of temper, which makes them so easily led to evil, make them as easy to be led towards good? Yes—here, away from courts, among a people who should bless me as their benefactor and deliverer—what golden days might be mine! And yet—is this but another angel's mask from that same cunning fiend ambition's stage? And will my house be indeed the house of God, the foundations of which are loyalty, and its bulwarks righteousness, and not the house of fame, whose walls are of the soap-bubble, and its floor a sea of glass mingled with fire? I would be good and great—When will the day come when I shall be content to be good, and yet not great, like this same simple Leigh, toiling on by my side to do his duty, with no more thought for the morrow than the birds of God? Greatness? I have tasted that cup within the last twelve months; do I not know that it is sweet in the mouth, but bitter in the belly? Greatness? And was not Essex great, and John of Austria great, and Desmond great, whose race, but three short years ago, had stood for ages higher than I shall ever hope to climb—castles, and lands, and slaves by thousands, and five hundred gentlemen of his name, who had vowed to forswear God before they forswore him and well have they kept their vow! And now, dead in a turf-hovel, like a coney in a burrow! Leigh, what noise was that?"

"An Irish howl, I fancied: but it came from off the bog; it may be only a plover's cry."

"Something not quite right, sir captain, to my mind," said the ancient. "They have ugly stories here of pucks and banshees, and what not of ghosts. There it was again, wailing just like a woman. They say the banshee cried all night before Desmond was slain."

"Perhaps, then, this one may be crying for Baltinglas; for his turn is likely to come next—not that I believe in such old wives' tales."

"Shamus, my man," said Amyas to the guide, "do you hear that cry in the bog?"

The guide put on the most stolid of faces, and answered in broken English—

"Shamus hear naught. Perhaps—what you call him?—fishing in ta pool."

"An otter, he means, and I believe he is right. Stay, no! Did you not hear it then, Shamus? It was a woman's voice."

"Shamus is shick in his ears ever since Christmas."

"Shamus will go after Desmond if he lies," said Amyas. "Ancient, we had better send a few men to see what it is; there may be a poor soul taken by robbers, or perhaps starving to death, as I have seen many a one."

"And I too, poor wretches; and by no fault of their own or ours either: but if their lords will fall to quarrelling, and then drive each other's cattle, and waste each other's lands, sir, you know—"

"I know," said Amyas, impatiently; "why dost not take the men, and go?"

"Cry you mercy, noble captain, but—I fear nothing born of woman."

"Well, what of that?" said Amyas, with a smile.

"But these pucks, sir. The wild Irish do say that they haunt the pools; and they do no manner of harm, sir, when you are coming up to them; but when you are past, sir, they jump on your back like to apes, sir,—and who can tackle that manner of fiend?"

"Why, then, by thine own showing, ancient," said Raleigh, "thou may'st go and see all safely enough, and then if the puck jumps on thee as thou comest back, just run in with him here, and I'll buy him of thee for a noble; or thou may'st keep him in a cage, and make money in London by showing him for a monster."

"Good heavens forefend, Captain Raleigh! but you talk rashly! But if I must, Captain Leigh—Lads, who'll follow me?"

"Thou askest for volunteers, as if thou wert to lead a forlorn hope. Pull away at the usquebaugh, man, and swallow Dutch courage, since thine English is oozed away. Stay, I'll go myself."

"And I with you," said Raleigh. "As the queen's true knight-errant, I am bound to be behindhand in no adventure. Who knows but we may find a wicked magician, just going to cut off the head of some saffron-mantled princess?" and he dismounted.

"Oh, sirs, sirs, to endanger your precious—"

"Pooh," said Raleigh. "I wear an amulet, and have a spell of art-magic at my tongue's end, whereby, sir ancient, neither can a ghost see me, nor I see them. Come with us, Yeo, the Desmond-slayer, and we will shame the devil, or be shamed by him."

"He may shame me, sir, but he will never frighten me," quoth Yeo; "but the bog, captains?"

"Tut! Devonshire men, and heath-trotters born, and not know our way over a peat moor!"

And the three strode away.

They splashed and scrambled for some quarter of a mile to the knoll, while the cry became louder and louder as they neared.

"That's neither ghost nor otter, sirs, but a true Irish howl, as Captain Leigh said; and I'll warrant Master Shamus knew as much long ago," said Yeo.

And in fact, they could now hear plainly the "Ochone, Ochonorie," of some wild woman; and scrambling over the boulders of the knoll, in another minute came full upon her.

She was a young girl, sluttish and unkempt, of course, but fair enough: her only covering, as usual, was the ample yellow mantle. There she sat upon a stone, tearing her black dishevelled hair, and every now and then throwing up her head, and bursting into a long mournful cry, "for all the world," as Yeo said, "like a dumb four-footed hound, and not a Christian soul."

On her knees lay the head of a man of middle age, in the long soutane of a Romish priest. One look at the attitude of his limbs told them that he was dead.

The two paused in awe; and Raleigh's spirit, susceptible of all poetical images, felt keenly that strange scene,—the bleak and bitter sky, the shapeless bog, the stunted trees, the savage girl alone with the corpse in that utter desolation. And as she bent her head over the still face, and called wildly to him who heard her not, and then, utterly unmindful of the intruders, sent up again that dreary wail into the dreary air, they felt a sacred horror, which almost made them turn away, and leave her unquestioned: but Yeo, whose nerves were of tougher fibre, asked quietly—

"Shall I go and search the fellow, captain?"

"Better, I think," said Amyas.

Raleigh went gently to the girl, and spoke to her in English. She looked up at him, his armor and his plume, with wide and wondering eyes, and then shook her head, and returned to her lamentation.

Raleigh gently laid his hand on her arm, and lifted her up, while Yeo and Amyas bent over the corpse.

It was the body of a large and coarse-featured man, but wasted and shrunk as if by famine to a very skeleton. The hands and legs were cramped up, and the trunk bowed together, as if the man had died of cold or famine. Yeo drew back the clothes from the thin bosom, while the girl screamed and wept, but made no effort to stop him.

"Ask her who it is? Yeo, you know a little Irish," said Amyas.

He asked, but the girl made no answer. "The stubborn jade won't tell, of course, sir. If she were but a man, I'd make her soon enough."

"Ask her who killed him?"

"No one, she says; and I believe she says true, for I can find no wound. The man has been starved, sirs, as I am a sinful man. God help him, though he is a priest; and yet he seems full enough down below. What's here? A big pouch, sirs, stuffed full of somewhat."

"Hand it hither."

The two opened the pouch; papers, papers, but no scrap of food. Then a parchment. They unrolled it.

"Latin," said Amyas; "you must construe, Don Scholar."

"Is it possible?" said Raleigh, after reading a moment. "This is indeed a prize! This is Saunders himself!"

Yeo sprang up from the body as if he had touched an adder. "Nick Saunders, the Legacy, sir?"

"Nicholas Saunders, the legate."

"The villain! why did not he wait for me to have the comfort of killing him? Dog!" and he kicked the corpse with his foot.

"Quiet! quiet! Remember the poor girl," said Amyas, as she shrieked at the profanation, while Raleigh went on, half to himself:

"Yes, this is Saunders. Misguided fool, and this is the end! To this thou hast come with thy plotting and thy conspiring, thy lying and thy boasting, consecrated banners and Pope's bulls, Agnus Deis and holy waters, the blessing of all saints and angels, and thy Lady of the Immaculate Conception! Thou hast called on the heavens to judge between thee and us, and here is their answer! What is that in his hand, Amyas? Give it me. A pastoral epistle to the Earl of Ormond, and all nobles of the realm of Ireland; 'To all who groan beneath the loathsome tyranny of an illegitimate adulteress, etc., Nicholas Saunders, by the grace of God, Legate, etc.' Bah! and this forsooth was thy last meditation! Incorrigible pedant! Victrix causa Diis placuit, sed victa Catoni!"

He ran his eye through various other documents, written in the usual strain: full of huge promises from the Pope and the king of Spain; frantic and filthy slanders against Elizabeth, Burghley, Leicester, Essex (the elder), Sidney, and every great and good man (never mind of which party) who then upheld the commonweal; bombastic attempts to terrify weak consciences, by denouncing endless fire against those who opposed the true faith; fulsome ascriptions of martyrdom and sanctity to every rebel and traitor who had been hanged for the last twenty years; wearisome arguments about the bull In Caena Domini, Elizabeth's excommunication, the nullity of English law, the sacred duty of rebellion, the right to kill a prince impenitently heretical, and the like insanities and villainies, which may be read at large in Camden, the Phoenix Britannicus, Fox's Martyrs, or, surest of all, in the writings of the worthies themselves.

With a gesture of disgust, Raleigh crammed the foul stuff back again into the pouch. Taking it with them, they walked back to the company, and then remounting, marched away once more towards the lands of the Desmonds; and the girl was left alone with the dead.

An hour had passed, when another Englishman was standing by the wailing girl, and round him a dozen shockheaded kernes, skene on thigh and javelin in hand, were tossing about their tawny rags, and adding their lamentations to those of the lonely watcher.

The Englishman was Eustace Leigh; a layman still, but still at his old work. By two years of intrigue and labor from one end of Ireland to the other, he had been trying to satisfy his conscience for rejecting "the higher calling" of the celibate; for mad hopes still lurked within that fiery heart. His brow was wrinkled now; his features harshened; the scar upon his face, and the slight distortion which accompanied it, was hidden by a bushy beard from all but himself; and he never forgot it for a day, nor forgot who had given it to him.

He had been with Desmond, wandering in moor and moss for many a month in danger of his life; and now he was on his way to James Fitz-Eustace, Lord Baltinglas, to bring him the news of Desmond's death; and with him a remnant of the clan, who were either too stout-hearted, or too desperately stained with crime, to seek peace from the English, and, as their fellows did, find it at once and freely.

There Eustace stood, looking down on all that was left of the most sacred personage of Ireland; the man who, as he once had hoped, was to regenerate his native land, and bring the proud island of the West once more beneath that gentle yoke, in which united Christendom labored for the commonweal of the universal Church. There he was, and with him all Eustace's dreams, in the very heart of that country which he had vowed, and believed as he vowed, was ready to rise in arms as one man, even to the baby at the breast (so he had said), in vengeance against the Saxon heretic, and sweep the hated name of Englishman into the deepest abysses of the surge which walled her coasts; with Spain and the Pope to back him, and the wealth of the Jesuits at his command; in the midst of faithful Catholics, valiant soldiers, noblemen who had pledged themselves to die for the cause, serfs who worshipped him as a demigod—starved to death in a bog! It was a pretty plain verdict on the reasonableness of his expectations; but not to Eustace Leigh.

It was a failure, of course; but it was an accident; indeed, to have been expected, in a wicked world whose prince and master, as all knew, was the devil himself; indeed, proof of the righteousness of the cause—for when had the true faith been other than persecuted and trampled under foot? If one came to think of it with eyes purified from the tears of carnal impatience, what was it but a glorious martyrdom?

"Blest Saunders!" murmured Eustace Leigh; "let me die the death of the righteous, and let my last end he like this! Ora pro me, most excellent martyr, while I dig thy grave upon this lonely moor, to wait there for thy translation to one of those stately shrines, which, cemented by the blood of such as thee, shall hereafter rise restored toward heaven, to make this land once more 'The Isle of Saints.'"

The corpse was buried; a few prayers said hastily; and Eustace Leigh was away again, not now to find Baltinglas; for it was more than his life was worth. The girl had told him of the English soldiers who had passed, and he knew that they would reach the earl probably before he did. The game was up; all was lost. So he retraced his steps, as a desperate resource, to the last place where he would be looked for, and after a month of disguising, hiding, and other expedients, found himself again in his native county of Devon, while Fitz-Eustace Viscount Baltinglas had taken ship for Spain, having got little by his famous argument to Ormond in behalf of his joining the Church of Rome, "Had not thine ancestor, blessed Thomas of Canterbury, died for the Church of Rome, thou hadst never been Earl of Ormond." The premises were certainly sounder than those of his party were wont to be; for it was to expiate the murder of that turbulent hero that the Ormond lands had been granted by Henry II.: but as for the conclusion therefrom, it was much on a par with the rest.

And now let us return to Raleigh and Amyas, as they jog along their weary road. They have many things to talk of; for it is but three days since they met.

Amyas, as you see, is coming fast into Raleigh's old opinion of Ireland. Raleigh, under the inspiration of a possible grant of Desmond's lands, looks on bogs and rocks transfigured by his own hopes and fancy, as if by the glory of a rainbow. He looked at all things so, noble fellow, even thirty years after, when old, worn out, and ruined; well for him had it been otherwise, and his heart had grown old with his head! Amyas, who knows nothing about Desmond's lands, is puzzled at the change.

"Why, what is this, Raleigh? You are like children sitting in the market-place, and nothing pleases you. You wanted to get to Court, and you have got there; and are lord and master, I hear, or something very like it, already—and as soon as fortune stuffs your mouth full of sweet-meats, do you turn informer on her?"

Raleigh laughed insignificantly, but was silent.

"And how is your friend Mr. Secretary Spenser, who was with us at Smerwick?"

"Spenser? He has thriven even as I have; and he has found, as I have, that in making one friend at Court you make ten foes; but 'Oderint dum metuant' is no more my motto than his, Leigh. I want to be great—great I am already, they say, if princes' favor can swell the frog into an ox; but I want to be liked, loved—I want to see people smile when I enter."

"So they do, I'll warrant," said Amyas.

"So do hyenas," said Raleigh; "grin because they are hungry, and I may throw them a bone; I'll throw you one now, old lad, or rather a good sirloin of beef, for the sake of your smile. That's honest, at least, I'll warrant, whosoever's else is not. Have you heard of my brother Humphrey's new project?"

"How should I hear anything in this waste howling wilderness?"

"Kiss hands to the wilderness, then, and come with me to Newfoundland!"

"You to Newfoundland?"

"Yes. I to Newfoundland, unless my little matter here is settled at once. Gloriana don't know it, and sha'n't till I'm off. She'd send me to the Tower, I think, if she caught me playing truant. I could hardly get leave to come hither; but I must out, and try my fortune. I am over ears in debt already, and sick of courts and courtiers. Humphrey must go next spring and take possession of his kingdom beyond seas, or his patent expires; and with him I go, and you too, my circumnavigating giant."

And then Raleigh expounded to Amyas the details of the great Newfoundland scheme, which whoso will may read in the pages of Hakluyt.

Sir Humphrey Gilbert, Raleigh's half-brother, held a patent for "planting" the lands of Newfoundland and "Meta Incognita" (Labrador). He had attempted a voyage thither with Raleigh in 1578, whereof I never could find any news, save that he came back again, after a heavy brush with some Spanish ships (in which his best captain, Mr. Morgan, was killed), having done nothing, and much impaired his own estate: but now he had collected a large sum; Sir Gilbert Peckham of London, Mr. Hayes of South Devon, and various other gentlemen, of whom more hereafter, had adventured their money; and a considerable colony was to be sent out the next year, with miners, assayers, and, what was more, Parmenius Budaeus, Frank's old friend, who had come to England full of thirst to see the wonders of the New World; and over and above this, as Raleigh told Amyas in strictest secrecy, Adrian Gilbert, Humphrey's brother, was turning every stone at Court for a patent of discovery in the North-West; and this Newfoundland colony, though it was to produce gold, silver, merchandise, and what not, was but a basis of operations, a halfway house from whence to work out the North-West passage to the Indies—that golden dream, as fatal to English valor as the Guiana one to Spanish—and yet hardly, hardly to be regretted, when we remember the seamanship, the science, the chivalry, the heroism, unequalled in the history of the English nation, which it has called forth among those our later Arctic voyagers, who have combined the knight-errantry of the middle age with the practical prudence of the modern, and dared for duty more than Cortez or Pizarro dared for gold.

Amyas, simple fellow, took all in greedily; he knew enough of the dangers of the Magellan passage to appreciate the boundless value of a road to the East Indies which would (as all supposed then) save half the distance, and be as it were a private possession of the English, safe from Spanish interference; and he listened reverently to Sir Humphrey's quaint proofs, half true, half fantastic, of such a passage, which Raleigh detailed to him—of the Primum Mobile, and its diurnal motion from east to west, in obedience to which the sea-current flowed westward ever round the Cape of Good Hope, and being unable to pass through the narrow strait between South America and the Antarctic Continent, rushed up the American shore, as the Gulf Stream, and poured northwestward between Greenland and Labrador towards Cathay and India; of that most crafty argument of Sir Humphrey's—how Aristotle in his book "De Mundo," and Simon Gryneus in his annotations thereon, declare that the world (the Old World) is an island, compassed by that which Homer calls the river Oceanus; ergo, the New World is an island also, and there is a North-West passage; of the three brothers (names unknown) who had actually made the voyage, and named what was afterwards called Davis's Strait after themselves; of the Indians who were cast ashore in Germany in the reign of Frederic Barbarossa who, as Sir Humphrey had learnedly proved per modum tollendi, could have come only by the North-West; and above all, of Salvaterra, the Spaniard, who in 1568 had told Sir Henry Sidney (Philip's father), there in Ireland, how he had spoken with a Mexican friar named Urdaneta, who had himself come from Mar del Zur (the Pacific) into Germany by that very North-West passage; at which last Amyas shook his head, and said that friars were liars, and seeing believing; "but if you must needs have an adventure, you insatiable soul you, why not try for the golden city of Manoa?"

"Manoa?" asked Raleigh, who had heard, as most had, dim rumors of the place. "What do you know of it?"

Whereon Amyas told him all that he had gathered from the Spaniard; and Raleigh, in his turn, believed every word.

"Humph!" said he after a long silence. "To find that golden emperor; offer him help and friendship from the queen of England; defend him against the Spaniards; if we became strong enough, conquer back all Peru from the Popish tyrants, and reinstate him on the throne of the Incas, with ourselves for his body-guard, as the Norman Varangians were to the effeminate emperors of Byzant—Hey, Amyas? You would make a gallant chieftain of Varangs. We'll do it, lad!"

"We'll try," said Amyas; "but we must be quick, for there's one Berreo sworn to carry out the quest to the death; and if the Spaniards once get thither, their plan of works will be much more like Pizarro's than like yours; and by the time we come, there will be neither gold nor city left."

"Nor Indians either, I'll warrant the butchers; but, lad, I am promised to Humphrey; I have a bark fitting out already, and all I have, and more, adventured in her; so Manoa must wait."

"It will wait well enough, if the Spaniards prosper no better on the Amazon than they have done; but must I come with you? To tell the truth, I am quite shore-sick, and to sea I must go. What will my mother say?"

"I'll manage thy mother," said Raleigh; and so he did; for, to cut a long story short, he went back the month after, and he not only took home letters from Amyas to his mother, but so impressed on that good lady the enormous profits and honors to be derived from Meta Incognita, and (which was most true) the advantage to any young man of sailing with such a general as Humphrey Gilbert, most pious and most learned of seamen and of cavaliers, beloved and honored above all his compeers by Queen Elizabeth, that she consented to Amyas's adventuring in the voyage some two hundred pounds which had come to him as his share of prize-money, after the ever memorable circumnavigation. For Mrs. Leigh, be it understood, was no longer at Burrough Court. By Frank's persuasion, she had let the old place, moved up to London with her eldest son, and taken for herself a lodging somewhere by Palace Stairs, which looked out upon the silver Thames (for Thames was silver then), with its busy ferries and gliding boats, across to the pleasant fields of Lambeth, and the Archbishop's palace, and the wooded Surrey hills; and there she spent her peaceful days, close to her Frank and to the Court. Elizabeth would have had her re-enter it, offering her a small place in the household: but she declined, saying that she was too old and heart-weary for aught but prayer. So by prayer she lived, under the sheltering shadow of the tall minster where she went morn and even to worship, and to entreat for the two in whom her heart was bound up; and Frank slipped in every day if but for five minutes, and brought with him Spenser, or Raleigh, or Dyer, or Budaeus or sometimes Sidney's self: and there was talk of high and holy things, of which none could speak better than could she; and each guest went from that hallowed room a humbler and yet a loftier man. So slipped on the peaceful months, and few and far between came Irish letters, for Ireland was then farther from Westminster than is the Black Sea now; but those were days in which wives and mothers had learned (as they have learned once more, sweet souls!) to walk by faith and not by sight for those they love: and Mrs. Leigh was content (though when was she not content?) to hear that Amyas was winning a good report as a brave and prudent officer, sober, just, and faithful, beloved and obeyed alike by English soldiers and Irish kernes.

Those two years, and the one which followed, were the happiest which she had known since her husband's death. But the cloud was fast coming up the horizon, though she saw it not. A little longer, and the sun would be hid for many a wintry day.

Amyas went to Plymouth (with Yeo, of course, at his heels), and there beheld, for the first time, the majestic countenance of the philosopher of Compton castle. He lodged with Drake, and found him not over-sanguine as to the success of the voyage.

"For learning and manners, Amyas, there's not his equal; and the queen may well love him, and Devon be proud of him: but book-learning is not business: book-learning didn't get me round the world; book-learning didn't make Captain Hawkins, nor his father neither, the best ship-builders from Hull to Cadiz; and book-learning, I very much fear, won't plant Newfoundland."

However, the die was cast, and the little fleet of five sail assembled in Cawsand Bay. Amyas was to go as a gentleman adventurer on board of Raleigh's bark; Raleigh himself, however, at the eleventh hour, had been forbidden by the queen to leave England. Ere they left, Sir Humphrey Gilbert's picture was painted by some Plymouth artist, to be sent up to Elizabeth in answer to a letter and a gift sent by Raleigh, which, as a specimen of the men and of the time, I here transcribe*—

"BROTHER—I have sent you a token from her Majesty, an anchor guided by a lady, as you see. And further, her Highness willed me to send you word, that she wisheth you as great good hap and safety to your ship as if she were there in person, desiring you to have care of yourself as of that which she tendereth and, therefore, for her sake, you must provide for it accordingly. Furthermore, she commandeth that you leave your picture with her. For the rest I leave till our meeting, or to the report of the bearer, who would needs be the messenger of this good news. So I commit you to the will and protection of God, who send us such life and death as he shall please, or hath appointed.

"Richmond, this Friday morning,

"Your true Brother,

"W. RALEIGH."

"Who would not die, sir, for such a woman?" said Sir Humphrey (and he said truly), as he showed that letter to Amyas.

"Who would not? But she bids you rather live for her."

"I shall do both, young man; and for God too, I trust. We are going in God's cause; we go for the honor of God's Gospel, for the deliverance of poor infidels led captive by the devil; for the relief of my distressed countrymen unemployed within this narrow isle; and to God we commit our cause. We fight against the devil himself; and stronger is He that is within us than he that is against us."

Some say that Raleigh himself came down to Plymouth, accompanied the fleet a day's sail to sea, and would have given her majesty the slip, and gone with them Westward-ho, but for Sir Humphrey's advice. It is likely enough: but I cannot find evidence for it. At all events, on the 11th June the fleet sailed out, having, says Mr. Hayes, "in number about 260 men, among whom we had of every faculty good choice, as shipwrights, masons, carpenters, smiths, and such like, requisite for such an action; also mineral men and refiners. Beside, for solace of our people and allurement of the savages, we were provided of musique in good variety; not omitting the least toys, as morris-dancers, hobby-horses, and May-like conceits, to delight the savage people, whom we intended to win by all fair means possible." An armament complete enough, even to that tenderness towards the Indians, which is so striking a feature of the Elizabethan seamen (called out in them, perhaps, by horror at the Spanish cruelties, as well as by their more liberal creed), and to the daily service of God on board of every ship, according to the simple old instructions of Captain John Hawkins to one of his little squadrons, "Keep good company; beware of fire; serve God daily; and love one another"—an armament, in short, complete in all but men. The sailors had been picked up hastily and anywhere, and soon proved themselves a mutinous, and, in the case of the bark Swallow, a piratical set. The mechanics were little better. The gentlemen-adventurers, puffed up with vain hopes of finding a new Mexico, became soon disappointed and surly at the hard practical reality; while over all was the head of a sage and an enthusiast, a man too noble to suspect others, and too pure to make allowances for poor dirty human weaknesses. He had got his scheme perfect upon paper; well for him, and for his company, if he had asked Francis Drake to translate it for him into fact! As early as the second day, the seeds of failure began to sprout above ground. The men of Raleigh's bark, the Vice-Admiral, suddenly found themselves seized, or supposed themselves seized, with a contagious sickness, and at midnight forsook the fleet, and went back to Plymouth; whereto Mr. Hayes can only say, "The reason I never could understand. Sure I am that Mr. Raleigh spared no cost in setting them forth. And so I leave it unto God!"

But Amyas said more. He told Butler the captain plainly that, if the bark went back, he would not; that he had seen enough of ships deserting their consorts; that it should never be said of him that he had followed Winter's example, and that, too, on a fair easterly wind; and finally that he had seen Doughty hanged for trying to play such a trick; and that he might see others hanged too before he died. Whereon Captain Butler offered to draw and fight, to which Amyas showed no repugnance; whereon the captain, having taken a second look at Amyas's thews and sinews, reconsidered the matter, and offered to put Amyas on board of Sir Humphrey's Delight, if he could find a crew to row him.

Amyas looked around.

"Are there any of Sir Francis Drake's men on board?"

"Three, sir," said Yeo. "Robert Drew, and two others."

"Pelicans!" roared Amyas, "you have been round the world, and will you turn back from Westward-ho?"

There was a moment's silence, and then Drew came forward.

"Lower us a boat, captain, and lend us a caliver to make signals with, while I get my kit on deck; I'll after Captain Leigh, if I row him aboard all alone to my own hands."

"If I ever command a ship, I will not forget you," said Amyas.

"Nor us either, sir, we hope; for we haven't forgotten you and your honest conditions," said both the other Pelicans; and so away over the side went all the five, and pulled away after the admiral's lantern, firing shots at intervals as signals. Luckily for the five desperadoes, the night was all but calm. They got on board before the morning, and so away into the boundless West.*

CHAPTER XII: HOW BIDEFORD BRIDGE DINED AT ANNERY HOUSE

Every one who knows Bideford cannot but know Bideford bridge; for it is the very omphalos, cynosure, and soul, around which the town, as a body, has organized itself; and as Edinburgh is Edinburgh by virtue of its castle, Rome Rome by virtue of its capitol, and Egypt Egypt by virtue of its pyramids, so is Bideford Bideford by virtue of its bridge. But all do not know the occult powers which have advanced and animated the said wondrous bridge for now five hundred years, and made it the chief wonder, according to Prince and Fuller, of this fair land of Devon: being first an inspired bridge, a soul-saving bridge, an alms-giving bridge, an educational bridge, a sentient bridge, and last, but not least, a dinner-giving bridge. All do not know how, when it began to be built some half mile higher up, hands invisible carried the stones down-stream each night to the present site; until Sir Richard Gurney, parson of the parish, going to bed one night in sore perplexity and fear of the evil spirit who seemed so busy in his sheepfold, beheld a vision of an angel, who bade build the bridge where he himself had so kindly transported the materials; for there alone was sure foundation amid the broad sheet of shifting sand. All do not know how Bishop Grandison of Exeter proclaimed throughout his diocese indulgences, benedictions, and "participation in all spiritual blessings for ever," to all who would promote the bridging of that dangerous ford; and so, consulting alike the interests of their souls and of their bodies, "make the best of both worlds."

All do not know, nor do I, that "though the foundation of the bridge is laid upon wool, yet it shakes at the slightest step of a horse;" or that, "though it has twenty-three arches, yet one Wm. Alford (another Milo) carried on his back for a wager four bushels salt-water measure, all the length thereof;" or that the bridge is a veritable esquire, bearing arms of its own (a ship and bridge proper on a plain field), and owning lands and tenements in many parishes, with which the said miraculous bridge has, from time to time, founded charities, built schools, waged suits at law, and finally (for this concerns us most) given yearly dinners, and kept for that purpose (luxurious and liquorish bridge that it was) the best stocked cellar of wines in all Devon.

To one of these dinners, as it happened, were invited in the year 1583 all the notabilities of Bideford, and beside them Mr. St. Leger of Annery close by, brother of the marshal of Munster, and of Lady Grenville; a most worthy and hospitable gentleman, who, finding riches a snare, parted with them so freely to all his neighbors as long as he lived, that he effectually prevented his children after him from falling into the temptations thereunto incident.

Between him and one of the bridge trustees arose an argument, whether a salmon caught below the bridge was better or worse than one caught above; and as that weighty question could only be decided by practical experiment, Mr. St. Leger vowed that as the bridge had given him a good dinner, he would give the bridge one; offered a bet of five pounds that he would find them, out of the pool below Annery, as firm and flaky a salmon as the Appledore one which they had just eaten; and then, in the fulness of his heart, invited the whole company present to dine with him at Annery three days after, and bring with them each a wife or daughter; and Don Guzman being at table, he was invited too.

So there was a mighty feast in the great hall at Annery, such as had seldom been since Judge Hankford feasted Edward the Fourth there; and while every one was eating their best and drinking their worst, Rose Salterne and Don Guzman were pretending not to see each other, and watching each other all the more. But Rose, at least, had to be very careful of her glances; for not only was her father at the table, but just opposite her sat none other than Messrs. William Cary and Arthur St. Leger, lieutenants in her majesty's Irish army, who had returned on furlough a few days before.

Rose Salterne and the Spaniard had not exchanged a word in the last six months, though they had met many times. The Spaniard by no means avoided her company, except in her father's house; he only took care to obey her carefully, by seeming always unconscious of her presence, beyond the stateliest of salutes at entering and departing. But he took care, at the same time, to lay himself out to the very best advantage whenever he was in her presence; to be more witty, more eloquent, more romantic, more full of wonderful tales than he ever yet had been. The cunning Don had found himself foiled in his first tactic; and he was now trying another, and a far more formidable one. In the first place, Rose deserved a very severe punishment, for having dared to refuse the love of a Spanish nobleman; and what greater punishment could he inflict than withdrawing the honor of his attentions, and the sunshine of his smiles? There was conceit enough in that notion, but there was cunning too; for none knew better than the Spaniard, that women, like the world, are pretty sure to value a man (especially if there be any real worth in him) at his own price; and that the more he demands for himself, the more they will give for him.

And now he would put a high price on himself, and pique her pride, as she was too much accustomed to worship, to be won by flattering it. He might have done that by paying attention to some one else: but he was too wise to employ so coarse a method, which might raise indignation, or disgust, or despair in Rose's heart, but would have never brought her to his feet—as it will never bring any woman worth bringing. So he quietly and unobtrusively showed her that he could do without her; and she, poor fool, as she was meant to do, began forthwith to ask herself—why? What was the hidden treasure, what was the reserve force, which made him independent of her, while she could not say that she was independent of him? Had he a secret? how pleasant to know it! Some huge ambition? how pleasant to share in it! Some mysterious knowledge? how pleasant to learn it! Some capacity of love beyond the common? how delicious to have it all for her own! He must be greater, wiser, richer-hearted than she was, as well as better-born. Ah, if his wealth would but supply her poverty! And so, step by step, she was being led to sue in forma pauperis to the very man whom she had spurned when he sued in like form to her. That temptation of having some mysterious private treasure, of being the priestess of some hidden sanctuary, and being able to thank Heaven that she was not as other women are, was becoming fast too much for Rose, as it is too much for most. For none knew better than the Spaniard how much more fond women are, by the very law of their sex, of worshipping than of being worshipped, and of obeying than of being obeyed; how their coyness, often their scorn, is but a mask to hide their consciousness of weakness; and a mask, too, of which they themselves will often be the first to tire.

And Rose was utterly tired of that same mask as she sat at table at Annery that day; and Don Guzman saw it in her uneasy and downcast looks, and thinking (conceited coxcomb) that she must be by now sufficiently punished, stole a glance at her now and then, and was not abashed when he saw that she dropped her eyes when they met his, because he saw her silence and abstraction increase, and something like a blush steal into her cheeks. So he pretended to be as much downcast and abstracted as she was, and went on with his glances, till he once found her, poor thing, looking at him to see if he was looking at her; and then he knew his prey was safe, and asked her, with his eyes, "Do you forgive me?" and saw her stop dead in her talk to her next neighbor, and falter, and drop her eyes, and raise them again after a minute in search of his, that he might repeat the pleasant question. And then what could she do but answer with all her face and every bend of her pretty neck, "And do you forgive me in turn?"

Whereon Don Guzman broke out jubilant, like nightingale on bough, with story, and jest, and repartee; and became forthwith the soul of the whole company, and the most charming of all cavaliers. And poor Rose knew that she was the cause of his sudden change of mood, and blamed herself for what she had done, and shuddered and blushed at her own delight, and longed that the feast was over, that she might hurry home and hide herself alone with sweet fancies about a love the reality of which she felt she dared not face.

It was a beautiful sight, the great terrace at Annery that afternoon; with the smart dames in their gaudy dresses parading up and down in twos and threes before the stately house; or looking down upon the park, with the old oaks, and the deer, and the broad land-locked river spread out like a lake beneath, all bright in the glare of the midsummer sun; or listening obsequiously to the two great ladies who did the honors, Mrs. St. Leger the hostess, and her sister-in-law, fair Lady Grenville. All chatted, and laughed, and eyed each other's dresses, and gossiped about each other's husbands and servants: only Rose Salterne kept apart, and longed to get into a corner and laugh or cry, she knew not which.

"Our pretty Rose seems sad," said Lady Grenville, coming up to her. "Cheer up, child! we want you to come and sing to us."

Rose answered she knew not what, and obeyed mechanically.

She took the lute, and sat down on a bench beneath the house, while the rest grouped themselves round her.

"What shall I sing?"

"Let us have your old song, 'Earl Haldan's Daughter.'"

Rose shrank from it. It was a loud and dashing ballad, which chimed in but little with her thoughts; and Frank had praised it too, in happier days long since gone by. She thought of him, and of others, and of her pride and carelessness; and the song seemed ominous to her: and yet for that very reason she dared not refuse to sing it, for fear of suspicion where no one suspected; and so she began per force—

I.

"It was Earl Haldan's daughter, She look'd across the sea; She look'd across the water, And long and loud laugh'd she; 'The locks of six princesses Must be my marriage-fee, So hey bonny boat, and ho bonny boat! Who comes a wooing me?'

II.

"It was Earl Haldan's daughter, She walk'd along the sand; When she was aware of a knight so fair, Come sailing to the land. His sails were all of velvet, His mast of beaten gold, And 'hey bonny boat, and ho bonny boat, Who saileth here so bold?'

III.

"'The locks of five princesses I won beyond the sea; I shore their golden tresses, To fringe a cloak for thee. One handful yet is wanting, But one of all the tale; So hey bonny boat, and ho bonny boat! Furl up thy velvet sail!'

IV.

"He leapt into the water, That rover young and bold; He gript Earl Haldan's daughter, He shore her locks of gold; 'Go weep, go weep, proud maiden, The tale is full to-day. Now hey bonny boat, and ho bonny boat! Sail Westward-ho, and away!'"

As she ceased, a measured voice, with a foreign accent, thrilled through her.

"In the East, they say the nightingale sings to the rose; Devon, more happy, has nightingale and rose in one."

"We have no nightingales in Devon, Don Guzman," said Lady Grenville; "but our little forest thrushes sing, as you hear, sweetly enough to content any ear. But what brings you away from the gentlemen so early?"

"These letters," said he, "which have just been put into my hand; and as they call me home to Spain, I was loath to lose a moment of that delightful company from which I must part so soon."

"To Spain?" asked half-a-dozen voices: for the Don was a general favorite.

"Yes, and thence to the Indies. My ransom has arrived, and with it the promise of an office. I am to be Governor of La Guayra in Caracas. Congratulate me on my promotion."

A mist was over Rose's eyes. The Spaniard's voice was hard and flippant. Did he care for her, after all? And if he did, was it nevertheless hopeless? How her cheeks glowed! Everybody must see it! Anything to turn away their attention from her, and in that nervous haste which makes people speak, and speak foolishly too, just because they ought to be silent, she asked—

"And where is La Guayra?"

"Half round the world, on the coast of the Spanish Main. The loveliest place on earth, and the loveliest governor's house, in a forest of palms at the foot of a mountain eight thousand feet high: I shall only want a wife there to be in paradise."

"I don't doubt that you may persuade some fair lady of Seville to accompany you thither," said Lady Grenville.

"Thanks, gracious madam: but the truth is, that since I have had the bliss of knowing English ladies, I have begun to think that they are the only ones on earth worth wooing."

"A thousand thanks for the compliment; but I fear none of our free English maidens would like to submit to the guardianship of a duenna. Eh, Rose? how should you like to be kept under lock and key all day by an ugly old woman with a horn on her forehead?"

Poor Rose turned so scarlet that Lady Grenville knew her secret on the spot, and would have tried to turn the conversation: but before she could speak, some burgher's wife blundered out a commonplace about the jealousy of Spanish husbands; and another, to make matters better, giggled out something more true than delicate about West Indian masters and fair slaves.

"Ladies," said Don Guzman, reddening, "believe me that these are but the calumnies of ignorance. If we be more jealous than other nations, it is because we love more passionately. If some of us abroad are profligate, it is because they, poor men, have no helpmate, which, like the amethyst, keeps its wearer pure. I could tell you stories, ladies, of the constancy and devotion of Spanish husbands, even in the Indies, as strange as ever romancer invented."

"Can you? Then we challenge you to give us one at least."

"I fear it would be too long, madam."

"The longer the more pleasant, senor. How can we spend an hour better this afternoon, while the gentlemen within are finishing their wine?"

Story-telling, in those old times, when books (and authors also, lucky for the public) were rarer than now, was a common amusement; and as the Spaniard's accomplishments in that line were well known, all the ladies crowded round him; the servants brought chairs and benches; and Don Guzman, taking his seat in the midst, with a proud humility, at Lady Grenville's feet, began—

"Your perfections, fair and illustrious ladies, must doubtless have heard, ere now, how Sebastian Cabota, some forty-five years ago, sailed forth with a commission from my late master, the Emperor Charles the Fifth, to discover the golden lands of Tarshish, Ophir, and Cipango; but being in want of provisions, stopped short at the mouth of that mighty South American river to which he gave the name of Rio de la Plata, and sailing up it, discovered the fair land of Paraguay. But you may not have heard how, on the bank of that river, at the mouth of the Rio Terceiro, he built a fort which men still call Cabot's Tower; nor have you, perhaps, heard of the strange tale which will ever make the tower a sacred spot to all true lovers.

"For when he returned to Spain the year after, he left in his tower a garrison of a hundred and twenty men, under the command of Nuno de Lara, Ruiz Moschera, and Sebastian da Hurtado, old friends and fellow-soldiers of my invincible grandfather Don Ferdinando da Soto; and with them a jewel, than which Spain never possessed one more precious, Lucia Miranda, the wife of Hurtado, who, famed in the court of the emperor no less for her wisdom and modesty than for her unrivalled beauty, had thrown up all the pomp and ambition of a palace, to marry a poor adventurer, and to encounter with him the hardships of a voyage round the world. Mangora, the cacique of the neighboring Timbuez Indians (with whom Lara had contrived to establish a friendship), cast his eyes on this fair creature, and no sooner saw than he coveted; no sooner coveted than he plotted, with the devilish subtilty of a savage, to seize by force what he knew he could never gain by right. She soon found out his passion (she was wise enough—what every woman is not—to know when she is loved), and telling her husband, kept as much as she could out of her new lover's sight; while the savage pressed Hurtado to come and visit him, and to bring his lady with him. Hurtado, suspecting the snare, and yet fearing to offend the cacique, excused himself courteously on the score of his soldier's duty; and the savage, mad with desire and disappointment, began plotting against Hurtado's life.

"So went on several weeks, till food grew scarce, and Don Hurtado and Don Ruiz Moschera, with fifty soldiers, were sent up the river on a foraging party. Mangora saw his opportunity, and leapt at it forthwith.

"The tower, ladies, as I have heard from those who have seen it, stands on a knoll at the meeting of the two rivers, while on the land side stretches a dreary marsh, covered with tall grass and bushes; a fit place for the ambuscade of four thousand Indians, which Mangora, with devilish cunning, placed around the tower, while he himself went boldly up to it, followed by thirty men, laden with grain, fruit, game, and all the delicacies which his forests could afford.

"There, with a smiling face, he told the unsuspecting Lara his sorrow for the Spaniards' want of food; besought him to accept the provision he had brought, and was, as he had expected, invited by Lara to come in and taste the wines of Spain.

"In went he and his thirty fellow-bandits, and the feast continued, with songs and libations, far into the night, while Mangora often looked round, and at last boldly asked for the fair Miranda: but she had shut herself into her lodging, pleading illness.

"A plea, fair ladies, which little availed that hapless dame, for no sooner had the Spaniards retired to rest, leaving (by I know not what madness) Mangora and his Indians within, than they were awakened by the cry of fire, the explosion of their magazine, and the inward rush of the four thousand from the marsh outside.

"Why pain your gentle ears with details of slaughter? A few fearful minutes sufficed to exterminate my bewildered and unarmed countrymen, to bind the only survivors, Miranda (innocent cause of the whole tragedy) and four other women with their infants, and to lead them away in triumph across the forest towards the Indian town.

"Stunned by the suddenness of the evils which had passed, and still more by the thought of those worse which were to come (as she too well foresaw), Miranda travelled all night through the forest, and was brought in triumph at day-dawn before the Indian king to receive her doom. Judge of her astonishment, when, on looking up, she saw that he was not Mangora.

"A ray of hope flashed across her, and she asked where he was.

"'He was slain last night,' said the king; 'and I, his brother Siripa, am now cacique of the Timbuez.'

"It was true; Lara, maddened with drink, rage, and wounds, had caught up his sword, rushed into the thick of the fight, singled out the traitor, and slain him on the spot; and then, forgetting safety in revenge, had continued to plunge his sword into the corpse, heedless of the blows of the savages, till he fell pierced with a hundred wounds.

"A ray of hope, as I said, flashed across the wretched Miranda for a moment; but the next she found that she had been freed from one bandit only to be delivered to another.

"'Yes,' said the new king, in broken Spanish; 'my brother played a bold stake, and lost it; but it was well worth the risk, and he showed his wisdom thereby. You cannot be his queen now: you must content yourself with being mine.'

"Miranda, desperate, answered him with every fierce taunt which she could invent against his treachery and his crime; and asked him, how he came to dream that the wife of a Christian

Spaniard would condescend to become the mistress of a heathen savage; hoping, unhappy lady, to exasperate him into killing her on the spot. But in vain; she only prolonged thereby her own misery. For, whether it was, ladies, that the novel sight of divine virtue and beauty awed (as it may have awed me ere now), where it had just before maddened; or whether some dream crossed the savage (as it may have crossed me ere now), that he could make the wisdom of a mortal angel help his ambition, as well as her beauty his happiness; or whether (which I will never believe of one of those dark children of the devil, though I can boldly assert it of myself) some spark of boldness within him made him too proud to take by force what he could not win by persuasion, certain it is, as the Indians themselves confessed afterwards, that the savage only answered her by smiles; and bidding his men unbind her, told her that she was no slave of his, and that it only lay with her to become the sovereign of him and all his vassals; assigned her a hut to herself, loaded her with savage ornaments, and for several weeks treated her with no less courtesy (so miraculous is the power of love) than if he had been a cavalier of Castile.

"Three months and more, ladies, as I have heard, passed in this misery, and every day Miranda grew more desperate of all deliverance, and saw staring her in the face, nearer and nearer, some hideous and shameful end; when one day going down with the wives of the cacique to draw water in the river, she saw on the opposite bank a white man in a tattered Spanish dress, with a drawn sword in his hand; who had no sooner espied her, than shrieking her name, he plunged into the stream, swam across, landed at her feet, and clasped her in his arms. It was no other, ladies, incredible as it may seem, than Don Sebastian himself, who had returned with Ruiz Moschera to the tower, and found it only a charred and bloodstained heap of ruins.

"He guessed, as by inspiration, what had passed, and whither his lady was gone; and without a thought of danger, like a true Spanish gentleman and a true Spanish lover, darted off alone into the forest, and guided only by the inspiration of his own loyal heart, found again his treasure, and found it still unstained and his own.

"Who can describe the joy, and who again the terror, of their meeting? The Indian women had fled in fear, and for the short ten minutes that the lovers were left together, life, to be sure, was one long kiss. But what to do they knew not. To go inland was to rush into the enemy's arms. He would have swum with her across the river, and attempted it; but his strength, worn out with hunger and travel, failed him; he drew her with difficulty on shore again, and sat down by her to await their doom with prayer, the first and last resource of virtuous ladies, as weapons are of cavaliers.

"Alas for them! May no true lovers ever have to weep over joys so soon lost, after having been so hardly found! For, ere a quarter of an hour was passed, the Indian women, who had fled at his approach, returned with all the warriors of the tribe. Don Sebastian, desperate, would fain have slain his wife and himself on the spot; but his hand sank again—and whose would not but an Indian's?—as he raised it against that fair and faithful breast; in a few minutes he was surrounded, seized from behind, disarmed, and carried in triumph into the village. And if you cannot feel for him in that misery, fair ladies, who have known no sorrow, yet I, a prisoner, can."

Don Guzman paused a moment, as if overcome by emotion; and I will not say that, as he paused, he did not look to see if Rose Salterne's eyes were on him, as indeed they were.

"Yes, I can feel with him; I can estimate, better than you, ladies, the greatness of that love which could submit to captivity; to the loss of his sword; to the loss of that honor, which, next to god and his mother, is the true Spaniard's deity. There are those who have suffered that shame at the hands of valiant gentlemen" (and again Don Guzman looked up at Rose), "and yet would have sooner died a thousand deaths; but he dared to endure it from the hands of villains, savages, heathens; for he was a true Spaniard, and therefore a true lover: but I will go on with my tale.

"This wretched pair, then, as I have been told by Ruiz Moschera himself, stood together before the cacique. He, like a true child of the devil, comprehending in a moment who Don Sebastian was, laughed with delight at seeing his rival in his power, and bade bind him at once to a tree, and shoot him to death with arrows.

"But the poor Miranda sprang forward, and threw herself at his feet, and with piteous entreaties besought for mercy from him who knew no mercy.

"And yet love and the sight of her beauty, and the terrible eloquence of her words, while she invoked on his head the just vengeance of Heaven, wrought even on his heart: nevertheless the pleasure of seeing her, who had so long scorned him, a suppliant at his feet, was too delicate to be speedily foregone; and not till she was all but blind with tears, and dumb with agony of pleading, did he make answer, that if she would consent to become his wife, her husband's life should be spared. She, in her haste and madness, sobbed out desperately I know not what consent. Don Sebastian, who understood, if not the language, still the meaning (so had love quickened his understanding), shrieked to her not to lose her precious soul for the sake of his worthless body; that death was nothing compared to the horror of that shame; and such other words as became a noble and valiant gentleman. She, shuddering now at her own frailty, would have recalled her promise; but Siripa kept her to it, vowing, if she disappointed him again, such a death to her husband as made her blood run cold to hear of; and the wretched woman could only escape for the present by some story, that it was not the custom of her race to celebrate nuptials till a month after the betrothment; that the anger of Heaven would be on her, unless she first performed in solitude certain religious rites; and lastly, that if he dared to lay hands on her husband, she would die so resolutely, that every drop of water should be deep enough to drown her, every thorn sharp enough to stab her to the heart: till fearing lest by demanding too much he should lose all, and awed too, as he had been at first by a voice and looks which seemed to be, in comparison with his own, divine, Siripa bade her go back to her hut, promising her husband life; but promising too, that if he ever found the two speaking together, even for a moment, he would pour out on them both all the cruelty of those tortures in which the devil, their father, has so perfectly instructed the Indians.

"So Don Sebastian, being stripped of his garments, and painted after the Indian fashion, was set to all mean and toilsome work, amid the buffetings and insults of the whole village. And this, ladies, he endured without a murmur, ay, took delight in enduring it, as he would have endured things worse a thousand times, only for the sake, like a true lover as he was, of being near the goddess whom he worshipped, and of seeing her now and then afar off, happy enough to be repaid even by that for all indignities.

"And yet, you who have loved may well guess, as I can, that ere a week had passed, Don Sebastian and the Lady Miranda had found means, in spite of all spiteful eyes, to speak to each other once and again; and to assure each other of their love; even to talk of escape, before the month's grace should be expired. And Miranda, whose heart was full of courage as long as she felt her husband near her, went so far as to plan a means of escape which seemed possible and hopeful.

"For the youngest wife of the cacique, who, till Miranda's coming, had been his favorite, often talked with the captive, insulting and tormenting her in her spite and jealousy, and receiving in return only gentle and conciliatory words. And one day when the woman had been threatening to kill her, Miranda took courage to say, 'Do you fancy that I shall not be as glad to be rid of your husband, as you to be rid of me? Why kill me needlessly, when all that you require is to get me forth of the place? Out of sight, out of mind. When I am gone, your husband will soon forget me, and you will be his favorite as before.' Soon, seeing that the girl was inclined to listen, she went on to tell her of her love to Don Sebastian, entreating and adjuring her, by the love which she bore the cacique, to pity and help her; and so won upon the girl, that she consented to be privy to Miranda's escape, and even offered to give her an opportunity of speaking to her husband about it; and at last was so won over by Miranda, that she consented to keep all intruders out of the way, while Don Sebastian that very night visited Miranda in her hut.

"The hapless husband, thirsting for his love, was in that hut, be sure, the moment that kind darkness covered his steps:—and what cheer these two made of each other, when they once found themselves together, lovers must fancy for themselves: but so it was, that after many a leave-taking, there was no departure; and when the night was well-nigh past, Sebastian and Miranda were still talking together as if they had never met before, and would never meet again.

"But it befell, ladies (would that I was not speaking truth, but inventing, that I might have invented something merrier for your ears), it befell that very night, that the young wife of the cacique, whose heart was lifted up with the thought that her rival was now at last disposed of, tried all her wiles to win back her faithless husband; but in vain. He only answered her caresses by indifference, then by contempt, then insults, then blows (for with the Indians, woman is always a slave, or rather a beast of burden), and went on to draw such cruel comparisons between her dark skin and the glorious fairness of the Spanish lady, that the wretched girl, beside herself with rage, burst out at last with her own secret. 'Fool that you are to madden yourself about a stranger who prizes one hair of her Spanish husband's head more than your whole body! Much does your new bride care for you! She is at this moment in her husband's arms!'

"The cacique screamed furiously to know what she meant; and she, her jealousy and hate of the guiltless lady boiling over once for all, bade him, if he doubted her, go see for himself.

"What use of many words? They were taken. Love, or rather lust, repelled, turned in a moment into devilish hate; and the cacique, summoning his Indians, bade them bind the wretched Don Sebastian to a tree, and there inflicted on him the lingering death to which he had at first been doomed. For Miranda he had more exquisite cruelty in store. And shall I tell it? Yes, ladies, for the honor of love and of Spain, and for a justification of those cruelties against the Indians which are so falsely imputed to our most Christian nation, it shall be told: he delivered the wretched lady over to the tender mercies of his wives; and what they were is neither fit for me to tell, nor you to hear.

"The two wretched lovers cast themselves upon each other's neck; drank each other's salt tears with the last kisses; accused themselves as the cause of each other's death; and then, rising above fear and grief, broke out into triumph at thus dying for and with each other; and proclaiming themselves the martyrs of love, commended their souls to God, and then stepped joyfully and proudly to their doom."

"And what was that?" asked half-a-dozen trembling voices.

"Don Sebastian, as I have said, was shot to death with arrows; but as for the Lady Miranda, the wretches themselves confessed afterwards, when they received due vengeance for their crimes (as they did receive it), that after all shameful and horrible indignities, she was bound to a tree, and there burned slowly in her husband's sight, stifling her shrieks lest they should wring his heart by one additional pang, and never taking her eyes, to the last, off that beloved face. And so died (but not unavenged) Sebastian de Hurtado and Lucia Miranda,—a Spanish husband and a Spanish wife."

The Don paused, and the ladies were silent awhile, for, indeed, there was many a gentle tear to be dried; but at last Mrs. St. Leger spoke, half, it seemed, to turn off the too painful impression of the over-true tale, the outlines whereof may be still read in old Charlevoix.

"You have told a sad and a noble tale, sir, and told it well; but, though your story was to set forth a perfect husband, it has ended rather by setting forth a perfect wife."

"And if I have forgotten, madam, in praising her to praise him also, have I not done that which would have best pleased his heroical and chivalrous spirit? He, be sure, would have forgotten his own virtue in the light of hers; and he would have wished me, I doubt not, to do the same also. And beside, madam, where ladies are the theme, who has time or heart to cast one thought upon their slaves?" And the Don made one of his deliberate and highly-finished bows.

"Don Guzman is courtier enough, as far as compliments go," said one of the young ladies; "but it was hardly courtier-like of him to find us so sad an entertainment, upon a merry evening."

"Yes," said another; "we must ask him for no more stories."

"Or songs either," said a third. "I fear he knows none but about forsaken maidens and despairing lovers."

"I know nothing at all about forsaken ladies, madam; because ladies are never forsaken in Spain."

"Nor about lovers despairing there, I suppose?"

"That good opinion of ourselves, madam, with which you English are pleased to twit us now and then, always prevents so sad a state of mind. For myself, I have had little to do with love; but I have had still less to do with despair, and intend, by help of Heaven, to have less."

"You are valiant, sir."

"You would not have me a coward, madam?" and so forth.

Now all this time Don Guzman had been talking at Rose Salterne, and giving her the very slightest hint, every now and then, that he was talking at her; till the poor girl's face was almost crimson with pleasure, and she gave herself up to the spell. He loved her still; perhaps he knew that she loved him: he must know some day. She felt now that there was no escape; she was almost glad to think that there was none.

The dark, handsome, stately face; the melodious voice, with its rich Spanish accent; the quiet grace of the gestures; the wild pathos of the story; even the measured and inflated style, as of one speaking of another and a loftier world; the chivalrous respect and admiration for woman, and for faithfulness to woman—what a man he was! If he had been pleasant heretofore, he was now enchanting. All the ladies round felt that, she could see, as much as she herself did; no, not quite as much, she hoped. She surely understood him, and felt for his loneliness more than any of them. Had she not been feeling for it through long and sad months? But it was she whom he was thinking of, she whom he was speaking to, all along. Oh, why had the tale ended so soon? She would gladly have sat and wept her eyes out till midnight over one melodious misery after another; but she was quite wise enough to keep her secret to herself; and sat behind the rest, with greedy eyes and demure lips, full of strange and new happiness—or misery; she knew not which to call it.

In the meanwhile, as it was ordained, Cary could see and hear through the window of the hall a good deal of what was going on.

"How that Spanish crocodile ogles the Rose!" whispered he to young St. Leger.

"What wonder? He is not the first by many a one."

"Ay—but—By heaven, she is making side-shots at him with those languishing eyes of hers, the little baggage!"

"What wonder? He is not the first, say I, and won't be the last. Pass the wine, man."

"I have had enough; between sack and singing, my head is as mazed as a dizzy sheep. Let me slip out."

"Not yet, man; remember you are bound for one song more."

So Cary, against his will, sat and sang another song; and in the meanwhile the party had broken up, and wandered away by twos and threes, among trim gardens and pleasaunces, and clipped yew-walks—

admiring the beauty of that stately place, long since passed into other hands, and fallen to decay, but then (if old Prince speaks true) one of the noblest mansions of the West.

At last Cary got away and out; sober, but just enough flushed with wine to be ready for any quarrel; and luckily for him, had not gone twenty yards along the great terrace before he met Lady Grenville.

"Has your ladyship seen Don Guzman?"

"Yes—why, where is he? He was with me not ten minutes ago. You know he is going back to Spain."

"Going! Has his ransom come?"

"Yes, and with it a governorship in the Indies."

"Governorship! Much good may it do the governed."

"Why not, then? He is surely a most gallant gentleman."

"Gallant enough—yes," said Cary, carelessly. "I must find him, and congratulate him on his honors."

"I will help you to find him," said Lady Grenville, whose woman's eye and ear had already suspected something. "Escort me, sir."

"It is but too great an honor to squire the Queen of Bideford," said Cary, offering his hand.

"If I am your queen, sir, I must be obeyed," answered she, in a meaning tone. Cary took the hint, and went on chattering cheerfully enough.

But Don Guzman was not to be found in garden or in pleasaunce.

"Perhaps," at last said a burgher's wife, with a toss of her head, "your ladyship may meet with him at Hankford's oak."

"At Hankford's oak! what should take him there?"

"Pleasant company, I reckon" (with another toss). "I heard him and Mistress Salterne talking about the oak just now."

Cary turned pale and drew in his breath.

"Very likely," said Lady Grenville, quietly. "Will you walk with me so far, Mr. Cary?"

"To the world's end, if your ladyship condescends so far." And off they went, Lady Grenville wishing that they were going anywhere else, but afraid to let Cary go alone; and suspecting, too, that some one or other ought to go.

So they went down past the herds of deer, by a trim-kept path into the lonely dell where stood the fatal oak; and, as they went, Lady Grenville, to avoid more unpleasant talk, poured into Cary's unheeding ears the story (which he probably had heard fifty times before) how old Chief-justice Hankford (whom some contradictory myths make the man who committed Prince Henry to prison for striking him on the bench), weary of life and sickened at the horrors and desolations of the Wars of the Roses, went down to his house at Annery there, and bade his keeper shoot any man who, passing through the deer-park at night, should refuse to stand when challenged; and then going down into that glen himself, and hiding himself beneath that oak, met willingly by his keeper's hand the death which his own dared not inflict: but ere the story was half done, Cary grasped Lady Grenville's hand so tightly that she gave a little shriek of pain.

"There they are!" whispered he, heedless of her; and pointed to the oak, where, half hidden by the tall fern, stood Rose and the Spaniard.

Her head was on his bosom. She seemed sobbing, trembling; he talking earnestly and passionately; but Lady Grenville's little shriek made them both look up. To turn and try to escape was to confess all; and the two, collecting themselves instantly, walked towards her, Rose wishing herself fathoms deep beneath the earth.

"Mind, sir," whispered Lady Grenville as they came up; "you have seen nothing."

"Madam?"

"If you are not on my ground, you are on my brother's. Obey me!"

Cary bit his lip, and bowed courteously to the Don.

"I have to congratulate you, I hear, senor, on your approaching departure."

"I kiss your hands, senor, in return; but I question whether it be a matter of congratulation, considering all that I leave behind."

"So do I," answered Cary, bluntly enough, and the four walked back to the house, Lady Grenville taking everything for granted with the most charming good humor, and chatting to her three silent companions till they gained the terrace once more, and found four or five of the gentlemen, with Sir Richard at their head, proceeding to the bowling-green.

Lady Grenville, in an agony of fear about the quarrel which she knew must come, would have gladly whispered five words to her husband: but she dared not do it before the Spaniard, and dreaded, too, a faint or a scream from the Rose, whose father was of the party. So she walked on with her fair prisoner, commanding Cary to escort them in, and the Spaniard to go to the bowling-green.

Cary obeyed: but he gave her the slip the moment she was inside the door, and then darted off to the gentlemen.

His heart was on fire: all his old passion for the Rose had flashed up again at the sight of her with a lover;—and that lover a Spaniard! He would cut his throat for him, if steel could do it! Only he recollected that Salterne was there, and shrank from exposing Rose; and shrank, too, as every gentleman should, from making a public quarrel in another man's house. Never mind. Where there was a will there was a way. He could get him into a corner, and quarrel with him privately about the cut of his beard, or the color of his ribbon. So in he went; and, luckily or unluckily, found standing together apart from the rest, Sir Richard, the Don, and young St. Leger.

"Well, Don Guzman, you have given us wine-bibbers the slip this afternoon. I hope you have been well employed in the meanwhile?"

"Delightfully to myself, senor," said the Don, who, enraged at being interrupted, if not discovered, was as ready to fight as Cary, but disliked, of course, an explosion as much as he did; "and to others, I doubt not."

"So the ladies say," quoth St. Leger. "He has been making them all cry with one of his stories, and robbing us meanwhile of the pleasure we had hoped for from some of his Spanish songs."

"The devil take Spanish songs!" said Cary, in a low voice, but loud enough for the Spaniard. Don Guzman clapt his hand on his sword-hilt instantly.

"Lieutenant Cary," said Sir Richard, in a stern voice, "the wine has surely made you forget yourself!"

"As sober as yourself, most worshipful knight; but if you want a Spanish song, here's one; and a very scurvy one it is, like its subject—

And he bowed low to the Spaniard.

The insult was too gross to require any spluttering.

"Senor Cary, we meet?"

"I thank your quick apprehension, Don Guzman Maria Magdalena Sotomayor de Soto. When, where, and with what weapons?"

"For God's sake, gentlemen! Nephew Arthur, Cary is your guest; do you know the meaning of this?"

St. Leger was silent. Cary answered for him.

"An old Irish quarrel, I assure you, sir. A matter of years' standing. In unlacing the senor's helmet, the evening that he was taken prisoner, I was unlucky enough to twitch his mustachios. You recollect the fact, of course, senor?"

"Perfectly," said the Spaniard; and then, half-amused and half-pleased, in spite of his bitter wrath, at Cary's quickness and delicacy in shielding Rose, he bowed, and—

"And it gives me much pleasure to find that he whom I trust to have the pleasure of killing tomorrow morning is a gentleman whose nice sense of honor renders him thoroughly worthy of the sword of a De Soto."

Cary bowed in return, while Sir Richard, who saw plainly enough that the excuse was feigned, shrugged his shoulders.

"What weapons, senor?" asked Will again.

"I should have preferred a horse and pistols," said Don Guzman after a moment, half to himself, and in Spanish; "they make surer work of it than bodkins; but" (with a sigh and one of his smiles) "beggars must not be choosers."

"The best horse in my stable is at your service, senor," said Sir Richard Grenville, instantly.

"And in mine also, senor," said Cary; "and I shall be happy to allow you a week to train him, if he does not answer at first to a Spanish hand."

"You forget in your courtesy, gentle sir, that the insult being with me, the time lies with me also. We wipe it off to-morrow morning with simple rapiers and daggers. Who is your second?"

"Mr. Arthur St. Leger here, senor: who is yours?"

The Spaniard felt himself alone in the world for one moment; and then answered with another of his smiles,—

"Your nation possesses the soul of honor. He who fights an Englishman needs no second."

"And he who fights among Englishmen will always find one," said Sir Richard. "I am the fittest second for my guest."

"You only add one more obligation, illustrious cavalier, to a two-years' prodigality of favors, which I shall never be able to repay."

"But, Nephew Arthur," said Grenville, "you cannot surely be second against your father's guest, and your own uncle."

"I cannot help it, sir; I am bound by an oath, as Will can tell you. I suppose you won't think it necessary to let me blood?"

"You half deserve it, sirrah!" said Sir Richard, who was very angry: but the Don interposed quickly.

"Heaven forbid, senors! We are no French duellists, who are mad enough to make four or six lives answer for the sins of two. This gentleman and I have quarrel enough between us, I suspect, to make a right bloody encounter."

"The dependence is good enough, sir," said Cary, licking his sinful lips at the thought. "Very well. Rapiers and shirts at three tomorrow morning—Is that the bill of fare? Ask Sir Richard where, Atty? It is against punctilio now for me to speak to him till after I am killed."

"On the sands opposite. The tide will be out at three. And now, gallant gentlemen, let us join the bowlers."

And so they went back and spent a merry evening, all except poor Rose, who, ere she went back, had poured all her sorrows into Lady Grenville's ear. For the kind woman, knowing that she was motherless and guileless, carried her off into Mrs. St. Leger's chamber, and there entreated her to tell the truth, and heaped her with pity but with no comfort. For indeed, what comfort was there to give?

Three o'clock, upon a still pure bright midsummer morning. A broad and yellow sheet of ribbed tide-sands, through which the shallow river wanders from one hill-foot to the other, whispering round dark knolls of rock, and under low tree-fringed cliffs, and banks of golden broom. A mile below, the long bridge and the white walled town, all sleeping pearly in the soft haze, beneath a cloudless vault of blue. The white glare of dawn, which last night hung high in the northwest, has travelled now to the northeast, and above the wooded wall of the hills the sky is flushing with rose and amber.

A long line of gulls goes wailing up inland; the rooks from Annery come cawing and sporting round the corner at Landcross, while high above them four or five herons flap solemnly along to find their breakfast on the shallows. The pheasants and partridges are clucking merrily in the long wet grass; every copse and hedgerow rings with the voice of birds, but the lark, who has been singing since midnight in the "blank height of the dark," suddenly hushes his carol and drops headlong among the corn, as a broad-winged buzzard swings from some wooded peak into the abyss of the valley, and hangs high-poised above the heavenward songster. The air is full of perfume; sweet clover, new-mown hay, the fragrant breath of kine, the dainty scent of sea-weed wreaths and fresh wet sand. Glorious day, glorious place, "bridal of earth and sky," decked well with bridal garlands, bridal perfumes, bridal songs,—What do those four cloaked figures there by the river brink, a dark spot on the fair face of the summer morn?

Yet one is as cheerful as if he too, like all nature round him, were going to a wedding; and that is Will Cary. He has been bathing down below, to cool his brain and steady his hand; and he intends to stop Don Guzman Maria Magdalena Sotomayor de Soto's wooing for ever and a day. The Spaniard is in a very different mood; fierce and haggard, he is pacing up and down the sand. He intends to kill Will Cary; but then? Will he be the nearer to Rose by doing so? Can he stay in Bideford? Will she go with him? Shall he stoop to stain his family by marrying a burgher's daughter? It is a confused, all but desperate business; and Don Guzman is certain but of one thing, that he is madly in love with this fair witch, and that if she refuse him, then, rather than see her accept another man, he would kill her with his own hands.

Sir Richard Grenville too is in no very pleasant humor, as St. Leger soon discovers, when the two seconds begin whispering over their arrangements.

"We cannot have either of them killed, Arthur."

"Mr. Cary swears he will kill the Spaniard, sir."

"He sha'n't. The Spaniard is my guest. I am answerable for him to Leigh, and for his ransom too. And how can Leigh accept the ransom if the man is not given up safe and sound? They won't pay for a dead carcass, boy! The man's life is worth two hundred pounds."

"A very bad bargain, sir, for those who pay the said two hundred for the rascal; but what if he kills Cary?"

"Worse still. Cary must not be killed. I am very angry with him, but he is too good a lad to be lost; and his father would never forgive us. We must strike up their swords at the first scratch."

"It will make them very mad, sir."

"Hang them! let them fight us then, if they don't like our counsel. It must be, Arthur."

"Be sure, sir," said Arthur, "that whatsoever you shall command I shall perform. It is only too great an honor to a young man as I am to find myself in the same duel with your worship, and to have the advantage of your wisdom and experience."

Sir Richard smiles, and says—"Now, gentlemen! are you ready?"

The Spaniard pulls out a little crucifix, and kisses it devoutly, smiting on his breast; crosses himself two or three times, and says—"Most willingly, senor."

Cary kisses no crucifix, but says a prayer nevertheless.

Cloaks and doublets are tossed off, the men placed, the rapiers measured hilt and point; Sir Richard and St. Leger place themselves right and left of the combatants, facing each other, the points of their drawn swords on the sand. Cary and the Spaniard stand for a moment quite upright, their sword-arms stretched straight before them, holding the long rapier horizontally, the left hand clutching the dagger close to their breasts. So they stand eye to eye, with clenched teeth and pale crushed lips, while men might count a score; St. Leger can hear the beating of his own heart; Sir Richard is praying inwardly that no life may be lost. Suddenly there is a quick turn of Cary's wrist and a leap forward. The Spaniard's dagger flashes, and the rapier is turned aside; Cary springs six feet back as the Spaniard rushes on him in turn. Parry, thrust, parry—the steel rattles, the sparks fly, the men breathe fierce and loud; the devil's game is begun in earnest.

Five minutes have the two had instant death a short six inches off from those wild sinful hearts of theirs, and not a scratch has been given. Yes! the Spaniard's rapier passes under Cary's left arm; he bleeds.

"A hit! a hit! Strike up, Atty!" and the swords are struck up instantly.

Cary, nettled by the smart, tries to close with his foe, but the seconds cross their swords before him.

"It is enough, gentlemen. Don Guzman's honor is satisfied!"

"But not my revenge, senor," says the Spaniard, with a frown. "This duel is a l'outrance, on my part; and, I believe, on Mr. Cary's also."

"By heaven, it is!" says Will, trying to push past. "Let me go, Arthur St. Leger; one of us must down. Let me go, I say!"

"If you stir, Mr. Cary, you have to do with Richard Grenville!" thunders the lion voice. "I am angry enough with you for having brought on this duel at all. Don't provoke me still further, young hot-head!"

Cary stops sulkily.

"You do not know all, Sir Richard, or you would not speak in this way."

"I do, sir, all; and I shall have the honor of talking it over with Don Guzman myself."

"Hey!" said the Spaniard. "You came here as my second, Sir Richard, as I understood, but not as my counsellor."

"Arthur, take your man away! Cary! obey me as you would your father, sir! Can you not trust Richard Grenville?"

"Come away, for God's sake!" says poor Arthur, dragging Cary's sword from him; "Sir Richard must know best!"

So Cary is led off sulking, and Sir Richard turns to the Spaniard,

"And now, Don Guzman, allow me, though much against my will, to speak to you as a friend to a friend. You will pardon me if I say that I cannot but have seen last night's devotion to—"

"You will be pleased, senor, not to mention the name of any lady to whom I may have shown devotion. I am not accustomed to have my little affairs talked over by any unbidden counsellors."

"Well, senor, if you take offence, you take that which is not given. Only I warn you, with all apologies for any seeming forwardness, that the quest on which you seem to be is one on which you will not be allowed to proceed."

"And who will stop me?" asked the Spaniard, with a fierce oath.

"You are not aware, illustrious senor," said Sir Richard, parrying the question, "that our English laity look upon mixed marriages with full as much dislike as your own ecclesiastics."

"Marriage, sir? Who gave you leave to mention that word to me?"

Sir Richard's brow darkened; the Spaniard, in his insane pride, had forced upon the good knight a suspicion which was not really just.

"Is it possible, then, Senor Don Guzman, that I am to have the shame of mentioning a baser word?"

"Mention what you will, sir. All words are the same to me; for, just or unjust, I shall answer them alike only by my sword."

"You will do no such thing, sir. You forget that I am your host."

"And do you suppose that you have therefore a right to insult me? Stand on your guard, sir!"

Grenville answered by slapping his own rapier home into the sheath with a quiet smile.

"Senor Don Guzman must be well enough aware of who Richard Grenville is, to know that he may claim the right of refusing duel to any man, if he shall so think fit."

"Sir!" cried the Spaniard, with an oath, "this is too much! Do you dare to hint that I am unworthy of your sword? Know, insolent Englishman, I am not merely a De Soto, though that, by St. James, were enough for you or any man. I am a Sotomayor, a Mendoza, a Bovadilla, a Losada, a—sir! I have blood royal in my veins, and you dare to refuse my challenge?"

"Richard Grenville can show quarterings, probably, against even Don Guzman Maria Magdalena Sotomayor de Soto, or against (with no offence to the unquestioned nobility of your pedigree) the bluest blood of Spain. But he can show, moreover, thank God, a reputation which raises him as much above the imputation of cowardice, as it does above that of discourtesy. If you think fit, senor, to forget what you have just, in very excusable anger, vented, and to return with me, you will find me still, as ever, your most faithful servant and host. If otherwise, you have only to name whither you wish your mails to be sent, and I shall, with unfeigned sorrow, obey your commands concerning them."

The Spaniard bowed stiffly, answered, "To the nearest tavern, senor," and then strode away. His baggage was sent thither. He took a boat down to Appledore that very afternoon, and vanished, none knew whither. A very courteous note to Lady Grenville, enclosing the jewel which he had been used to wear round his neck, was the only memorial he left behind him: except, indeed, the scar on Cary's arm, and poor Rose's broken heart.

Now county towns are scandalous places at best; and though all parties tried to keep the duel secret, yet, of course, before noon all Bideford knew what had happened, and a great deal more; and what was even worse, Rose, in an agony of terror, had seen Sir Richard Grenville enter her father's private room, and sit there closeted with him for an hour and more; and when he went, upstairs came old Salterne, with his stick in his hand, and after rating her soundly for far worse than a flirt, gave her (I am sorry to have to say it, but such was the mild fashion of paternal rule in those times, even over such daughters as Lady Jane Grey, if Roger Ascham is to be believed) such a beating that her poor sides were black and blue for many a day; and then putting her on a pillion behind him, carried her off twenty miles to her old prison at Stow mill, commanding her aunt to tame down her saucy blood with bread of affliction and water of affliction. Which commands were willingly enough fulfilled by the old dame, who had always borne a grudge against Rose for being rich while she was poor, and pretty while her daughter was plain; so that between flouts, and sneers, and watchings, and pretty open hints that she was a disgrace to her family, and no better than she should be, the poor innocent child watered her couch with her tears for a fortnight or more, stretching out her hands to the wide Atlantic, and calling wildly to Don Guzman to return and take her where he would, and she would live for him and die for him; and perhaps she did not call in vain.

CHAPTER XIII: HOW THE GOLDEN HIND CAME HOME AGAIN

"So you see, my dear Mrs. Hawkins, having the silver, as your own eyes show you, beside the ores of lead, manganese, and copper, and above all this gossan (as the Cornish call it), which I suspect to be not merely the matrix of the ore, but also the very crude form and materia prima of all metals—you mark me?—If my recipes, which I had from Doctor Dee, succeed only half so well as I expect, then I refine out the luna, the silver, lay it by, and transmute the remaining ores into sol, gold. Whereupon Peru and Mexico become superfluities, and England the mistress of the globe. Strange, no doubt; distant, no doubt: but possible, my dear madam, possible!"

"And what good to you if it be, Mr. Gilbert? If you could find a philosopher's stone to turn sinners into saints, now—but naught save God's grace can do that; and that last seems ofttimes over long in coming." And Mrs. Hawkins sighed.

"But indeed, my dear madam, conceive now.—The Comb Martin mine thus becomes a gold mine, perhaps inexhaustible; yields me wherewithal to carry out my North-West patent; meanwhile my brother Humphrey holds Newfoundland, and builds me fresh ships year by year (for the forests of pine are boundless) for my China voyage."

"Sir Humphrey has better thoughts in his dear heart than gold, Mr. Adrian; a very close and gracious walker he has been this seven year. I wish my Captain John were so too."

"And how do you know I have naught better in my mind's eye than gold? Or, indeed, what better could I have? Is not gold the Spaniard's strength—the very mainspring of Antichrist? By gold only, therefore, can we out-wrestle him. You shake your head, but say, dear madam (for gold England must have), which is better, to make gold bloodlessly at home, or take it bloodily abroad?"

"Oh, Mr. Gilbert, Mr. Gilbert! is it not written, that those who make haste to be rich, pierce themselves through with many sorrows? Oh, Mr. Gilbert! God's blessing is not on it all."

"Not on you, madam? Be sure that brave Captain John Hawkins's star told me a different tale, when I cast his nativity for him.—Born under stormy planets, truly, but under right royal and fortunate ones."

"Ah, Mr. Adrian! I am a simple body, and you a great philosopher, but I hold there is no star for the seaman like the Star of Bethlehem; and that goes with 'peace on earth and good will to men,' and not with such arms as that, Mr. Adrian. I can't abide to look upon them."

And she pointed up to one of the bosses of the ribbed oak-roof, on which was emblazoned the fatal crest which Clarencieux Hervey had granted years before to her husband, the "Demi-Moor proper, bound."

"Ah, Mr. Gilbert! since first he went to Guinea after those poor negroes, little lightness has my heart known; and the very day that that crest was put up in our grand new house, as the parson read the first lesson, there was this text in it, Mr. Gilbert, 'Woe to him that buildeth his house by iniquity, and his chambers by wrong. Shalt thou live because thou closest thyself in cedar?' And it went into my ears like fire, Mr. Gilbert, and into my heart like lead; and when the parson went on, 'Did not thy father eat and drink, and do judgment and justice? Then it was well with him,' I thought of good old Captain Will; and—I tell you, Mr. Gilbert, those negroes are on my soul from morning until night! We are all mighty grand now, and money comes in fast, but the Lord will require the blood of them at our hands yet, He will!"

"My dearest madam, who can prosper more than you? If your husband copied the Dons too closely once or twice in the matter of those negroes (which I do not deny,) was he not punished at once when he lost ships, men, all but life, at St. Juan d'Ulloa?"

"Ay, yes," she said; "and that did give me a bit of comfort, especially when the queen—God save her tender heart!—was so sharp with him for pity of the poor wretches, but it has not mended him. He is growing fast like the rest now, Mr. Gilbert, greedy to win, and niggardly to spend (God forgive him!) and always fretting and plotting for some new gain, and envying and grudging at Drake, and all who are deeper in the snare of prosperity than he is. Gold, gold, nothing but gold in every mouth—there it is! Ah! I mind when Plymouth was a quiet little God-fearing place as God could smile upon: but ever since my John, and Sir Francis, and poor Mr. Oxenham found out the way to the Indies, it's been a sad place. Not a sailor's wife but is crying 'Give, give,' like the daughters of the horse-leech; and every woman must drive her husband out across seas to bring her home money to squander on hoods and farthingales, and go mincing with outstretched necks and wanton eyes; and they will soon learn to do worse than that, for the sake of gain. But the Lord's hand will be against their tires and crisping-pins, their mufflers and farthingales, as it was against the Jews of old. Ah, dear me!"

The two interlocutors in this dialogue were sitting in a low oak-panelled room in Plymouth town, handsomely enough furnished, adorned with carving and gilding and coats of arms, and noteworthy for many strange knickknacks, Spanish gold and silver vessels on the sideboard; strange birds and skins, and charts and rough drawings of coast which hung about the room; while over the fireplace, above the portrait of old Captain Will Hawkins, pet of Henry the Eighth, hung the Spanish ensign which Captain John had taken in fair fight at Rio de la Hacha fifteen years before, when, with two hundred men, he seized the town in despite of ten hundred Spanish soldiers, and watered his ship triumphantly at the enemy's wells.

The gentleman was a tall fair man, with a broad and lofty forehead, wrinkled with study, and eyes weakened by long poring over the crucible and the furnace.

The lady had once been comely enough, but she was aged and worn, as sailors' wives are apt to be, by many sorrows. Many a sad day had she had already; for although John Hawkins, port-admiral of Plymouth, and patriarch of British shipbuilders, was a faithful husband enough, and as ready to forgive as he was to quarrel, yet he was obstinate and ruthless, and in spite of his religiosity (for all men were religious then) was by no means a "consistent walker."

And sadder days were in store for her, poor soul. Nine years hence she would be asked to name her son's brave new ship, and would christen it The Repentance, giving no reason in her quiet steadfast way (so says her son Sir Richard) but that "Repentance was the best ship in which we could sail to the harbor of heaven;" and she would hear that Queen Elizabeth, complaining of the name for an unlucky one, had re-christened her The Dainty, not without some by-quip, perhaps, at the character of her most dainty captain, Richard Hawkins, the complete seaman and Euphuist afloat, of whom, perhaps, more hereafter.

With sad eyes Mrs. (then Lady) Hawkins would see that gallant bark sail Westward-ho, to go the world around, as many another ship sailed; and then wait, as many a mother beside had waited, for the sail which never returned; till, dim and uncertain, came tidings of her boy fighting for four days three great Armadas (for the coxcomb had his father's heart in him after all), a prisoner, wounded, ruined, languishing for weary years in Spanish prisons. And a sadder day than that was in store, when a gallant fleet should round the Ram Head, not with drum and trumpet, but with solemn minute-guns, and all flags half-mast high, to tell her that her terrible husband's work was done, his terrible heart broken by failure and fatigue, and his body laid by Drake's beneath the far-off tropic seas.

And if, at the close of her eventful life, one gleam of sunshine opened for a while, when her boy Richard returned to her bosom from his Spanish prison, to be knighted for his valor, and made a privy councillor for his wisdom; yet soon, how soon, was the old cloud to close in again above her, until her weary eyes should open in the light of Paradise. For that son dropped dead, some say at the very council-table, leaving behind him naught but broken fortunes, and huge purposes which never were fulfilled; and the stormy star of that bold race was set forever, and Lady Hawkins bowed her weary head and died, the groan of those stolen negroes ringing in her ears, having lived long enough to see her husband's youthful sin become a national institution, and a national curse for generations yet unborn.

I know not why she opened her heart that night to Adrian Gilbert, with a frankness which she would hardly have dared to use to her own family. Perhaps it was that Adrian, like his great brothers, Humphrey and Raleigh, was a man full of all lofty and delicate enthusiasms, tender and poetical, such as women cling to when their hearts are lonely; but so it was; and Adrian, half ashamed of his own ambitious dreams, sate looking at her a while in silence; and then—

"The Lord be with you, dearest lady. Strange, how you women sit at home to love and suffer, while we men rush forth to break our hearts and yours against rocks of our own seeking! Ah well! were it not for Scripture, I should have thought that Adam, rather than Eve, had been the one who plucked the fruit of the forbidden tree."

"We women, I fear; did the deed nevertheless; for we bear the doom of it our lives long."

"You always remind me, madam, of my dear Mrs. Leigh of Burrough, and her counsels."

"Do you see her often? I hear of her as one of the Lord's most precious vessels."

"I would have done more ere now than see her," said he with a blush, "had she allowed me: but she lives only for the memory of her husband and the fame of her noble sons."

As he spoke the door opened, and in walked, wrapped in his rough sea-gown, none other than one of those said noble sons.

Adrian turned pale.

"Amyas Leigh! What brings you hither? how fares my brother? Where is the ship?"

"Your brother is well, Mr. Gilbert. The Golden Hind is gone on to Dartmouth, with Mr. Hayes. I came ashore here, meaning to go north to Bideford, ere I went to London. I called at Drake's just now, but he was away."

"The Golden Hind? What brings her home so soon?"

"Yet welcome ever, sir," said Mrs. Hawkins. "This is a great surprise, though. Captain John did not look for you till next year."

Amyas was silent.

"Something is wrong!" cried Adrian. "Speak!"

Amyas tried, but could not.

"Will you drive a man mad, sir? Has the adventure failed? You said my brother was well."

"He is well."

"Then what—Why do you look at me in that fashion, sir?" and springing up, Adrian rushed forward, and held the candle to Amyas's face.

Amyas's lip quivered, as he laid his hand on Adrian's shoulder.

"Your great and glorious brother, sir, is better bestowed than in settling Newfoundland."

"Dead?" shrieked Adrian.

"He is with the God whom he served!"

"He was always with Him, like Enoch: parable me no parables, if you love me, sir!"

"And, like Enoch, he was not; for God took him."

Adrian clasped his hands over his forehead, and leaned against the table.

"Go on, sir, go on. God will give me strength to hear all."

And gradually Amyas opened to Adrian that tragic story, which Mr. Hayes has long ago told far too well to allow a second edition of it from me: of the unruliness of the men, ruffians, as I said before, caught up at hap-hazard; of conspiracies to carry off the ships, plunder of fishing vessels, desertions multiplying daily; licenses from the general to the lazy and fearful to return home: till Adrian broke out with a groan—

"From him? Conspired against him? Deserted from him? Dotards, buzzards! Where would they have found such another leader?"

"Your illustrious brother, sir," said Amyas, "if you will pardon me, was a very great philosopher, but not so much of a general."

"General, sir? Where was braver man?"

"Not on God's earth, but that does not make a general, sir. If Cortez had been brave and no more, Mexico would have been Mexico still. The truth is, sir, Cortez, like my Captain Drake, knew when to hang a man; and your great brother did not."

Amyas, as I suppose, was right. Gilbert was a man who could be angry enough at baseness or neglect, but who was too kindly to punish it; he was one who could form the wisest and best-digested plans, but who could not stoop to that hail-fellow-well-met drudgery among his subordinates which has been the talisman of great captains.

Then Amyas went on to tell the rest of his story; the setting sail from St. John's to discover the southward coast; Sir Humphrey's chivalrous determination to go in the little Squirrel of only ten tons, and "overcharged with nettings, fights, and small ordnance," not only because she was more fit to examine the creeks, but because he had heard of some taunt against him among the men, that he was afraid of the sea.

After that, woe on woe; how, seven days after they left Cape Raz, their largest ship, the Delight, after she had "most part of the night" (I quote Hayes), "like the swan that singeth before her death, continued in sounding of trumpets, drums, and fifes, also winding of the comets and hautboys, and, in the end of their jollity, left off with the battle and doleful knells," struck the next day (the Golden Hind and the Squirrel sheering off just in time) upon unknown shoals; where were lost all but fourteen, and among them Frank's philosopher friend, poor Budaeus; and those who escaped, after all horrors of cold and famine, were cast on shore in Newfoundland. How, worn out with hunger and want of clothes, the crews of the two remaining ships persuaded Sir Humphrey to sail toward England on the 31st of August; and on "that very instant, even in winding about," beheld close alongside "a very lion in shape, hair, and color, not swimming, but sliding on the water, with his whole body; who passed along, turning his head to and fro, yawning and gaping wide, with ugly demonstration of long teeth and glaring eyes; and to bid us farewell (coming right against the Hind) he sent forth a horrible voice, roaring or bellowing as doth a lion." "What opinion others had thereof, and chiefly the general himself, I forbear to deliver; but he took it for bonum omen, rejoicing that he was to war against such an enemy, if it were the devil."

"And the devil it was, doubtless," said Adrian, "the roaring lion who goes about seeking whom he may devour."

"He has not got your brother, at least," quoth Amyas.

"No," rejoined Mrs. Hawkins (smile not, reader, for those were days in which men believed in the devil); "he roared for joy to think how many poor souls would be left still in heathen darkness by Sir Humphrey's death. God be with that good knight, and send all mariners where he is now!"

Then Amyas told the last scene; how, when they were off the Azores, the storms came on heavier than ever, with "terrible seas, breaking short and pyramid-wise," till, on the 9th September, the tiny Squirrel nearly foundered and yet recovered; "and the general, sitting abaft with a book in his hand, cried out to us in the Hind so oft as we did approach within hearing, 'We are as near heaven by sea as by land,' reiterating the same speech, well beseeming a soldier resolute in Jesus Christ, as I can testify he was.

"The same Monday, about twelve of the clock, or not long after, the frigate (the Squirrel) being ahead of us in the Golden Hind, suddenly her lights were out; and withal our watch cried, the general was cast away, which was true; for in that moment the frigate was devoured and swallowed up of the sea."

And so ended (I have used Hayes' own words) Amyas Leigh's story.

"Oh, my brother! my brother!" moaned poor Adrian; "the glory of his house, the glory of Devon!"

"Ah! what will the queen say?" asked Mrs. Hawkins through her tears.

"Tell me," asked Adrian, "had he the jewel on when he died?"

"The queen's jewel? He always wore that, and his own posy too, 'Mutare vel timere sperno.' He wore it; and he lived it."

"Ay," said Adrian, "the same to the last!"

"Not quite that," said Amyas. "He was a meeker man latterly than he used to be. As he said himself once, a better refiner than any whom he had on board had followed him close all the seas over, and purified him in the fire. And gold seven times tried he was, when God, having done His work in him, took him home at last."

And so the talk ended. There was no doubt that the expedition had been an utter failure; Adrian was a ruined man; and Amyas had lost his venture.

Adrian rose, and begged leave to retire; he must collect himself.

"Poor gentleman!" said Mrs. Hawkins; "it is little else he has left to collect."

"Or I either," said Amyas. "I was going to ask you to lend me one of your son's shirts, and five pounds to get myself and my men home."

"Five? Fifty, Mr. Leigh! God forbid that John Hawkins's wife should refuse her last penny to a distressed mariner, and he a gentleman born. But you must eat and drink."

"It's more than I have done for many a day worth speaking of."

And Amyas sat down in his rags to a good supper, while Mrs. Hawkins told him all the news which she could of his mother, whom Adrian Gilbert had seen a few months before in London; and then went on, naturally enough, to the Bideford news.

"And by the by, Captain Leigh, I've sad news for you from your place; and I had it from one who was there at the time. You must know a Spanish captain, a prisoner—"

"What, the one I sent home from Smerwick?"

"You sent? Mercy on us! Then, perhaps, you've heard—"

"How can I have heard? What?"

"That he's gone off, the villain?"

"Without paying his ransom?"

"I can't say that; but there's a poor innocent young maid gone off with him, one Salterne's daughter—the Popish serpent!"

"Rose Salterne, the mayor's daughter, the Rose of Torridge!"

"That's her. Bless your dear soul, what ails you?"

Amyas had dropped back in his seat as if he had been shot; but he recovered himself before kind Mrs. Hawkins could rush to the cupboard for cordials.

"You'll forgive me, madam; but I'm weak from the sea; and your good ale has turned me a bit dizzy, I think."

"Ay, yes, 'tis too, too heavy, till you've been on shore a while. Try the aqua vitae; my Captain John has it right good; and a bit too fond of it too, poor dear soul, between whiles, Heaven forgive him!"

So she poured some strong brandy and water down Amyas's throat, in spite of his refusals, and sent him to bed, but not to sleep; and after a night of tossing, he started for Bideford, having obtained the means for so doing from Mrs. Hawkins.

CHAPTER XIV: HOW SALVATION YEO SLEW THE KING OF THE GUBBINGS

Now I am sorry to say, for the honor of my country, that it was by no means a safe thing in those days to travel from Plymouth to the north of Devon; because, to get to your journey's end, unless you were minded to make a circuit of many miles, you must needs pass through the territory of a foreign and hostile potentate, who had many times ravaged the dominions, and defeated the forces of her Majesty Queen Elizabeth, and was named (behind his back at least) the King of the Gubbings. "So now I dare call them," says Fuller, "secured by distance, which one of more valor durst not do to their face, for fear their fury fall upon him. Yet hitherto have I met with none who could render a reason of their name. We call the shavings of fish (which are little worth) gubbings; and sure it is that they are sensible that the word importeth shame and disgrace.

"As for the suggestion of my worthy and learned friend, Mr. Joseph Maynard, that such as did inhabitare montes gibberosos, were called Gubbings, such will smile at the ingenuity who dissent from the truth of the etymology.

"I have read of an England beyond Wales, but the Gubbings land is a Scythia within England, and they pure heathens therein. It lieth nigh Brent. For in the edge of Dartmoor it is reported that, some two hundred years since, two bad women, being with child, fled thither to hide themselves; to whom certain lewd fellows resorted, and this was their first original. They are a peculiar of their own making, exempt from bishop, archdeacon, and all authority, either ecclesiastical or civil. They live in cots (rather holes than houses) like swine, having all in common, multiplied without marriage into many hundreds. Their language is the dross of the dregs of the vulgar Devonian; and the more learned a man is, the worse he can understand them. During our civil wars no soldiers were quartered upon them, for fear of being quartered amongst them. Their wealth consisteth in other men's goods; they live by stealing the sheep on the moors; and vain is it for any to search their houses, being a work beneath the pains of any sheriff, and above the power of any constable. Such is their fleetness, they will outrun many horses; vivaciousness, they outlive most men; living in an ignorance of luxury, the extinguisher of life. They hold together like bees; offend one, and all will revenge his quarrel.

"But now I am informed that they begin to be civilized, and tender their children to baptism, and return to be men, yea, Christians again. I hope no CIVIL people amongst us will turn barbarians, now these barbarians begin to be civilized."*

With which quip against the Anabaptists of his day, Fuller ends his story; and I leave him to set forth how Amyas, in fear of these same Scythians and heathens, rode out of Plymouth on a right good horse, in his full suit of armor, carrying lance and sword, and over and above two great dags, or horse-pistols; and behind him Salvation Yeo, and five or six north Devon men (who had served with him in Ireland, and were returning on furlough), clad in head-pieces and quilted jerkins, each man with his pike and sword, and Yeo with arquebuse and match, while two sumpter ponies carried the baggage of this formidable troop.

They pushed on as fast as they could, through Tavistock, to reach before nightfall Lydford, where they meant to sleep; but what with buying the horses, and other delays, they had not been able to start before noon; and night fell just as they reached the frontiers of the enemy's country. A dreary place enough it was, by the wild glare of sunset. A high tableland of heath, banked on the right by the crags and hills of Dartmoor, and sloping away to the south and west toward the foot of the great cone of Brent-Tor, which towered up like an extinct volcano (as some say that it really is), crowned with the tiny church, the votive offering of some Plymouth merchant of old times, who vowed in sore distress to build a church to the Blessed Virgin on the first point of English land which he should see. Far away, down those waste slopes, they could see the tiny threads of blue smoke rising from the dens of the Gubbings; and more than once they called a halt, to examine whether distant furze-bushes and ponies might not be the patrols of an advancing army. It is all very well to laugh at it now, in the nineteenth century, but it was no laughing matter then; as they found before they had gone two miles farther.

On the middle of the down stood a wayside inn; a desolate and villainous-looking lump of lichen-spotted granite, with windows paper-patched, and rotting thatch kept down by stones and straw-banks; and at the back a rambling court-ledge of barns and walls, around which pigs and barefoot children grunted in loving communion of dirt. At the door, rapt apparently in the contemplation of the mountain peaks which glowed rich orange in the last lingering sun-rays, but really watching which way the sheep on the moor were taking, stood the innkeeper, a brawny, sodden-visaged, blear-eyed six feet of brutishness, holding up his hose with one hand, for want of points, and clawing with the other his elf-locks, on which a fair sprinkling of feathers might denote: first, that he was just out of bed, having been out sheep-stealing all the night before; and secondly, that by natural genius he had anticipated the opinion of that great apostle of sluttishness, Fridericus Dedekind, and his faithful disciple Dekker, which last speaks thus to all gulls and grobians: "Consider that as those trees of cobweb lawn, woven by spinners in the fresh May mornings, do dress the curled heads of the mountains, and adorn the swelling bosoms of the valleys; or as those snowy fleeces, which the naked briar steals from the innocent sheep to make himself a warm winter livery, are, to either of them both, an excellent ornament; so make thou account, that to have feathers sticking here and there on thy head will embellish thee, and set thy crown out rarely. None dare upbraid thee, that like a beggar thou hast lain on straw, or like a travelling pedlar upon musty flocks; for those feathers will rise up as witnesses to choke him that says so, and to prove thy bed to have been of the softest down." Even so did those feathers bear witness that the possessor of Rogues' Harbor Inn, on Brent-Tor Down, whatever else he lacked, lacked not geese enough to keep him in soft lying.

Presently he spies Amyas and his party coming slowly over the hill, pricks up his ears, and counts them; sees Amyas's armor; shakes his head and grunts; and then, being a man of few words, utters a sleepy howl—

"Mirooi!—Fushing pooale!"

A strapping lass—whose only covering (for country women at work in those days dispensed with the ornament of a gown) is a green bodice and red petticoat, neither of them over ample—brings out his fishing-rod and basket, and the man, having tied up his hose with some ends of string, examines the footlink.

"Don vlies' gone!"

"May be," says Mary; "shouldn't hay' left mun out to coort. May be old hen's ate mun off. I see her chocking about a while agone."

The host receives this intelligence with an oath, and replies by a violent blow at Mary's head, which she, accustomed to such slight matters, dodges, and then returns the blow with good effect on the shock head.

Whereon mine host, equally accustomed to such slight matters, quietly shambles off, howling as he departs—

"Tell Patrico!"

Mary runs in, combs her hair, slips a pair of stockings and her best gown over her dirt, and awaits the coming guests, who make a few long faces at the "mucksy sort of a place," but prefer to spend the night there than to bivouac close to the enemy's camp.

So the old hen who has swallowed the dun fly is killed, plucked, and roasted, and certain "black Dartmoor mutton" is put on the gridiron, and being compelled to confess the truth by that fiery torment, proclaims itself to all noses as red-deer venison. In the meanwhile Amyas has put his horse and the ponies into a shed, to which he can find neither lock nor key, and therefore returns grumbling, not without fear for his steed's safety. The baggage is heaped in a corner of the room, and Amyas stretches his legs before a turf fire; while Yeo, who has his notions about the place, posts himself at the door, and the men are seized with a desire to superintend the cooking, probably to be attributed to the fact that Mary is cook.

Presently Yeo comes in again.

"There's a gentleman just coming up, sir, all alone."

"Ask him to make one of our party, then, with my compliments." Yeo goes out, and returns in five minutes.

"Please, sir, he's gone in back ways, by the court."

"Well, he has an odd taste, if he makes himself at home here."

Out goes Yeo again, and comes back once more after five minutes, in high excitement.

"Come out, sir; for goodness' sake come out. I've got him. Safe as a rat in a trap, I have!"

"Who?"

"A Jesuit, sir."

"Nonsense, man!"

"I tell you truth, sir. I went round the house, for I didn't like the looks of him as he came up. I knew he was one of them villains the minute he came up, by the way he turned in his toes, and put down his feet so still and careful, like as if he was afraid of offending God at every step. So I just put my eye between the wall and the dern of the gate, and I saw him come up to the back door and knock, and call 'Mary!' quite still, like any Jesuit; and the wench flies out to him ready to eat him; and 'Go away,' I heard her say, 'there's a dear man;' and then something about a 'queer cuffin' (that's a justice in these canters' thieves' Latin); and with that he takes out a somewhat—I'll swear it was one of those Popish Agnuses—and gives it her; and she kisses it, and crosses herself, and asks him if that's the right way, and then puts it into her bosom, and he says, 'Bless you, my daughter;' and then I was sure of the dog: and he slips quite still to the stable, and peeps in, and when he sees no one there, in he goes, and out I go, and shut to the door, and back a cart that was there up against it, and call out one of the men to watch the stable, and the girl's crying like mad."

"What a fool's trick, man! How do you know that he is not some honest gentleman, after all?"

"Fool or none, sir; honest gentlemen don't give maidens Agnuses. I've put him in; and if you want him let out again, you must come and do it yourself, for my conscience is against it, sir. If the Lord's enemies are delivered into my hand, I'm answerable, sir," went on Yeo as Amyas hurried out with him. "'Tis written, 'If any let one of them go, his life shall be for the life of him.'"

So Amyas ran out, pulled back the cart grumbling, opened the door, and began a string of apologies to—his cousin Eustace.

Yes, here he was, with such a countenance, half foolish, half venomous, as reynard wears when the last spadeful of earth is thrown back, and he is revealed sitting disconsolately on his tail within a yard of the terriers' noses.

Neither cousin spoke for a minute or two. At last Amyas—

"Well, cousin hide-and-seek, how long have you added horse-stealing to your other trades?"

"My dear Amyas," said Eustace, very meekly, "I may surely go into an inn stable without intending to steal what is in it."

"Of course, old fellow," said Amyas, mollified, "I was only in jest. But what brings you here? Not prudence, certainly."

"I am bound to know no prudence save for the Lord's work."

"That's giving away Agnus Deis, and deceiving poor heathen wenches, I suppose," said Yeo.

Eustace answered pretty roundly—

"Heathens? Yes, truly; you Protestants leave these poor wretches heathens, and then insult and persecute those who, with a devotion unknown to you, labor at the danger of their lives to make them Christians. Mr. Amyas Leigh, you can give me up to be hanged at Exeter, if it shall so please you to disgrace your own family; but from this spot neither you, no, nor all the myrmidons of your queen, shall drive me, while there is a soul here left unsaved."

"Come out of the stable, at least," said Amyas; "you don't want to make the horses Papists, as well as the asses, do you? Come out, man, and go to the devil your own way. I sha'n't inform against you; and Yeo here will hold his tongue if I tell him, I know."

"It goes sorely against my conscience, sir; but being that he is your cousin, of course—"

"Of course; and now come in and eat with me; supper's just ready, and bygones shall be bygones, if you will have them so."

How much forgiveness Eustace felt in his heart, I know not: but he knew, of course, that he ought to forgive; and to go in and eat with Amyas was to perform an act of forgiveness, and for the best of motives, too, for by it the cause of the Church might be furthered; and acts and motives being correct, what more was needed? So in he went; and yet he never forgot that scar upon his cheek; and Amyas could not look him in the face but Eustace must fancy that his eyes were on the scar, and peep up from under his lids to see if there was any smile of triumph on that honest visage. They talked away over the venison, guardedly enough at first; but as they went on, Amyas's straightforward kindliness warmed poor Eustace's frozen heart; and ere they were aware, they found themselves talking over old haunts and old passages of their boyhood—uncles, aunts, and cousins; and Eustace, without any sinister intention, asked Amyas why he was going to Bideford, while Frank and his mother were in London.

"To tell you the truth, I cannot rest till I have heard the whole story about poor Rose Salterne."

"What about her?" cried Eustace.

"Do you not know?"

"How should I know anything here? For heaven's sake, what has happened?"

Amyas told him, wondering at his eagerness, for he had never had the least suspicion of Eustace's love.

Eustace shrieked aloud.

"Fool, fool that I have been! Caught in my own trap! Villain, villain that he is! After all he promised me at Lundy!"

And springing up, Eustace stamped up and down the room, gnashing his teeth, tossing his head from side to side, and clutching with outstretched hands at the empty air, with the horrible gesture (Heaven grant that no reader has ever witnessed it!) of that despair which still seeks blindly for the object which it knows is lost forever.

Amyas sat thunderstruck. His first impulse was to ask, "Lundy? What knew you of him? What had he or you to do at Lundy?" but pity conquered curiosity.

"Oh, Eustace! And you then loved her too?"

"Don't speak to me! Loved her? Yes, sir, and had as good a right to love her as any one of your precious Brotherhood of the Rose. Don't speak to me, I say, or I shall do you a mischief!"

So Eustace knew of the brotherhood too! Amyas longed to ask him how; but what use in that? If he knew it, he knew it; and what harm? So he only answered:

"My good cousin, why be wroth with me? If you really love her, now is the time to take counsel with me how best we shall—"

Eustace did not let him finish his sentence. Conscious that he had betrayed himself upon more points than one, he stopped short in his walk, suddenly collected himself by one great effort, and eyed Amyas from underneath his brows with the old down look.

"How best we shall do what, my valiant cousin?" said he, in a meaning and half-scornful voice. "What does your most chivalrous Brotherhood of the Rose purpose in such a case?"

Amyas, a little nettled, stood on his guard in return, and answered bluntly—

"What the Brotherhood of the Rose will do, I can't yet say. What it ought to do, I have a pretty sure guess."

"So have I. To hunt her down as you would an outlaw, because forsooth she has dared to love a Catholic; to murder her lover in her arms, and drag her home again stained with his blood, to be forced by threats and persecution to renounce that Church into whose maternal bosom she has doubtless long since found rest and holiness!"

"If she has found holiness, it matters little to me where she has found it, Master Eustace, but that is the very point that I should be glad to know for certain."

"And you will go and discover for yourself?"

"Have you no wish to discover it also?"

"And if I had, what would that be to you?"

"Only," said Amyas, trying hard to keep his temper, "that, if we had the same purpose, we might sail in the same ship."

"You intend to sail, then?"

"I mean simply, that we might work together."

"Our paths lie on very different roads, sir!"

"I am afraid you never spoke a truer word, sir. In the meanwhile, ere we part, be so kind as to tell me what you meant by saying that you had met this Spaniard at Lundy?"

"I shall refuse to answer that."

"You will please to recollect, Eustace, that however good friends we have been for the last half-hour, you are in my power. I have a right to know the bottom of this matter; and, by heaven, I will know it."

"In your power? See that you are not in mine! Remember, sir, that you are within a—within a few miles, at least, of those who will obey me, their Catholic benefactor, but who owe no allegiance to those Protestant authorities who have left them to the lot of the beasts which perish."

Amyas was very angry. He wanted but little more to make him catch Eustace by the shoulders, shake the life out of him, and deliver him into the tender guardianship of Yeo; but he knew that to take him at all was to bring certain death on him, and disgrace on the family; and remembering Frank's conduct on that memorable night at Clovelly, he kept himself down.

"Take me," said Eustace, "if you will, sir. You, who complain of us that we keep no faith with heretics, will perhaps recollect that you asked me into this room as your guest, and that in your good faith I trusted when I entered it."

The argument was a worthless one in law; for Eustace had been a prisoner before he was a guest, and Amyas was guilty of something very like misprision of treason in not handing him over to the nearest justice. However, all he did was, to go to the door, open it, and bowing to his cousin, bid him walk out and go to the devil, since he seemed to have set his mind on ending his days in the company of that personage.

Whereon Eustace vanished.

"Pooh!" said Amyas to himself, "I can find out enough, and too much, I fear, without the help of such crooked vermin. I must see Cary; I must see Salterne; and I suppose, if I am ready to do my duty, I shall learn somehow what it is. Now to sleep; to-morrow up and away to what God sends."

"Come in hither, men," shouted he down the passage, "and sleep here. Haven't you had enough of this villainous sour cider?"

The men came in yawning, and settled themselves to sleep on the floor.

"Where's Yeo?"

No one knew; he had gone out to say his prayers, and had not returned.

"Never mind," said Amyas, who suspected some plot on the old man's part. "He'll take care of himself, I'll warrant him."

"No fear of that, sir;" and the four tars were soon snoring in concert round the fire, while Amyas laid himself on the settle, with his saddle for a pillow.

It was about midnight, when Amyas leaped to his feet, or rather fell upon his back, upsetting saddle, settle, and finally, table, under the notion that ten thousand flying dragons were bursting in the window close to his ear, with howls most fierce and fell. The flying dragons past, however, being only a flock of terror-stricken geese, which flew flapping and screaming round the corner of the house; but the noise which had startled them did not pass; and another minute made it evident that a sharp fight was going on in the courtyard, and that Yeo was hallooing lustily for help.

Out turned the men, sword in hand, burst the back door open, stumbling over pails and pitchers, and into the courtyard, where Yeo, his back against the stable-door, was holding his own manfully with sword and buckler against a dozen men.

Dire and manifold was the screaming; geese screamed, chickens screamed, pigs screamed, donkeys screamed, Mary screamed from an upper window; and to complete the chorus, a flock of plovers, attracted by the noise, wheeled round and round overhead, and added their screams also to that Dutch concert.

The screaming went on, but the fight ceased; for, as Amyas rushed into the yard, the whole party of ruffians took to their heels, and vanished over a low hedge at the other end of the yard.

"Are you hurt, Yeo?"

"Not a scratch, thank Heaven! But I've got two of them, the ringleaders, I have. One of them's against the wall. Your horse did for t'other."

The wounded man was lifted up; a huge ruffian, nearly as big as Amyas himself. Yeo's sword had passed through his body. He groaned and choked for breath.

"Carry him indoors. Where is the other?"

"Dead as a herring, in the straw. Have a care, men, have a care how you go in! the horses are near mad!"

However, the man was brought out after a while. With him all was over. They could feel neither pulse nor breath.

"Carry him in too, poor wretch. And now, Yeo, what is the meaning of all this?"

Yeo's story was soon told. He could not get out of his Puritan head the notion (quite unfounded, of course) that Eustace had meant to steal the horses. He had seen the inn-keeper sneak off at their approach; and expecting some night-attack, he had taken up his lodging for the night in the stable.

As he expected, an attempt was made. The door was opened (how, he could not guess, for he had fastened it inside), and two fellows came in, and began to loose the beasts. Yeo's account was, that he seized the big fellow, who drew a knife on him, and broke loose; the horses, terrified at the scuffle, kicked right and left; one man fell, and the other ran out, calling for help, with Yeo at his heels; "Whereon," said Yeo, "seeing a dozen more on me with clubs and bows, I thought best to shorten the number while I could, ran the rascal through, and stood on my ward; and only just in time I was, what's more; there's two arrows in the house wall, and two or three more in my buckler, which I caught up as I went out, for I had hung it close by the door, you see, sir, to be all ready in case," said the cunning old Philistine-slayer, as they went in after the wounded man.

But hardly had they stumbled through the low doorway into the back-kitchen when a fresh hubbub arose inside—more shouts for help. Amyas ran forward breaking his head against the doorway, and beheld, as soon as he could see for the flashes in his eyes, an old acquaintance, held on each side by a sturdy sailor.

With one arm in the sleeve of his doublet, and the other in a not over spotless shirt; holding up his hose with one hand, and with the other a candle, whereby he had lighted himself to his own confusion; foaming with rage, stood Mr. Evan Morgans, alias Father Parsons, looking, between his confused habiliments and his fiery visage (as Yeo told him to his face), "the very moral of a half-plucked turkey-cock." And behind him, dressed, stood Eustace Leigh.

"We found the maid letting these here two out by the front door," said one of the captors.

"Well, Mr. Parsons," said Amyas; "and what are you about here? A pretty nest of thieves and Jesuits we seem to have routed out this evening."

"About my calling, sir," said Parsons, stoutly. "By your leave, I shall prepare this my wounded lamb for that account to which your man's cruelty has untimely sent him."

The wounded man, who lay upon the floor, heard Parsons' voice, and moaned for the "Patrico."

"You see, sir," said he, pompously, "the sheep know their shepherd's voice."

"The wolves you mean, you hypocritical scoundrel!" said Amyas, who could not contain his disgust. "Let the fellow truss up his points, lads, and do his work. After all, the man is dying."

"The requisite matters, sir, are not at hand," said Parsons, unabashed.

"Eustace, go and fetch his matters for him; you seem to be in all his plots."

Eustace went silently and sullenly.

"What's that fresh noise at the back, now?"

"The maid, sir, a wailing over her uncle; the fellow that we saw sneak away when we came up. It was him the horse killed."

It was true. The wretched host had slipped off on their approach, simply to call the neighboring outlaws to the spoil; and he had been filled with the fruit of his own devices.

"His blood be on his own head," said Amyas.

"I question, sir," said Yeo, in a low voice, "whether some of it will not be on the heads of those proud prelates who go clothed in purple and fine linen, instead of going forth to convert such as he, and then wonder how these Jesuits get hold of them. If they give place to the devil in their sheepfolds, sure he'll come in and lodge there. Look, sir, there's a sight in a gospel land!"

And, indeed, the sight was curious enough. For Parsons was kneeling by the side of the dying man, listening earnestly to the confession which the man sobbed out in his gibberish, between the spasms of his wounded chest. Now and then Parsons shook his head; and when Eustace returned with the holy wafer, and the oil for extreme unction, he asked him, in a low voice, "Ballard, interpret for me."

And Eustace knelt down on the other side of the sufferer, and interpreted his thieves' dialect into Latin; and the dying man held a hand of each, and turned first to one and then to the other stupid eyes,—not without affection, though, and gratitude.

"I can't stand this mummery any longer," said Yeo. "Here's a soul perishing before my eyes, and it's on my conscience to speak a word in season."

"Silence!" whispered Amyas, holding him back by the arm; "he knows them, and he don't know you; they are the first who ever spoke to him as if he had a soul to be saved, and first come, first served; you can do no good. See, the man's face is brightening already."

"But, sir, 'tis a false peace."

"At all events he is confessing his sins, Yeo; and if that's not good for him, and you, and me, what is?"

"Yea, Amen! sir; but this is not to the right person."

"How do you know his words will not go to the right person, after all, though he may not send them there? By heaven! the man is dead!"

It was so. The dark catalogue of brutal deeds had been gasped out; but ere the words of absolution could follow, the head had fallen back, and all was over.

"Confession in extremis is sufficient," said Parsons to Eustace ("Ballard," as Parsons called him, to Amyas's surprise), as he rose. "As for the rest, the intention will be accepted instead of the act."

"The Lord have mercy on his soul!" said Eustace.

"His soul is lost before our very eyes," said Yeo.

"Mind your own business," said Amyas.

"Humph; but I'll tell you, sir, what our business is, if you'll step aside with me. I find that poor fellow that lies dead is none other than the leader of the Gubbings; the king of them, as they dare to call him."

"Well, what of that?"

"Mark my words, sir, if we have not a hundred stout rogues upon us before two hours are out; forgive us they never will; and if we get off with our lives, which I don't much expect, we shall leave our horses behind; for we can hold the house, sir, well enough till morning, but the courtyard we can't, that's certain!"

"We had better march at once, then."

"Think, sir; if they catch us up—as they are sure to do, knowing the country better than we—how will our shot stand their arrows?"

"True, old wisdom; we must keep the road; and we must keep together; and so be a mark for them, while they will be behind every rock and bank; and two or three flights of arrows will do our business for us. Humph! stay, I have a plan." And stepping forward he spoke—

"Eustace, you will be so kind as to go back to your lambs; and tell them, that if they meddle with us cruel wolves again to-night, we are ready and willing to fight to the death, and have plenty of shot and powder at their service. Father Parsons, you will be so kind as to accompany us; it is but fitting that the shepherd should be hostage for his sheep."

"If you carry me off this spot, sir, you carry my corpse only," said Parsons. "I may as well die here as be hanged elsewhere, like my martyred brother Campian."

"If you take him, you must take me too," said Eustace.

"What if we won't?"

"How will you gain by that? you can only leave me here. You cannot make me go to the Gubbings, if I do not choose."

Amyas uttered sotto voce an anathema on Jesuits, Gubbings, and things in general. He was in a great hurry to get to Bideford, and he feared that this business would delay him, as it was, a day or two. He wanted to hang Parsons, he did not want to hang Eustace; and Eustace, he knew, was well aware of that latter fact, and played his game accordingly; but time ran on, and he had to answer sulkily enough:

"Well then; if you, Eustace, will go and give my message to your converts, I will promise to set Mr. Parsons free again before we come to Lydford town; and I advise you, if you have any regard for his life, to see that your eloquence be persuasive enough; for as sure as I am an Englishman, and he none, if the Gubbings attack us, the first bullet that I shall fire at them will have gone through his scoundrelly brains."

Parsons still kicked.

"Very well, then, my merry men all. Tie this gentleman's hands behind his back, get the horses out, and we'll right away up into Dartmoor, find a good high tor, stand our ground there till morning, and then carry him into Okehampton to the nearest justice. If he chooses to delay me in my journey, it is fair that I should make him pay for it."

Whereon Parsons gave in, and being fast tied by his arm to Amyas's saddle, trudged alongside his horse for several weary miles, while Yeo walked by his side, like a friar by a condemned criminal; and in order to keep up his spirits, told him the woful end of Nicholas Saunders the Legate, and how he was found starved to death in a bog.

"And if you wish, sir, to follow in his blessed steps, which I heartily hope you will do, you have only to go over that big cow-backed hill there on your right hand, and down again the other side to Crawmere pool, and there you'll find as pretty a bog to die in as ever Jesuit needed; and your ghost may sit there on a grass tummock, and tell your beads without any one asking for you till the day of judgment; and much good may it do you!"

At which imagination Yeo was actually heard, for the first and last time in this history, to laugh most heartily.

His ho-ho's had scarcely died away when they saw shining under the moon the old tower of Lydford castle.

"Cast the fellow off now," said Amyas.

"Ay, ay, sir!" and Yeo and Simon Evans stopped behind, and did not come up for ten minutes after.

"What have you been about so long?"

"Why, sir," said Evans, "you see the man had a very fair pair of hose on, and a bran-new kersey doublet, very warm-lined; and so, thinking it a pity good clothes should be wasted on such noxious trade, we've just brought them along with us."

"Spoiling the Egyptians," said Yeo as comment.

"And what have you done with the man?"

"Hove him over the bank, sir; he pitched into a big furze-bush, and for aught I know, there he'll bide."

"You rascal, have you killed him?

"Never fear, sir," said Yeo, in his cool fashion. "A Jesuit has as many lives as a cat, and, I believe, rides broomsticks post, like a witch. He would be at Lydford now before us, if his master Satan had any business for him there."

Leaving on their left Lydford and its ill-omened castle (which, a century after, was one of the principal scenes of Judge Jeffreys's cruelty), Amyas and his party trudged on through the mire toward Okehampton till sunrise; and ere the vapors had lifted from the mountain tops, they were descending the long slopes from Sourton down, while Yestor and Amicombe slept steep and black beneath their misty pall; and roaring far below unseen,

The voice of the stream recalled these words to Amyas's mind. The nymph of Torridge had spoken them upon the day of his triumph. He recollected, too, his vexation on that day at not seeing Rose Salterne. Why, he had never seen her since. Never seen her now for six years and more! Of her ripened beauty he knew only by hearsay; she was still to him the lovely fifteen years' girl for whose sake he had smitten the Barnstaple draper over the quay. What a chain of petty accidents had kept them from meeting, though so often within a mile of each other! "And what a lucky one!" said practical old Amyas to himself. "If I had seen her as she is now, I might have loved her as Frank does—poor Frank! what will he say? What does he say, for he must know it already? And what ought I to say—to do rather, for talking is no use on this side the grave, nor on the other either, I expect!" And then he asked himself whether his old oath meant nothing or something; whether it was a mere tavern frolic, or a sacred duty. And he held, the more that he looked at it, that it meant the latter.

But what could he do? He had nothing on earth but his sword, so he could not travel to find her. After all, she might not be gone far. Perhaps not gone at all. It might be a mistake, an exaggerated scandal. He would hope so. And yet it was evident that there had been some passages between her and Don Guzman. Eustace's mysterious words about the promise at Lundy proved that. The villain! He had felt all along that he was a villain; but just the one to win a woman's heart, too. Frank had been away—all the Brotherhood away. What a fool he had been, to turn the wolf loose into the sheepfold! And yet who would have dreamed of it? . . .

"At all events," said Amyas, trying to comfort himself, "I need not complain. I have lost nothing. I stood no more chance of her against Frank than I should have stood against the Don. So there is no use for me to cry about the matter." And he tried to hum a tune concerning the general frailty of women, but nevertheless, like Sir Hugh, felt that "he had a great disposition to cry."

He never had expected to win her, and yet it seemed bitter to know that she was lost to him forever. It was not so easy for a heart of his make to toss away the image of a first love; and all the less easy because that image was stained and ruined.

"Curses on the man who had done that deed! I will yet have his heart's blood somehow, if I go round the world again to find him. If there's no law for it on earth, there's law in heaven, or I'm much mistaken."

With which determination he rode into the ugly, dirty, and stupid town of Okehampton, with which fallen man (by some strange perversity) has chosen to defile one of the loveliest sites in the pleasant land of Devon. And heartily did Amyas abuse the old town that day; for he was detained there, as he expected, full three hours, while the Justice Shallow of the place was sent for from his farm (whither he had gone at sunrise, after the early-rising fashion of those days) to take Yeo's deposition concerning last night's affray. Moreover, when Shallow came, he refused to take the depositions, because they ought to have been made before a brother Shallow at Lydford; and in the wrangling which ensued, was very near finding out what Amyas (fearing fresh loss of time and worse evils beside) had commanded to be concealed, namely, the presence of Jesuits in that Moorland Utopia. Then, in broadest Devon—

"And do you call this Christian conduct, sir, to set a quiet man like me upon they Gubbings, as if I was going to risk my precious life—no, nor ever a constable to Okehampton neither? Let Lydfor' men mind Lydfor' roogs, and by Lydfor' law if they will, hang first and try after; but as for me, I've rade my Bible, and 'He that meddleth with strife is like him that taketh a dog by the ears.' So if you choose to sit down and ate your breakfast with me, well and good: but depositions I'll have none. If your man is enquired for, you'll be answerable for his appearing, in course; but I expect mortally" (with a wink), "you wain't hear much more of the matter from any hand. 'Leave well alone is a good rule, but leave ill alone is a better.'—So we says round about here; and so you'll say, captain, when you be so old as I."

So Amyas sat down and ate his breakfast, and went on afterwards a long and weary day's journey, till he saw at last beneath him the broad shining river, and the long bridge, and the white houses piled up the hill-side; and beyond, over Raleigh downs, the dear old tower of Northam Church.

Alas! Northam was altogether a desert to him then; and Bideford, as it turned out, hardly less so. For when he rode up to Sir Richard's door, he found that the good knight was still in Ireland, and Lady Grenville at Stow. Whereupon he rode back again down the High Street to that same bow-windowed Ship Tavern where the Brotherhood of the Rose made their vow, and settled himself in the very room where they had supped.

"Ah! Mr. Leigh—Captain Leigh now, I beg pardon," quoth mine host. "Bideford is an empty place now-a-days, and nothing stirring, sir. What with Sir Richard to Ireland, and Sir John to London, and all the young gentlemen to the wars, there's no one to buy good liquor, and no one to court the young ladies, neither. Sack, sir? I hope so. I haven't brewed a gallon of it this fortnight, if you'll believe me; ale, sir, and aqua vitae, and such low-bred trade, is all I draw now-a-days. Try a pint of sherry, sir, now, to give you an appetite. You mind my sherry of old? Jane!

Sherry and sugar, quick, while I pull off the captain's boots."

Amyas sat weary and sad, while the innkeeper chattered on.

"Ah, sir! two or three like you would set the young ladies all alive again. By-the-by, there's been strange doings among them since you were here last. You mind Mistress Salterne!"

"For God's sake, don't let us have that story, man! I heard enough of it at Plymouth!" said Amyas, in so disturbed a tone that mine host looked up, and said to himself—

"Ah, poor young gentleman, he's one of the hard-hit ones."

"How is the old man?" asked Amyas, after a pause.

"Bears it well enough, sir; but a changed man. Never speaks to a soul, if he can help it. Some folk say he's not right in his head; or turned miser, or somewhat, and takes naught but bread and water, and sits up all night in the room as was hers, turning over her garments. Heaven knows what's on his mind—they do say he was over hard on her, and that drove her to it. All I know is, he has never been in here for a drop of liquor (and he came as regular every evening as the town clock, sir) since she went, except a ten days ago, and then he met young Mr. Cary at the door, and I heard him ask Mr. Cary when you would be home, sir."

"Put on my boots again. I'll go and see him."

"Bless you, sir! What, without your sack?"

"Drink it yourself, man."

"But you wouldn't go out again this time o' night on an empty stomach, now?"

"Fill my men's stomachs for them, and never mind mine. It's market-day, is it not? Send out, and see whether Mr. Cary is still in town;" and Amyas strode out, and along the quay to Bridgeland Street, and knocked at Mr. Salterne's door.

Salterne himself opened it, with his usual stern courtesy.

"I saw you coming up the street, sir. I have been expecting this honor from you for some time past. I dreamt of you only last night, and many a night before that too. Welcome, sir, into a lonely house. I trust the good knight your general is well."

"The good knight my general is with God who made him, Mr. Salterne."

"Dead, sir?"

"Foundered at sea on our way home; and the Delight lost too."

"Humph!" growled Salterne, after a minute's silence. "I had a venture in her. I suppose it's gone. No matter—I can afford it, sir, and more, I trust. And he was three years younger than I! And Draper Heard was buried yesterday, five years younger.—How is it that every one can die, except me? Come in, sir, come in; I have forgotten my manners."

And he led Amyas into his parlor, and called to the apprentices to run one way, and to the cook to run another.

"You must not trouble yourself to get me supper, indeed."

"I must though, sir, and the best of wine too; and old Salterne had a good tap of Alicant in old time, old time, old time, sir! and you must drink it now, whether he does or not!" and out he bustled.

Amyas sat still, wondering what was coming next, and puzzled at the sudden hilarity of the man, as well as his hospitality, so different from what the innkeeper had led him to expect.

In a minute more one of the apprentices came in to lay the cloth, and Amyas questioned him about his master.

"Thank the Lord that you are come, sir," said the lad.

"Why, then?"

"Because there'll be a chance of us poor fellows getting a little broken meat. We'm half-starved this three months—bread and dripping, bread and dripping, oh dear, sir! And now he's sent out to the inn for chickens, and game, and salads, and all that money can buy, and down in the cellar haling out the best of wine."—And the lad smacked his lips audibly at the thought.

"Is he out of his mind?"

"I can't tell; he saith as how he must save mun's money now-a-days; for he've a got a great venture on hand: but what a be he tell'th no man. They call'th mun 'bread and dripping' now, sir, all town over," said the prentice, confidentially, to Amyas.

"They do, do they, sirrah! Then they will call me bread and no dripping to-morrow!" and old Salterne, entering from behind, made a dash at the poor fellow's ears: but luckily thought better of it, having a couple of bottles in each hand.

"My dear sir," said Amyas, "you don't mean us to drink all that wine?"

"Why not, sir?" answered Salterne, in a grim, half-sneering tone, thrusting out his square-grizzled beard and chin. "Why not, sir? why should I not make merry when I have the honor of a noble captain in my house? one who has sailed the seas, sir, and cut Spaniards' throats; and may cut them again too; eh, sir? Boy, where's the kettle and the sugar?"

"What on earth is the man at?" quoth Amyas to himself—"flattering me, or laughing at me?"

"Yes," he ran on, half to himself, in a deliberate tone, evidently intending to hint more than he said, as he began brewing the sack—in plain English, hot negus; "Yes, bread and dripping for those who can't fight Spaniards; but the best that money can buy for those who can. I heard of you at Smerwick, sir—Yes, bread and dripping for me too—I can't fight Spaniards: but for such as you. Look here, sir; I should like to feed a crew of such up, as you'd feed a main of fighting-cocks, and then start them with a pair of Sheffield spurs a-piece—you've a good one there to your side, sir: but don't you think a man might carry two now, and fight as they say those Chineses do, a sword to each hand? You could kill more that way, Captain Leigh, I reckon?"

Amyas half laughed.

"One will do, Mr. Salterne, if one is quick enough with it."

"Humph!—Ah—No use being in a hurry. I haven't been in a hurry. No—I waited for you; and here you are and welcome, sir! Here comes supper, a light matter, sir, you see. A capon and a brace of partridges. I had no time to feast you as you deserve."

And so he ran on all supper-time, hardly allowing Amyas to get a word in edge-ways; but heaping him with coarse flattery, and urging him to drink, till after the cloth was drawn, and the two left alone, he grew so outrageous that Amyas was forced to take him to task good-humoredly.

"Now, my dear sir, you have feasted me royally, and better far than I deserve, but why will you go about to make me drunk twice over, first with vainglory and then with wine?"

Salterne looked at him a while fixedly, and then, sticking out his chin—"Because, Captain Leigh, I am a man who has all his life tried the crooked road first, and found the straight one the safer after all."

"Eh, sir? That is a strange speech for one who bears the character of the most upright man in Bideford."

"Humph. So I thought myself once, sir; and well I have proved it. But I'll be plain with you, sir. You've heard how—how I've fared since you saw me last?"

Amyas nodded his head.

"I thought so. Shame rides post. Now then, Captain Leigh, listen to me. I, being a plain man and a burgher, and one that never drew iron in my life except to mend a pen, ask you, being a gentleman and a captain and a man of honor, with a weapon to your side, and harness to your back—what would you do in my place?"

"Humph!" said Amyas, "that would very much depend on whether 'my place' was my own fault or not."

"And what if it were, sir? What if all that the charitable folks of Bideford—(Heaven reward them for their tender mercies!)—have been telling you in the last hour be true, sir,—true! and yet not half the truth?"

Amyas gave a start.

"Ah, you shrink from me! Of course a man is too righteous to forgive those who repent, though God is not."

"God knows, sir—"

"Yes, sir, God does know—all; and you shall know a little—as much as I can tell—or you understand. Come upstairs with me, sir, as you'll drink no more; I have a liking for you. I have watched you from your boyhood, and I can trust you, and I'll show you what I never showed to mortal man but one."

And, taking up a candle, he led the way upstairs, while Amyas followed wondering.

He stopped at a door, and unlocked it.

"There, come in. Those shutters have not been opened since she—" and the old man was silent.

Amyas looked round the room. It was a low wainscoted room, such as one sees in old houses: everything was in the most perfect neatness. The snow-white sheets on the bed were turned down as if ready for an occupant. There were books arranged on the shelves, fresh flowers on the table; the dressing-table had all its woman's mundus of pins, and rings, and brushes; even the dressing-gown lay over the chair-back. Everything was evidently just as it had been left.

"This was her room, sir," whispered the old man.

Amyas nodded silently, and half drew back.

"You need not be modest about entering it now, sir," whispered he, with a sort of sneer. "There has been no frail flesh and blood in it for many a day."

Amyas sighed.

"I sweep it out myself every morning, and keep all tidy. See here!" and he pulled open a drawer. "Here are all her gowns, and there are her hoods; and there—I know 'em all by heart now, and the place of every one. And there, sir—"

And he opened a cupboard, where lay in rows all Rose's dolls, and the worn-out playthings of her childhood.

"That's the pleasantest place of all in the room to me," said he, whispering still, "for it minds me of when—and maybe, she may become a little child once more, sir; it's written in the Scripture, you know—"

"Amen!" said Amyas, who felt, to his own wonder, a big tear stealing down each cheek.

"And now," he whispered, "one thing more. Look here!"—and pulling out a key, he unlocked a chest, and lifted up tray after tray of necklaces and jewels, furs, lawns, cloth of gold. "Look there! Two thousand pound won't buy that chest. Twenty years have I been getting those things together. That's the cream of many a Levant voyage, and East Indian voyage, and West Indian voyage. My Lady Bath can't match those pearls in her grand house at Tawstock; I got 'em from a Genoese, though, and paid for 'em. Look at that embroidered lawn! There's not such a piece in London; no, nor in Alexandria, I'll warrant; nor short of Calicut, where it came from. . . . Look here again, there's a golden cup! I bought that of one that was out with Pizarro in Peru. And look here, again!"—and the old man gloated over the treasure.

"And whom do you think I kept all these for? These were for her wedding-day—for her wedding-day. For your wedding-day, if you'd been minded, sir! Yes, yours, sir! And yet, I believe, I was so ambitious that I would not have let her marry under an earl, all the while I was pretending to be too proud to throw her at the head of a squire's son. Ah, well! There was my idol, sir. I made her mad, I pampered her up with gewgaws and vanity; and then, because my idol was just what I had made her, I turned again and rent her.

"And now," said he, pointing to the open chest, "that was what I meant; and that" (pointing to the empty bed) "was what God meant. Never mind. Come downstairs and finish your wine. I see you don't care about it all. Why should you! you are not her father, and you may thank God you are not. Go, and be merry while you can, young sir! . . . And yet, all this might have been yours. And—but I don't suppose you are one to be won by money—but all this may be yours still, and twenty thousand pounds to boot."

"I want no money, sir, but what I can earn with my own sword."

"Earn my money, then!"

"What on earth do you want of me!"

"To keep your oath," said Salterne, clutching his arm, and looking up into his face with searching eyes.

"My oath! How did you know that I had one?"

"Ah! you were well ashamed of it, I suppose, next day! A drunken frolic all about a poor merchant's daughter! But there is nothing hidden that shall not be revealed, nor done in the closet that is not proclaimed on the house-tops."

"Ashamed of it, sir, I never was: but I have a right to ask how you came to know it?"

"What if a poor fat squinny rogue, a low-born fellow even as I am, whom you had baffled and made a laughing-stock, had come to me in my loneliness and sworn before God that if you honorable gentlemen would not keep your words, he the clown would?"

"John Brimblecombe?"

"And what if I had brought him where I have brought you, and shown him what I have shown you, and, instead of standing as stiff as any Spaniard, as you do, he had thrown himself on his knees by that bedside, and wept and prayed, sir, till he opened my hard heart for the first and last time, and I fell down on my sinful knees and wept and prayed by him?"

"I am not given to weeping, Mr. Salterne," said Amyas; "and as for praying, I don't know yet what I have to pray for, on her account: my business is to work. Show me what I can do; and when you have done that, it will be full time to upbraid me with not doing it."

"You can cut that fellow's throat."

"It will take a long arm to reach him."

"I suppose it is as easy to sail to the Spanish Main as it was to sail round the world."

"My good sir," said Amyas, "I have at this moment no more worldly goods than my clothes and my sword, so how to sail to the Spanish Main, I don't quite see."

"And do you suppose, sir, that I should hint to you of such a voyage if I meant you to be at the charge of it? No, sir; if you want two thousand pounds, or five, to fit a ship, take it! Take it, sir! I hoarded money for my child: and now I will spend it to avenge her."

Amyas was silent for a while; the old man still held his arm, still looked up steadfastly and fiercely in his face.

"Bring me home that man's head, and take ship, prizes—all! Keep the gain, sir, and give me the revenge!"

"Gain? Do you think I need bribing, sir? What kept me silent was the thought of my mother. I dare not go without her leave."

Salterne made a gesture of impatience.

"I dare not, sir; I must obey my parent, whatever else I do."

"Humph!" said he. "If others had obeyed theirs as well!—But you are right, Captain Leigh, right. You will prosper, whoever else does not. Now, sir, good-night, if you will let me be the first to say so. My old eyes grow heavy early now-a-days. Perhaps it's old age, perhaps it's sorrow."

So Amyas departed to the inn, and there, to his great joy, found Cary waiting for him, from whom he learnt details, which must be kept for another chapter, and which I shall tell, for convenience' sake, in my own words and not in his.

CHAPTER XV: HOW MR. JOHN BRIMBLECOMBE UNDERSTOOD THE NATURE OF AN OATH

About six weeks after the duel, the miller at Stow had come up to the great house in much tribulation, to borrow the bloodhounds. Rose Salterne had vanished in the night, no man knew whither.

Sir Richard was in Bideford: but the old steward took on himself to send for the keepers, and down went the serving-men to the mill with all the idle lads of the parish at their heels, thinking a maiden-hunt very good sport; and of course taking a view of the case as favorable as possible to Rose.

They reviled the miller and his wife roundly for hard-hearted old heathens; and had no doubt that they had driven the poor maid to throw herself over cliff, or drown herself in the sea; while all the women of Stow, on the other hand, were of unanimous opinion that the hussy had "gone off" with some bad fellow; and that pride was sure to have a fall, and so forth.

The facts of the case were, that all Rose's trinkets were left behind, so that she had at least gone off honestly; and nothing seemed to be missing, but some of her linen, which old Anthony the steward broadly hinted was likely to be found in other people's boxes. The only trace was a little footmark under her bedroom window. On that the bloodhound was laid (of course in leash), and after a premonitory whimper, lifted up his mighty voice, and started bell-mouthed through the garden gate, and up the lane, towing behind him the panting keeper, till they reached the downs above, and went straight away for Marslandmouth, where the whole posse comitatus pulled up breathless at the door of Lucy Passmore.

Lucy, as perhaps I should have said before, was now a widow, and found her widowhood not altogether contrary to her interest. Her augury about her old man had been fulfilled; he had never returned since the night on which he put to sea with Eustace and the Jesuits.

as many of them, at least, as were not required for purposes of business; and then determined to prevent suspicion by a bold move; she started off to Stow, and told Lady Grenville a most pathetic tale: how her husband had gone out to pollock fishing, and never returned: but how she had heard horsemen gallop past her window in the dead of night, and was sure they must have been the Jesuits, and that they had carried off her old man by main force, and probably, after making use of his services, had killed and salted him down for provision on their voyage back to the Pope at Rome; after which she ended by entreating protection against those "Popish skulkers up to Chapel," who were sworn to do her a mischief; and by an appeal to Lady Grenville's sense of justice, as to whether the queen ought not to allow her a pension, for having had her heart's love turned into a sainted martyr by the hands of idolatrous traitors.

Lady Grenville (who had a great opinion of Lucy's medical skill, and always sent for her if one of the children had a "housty," i. e. sore throat) went forth and pleaded the case before Sir Richard with such effect, that Lucy was on the whole better off than ever for the next two or three years. But now—what had she to do with Rose's disappearance? and, indeed, where was she herself? Her door was fast; and round it her flock of goats stood, crying in vain for her to come and milk them; while from the down above, her donkeys, wandering at their own sweet will, answered the bay of the bloodhound with a burst of harmony.

"They'm laughing at us, keper, they neddies; sure enough, we'm lost our labor here."

But the bloodhound, after working about the door a while, turned down the glen, and never stopped till he reached the margin of the sea.

"They'm taken water. Let's go back, and rout out the old witch's house."

"'Tis just like that old Lucy, to lock a poor maid into shame."

And returning, they attacked the cottage, and by a general plebiscitum, ransacked the little dwelling, partly in indignation, and partly, if the truth be told, in the hope of plunder; but plunder there was none. Lucy had decamped with all her movable wealth, saving the huge black cat among the embers, who at the sight of the bloodhound vanished up the chimney (some said with a strong smell of brimstone), and being viewed outside, was chased into the woods, where she lived, I doubt not, many happy years, a scourge to all the rabbits of the glen.

The goats and donkeys were driven off up to Stow; and the mob returned, a little ashamed of themselves when their brief wrath was past; and a little afraid, too, of what Sir Richard might say.

He, when he returned, sold the donkeys and goats, and gave the money to the poor, promising to refund the same, if Lucy returned and gave herself up to justice. But Lucy did not return; and her cottage, from which the neighbors shrank as from a haunted place, remained as she had left it, and crumbled slowly down to four fern-covered walls, past which the little stream went murmuring on from pool to pool—the only voice, for many a year to come, which broke the silence of that lonely glen.

A few days afterwards, Sir Richard, on his way from Bideford to Stow, looked in at Clovelly Court, and mentioned, with a "by the by," news which made Will Cary leap from his seat almost to the ceiling. What it was we know already.

"And there is no clue?" asked old Cary; for his son was speechless.

"Only this; I hear that some fellow prowling about the cliffs that night saw a pinnace running for Lundy."

Will rose, and went hastily out of the room.

In half an hour he and three or four armed servants were on board a trawling-skiff, and away to Lundy. He did not return for three days, and then brought news: that an elderly man, seemingly a foreigner, had been lodging for some months past in a part of the ruined Moresco Castle, which was tenanted by one John Braund; that a few weeks since a younger man, a foreigner also, had joined him from on board a ship: the ship a Flushinger, or Easterling of some sort. The ship came and went more than once; and the young man in her. A few days since, a lady and her maid, a stout woman, came with him up to the castle, and talked with the elder man a long while in secret; abode there all night; and then all three sailed in the morning. The fishermen on the beach had heard the young man call the other father. He was a very still man, much as a mass-priest might be. More they did not know, or did not choose to know.

Whereon old Cary and Sir Richard sent Will on a second trip with the parish constable of

Hartland (in which huge parish, for its sins, is situate the Isle of Lundy, ten miles out at sea); who returned with the body of the hapless John Braund, farmer, fisherman, smuggler, etc.; which worthy, after much fruitless examination (wherein examinate was afflicted with extreme deafness and loss of memory), departed to Exeter gaol, on a charge of "harboring priests, Jesuits, gipsies, and other suspect and traitorous persons."

 Poor John Braund, whose motive for entertaining the said ugly customers had probably been not treason, but a wife, seven children, and arrears of rent, did not thrive under the change from the pure air of Lundy to the pestiferous one of Exeter gaol, made infamous, but two years after (if I recollect right), by a "black assizes," nearly as fatal as that more notorious one at Oxford; for in it, "whether by the stench of the prisoners, or by a stream of foul air," judge, jury, counsel, and bystanders, numbering among them many members of the best families in Devon, sickened in court, and died miserably within a few days.

 John Braund, then, took the gaol-fever in a week, and died raving in that noisome den: his secret, if he had one, perished with him, and nothing but vague suspicion was left as to Rose Salterne's fate. That she had gone off with the Spaniard, few doubted; but whither, and in what character? On that last subject, be sure, no mercy was shown to her by many a Bideford dame, who had hated the poor girl simply for her beauty; and by many a country lady, who had "always expected that the girl would be brought to ruin by the absurd notice, beyond what her station had a right to, which was taken of her," while every young maiden aspired to fill the throne which Rose had abdicated. So that, on the whole, Bideford considered itself as going on as well without poor Rose as it had done with her, or even better. And though she lingered in some hearts still as a fair dream, the business and the bustle of each day soon swept that dream away, and her place knew her no more.

 And Will Cary?

 He was for a while like a man distracted. He heaped himself with all manner of superfluous reproaches, for having (as he said) first brought the Rose into disgrace, and then driven her into the arms of the Spaniard; while St. Leger, who was a sensible man enough, tried in vain to persuade him that the fault was not his at all; that the two must have been attached to each other long before the quarrel; that it must have ended so, sooner or later; that old Salterne's harshness, rather than Cary's wrath, had hastened the catastrophe; and finally, that the Rose and her fortunes were, now that she had eloped with a Spaniard, not worth troubling their heads about. Poor Will would not be so comforted. He wrote off to Frank at Whitehall, telling him the whole truth, calling himself all fools and villains, and entreating Frank's forgiveness; to which he received an answer, in which Frank said that Will had no reason to accuse himself; that these strange attachments were due to a synastria, or sympathy of the stars, which ruled the destinies of each person, to fight against which was to fight against the heavens themselves; that he, as a brother of the Rose, was bound to believe, nay, to assert at the sword's point if need were, that the incomparable Rose of Torridge could make none but a worthy and virtuous choice; and that to the man whom she had honored by her affection was due on their part, Spaniard and Papist though he might be, all friendship, worship, and loyal faith for evermore.

And honest Will took it all for gospel, little dreaming what agony of despair, what fearful suspicions, what bitter prayers, this letter had cost to the gentle heart of Francis Leigh.

He showed the letter triumphantly to St. Leger; and he was quite wise enough to gainsay no word of it, at least aloud; but quite wise enough, also, to believe in secret that Frank looked on the matter in quite a different light; however, he contented himself with saying:

"The man is an angel as his mother is!" and there the matter dropped for a few days, till one came forward who had no mind to let it drop, and that was Jack Brimblecombe, now curate of Hartland town, and "passing rich on forty pounds a year.

"I hope no offence, Mr. William; but when are you and the rest going after—after her?" The name stuck in his throat.

Cary was taken aback.

"What's that to thee, Catiline the blood-drinker?" asked he, trying to laugh it off.

"What? Don't laugh at me, sir, for it's no laughing matter. I drank that night naught worse, I expect, than red wine. Whatever it was, we swore our oaths, Mr. Cary; and oaths are oaths, say I."

"Of course, Jack, of course; but to go to look for her—and when we've found her, cut her lover's throat. Absurd, Jack, even if she were worth looking for, or his throat worth cutting. Tut, tut, tut—"

But Jack looked steadfastly in his face, and after some silence:

How far is it to the Caracas, then, sir?"

"What is that to thee, man?"

"Why, he was made governor thereof, I hear; so that would be the place to find her?"

"You don't mean to go thither to seek her?" shouted Cary, forcing a laugh.

"That depends on whether I can go, sir; but if I can scrape the money together, or get a berth on board some ship, why, God's will must be done."

Will looked at him, to see if he had been drinking, or gone mad; but the little pigs' eyes were both sane and sober.

Will knew no answer. To laugh at the poor fellow was easy enough; to deny that he was right, that he was a hero and cavalier, outdoing romance itself in faithfulness, not so easy; and Cary, in the first impulse, wished him at the bottom of the bay for shaming him. Of course, his own plan of letting ill alone was the rational, prudent, irreproachable plan, and just what any gentleman in his senses would have done; but here was a vulgar, fat curate, out of his senses, determined not to let ill alone, but to do something, as Cary felt in his heart, of a far diviner stamp.

"Well," said Jack, in his stupid steadfast way, "it's a very bad look-out; but mother's pretty well off, if father dies, and the maidens are stout wenches enough, and will make tidy servants, please the Lord. And you'll see that they come to no harm, Mr. William, for old acquaintance' sake, if I never come back."

Cary was silent with amazement.

"And, Mr. William, you know me for an honest man, I hope. Will you lend me a five pound, and take my books in pawn for them, just to help me out?"

"Are you mad, or in a dream? You will never find her!"

"That's no reason why I shouldn't do my duty in looking for her, Mr. William."

"But, my good fellow, even if you get to the Indies, you will be clapt into the Inquisition, and burnt alive, as sure as your name is Jack."

"I know that," said he, in a doleful tone; "and a sore struggle of the flesh I have had about it; for I am a great coward, Mr. William, a dirty coward, and always was, as you know: but maybe the Lord will take care of me, as He does of little children and drunken men; and if not, Mr. Will, I'd sooner burn, and have it over, than go on this way any longer, I would!" and Jack burst out blubbering.

"What way, my dear old lad?" said Will, softened as he well might be.

"Why, not—not to know whether—whether—whether she's married to him or not—her that I looked up to as an angel of God, as pure as the light of day; and knew she was too good for a poor pot-head like me; and prayed for her every night, God knows, that she might marry a king, if there was one fit for her—and I not to know whether she's living in sin or not, Mr. William.—It's more than I can bear, and there's an end of it. And if she is married to him they keep no faith with heretics; they can dissolve the marriage, or make away with her into the Inquisition; burn her, Mr. Cary, as soon as burn me, the devils incarnate!"

Cary shuddered; the fact, true and palpable as it was, had never struck him before.

"Yes! or make her deny her God by torments, if she hasn't done it already for love to that—I know how love will make a body sell his soul, for I've been in love. Don't you laugh at me, Mr. Will, or I shall go mad!"

"God knows, I was never less inclined to laugh at you in my life, my brave old Jack."

"Is it so, then? Bless you for that word!" and Jack held out his hand. "But what will become of my soul, after my oath, if I don't seek her out, just to speak to her, to warn her, for God's sake, even if it did no good; just to set before her the Lord's curse on idolatry and Antichrist, and those who deny Him for the sake of any creature, though I can't think he would be hard on her,—for who could? But I must speak all the same. The Lord has laid the burden on me, and done it must be. God help me!"

"Jack," said Cary, "if this is your duty, it is others'."

"No, sir, I don't say that; you're a layman, but I am a deacon, and the chaplain of you all, and sworn to seek out Christ's sheep scattered up and down this naughty world, and that innocent lamb first of all."

"You have sheep at Hartland, Jack, already."

"There's plenty better than I will tend them, when I am gone; but none that will tend her, because none love her like me, and they won't venture. Who will? It can't be expected, and no shame to them?"

"I wonder what Amyas Leigh would say to all this, if he were at home?"

"Say? He'd do. He isn't one for talking. He'd go through fire and water for her, you trust him, Will Cary; and call me an ass if he won't."

"Will you wait, then, till he comes back, and ask him?"

"He may not be back for a year and more."

"Hear reason, Jack. If you will wait like a rational and patient man, instead of rushing blindfold on your ruin, something may be done."

"You think so!"

"I cannot promise; but—"

"But promise me one thing. Do you tell Mr. Frank what I say—or rather, I'll warrant, if I knew the truth, he has said the very same thing himself already."

"You are out there, old man; for here is his own handwriting."

Jack read the letter and sighed bitterly. "Well, I did take him for another guess sort of fine gentleman. Still, if my duty isn't his, it's mine all the same. I judge no man; but I go, Mr. Cary."

"But go you shall not till Amyas returns. As I live, I will tell your father, Jack, unless you promise; and you dare not disobey him."

"I don't know even that, for conscience' sake," said Jack, doubtfully.

"At least, you stay and dine here, old fellow, and we will settle whether you are to break the fifth commandment or not, over good brewed sack."

Now a good dinner was (as we know) what Jack loved, and loved too oft in vain; so he submitted for the nonce, and Cary thought, ere he went, that he had talked him pretty well round. At least he went home, and was seen no more for a week.

But at the end of that time he returned, and said with a joyful voice—

"I have settled all, Mr. Will. The parson of Welcombe will serve my church for two Sundays, and I am away for London town, to speak to Mr. Frank."

"To London? How wilt get there?"

"On Shanks his mare," said Jack, pointing to his bandy legs. "But I expect I can get a lift on board of a coaster so far as Bristol, and it's no way on to signify, I hear."

Cary tried in vain to dissuade him; and then forced on him a small loan, with which away went Jack, and Cary heard no more of him for three weeks.

At last he walked into Clovelly Court again just before supper-time, thin and leg-weary, and sat himself down among the serving-men till Will appeared.

Will took him up above the salt, and made much of him (which indeed the honest fellow much needed), and after supper asked him in private how he had sped.

"I have learnt a lesson, Mr. William. I've learnt that there is one on earth loves her better than I, if she had but had the wit to have taken him."

"But what says he of going to seek her?"

"He says what I say, Go! and he says what you say, Wait."

"Go? Impossible! How can that agree with his letter?"

"That's no concern of mine. Of course, being nearer heaven than I am, he sees clearer what he should say and do than I can see for him. Oh, Mr. Will, that's not a man, he's an angel of God; but he's dying, Mr. Will."

"Dying?"

"Yes, faith, of love for her. I can see it in his eyes, and hear it in his voice; but I am of tougher hide and stiffer clay, and so you see I can't die even if I tried. But I'll obey my betters, and wait."

And so Jack went home to his parish that very evening, weary as he was, in spite of all entreaties to pass the night at Clovelly. But he had left behind him thoughts in Cary's mind, which gave their owner no rest by day or night, till the touch of a seeming accident made them all start suddenly into shape, as a touch of the freezing water covers it in an instant with crystals of ice.

He was lounging (so he told Amyas) one murky day on Bideford quay, when up came Mr. Salterne. Cary had shunned him of late, partly from delicacy, partly from dislike of his supposed hard-heartedness. But this time they happened to meet full; and Cary could not pass without speaking to him.

"Well, Mr. Salterne, and how goes on the shipping trade?"

"Well enough, sir, if some of you young gentlemen would but follow Mr. Leigh's example, and go forth to find us stay-at-homes new markets for our ware."

"What? you want to be rid of us, eh?"

"I don't know why I should, sir. We sha'n't cross each other now, sir, whatever might have been once. But if I were you, I should be in the Indies about now, if I were not fighting the queen's battles nearer home."

"In the Indies? I should make but a poor hand of Drake's trade." And so the conversation dropped; but Cary did not forget the hint.

"So, lad, to make an end of a long story," said he to Amyas; "if you are minded to take the old man's offer, so am I: and Westward-ho with you, come foul come fair."

"It will be but a wild-goose chase, Will."

"If she is with him, we shall find her at La Guayra. If she is not, and the villain has cast her off down the wind, that will be only an additional reason for making an example of him."

"And if neither of them are there, Will, the Plate-fleets will be; so it will be our own shame if we come home empty-handed. But will your father let you run such a risk?"

"My father!" said Cary, laughing. "He has just now so good hope of a long string of little Carys to fill my place, that he will be in no lack of an heir, come what will."

"Little Carys?"

"I tell you truth. I think he must have had a sly sup of that fountain of perpetual youth, which our friend Don Guzman's grandfather went to seek in Florida; for some twelvemonth since, he must needs marry a tenant's buxom daughter; and Mistress Abishag Jewell has brought him one fat baby already. So I shall go, back to Ireland, or with you: but somewhere. I can't abide the thing's squalling, any more than I can seeing Mistress Abishag sitting in my poor dear mother's place, and informing me every other day that she is come of an illustrious house, because she is (or is not) third cousin seven times removed to my father's old friend, Bishop Jewell of glorious memory. I had three-parts of a quarrel with the dear old man the other day; for after one of her peacock-bouts, I couldn't for the life of me help saying, that as the Bishop had written an Apology for the people of England, my father had better conjure up his ghost to write an apology for him, and head it, 'Why green heads should grow on gray shoulders.'"

"You impudent villain! And what did he say?"

Laughed till he cried again, and told me if I did not like it I might leave it; which is just what I intend to do. Only mind, if we go, we must needs take Jack Brimblecombe with us, or he will surely heave himself over Harty Point, and his ghost will haunt us to our dying day."

"Jack shall go. None deserves it better."

After which there was a long consultation on practical matters, and it was concluded that Amyas should go up to London and sound Frank and his mother before any further steps were taken. The other brethren of the Rose were scattered far and wide, each at his post, and St. Leger had returned to his uncle, so that it would be unfair to them, as well as a considerable delay, to demand of them any fulfilment of their vow. And, as Amyas sagely remarked, "Too many cooks spoil the broth, and half-a-dozen gentlemen aboard one ship are as bad as two kings of Brentford."

With which maxim he departed next morning for London, leaving Yeo with Cary.

CHAPTER XVI: THE MOST CHIVALROUS ADVENTURE OF THE GOOD SHIP ROSE

Let us take boat, as Amyas did, at Whitehall-stairs, and slip down ahead of him under old London Bridge, and so to Deptford Creek, where remains, as it were embalmed, the famous ship Pelican, in which Drake had sailed round the world. There she stands, drawn up high and dry upon the sedgy bank of Thames, like an old warrior resting after his toil. Nailed upon her mainmast are epigrams and verses in honor of her and of her captain, three of which, by the Winchester scholar, Camden gives in his History; and Elizabeth's self consecrated her solemnly, and having banqueted on board, there and then honored Drake with the dignity of knighthood. "At which time a bridge of planks, by which they came on board, broke under the press of people, and fell down with a hundred men upon it, who, notwithstanding, had none of them any harm. So as that ship may seem to have been built under a lucky planet."

There she has remained since as a show, and moreover as a sort of dining-hall for jovial parties from the city; one of which would seem to be on board this afternoon, to judge from the flags which bedizen the masts, the sounds of revelry and savory steams which issue from those windows which once were portholes, and the rushing to and fro along the river brink, and across that lucky bridge, of white-aproned waiters from the neighboring Pelican Inn. A great feast is evidently toward, for with those white-aproned waiters are gay serving men, wearing on their shoulders the city-badge. The lord mayor is giving a dinner to certain gentlemen of the Leicester house party, who are interested in foreign discoveries; and what place so fit for such a feast as the Pelican itself?

Look at the men all round; a nobler company you will seldom see. Especially too, if you be Americans, look at their faces, and reverence them; for to them and to their wisdom you owe the existence of your mighty fatherland.

At the head of the table sits the lord mayor; whom all readers will recognize at once, for he is none other than that famous Sir Edward Osborne, clothworker, and ancestor of the dukes of Leeds, whose romance now-a-days is in every one's hands. He is aged, but not changed, since he leaped from the window upon London Bridge into the roaring tide below, to rescue the infant who is now his wife. The chivalry and promptitude of the 'prentice boy have grown and hardened into the thoughtful daring of the wealthy merchant adventurer. There he sits, a right kingly man, with my lord Earl of Cumberland on his right hand, and Walter Raleigh on his left; the three talk together in a low voice on the chance of there being vast and rich countries still undiscovered between Florida and the River of Canada. Raleigh's half-scientific declamation and his often quotations of Doctor Dee the conjuror, have less effect on Osborne than on Cumberland (who tried many an adventure to foreign parts, and failed in all of them; apparently for the simple reason that, instead of going himself, he sent other people), and Raleigh is fain to call to his help the quiet student who sits on his left hand, Richard Hakluyt, of Oxford. But he is deep in talk with a reverend elder, whose long white beard flows almost to his waist, and whose face is furrowed by a thousand storms; Anthony Jenkinson by name, the great Asiatic traveller, who is discoursing to the Christ-church virtuoso of reindeer sledges and Siberian steppes, and of the fossil ivory, plain proof of Noah's flood, which the Tungoos dig from the ice-cliffs of the Arctic sea. Next to him is Christopher Carlile, Walsingham's son-in-law (as Sidney also is now), a valiant captain, afterwards general of the soldiery in Drake's triumphant West Indian raid of 1585, with whom a certain Bishop of Carthagena will hereafter drink good wine. He is now busy talking with Alderman Hart the grocer, Sheriff Spencer the clothworker, and Charles Leigh (Amyas's merchant-cousin), and with Aldworth the mayor of Bristol, and William Salterne, alderman thereof, and cousin of our friend at Bideford. For Carlile, and Secretary Walsingham also, have been helping them heart and soul for the last two years to collect money for Humphrey and Adrian Gilbert's great adventures to the North-West, on one of which Carlile was indeed to have sailed himself, but did not go after all; I never could discover for what reason.

On the opposite side of the table is a group, scarcely less interesting. Martin Frobisher and John Davis, the pioneers of the North-West passage, are talking with Alderman Sanderson, the great geographer and "setter forth of globes;" with Mr. Towerson, Sir Gilbert Peckham, our old acquaintance Captain John Winter, and last, but not least, with Philip Sidney himself, who, with his accustomed courtesy; has given up his rightful place toward the head of the table that he may have a knot of virtuosi all to himself; and has brought with him, of course, his two especial intimates, Mr. Edward Dyer and Mr. Francis Leigh. They too are talking of the North-West passage: and Sidney is lamenting that he is tied to diplomacy and courts, and expressing his envy of old Martin Frobisher in all sorts of pretty compliments; to which the other replies that,

"It's all very fine to talk of here, a sailing on dry land with a good glass of wine before you; but you'd find it another guess sort of business, knocking about among the icebergs with your beard frozen fast to your ruff, Sir Philip, specially if you were a bit squeamish about the stomach."

"That were a slight matter to endure, my dear sir, if by it I could win the honor which her majesty bestowed on you, when her own ivory hand waved a farewell 'kerchief to your ship from the windows of Greenwich Palace."

"Well, sir, folks say you have no reason to complain of lack of favors, as you have no reason to deserve lack; and if you can get them by staying ashore, don't you go to sea to look for more, say I. Eh, Master Towerson?"

Towerson's gray beard, which has stood many a foreign voyage, both fair and foul, wags grim assent. But at this moment a Waiter enters, and—

"Please my lord mayor's worship, there is a tall gentleman outside, would speak with the Right Honorable Sir Walter Raleigh."

"Show him in, man. Sir Walter's friends are ours."

Amyas enters, and stands hesitating in the doorway.

"Captain Leigh!" cry half a-dozen voices.

"Why did you not walk in, sir?" says Osborne. "You should know your way well enough between these decks."

"Well enough, my lords and gentlemen. But, Sir Walter—you will excuse me"—and he gave Raleigh a look which was enough for his quick wit. Turning pale as death, he rose, and followed

Amyas into an adjoining cabin. They were five minutes together; and then Amyas came out alone.

In few words he told the company the sad story which we already know. Ere it was ended, noble tears were glistening on some of those stern faces.

"The old Egyptians," said Sir Edward Osborne, "when they banqueted, set a corpse among their guests, for a memorial of human vanity. Have we forgotten God and our own weakness in this our feast, that He Himself has sent us thus a message from the dead?"

"Nay, my lord mayor," said Sidney, "not from the dead, but from the realm of everlasting life."

"Amen!" answered Osborne. "But, gentlemen, our feast is at an end. There are those here who would drink on merrily, as brave men should, in spite of the private losses of which they have just had news; but none here who can drink with the loss of so great a man still ringing in his ears."

It was true. Though many of the guests had suffered severely by the failure of the expedition, they had utterly forgotten that fact in the awful news of Sir Humphrey's death; and the feast broke up sadly and hurriedly, while each man asked his neighbor, "What will the queen say?"

Raleigh re-entered in a few minutes, but was silent, and pressing many an honest hand as he passed, went out to call a wherry, beckoning Amyas to follow him. Sidney, Cumberland, and Frank went with them in another boat, leaving the two to talk over the sad details.

They disembarked at Whitehall-stairs; Raleigh, Sidney, and Cumberland went to the palace; and the two brothers to their mother's lodgings.

Amyas had prepared his speech to Frank about Rose Salterne, but now that it was come to the point, he had not courage to begin, and longed that Frank would open the matter. Frank, too, shrank from what he knew must come, and all the more because he was ignorant that Amyas had been to Bideford, or knew aught of the Rose's disappearance.

So they went upstairs; and it was a relief to both of them to find that their mother was at the Abbey; for it was for her sake that both dreaded what was coming. So they went and stood in the bay-window which looked out upon the river, and talked of things indifferent, and looked earnestly at each other's faces by the fading light, for it was now three years since they had met.

Years and events had deepened the contrast between the two brothers; and Frank smiled with affectionate pride as he looked up in Amyas's face, and saw that he was no longer merely the rollicking handy sailor-lad, but the self-confident and stately warrior, showing in every look and gesture,

worthy of one whose education had been begun by such men as Drake and Grenville, and finished by such as Raleigh and Gilbert. His long locks were now cropped close to the head; but as a set-off, the lips and chin were covered with rich golden beard; his face was browned by a thousand suns and storms; a long scar, the trophy of some Irish fight, crossed his right temple; his huge figure had gained breadth in proportion to its height; and his hand, as it lay upon the window-sill, was hard and massive as a smith's. Frank laid his own upon it, and sighed; and Amyas looked down, and started at the contrast between the two—so slender, bloodless, all but transparent, were the delicate fingers of the courtier. Amyas looked anxiously into his brother's face. It was changed, indeed, since they last met. The brilliant red was still on either cheek, but the white had become dull and opaque; the lips were pale, the features sharpened; the eyes glittered with unnatural fire: and when Frank told Amyas that he looked aged, Amyas could not help thinking that the remark was far more true of the speaker himself.

Trying to shut his eyes to the palpable truth, he went on with his chat, asking the names of one building after another.

"And so this is old Father Thames, with his bank of palaces?"

"Yes. His banks are stately enough; yet, you see, he cannot stay to look at them. He hurries down to the sea; and the sea into the ocean; and the ocean Westward-ho, forever. All things move Westward-ho. Perhaps we may move that way ourselves some day, Amyas."

"What do you mean by that strange talk?"

"Only that the ocean follows the primum mobile of the heavens, and flows forever from east to west. Is there anything so strange in my thinking of that, when I am just come from a party where we have been drinking success to Westward-ho?"

"And much good has come of it! I have lost the best friend and the noblest captain upon earth, not to mention all my little earnings, in that same confounded gulf of Westward-ho."

"Yes, Sir Humphrey Gilbert's star has set in the West—why not? Sun, moon, and planets sink into the West: why not the meteors of this lower world? why not a will-o'-the-wisp like me, Amyas?"

"God forbid, Frank!"

"Why, then? Is not the West the land of peace, and the land of dreams? Do not our hearts tell us so each time we look upon the setting sun, and long to float away with him upon the golden-cushioned clouds? They bury men with their faces to the East. I should rather have mine turned to the West, Amyas, when I die; for I cannot but think it some divine instinct which made the ancient poets guess that Elysium lay beneath the setting sun. It is bound up in the heart of man, that longing for the West. I complain of no one for fleeing away thither beyond the utmost sea, as David wished to flee, and be at peace."

"Complain of no one for fleeing thither?" asked Amyas. "That is more than I do."

Frank looked inquiringly at him; and then—

"No. If I had complained of any one, it would have been of you just now, for seeming to be tired of going Westward-ho."

"Do you wish me to go, then?"

"God knows," said Frank, after a moment's pause. "But I must tell you now, I suppose, once and for all. That has happened at Bideford which—"

"Spare us both, Frank; I know all. I came through Bideford on my way hither; and came hither not merely to see you and my mother, but to ask your advice and her permission."

"True heart! noble heart!" cried Frank. "I knew you would be stanch!"

"Westward-ho it is, then?"

"Can we escape?"

"We?"

"Amyas, does not that which binds you bind me?"

Amyas started back, and held Frank by the shoulders at arm's length; as he did so, he could feel through, that his brother's arms were but skin and bone.

"You? Dearest man, a month of it would kill you!"

Frank smiled, and tossed his head on one side in his pretty way.

"I belong to the school of Thales, who held that the ocean is the mother of all life; and feel no more repugnance at returning to her bosom again than Humphrey Gilbert did."

"But, Frank,—my mother?"

"My mother knows all; and would not have us unworthy of her."

"Impossible! She will never give you up!"

"All things are possible to them that believe in God, my brother; and she believes. But, indeed, Doctor Dee, the wise man, gave her but this summer I know not what of prognostics and diagnostics concerning me. I am born, it seems, under a cold and watery planet, and need, if I am to be long-lived, to go nearer to the vivifying heat of the sun, and there bask out my little life, like fly on wall. To tell truth, he has bidden me spend no more winters here in the East; but return to our native sea-breezes, there to warm my frozen lungs; and has so filled my mother's fancy with stories of sick men, who were given up for lost in Germany and France, and yet renewed their youth, like any serpent or eagle, by going to Italy, Spain, and the Canaries, that she herself will be more ready to let me go than I to leave her all alone. And yet I must go, Amyas. It is not merely that my heart pants, as Sidney's does, as every gallant's ought, to make one of your noble choir of Argonauts, who are now replenishing the earth and subduing it for God and for the queen; it is not merely, Amyas, that love calls me,—love tyrannous and uncontrollable, strengthened by absence, and deepened by despair; but honor, Amyas—my oath—"

And he paused for lack of breath, and bursting into a violent fit of coughing, leaned on his brother's shoulder, while Amyas cried,

"Fools, fools that we were—that I was, I mean—to take that fantastical vow!"

"Not so," answered a gentle voice from behind: "you vowed for the sake of peace on earth, and good-will toward men, and 'Blessed are the peacemakers, for they shall be called the children of God.' No my sons, be sure that such self-sacrifice as you have shown will meet its full reward at the hand of Him who sacrificed Himself for you."

"Oh, mother! mother!" said Amyas, "and do you not hate the very sight of me—come here to take away your first-born?"

"My boy, God takes him, and not you. And if I dare believe in such predictions, Doctor Dee assured me that some exceeding honor awaited you both in the West, to each of you according to your deserts."

"Ah!" said Amyas. "My blessing, I suppose, will be like Esau's, to live by my sword; while Jacob here, the spiritual man, inherits the kingdom of heaven, and an angel's crown."

"Be it what it may, it will surely be a blessing, as long as you are such, my children, as you have been. At least my Frank will be safe from the intrigues of court, and the temptations of the world. Would that I too could go with you, and share in your glory! Come, now," said she, laying her head upon Amyas's breast, and looking up into his face with one of her most winning smiles, "I have heard of heroic mothers ere now who went forth with their sons to battle, and cheered them on to victory. Why should I not go with you on a more peaceful errand? I could nurse the sick, if there were any; I could perhaps have speech of that poor girl, and win her back more easily than you. She might listen to words from a woman—a woman, too, who has loved—which she could not hear from men. At least I could mend and wash for you. I suppose it is as easy to play the good housewife afloat as on shore? Come, now!"

Amyas looked from one to the other.

"God only knows which of the two is less fit to go. Mother! mother! you know not what you ask. Frank! Frank! I do not want you with me. This is a sterner matter than either of you fancy it to be; one that must be worked out, not with kind words, but with sharp shot and cold steel."

"How?" cried both together, aghast.

"I must pay my men, and pay my fellow-adventurers; and I must pay them with Spanish gold. And what is more, I cannot, as a loyal subject of the queen's, go to the Spanish Main with a clear conscience on my own private quarrel, unless I do all the harm that my hand finds to do, by day and night, to her enemies, and the enemies of God."

"What nobler knight-errantry?" said Frank, cheerfully; but Mrs. Leigh shuddered.

"What! Frank too?" she said, half to herself; but her sons knew what she meant. Amyas's warlike life, honorable and righteous as she knew it to be, she had borne as a sad necessity: but that Frank as well should become "a man of blood," was more than her gentle heart could face at first sight. That one youthful duel of his he had carefully concealed from her, knowing her feeling on such matters. And it seemed too dreadful to her to associate that gentle spirit with all the ferocities and the carnage of a battlefield. "And yet," said she to herself, "is this but another of the self-willed idols which I must renounce one by one?" And then, catching at a last hope, she answered—

"Frank must at least ask the queen's leave to go; and if she permits, how can I gainsay her wisdom?"

And so the conversation dropped, sadly enough.

But now began a fresh perplexity in Frank's soul, which amused Amyas at first, when it seemed merely jest, but nettled him a good deal when he found it earnest. For Frank looked forward to asking the queen's permission for his voyage with the most abject despondency and terror. Two or three days passed before he could make up his mind to ask for an interview with her; and he spent the time in making as much interest with Leicester, Hatton, and Sidney, as if he were about to sue for a reprieve from the scaffold.

So said Amyas, remarking, further, that the queen could not cut his head off for wanting to go to sea.

"But what axe so sharp as her frown?" said Frank in most lugubrious tone.

Amyas began to whistle in a very rude way.

"Ah, my brother, you cannot comprehend the pain of parting from her."

"No, I can't. I would die for the least hair of her royal head, God bless it! but I could live very well from now till Doomsday without ever setting eyes on the said head."

"Plato's Troglodytes regretted not that sunlight which they had never beheld."

Amyas, not understanding this recondite conceit, made no answer to it, and there the matter ended for the time. But at last Frank obtained his audience; and after a couple of hours' absence returned quite pale and exhausted.

"Thank Heaven, it is over! She was very angry at first—what else could she be?—and upbraided me with having set my love so low. I could only answer, that my fatal fault was committed before the sight of her had taught me what was supremely lovely, and only worthy of admiration. Then she accused me of disloyalty in having taken an oath which bound me to the service of another than her. I confessed my sin with tears, and when she threatened punishment, pleaded that the offence had avenged itself heavily already,—for what worse punishment than exile from the sunlight of her presence, into the outer darkness which reigns where she is not? Then she was pleased to ask me, how I could dare, as her sworn servant, to desert her side in such dangerous times as these; and asked me how I should reconcile it to my conscience, if on my return I found her dead by the assassin's knife? At which most pathetic demand I could only throw myself at once on my own knees and her mercy, and so awaited my sentence. Whereon, with that angelic pity which alone makes her awfulness endurable, she turned to Hatton and asked, 'What say you, Mouton? Is he humbled sufficiently?' and so dismissed me."

"Heigh-ho!" yawned Amyas;

"Amyas! Amyas!" quoth Frank, solemnly, "you know not what power over the soul has the native and God-given majesty of royalty (awful enough in itself) when to it is superadded the wisdom of the sage, and therewithal the tenderness of the woman. Had I my will, there should be in every realm not a salique, but an anti-salique law: whereby no kings, but only queens should rule mankind. Then would weakness and not power be to man the symbol of divinity; love, and not cunning, would be the arbiter of every cause; and chivalry, not fear, the spring of all obedience."

"Humph! There's some sense in that," quoth Amyas. "I'd run a mile for a woman when I would not walk a yard for a man; and—Who is this our mother is bringing in? The handsomest fellow I ever saw in my life!"

Amyas was not far wrong; for Mrs. Leigh's companion was none other than Mr. Secretary, Amyas's Smerwick Fort acquaintance; alias Colin Clout, alias Immerito, alias Edmund Spenser. Some half-jesting conversation had seemingly been passing between the poet and the saint; for as they came in she said with a smile (which was somewhat of a forced one)—"Well, my dear sons, you are sure of immortality, at least on earth; for Mr. Spenser has been vowing to me to give your adventure a whole canto to itself in his 'Faerie Queene'."

"And you no less, madam," said Spenser. "What were the story of the Gracchi worth without the figure of Cornelia? If I honor the fruit, I must not forget the stem which bears it. Frank, I congratulate you."

"Then you know the result of my interview, mother?"

"I know everything, and am content," said Mrs. Leigh.

"Mrs. Leigh has reason to be content," said Spenser, "with that which is but her own likeness."

"Spare your flattery to an old woman, Mr. Spenser. When, pray, did I" (with a most loving look at Frank) "refuse knighthood for duty's sake?"

"Knighthood?" cried Amyas. "You never told me that, Frank!"

"That may well be, Captain Leigh," said Spenser; "but believe me, her majesty (so Hatton assures me) told him this day, no less than that by going on this quest he deprived himself of that highest earthly honor, which crowned heads are fain to seek from their own subjects."

Spenser did not exaggerate. Knighthood was then the prize of merit only; and one so valuable, that Elizabeth herself said, when asked why she did not bestow a peerage upon some favorite, that having already knighted him, she had nothing better to bestow. It remained for young Essex to begin the degradation of the order in his hapless Irish campaign, and for James to complete that degradation by his novel method of raising money by the sale of baronetcies; a new order of hereditary knighthood which was the laughing-stock of the day, and which (however venerable it may have since become) reflects anything but honor upon its first possessors.

"I owe you no thanks, Colin," said Frank, "for having broached my secret: but I have lost nothing after all. There is still an order of knighthood in which I may win my spurs, even though her majesty refuse me the accolade."

"What, then? you will not take it from a foreign prince?"

Frank smiled.

"Have you never read of that knighthood which is eternal in the heavens, and of those true cavaliers whom John saw in Patmos, riding on white horses, clothed in fine linen, white and clean, knights-errant in the everlasting war against the False Prophet and the Beast? Let me but become worthy of their ranks hereafter, what matter whether I be called Sir Frank on earth?"

"My son," said Mrs. Leigh, "remember that they follow One whose vesture is dipped, not in the blood of His enemies, but in His own."

"I have remembered it for many a day; and remembered, too, that the garments of the knights may need the same tokens as their captain's."

"Oh, Frank! Frank! is not His precious blood enough to cleanse all sin, without the sacrifice of our own?"

"We may need no more than His blood, mother, and yet He may need ours," said Frank.

How that conversation ended I know not, nor whether Spenser fulfilled his purpose of introducing the two brothers and their mother into his "Faerie Queene." If so, the manuscripts must have been lost among those which perished (along with Spenser's baby) in the sack of Kilcolman by the Irish in 1598. But we need hardly regret the loss of them; for the temper of the Leighs and their mother is the same which inspires every canto of that noblest of poems; and which inspired, too, hundreds in those noble days, when the chivalry of the Middle Ages was wedded to the free thought and enterprise of the new.

So mother and sons returned to Bideford, and set to work. Frank mortgaged a farm; Will Cary did the same (having some land of his own from his mother). Old Salterne grumbled at any man save himself spending a penny on the voyage, and forced on the adventurers a good ship of two hundred tons burden, and five hundred pounds toward fitting her out; Mrs. Leigh worked day and night at clothes and comforts of every kind; Amyas had nothing to give but his time and his brains: but, as Salterne said, the rest would have been of little use without them; and day after day he and the old merchant were on board the ship, superintending with their own eyes the fitting of every rope and nail. Cary went about beating up recruits; and made, with his jests and his frankness, the best of crimps: while John Brimblecombe, beside himself with joy, toddled about after him from tavern to tavern, and quay to quay, exalted for the time being (as Cary told him) into a second Peter the Hermit; and so fiercely did he preach a crusade against the Spaniards, through Bideford and Appledore, Clovelly and Ilfracombe, that Amyas might have had a hundred and fifty loose fellows in the first fortnight. But he knew better: still smarting from the effects of a similar haste in the Newfoundland adventure, he had determined to take none but picked men; and by dint of labor he obtained them.

    Only one scapegrace did he take into his crew, named Parracombe; and by that scapegrace hangs a tale. He was an old schoolfellow of his at Bideford, and son of a merchant in that town—one of those unlucky members who are "nobody's enemy but their own"—a handsome, idle, clever fellow, who used his scholarship, of which he had picked up some smattering, chiefly to justify his own escapades, and to string songs together. Having drunk all that he was worth at home, he had in a penitent fit forsworn liquor, and tormented Amyas into taking him to sea, where he afterwards made as good a sailor as any one else, but sorely scandalized John Brimblecombe by all manner of heretical arguments, half Anacreontic, half smacking of the rather loose doctrines of that "Family of Love" which tormented the orthodoxy and morality of more than one Bishop of Exeter. Poor Will Parracombe! he was born a few centuries too early. Had he but lived now, he might have published a volume or two of poetry, and then settled down on the staff of a newspaper. Had he even lived thirty years later than he did, he might have written frantic tragedies or filthy comedies for the edification of James's profligate metropolis, and roistered it in taverns with Marlowe, to die as Marlowe did, by a footman's sword in a drunken brawl. But in those stern days such weak and hysterical spirits had no fair vent for their "humors," save in being reconciled to the Church of Rome, and plotting with Jesuits to assassinate the queen, as Parry and Somerville, and many other madmen, did.

    So, at least, some Jesuit or other seems to have thought, shortly after Amyas had agreed to give the spendthrift a berth on board. For one day Amyas, going down to Appledore about his business, was called into the little Mariners' Rest inn, to extract therefrom poor Will Parracombe, who (in spite of his vow) was drunk and outrageous, and had vowed the death of the landlady and all her kin. So Amyas fetched him out by the collar, and walked him home thereby to Bideford; during which walk Will told him a long and confused story; how an Egyptian rogue had met him that morning on the sands by Boathythe, offered to tell his fortune, and prophesied to him great wealth and honor, but not from the Queen of England; had coaxed him to the Mariners' Rest, and gambled with him for liquor, at which it seemed Will always won, and of course drank his winnings on the spot; whereon the Egyptian began asking him all sorts of questions about the projected voyage of the Rose—a good many of which, Will confessed, he had answered before he saw the fellow's drift; after which the Egyptian had offered him a vast sum of money to do some desperate villainy; but whether it was to murder Amyas or the queen, whether to bore a hole in the bottom of the good ship Rose or to set the Torridge on fire by art-magic, he was too drunk to recollect exactly. Whereon Amyas treated three-quarters of the story as a tipsy dream, and contented himself by getting a warrant against the landlady for harboring "Egyptians," which was then a heavy offence—a gipsy disguise being a favorite one with Jesuits and their emissaries. She of course denied that any gipsy had been there; and though there were some who thought they had seen such a man come in, none had seen him go out again. On which Amyas took occasion to ask, what had become of the suspicious Popish ostler whom he had seen at the Mariners' Rest three years before; and discovered, to his surprise, that the said ostler had vanished from the very day of Don Guzman's departure from Bideford. There was evidently a mystery somewhere: but nothing could be proved; the landlady was dismissed with a reprimand, and Amyas soon forgot the whole matter, after rating Parracombe soundly. After all, he could not have told the gipsy (if one existed) anything important; for the special destination of the voyage (as was the custom in those times, for fear of Jesuits playing into the hands of Spain) had been carefully kept secret among the adventurers themselves, and, except Yeo and Drew, none of the men had any suspicion that La Guayra was to be their aim.

And Salvation Yeo?

Salvation was almost wild for a few days, at the sudden prospect of going in search of his little maid, and of fighting Spaniards once more before he died. I will not quote the texts out of Isaiah and the Psalms with which his mouth was filled from morning to night, for fear of seeming irreverent in the eyes of a generation which does not believe, as Yeo believed, that fighting the Spaniards was as really fighting in God's battle against evil as were the wars of Joshua or David. But the old man had his practical hint too, and entreated to be sent back to Plymouth to look for men.

"There's many a man of the old Pelican, sir, and of Captain Hawkins's Minion that knows the Indies as well as I, and longs to be back again. There's Drew, sir, that we left behind (and no better sailing-master for us in the West-country, and has accounts against the Spaniards, too; for it was his brother, the Barnstaple man, that was factor aboard of poor Mr. Andrew Barker, and got clapt into the Inquisition at the Canaries); you promised him, sir, that night he stood by you on board the Raleigh: and if you'll be as good as your word, he'll be as good as his; and bring a score more brave fellows with him."

So off went Yeo to Plymouth, and returned with Drew and a score of old never-strikes. One look at their visages, as Yeo proudly ushered them into the Ship Tavern, showed Amyas that they were of the metal which he wanted, and that, with the four North-Devon men who had gone round the world with him in the Pelican (who all joined in the first week), he had a reserve-force on which he could depend in utter need; and that utter need might come he knew as well as any.

Nor was this all which Yeo had brought; for he had with him a letter from Sir Francis Drake, full of regrets that he had not seen "his dear lad" as he went through Plymouth. "But indeed I was up to Dartmoor, surveying with cross-staff and chain, over my knees in bog for a three weeks or more. For I have a project to bring down a leat of fair water from the hill-tops right into Plymouth town, cutting off the heads of Tavy, Meavy, Wallcomb, and West Dart, and thereby purging Plymouth harbor from the silt of the mines whereby it has been choked of late years, and giving pure drink not only to the townsmen, but to the fleets of the queen's majesty; which if I do, I shall both make some poor return to God for all His unspeakable mercies, and erect unto myself a monument better than of brass or marble, not merely honorable to me, but useful to my countrymen."* Whereon Frank sent Drake a pretty epigram, comparing Drake's projected leat to that river of eternal life whereof the just would drink throughout eternity, and quoting (after the fashion of those days) John vii. 38; while Amyas took more heed of a practical appendage to the same letter, which was a list of hints scrawled for his use by Captain John Hawkins himself, on all sea matters, from the mounting of ordnance to the use of vitriol against the scurvy, in default of oranges and "limmons;" all which stood Amyas in good stead during the ensuing month, while Frank grew more and more proud of his brother, and more and more humble about himself.

For he watched with astonishment how the simple sailor, without genius, scholarship, or fancy, had gained, by plain honesty, patience, and common sense, a power over the human heart, and a power over his work, whatsoever it might be, which Frank could only admire afar off. The men looked up to him as infallible, prided themselves on forestalling his wishes, carried out his slightest hint, worked early and late to win a smile from him; while as for him, no detail escaped him, no drudgery sickened him, no disappointment angered him, till on the 15th of November, 1583, dropped down from Bideford Quay to Appledore Pool the tall ship Rose, with a hundred men on board (for sailors packed close in those days), beef, pork, biscuit, and good ale (for ale went to sea always then) in abundance, four culverins on her main deck, her poop and forecastle well fitted with swivels of every size, and her racks so full of muskets, calivers, long bows, pikes, and swords, that all agreed so well-appointed a ship had never sailed "out over Bar."

The next day being Sunday, the whole crew received the Communion together at Northam Church, amid a mighty crowd; and then going on board again, hove anchor and sailed out over the Bar before a soft east wind, to the music of sacbut, fife, and drum, with discharge of all ordnance, great and small, with cheering of young and old from cliff and strand and quay, and with many a tearful prayer and blessing upon that gallant bark, and all brave hearts on board.

And Mrs. Leigh who had kissed her sons for the last time after the Communion at the altar-steps (and what more fit place for a mother's kiss?) went to the rocky knoll outside the churchyard wall, and watched the ship glide out between the yellow denes, and lessen slowly hour by hour into the boundless West, till her hull sank below the dim horizon, and her white sails faded away into the gray Atlantic mist, perhaps forever.

And Mrs. Leigh gathered her cloak about her, and bowed her head and worshipped; and then went home to loneliness and prayer.

CHAPTER XVII: HOW THEY CAME TO BARBADOS, AND FOUND NO MEN THEREIN

Land! land! land! Yes, there it was, far away to the south and west, beside the setting sun, a long blue bar between the crimson sea and golden sky. Land at last, with fresh streams, and cooling fruits, and free room for cramped and scurvy-weakened limbs. And there, too, might be gold, and gems, and all the wealth of Ind. Who knew? Why not? The old world of fact and prose lay thousands of miles behind them, and before them and around them was the realm of wonder and fable, of boundless hope and possibility. Sick men crawled up out of their stifling hammocks; strong men fell on their knees and gave God thanks; and all eyes and hands were stretched eagerly toward the far blue cloud, fading as the sun sank down, yet rising higher and broader as the ship rushed on before the rich trade-wind, which whispered lovingly round brow and sail, "I am the faithful friend of those who dare!" "Blow freshly, freshlier yet, thou good trade-wind, of whom it is written that He makes the winds His angels, ministering breaths to the heirs of His salvation. Blow freshlier yet, and save, if not me from death, yet her from worse than death. Blow on, and land me at her feet, to call the lost lamb home, and die!"

So murmured Frank to himself, as with straining eyes he gazed upon that first outlier of the New World which held his all. His cheeks were thin and wasted, and the hectic spot on each glowed crimson in the crimson light of the setting sun. A few minutes more, and the rainbows of the West were gone; emerald and topaz, amethyst and ruby, had faded into silver-gray; and overhead, through the dark sapphire depths, the Moon and Venus reigned above the sea.

"That should be Barbados, your worship," said Drew, the master; "unless my reckoning is far out, which, Heaven knows, it has no right to be, after such a passage, and God be praised."

"Barbados? I never heard of it."

"Very like, sir: but Yeo and I were here with Captain Drake, and I was here after, too, with poor Captain Barlow; and there is good harborage to the south and west of it, I remember."

"And neither Spaniard, cannibal, or other evil beast," said Yeo. "A very garden of the Lord, sir, hid away in the seas, for an inheritance to those who love Him. I heard Captain Drake talk of planting it, if ever he had a chance."

"I recollect now," said Amyas, "some talk between him and poor Sir Humphrey about an island here. Would God he had gone thither instead of to Newfoundland!"

"Nay, then," said Yeo, "he is in bliss now with the Lord; and you would not have kept him from that, sir?"

"He would have waited as willingly as he went, if he could have served his queen thereby. But what say you, my masters? How can we do better than to spend a few days here, to get our sick round, before we make the Main, and set to our work?"

All approved the counsel except Frank, who was silent.

"Come, fellow-adventurer," said Cary, "we must have your voice too."

"To my impatience, Will," said he, aside in a low voice, "there is but one place on earth, and I am all day longing for wings to fly thither: but the counsel is right. I approve it."

So the verdict was announced, and received with a hearty cheer by the crew; and long before morning they had run along the southern shore of the island, and were feeling their way into the bay where Bridgetown now stands. All eyes were eagerly fixed on the low wooded hills which slept in the moonlight, spangled by fireflies, with a million dancing stars; all nostrils drank greedily the fragrant air, which swept from the land, laden with the scent of a thousand flowers; all ears welcomed, as a grateful change from the monotonous whisper and lap of the water, the hum of insects, the snore of the tree-toads, the plaintive notes of the shore-fowl, which fill a tropic night with noisy life.

At last she stopped; at last the cable rattled through the hawsehole; and then, careless of the chance of lurking Spaniard or Carib, an instinctive cheer burst from every throat. Poor fellows! Amyas had much ado to prevent them going on shore at once, dark as it was, by reminding them that it wanted but two hours of day.

"Never were two such long hours," said one young lad, fidgeting up and down.

"You never were in the Inquisition," said Yeo, "or you'd know better how slow time can run. Stand you still, and give God thanks you're where you are."

"I say, Gunner, be there goold to that island?"

"Never heard of none; and so much the better for it," said Yeo, dryly.

"But, I say, Gunner," said a poor scurvy-stricken cripple, licking his lips, "be there oranges and limmons there?"

"Not of my seeing; but plenty of good fruit down to the beach, thank the Lord. There comes the dawn at last."

Up flushed the rose, up rushed the sun, and the level rays glittered on the smooth stems of the palm-trees, and threw rainbows across the foam upon the coral-reefs, and gilded lonely uplands far away, where now stands many a stately country-seat and busy engine-house. Long lines of pelicans went clanging out to sea; the hum of the insects hushed, and a thousand birds burst into jubilant song; a thin blue mist crept upward toward the inner downs, and vanished, leaving them to quiver in the burning glare; the land-breeze, which had blown fresh out to sea all night, died away into glassy calm, and the tropic day was begun.

The sick were lifted over the side, and landed boat-load after boat-load on the beach, to stretch themselves in the shade of the palms; and in half-an-hour the whole crew were scattered on the shore, except some dozen worthy men, who had volunteered to keep watch and ward on board till noon.

And now the first instinctive cry of nature was for fruit! fruit! fruit! The poor lame wretches crawled from place to place plucking greedily the violet grapes of the creeping shore vine, and staining their mouths and blistering their lips with the prickly pears, in spite of Yeo's entreaties and warnings against the thorns. Some of the healthy began hewing down cocoa-nut trees to get at the nuts, doing little thereby but blunt their hatchets; till Yeo and Drew, having mustered half-a-dozen reasonable men, went off inland, and returned in an hour laden with the dainties of that primeval orchard,—with acid junipa-apples, luscious guavas, and crowned ananas, queen of all the fruits, which they had found by hundreds on the broiling ledges of the low tufa-cliffs; and then all, sitting on the sandy turf, defiant of galliwasps and jackspaniards, and all the weapons of the insect host, partook of the equal banquet, while old blue land-crabs sat in their house-doors and brandished their fists in defiance at the invaders, and solemn cranes stood in the water on the shoals with their heads on one side, and meditated how long it was since they had seen bipeds without feathers breaking the solitude of their isle.

And Frank wandered up and down, silent, but rather in wonder than in sadness, while great Amyas walked after him, his mouth full of junipa-apples, and enacted the part of showman, with a sort of patronizing air, as one who had seen the wonders already, and was above being astonished at them.

"New, new; everything new!" said Frank, meditatively. "Oh, awful feeling! All things changed around us, even to the tiniest fly and flower; yet we the same, the same forever!"

Amyas, to whom such utterances were altogether sibylline and unintelligible, answered by:

"Look, Frank, that's a colibri. You 've heard of colibris?"

Frank looked at the living gem, which hung, loud humming, over some fantastic bloom, and then dashed away, seemingly to call its mate, and whirred and danced with it round and round the flower-starred bushes, flashing fresh rainbows at every shifting of the lights.

Frank watched solemnly awhile, and then:

"Qualis Natura formatrix, si talis formata? Oh my God, how fair must be Thy real world, if even Thy phantoms are so fair!"

"Phantoms?" asked Amyas, uneasily. "That's no ghost, Frank, but a jolly little honey-sucker, with a wee wife, and children no bigger than peas, but yet solid greedy little fellows enough, I'll warrant."

"Not phantoms in thy sense, good fellow, but in the sense of those who know the worthlessness of all below."

"I'll tell you what, brother Frank, you are a great deal wiser than me, I know; but I can't abide to see you turn up your nose as it were at God's good earth. See now, God made all these things; and never a man, perhaps, set eyes on them till fifty years agone; and yet they were as pretty as they are now, ever since the making of the world. And why do you think God could have put them here, then, but to please Himself"—and Amyas took off his hat—"with the sight of them? Now, I say, brother Frank, what's good enough to please God, is good enough to please you and me."

"Your rebuke is just, dear old simple-hearted fellow; and God forgive me, if with all my learning, which has brought me no profit, and my longings, which have brought me no peace, I presume at moments, sinner that I am, to be more dainty than the Lord Himself. He walked in Paradise among the trees of the garden, Amyas; and so will we, and be content with what He sends. Why should we long for the next world, before we are fit even for this one?"

"And in the meanwhile," said Amyas, "this earth's quite good enough, at least here in Barbados."

"Do you believe," asked Frank, trying to turn his own thoughts, "in those tales of the Spaniards, that the Sirens and Tritons are heard singing in these seas?"

"I can't tell. There's more fish in the water than ever came out of it, and more wonders in the world, I'll warrant, than we ever dreamt of; but I was never in these parts before; and in the South Sea, I must say, I never came across any, though Yeo says he has heard fair music at night up in the Gulf, far away from land."

"The Spaniards report that at certain seasons choirs of these nymphs assemble in the sea, and with ravishing music sing their watery loves. It may be so. For Nature, which has peopled the land with rational souls, may not have left the sea altogether barren of them; above all, when we remember that the ocean is as it were the very fount of all fertility, and its slime (as the most learned hold with Thales of Miletus) that prima materia out of which all things were one by one concocted. Therefore, the ancients feigned wisely that Venus, the mother of all living things, whereby they designed the plastic force of nature, was born of the sea-foam, and rising from the deep, floated ashore upon the isles of Greece."

"I don't know what plastic force is; but I wish I had had the luck to be by when the pretty poppet came up: however, the nearest thing I ever saw to that was maidens swimming alongside of us when we were in the South Seas, and would have come aboard, too; but Drake sent them all off again for a lot of naughty packs, and I verily believe they were no better. Look at the butterflies, now! Don't you wish you were a boy again, and not too proud to go catching them in your cap?"

And so the two wandered on together through the glorious tropic woods, and then returned to the beach to find the sick already grown cheerful, and many who that morning could not stir from their hammocks, pacing up and down, and gaining strength with every step.

"Well done, lads!" cried Amyas, "keep a cheerful mind. We will have the music ashore after dinner, for want of mermaids to sing to us, and those that can dance may."

And so those four days were spent; and the men, like schoolboys on a holiday, gave themselves up to simple merriment, not forgetting, however, to wash the clothes, take in fresh water, and store up a good supply of such fruit as seemed likely to keep; until, tired with fruitless rambles after gold, which they expected to find in every bush, in spite of Yeo's warnings that none had been heard of on the island, they were fain to lounge about, full-grown babies, picking up shells and sea-fans to take home to their sweethearts, smoking agoutis out of the hollow trees, with shout and laughter, and tormenting every living thing they could come near, till not a land-crab dare look out of his hole, or an armadillo unroll himself, till they were safe out of the bay, and off again to the westward, unconscious pioneers of all the wealth, and commerce, and beauty, and science which has in later centuries made that lovely isle the richest gem of all the tropic seas.

CHAPTER XVIII: HOW THEY TOOK THE PEARLS AT MARGARITA

They had slipped past the southern point of Grenada in the night, and were at last within that fairy ring of islands, on which nature had concentrated all her beauty, and man all his sin. If Barbados had been invested in the eyes of the newcomers with some strange glory, how much more the seas on which they now entered, which smile in almost perpetual calm, untouched by the hurricane which roars past them far to northward! Sky, sea, and islands were one vast rainbow; though little marked, perhaps, by those sturdy practical sailors, whose main thought was of Spanish gold and pearls; and as little by Amyas, who, accustomed to the scenery of the tropics, was speculating inwardly on the possibility of extirpating the Spaniards, and annexing the West Indies to the domains of Queen Elizabeth. And yet even their unpoetic eyes could not behold without awe and excitement lands so famous and yet so new, around which all the wonder, all the pity, and all the greed of the age had concentrated itself. It was an awful thought, and yet inspiring, that they were entering regions all but unknown to Englishmen, where the penalty of failure would be worse than death—the torments of the Inquisition. Not more than five times before, perhaps, had those mysterious seas been visited by English keels; but there were those on board who knew them well, and too well; who, first of all British mariners, had attempted under Captain John Hawkins to trade along those very coasts, and, interdicted from the necessaries of life by Spanish jealousy, had, in true English fashion, won their markets at the sword's point, and then bought and sold honestly and peaceably therein. The old mariners of the Pelican and the Minion were questioned all day long for the names of every isle and cape, every fish and bird; while Frank stood by, listening serious and silent.

A great awe seemed to have possessed his soul; yet not a sad one: for his face seemed daily to drink in glory from the glory round him; and murmuring to himself at whiles, "This is the gate of heaven," he stood watching all day long, careless of food and rest, as every forward plunge of the ship displayed some fresh wonder. Islands and capes hung high in air, with their inverted images below them; long sand-hills rolled and weltered in the mirage; and the yellow flower-beds, and huge thorny cacti like giant candelabra, which clothed the glaring slopes, twisted, tossed, and flickered, till the whole scene seemed one blazing phantom-world, in which everything was as unstable as it was fantastic, even to the sun itself, distorted into strange oval and pear-shaped figures by the beds of crimson mist through which he sank to rest. But while Frank wondered, Yeo rejoiced; for to the southward of that setting sun a cluster of tall peaks rose from the sea; and they, unless his reckonings were wrong, were the mountains of Macanao, at the western end of Margarita, the Isle of Pearls, then famous in all the cities of the Mediterranean, and at the great German fairs, and second only in richness to that pearl island in the gulf of Panama, which fifteen years before had cost John Oxenham his life.

The next day saw them running along the north side of the island, having passed undiscovered (as far as they could see) the castle which the Spaniards had built at the eastern end for the protection of the pearl fisheries.

At last they opened a deep and still bight, wooded to the water's edge; and lying in the roadstead a caravel, and three boats by her. And at that sight there was not a man but was on deck at once, and not a mouth but was giving its opinion of what should be done. Some were for sailing right into the roadstead, the breeze blowing fresh toward the shore (as it usually does throughout those islands in the afternoon). However, seeing the billows break here and there off the bay's mouth, they thought it better, for fear of rocks, to run by quietly, and then send in the pinnace and the boat. Yeo would have had them show Spanish colors, for fear of alarming the caravel; but Amyas stoutly refused, "counting it," he said, "a mean thing to tell a lie in that way, unless in extreme danger, or for great ends of state."

So holding on their course till they were shut out by the next point, they started; Cary in the largest boat with twenty men, and Amyas in the smaller one with fifteen more; among whom was John Brimblecombe, who must needs come in his cassock and bands, with an old sword of his uncle's which he prized mightily.

When they came to the bight's mouth, they found, as they had expected, coral rocks, and too many of them; so that they had to run along the edge of the reef a long way before they could find a passage for the boats. While they were so doing, and those of them who were new to the Indies were admiring through the clear element those living flower-beds, and subaqueous gardens of Nereus and Amphitrite, there suddenly appeared below what Yeo called "a school of sharks," some of them nearly as long as the boat, who looked up at them wistfully enough out of their wicked scowling eyes.

"Jack," said Amyas, who sat next to him, "look how that big fellow eyes thee: he has surely taken a fancy to that plump hide of thine, and thinks thou wouldst eat as tender as any sucking porker."

Jack turned very pale, but said nothing.

Now, as it befell, just then that very big fellow, seeing a parrot-fish come out of a cleft of the coral, made at him from below, as did two or three more; the poor fish finding no other escape, leaped clean into the air, and almost aboard the boat; while just where he had come out of the water, three or four great brown shagreened noses clashed together within two yards of Jack as he sat, each showing its horrible rows of saw teeth, and then sank sulkily down again, to watch for a fresh bait. At which Jack said very softly, "In manus tuas, Domine!" and turning his eyes in board, had no lust to look at sharks any more.

So having got through the reef, in they ran with a fair breeze, the caravel not being now a musket-shot off. Cary laid her aboard before the Spaniards had time to get to their ordnance; and standing up in the stern-sheets, shouted to them to yield. The captain asked boldly enough, in whose name? "In the name of common sense, ye dogs," cries Will; "do you not see that you are but fifty strong to our twenty?" Whereon up the side he scrambled, and the captain fired a pistol at him. Cary knocked him over, unwilling to shed needless blood; on which all the crew yielded, some falling on their knees, some leaping overboard; and the prize was taken.

In the meanwhile, Amyas had pulled round under her stern, and boarded the boat which was second from her, for the nearest was fast alongside, and so a sure prize. The Spaniards in her yielded without a blow, crying "Misericordia;" and the negroes, leaping overboard, swam ashore like sea-dogs. Meanwhile, the third boat, which was not an oar's length off, turned to pull away. Whereby befell a notable adventure: for John Brimblecombe, casting about in a valiant mind how he should distinguish himself that day, must needs catch up a boat-hook, and claw on to her stern, shouting, "Stay, ye Papists! Stay, Spanish dogs!"—by which, as was to be expected, they being ten to his one, he was forthwith pulled overboard, and fell all along on his nose in the sea, leaving the hook fast in her stern.

Where, I know not how, being seized with some panic fear (his lively imagination filling all the sea with those sharks which he had just seen), he fell a-roaring like any town-bull, and in his confusion never thought to turn and get aboard again, but struck out lustily after the Spanish boat, whether in hope of catching hold of the boat-hook which trailed behind her, or from a very madness of valor, no man could divine; but on he swam, his cassock afloat behind him, looking for all the world like a great black monk-fish, and howling and puffing, with his mouth full of salt water, "Stay, ye Spanish dogs! Help, all good fellows! See you not that I am a dead man? They are nuzzling already at my toes! He hath hold of my leg! My right thigh is bitten clean off! Oh that I were preaching in Hartland pulpit! Stay, Spanish dogs! Yield, Papist cowards, least I make mincemeat of you; and take me aboard! Yield, I say, or my blood be on your heads! I am no Jonah; if he swallow me, he will never cast me up again! it is better to fall into the hands of man, than into the hands of devils with three rows of teeth apiece. In manus tuas. Orate pro anima—!"

And so forth, in more frantic case than ever was Panurge in that his ever-memorable seasickness; till the English, expecting him every minute to be snapped up by sharks, or brained by the Spaniard's oars, let fly a volley into the fugitives, on which they all leaped overboard like their fellows; whereon Jack scrambled into the boat, and drawing sword with one hand, while he wiped the water out of his eyes with the other, began to lay about him like a very lion, cutting the empty air, and crying, "Yield, idolaters! Yield, Spanish dogs!" However, coming to himself after a while, and seeing that there was no one on whom to flesh his maiden steel, he sits down panting in the sternsheets, and begins stripping off his hose. On which Amyas, thinking surely that the good fellow had gone mad with some stroke of the sun, or by having fallen into the sea after being overheated with his rowing, bade pull alongside, and asked him in heaven's name what he was doing with his nether tackle. On which Jack, amid such laughter as may be conceived, vowed and swore that his right thigh was bitten clean through, and to the bone; yea, and that he felt his hose full of blood; and so would have swooned away for imaginary loss of blood (so strong was the delusion on him) had not his friends, after much arguing on their part, and anger on his, persuaded him that he was whole and sound.

After which they set to work to overhaul their maiden prize, which they found full of hides and salt-pork; and yet not of that alone; for in the captain's cabin, and also in the sternsheets of the boat which Brimblecombe had so valorously boarded, were certain frails of leaves packed neatly enough, which being opened were full of goodly pearls, though somewhat brown (for the Spaniards used to damage the color in their haste and greediness, opening the shells by fire, instead of leaving them to decay gradually after the Arabian fashion); with which prize, though they could not guess its value very exactly, they went off content enough, after some malicious fellow had set the ship on fire, which, being laden with hides, was no nosegay as it burnt.

Amyas was very angry at this wanton damage, in which his model, Drake, had never indulged; but Cary had his jest ready. "Ah!" said he, "'Lutheran devils' we are, you know; so we are bound to vanish, like other fiends, with an evil savor."

As soon, however, as Amyas was on board again, he rounded his friend Mr. Brimblecombe in the ear, and told him he had better play the man a little more, roaring less before he was hurt, and keeping his breath to help his strokes, if he wished the crew to listen much to his discourses. Frank, hearing this, bade Amyas leave the offender to him, and so began upon him with—

"Come hither, thou recreant Jack, thou lily-livered Jack, thou hysterical Jack. Tell me now, thou hast read Plato's Dialogues, and Aristotle's Logic?"

To which Jack very meekly answered, "Yes."

"Then I will deal with thee after the manner of those ancient sages, and ask whether the greater must not contain the less?"

Jack. Yes, sure.

Frank. And that which is more than a part, contain that part, more than which it is?

Jack. Yes, sure.

Frank. Then tell me, is not a priest more than a layman?

Jack (who was always very loud about the dignity of the priesthood, as many of his cloth are, who have no other dignity whereon to stand) answered very boldly, "Of course."

Frank. Then a priest containeth a man, and is a man, and something over—viz, his priesthood?

Jack (who saw whither this would lead). I suppose so.

Frank. Then, if a priest show himself no man, he shows himself all the more no priest?

"I'll tell you what, Master Frank," says Jack, "you may be right by logic; but sharks aren't logic, nor don't understand it neither."

Frank. Nay but, my recalcitrant Jack, my stiff-necked Jack, is it the part of a man to howl like a pig in a gate, because he thinks that is there which is not there?

Jack had not a word to say.

Frank. And still more, when if that had been there, it had been the duty of a brave man to have kept his mouth shut, if only to keep salt water out, and not add the evil of choking to that of being eaten?

"Ah!" says Jack, "that's all very fine; but you know as well as I that it was not the Spaniards I was afraid of. They were Heaven's handiwork, and I knew how to deal with them; but as for those fiends' spawn of sharks, when I saw that fellow take the fish alongside, it upset me clean, and there's an end of it!"

Frank. Oh, Jack, Jack, behold how one sin begets another! Just now thou wert but a coward, and now thou art a Manichee. For thou hast imputed to an evil creator that which was formed only for a good end, namely, sharks, which were made on purpose to devour useless carcasses like thine. Moreover, as a brother of the Rose, thou wert bound by the vow of thy brotherhood to have leaped joyfully down that shark's mouth.

Jack. Ay, very likely, if Mistress Rose had been in his stomach; but I wanted to fight Spaniards just then, not to be shark-bitten.

Frank. Jack, thy answer savors of self-will. If it is ordained that thou shouldst advance the ends of the Brotherhood by being shark-bitten, or flea-bitten, or bitten by sharpers, to the detriment of thy carnal wealth, or, shortly, to suffer any shame or torment whatsoever, even to strappado and scarpines, thou art bound to obey thy destiny, and not, after that vain Roman conceit, to choose the manner of thine own death, which is indeed only another sort of self-murder. We therefore consider thee as a cause of scandal, and a rotten and creaking branch, to be excised by the spiritual arm, and do hereby excise thee, and cut thee off.

Jack. Nay faith, that's a little too much, Master Frank. How long have you been Bishop of Exeter?

Frank. Jack, thy wit being blinded, and full of gross vapors, by reason of the perturbations of fear (which, like anger, is a short madness, and raises in the phantasy vain spectres,—videlicet, of sharks and Spaniards), mistakes our lucidity. For thy Manicheeism, let his lordship of Exeter deal with it. For thy abominable howling and caterwauling, offensive in a chained cur, but scandalous in a preacher and a brother of the Rose, we do hereby deprive thee of thine office of chaplain to the Brotherhood; and warn thee, that unless within seven days thou do some deed equal to the Seven Champions, or Ruggiero and Orlando's self, thou shalt be deprived of sword and dagger, and allowed henceforth to carry no more iron about thee than will serve to mend thy pen.

"And now, Jack," said Amyas, "I will give thee a piece of news. No wonder that young men, as the parsons complain so loudly, will not listen to the Gospel, while it is preached to them by men on whom they cannot but look down; a set of softhanded fellows who cannot dig, and are ashamed to beg; and, as my brother has it, must needs be parsons before they are men.

"Frank. Ay, and even though we may excuse that in Popish priests and friars, who are vowed not to be men, and get their bread shamefully and rascally by telling sinners who owe a hundred measures to sit down quickly and take their bill and write fifty: yet for a priest of the Church of England (whose business is not merely to smuggle sinful souls up the backstairs into heaven, but to make men good Christians by making them good men, good gentlemen, and good Englishmen) to show the white feather in the hour of need, is to unpreach in one minute all that he had been preaching his life long.

"I tell thee," says Amyas, "if I had not taken thee for another guess sort of man, I had never let thee have the care of a hundred brave lads' immortal souls—"

And so on, both of them boarding him at once with their heavy shot, larboard and starboard, till he fairly clapped his hands to his ears and ran for it, leaving poor Frank laughing so heartily, that Amyas was after all glad the thing had happened, for the sake of the smile which it put into his sad and steadfast countenance.

The next day was Sunday; on which, after divine service (which they could hardly persuade Jack to read, so shamefaced was he; and as for preaching after it, he would not hear of such a thing), Amyas read aloud, according to custom, the articles of their agreement; and then seeing abreast of them a sloping beach with a shoot of clear water running into the sea, agreed that they should land there, wash the clothes, and again water the ship; for they had found water somewhat scarce at Barbados. On this party Jack Brimblecombe must needs go, taking with him his sword and a great arquebuse; for he had dreamed last night (he said) that he was set upon by Spaniards, and was sure that the dream would come true; and moreover, that he did not very much care if they did, or if he ever got back alive; "for it was better to die than be made an ape, and a scarecrow, and laughed at by the men, and badgered with Ramus his logic, and Plato his dialectical devilries, to confess himself a Manichee, and, for aught he knew, a turbaned Turk, or Hebrew Jew," and so flung into the boat like a man desperate.

So they went ashore, after Amyas had given strict commands against letting off firearms, for fear of alarming the Spaniards. There they washed their clothes, and stretched their legs with great joy, admiring the beauty of the place, and then began to shoot the seine which they had brought on shore with them. "In which," says the chronicler, "we caught many strange fishes, and beside them, a sea-cow full seven feet long, with limpets and barnacles on her back, as if she had been a stick of drift-timber. This is a fond and foolish beast: and yet pious withal; for finding a corpse, she watches over it day and night until it decay or be buried. The Indians call her manati; who carries her young under her arm, and gives it suck like a woman; and being wounded, she lamenteth aloud with a human voice, and is said at certain seasons to sing very melodiously; which melody, perhaps, having been heard in those seas, is that which Mr. Frank reported to be the choirs of the Sirens and Tritons. The which I do not avouch for truth, neither rashly deny, having seen myself such fertility of Nature's wonders that I hold him who denieth aught merely for its strangeness to be a ribald and an ignoramus. Also one of our men brought in two great black fowls which he had shot with a crossbow, bodied and headed like a capon, but bigger than any eagle, which the Spaniards call curassos; which, with that sea-cow, afterwards made us good cheer, both roast and sodden, for the cow was very dainty meat, as good as a four-months' calf, and tender and fat withal."

After that they set to work filling the casks and barricos, having laid the boat up to the outflow of the rivulet. And lucky for them it was, as it fell out, that they were all close together at that work, and not abroad skylarking as they had been half-an-hour before.

Now John Brimblecombe had gone apart as soon as they landed, with a shamefaced and doleful countenance; and sitting down under a great tree, plucked a Bible from his bosom, and read steadfastly, girded with his great sword, and his arquebuse lying by him. This too was well for him, and for the rest; for they had not yet finished their watering, when there was a cry that the enemy was on them; and out of the wood, not twenty yards from the good parson, came full fifty shot, with a multitude of negroes behind them, and an officer in front on horseback, with a great plume of feathers in his hat, and his sword drawn in his hand.

"Stand, for your lives!" shouted Amyas: and only just in time; for there was ten good minutes lost in running up and down before he could get his men into some order of battle. But when Jack beheld the Spaniards, as if he had expected their coming, he plucked a leaf and put it into the page of his book for a mark, laid the book down soberly, caught up his arquebuse, ran like a mad dog right at the Spanish captain, shot him through the body stark dead, and then, flinging the arquebuse at the head of him who stood next, fell on with his sword like a very Colbrand, breaking in among the arquebuses, and striking right and left such ugly strokes, that the Spaniards (who thought him a very fiend, or Luther's self come to life to plague them) gave back pell-mell, and shot at him five or six at once with their arquebuses: but whether from fear of him, or of wounding each other, made so bad play with their pieces, that he only got one shrewd gall in his thigh, which made him limp for many a day. But as fast as they gave back he came on; and the rest by this time ran up in good order, and altogether nearly forty men well armed. On which the Spaniards turned, and went as fast as they had come, while Cary hinted that, "The dogs had had such a taste of the parson, that they had no mind to wait for the clerk and people."

"Come back, Jack! are you mad?" shouted Amyas.

But Jack (who had not all this time spoken one word) followed them as fiercely as ever, till, reaching a great blow at one of the arquebusiers, he caught his foot in a root; on which down he went, and striking his head against the ground, knocked out of himself all the breath he had left (which between fatness and fighting was not much), and so lay. Amyas, seeing the Spaniards gone, did not care to pursue them: but picked up Jack, who, staring about, cried, "Glory be! glory be!—How many have I killed? How many have I killed?"

"Nineteen, at the least," quoth Cary, "and seven with one back stroke;" and then showed Brimblecombe the captain lying dead, and two arquebusiers, one of which was the fugitive by whom he came to his fall, beside three or four more who were limping away wounded, some of them by their fellows' shot.

"There!" said Jack, pausing and blowing, "will you laugh at me any more, Mr. Cary; or say that I cannot fight, because I am a poor parson's son?"

Cary took him by the hand, and asked pardon of him for his scoffing, saying that he had that day played the best man of all of them; and Jack, who never bore malice, began laughing in his turn, and—

"Oh, Mr. Cary, we have all known your pleasant ways, ever since you used to put drumble-drones into my desk to Bideford school." And so they went to the boats, and pulled off, thanking God (as they had need to do) for their great deliverance: while all the boats' crew rejoiced over Jack, who after a while grew very faint (having bled a good deal without knowing it), and made as little of his real wound as he made much the day before of his imaginary one.

Frank asked him that evening how he came to show so cool and approved a valor in so sudden a mishap.

"Well, my masters," said Jack, "I don't deny that I was very downcast on account of what you said, and the scandal which I had given to the crew; but as it happened, I was reading there under the tree, to fortify my spirits, the history of the ancient worthies, in St. Paul his eleventh chapter to the Hebrews; and just as I came to that, 'out of weakness were made strong, waxed valiant in fight, turned to flight the armies of the aliens,' arose the cry of the Spaniards. At which, gentlemen, thinking in myself that I fought in just so good a cause as they, and, as I hoped, with like faith, there came upon me so strange an assurance of victory, that I verily believed in myself that if there had been a ten thousand of them, I should have taken no hurt. Wherefore," said Jack, modestly, "there is no credit due to me, for there was no valor in me whatsoever, but only a certainty of safety; and any coward would fight if he knew that he were to have all the killing and none of the scratches."

Which words he next day, being Sunday, repeated in his sermon which he made on that chapter, with which all, even Salvation Yeo himself, were well content and edified, and allowed him to be as godly a preacher as he was (in spite of his simple ways) a valiant and true-hearted comrade.

They brought away the Spanish officer's sword (a very good blade), and also a great chain of gold which he wore about his neck; both of which were allotted to Brimblecombe as his fair prize; but he, accepting the sword, steadfastly refused the chain, entreating Amyas to put it into the common stock; and when Amyas refused, he cut it into links and distributed it among those of the boat's crew who had succored him, winning thereby much good-will. "And indeed" (says the chronicler), "I never saw in that worthy man, from the first day of our school-fellowship till he was laid in his parish church of Hartland (where he now sleeps in peace), any touch of that sin of covetousness which has in all ages, and in ours no less than others, beset especially (I know not why) them who minister about the sanctuary. But this man, though he was ugly and lowly in person, and in understanding simple, and of breeding but a poor parson's son, had yet in him a spirit so loving and cheerful, so lifted from base and selfish purposes to the worship of duty, and to a generosity rather knightly than sacerdotal, that all through his life he seemed to think only that it was more blessed to give than to receive. And all that wealth which he gained in the wars he dispersed among his sisters and the poor of his parish, living unmarried till his death like a true lover and constant mourner (as shall be said in place), and leaving hardly wherewith to bring his body to the grave. At whom if we often laughed once, we should now rather envy him, desiring to be here what he was, that we may be hereafter where he is. Amen."

CHAPTER XIX: WHAT BEFELL AT LA GUAYRA

The men would gladly have hawked awhile round Margarita and Cubagua for another pearl prize. But Amyas having, as he phrased it, "fleshed his dogs," was loth to hang about the islands after the alarm had been given. They ran, therefore, south-west across the mouth of that great bay which stretches from the Peninsula of Paria to Cape Codera, leaving on their right hand Tortuga, and on their left the meadow-islands of the Piritoos, two long green lines but a few inches above the tideless sea. Yeo and Drew knew every foot of the way, and had good reason to know it; for they, the first of all English mariners, had tried to trade along this coast with Hawkins. And now, right ahead, sheer out of the sea from base to peak, arose higher and higher the mighty range of the Caracas mountains; beside which all hills which most of the crew had ever seen seemed petty mounds. Frank, of course, knew the Alps; and Amyas the Andes; but Cary's notions of height were bounded by M'Gillicuddy's Reeks, and Brimblecombe's by Exmoor; and the latter, to Cary's infinite amusement, spent a whole day holding on by the rigging, and staring upwards with his chin higher than his nose, till he got a stiff neck. Soon the sea became rough and chopping, though the breeze was fair and gentle; and ere they were abreast of the Cape, they became aware of that strong eastward current which, during the winter months, so often baffles the mariner who wishes to go to the westward. All night long they struggled through the billows, with the huge wall of Cape Codera a thousand feet above their heads to the left, and beyond it again, bank upon bank of mountain, bathed in the yellow moonlight.

Morning showed them a large ship, which had passed them during the night upon the opposite course, and was now a good ten miles to the eastward. Yeo was for going back and taking her. Of the latter he made a matter of course; and the former was easy enough, for the breeze blowing dead off the land, was a "soldier's wind, there and back again," for either ship; but Amyas and Frank were both unwilling.

"Why, Yeo, you said that one day more would bring us to La Guayra."

"All the more reason, sir, for doing the Lord's work thoroughly, when He has brought us safely so far on our journey."

"She can pass well enough, and no loss."

"Ah, sirs, sirs, she is delivered into your hands, and you will have to give an account of her."

"My good Yeo," said Frank, "I trust we shall give good account enough of many a tall Spaniard before we return: but you know surely that La Guayra, and the salvation of one whom we believe dwells there, was our first object in this adventure."

Yeo shook his head sadly. "Ah, sirs, a lady brought Captain Oxenham to ruin."

"You do not dare to compare her with this one?" said Frank and Cary, both in a breath.

"God forbid, gentlemen: but no adventure will prosper, unless there is a single eye to the Lord's work; and that is, as I take it, to cripple the Spaniard, and exalt her majesty the queen. And I had thought that nothing was more dear than that to Captain Leigh's heart."

Amyas stood somewhat irresolute. His duty to the queen bade him follow the Spanish vessel: his duty to his vow, to go on to La Guayra. It may seem a far-fetched dilemma. He found it a practical one enough.

However, the counsel of Frank prevailed, and on to La Guayra he went. He half hoped that the Spaniard would see and attack them. However, he went on his way to the eastward; which if he had not done, my story had had a very different ending.

About mid-day a canoe, the first which they had seen, came staggering toward them under a huge three-cornered sail. As it came near, they could see two Indians on board.

"Metal floats in these seas, you see," quoth Cary. "There's a fresh marvel, for you, Frank."

"Expound," quoth Frank, who was really ready to swallow any fresh marvel, so many had he seen already.

"Why, how else would those two bronze statues dare to go to sea in such a cockleshell, eh? Have I given you the dor now, master courtier!"

"I am long past dors, Will. But what noble creatures they are! and how fearlessly they are coming alongside! Can they know that we are English, and the avengers of the Indians?"

"I suspect they just take us for Spaniards, and want to sell their cocoa-nuts. See, the canoe is laden with vegetables."

"Hail them, Yeo!" said Amyas. "You talk the best Spanish, and I want speech of one of them."

Yeo did so; the canoe, without more ado, ran alongside, and lowered her felucca sail, while a splendid Indian scrambled on board like a cat.

He was full six feet high, and as bold and graceful of bearing as Frank or Amyas's self. He looked round for the first moment smilingly, showing his white teeth; but the next, his countenance changed; and springing to the side, he shouted to his comrade in Spanish—

"Treachery! No Spaniard," and would have leaped overboard, but a dozen strong fellows caught him ere he could do so.

It required some trouble to master him, so strong was he, and so slippery his naked limbs; Amyas, meanwhile, alternately entreated the men not to hurt the Indian, and the Indian to be quiet, and no harm should happen to him; and so, after five minutes' confusion, the stranger gave in sulkily.

"Don't bind him. Let him loose, and make a ring round him. Now, my man, there's a dollar for you."

The Indian's eyes glistened, and he took the coin.

"All I want of you is, first, to tell me what ships are in La Guayra, and next, to go thither on board of me, and show me which is the governor's house, and which the custom-house."

The Indian laid the coin down on the deck, and crossing himself, looked Amyas in the face.

"No, senor! I am a freeman and a cavalier, a Christian Guayqueria, whose forefathers, first of all the Indians, swore fealty to the King of Spain, and whom he calls to this day in all his proclamations his most faithful, loyal, and noble Guayquerias. God forbid, therefore, that I should tell aught to his enemies, who are my enemies likewise."

A growl arose from those of the men who understood him; and more than one hinted that a cord twined round the head, or a match put between the fingers, would speedily extract the required information.

"God forbid!" said Amyas; "a brave and loyal man he is, and as such will I treat him. Tell me, my brave fellow, how do you know us to be his Catholic majesty's enemies?"

The Indian, with a shrewd smile, pointed to half-a-dozen different objects, saying to each, "Not Spanish."

"Well, and what of that?"

"None but Spaniards and free Guayquerias have a right to sail these seas."

Amyas laughed.

"Thou art a right valiant bit of copper. Pick up thy dollar, and go thy way in peace. Make room for him, men. We can learn what we want without his help."

The Indian paused, incredulous and astonished. "Overboard with you!" quoth Amyas. "Don't you know when you are well off?"

"Most illustrious senor," began the Indian, in the drawling sententious fashion of his race (when they take the trouble to talk at all), "I have been deceived. I heard that you heretics roasted and ate all true Catholics (as we Guayquerias are), and that all your padres had tails."

"Plague on you, sirrah!" squeaked Jack Brimblecombe. "Have I a tail? Look here!"

"Quien sabe? Who knows?" quoth the Indian through his nose.

"How do you know we are heretics?" said Amyas.

"Humph! But in repayment for your kindness, I would warn you, illustrious senor, not to go on to La Guayra. There are ships of war there waiting for you; and moreover, the governor Don Guzman sailed to the eastward only yesterday to look for you; and I wonder much that you did not meet him."

"To look for us! On the watch for us!" said Cary. "Impossible; lies! Amyas, this is some trick of the rascal's to frighten us away."

"Don Guzman came out but yesterday to look for us? Are you sure you spoke truth?"

"As I live, senor, he and another ship, for which I took yours."

Amyas stamped upon the deck: that then was the ship which they had passed!

"Fool that I was to have been close to my enemy, and let my opportunity slip! If I had but done my duty, all would have gone right!"

But it was too late to repine; and after all, the Indian's story was likely enough to be false.

"Off with you!" said he; and the Indian bounded over the side into his canoe, leaving the whole crew wondering at the stateliness and courtesy of this bold sea-cavalier.

So Westward-ho they ran, beneath the mighty northern wall, the highest cliff on earth, some seven thousand feet of rock parted from the sea by a narrow strip of bright green lowland. Here and there a patch of sugar-cane, or a knot of cocoa-nut trees, close to the water's edge, reminded them that they were in the tropics; but above, all was savage, rough, and bare as an Alpine precipice. Sometimes deep clefts allowed the southern sun to pour a blaze of light down to the sea marge, and gave glimpses far above of strange and stately trees lining the glens, and of a veil of perpetual mist which shrouded the inner summits; while up and down, between them and the mountain side, white fleecy clouds hung motionless in the burning air, increasing the impression of vastness and of solemn rest, which was already overpowering.

"Within those mountains, three thousand feet above our heads," said Drew, the master, "lies Saint Yago de Leon, the great city which the Spaniards founded fifteen years agone."

"Is it a rich place?" asked Cary.

"Very, they say."

"Is it a strong place?" asked Amyas.

"No forts to it at all, they say. The Spaniards boast, that Heaven has made such good walls to it already, that man need make none."

"I don't know," quoth Amyas. "Lads, could you climb those hills, do you think?"

"Rather higher than Harty Point, sir: but it depends pretty much on what's behind them."

And now the last point is rounded, and they are full in sight of the spot in quest of which they have sailed four thousand miles of sea. A low black cliff, crowned by a wall; a battery at either end. Within, a few narrow streets of white houses, running parallel with the sea, upon a strip of flat, which seemed not two hundred yards in breadth; and behind, the mountain wall, covering the whole in deepest shade. How that wall was ever ascended to the inland seemed the puzzle; but Drew, who had been off the place before, pointed out to them a narrow path, which wound upwards through a glen, seemingly sheer perpendicular. That was the road to the capital, if any man dare try it. In spite of the shadow of the mountain, the whole place wore a dusty and glaring look. The breaths of air which came off the land were utterly stifling; and no wonder, for La Guayra, owing to the radiation of that vast fire-brick of heated rock, is one of the hottest spots upon the face of the whole earth.

Where was the harbor? There was none. Only an open roadstead, wherein lay tossing at anchor five vessels. The two outer ones were small merchant caravels. Behind them lay two long, low, ugly-looking craft, at sight of which Yeo gave a long whew.

"Galleys, as I'm a sinful saint! And what's that big one inside of them, Robert Drew? She has more than hawseholes in her idolatrous black sides, I think."

"We shall open her astern of the galleys in another minute," said Amyas. "Look out, Cary, your eyes are better than mine."

"Six round portholes on the main deck," quoth Will.

"And I can see the brass patararoes glittering on her poop," quoth Amyas. "Will, we're in for it."

"In for it we are, captain.

"Let's go in, nevertheless, and pound the Don's ribs, my old lad of Smerwick. Eh? Three to one is very fair odds."

"Not underneath those fort guns, I beg leave to say," quoth Yeo. "If the Philistines will but come out unto us, we will make them like unto Zeba and Zalmunna."

"Quite true," said Amyas. "Game cocks are game cocks, but reason's reason."

"If the Philistines are not coming out, they are going to send a messenger instead," quoth Cary. "Look out, all thin skulls!"

And as he spoke, a puff of white smoke rolled from the eastern fort, and a heavy ball plunged into the water between it and the ship.

"I don't altogether like this," quoth Amyas. "What do they mean by firing on us without warning? And what are these ships of war doing here? Drew, you told me the armadas never lay here."

"No more, I believe, they do, sir, on account of the anchorage being so bad, as you may see. I'm mortal afeared that rascal's story was true, and that the Dons have got wind of our coming."

"Run up a white flag, at all events. If they do expect us, they must have known some time since, or how could they have got their craft hither?"

"True, sir. They must have come from Santa Marta, at the least; perhaps from Cartagena. And that would take a month at least going and coming."

Amyas suddenly recollected Eustace's threat in the wayside inn. Could he have betrayed their purpose? Impossible!

"Let us hold a council of war, at all events, Frank."

Frank was absorbed in a very different matter. A half-mile to the eastward of the town, two or three hundred feet up the steep mountain side, stood a large, low, white house embosomed in trees and gardens. There was no other house of similar size near; no place for one. And was not that the royal flag of Spain which flaunted before it? That must be the governor's house; that must be the abode of the Rose of Torridge! And Frank stood devouring it with wild eyes, till he had persuaded himself that he could see a woman's figure walking upon the terrace in front, and that the figure was none other than hers whom he sought. Amyas could hardly tear him away to a council of war, which was a sad, and only not a peevish one.

The three adventurers, with Brimblecombe, Yeo, and Drew, went apart upon the poop; and each looked the other in the face awhile. For what was to be done? The plans and hopes of months were brought to naught in an hour.

"It is impossible, you see," said Amyas, at last, "to surprise the town by land, while these ships are here; for if we land our men, we leave our ship without defence."

"As impossible as to challenge Don Guzman while he is not here," said Cary.

"I wonder why the ships have not opened on us already," said Drew.

"Perhaps they respect our flag of truce," said Cary. "Why not send in a boat to treat with them, and to inquire for—"

"For her?" interrupted Frank. "If we show that we are aware of her existence, her name is blasted in the eyes of those jealous Spaniards."

"And as for respecting our flag of truce, gentlemen," said Yeo, "if you will take an old man's advice, trust them not. They will keep the same faith with us as they kept with Captain Hawkins at San Juan d'Ulloa, in that accursed business which was the beginning of all the wars; when we might have taken the whole plate-fleet, with two hundred thousand pounds' worth of gold on board, and did not, but only asked license to trade like honest men. And yet, after they had granted us license, and deceived us by fair speech into landing ourselves and our ordnance, the governor and all the fleet set upon us, five to one, and gave no quarter to any soul whom he took. No, sir; I expect the only reason why they don't attack us is, because their crews are not on board."

"They will be, soon enough, then," said Amyas. "I can see soldiers coming down the landing-stairs."

And, in fact, boats full of armed men began to push off to the ships.

"We may thank Heaven," said Drew, "that we were not here two hours agone. The sun will be down before they are ready for sea, and the fellows will have no stomach to go looking for us by night."

"So much the worse for us. If they will but do that, we may give them the slip, and back again to the town, and there try our luck; for I cannot find it in my heart to leave the place without having one dash at it."

Yeo shook his head. "There are plenty more towns along the coast more worth trying than this, sir: but Heaven's will be done!"

And as they spoke, the sun plunged into the sea, and all was dark.

At last it was agreed to anchor, and wait till midnight. If the ships of war came out, they were to try to run in past them, and, desperate as the attempt might be, attempt their original plan of landing to the westward of the town, taking it in flank, plundering the government storehouses, which they saw close to the landing-place, and then fighting their way back to their boats, and out of the roadstead. Two hours would suffice if the armada and the galleys were but once out of the way.

Amyas went forward, called the men together, and told them the plan. It was not very cheerfully received: but what else was there to be done!

They ran down about a mile and a half to the westward, and anchored.

The night wore on, and there was no sign of stir among the shipping; for though they could not see the vessels themselves, yet their lights (easily distinguished by their relative height from those in the town above) remained motionless; and the men fretted and fumed for weary hours at thus seeing a rich prize (for of course the town was paved with gold) within arm's reach, and yet impossible.

Let Amyas and his men have patience. Some short five years more, and the great Armada will have come and gone; and then that avenging storm, of which they, like Oxenham, Hawkins, and Drake, are but the avant-couriers, will burst upon every Spanish port from Corunna to Cadiz, from the Canaries to Havana, and La Guayra and St. Yago de Leon will not escape their share. Captain Amyas Preston and Captain Sommers, the colonist of the Bermudas, or Sommers' Islands, will land, with a force tiny enough, though larger far than Leigh's, where Leigh dare not land; and taking the fort of Guayra, will find, as Leigh found, that their coming has been expected, and that the Pass of the Venta, three thousand feet above, has been fortified with huge barricadoes, abattis, and cannon, making the capital, amid its ring of mountain-walls, impregnable—to all but Englishmen or Zouaves. For up that seven thousand feet of precipice, which rises stair on stair behind the town, those fierce adventurers will climb hand over hand, through rain and fog, while men lie down, and beg their officers to kill them, for no farther can they go. Yet farther they will go, hewing a path with their swords through woods of wild plantain, and rhododendron thickets, over (so it seems, however incredible) the very saddle of the Silla,* down upon the astonished "Mantuanos" of St. Jago, driving all before them; and having burnt the city in default of ransom, will return triumphant by the right road, and pass along the coast, the masters of the deep.

I know not whether any men still live who count their descent from those two valiant captains; but if such there be, let them be sure that the history of the English navy tells no more Titanic victory over nature and man than that now forgotten raid of Amyas Preston and his comrade, in the year of grace 1595.

But though a venture on the town was impossible, yet there was another venture which Frank was unwilling to let slip. A light which now shone brightly in one of the windows of the governor's house was the lodestar to which all his thoughts were turned; and as he sat in the cabin with Amyas, Cary, and Jack, he opened his heart to them.

"And are we, then," asked he, mournfully, "to go without doing the very thing for which we came?"

All were silent awhile. At last John Brimblecombe spoke.

"Show me the way to do it, Mr. Frank, and I will go."

"My dearest man," said Amyas, "what would you have? Any attempt to see her, even if she be here, would be all but certain death."

"And what if it were? What if it were, my brother Amyas? Listen to me. I have long ceased to shrink from Death; but till I came into these magic climes, I never knew the beauty of his face."

"Of death?" said Cary. "I should have said, of life. God forgive me! but man might wish to live forever, if he had such a world as this wherein to live."

"And do you forget, Cary, that the more fair this passing world of time, by so much the more fair is that eternal world, whereof all here is but a shadow and a dream; by so much the more fair is He before whose throne the four mystic beasts, the substantial ideas of Nature and her powers, stand day and night, crying, 'Holy, holy, holy, Lord God of hosts, Thou hast made all things, and for Thy pleasure they are and were created!' My friends, if He be so prodigal of His own glory as to have decked these lonely shores, all but unknown since the foundation of the world, with splendors beyond all our dreams, what must be the glory of His face itself! I have done with vain shadows. It is better to depart and to be with Him, where shall be neither desire nor anger, self-deception nor pretence, but the eternal fulness of reality and truth. One thing I have to do before I die, for God has laid it on me. Let that be done to-night, and then, farewell!"

"Frank! Frank! remember our mother!"

"I do remember her. I have talked over these things with her many a time; and where I would fain be, she would fain be also. She sent me out with my virgin honor, as the Spartan mother did her boy with the shield, saying, 'Come back either with this, or upon this;' and one or the other I must do, if I would meet her either in this life or in the next. But in the meanwhile do not mistake me; my life is God's, and I promise not to cast it away rashly."

"What would you do, then?"

"Go up to that house, Amyas, and speak with her, if Heaven gives me an opportunity, as Heaven, I feel assured, will give."

"And do you call that no rashness?"

"Is any duty rashness? Is it rash to stand amid the flying bullets, if your queen has sent you? Is it more rash to go to seek Christ's lost lamb, if God and your own oath hath sent you? John Brimblecombe answered that question for us long ago."

"If you go, I go with you!" said all three at once.

"No. Amyas, you owe a duty to our mother and to your ship. Cary, you are heir to great estates, and are bound thereby to your country and to your tenants. John Brimblecombe—"

"Ay!" squeaked Jack. "And what have you to say, Mr. Frank, against my going?—I, who have neither ship nor estates—except, I suppose, that I am not worthy to travel in such good company?"

"Think of your old parents, John, and all your sisters."

"I thought of them before I started, sir, as Mr. Cary knows, and you know too. I came here to keep my vow, and I am not going to turn renegade at the very foot of the cross."

"Some one must go with you, Frank," said Amyas; "if it were only to bring back the boat's crew in case—" and he faltered.

"In case I fall," replied Frank, with a smile. "I will finish your sentence for you, lad; I am not afraid of it, though you may be for me. Yet some one, I fear, must go. Unhappy me! that I cannot risk my own worthless life without risking your more precious lives!"

"Not so, Mr. Frank! Your oath is our oath, and your duty ours!" said John. "I will tell you what we will do, gentlemen all. We three will draw cuts for the honor of going with him."

"Lots?" said Amyas. "I don't like leaving such grave matters to chance, friend John."

"Chance, sir? When you have used all your own wit, and find it fail you, then what is drawing lots but taking the matter out of your own weak hands, and laying it in God's strong hands?"

"Right, John!" said Frank. "So did the apostles choose their successor, and so did holy men of old decide controversies too subtle for them; and we will not be ashamed to follow their example. For my part, I have often said to Sidney and to Spenser, when we have babbled together of Utopian governments in days which are now dreams to me, that I would have all officers of state chosen by lot out of the wisest and most fit; so making sure that they should be called by God, and not by man alone. Gentlemen, do you agree to Sir John's advice?"

They agreed, seeing no better counsel, and John put three slips of paper into Frank's hand, with the simple old apostolic prayer—

"Show which of us three Thou hast chosen."

The lot fell upon Amyas Leigh.

Frank shuddered, and clasped his hands over his face.

"Well," said Cary, "I have ill-luck to-night: but Frank goes at least in good company."

"Ah, that it had been I!" said Jack; "though I suppose I was too poor a body to have such an honor fall on me. And yet it is hard for flesh and blood; hard indeed to have come all this way, and not to see her after all!"

"Jack," said Frank, "you are kept to do better work than this, doubt not. But if the lot had fallen on you—ay, if it had fallen on a three years' child, I would have gone up as cheerfully with that child to lead me, as I do now with this my brother! Amyas, can we have a boat, and a crew? It is near midnight already."

Amyas went on deck, and asked for six volunteers. Whosoever would come, Amyas would double out of his own purse any prize-money which might fall to that man's share.

One of the old Pelican's crew, Simon Evans of Clovelly, stepped out at once.

"Why six only, captain? Give the word, and any and all of us will go up with you, sack the house, and bring off the treasure and the lady, before two hours are out."

"No, no, my brave lads! As for treasure, if there be any, it is sure to have been put all safe into the forts, or hidden in the mountains; and as for the lady, God forbid that we should force her a step without her own will."

The honest sailor did not quite understand this punctilio: but—

"Well, captain," quoth he, "as you like; but no man shall say that you asked for a volunteer, were it to jump down a shark's throat, but what you had me first of all the crew."

After this sort of temper had been exhibited, three or four more came forward—Yeo was very anxious to go, but Amyas forbade him.

"I'll volunteer, sir, without reward, for this or anything; though" (added he in a lower tone) "I would to Heaven that the thought had never entered your head."

"And so would I have volunteered," said Simon Evans, "if it were the ship's quarrel, or the queen's; but being it's a private matter of the captain's, and I've a wife and children at home, why, I take no shame to myself for asking money for my life."

So the crew was made up; but ere they pushed off, Amyas called Cary aside—

"If I perish, Will—"

"Don't talk of such things, dear old lad."

"I must. Then you are captain. Do nothing without Yeo and Drew. But if they approve, go right north away for San Domingo and Cuba, and try the ports; they can have no news of us there, and there is booty without end. Tell my mother that I died like a gentleman; and mind—mind, dear lad, to keep your temper with the men, let the poor fellows grumble as they may. Mind but that, and fear God, and all will go well."

The tears were glistening in Cary's eyes as he pressed Amyas's hand, and watched the two brothers down over the side upon their desperate errand.

They reached the pebble beach. There seemed no difficulty about finding the path to the house—so bright was the moon, and so careful a survey of the place had Frank taken. Leaving the men with the boat (Amyas had taken care that they should be well armed), they started up the beach, with their swords only. Frank assured Amyas that they would find a path leading from the beach up to the house, and he was not mistaken. They found it easily, for it was made of white shell sand; and following it, struck into a "tunal," or belt of tall thorny cactuses. Through this the path wound in zigzags up a steep rocky slope, and ended at a wicket-gate. They tried it, and found it open.

"She may expect us," whispered Frank.

"Impossible!"

"Why not? She must have seen our ship; and if, as seems, the townsfolk know who we are, how much more must she! Yes, doubt it not, she still longs to hear news of her own land, and some secret sympathy will draw her down towards the sea to-night. See! the light is in the window still!"

"But if not," said Amyas, who had no such expectation, "what is your plan?"

"I have none."

"None?"

"I have imagined twenty different ones in the last hour; but all are equally uncertain, impossible. I have ceased to struggle—I go where I am called, love's willing victim. If Heaven accept the sacrifice, it will provide the altar and the knife."

Aymas was at his wits' end. Judging of his brother by himself, he had taken for granted that Frank had some well-concocted scheme for gaining admittance to the Rose; and as the wiles of love were altogether out of his province, he had followed in full faith such a sans-appel as he held Frank to be. But now he almost doubted of his brother's sanity, though Frank's manner was perfectly collected and his voice firm. Amyas, honest fellow, had no understanding of that intense devotion, which so many in those days (not content with looking on it as a lofty virtue, and yet one to be duly kept in its place by other duties) prided themselves on pampering into the most fantastic and self-willed excesses.

Beautiful folly! the death-song of which two great geniuses were composing at that very moment, each according to his light. For, while Spenser was embalming in immortal verse all that it contained of noble and Christian elements, Cervantes sat, perhaps, in his dungeon, writing with his left hand Don Quixote, saddest of books, in spite of all its wit; the story of a pure and noble soul, who mistakes this actual life for that ideal one which he fancies (and not so wrongly either) eternal in the heavens: and finding instead of a battlefield for heroes in God's cause, nothing but frivolity, heartlessness, and godlessness, becomes a laughing-stock,—and dies. One of the saddest books, I say again, which man can read.

Amyas hardly dare trust himself to speak, for fear of saying too much; but he could not help saying—

"You are going to certain death, Frank."

"Did I not entreat," answered he, very quietly, "to go alone?"

Amyas had half a mind to compel him to return: but he feared Frank's obstinacy; and feared, too, the shame of returning on board without having done anything; so they went up through the wicket-gate, along a smooth turf walk, into what seemed a pleasure-garden, formed by the hand of man, or rather of woman. For by the light, not only of the moon, but of the innumerable fireflies, which flitted to and fro across the sward like fiery imps sent to light the brothers on their way, they could see that the bushes on either side, and the trees above their heads, were decked with flowers of such strangeness and beauty, that, as Frank once said of Barbados, "even the gardens of Wilton were a desert in comparison." All around were orange and lemon trees (probably the only addition which man had made to Nature's prodigality), the fruit of which, in that strange colored light of the fireflies, flashed in their eyes like balls of burnished gold and emerald; while great white tassels swinging from every tree in the breeze which swept down the glade, tossed in their faces a fragrant snow of blossoms, and glittering drops of perfumed dew.

"What a paradise!" said Amyas to Frank, "with the serpent in it, as of old. Look!"

And as he spoke, there dropped slowly down from a bough, right before them, what seemed a living chain of gold, ruby, and sapphire. Both stopped, and another glance showed the small head and bright eyes of a snake, hissing and glaring full in their faces.

"See!" said Frank. "And he comes, as of old, in the likeness of an angel of light. Do not strike it. There are worse devils to be fought with to-night than that poor beast." And stepping aside, they passed the snake safely, and arrived in front of the house.

It was, as I have said, a long low house, with balconies along the upper story, and the under part mostly open to the wind. The light was still burning in the window.

"Whither now?" said Amyas, in a tone of desperate resignation.

"Thither! Where else on earth?" and Frank pointed to the light, trembling from head to foot, and pushed on.

"For Heaven's sake! Look at the negroes on the barbecue!"

It was indeed time to stop; for on the barbecue, or terrace of white plaster, which ran all round the front, lay sleeping full twenty black figures.

"What will you do now? You must step over them to gain an entrance."

"Wait here, and I will go up gently towards the window. She may see me. She will see me as I step into the moonlight. At least I know an air by which she will recognize me, if I do but hum a stave."

"Why, you do not even know that that light is hers!—Down, for your life!"

And Amyas dragged him down into the bushes on his left hand; for one of the negroes, wakening suddenly with a cry, had sat up, and began crossing himself four or five times, in fear of "Duppy," and mumbling various charms, ayes, or what not.

The light above was extinguished instantly.

"Did you see her?" whispered Frank.

"No."

"I did—the shadow of the face, and the neck! Can I be mistaken?" And then, covering his face with his hands, he murmured to himself, "Misery! misery! So near and yet impossible?"

"Would it be the less impossible were you face to face? Let us go back. We cannot go up without detection, even if our going were of use. Come back, for God's sake, ere all is lost! If you have seen her, as you say, you know at least that she is alive, and safe in his house—"

"As his mistress? or as his wife? Do I know that yet, Amyas, and can I depart until I know?"

There was a few minutes' silence, and then Amyas, making one last attempt to awaken Frank to the absurdity of the whole thing, and to laugh him, if possible, out of it, as argument had no effect—

"My dear fellow, I am very hungry and sleepy; and this bush is very prickly; and my boots are full of ants—"

"So are mine.—Look!" and Frank caught Amyas's arm, and clenched it tight.

For round the farther corner of the house a dark cloaked figure stole gently, turning a look now and then upon the sleeping negroes, and came on right toward them.

"Did I not tell you she would come?" whispered Frank, in a triumphant tone.

Amyas was quite bewildered; and to his mind the apparition seemed magical, and Frank prophetic; for as the figure came nearer, incredulous as he tried to be, there was no denying that the shape and the walk were exactly those of her, to find whom they had crossed the Atlantic. True, the figure was somewhat taller; but then, "she must be grown since I saw her," thought Amyas; and his heart for the moment beat as fiercely as Frank's.

But what was that behind her? Her shadow against the white wall of the house. Not so. Another figure, cloaked likewise, but taller far, was following on her steps. It was a man's. They could see that he wore a broad sombrero. It could not be Don Guzman, for he was at sea. Who then? Here was a mystery; perhaps a tragedy. And both brothers held their breaths, while Amyas felt whether his sword was loose in the sheath.

The Rose (if indeed it was she) was within ten yards of them, when she perceived that she was followed. She gave a little shriek. The cavalier sprang forward, lifted his hat courteously, and joined her, bowing low. The moonlight was full upon his face.

"It is Eustace, our cousin! How came he here, in the name of all the fiends?"

"Eustace! Then that is she, after all!" said Frank, forgetting everything else in her.

And now flashed across Amyas all that had passed between him and Eustace in the moorland inn, and Parracombe's story, too, of the suspicious gipsy. Eustace had been beforehand with them, and warned Don Guzman! All was explained now: but how had he got hither?

"The devil, his master, sent him hither on a broomstick, I suppose: or what matter how? Here he is; and here we are, worse luck!" And, setting his teeth, Amyas awaited the end.

The two came on, talking earnestly, and walking at a slow pace, so that the brothers could hear every word.

"What shall we do now?" said Frank. "We have no right to be eavesdroppers."

"But we must be, right or none." And Amyas held him down firmly by the arm.

"But whither are you going, then, my dear madam?" they heard Eustace say in a wheedling tone. "Can you wonder if such strange conduct should cause at least sorrow to your admirable and faithful husband?"

"Husband!" whispered Frank faintly to Amyas. "Thank God, thank God! I am content. Let us go."

But to go was impossible; for, as fate would have it, the two had stopped just opposite them.

"The inestimable Senor Don Guzman—" began Eustace again.

"What do you mean by praising him to me in this fulsome way, sir? Do you suppose that I do not know his virtues better than you?"

"If you do, madam" (this was spoken in a harder tone), "it were wise for you to try them less severely, than by wandering down towards the beach on the very night that you know his most deadly enemies are lying in wait to slay him, plunder his house, and most probably to carry you off from him."

"Carry me off? I will die first!"

"Who can prove that to him? Appearances are at least against you."

"My love to him, and his trust for me, sir!"

"His trust? Have you forgotten, madam, what passed last week, and why he sailed yesterday?"

The only answer was a burst of tears. Eustace stood watching her with a terrible eye; but they could see his face writhing in the moonlight.

"Oh!" sobbed she at last. "And if I have been imprudent, was it not natural to wish to look once more upon an English ship? Are you not English as well as I? Have you no longing recollections of the dear old land at home?"

Eustace was silent; but his face worked more fiercely than ever.

"How can he ever know it?"

"Why should he not know it?"

"Ah!" she burst out passionately, "why not, indeed, while you are here? You, sir, the tempter, you the eavesdropper, you the sunderer of loving hearts! You, serpent, who found our home a paradise, and see it now a hell!"

"Do you dare to accuse me thus, madam, without a shadow of evidence?"

"Dare? I dare anything, for I know all! I have watched you, sir, and I have borne with you too long."

"Me, madam, whose only sin towards you, as you should know by now, is to have loved you too well? Rose! Rose! have you not blighted my life for me—broken my heart? And how have I repaid you? How but by sacrificing myself to seek you over land and sea, that I might complete your conversion to the bosom of that Church where a Virgin Mother stands stretching forth soft arms to embrace her wandering daughter, and cries to you all day long, 'Come unto me, ye that are weary and heavy laden, and I will give you rest!' And this is my reward!"

"Depart with your Virgin Mother, sir, and tempt me no more! You have asked me what I dare; and I dare this, upon my own ground, and in my own garden, I, Donna Rosa de Soto, to bid you leave this place now and forever, after having insulted me by talking of your love, and tempted me to give up that faith which my husband promised me he would respect and protect. Go, sir!"

The brothers listened breathless with surprise as much as with rage. Love and conscience, and perhaps, too, the pride of her lofty alliance, had converted the once gentle and dreamy Rose into a very Roxana; but it was only the impulse of a moment. The words had hardly passed her lips, when, terrified at what she had said, she burst into a fresh flood of tears; while Eustace answered calmly:

"I go, madam: but how know you that I may not have orders, and that, after your last strange speech, my conscience may compel me to obey those orders, to take you with me?"

"Me? with you?"

"My heart has bled for you, madam, for many a year. It longs now that it had bled itself to death, and never known the last worst agony of telling you—"

And drawing close to her he whispered in her ear—what, the brothers heard not—but her answer was a shriek which rang through the woods, and sent the night-birds fluttering up from every bough above their heads.

"By Heaven!" said Amyas, "I can stand this no longer. Cut that devil's throat I must—"

"She is lost if his dead body is found by her."

"We are lost if we stay here, then," said Amyas; "for those negroes will hurry down at her cry, and then found we must be."

"Are you mad, madam, to betray yourself by your own cries? The negroes will be here in a moment. I give you one last chance for life, then:" and Eustace shouted in Spanish at the top of his voice, "Help, help, servants! Your mistress is being carried off by bandits!"

"What do you mean, sir?"

"Let your woman's wit supply the rest: and forget not him who thus saves you from disgrace."

Whether the brothers heard the last words or not, I know not; but taking for granted that Eustace had discovered them, they sprang to their feet at once, determined to make one last appeal, and then to sell their lives as dearly as they could.

Eustace started back at the unexpected apparition; but a second glance showed him Amyas's mighty bulk; and he spoke calmly—

"You see, madam, I did not call without need. Welcome, good cousins. My charity, as you perceive, has found means to outstrip your craft; while the fair lady, as was but natural, has been true to her assignation!"

"Liar!" cried Frank. "She never knew of our being—"

"Credat Judaeus!" answered Eustace; but, as he spoke, Amyas burst through the bushes at him. There was no time to be lost; and ere the giant could disentangle himself from the boughs and shrubs, Eustace had slipped off his long cloak, thrown it over Amyas's head, and ran up the alley shouting for help.

Mad with rage, Amyas gave chase: but in two minutes more Eustace was safe among the ranks of the negroes, who came shouting and jabbering down the path.

He rushed back. Frank was just ending some wild appeal to Rose—

"Your conscience! your religion!—"

"No, never! I can face the chance of death, but not the loss of him. Go! for God's sake, leave me!"

"You are lost, then,—and I have ruined you!"

"Come off, now or never," cried Amyas, clutching him by the arm, and dragging him away like a child.

"You forgive me?" cried he.

"Forgive you?" and she burst into tears again.

Frank burst into tears also.

"Let me go back, and die with her—Amyas!—my oath!—my honor!" and he struggled to turn back.

Amyas looked back too, and saw her standing calmly, with her hands folded across her breast, awaiting Eustace and the servants; and he half turned to go back also. Both saw how fearfully appearances had put her into Eustace's power. Had he not a right to suspect that they were there by her appointment; that she was going to escape with them? And would not Eustace use his power? The thought of the Inquisition crossed their minds. "Was that the threat which Eustace had whispered?" asked he of Frank.

"It was," groaned Frank, in answer.

For the first and last time in his life, Amyas Leigh stood irresolute.

"Back, and stab her to the heart first!" said Frank, struggling to escape from him.

Oh, if Amyas were but alone, and Frank safe home in England! To charge the whole mob, kill her, kill Eustace, and then cut his way back again to the ship, or die,—what matter? as he must die some day,—sword in hand! But Frank!—and then flashed before his eyes his mother's hopeless face; then rang in his ears his mother's last bequest to him of that frail treasure. Let Rose, let honor, let the whole world perish, he must save Frank. See! the negroes were up with her now—past her—away for life! and once more he dragged his brother down the hill, and through the wicket, only just in time; for the whole gang of negroes were within ten yards of them in full pursuit.

"Frank," said he, sharply, "if you ever hope to see your mother again, rouse yourself, man, and fight!" And, without waiting for an answer, he turned, and charged up-hill upon his pursuers, who saw the long bright blade, and fled instantly.

Again he hurried Frank down the hill; the path wound in zigzags, and he feared that the negroes would come straight over the cliff, and so cut off his retreat: but the prickly cactuses were too much for them, and they were forced to follow by the path, while the brothers (Frank having somewhat regained his senses) turned every now and then to menace them: but once on the rocky path, stones began to fly fast; small ones fortunately, and wide and wild for want of light—but when they reached the pebble-beach? Both were too proud to run; but, if ever Amyas prayed in his life, he prayed for the last twenty yards before he reached the water-mark.

"Now, Frank! down to the boat as hard as you can run, while I keep the curs back."

"Amyas! what do you take me for? My madness brought you hither: your devotion shall not bring me back without you."

"Together, then!"

And putting Frank's arm through his, they hurried down, shouting to their men.

The boat was not fifty yards off: but fast travelling over the pebbles was impossible, and long ere half the distance was crossed, the negroes were on the beach, and the storm burst. A volley of great quartz pebbles whistled round their heads.

"Come on, Frank! for life's sake! Men, to the rescue! Ah! what was that?"

The dull crash of a pebble against Frank's fair head! Drooping like Hyacinthus beneath the blow of the quoit, he sank on Amyas's arm. The giant threw him over his shoulder, and plunged blindly on,—himself struck again and again.

"Fire, men! Give it the black villains!"

The arquebuses crackled from the boat in front. What were those dull thuds which answered from behind? Echoes? No. Over his head the caliver-balls went screeching. The governors' guard have turned out, followed them to the beach, fixed their calivers, and are firing over the negroes' heads, as the savages rush down upon the hapless brothers.

If, as all say, there are moments which are hours, how many hours was Amyas Leigh in reaching that boat's bow? Alas! the negroes are there as soon as he, and the guard, having left their calivers, are close behind them, sword in hand. Amyas is up to his knees in water—battered with stones—blinded with blood. The boat is swaying off and on against the steep pebble-bank: he clutches at it—misses—falls headlong—rises half-choked with water: but Frank is still in his arms. Another heavy blow—a confused roar of shouts, shots, curses—a confused mass of negroes and English, foam and pebbles—and he recollects no more.

He is lying in the stern-sheets of the boat; stiff, weak, half blind with blood. He looks up; the moon is still bright overhead: but they are away from the shore now, for the wave-crests are dancing white before the land-breeze, high above the boat's side. The boat seems strangely empty. Two men are pulling instead of six! And what is this lying heavy across his chest? He pushes, and is answered by a groan. He puts his hand down to rise, and is answered by another groan.

"What's this?"

"All that are left of us," says Simon Evans of Clovelly.

"All?" The bottom of the boat seemed paved with human bodies. "Oh God! oh God!" moans Amyas, trying to rise. "And where—where is Frank? Frank!"

"Mr. Frank!" cries Evans. There is no answer.

"Dead?" shrieks Amyas. "Look for him, for God's sake, look!" and struggling from under his living load, he peers into each pale and bleeding face.

"Where is he? Why don't you speak, forward there?"

"Because we have naught to say, sir," answers Evans, almost surlily.

Frank was not there.

"Put the boat about! To the shore!" roars Amyas.

"Look over the gunwale, and judge for yourself, sir!"

The waves are leaping fierce and high before a furious land-breeze. Return is impossible.

"Cowards! villains! traitors! hounds! to have left him behind."

"Listen you to me, Captain Amyas Leigh," says Simon Evans, resting on his oar; "and hang me for mutiny, if you will, when we're aboard, if we ever get there. Isn't it enough to bring us out to death (as you knew yourself, sir, for you're prudent enough) to please that poor young gentleman's fancy about a wench; but you must call coward an honest man that have saved your life this night, and not a one of us but has his wound to show?"

Amyas was silent; the rebuke was just.

"I tell you, sir, if we've hove a stone out of this boat since we got off, we've hove two hundredweight, and, if the Lord had not fought for us, she'd have been beat to noggin-staves there on the beach."

"How did I come here, then?"

"Tom Hart dragged you in out of five feet water, and then thrust the boat off, and had his brains beat out for reward. All were knocked down but us two. So help me God, we thought that you had hove Mr. Frank on board just as you were knocked down, and saw William Frost drag him in."

But William Frost was lying senseless in the bottom of the boat. There was no explanation. After all, none was needed.

"And I have three wounds from stones, and this man behind me as many more, beside a shot through his shoulder. Now, sir, be we cowards?"

"You have done your duty," said Amyas, and sank down in the boat, and cried as if his heart would break; and then sprang up, and, wounded as he was, took the oar from Evans's hands. With weary work they made the ship, but so exhausted that another boat had to be lowered to get them alongside.

The alarm being now given, it was hardly safe to remain where they were; and after a stormy and sad argument, it was agreed to weigh anchor and stand off and on till morning; for Amyas refused to leave the spot till he was compelled, though he had no hope (how could he have?) that Frank might still be alive. And perhaps it was well for them, as will appear in the next chapter, that morning did not find them at anchor close to the town.

However that may be, so ended that fatal venture of mistaken chivalry.

CHAPTER XX: SPANISH BLOODHOUNDS AND ENGLISH MASTIFFS

When the sun leaped up the next morning, and the tropic light flashed suddenly into the tropic day, Amyas was pacing the deck, with dishevelled hair and torn clothes, his eyes red with rage and weeping, his heart full—how can I describe it? Picture it to yourselves, picture it to yourselves, you who have ever lost a brother; and you who have not, thank God that you know nothing of his agony. Full of impossible projects, he strode and staggered up and down, as the ship thrashed close-hauled through the rolling seas. He would go back and burn the villa. He would take Guayra, and have the life of every man in it in return for his brother's. "We can do it, lads!" he shouted. "If Drake took Nombre de Dios, we can take La Guayra." And every voice shouted, "Yes."

"We will have it, Amyas, and have Frank too, yet," cried Cary; but Amyas shook his head. He knew, and knew not why he knew, that all the ports in New Spain would never restore to him that one beloved face.

"Yes, he shall be well avenged. And look there! There is the first crop of our vengeance. And he pointed toward the shore, where between them and the now distant peaks of the Silla, three sails appeared, not five miles to windward.

"There are the Spanish bloodhounds on our heels, the same ships which we saw yesterday off Guayra. Back, lads, and welcome them, if they were a dozen."

There was a murmur of applause from all around; and if any young heart sank for a moment at the prospect of fighting three ships at once, it was awed into silence by the cheer which rose from all the older men, and by Salvation Yeo's stentorian voice.

"If there were a dozen, the Lord is with us, who has said, 'One of you shall chase a thousand.' Clear away, lads, and see the glory of the Lord this day."

"Amen!" cried Cary; and the ship was kept still closer to the wind.

Amyas had revived at the sight of battle. He no longer felt his wounds, or his great sorrow; even Frank's last angel's look grew dimmer every moment as he bustled about the deck; and ere a quarter of an hour had passed, his voice cried firmly and cheerfully as of old—

"Now, my masters, let us serve God, and then to breakfast, and after that clear for action."

Jack Brimblecombe read the daily prayers, and the prayers before a fight at sea, and his honest voice trembled, as, in the Prayer for all Conditions of Men (in spite of Amyas's despair), he added, "and especially for our dear brother Mr. Francis Leigh, perhaps captive among the idolaters;" and so they rose.

"Now, then," said Amyas, "to breakfast. A Frenchman fights best fasting, a Dutchman drunk, an Englishman full, and a Spaniard when the devil is in him, and that's always."

"And good beef and the good cause are a match for the devil," said Cary. "Come down, captain; you must eat too."

Amyas shook his head, took the tiller from the steersman, and bade him go below and fill himself. Will Cary went down, and returned in five minutes, with a plate of bread and beef, and a great jack of ale, coaxed them down Amyas's throat, as a nurse does with a child, and then scuttled below again with tears hopping down his face.

Amyas stood still steering. His face was grown seven years older in the last night. A terrible set calm was on him. Woe to the man who came across him that day!

"There are three of them, you see, my masters," said he, as the crew came on deck again. "A big ship forward, and two galleys astern of her. The big ship may keep; she is a race ship, and if we can but recover the wind of her, we will see whether our height is not a match for her length. We must give her the slip, and take the galleys first."

"I thank the Lord," said Yeo, "who has given so wise a heart to so young a general; a very David and Daniel, saving his presence, lads; and if any dare not follow him, let him be as the men of Meroz and of Succoth. Amen! Silas Staveley, smite me that boy over the head, the young monkey; why is he not down at the powder-room door?"

And Yeo went about his gunnery, as one who knew how to do it, and had the most terrible mind to do it thoroughly, and the most terrible faith that it was God's work.

So all fell to; and though there was comparatively little to be done, the ship having been kept as far as could be in fighting order all night, yet there was "clearing of decks, lacing of nettings, making of bulwarks, fitting of waist-cloths, arming of tops, tallowing of pikes, slinging of yards, doubling of sheets and tacks," enough to satisfy even the pedantical soul of Richard Hawkins himself. Amyas took charge of the poop, Cary of the forecastle, and Yeo, as gunner, of the main-deck, while Drew, as master, settled himself in the waist; and all was ready, and more than ready, before the great ship was within two miles of them.

And now while the mastiffs of England and the bloodhounds of Spain are nearing and nearing over the rolling surges, thirsting for each other's blood, let us spend a few minutes at least in looking at them both, and considering the causes which in those days enabled the English to face and conquer armaments immensely superior in size and number of ships, and to boast that in the whole Spanish war but one queen's ship, the Revenge, and (if I recollect right) but one private man-of-war, Sir Richard Hawkins's Dainty, had ever struck their colors to the enemy.

What was it which enabled Sir Richard Grenville's Revenge, in his last fearful fight off the Azores, to endure, for twelve hours before she struck, the attack of eight Spanish armadas, of which two (three times her own burden) sank at her side; and after all her masts were gone, and she had been boarded three times without success, to defy to the last the whole fleet of fifty-four sail, which lay around her, waiting for her to sink, "like dogs around the dying forest king"?

What enabled young Richard Hawkins's Dainty, though half her guns were useless through the carelessness or treachery of the gunner, to maintain for three days a running fight with two Spaniards of equal size with her, double the weight of metal, and ten times the number of men?

What enabled Sir George Cary's illustrious ship, the Content, to fight, single-handed, from seven in the morning till eleven at night, with four great armadas and two galleys, though her heaviest gun was but one nine-pounder, and for many hours she had but thirteen men fit for service?

What enabled, in the very year of which I write, those two "valiant Turkey Merchantmen of London, the Merchant Royal and the Tobie," with their three small consorts, to cripple, off

Pantellaria in the Mediterranean, the whole fleet of Spanish galleys sent to intercept them, and return triumphant through the Straits of Gibraltar?

And lastly, what in the fight of 1588, whereof more hereafter, enabled the English fleet to capture, destroy, and scatter that Great Armada, with the loss (but not the capture) of one pinnace, and one gentleman of note?

There were more causes than one: the first seems to have lain in the build of the English ships; the second in their superior gunnery and weight of metal; the third (without which the first would have been useless) in the hearts of the English men.

The English ship was much shorter than the Spanish; and this (with the rig of those days) gave them an ease in manoeuvring, which utterly confounded their Spanish foes. "The English ships in the fight of 1588," says Camden, "charged the enemy with marvellous agility, and having discharged their broadsides, flew forth presently into the deep, and levelled their shot directly, without missing, at those great ships of the Spaniards, which were altogether heavy and unwieldy." Moreover, the Spanish fashion, in the West Indies at least, though not in the ships of the Great Armada, was, for the sake of carrying merchandise, to build their men-of-war flush-decked, or as it was called "race" (razes), which left those on deck exposed and open; while the English fashion was to heighten the ship as much as possible at stem and stern, both by the sweep of her lines, and also by stockades ("close fights and cage-works") on the poop and forecastle, thus giving to the men a shelter, which was further increased by strong bulkheads ("cobridgeheads") across the main-deck below, dividing the ship thus into a number of separate forts, fitted with swivels ("bases, fowlers, and murderers") and loopholed for musketry and arrows.

But the great source of superiority was, after all, in the men themselves. The English sailor was then, as now, a quite amphibious and all-cunning animal, capable of turning his hand to everything, from needlework and carpentry to gunnery or hand-to-hand blows; and he was, moreover, one of a nation, every citizen of which was not merely permitted to carry arms, but compelled by law to practise from childhood the use of the bow, and accustomed to consider sword-play and quarter-staff as a necessary part and parcel of education, and the pastime of every leisure hour. The "fiercest nation upon earth," as they were then called, and the freest also, each man of them fought for himself with the self-help and self-respect of a Yankee ranger, and once bidden to do his work, was trusted to carry it out by his own wit as best he could. In one word, he was a free man.

The English officers, too, as now, lived on terms of sympathy with their men unknown to the Spaniards, who raised between the commander and the commanded absurd barriers of rank and blood, which forbade to his pride any labor but that of fighting. The English officers, on the other hand, brought up to the same athletic sports, the same martial exercises, as their men, were not ashamed to care for them, to win their friendship, even on emergency to consult their judgment; and used their rank, not to differ from their men, but to outvie them; not merely to command and be obeyed, but, like Homer's heroes, or the old Norse Vikings, to lead and be followed. Drake touched the true mainspring of English success when he once (in his voyage round the world) indignantly rebuked some coxcomb gentlemen-adventurers with—"I should like to see the gentleman that will refuse to set his hand to a rope. I must have the gentlemen to hale and draw with the mariners." But those were days in which her majesty's service was as little overridden by absurd rules of seniority, as by that etiquette which is at once the counterfeit and the ruin of true discipline. Under Elizabeth and her ministers, a brave and a shrewd man was certain of promotion, let his rank or his age be what they might; the true honor of knighthood covered once and for all any lowliness of birth; and the merchant service (in which all the best sea-captains, even those of noble blood, were more or less engaged) was then a nursery, not only for seamen, but for warriors, in days when Spanish and Portuguese traders (whenever they had a chance) got rid of English competition by salvos of cannon-shot.

Hence, as I have said, that strong fellow-feeling between officers and men; and hence mutinies (as Sir Richard Hawkins tells us) were all but unknown in the English ships, while in the Spanish they broke out on every slight occasion. For the Spaniards, by some suicidal pedantry, had allowed their navy to be crippled by the same despotism, etiquette, and official routine, by which the whole nation was gradually frozen to death in the course of the next century or two; forgetting that, fifty years before, Cortez, Pizarro, and the early Conquistadores of America had achieved their miraculous triumphs on the exactly opposite method by that very fellow-feeling between commander and commanded by which the English were now conquering them in their turn.

Their navy was organized on a plan complete enough; but on one which was, as the event proved, utterly fatal to their prowess and unanimity, and which made even their courage and honor useless against the assaults of free men. "They do, in their armadas at sea, divide themselves into three bodies; to wit, soldiers, mariners, and gunners. The soldiers and officers watch and ward as if on shore; and this is the only duty they undergo, except cleaning their arms, wherein they are not over curious. The gunners are exempted from all labor and care, except about the artillery; and these are either Almaines, Flemings, or strangers; for the Spaniards are but indifferently practised in this art. The mariners are but as slaves to the rest, to moil and to toil day and night; and those but few and bad, and not suffered to sleep or harbor under the decks. For in fair or foul weather, in storms, sun, or rain, they must pass void of covert or succor."

This is the account of one who was long prisoner on board their ships; let it explain itself, while I return to my tale. For the great ship is now within two musket-shots of the Rose, with the golden flag of Spain floating at her poop; and her trumpets are shouting defiance up the breeze, from a dozen brazen throats, which two or three answer lustily from the Rose, from whose poop flies the flag of England, and from her fore the arms of Leigh and Cary side by side, and over them the ship and bridge of the good town of Bideford. And then Amyas calls:

"Now, silence trumpets, waits, play up! 'Fortune my foe!' and God and the Queen be with us!"

Whereon (laugh not, reader, for it was the fashion of those musical as well as valiant days) up rose that noble old favorite of good Queen Bess, from cornet and sackbut, fife and drum; while Parson Jack, who had taken his stand with the musicians on the poop, worked away lustily at his violin, and like Volker of the Nibelungen Lied.

"Well played, Jack; thy elbow flies like a lamb's tail," said Amyas, forcing a jest.

"It shall fly to a better fiddle-bow presently, sir, an I have the luck—"

"Steady, helm!" said Amyas. "What is he after now?"

The Spaniard, who had been coming upon them right down the wind under a press of sail, took in his light canvas.

"He don't know what to make of our waiting for him so bold," said the helmsman.

"He does though, and means to fight us," cried another. "See, he is hauling up the foot of his mainsail, but he wants to keep the wind of us."

"Let him try, then," quoth Amyas. "Keep her closer still. Let no one fire till we are about. Man the starboard guns; to starboard, and wait, all small arm men. Pass the order down to the gunner, and bid all fire high, and take the rigging."

Bang went one of the Spaniard's bow guns, and the shot went wide. Then another and another, while the men fidgeted about, looking at the priming of their muskets, and loosened their arrows in the sheaf.

"Lie down, men, and sing a psalm. When I want you, I'll call you. Closer still, if you can, helmsman, and we will try a short ship against a long one. We can sail two points nearer the wind than he."

As Amyas had calculated, the Spaniard would gladly enough have stood across the Rose's bows, but knowing the English readiness, dare not for fear of being raked; so her only plan, if she did not intend to shoot past her foe down to leeward, was to put her head close to the wind, and wait for her on the same tack.

Amyas laughed to himself. "Hold on yet awhile. More ways of killing a cat than choking her with cream. Drew, there, are your men ready?"

"Ay, ay, sir!" and on they went, closing fast with the Spaniard, till within a pistol-shot.

"Ready about!" and about she went like an eel, and ran upon the opposite tack right under the Spaniard's stern. The Spaniard, astounded at the quickness of the manoeuvre, hesitated a moment, and then tried to get about also, as his only chance; but it was too late, and while his lumbering length was still hanging in the wind's eye, Amyas's bowsprit had all but scraped his quarter, and the Rose passed slowly across his stern at ten yards' distance.

"Now, then!" roared Amyas. "Fire, and with a will! Have at her, archers: have at her, muskets all!" and in an instant a storm of bar and chain-shot, round and canister, swept the proud Don from stem to stern, while through the white cloud of smoke the musket-balls, and the still deadlier cloth-yard arrows, whistled and rushed upon their venomous errand. Down went the steersman, and every soul who manned the poop. Down went the mizzen topmast, in went the stern-windows and quarter-galleries; and as the smoke cleared away, the gorgeous painting of the Madre Dolorosa, with her heart full of seven swords, which, in a gilded frame, bedizened the Spanish stern, was shivered in splinters; while, most glorious of all, the golden flag of Spain, which the last moment flaunted above their heads, hung trailing in the water. The ship, her tiller shot away, and her helmsman killed, staggered helplessly a moment, and then fell up into the wind.

"Well done, men of Devon!" shouted Amyas, as cheers rent the welkin.

"She has struck," cried some, as the deafening hurrahs died away.

"Not a bit," said Amyas. "Hold on, helmsman, and leave her to patch her tackle while we settle the galleys."

On they shot merrily, and long ere the armada could get herself to rights again, were two good miles to windward, with the galleys sweeping down fast upon them.

And two venomous-looking craft they were, as they shot through the short chopping sea upon some forty oars apiece, stretching their long sword-fish snouts over the water, as if snuffing for their prey. Behind this long snout, a strong square forecastle was crammed with soldiers, and the muzzles of cannon grinned out through portholes, not only in the sides of the forecastle, but forward in the line of the galley's course, thus enabling her to keep up a continual fire on a ship right ahead.

The long low waist was packed full of the slaves, some five or six to each oar, and down the centre, between the two banks, the English could see the slave-drivers walking up and down a long gangway, whip in hand. A raised quarter-deck at the stern held more soldiers, the sunlight flashing merrily upon their armor and their gun-barrels; as they neared, the English could hear plainly the cracks of the whips, and the yells as of wild beasts which answered them; the roll and rattle of the oars, and the loud "Ha!" of the slaves which accompanied every stroke, and the oaths and curses of the drivers; while a sickening musky smell, as of a pack of kennelled hounds, came down the wind from off those dens of misery. No wonder if many a young heart shuddered as it faced, for the first time, the horrible reality of those floating hells, the cruelties whereof had rung so often in English ears, from the stories of their own countrymen, who had passed them, fought them, and now and then passed years of misery on board of them. Who knew but what there might be English among those sun-browned half-naked masses of panting wretches?

"Must we fire upon the slaves?" asked more than one, as the thought crossed him.

Amyas sighed.

"Spare them all you can, in God's name; but if they try to run us down, rake them we must, and God forgive us."

The two galleys came on abreast of each other, some forty yards apart. To outmanoeuvre their oars as he had done the ship's sails, Amyas knew was impossible. To run from them was to be caught between them and the ship.

He made up his mind, as usual, to the desperate game.

"Lay her head up in the wind, helmsman, and we will wait for them."

They were now within musket-shot, and opened fire from their bow-guns; but, owing to the chopping sea, their aim was wild. Amyas, as usual, withheld his fire.

The men stood at quarters with compressed lips, not knowing what was to come next. Amyas, towering motionless on the quarter-deck, gave his orders calmly and decisively. The men saw that he trusted himself, and trusted him accordingly.

The Spaniards, seeing him wait for them, gave a shout of joy—was the Englishman mad? And the two galleys converged rapidly, intending to strike him full, one on each bow.

They were within forty yards—another minute, and the shock would come. The Englishman's helm went up, his yards creaked round, and gathering way, he plunged upon the larboard galley.

"A dozen gold nobles to him who brings down the steersman!" shouted Cary, who had his cue. And a flight of arrows from the forecastle rattled upon the galley's quarter-deck.

Hit or not hit, the steersman lost his nerve, and shrank from the coming shock. The galley's helm went up to port, and her beak slid all but harmless along Amyas's bow; a long dull grind, and then loud crack on crack, as the Rose sawed slowly through the bank of oars from stem to stern, hurling the wretched slaves in heaps upon each other; and ere her mate on the other side could swing round, to strike him in his new position, Amyas's whole broadside, great and small, had been poured into her at pistol-shot, answered by a yell which rent their ears and hearts.

"Spare the slaves! Fire at the soldiers!" cried Amyas; but the work was too hot for much discrimination; for the larboard galley, crippled but not undaunted, swung round across his stern, and hooked herself venomously on to him.

It was a move more brave than wise; for it prevented the other galley from returning to the attack without exposing herself a second time to the English broadside; and a desperate attempt of the Spaniards to board at once through the stern-ports and up the quarter was met with such a demurrer of shot and steel, that they found themselves in three minutes again upon the galley's poop, accompanied, to their intense disgust, by Amyas Leigh and twenty English swords.

Five minutes' hard cutting, hand to hand, and the poop was clear. The soldiers in the forecastle had been able to give them no assistance, open as they lay to the arrows and musketry from the Rose's lofty stern. Amyas rushed along the central gangway, shouting in Spanish, "Freedom to the slaves! death to the masters!" clambered into the forecastle, followed close by his swarm of wasps, and set them so good an example how to use their stings, that in three minutes more there was not a Spaniard on board who was not dead or dying.

"Let the slaves free!" shouted he. "Throw us a hammer down, men. Hark! there's an English voice!"

There is indeed. From amid the wreck of broken oars and writhing limbs, a voice is shrieking in broadest Devon to the master, who is looking over the side.

"Oh, Robert Drew! Robert Drew! Come down, and take me out of hell!"

"Who be you, in the name of the Lord!"

"Don't you mind William Prust, that Captain Hawkins left behind in the Honduras, years and years agone? There's nine of us aboard, if your shot hasn't put 'em out of their misery. Come down, if you've a Christian heart, come down!"

Utterly forgetful of all discipline, Drew leaps down hammer in hand, and the two old comrades rush into each other's arms.

Why make a long story of what took but five minutes to do? The nine men (luckily none of them wounded) are freed, and helped on board, to be hugged and kissed by old comrades and young kinsmen; while the remaining slaves, furnished with a couple of hammers, are told to free themselves and help the English. The wretches answer by a shout; and Amyas, once more safe on board again, dashes after the other galley, which has been hovering out of reach of his guns:

but there is no need to trouble himself about her; sickened with what she has got, she is struggling right up wind, leaning over to one side, and seemingly ready to sink.

"Are there any English on board of her?" asks Amyas, loath to lose the chance of freeing a countryman.

"Never a one, sir, thank God."

So they set to work to repair damages; while the liberated slaves, having shifted some of the galley's oars, pull away after their comrade; and that with such a will, that in ten minutes they have caught her up, and careless of the Spaniard's fire, boarded her en masse, with yells as of a thousand wolves. There will be fearful vengeance taken on those tyrants, unless they play the man this day.

And in the meanwhile half the crew are clothing, feeding, questioning, caressing those nine poor fellows thus snatched from living death; and Yeo, hearing the news, has rushed up on deck to welcome his old comrades, and—

"Is Michael Heard, my cousin, here among you?"

Yes, Michael Heard is there, white-headed rather from misery than age; and the embracings and questionings begin afresh.

"Where is my wife, Salvation Yeo?"

"With the Lord."

"Amen!" says the old man, with a short shudder. "I thought so much; and my two boys?"

"With the Lord."

The old man catches Yeo by the arm.

"How, then?" It is Yeo's turn to shudder now.

"Killed in Panama, fighting the Spaniards; sailing with Mr. Oxenham; and 'twas I led 'em into it. May God and you forgive me!"

"They couldn't die better, cousin Yeo. Where's my girl Grace?"

"Died in childbed."

"Any childer?"

"No."

The old man covers his face with his hands for a while.

"Well, I've been alone with the Lord these fifteen years, so I must not whine at being alone a while longer—'t won't be long."

"Put this coat on your back, uncle," says some one.

"No; no coats for me. Naked came I into the world, and naked I go out of it this day, if I have a chance. You'm better to go to your work, lads, or the big one will have the wind of you yet."

"So she will," said Amyas, who has overheard; but so great is the curiosity on all hands, that he has some trouble in getting the men to quarters again; indeed, they only go on condition of parting among themselves with them the new-comers, each to tell his sad and strange story. How after Captain Hawkins, constrained by famine, had put them ashore, they wandered in misery till the Spaniards took them; how, instead of hanging them (as they at first intended), the Dons fed and clothed them, and allotted them as servants to various gentlemen about Mexico, where they throve, turned their hands (like true sailors) to all manner of trades, and made much money, and some of them were married, even to women of wealth; so that all went well, until the fatal year 1574, when, "much against the minds of many of the Spaniards themselves, that cruel and bloody Inquisition was established for the first time in the Indies;" and how from that moment their lives were one long tragedy; how they were all imprisoned for a year and a half, not for proselytizing, but simply for not believing in transubstantiation; racked again and again, and at last adjudged to receive publicly, on Good Friday, 1575, some three hundred, some one hundred stripes, and to serve in the galleys for six or ten years each; while, as the crowning atrocity of the Moloch sacrifice, three of them were burnt alive in the market-place of Mexico; a story no less hideous than true, the details whereof whoso list may read in Hakluyt's third volume, as told by Philip Miles, one of that hapless crew; as well as the adventures of Job Hortop, a messmate of his, who, after being sent to Spain, and seeing two more of his companions burnt alive at Seville, was sentenced to row in the galleys ten years, and after that to go to the "everlasting prison remediless;" from which doom, after twenty-three years of slavery, he was delivered by the galleon Dudley, and came safely home to Redriff.

The fate of Hortop and his comrades was, of course, still unknown to the rescued men; but the history even of their party was not likely to improve the good feeling of the crew toward the Spanish ship which was two miles to leeward of them, and which must be fought with, or fled from, before a quarter of an hour was past. So, kneeling down upon the deck, as many a brave crew in those days did in like case, they "gave God thanks devoutly for the favor they had found;" and then with one accord, at Jack's leading, sang one and all the Ninety-fourth Psalm:*

And then again to quarters; for half the day's work, or more than half, still remained to be done; and hardly were the decks cleared afresh, and the damage repaired as best it could be, when she came ranging up to leeward, as closehauled as she could.

She was, as I said, a long flush-decked ship of full five hundred tons, more than double the size, in fact, of the Rose, though not so lofty in proportion; and many a bold heart beat loud, and no shame to them, as she began firing away merrily, determined, as all well knew, to wipe out in English blood the disgrace of her late foil.

"Never mind, my merry masters," said Amyas, "she has quantity and we quality."

"That's true," said one, "for one honest man is worth two rogues."

"And one culverin three of their footy little ordnance," said another. "So when you will, captain, and have at her."

"Let her come abreast of us, and don't burn powder. We have the wind, and can do what we like with her. Serve the men out a horn of ale all round, steward, and all take your time."

So they waited for five minutes more, and then set to work quietly, after the fashion of English mastiffs, though, like those mastiffs, they waxed right mad before three rounds were fired, and the white splinters (sight beloved) began to crackle and fly.

Amyas, having, as he had said, the wind, and being able to go nearer it than the Spaniard, kept his place at easy point-blank range for his two eighteen-pounder culverins, which Yeo and his mate worked with terrible effect.

"We are lacking her through and through every shot," said he. "Leave the small ordnance alone yet awhile, and we shall sink her without them."

"Whing, whing," went the Spaniard's shot, like so many humming-tops, through the rigging far above their heads; for the ill-constructed ports of those days prevented the guns from hulling an enemy who was to windward, unless close alongside.

"Blow, jolly breeze," cried one, "and lay the Don over all thou canst.—What the murrain is gone, aloft there?"

Alas! a crack, a flap, a rattle; and blank dismay! An unlucky shot had cut the foremast (already wounded) in two, and all forward was a mass of dangling wreck.

"Forward, and cut away the wreck!" said Amyas, unmoved. "Small arm men, be ready. He will be aboard of us in five minutes!"

It was too true. The Rose, unmanageable from the loss of her head-sail, lay at the mercy of the Spaniard; and the archers and musqueteers had hardly time to range themselves to leeward, when the Madre Dolorosa's chains were grinding against the Rose's, and grapples tossed on board from stem to stern.

"Don't cut them loose!" roared Amyas. "Let them stay and see the fun! Now, dogs of Devon, show your teeth, and hurrah for God and the queen!"

And then began a fight most fierce and fell: the Spaniards, according to their fashion, attempting to board, the English, amid fierce shouts of "God and the queen!" "God and St. George for England!" sweeping them back by showers of arrows and musquet balls, thrusting them down with pikes, hurling grenades and stink-pots from the tops; while the swivels on both sides poured their grape, and bar, and chain, and the great main-deck guns, thundering muzzle to muzzle, made both ships quiver and recoil, as they smashed the round shot through and through each other.

So they roared and flashed, fast clenched to each other in that devil's wedlock, under a cloud of smoke beneath the cloudless tropic sky; while all around, the dolphins gambolled, and the flying-fish shot on from swell to swell, and the rainbow-hued jellies opened and shut their cups of living crystal to the sun, as merrily as if man had never fallen, and hell had never broken loose on earth.

So it raged for an hour or more, till all arms were weary, and all tongues clove to the mouth. And sick men, rotting with scurvy, scrambled up on deck, and fought with the strength of madness; and tiny powder-boys, handing up cartridges from the hold, laughed and cheered as the shots ran past their ears; and old Salvation Yeo, a text upon his lips, and a fury in his heart as of Joshua or Elijah in old time, worked on, calm and grim, but with the energy of a boy at play. And now and then an opening in the smoke showed the Spanish captain, in his suit of black steel armor, standing cool and proud, guiding and pointing, careless of the iron hail, but too lofty a gentleman to soil his glove with aught but a knightly sword-hilt: while Amyas and Will, after the fashion of the English gentlemen, had stripped themselves nearly as bare as their own sailors, and were cheering, thrusting, hewing, and hauling, here, there, and everywhere, like any common mariner, and filling them with a spirit of self-respect, fellow-feeling, and personal daring, which the discipline of the Spaniards, more perfect mechanically, but cold and tyrannous, and crushing spiritually, never could bestow. The black-plumed senor was obeyed; but the golden-locked Amyas was followed, and would have been followed through the jaws of hell.

The Spaniards, ere five minutes had passed, poured en masse into the Rose's waist, but only to their destruction. Between the poop and forecastle (as was then the fashion) the upper-deck beams were left open and unplanked, with the exception of a narrow gangway on either side; and off that fatal ledge the boarders, thrust on by those behind, fell headlong between the beams to the main-deck below, to be slaughtered helpless in that pit of destruction, by the double fire from the bulkheads fore and aft; while the few who kept their footing on the gangway, after vain attempts to force the stockades on poop and forecastle, leaped overboard again amid a shower of shot and arrows. The fire of the English was as steady as it was quick; and though three-fourths of the crew had never smelt powder before, they proved well the truth of the old chronicler's saying (since proved again more gloriously than ever, at Alma, Balaklava, and Inkerman), that "the English never fight better than in their first battle."

Thrice the Spaniards clambered on board, and thrice surged back before that deadly hail. The decks on both sides were very shambles; and Jack Brimblecombe, who had fought as long as his conscience would allow him, found, when he turned to a more clerical occupation, enough to do in carrying poor wretches to the surgeon, without giving that spiritual consolation which he longed to give, and they to receive. At last there was a lull in that wild storm. No shot was heard from the Spaniard's upper-deck.

Amyas leaped into the mizzen rigging, and looked through the smoke. Dead men he could descry through the blinding veil, rolled in heaps, laid flat; dead men and dying: but no man upon his feet. The last volley had swept the deck clear; one by one had dropped below to escape that fiery shower: and alone at the helm, grinding his teeth with rage, his mustachios curling up to his very eyes, stood the Spanish captain.

Now was the moment for a counter-stroke. Amyas shouted for the boarders, and in two minutes more he was over the side, and clutching at the Spaniard's mizzen rigging.

What was this? The distance between him and the enemy's side was widening. Was she sheering off? Yes—and rising too, growing bodily higher every moment, as if by magic. Amyas looked up in astonishment and saw what it was. The Spaniard was heeling fast over to leeward away from him. Her masts were all sloping forward, swifter and swifter—the end was come, then!

"Back! in God's name back, men! She is sinking by the head!" And with much ado some were dragged back, some leaped back—all but old Michael Heard.

With hair and beard floating in the wind, the bronzed naked figure, like some weird old Indian fakir, still climbed on steadfastly up the mizzen-chains of the Spaniard, hatchet in hand.

"Come back, Michael! Leap while you may!" shouted a dozen voices. Michael turned—

"And what should I come back for, then, to go home where no one knoweth me? I'll die like an Englishman this day, or I'll know the rason why!" and turning, he sprang in over the bulwarks, as the huge ship rolled up more and more, like a dying whale, exposing all her long black hulk almost down to the keel, and one of her lower-deck guns, as if in defiance, exploded upright into the air, hurling the ball to the very heavens.

In an instant it was answered from the Rose by a column of smoke, and the eighteen-pound ball crashed through the bottom of the defenceless Spaniard.

"Who fired? Shame to fire on a sinking ship!"

"Gunner Yeo, sir," shouted a voice up from the main-deck. "He's like a madman down here."

"Tell him if he fires again, I'll put him in irons, if he were my own brother. Cut away the grapples aloft, men. Don't you see how she drags us over? Cut away, or we shall sink with her."

They cut away, and the Rose, released from the strain, shook her feathers on the wave-crest like a freed sea-gull, while all men held their breaths.

Suddenly the glorious creature righted herself, and rose again, as if in noble shame, for one last struggle with her doom. Her bows were deep in the water, but her after-deck still dry. Righted: but only for a moment, long enough to let her crew come pouring wildly up on deck, with cries and prayers, and rush aft to the poop, where, under the flag of Spain, stood the tall captain, his left hand on the standard-staff, his sword pointed in his right.

"Back, men!" they heard him cry, "and die like valiant mariners."

Some of them ran to the bulwarks, and shouted "Mercy! We surrender!" and the English broke into a cheer and called to them to run her alongside.

"Silence!" shouted Amyas. "I take no surrender from mutineers. Senor," cried he to the captain, springing into the rigging and taking off his hat, "for the love of God and these men, strike! and surrender a buena querra."

The Spaniard lifted his hat and bowed courteously, and answered, "Impossible, senor. No querra is good which stains my honor."

"God have mercy on you, then!"

"Amen!" said the Spaniard, crossing himself.

She gave one awful lounge forward, and dived under the coming swell, hurling her crew into the eddies. Nothing but the point of her poop remained, and there stood the stern and steadfast Don, cap-a-pie in his glistening black armor, immovable as a man of iron, while over him the flag, which claimed the empire of both worlds, flaunted its gold aloft and upwards in the glare of the tropic noon.

"He shall not carry that flag to the devil with him; I will have it yet, if I die for it!" said Will Cary, and rushed to the side to leap overboard, but Amyas stopped him.

"Let him die as he has lived, with honor."

A wild figure sprang out of the mass of sailors who struggled and shrieked amid the foam, and rushed upward at the Spaniard. It was Michael Heard. The Don, who stood above him, plunged his sword into the old man's body: but the hatchet gleamed, nevertheless: down went the blade through headpiece and through head; and as Heard sprang onward, bleeding, but alive, the steel-clad corpse rattled down the deck into the surge. Two more strokes, struck with the fury of a dying man, and the standard-staff was hewn through. Old Michael collected all his strength, hurled the flag far from the sinking ship, and then stood erect one moment and shouted, "God save Queen Bess!" and the English answered with a "Hurrah!" which rent the welkin.

Another moment and the gulf had swallowed his victim, and the poop, and him; and nothing remained of the Madre Dolorosa but a few floating spars and struggling wretches, while a great awe fell upon all men, and a solemn silence, broken only by the cry

And then, suddenly collecting themselves, as men awakened from a dream, half-a-dozen desperate gallants, reckless of sharks and eddies, leaped overboard, swam towards the flag, and towed it alongside in triumph.

"Ah!" said Salvation Yeo, as he helped the trophy up over the side; "ah! it was not for nothing that we found poor Michael! He was always a good comrade—nigh as good a one as William Penberthy of Marazion, whom the Lord grant I meet in bliss! And now, then, my masters, shall we inshore again and burn La Guayra?"

"Art thou never glutted with Spanish blood, thou old wolf?" asked Will Cary.

"Never, sir," answered Yeo.

"To St. Jago be it," said Amyas, "if we can get there; but—God help us!"

And he looked round sadly enough; while no one needed that he should finish his sentence, or explain his "but."

The foremast was gone, the main-yard sprung, the rigging hanging in elf-locks, the hull shot through and through in twenty places, the deck strewn with the bodies of nine good men, beside sixteen wounded down below; while the pitiless sun, right above their heads, poured down a flood of fire upon a sea of glass.

And it would have been well if faintness and weariness had been all that was the matter; but now that the excitement was over, the collapse came; and the men sat down listlessly and sulkily by twos and threes upon the deck, starting and wincing when they heard some poor fellow below cry out under the surgeon's knife; or murmuring to each other that all was lost. Drew tried in vain to rouse them, telling them that all depended on rigging a jury-mast forward as soon as possible. They answered only by growls; and at last broke into open reproaches. Even Will Cary's volatile nature, which had kept him up during the fight, gave way, when Yeo and the carpenter came aft, and told Amyas in a low voice—

"We are hit somewhere forward, below the water-line, sir. She leaks a terrible deal, and the Lord will not vouchsafe to us to lay our hands on the place, for all our searching."

"What are we to do now, Amyas, in the devil's name?" asked Cary, peevishly.

"What are we to do, in God's name, rather," answered Amyas, in a low voice. "Will, Will, what did God make you a gentleman for, but to know better than those poor fickle fellows forward, who blow hot and cold at every change of weather!"

"I wish you'd come forward and speak to them, sir," said Yeo, who had overheard the last words, "or we shall get naught done."

Amyas went forward instantly.

"Now then, my brave lads, what's the matter here, that you are all sitting on your tails like monkeys?"

"Ugh!" grunts one. "Don't you think our day's work has been long enough yet, captain?"

"You don't want us to go in to La Guayra again, sir? There are enough of us thrown away already, I reckon, about that wench there."

"Best sit here, and sink quietly. There's no getting home again, that's plain."

"Why were we brought out here to be killed?"

"For shame, men!" cries Yeo; "you're no better than a set of stiff-necked Hebrew Jews, murmuring against Moses the very minute after the Lord has delivered you from the Egyptians."

Now I do not wish to set Amyas up as a perfect man; for he had his faults, like every one else; nor as better, thank God, than many and many a brave and virtuous captain in her majesty's service at this very day: but certainly he behaved admirably under that trial. Drake had trained him, as he trained many another excellent officer, to be as stout in discipline, and as dogged of purpose, as he himself was: but he had trained him also to feel with and for his men, to make allowances for them, and to keep his temper with them, as he did this day. True, he had seen Drake in a rage; he had seen him hang one man for a mutiny (and that man his dearest friend), and threaten to hang thirty more; but Amyas remembered well that that explosion took place when having, as Drake said publicly himself, "taken in hand that I know not in the world how to go through with; it passeth my capacity; it hath even bereaved me of my wits to think of it," . . . and having "now set together by the ears three mighty princes, her majesty and the kings of Spain and Portugal," he found his whole voyage ready to come to naught, "by mutinies and discords, controversy between the sailors and gentlemen, and stomaching between the gentlemen and sailors." "But, my masters" (quoth the self-trained hero, and Amyas never forgot his words), "I must have it left; for I must have the gentlemen to haul and draw with the mariner, and the mariner with the gentlemen. I would like to know him that would refuse to set his hand to a rope!"

And now Amyas's conscience smote him (and his simple and pious soul took the loss of his brother as God's verdict on his conduct), because he had set his own private affection, even his own private revenge, before the safety of his ship's company, and the good of his country.

"Ah," said he to himself, as he listened to his men's reproaches, "if I had been thinking, like a loyal soldier, of serving my queen, and crippling the Spaniard, I should have taken that great bark three days ago, and in it the very man I sought!"

So "choking down his old man," as Yeo used to say, he made answer cheerfully—

"Pooh! pooh! brave lads! For shame, for shame! You were lions half-an-hour ago; you are not surely turned sheep already! Why, but yesterday evening you were grumbling because I would not run in and fight those three ships under the batteries of La Guayra, and now you think it too much to have fought them fairly out at sea? What has happened but the chances of war, which might have happened anywhere? Nothing venture, nothing win; and nobody goes bird-nesting without a fall at times. If any one wants to be safe in this life, he'd best stay at home and keep his bed; though even there, who knows but the roof might fall through on him?"

"Ah, it's all very well for you, captain," said some grumbling younker, with a vague notion that Amyas must be better off than he, because he was a gentleman. Amyas's blood rose.

"Yes, sirrah! it is very well for me, as long as God is with me: but He is with every man in this ship, I would have you to know, as much as He is with me. Do you fancy that I have nothing to lose? I who have adventured in this voyage all I am worth, and more; who, if I fail, must return to beggary and scorn? And if I have ventured rashly, sinfully, if you will, the lives of any of you in my own private quarrel, am I not punished? Have I not lost—?"

His voice trembled and stopped there, but he recovered himself in a moment.

"Pish! I can't stand here chattering. Carpenter! an axe! and help me to cast these spars loose. Get out of my way, there! lumbering the scuppers up like so many moulting fowls! Here, all old friends, lend a hand! Pelican's men, stand by your captain! Did we sail round the world for nothing?"

This last appeal struck home, and up leaped half-a-dozen of the old Pelicans, and set to work at his side manfully to rig the jury-mast.

"Come along!" cried Cary to the malcontents; "we're raw longshore fellows, but we won't be outdone by any old sea-dog of them all." And setting to work himself, he was soon followed by one and another, till order and work went on well enough.

"And where are we going, when the mast's up?" shouted some saucy hand from behind.

"Where you daren't follow us alone by yourself, so you had better keep us company," replied Yeo.

"I'll tell you where we are going, lads," said Amyas, rising from his work. "Like it or leave it as you will, I have no secrets from my crew. We are going inshore there to find a harbor, and careen the ship."

There was a start and a murmur.

"Inshore? Into the Spaniards' mouths?"

"All in the Inquisition in a week's time."

"Better stay here, and be drowned."

"You're right in that last," shouts Cary. "That's the right death for blind puppies. Look you! I don't know in the least where we are, and I hardly know stem from stern aboard ship; and the captain may be right or wrong—that's nothing to me; but this I know, that I am a soldier, and will obey orders; and where he goes, I go; and whosoever hinders me must walk up my sword to do it."

Amyas pressed Cary's hand, and then—

"And here's my broadside next, men. I'll go nowhere, and do nothing without the advice of Salvation Yeo and Robert Drew; and if any man in the ship knows better than these two, let him up, and we'll give him a hearing. Eh, Pelicans?"

There was a grunt of approbation from the Pelicans; and Amyas returned to the charge.

"We have five shot between wind and water, and one somewhere below. Can we face a gale of wind in that state, or can we not?"

Silence.

"Can we get home with a leak in our bottom?"

Silence.

"Then what can we do but run inshore, and take our chance? Speak! It's a coward's trick to do nothing because what we must do is not pleasant. Will you be like children, that would sooner die than take nasty physic, or will you not?"

Silence still.

"Come along now! Here's the wind again round with the sun, and up to the north-west. In with her!"

Sulkily enough, but unable to deny the necessity, the men set to work, and the vessel's head was put toward the land; but when she began to slip through the water, the leak increased so fast, that they were kept hard at work at the pumps for the rest of the afternoon.

The current had by this time brought them abreast of the bay of Higuerote; and, luckily for them, safe out of the short heavy swell which it causes round Cape Codera. Looking inland, they had now to the south-west that noble headland, backed by the Caracas Mountains, range on range, up to the Silla and the Neguater; while, right ahead of them to the south, the shore sank suddenly into a low line of mangrove-wood, backed by primaeval forest. As they ran inward, all eyes were strained greedily to find some opening in the mangrove belt; but none was to be seen for some time. The lead was kept going; and every fresh heave announced shallower water.

"We shall have very shoal work off those mangroves, Yeo," said Amyas; "I doubt whether we shall do aught now, unless we find a river's mouth."

"If the Lord thinks a river good for us, sir, He'll show us one." So on they went, keeping a south-east course, and at last an opening in the mangrove belt was hailed with a cheer from the older hands, though the majority shrugged their shoulders, as men going open-eyed to destruction.

Off the mouth they sent in Drew and Cary with a boat, and watched anxiously for an hour. The boat returned with a good report of two fathoms of water over the bar, impenetrable forests for two miles up, the river sixty yards broad, and no sign of man. The river's banks were soft and sloping mud, fit for careening.

"Safe quarters, sir," said Yeo, privately, "as far as Spaniards go. I hope in God it may be as safe from calentures and fevers."

"Beggars must not be choosers," said Amyas. So in they went.

They towed the ship up about half-a-mile to a point where she could not be seen from the seaward; and there moored her to the mangrove-stems. Amyas ordered a boat out, and went up the river himself to reconnoitre. He rowed some three miles, till the river narrowed suddenly, and was all but covered in by the interlacing boughs of mighty trees. There was no sign that man had been there since the making of the world.

He dropped down the stream again, thoughtfully and sadly. How many years ago was it that he passed this river's mouth? Three days. And yet how much had passed in them! Don Guzman found and lost—Rose found and lost—a great victory gained, and yet lost—perhaps his ship lost—above all, his brother lost.

Lost! O God, how should he find his brother?

Some strange bird out of the woods made mournful answer—"Never, never, never!"

How should he face his mother?

"Never, never, never!" wailed the bird again; and Amyas smiled bitterly, and said "Never!" likewise.

The night mist began to steam and wreathe upon the foul beer-colored stream. The loathy floor of liquid mud lay bare beneath the mangrove forest. Upon the endless web of interarching roots great purple crabs were crawling up and down. They would have supped with pleasure upon Amyas's corpse; perhaps they might sup on him after all; for a heavy sickening graveyard smell made his heart sink within him, and his stomach heave; and his weary body, and more weary soul, gave themselves up helplessly to the depressing influence of that doleful place. The black bank of dingy leathern leaves above his head, the endless labyrinth of stems and withes (for every bough had lowered its own living cord, to take fresh hold of the foul soil below); the web of roots, which stretched away inland till it was lost in the shades of evening—all seemed one horrid complicated trap for him and his; and even where, here and there, he passed the mouth of a lagoon, there was no opening, no relief—nothing but the dark ring of mangroves, and here and there an isolated group of large and small, parents and children, breeding and spreading, as if in hideous haste to choke out air and sky. Wailing sadly, sad-colored mangrove-hens ran off across the mud into the dreary dark. The hoarse night-raven, hid among the roots, startled the voyagers with a sudden shout, and then all was again silent as a grave. The loathly alligators, lounging in the slime, lifted their horny eyelids lazily, and leered upon him as he passed with stupid savageness. Lines of tall herons stood dimly in the growing gloom, like white fantastic ghosts, watching the passage of the doomed boat. All was foul, sullen, weird as witches' dream. If Amyas had seen a crew of skeletons glide down the stream behind him, with Satan standing at the helm, he would have scarcely been surprised. What fitter craft could haunt that Stygian flood?

That night every man of the boat's crew, save Amyas, was down with raging fever; before ten the next morning, five more men were taken, and others sickening fast.

CHAPTER XXI: HOW THEY TOOK THE COMMUNION UNDER THE TREE AT HIGUEROTE

Amyas would have certainly taken the yellow fever, but for one reason, which he himself gave to Cary. He had no time to be sick while his men were sick; a valid and sufficient reason (as many a noble soul in the Crimea has known too well), as long as the excitement of work is present, but too apt to fail the hero, and to let him sink into the pit which he has so often over-leapt, the moment that his work is done.

He called a council of war, or rather a sanitary commission, the next morning; for he was fairly at his wits' end. The men were panic-stricken, ready to mutiny: Amyas told them that he could not see any possible good which could accrue to them by killing him, or—(for there were two sides to every question)—being killed by him; and then went below to consult. The doctor talked mere science, or nonscience, about humors, complexions, and animal spirits. Jack Brimblecombe, mere pulpit, about its being the visitation of God. Cary, mere despair, though he jested over it with a smile. Yeo, mere stoic fatalism, though he quoted Scripture to back the same. Drew, the master, had nothing to say. His "business was to sail the ship, and not to cure calentures."

Whereon Amyas clutched his locks, according to custom; and at last broke forth—"Doctor! a fig for your humors and complexions! Can you cure a man's humors, or change his complexion? Can an Ethiopian change his skin, or a leopard his spots? Don't shove off your ignorance on God, sir. I ask you what's the reason of this sickness, and you don't know. Jack Brimblecombe, don't talk to me about God's visitation; this looks much more like the devil's visitation, to my mind. We are doing God's work, Sir John, and He is not likely to hinder us. So down with the devil, say I. Cary, laughing killed the cat, but it won't cure a Christian. Yeo, when an angel tells me that it's God's will that we should all die like dogs in a ditch, I'll call this God's will; but not before. Drew, you say your business is to sail the ship; then sail her out of this infernal poison-trap this very morning, if you can, which you can't. The mischief's in the air, and nowhere else. I felt it run through me coming down last night, and smelt it like any sewer: and if it was not in the air, why was my boat's crew taken first, tell me that?"

There was no answer.

"Then I'll tell you why they were taken first: because the mist, when we came through it, only rose five or six feet above the stream, and we were in it, while you on board were above it. And those that were taken on board this morning, every one of them, slept on the main-deck, and every one of them, too, was in fear of the fever, whereby I judge two things,—Keep as high as you can, and fear nothing but God, and we're all safe yet."

"But the fog was up to our round-tops at sunrise this morning," said Cary.

"I know it: but we who were on the half-deck were not in it so long as those below, and that may have made the difference, let alone our having free air. Beside, I suspect the heat in the evening draws the poison out more, and that when it gets cold toward morning, the venom of it goes off somehow."

How it went off Amyas could not tell (right in his facts as he was), for nobody on earth knew I suppose, at that day; and it was not till nearly two centuries of fatal experience that the settlers in America discovered the simple laws of these epidemics which now every child knows, or ought to know. But common sense was on his side; and Yeo rose and spoke—

"As I have said before, many a time, the Lord has sent us a very young Daniel for judge. I remember now to have heard the Spaniards say, how these calentures lay always in the low ground, and never came more than a few hundred feet above the sea."

"Let us go up those few hundred feet, then."

Every man looked at Amyas, and then at his neighbor.

"Gentlemen, 'Look the devil straight in the face, if you would hit him in the right place.' We cannot get the ship to sea as she is; and if we could, we cannot go home empty-handed; and we surely cannot stay here to die of fever.—We must leave the ship and go inland."

"Inland?" answered every voice but Yeo's.

"Up those hundred feet which Yeo talks of. Up to the mountains; stockade a camp, and get our sick and provisions thither."

"And what next?"

"And when we are recruited, march over the mountains, and surprise St. Jago de Leon."

Cary swore a great oath. "Amyas! you are a daring fellow!"

"Not a bit. It's the plain path of prudence."

"So it is, sir," said old Yeo, "and I follow you in it."

"And so do I," squeaked Jack Brimblecombe.

"Nay, then, Jack, thou shalt not outrun me. So I say yes too," quoth Cary.

"Mr. Drew?"

"At your service, sir, to live or die. I know naught about stockading; but Sir Francis would have given the same counsel, I verily believe, if he had been in your place."

"Then tell the men that we start in an hour's time. Win over the Pelicans, Yeo and Drew; and the rest must follow, like sheep over a hedge."

The Pelicans, and the liberated galley-slaves, joined the project at once; but the rest gave Amyas a stormy hour. The great question was, where were the hills? In that dense mangrove thicket they could not see fifty yards before them.

"The hills are not three miles to the south-west of you at this moment," said Amyas. "I marked every shoulder of them as we ran in."

"I suppose you meant to take us there?"

The question set a light to a train—and angry suspicions were blazing up one after another, but Amyas silenced them with a countermine.

"Fools! if I had not wit enow to look ahead a little farther than you do, where would you be? Are you mad as well as reckless, to rise against your own captain because he has two strings to his bow? Go my way, I say, or, as I live, I'll blow up the ship and every soul on board, and save you the pain of rotting here by inches."

The men knew that Amyas never said what he did not intend to do; not that Amyas intended to do this, because he knew that the threat would be enough. So they, agreed to go; and were reassured by seeing that the old Pelican's men turned to the work heartily and cheerfully.

There is no use keeping the reader for five or six weary hours, under a broiling (or rather stewing) sun, stumbling over mangrove roots, hewing his way through thorny thickets, dragging sick men and provisions up mountain steeps, amid disappointment, fatigue, murmurs, curses, snakes, mosquitoes, false alarms of Spaniards, and every misery, save cold, which flesh is heir to. Suffice it that by sunset that evening they had gained a level spot, a full thousand feet above the sea, backed by an inaccessible cliff which formed the upper shoulder of a mighty mountain, defended below by steep wooded slopes, and needing but the felling of a few trees to make it impregnable.

Amyas settled the sick under the arched roots of an enormous cottonwood tree, and made a second journey to the ship, to bring up hammocks and blankets for them; while Yeo's wisdom and courage were of inestimable value. He, as pioneer, had found the little brook up which they forced their way; he had encouraged them to climb the cliffs over which it fell, arguing rightly that on its course they were sure to find some ground fit for encampment within the reach of water; he had supported Amyas, when again and again the weary crew entreated to be dragged no farther, and had gone back again a dozen times to cheer them upward; while Cary, who brought up the rear, bullied and cheered on the stragglers who sat down and refused to move, drove back at the sword's point more than one who was beating a retreat, carried their burdens for them, sang them songs on the halt; in all things approving himself the gallant and hopeful soul which he had always been: till Amyas, beside himself with joy at finding that the two men on whom he had counted most were utterly worthy of his trust, went so far as to whisper to them both, in confidence, that very night—

"Cortez burnt his ships when he landed. Why should not we?"

Yeo leapt upright; and then sat down again, and whispered—

"Do you say that, captain? 'Tis from above, then, that's certain; for it's been hanging on my mind too all day."

"There's no hurry," quoth Amyas; "we must clear her out first, you know," while Cary sat silent and musing. Amyas had evidently more schemes in his head than he chose to tell.

The men were too tired that evening to do much, but ere the sun rose next morning Amyas had them hard at work fortifying their position. It was, as I said, strong enough by nature; for though it was commanded by high cliffs on three sides, yet there was no chance of an enemy coming over the enormous mountain-range behind them, and still less chance that, if he came, he would discover them through the dense mass of trees which crowned the cliff, and clothed the hills for a thousand feet above. The attack, if it took place, would come from below; and against that Amyas guarded by felling the smaller trees, and laying them with their boughs outward over the crest of the slope, thus forming an abatis (as every one who has shot in thick cover knows to his cost) warranted to bring up in two steps, horse, dog, or man. The trunks were sawn into logs, laid lengthwise, and steadied by stakes and mould; and three or four hours' hard work finished a stockade which would defy anything but artillery. The work done, Amyas scrambled up into the boughs of the enormous ceiba-tree, and there sat inspecting his own handiwork, looking out far and wide over the forest-covered plains and the blue sea beyond, and thinking, in his simple straightforward way, of what was to be done next.

To stay there long was impossible; to avenge himself upon La Guayra was impossible; to go until he had found out whether Frank was alive or dead seemed at first equally impossible. But were Brimblecombe, Cary, and those eighty men to be sacrificed a second time to his private interest? Amyas wept with rage, and then wept again with earnest, honest prayer, before he could make up his mind. But he made it up. There were a hundred chances to one that Frank was dead; and if not, he was equally past their help; for he was—Amyas knew that too well—by this time in the hands of the Inquisition. Who could lift him from that pit? Not Amyas, at least! And crying aloud in his agony, "God help him! for I cannot!" Amyas made up his mind to move. But whither? Many an hour he thought and thought alone, there in his airy nest; and at last he went down, calm and cheerful, and drew Cary and Yeo aside. They could not, he said, refit the ship without dying of fever during the process; an assertion which neither of his hearers was bold enough to deny. Even if they refitted her, they would be pretty certain to have to fight the Spaniards again; for it was impossible to doubt the Indian's story, that they had been forewarned of the Rose's coming, or to doubt, either, that Eustace had been the traitor.

"Let us try St. Jago, then; sack it, come down on La Guayra in the rear, take a ship there, and so get home."

"Nay, Will. If they have strengthened themselves against us at La Guayra, where they had little to lose, surely they have done so at St. Jago, where they have much. I hear the town is large, though new; and besides, how can we get over these mountains without a guide?"

"Or with one?" said Cary, with a sigh, looking up at the vast walls of wood and rock which rose range on range for miles. "But it is strange to find you, at least, throwing cold water on a daring plot."

"What if I had a still more daring one? Did you ever hear of the golden city of Manoa?"

Yeo laughed a grim but joyful laugh. "I have, sir; and so have the old hands from the Pelican and the Jesus of Lubec, I doubt not."

"So much the better;" and Amyas began to tell Cary all which he had learned from the Spaniard, while Yeo capped every word thereof with rumors and traditions of his own gathering. Cary sat half aghast as the huge phantasmagoria unfolded itself before his dazzled eyes; and at last—

"So that was why you wanted to burn the ship! Well, after all, nobody needs me at home, and one less at table won't be missed. So you want to play Cortez, eh?"

"We shall never need to play Cortez (who was not such a bad fellow after all, Will), because we shall have no such cannibal fiends' tyranny to rid the earth of, as he had. And I trust we shall fear God enough not to play Pizarro."

So the conversation dropped for the time, but none of them forgot it.

In that mountain-nook the party spent some ten days and more. Several of the sick men died, some from the fever superadded to their wounds; some, probably, from having been bled by the surgeon; the others mended steadily, by the help of certain herbs which Yeo administered, much to the disgust of the doctor, who, of course, wanted to bleed the poor fellows all round, and was all but mutinous when Amyas stayed his hand. In the meanwhile, by dint of daily trips to the ship, provisions were plentiful enough,—beside the raccoons, monkeys, and other small animals, which Yeo and the veterans of Hawkins's crew knew how to catch, and the fruit and vegetables; above all, the delicious mountain cabbage of the Areca palm, and the fresh milk of the cow-tree, which they brought in daily, paying well thereby for the hospitality they received.

All day long a careful watch was kept among the branches of the mighty ceiba-tree. And what a tree that was! The hugest English oak would have seemed a stunted bush beside it. Borne up on roots, or rather walls, of twisted board, some twelve feet high, between which the whole crew, their ammunitions, and provisions, were housed roomily, rose the enormous trunk full forty feet in girth, towering like some tall lighthouse, smooth for a hundred feet, then crowned with boughs, each of which was a stately tree, whose topmost twigs were full two hundred and fifty feet from the ground. And yet it was easy for the sailors to ascend; so many natural ropes had kind Nature lowered for their use, in the smooth lianes which hung to the very earth, often without a knot or leaf. Once in the tree, you were within a new world, suspended between heaven and earth, and as Cary said, no wonder if, like Jack when he climbed the magic bean-stalk, you had found a castle, a giant, and a few acres of well-stocked park, packed away somewhere amid that labyrinth of timber. Flower-gardens at least were there in plenty; for every limb was covered with pendent cactuses, gorgeous orchises, and wild pines; and while one-half the tree was clothed in rich foliage, the other half, utterly leafless, bore on every twig brilliant yellow flowers, around which humming-birds whirred all day long. Parrots peeped in and out of every cranny, while, within the airy woodland, brilliant lizards basked like living gems upon the bark, gaudy finches flitted and chirruped, butterflies of every size and color hovered over the topmost twigs, innumerable insects hummed from morn till eve; and when the sun went down, tree-toads came out to snore and croak till dawn. There was more life round that one tree than in a whole square mile of English soil.

And Amyas, as he lounged among the branches, felt at moments as if he would be content to stay there forever, and feed his eyes and ears with all its wonders—and then started sighing from his dream, as he recollected that a few days must bring the foe upon them, and force him to decide upon some scheme at which the bravest heart might falter without shame. So there he sat (for he often took the scout's place himself), looking out over the fantastic tropic forest at his feet, and the flat mangrove-swamps below, and the white sheet of foam-flecked blue; and yet no sail appeared; and the men, as their fear of fever subsided, began to ask when they would go down and refit the ship, and Amyas put them off as best he could, till one noon he saw slipping along the shore from the westward, a large ship under easy sail, and recognized in her, or thought he did so, the ship which they had passed upon their way.

If it was she, she must have run past them to La Guayra in the night, and have now returned, perhaps, to search for them along the coast.

She crept along slowly. He was in hopes that she might pass the river's mouth: but no. She lay-to close to the shore; and, after a while, Amyas saw two boats pull in from her, and vanish behind the mangroves.

Sliding down a liane, he told what he had seen. The men, tired of inactivity, received the news with a shout of joy, and set to work to make all ready for their guests. Four brass swivels, which they had brought up, were mounted, fixed in logs, so as to command the path; the musketeers and archers clustered round them with their tackle ready, and half-a-dozen good marksmen volunteered into the cotton-tree with their arquebuses, as a post whence "a man might have very pretty shooting." Prayers followed as a matter of course, and dinner as a matter of course also; but two weary hours passed before there was any sign of the Spaniards.

Presently a wreath of white smoke curled up from the swamp, and then the report of a caliver. Then, amid the growls of the English, the Spanish flag ran up above the trees, and floated— horrible to behold—at the mast-head of the Rose. They were signalling the ship for more hands; and, in effect, a third boat soon pushed off and vanished into the forest.

Another hour, during which the men had thoroughly lost their temper, but not their hearts, by waiting; and talked so loud, and strode up and down so wildly, that Amyas had to warn them that there was no need to betray themselves; that the Spaniards might not find them after all; that they might pass the stockade close without seeing it; that, unless they hit off the track at once, they would probably return to their ship for the present; and exacted a promise from them that they would be perfectly silent till he gave the word to fire.

Which wise commands had scarcely passed his lips, when, in the path below, glanced the headpiece of a Spanish soldier, and then another and another.

"Fools!" whispered Amyas to Cary; "they are coming up in single file, rushing on their own death. Lie close, men!"

The path was so narrow that two could seldom come up abreast, and so steep that the enemy had much ado to struggle and stumble upwards. The men seemed half unwilling to proceed, and hung back more than once; but Amyas could hear an authoritative voice behind, and presently there emerged to the front, sword in hand, a figure at which Amyas and Cary both started.

"Is it he?"

"Surely I know those legs among a thousand, though they are in armor."

"It is my turn for him, now, Cary, remember! Silence, silence, men!"

The Spaniards seemed to feel that they were leading a forlorn hope. Don Guzman (for there was little doubt that it was he) had much ado to get them on at all.

"The fellows have heard how gently we handled the Guayra squadron," whispers Cary, "and have no wish to become fellow-martyrs with the captain of the Madre Dolorosa."

At last the Spaniards get up the steep slope to within forty yards of the stockade, and pause, suspecting a trap, and puzzled by the complete silence. Amyas leaps on the top of it, a white flag in his hand; but his heart beats so fiercely at the sight of that hated figure, that he can hardly get out the words—

"Don Guzman, the quarrel is between you and me, not between your men and mine. I would have sent in a challenge to you at La Guayra, but you were away; I challenge you now to single combat."

"Lutheran dog, I have a halter for you, but no sword! As you served us at Smerwick, we will serve you now. Pirate and ravisher, you and yours shall share Oxenham's fate, as you have copied his crimes, and learn what it is to set foot unbidden on the dominions of the king of Spain."

"The devil take you and the king of Spain together!" shouts Amyas, laughing loudly. "This ground belongs to him no more than it does to me, but to the Queen Elizabeth, in whose name I have taken as lawful possession of it as you ever did of Caracas. Fire, men! and God defend the right!"

Both parties obeyed the order; Amyas dropped down behind the stockade in time to let a caliver bullet whistle over his head; and the Spaniards recoiled as the narrow face of the stockade burst into one blaze of musketry and swivels, raking their long array from front to rear.

The front ranks fell over each other in heaps; the rear ones turned and ran; overtaken, nevertheless, by the English bullets and arrows, which tumbled them headlong down the steep path.

"Out, men, and charge them. See! the Don is running like the rest!" And scrambling over the abattis, Amyas and about thirty followed them fast; for he had hope of learning from some prisoner his brother's fate.

Amyas was unjust in his last words. Don Guzman, as if by miracle, had been only slightly wounded; and seeing his men run, had rushed back and tried to rally them, but was borne away by the fugitives.

However, the Spaniards were out of sight among the thick bushes before the English could overtake them; and Amyas, afraid lest they should rally and surround his small party, withdrew sorely against his will, and found in the pathway fourteen Spaniards, but all dead. For one of the wounded, with more courage than wisdom, had fired on the English as he lay; and Amyas's men, whose blood was maddened both by their desperate situation, and the frightful stories of the rescued galley-slaves, had killed them all before their captain could stop them.

"Are you mad?" cries Amyas, as he strikes up one fellow's sword. "Will you kill an Indian?"

And he drags out of the bushes an Indian lad of sixteen, who, slightly wounded, is crawling away like a copper snake along the ground.

"The black vermin has sent an arrow through my leg; and poisoned too, most like."

"God grant not: but an Indian is worth his weight in gold to us now," said Amyas, tucking his prize under his arm like a bundle. The lad, as soon as he saw there was no escape, resigned himself to his fate with true Indian stoicism, was brought in, and treated kindly enough, but refused to eat. For which, after much questioning, he gave as a reason, that he would make them kill him at once; for fat him they should not; and gradually gave them to understand that the English always (so at least the Spaniards said) fatted and ate their prisoners like the Caribs; and till he saw them go out and bury the bodies of the Spaniards, nothing would persuade him that the corpses were not to be cooked for supper.

However, kind words, kind looks, and the present of that inestimable treasure—a knife, brought him to reason; and he told Amyas that he belonged to a Spaniard who had an "encomienda" of Indians some fifteen miles to the south-west; that he had fled from his master, and lived by hunting for some months past; and having seen the ship where she lay moored, and boarded her in hope of plunder, had been surprised therein by the Spaniards, and forced by threats to go with them as a guide in their search for the English. But now came a part of his story which filled the soul of Amyas with delight. He was an Indian of the Llanos, or great savannahs which lay to the southward beyond the mountains, and had actually been upon the Orinoco. He had been stolen as a boy by some Spaniards, who had gone down (as was the fashion of the Jesuits even as late as 1790) for the pious purpose of converting the savages by the simple process of catching, baptizing, and making servants of those whom they could carry off, and murdering those who resisted their gentle method of salvation. Did he know the way back again? Who could ask such a question of an Indian? And the lad's black eyes flashed fire, as Amyas offered him liberty and iron enough for a dozen Indians, if he would lead them through the passes of the mountains, and southward to the mighty river, where lay their golden hopes. Hernando de Serpa, Amyas knew, had tried the same course, which was supposed to be about one hundred and twenty leagues, and failed, being overthrown utterly by the Wikiri Indians; but Amyas knew enough of the Spaniards' brutal method of treating those Indians, to be pretty sure that they had brought that catastrophe upon themselves, and that he might avoid it well enough by that common justice and mercy toward the savages which he had learned from his incomparable tutor, Francis Drake.

Now was the time to speak; and, assembling his men around him, Amyas opened his whole heart, simply and manfully. This was their only hope of safety. Some of them had murmured that they should perish like John Oxenham's crew. This plan was rather the only way to avoid perishing like them. Don Guzman would certainly return to seek them; and not only he, but land-forces from St. Jago. Even if the stockade was not forced, they would be soon starved out; why not move at once, ere the Spaniards could return, and begin a blockade? As for taking St. Jago, it was impossible. The treasure would all be safely hidden, and the town well prepared to meet them. If they wanted gold and glory, they must seek it elsewhere. Neither was there any use in marching along the coast, and trying the ports: ships could outstrip them, and the country was already warned. There was but this one chance; and on it Amyas, the first and last time in his life, waxed eloquent, and set forth the glory of the enterprise, the service to the queen, the salvation of heathens, and the certainty that, if successful, they should win honor and wealth and everlasting fame, beyond that of Cortez or Pizarro, till the men, sulky at first, warmed every moment; and one old Pelican broke out with—

"Yes, sir! we didn't go round the world with you for naught; and watched your works and ways, which was always those of a gentleman, as you are—who spoke a word for a poor fellow when he was in a scrape, and saw all you ought to see, and naught that you ought not. And we'll follow you, sir, all alone to ourselves; and let those that know you worse follow after when they're come to their right mind."

Man after man capped this brave speech; the minority, who, if they liked little to go, liked still less to be left behind, gave in their consent perforce; and, to make a long story short, Amyas conquered, and the plan was accepted.

"This," said Amyas, "is indeed the proudest day of my life! I have lost one brother, but I have gained fourscore. God do so to me and more also, if I do not deal with you according to the trust which you have put in me this day!"

We, I suppose, are to believe that we have a right to laugh at Amyas's scheme as frantic and chimerical. It is easy to amuse ourselves with the premises, after the conclusion has been found for us. We know, now, that he was mistaken: but we have not discovered his mistake for ourselves, and have no right to plume ourselves on other men's discoveries. Had we lived in Amyas's days, we should have belonged either to the many wise men who believed as he did, or to the many foolish men, who not only sneered at the story of Manoa, but at a hundred other stories, which we now know to be true. Columbus was laughed at: but he found a new world, nevertheless. Cortez was laughed at: but he found Mexico. Pizarro: but he found Peru. I ask any fair reader of those two charming books, Mr. Prescott's Conquest of Mexico and his Conquest of Peru, whether the true wonders in them described do not outdo all the false wonders of Manoa.

But what reason was there to think them false? One quarter, perhaps, of America had been explored, and yet in that quarter two empires had been already found, in a state of mechanical, military, and agricultural civilization superior, in many things, to any nation of Europe. Was it not most rational to suppose that in the remaining three-quarters similar empires existed? If a second Mexico had been discovered in the mountains of Parima, and a second Peru in those of Brazil, what right would any man have had to wonder? As for the gold legends, nothing was told of Manoa which had not been seen in Peru and Mexico by the bodily eyes of men then living. Why should not the rocks of Guiana have been as full of the precious metals (we do not know yet that they are not) as the rocks of Peru and Mexico were known to be? Even the details of the story, its standing on a lake, for instance, bore a probability with them. Mexico actually stood in the centre of a lake—why should not Manoa? The Peruvian worship centred round a sacred lake—why not that of Manoa? Pizarro and Cortez, again, were led on to their desperate enterprises by the sight of small quantities of gold among savages, who told them of a civilized gold-country near at hand; and they found that those savages spoke truth. Why was the unanimous report of the Carib tribes of the Orinoco to be disbelieved, when they told a similar tale? Sir Richard Schomburgk's admirable preface to Raleigh's Guiana proves, surely, that the Indians themselves were deceived, as well as deceivers. It was known, again, that vast quantities of the Peruvian treasure had been concealed by the priests, and that members of the Inca family had fled across the Andes, and held out against the Spaniards. Barely fifty years had elapsed since then;—what more probable than that this remnant of the Peruvian dynasty and treasure still existed? Even the story of the Amazons, though it may serve Hume as a point for his ungenerous and untruthful attempt to make Raleigh out either fool or villain, has come from Spaniards, who had with their own eyes seen the Indian women fighting by their husbands' sides, and from Indians, who asserted the existence of an Amazonian tribe. What right had Amyas, or any man, to disbelieve the story? The existence of the Amazons in ancient Asia, and of their intercourse with Alexander the Great, was then an accredited part of history, which it would have been gratuitous impertinence to deny. And what if some stories connected these warlike women with the Emperor of Manoa, and the capital itself? This generation ought surely to be the last to laugh at such a story, at least as long as the Amazonian guards of the King of Dahomey continue to outvie the men in that relentless ferocity, with which they have subdued every neighboring tribe, save the Christians of Abbeokuta. In this case, as in a hundred more, fact not only outdoes, but justifies imagination; and Amyas spoke common sense when he said to his men that day—

"Let fools laugh and stay at home. Wise men dare and win. Saul went to look for his father's asses, and found a kingdom; and Columbus, my men, was called a madman for only going to seek China, and never knew, they say, until his dying day, that he had found a whole new world instead of it. Find Manoa? God only, who made all things, knows what we may find beside!"

So underneath that giant ceiba-tree, those valiant men, reduced by battle and sickness to some eighty, swore a great oath, and kept that oath like men. To search for the golden city for two full years to come, whatever might befall; to stand to each other for weal or woe; to obey their officers to the death; to murmur privately against no man, but bring all complaints to a council of war; to use no profane oaths, but serve God daily with prayer; to take by violence from no man, save from their natural enemies the Spaniards; to be civil and merciful to all savages, and chaste and courteous to all women; to bring all booty and all food into the common stock, and observe to the utmost their faith with the adventurers who had fitted out the ship; and finally, to march at sunrise the next morning toward the south, trusting in God to be their guide.

"It is a great oath, and a hard one," said Brimblecombe; "but God will give us strength to keep it." And they knelt all together and received the Holy Communion, and then rose to pack provisions and ammunition, and lay down again to sleep and to dream that they were sailing home up Torridge stream—as Cavendish, returning from round the world, did actually sail home up Thames but five years afterwards—"with mariners and soldiers clothed in silk, with sails of damask, and topsails of cloth of gold, and the richest prize which ever was brought at one time unto English shores."

The Cross stands upright in the southern sky. It is the middle of the night. Cary and Yeo glide silently up the hill and into the camp, and whisper to Amyas that they have done the deed. The sleepers are awakened, and the train sets forth.

Upward and southward ever: but whither, who can tell? They hardly think of the whither; but go like sleep-walkers, shaken out of one land of dreams, only to find themselves in another and stranger one. All around is fantastic and unearthly; now each man starts as he sees the figures of his fellows, clothed from head to foot in golden filigree; looks up, and sees the yellow moonlight through the fronds of the huge tree-ferns overhead, as through a cloud of glittering lace. Now they are hewing their way through a thicket of enormous flags; now through bamboos forty feet high; now they are stumbling over boulders, waist-deep in cushions of club-moss; now they are struggling through shrubberies of heaths and rhododendrons, and woolly incense-trees, where every leaf, as they brush past, dashes some fresh scent into their faces, and

Now they open upon some craggy brow, from whence they can see far below an ocean of soft cloud, whose silver billows, girdled by the mountain sides, hide the lowland from their sight.

And from beneath the cloud strange voices rise; the screams of thousand night-birds, and wild howls, which they used at first to fancy were the cries of ravenous beasts, till they found them to proceed from nothing fiercer than an ape. But what is that deeper note, like a series of muffled explosions,—arquebuses fired within some subterranean cavern,—the heavy pulse of which rolls up through the depths of the unseen forest? They hear it now for the first time, but they will hear it many a time again; and the Indian lad is hushed, and cowers close to them, and then takes heart, as he looks upon their swords and arquebuses; for that is the roar of the jaguar, "seeking his meat from God."

But what is that glare away to the northward? The yellow moon is ringed with gay rainbows; but that light is far too red to be the reflection of any beams of hers. Now through the cloud rises a column of black and lurid smoke; the fog clears away right and left around it, and shows beneath, a mighty fire.

The men look at each other with questioning eyes, each half suspecting, and yet not daring to confess their own suspicions; and Amyas whispers to Yeo—

"You took care to flood the powder?"

"Ay, ay, sir, and to unload the ordnance too. No use in making a noise to tell the Spaniards our whereabouts."

Yes; that glare rises from the good ship Rose. Amyas, like Cortez of old, has burnt his ship, and retreat is now impossible. Forward into the unknown abyss of the New World, and God be with them as they go!

The Indian knows a cunning path: it winds along the highest ridges of the mountains; but the travelling is far more open and easy.

They have passed the head of a valley which leads down to St. Jago. Beneath that long shining river of mist, which ends at the foot of the great Silla, lies (so says the Indian lad) the rich capital of Venezuela; and beyond, the gold-mines of Los Teques and Baruta, which first attracted the founder Diego de Losada; and many a longing eye is turned towards it as they pass the saddle at the valley head; but the attempt is hopeless, they turn again to the left, and so down towards the rancho, taking care (so the prudent Amyas had commanded) to break down, after crossing, the frail rope bridge which spans each torrent and ravine.

They are at the rancho long before daybreak, and have secured there, not only fourteen mules, but eight or nine Indians stolen from off the Llanos, like their guide, who are glad enough to escape from their tyrants by taking service with them. And now southward and away, with lightened shoulders and hearts; for they are all but safe from pursuit. The broken bridges prevent the news of their raid reaching St. Jago until nightfall; and in the meanwhile, Don Guzman returns to the river mouth the next day to find the ship a blackened wreck, and the camp empty; follows their trail over the hills till he is stopped by a broken bridge; surmounts that difficulty, and meets a second; his men are worn out with heat, and a little afraid of stumbling on the heretic desperadoes, and he returns by land to St. Jago; and when he arrives there, has news from home which gives him other things to think of than following those mad Englishmen, who have vanished into the wilderness. "What need, after all, to follow them?" asked the Spaniards of each other. "Blinded by the devil, whom they serve, they rush on in search of certain death, as many a larger company has before them, and they will find it, and will trouble La Guayra no more forever." "Lutheran dogs and enemies of God," said Don Guzman to his soldiers, "they will leave their bones to whiten on the Llanos, as may every heretic who sets foot on Spanish soil!"

Will they do so, Don Guzman? Or wilt thou and Amyas meet again upon a mightier battlefield, to learn a lesson which neither of you yet has learned?

CHAPTER XXII: THE INQUISITION IN THE INDIES

My next chapter is perhaps too sad; it shall be at least as short as I can make it; but it was needful to be written, that readers may judge fairly for themselves what sort of enemies the English nation had to face in those stern days.

Three weeks have passed, and the scene is shifted to a long, low range of cells in a dark corridor in the city of Cartagena. The door of one is open; and within stand two cloaked figures, one of whom we know. It is Eustace Leigh. The other is a familiar of the Holy Office.

He holds in his hand a lamp, from which the light falls on a bed of straw, and on the sleeping figure of a man. The high white brow, the pale and delicate features—them too we know, for they are those of Frank. Saved half-dead from the fury of the savage negroes, he has been reserved for the more delicate cruelty of civilized and Christian men. He underwent the question but this afternoon; and now Eustace, his betrayer, is come to persuade him—or to entrap him? Eustace himself hardly knows whether of the two.

And yet he would give his life to save his cousin.

His life? He has long since ceased to care for that. He has done what he has done, because it is his duty; and now he is to do his duty once more, and wake the sleeper, and argue, coax, threaten him into recantation while "his heart is still tender from the torture," so Eustace's employers phrase it.

And yet how calmly he is sleeping! Is it but a freak of the lamplight, or is there a smile upon his lips? Eustace takes the lamp and bends over him to see; and as he bends he hears Frank whispering in his dreams his mother's name, and a name higher and holier still.

Eustace cannot find the heart to wake him.

"Let him rest," whispers he to his companion. "After all, I fear my words will be of little use."

"I fear so too, sir. Never did I behold a more obdurate heretic. He did not scruple to scoff openly at their holinesses."

"Ah!" said Eustace; "great is the pravity of the human heart, and the power of Satan! Let us go for the present."

"Where is she?"

"The elder sorceress, or the younger?"

"The younger—the—"

"The Senora de Soto? Ah, poor thing! One could be sorry for her, were she not a heretic." And the man eyed Eustace keenly, and then quietly added, "She is at present with the notary; to the benefit of her soul, I trust—"

Eustace half stopped, shuddering. He could hardly collect himself enough to gasp out an "Amen!"

"Within there," said the man, pointing carelessly to a door as they went down the corridor. "We can listen a moment, if you like; but don't betray me, senor."

Eustace knows well enough that the fellow is probably on the watch to betray him, if he shows any signs of compunction; at least to report faithfully to his superiors the slightest expression of sympathy with a heretic; but a horrible curiosity prevails over fear, and he pauses close to the fatal door. His face is all of a flame, his knees knock together, his ears are ringing, his heart bursting through his ribs, as he supports himself against the wall, hiding his convulsed face as well as he can from his companion.

A man's voice is plainly audible within; low, but distinct. The notary is trying that old charge of witchcraft, which the Inquisitors, whether to justify themselves to their own consciences, or to whiten their villainy somewhat in the eyes of the mob, so often brought against their victims. And then Eustace's heart sinks within him as he hears a woman's voice reply, sharpened by indignation and agony—

"Witchcraft against Don Guzman? What need of that, oh God! what need?"

"You deny it then, senora? we are sorry for you; but—"

A confused choking murmur from the victim, mingled with words which might mean anything or nothing.

"She has confessed!" whispered Eustace; "saints, I thank you!—she—"

A wail which rings through Eustace's ears, and brain, and heart! He would have torn at the door to open it; but his companion forces him away. Another, and another wail, while the wretched man hurries off, stopping his ears in vain against those piercing cries, which follow him, like avenging angels, through the dreadful vaults.

He escaped into the fragrant open air, and the golden tropic moonlight, and a garden which might have served as a model for Eden; but man's hell followed into God's heaven, and still those wails seemed to ring through his ears.

"Oh, misery, misery, misery!" murmured he to himself through grinding teeth; "and I have brought her to this! I have had to bring her to it! What else could I? Who dare blame me? And yet what devilish sin can I have committed, that requires to be punished thus? Was there no one to be found but me? No one? And yet it may save her soul. It may bring her to repentance!"

"It may, indeed; for she is delicate, and cannot endure much. You ought to know as well as I, senor, the merciful disposition of the Holy Office."

"I know it, I know it," interrupted poor Eustace, trembling now for himself. "All in love—all in love.—A paternal chastisement—"

"And the proofs of heresy are patent, beside the strong suspicion of enchantment, and the known character of the elder sorceress. You yourself, you must remember, senor, told us that she had been a notorious witch in England, before the senora brought her hither as her attendant."

"Of course she was; of course. Yes; there was no other course open. And though the flesh may be weak, sir, in my case, yet none can have proved better to the Holy Office how willing is the spirit!"

And so Eustace departed; and ere another sun had set, he had gone to the principal of the Jesuits; told him his whole heart, or as much of it, poor wretch, as he dare tell to himself; and entreated to be allowed to finish his novitiate, and enter the order, on the understanding that he was to be sent at once back to Europe, or anywhere else; "Otherwise," as he said frankly, "he should go mad, even if he were not mad already." The Jesuit, who was a kindly man enough, went to the Holy Office, and settled all with the Inquisitors, recounting to them, to set him above all suspicion, Eustace's past valiant services to the Church. His testimony was no longer needed; he left Cartagena for Nombre that very night, and sailed the next week I know not whither.

I say, I know not whither. Eustace Leigh vanishes henceforth from these pages. He may have ended as General of his Order. He may have worn out his years in some tropic forest, "conquering the souls" (including, of course, the bodies) of Indians; he may have gone back to his old work in England, and been the very Ballard who was hanged and quartered three years afterwards for his share in Babington's villainous conspiracy: I know not. This book is a history of men,—of men's virtues and sins, victories and defeats; and Eustace is a man no longer: he is become a thing, a tool, a Jesuit; which goes only where it is sent, and does good or evil indifferently as it is bid; which, by an act of moral suicide, has lost its soul, in the hope of saving it; without a will, a conscience, a responsibility (as it fancies), to God or man, but only to "The Society." In a word, Eustace, as he says himself, is "dead." Twice dead, I fear. Let the dead bury their dead. We have no more concern with Eustace Leigh.

CHAPTER XXIII: THE BANKS OF THE META

Nearly three years are past and gone since that little band had knelt at evensong beneath the giant tree of Guayra—years of seeming blank, through which they are to be tracked only by scattered notes and mis-spelt names. Through untrodden hills and forests, over a space of some eight hundred miles in length by four hundred in breadth, they had been seeking for the Golden City, and they had sought in vain. They had sought it along the wooded banks of the Orinoco, and beyond the roaring foam-world of Maypures, and on the upper waters of the mighty Amazon. They had gone up the streams even into Peru itself, and had trodden the cinchona groves of Loxa, ignorant, as all the world was then, of their healing virtues. They had seen the virgin snows of Chimborazo towering white above the thundercloud, and the giant cone of Cotopaxi blackening in its sullen wrath, before the fiery streams rolled down its sides. Foiled in their search at the back of the Andes, they had turned eastward once more, and plunged from the alpine cliffs into "the green and misty ocean of the Montana." Slowly and painfully they had worked their way northward again, along the eastern foot of the inland Cordillera, and now they were bivouacking, as it seems, upon one of the many feeders of the Meta, which flow down from the Suma Paz into the forest-covered plains. There they sat, their watch-fires glittering on the stream, beneath the shadow of enormous trees, Amyas and Cary, Brimblecombe, Yeo, and the Indian lad, who has followed them in all their wanderings, alive and well: but as far as ever from Manoa, and its fairy lake, and golden palaces, and all the wonders of the Indian's tale. Again and again in their wanderings they had heard faint rumors of its existence, and started off in some fresh direction, to meet only a fresh disappointment, and hope deferred, which maketh sick the heart.

There they sit at last—four-and-forty men out of the eighty-four who left the tree of Guayra:—where are the rest?

Drew, the master, lies on the banks of the Rio Negro, and five brave fellows by him, slain in fight by the poisoned arrows of the Indians, in a vain attempt to penetrate the mountain-gorges of the Parima. Two more lie amid the valleys of the Andes, frozen to death by the fierce slaty hail which sweeps down from the condor's eyrie; four more were drowned at one of the rapids of the Orinoco; five or six more wounded men are left behind at another rapid among friendly Indians, to be recovered when they can be: perhaps never. Fever, snakes, jaguars, alligators, cannibal fish, electric eels, have thinned their ranks month by month, and of their march through the primeval wilderness no track remains, except those lonely graves.

And there the survivors sit, beside the silent stream, beneath the tropic moon; sun-dried and lean, but strong and bold as ever, with the quiet fire of English courage burning undimmed in every eye, and the genial smile of English mirth fresh on every lip; making a jest of danger and a sport of toil, as cheerily as when they sailed over the bar of Bideford, in days which seem to belong to some antenatal life. Their beards have grown down upon their breasts; their long hair is knotted on their heads, like women's, to keep off the burning sunshine; their leggings are of the skin of the delicate Guazu-puti deer; their shirts are patched with Indian cotton web; the spoils of jaguar, puma, and ape hang from their shoulders. Their ammunition is long since spent, their muskets, spoilt by the perpetual vapor-bath of the steaming woods, are left behind as useless in a cave by some cataract of the Orinoco: but their swords are bright and terrible as ever; and they carry bows of a strength which no Indian arm can bend, and arrows pointed with the remnants of their armor; many of them, too, are armed with the pocuna or blowgun of the Indians—more deadly, because more silent, than the firearms which they have left behind them. So they have wandered, and so they will wander still, the lords of the forest and its beasts; terrible to all hostile Indians, but kindly, just, and generous to all who will deal faithfully with them; and many a smooth-chinned Carib and Ature, Solimo and Guahiba, recounts with wonder and admiration the righteousness of the bearded heroes, who proclaimed themselves the deadly foes of the faithless and murderous Spaniard, and spoke to them of the great and good queen beyond the seas, who would send her warriors to deliver and avenge the oppressed Indian.

The men are sleeping among the trees, some on the ground, and some in grass-hammocks slung between the stems. All is silent, save the heavy plunge of the tapir in the river, as he tears up the water-weeds for his night's repast. Sometimes, indeed, the jaguar, as he climbs from one tree-top to another after his prey, wakens the monkeys clustered on the boughs, and they again arouse the birds, and ten minutes of unearthly roars, howls, shrieks, and cacklings make the forest ring as if all pandemonium had broke loose; but that soon dies away again; and, even while it lasts, it is too common a matter to awaken the sleepers, much less to interrupt the council of war which is going on beside the watch-fire, between the three adventurers and the faithful Yeo. A hundred times have they held such a council, and in vain; and, for aught they know, this one will be as fruitless as those which have gone before it. Nevertheless, it is a more solemn one than usual; for the two years during which they had agreed to search for Manoa are long past, and some new place must be determined on, unless they intend to spend the rest of their lives in that green wilderness.

"Well," says Will Cary, taking his cigar out of his mouth, "at least we have got something out of those last Indians. It is a comfort to have a puff at tobacco once more, after three weeks' fasting."

"For me," said Jack Brimblecombe, "Heaven forgive me! but when I get the magical leaf between my teeth again, I feel tempted to sit as still as a chimney, and smoke till my dying day, without stirring hand or foot."

"Then I shall forbid you tobacco, Master Parson," said Amyas; "for we must be up and away again to-morrow. We have been idling here three mortal days, and nothing done."

"Shall we ever do anything? I think the gold of Manoa is like the gold which lies where the rainbow touches the ground, always a field beyond you."

Amyas was silent awhile, and so were the rest. There was no denying that their hopes were all but gone. In the immense circuit which they had made, they had met with nothing but disappointment.

"There is but one more chance," said he at length, "and that is, the mountains to the east of the Orinoco, where we failed the first time. The Incas may have moved on to them when they escaped."

"Why not?" said Cary; "they would so put all the forests, beside the Llanos and half-a-dozen great rivers, between them and those dogs of Spaniards."

"Shall we try it once more?" said Amyas. "This river ought to run into the Orinoco; and once there, we are again at the very foot of the mountains. What say you, Yeo?"

"I cannot but mind, your worship, that when we came up the Orinoco, the Indians told us terrible stories of those mountains, how far they stretched, and how difficult they were to cross, by reason of the cliffs aloft, and the thick forests in the valleys. And have we not lost five good men there already?"

"What care we? No forests can be thicker than those we have bored through already; why, if one had had but a tail, like a monkey, for an extra warp, one might have gone a hundred miles on end along the tree-tops, and found it far pleasanter walking than tripping in withes, and being eaten up with creeping things, from morn till night."

"But remember, too," said Jack, "how they told us to beware of the Amazons."

"What, Jack, afraid of a parcel of women?"

"Why not?" said Jack, "I wouldn't run from a man, as you know; but a woman—it's not natural, like. They must be witches or devils. See how the Caribs feared them. And there were men there without necks, and with their eyes in their breasts, they said. Now how could a Christian tackle such customers as them?"

"He couldn't cut off their heads, that's certain; but, I suppose, a poke in the ribs will do as much for them as for their neighbors."

"Well," said Jack, "if I fight, let me fight honest flesh and blood, that's all, and none of these outlandish monsters. How do you know but that they are invulnerable by art-magic?"

"How do you know that they are? And as for the Amazons," said Cary, "woman's woman, all the world over. I'll bet that you may wheedle them round with a compliment or two, just as if they were so many burghers' wives. Pity I have not a court-suit and a Spanish hat. I would have taken an orange in one hand and a handkerchief in the other, gone all alone to them as ambassador, and been in a week as great with Queen Blackfacealinda as ever Raleigh is at Whitehall."

"Gentlemen!" said Yeo, "where you go, I go; and not only I, but every man of us, I doubt not; but we have lost now half our company, and spent our ammunition, so we are no better men, were it not for our swords, than these naked heathens round us. Now it was, as you all know, by the wonder and noise of their ordnance (let alone their horses, which is a break-neck beast I put no faith in) that both Cortez and Pizarro, those imps of Satan, made their golden conquests, with which if we could have astounded the people of Manoa—"

"Having first found the said people," laughed Amyas. "It is like the old fable. Every craftsman thinks his own trade the one pillar of the commonweal."

"Well! your worship," quoth Yeo, "it may be that being a gunner I overprize guns. But it don't need slate and pencil to do this sum—Are forty men without shot as good as eighty with?"

"Thou art right, old fellow, right enough, and I was only jesting for very sorrow, and must needs laugh about it lest I weep about it. Our chance is over, I believe, though I dare not confess as much to the men."

"Sir," said Yeo, "I have a feeling on me that the Lord's hand is against us in this matter. Whether He means to keep this wealth for worthier men than us, or whether it is His will to hide this great city in the secret place of His presence from the strife of tongues, and so to spare them from sinful man's covetousness, and England from that sin and luxury which I have seen gold beget among the Spaniards, I know not, sir; for who knoweth the counsels of the Lord? But I have long had a voice within which saith, 'Salvation Yeo, thou shalt never behold the Golden City which is on earth, where heathens worship sun and moon and the hosts of heaven; be content, therefore, to see that Golden City which is above, where is neither sun nor moon, but the Lord God and the Lamb are the light thereof."

There was a simple majesty about old Yeo when he broke forth in utterances like these, which made his comrades, and even Amyas and Cary, look on him as Mussulmans look on madmen, as possessed of mysterious knowledge and flashes of inspiration; and Brimblecombe, whose pious soul looked up to the old hero with a reverence which had overcome all his Churchman's prejudices against Anabaptists, answered gently,—

"Amen! amen! my masters all: and it has been on my mind, too, this long time, that there is a providence against our going east; for see how this two years past, whenever we have pushed eastward, we have fallen into trouble, and lost good men; and whenever we went Westward-ho, we have prospered; and do prosper to this day."

"And what is more, gentlemen," said Yeo, "if, as Scripture says, dreams are from the Lord, I verily believe mine last night came from Him; for as I lay by the fire, sirs, I heard my little maid's voice calling of me, as plain as ever I heard in my life; and the very same words, sirs, which she learned from me and my good comrade William Penberthy to say, 'Westward-ho! jolly mariners all!' a bit of an ungodly song, my masters, which we sang in our wild days; but she stood and called it as plain as ever mortal ears heard, and called again till I answered, 'Coming! my maid, coming!' and after that the dear chuck called no more—God grant I find her yet!—and so I woke."

Cary had long since given up laughing at Yeo about the "little maid;" and Amyas answered,—

"So let it be, Yeo, if the rest agree: but what shall we do to the westward?"

"Do?" said Cary; "there's plenty to do; for there's plenty of gold, and plenty of Spaniards, too, they say, on the other side of these mountains: so that our swords will not rust for lack of adventures, my gay knights-errant all."

So they chatted on; and before night was half through a plan was matured, desperate enough—but what cared those brave hearts for that? They would cross the Cordillera to Santa Fe de Bogota, of the wealth whereof both Yeo and Amyas had often heard in the Pacific: try to seize either the town or some convoy of gold going from it; make for the nearest river (there was said to be a large one which ran northward thence), build canoes, and try to reach the Northern Sea once more; and then, if Heaven prospered them, they might seize a Spanish ship, and make their way home to England, not, indeed, with the wealth of Manoa, but with a fair booty of Spanish gold. This was their new dream. It was a wild one: but hardly more wild than the one which Drake had fulfilled, and not as wild as the one which Oxenham might have fulfilled, but for his own fatal folly.

Amyas sat watching late that night, sad of heart. To give up the cherished dream of years was hard; to face his mother, harder still: but it must be done, for the men's sake. So the new plan was proposed next day, and accepted joyfully. They would go up to the mountains and rest awhile; if possible, bring up the wounded whom they had left behind; and then, try a new venture, with new hopes, perhaps new dangers; they were inured to the latter.

They started next morning cheerfully enough, and for three hours or more paddled easily up the glassy and windless reaches, between two green flower-bespangled walls of forest, gay with innumerable birds and insects; while down from the branches which overhung the stream long trailers hung to the water's edge, and seemed admiring in the clear mirror the images of their own gorgeous flowers. River, trees, flowers, birds, insects,—it was all a fairy-land: but it was a colossal one; and yet the voyagers took little note of it. It was now to them an everyday occurrence, to see trees full two hundred feet high one mass of yellow or purple blossom to the highest twigs, and every branch and stem one hanging garden of crimson and orange orchids or vanillas. Common to them were all the fantastic and enormous shapes with which Nature bedecks her robes beneath the fierce suns and fattening rains of the tropic forest. Common were forms and colors of bird, and fish, and butterfly, more strange and bright than ever opium-eater dreamed. The long processions of monkeys, who kept pace with them along the tree-tops, and proclaimed their wonder in every imaginable whistle, and grunt, and howl, had ceased to move their laughter, as much as the roar of the jaguar and the rustle of the boa had ceased to move their fear; and when a brilliant green and rose-colored fish, flat-bodied like a bream, flab-finned like a salmon, and saw-toothed like a shark, leapt clean on board of the canoe to escape the rush of the huge alligator (whose loathsome snout, ere he could stop, actually rattled against the canoe within a foot of Jack Brimblecombe's hand), Jack, instead of turning pale, as he had done at the sharks upon a certain memorable occasion, coolly picked up the fish, and said, "He's four pound weight! If you can catch 'pirai' for us like that, old fellow, just keep in our wake, and we'll give you the cleanings for wages."

Yes. The mind of man is not so "infinite," in the vulgar sense of that word, as people fancy; and however greedy the appetite for wonder may be, while it remains unsatisfied in everyday European life, it is as easily satiated as any other appetite, and then leaves the senses of its possessor as dull as those of a city gourmand after a lord mayor's feast. Only the highest minds— our Humboldts, and Bonplands, and Schomburgks (and they only when quickened to an almost unhealthy activity by civilization)—can go on long appreciating where Nature is insatiable, imperious, maddening, in her demands on our admiration. The very power of observing wears out under the rush of ever new objects; and the dizzy spectator is fain at last to shut the eyes of his soul, and take refuge (as West Indian Spaniards do) in tobacco and stupidity. The man, too, who has not only eyes but utterance,—what shall he do where all words fail him? Superlatives are but inarticulate, after all, and give no pictures even of size any more than do numbers of feet and yards: and yet what else can we do, but heap superlative on superlative, and cry, "Wonderful, wonderful!" and after that, "wonderful, past all whooping"? What Humboldt's self cannot paint, we will not try to daub. The voyagers were in a South American forest, readers. Fill up the meaning of those words, each as your knowledge enables you, for I cannot do it for you.

Certainly those adventurers could not. The absence of any attempt at word-painting, even of admiration at the glorious things which they saw, is most remarkable in all early voyagers, both Spanish and English. The only two exceptions which I recollect are Columbus—(but then all was new, and he was bound to tell what he had seen)—and Raleigh; the two most gifted men, perhaps, with the exception of Humboldt, who ever set foot in tropical America; but even they dare nothing but a few feeble hints in passing. Their souls had been dazzled and stunned by a great glory. Coming out of our European Nature into that tropic one, they had felt like Plato's men, bred in the twilight cavern, and then suddenly turned round to the broad blaze of day; they had seen things awful and unspeakable: why talk of them, except to say with the Turks, "God is great!"

So it was with these men. Among the higher-hearted of them, the grandeur and the glory around had attuned their spirits to itself, and kept up in them a lofty, heroical, reverent frame of mind; but they knew as little about the trees and animals in an "artistic" or "critical" point of view, as in a scientific one. This tree the Indians called one unpronounceable name, and it made good bows; that, some other name, and it made good canoes; of that, you could eat the fruit; that produced the caoutchouc gum, useful for a hundred matters; that was what the Indians (and they likewise) used to poison their arrows with; from the ashes of those palm-nuts you could make good salt; that tree, again, was full of good milk if you bored the stem: they drank it, and gave God thanks, and were not astonished. God was great: but that they had discovered long before they came into the tropics. Noble old child-hearted heroes, with just romance and superstition enough about them to keep them from that prurient hysterical wonder and enthusiasm, which is simply, one often fears, a product of our scepticism! We do not trust enough in God, we do not really believe His power enough, to be ready, as they were, as every one ought to be on a God-made earth, for anything and everything being possible; and then, when a wonder is discovered, we go into ecstasies and shrieks over it, and take to ourselves credit for being susceptible of so lofty a feeling, true index, forsooth, of a refined and cultivated mind.

They paddled onward hour after hour, sheltering themselves as best they could under the shadow of the southern bank, while on their right hand the full sun-glare lay upon the enormous wall of mimosas, figs, and laurels, which formed the northern forest, broken by the slender shafts of bamboo tufts, and decked with a thousand gaudy parasites; bank upon bank of gorgeous bloom piled upward to the sky, till where its outline cut the blue, flowers and leaves, too lofty to be distinguished by the eye, formed a broken rainbow of all hues quivering in the ascending streams of azure mist, until they seemed to melt and mingle with the very heavens.

And as the sun rose higher and higher, a great stillness fell upon the forest. The jaguars and the monkeys had hidden themselves in the darkest depths of the woods. The birds' notes died out one by one; the very butterflies ceased their flitting over the tree-tops, and slept with outspread wings upon the glossy leaves, undistinguishable from the flowers around them. Now and then a colibri whirred downward toward the water, hummed for a moment around some pendent flower, and then the living gem was lost in the deep blackness of the inner wood, among tree-trunks as huge and dark as the pillars of some Hindoo shrine; or a parrot swung and screamed at them from an overhanging bough; or a thirsty monkey slid lazily down a liana to the surface of the stream, dipped up the water in his tiny hand, and started chattering back, as his eyes met those of some foul alligator peering upward through the clear depths below. In shaded nooks beneath the boughs, the capybaras, rabbits as large as sheep, went paddling sleepily round and round, thrusting up their unwieldy heads among the blooms of the blue water-lilies; while black and purple water-hens ran up and down upon the rafts of floating leaves. The shining snout of a freshwater dolphin rose slowly to the surface; a jet of spray whirred up; a rainbow hung upon it for a moment; and the black snout sank lazily again. Here and there, too, upon some shallow pebbly shore, scarlet flamingoes stood dreaming knee-deep, on one leg; crested cranes pranced up and down, admiring their own finery; and ibises and egrets dipped their bills under water in search of prey: but before noon even those had slipped away, and there reigned a stillness which might be heard—such a stillness (to compare small things with great) as broods beneath the rich shadows of Amyas's own Devon woods, or among the lonely sweeps of Exmoor, when the heather is in flower—a stillness in which, as Humboldt says, "If beyond the silence we listen for the faintest undertones, we detect a stifled, continuous hum of insects, which crowd the air close to the earth; a confused swarming murmur which hangs round every bush, in the cracked bark of trees, in the soil undermined by lizards, millepedes, and bees; a voice proclaiming to us that all Nature breathes, that under a thousand different forms life swarms in the gaping and dusty earth, as much as in the bosom of the waters, and the air which breathes around."

At last a soft and distant murmur, increasing gradually to a heavy roar, announced that they were nearing some cataract; till turning a point, where the deep alluvial soil rose into a low cliff fringed with delicate ferns, they came full in sight of a scene at which all paused: not with astonishment, but with something very like disgust.

"Rapids again!" grumbled one. "I thought we had had enough of them on the Orinoco."

"We shall have to get out, and draw the canoes overland, I suppose. Three hours will be lost, and in the very hottest of the day, too."

"There's worse behind; don't you see the spray behind the palms?"

"Stop grumbling, my masters, and don't cry out before you are hurt. Paddle right up to the largest of those islands, and let us look about us."

In front of them was a snow-white bar of raging foam, some ten feet high, along which were ranged three or four islands of black rock. Each was crested with a knot of lofty palms, whose green tops stood out clear against the bright sky, while the lower half of their stems loomed hazy through a luminous veil of rainbowed mist. The banks right and left of the fall were so densely fringed with a low hedge of shrubs, that landing seemed all but impossible; and their Indian guide, suddenly looking round him and whispering, bade them beware of savages; and pointed to a canoe which lay swinging in the eddies under the largest island, moored apparently to the root of some tree.

"Silence all!" cried Amyas, "and paddle up thither and seize the canoe. If there be an Indian on the island, we will have speech of him: but mind and treat him friendly; and on your lives, neither strike nor shoot, even if he offers to fight."

So, choosing a line of smooth backwater just in the wake of the island, they drove their canoes up by main force, and fastened them safely by the side of the Indian's, while Amyas, always the foremost, sprang boldly on shore, whispering to the Indian boy to follow him.

Once on the island, Amyas felt sure enough, that if its wild tenant had not seen them approach, he certainly had not heard them, so deafening was the noise which filled his brain, and seemed to make the very leaves upon the bushes quiver, and the solid stone beneath his feet to reel and ring. For two hundred yards and more above the fall nothing met his eye but one white waste of raging foam, with here and there a transverse dyke of rock, which hurled columns of spray and surges of beaded water high into the air,—strangely contrasting with the still and silent cliffs of green leaves which walled the river right and left, and more strangely still with the knots of enormous palms upon the islets, which reared their polished shafts a hundred feet into the air, straight and upright as masts, while their broad plumes and golden-clustered fruit slept in the sunshine far aloft, the image of the stateliest repose amid the wildest wrath of Nature.

He looked round anxiously for the expected Indian; but he was nowhere to be seen; and, in the meanwhile, as he stept cautiously along the island, which was some fifty yards in length and breadth, his senses, accustomed as they were to such sights, could not help dwelling on the exquisite beauty of the scene; on the garden of gay flowers, of every imaginable form and hue, which fringed every boulder at his feet, peeping out amid delicate fern-fans and luxuriant cushions of moss; on the chequered shade of the palms, and the cool air, which wafted down from the cataracts above the scents of a thousand flowers. Gradually his ear became accustomed to the roar, and, above its mighty undertone, he could hear the whisper of the wind among the shrubs, and the hum of myriad insects; while the rock manakin, with its saffron plumage, flitted before him from stone to stone, calling cheerily, and seeming to lead him on. Suddenly, scrambling over the rocky flower-beds to the other side of the isle, he came upon a little shady beach, which, beneath a bank of stone some six feet high, fringed the edge of a perfectly still and glassy bay. Ten yards farther, the cataract fell sheer in thunder: but a high fern-fringed rock turned its force away from that quiet nook. In it the water swung slowly round and round in glassy dark-green rings, among which dimpled a hundred gaudy fish, waiting for every fly and worm which spun and quivered on the eddy. Here, if anywhere, was the place to find the owner of the canoe. He leapt down upon the pebbles; and as he did so, a figure rose from behind a neighboring rock, and met him face to face.

It was an Indian girl; and yet, when he looked again,—was it an Indian girl? Amyas had seen hundreds of those delicate dark-skinned daughters of the forest, but never such a one as this. Her stature was taller, her limbs were fuller and more rounded; her complexion, though tanned by light, was fairer by far than his own sunburnt face; her hair, crowned with a garland of white flowers, was not lank, and straight, and black, like an Indian's, but of a rich, glossy brown, and curling richly and crisply from her very temples to her knees. Her forehead, though low, was upright and ample; her nose was straight and small; her lips, the lips of a European; her whole face of the highest and richest type of Spanish beauty; a collar of gold mingled with green beads hung round her neck, and golden bracelets were on her wrists. All the strange and dim legends of white Indians, and of nations of a higher race than Carib, or Arrowak, or Solimo, which Amyas had ever heard, rose up in his memory. She must be the daughter of some great cacique, perhaps of the lost Incas themselves—why not? And full of simple wonder, he gazed upon that fairy vision, while she, unabashed in her free innocence, gazed fearlessly in return, as Eve might have done in Paradise, upon the mighty stature, and the strange garments, and above all, on the bushy beard and flowing yellow locks of the Englishman.

He spoke first, in some Indian tongue, gently and smilingly, and made a half-step forward; but quick as light she caught up from the ground a bow, and held it fiercely toward him, fitted with the long arrow, with which, as he could see, she had been striking fish, for a line of twisted grass hung from its barbed head. Amyas stopped, laid down his own bow and sword, and made another step in advance, smiling still, and making all Indian signs of amity: but the arrow was still pointed straight at his breast, and he knew the mettle and strength of the forest nymphs well enough to stand still and call for the Indian boy; too proud to retreat, but in the uncomfortable expectation of feeling every moment the shaft quivering between his ribs.

The boy, who had been peering from above, leaped down to them in a moment; and began, as the safest method, grovelling on his nose upon the pebbles, while he tried two or three dialects; one of which at last she seemed to understand, and answered in a tone of evident suspicion and anger.

"What does she say?"

"That you are a Spaniard and a robber, because you have a beard."

"Tell her that we are no Spaniards, but that we hate them; and are come across the great waters to help the Indians to kill them."

The boy translated his speech. The nymph answered by a contemptuous shake of the head.

"Tell her, that if she will send her tribe to us, we will do them no harm. We are going over the mountains to fight the Spaniards, and we want them to show us the way."

The boy had no sooner spoken, than, nimble as a deer, the nymph had sprung up the rocks, and darted between the palm-stems to her canoe. Suddenly she caught sight of the English boat, and stopped with a cry of fear and rage.

"Let her pass!" shouted Amyas, who had followed her close. "Push your boat off, and let her pass. Boy, tell her to go on; they will not come near her."

But she hesitated still, and with arrow drawn to the head, faced first on the boat's crew, and then on Amyas, till the Englishmen had shoved off full twenty yards.

Then, leaping into her tiny piragua, she darted into the wildest whirl of the eddies, shooting along with vigorous strokes, while the English trembled as they saw the frail bark spinning and leaping amid the muzzles of the alligators, and the huge dog-toothed trout: but with the swiftness of an arrow she reached the northern bank, drove her canoe among the bushes, and leaping from it, darted through some narrow opening in the bush, and vanished like a dream.

"What fair virago have you unearthed?" cried Cary, as they toiled up again to the landing-place.

"Beshrew me," quoth Jack, "but we are in the very land of the nymphs, and I shall expect to see Diana herself next, with the moon on her forehead."

"Take care, then, where you wander hereabouts, Sir John: lest you end as Actaeon did, by turning into a stag, and being eaten by a jaguar."

"Actaeon was eaten by his own hounds, Mr. Cary, so the parallel don't hold. But surely she was a very wonder of beauty!"

Why was it that Amyas did not like this harmless talk? There had come over him the strangest new feeling; as if that fair vision was his property, and the men had no right to talk about her, no right to have even seen her. And he spoke quite surlily as he said—

"You may leave the women to themselves, my masters; you'll have to deal with the men ere long: so get your canoes up on the rock, and keep good watch."

"Hillo!" shouted one in a few minutes, "here's fresh fish enough to feed us all round. I suppose that young cat-a-mountain left it behind her in her hurry. I wish she had left her golden chains and ouches into the bargain."

"Well," said another, "we'll take it as fair payment, for having made us drop down the current again to let her ladyship pass."

"Leave that fish alone," said Amyas; "it is none of yours."

"Why, sir!" quoth the finder in a tone of sulky deprecation.

"If we are to make good friends with the heathens, we had better not begin by stealing their goods. There are plenty more fish in the river; go and catch them, and let the Indians have their own."

The men were accustomed enough to strict and stern justice in their dealings with the savages: but they could not help looking slyly at each other, and hinting, when out of sight, that the captain seemed in a mighty fuss about his new acquaintance.

However, they were expert by this time in all the Indian's fishing methods; and so abundant was the animal life which swarmed around every rock, that in an hour fish enough lay on the beach to feed them all; whose forms and colors, names and families, I must leave the reader to guess from the wondrous pages of Sir Richard Schomburgk, for I know too little of them to speak without the fear of making mistakes.

A full hour passed before they saw anything more of their Indian neighbors; and then from under the bushes shot out a canoe, on which all eyes were fixed in expectation.

Amyas, who expected to find there some remnant of a higher race, was disappointed enough at seeing on board only the usual half-dozen of low-browed, dirty Orsons, painted red with arnotto: but a gray-headed elder at the stern seemed, by his feathers and gold ornaments, to be some man of note in the little woodland community.

The canoe came close up to the island; Amyas saw that they were unarmed, and, laying down his weapons, advanced alone to the bank, making all signs of amity. They were returned with interest by the old man, and Amyas's next care was to bring forward the fish which the fair nymph had left behind, and, through the medium of the Indian lad, to give the cacique (for so he seemed to be) to understand that he wished to render every one his own. This offer was received, as Amyas expected, with great applause, and the canoe came alongside; but the crew still seemed afraid to land. Amyas bade his men throw the fish one by one into the boat; and then proclaimed by the boy's mouth, as was his custom with all Indians, that he and his were enemies of the Spaniards, and on their way to make war against them,—and that all which they desired was a peaceable and safe passage through the dominions of the mighty potentate and renowned warrior whom they beheld before them; for Amyas argued rightly enough, that even if the old fellow aft was not the cacique, he would be none the less pleased at being mistaken for him.

Whereon the ancient worthy, rising in the canoe, pointed to heaven, earth, and the things under, and commenced a long sermon, in tone, manner, and articulation, very like one of those which the great black-bearded apes were in the habit of preaching every evening when they could get together a congregation of little monkeys to listen, to the great scandal of Jack, who would have it that some evil spirit set them on to mimic him; which sermon, being partly interpreted by the Indian lad, seemed to signify, that the valor and justice of the white men had already reached the ears of the speaker, and that he was sent to welcome them into those regions by the Daughter of the Sun.

"The Daughter of the Sun!" quoth Amyas; "then we have found the lost Incas after all."

"We have found something," said Cary; "I only hope it may not be a mare's nest, like many another of our finding."

"Or an adder's," said Yeo. "We must beware of treachery."

"We must beware of no such thing," said Amyas, pretty sharply. "Have I not told you fifty times, that if they see that we trust them, they will trust us, and if they see that we suspect them, they will suspect us? And when two parties are watching to see who strikes the first blow, they are sure to come to fisticuffs from mere dirty fear of each other."

Amyas spoke truth; for almost every atrocity against savages which had been committed by the Spaniards, and which was in later and worse times committed by the English, was wont to be excused in that same base fear of treachery. Amyas's plan, like that of Drake, and Cook, and all great English voyagers, had been all along to inspire at once awe and confidence, by a frank and fearless carriage; and he was not disappointed here. He bade the men step boldly into their canoes, and follow the old Indian whither he would. The simple children of the forest bowed themselves reverently before the mighty strangers, and then led them smilingly across the stream, and through a narrow passage in the covert, to a hidden lagoon, on the banks of which stood, not Manoa, but a tiny Indian village.

CHAPTER XXIV: HOW AMYAS WAS TEMPTED OF THE DEVIL

Humboldt has somewhere a curious passage; in which, looking on some wretched group of Indians, squatting stupidly round their fires, besmeared with grease and paint, and devouring ants and clay, he somewhat naively remarks, that were it not for science, which teaches us that such is the crude material of humanity, and this the state from which we all have risen, he should have been tempted rather to look upon those hapless beings as the last degraded remnants of some fallen and dying race. One wishes that the great traveller had been bold enough to yield to that temptation, which his own reason and common sense presented to him as the real explanation of the sad sight, instead of following the dogmas of a so-called science, which has not a fact whereon to base its wild notion, and must ignore a thousand facts in asserting it. His own good sense, it seems, coincided instinctively with the Bible doctrine, that man in a state of nature is a fallen being, doomed to death—a view which may be a sad one, but still one more honorable to poor humanity than the theory, that we all began as some sort of two-handed apes. It is surely more hopeful to believe that those poor Otomacs or Guahibas were not what they ought to be, than to believe that they were. It is certainly more complimentary to them to think that they had been somewhat nobler and more prudent in centuries gone by, than that they were such blockheads as to have dragged on, the son after the father, for all the thousands of years which have elapsed since man was made, without having had wit enough to discover any better food than ants and clay.

Our voyagers, however, like those of their time, troubled their heads with no such questions. Taking the Bible story as they found it, they agreed with Humboldt's reason, and not with his science; or, to speak correctly, agreed with Humboldt's self, and not with the shallow anthropologic theories which happened to be in vogue fifty years ago; and their new hosts were in their eyes immortal souls like themselves, "captivated by the devil at his will," lost there in the pathless forests, likely to be lost hereafter.

And certainly facts seemed to bear out their old-fashioned theories; although these Indians had sunk by no means so low as the Guahibas whom they had met upon the lower waters of the same river.

They beheld, on landing, a scattered village of palm-leaf sheds, under which, as usual, the hammocks were slung from tree to tree. Here and there, in openings in the forest, patches of cassava and indigo appeared; and there was a look of neatness and comfort about the little settlement superior to the average.

But now for the signs of the evil spirit. Certainly it was no good spirit who had inspired them with the art of music; or else (as Cary said) Apollo and Mercury (if they ever visited America) had played their forefathers a shabby trick, and put them off with very poor instruments, and still poorer taste. For on either side of the landing-place were arranged four or five stout fellows, each with a tall drum, or long earthen trumpet, swelling out in the course of its length into several hollow balls from which arose, the moment the strangers set foot on shore, so deafening a cacophony of howls, and groans, and thumps, as fully to justify Yeo's remark, "They are calling upon their devil, sir." To which Cary answered, with some show of reason, that "they were the less likely to be disappointed, for none but Sir Urian would ever come to listen to such a noise."

"And you mark, sirs," said Yeo, "there's some feast or sacrifice toward. I'm not overconfident of them yet."

"Nonsense!" said Amyas, "we could kill every soul of them in half-an-hour, and they know that as well as we."

But some great demonstration was plainly toward; for the children of the forest were arrayed in two lines, right and left of the open space, the men in front, and the women behind; and all bedizened, to the best of their power, with arnotto, indigo, and feathers.

Next, with a hideous yell, leapt into the centre of the space a personage who certainly could not have complained if any one had taken him for the devil, for he had dressed himself up carefully for that very intent, in a jaguar-skin with a long tail, grinning teeth, a pair of horns, a plume of black and yellow feathers, and a huge rattle.

"Here's the Piache, the rascal," says Amyas.

"Ay," says Yeo, "in Satan's livery, and I've no doubt his works are according, trust him for it."

"Don't be frightened, Jack," says Cary, backing up Brimblecombe from behind. "It's your business to tackle him, you know. At him boldly, and he'll run."

Whereat all the men laughed; and the Piache, who had intended to produce a very solemn impression, hung fire a little. However, being accustomed to get his bread by his impudence, he soon recovered himself, advanced, smote one of the musicians over the head with his rattle to procure silence; and then began a harangue, to which Amyas listened patiently, cigar in mouth.

"What's it all about, boy?"

"He wants to know whether you have seen Amalivaca on the other shore of the great water?"

Amyas was accustomed to this inquiry after the mythic civilizer of the forest Indians, who, after carving the mysterious sculptures which appear upon so many inland cliffs of that region, returned again whence he came, beyond the ocean. He answered, as usual, by setting forth the praises of Queen Elizabeth.

To which the Piache replied, that she must be one of Amalivaca's seven daughters, some of whom he took back with him, while he broke the legs of the rest to prevent their running away, and left them to people the forests.

To which Amyas replied, that his queen's legs were certainly not broken; for she was a very model of grace and activity, and the best dancer in all her dominions; but that it was more important to him to know whether the tribe would give them cassava bread, and let them stay peaceably on that island, to rest a while before they went on to fight the clothed men (the Spaniards), on the other side of the mountains.

On which the Piache, after capering and turning head over heels with much howling, beckoned Amyas and his party to follow him; they did so, seeing that the Indians were all unarmed, and evidently in the highest good humor.

The Piache went toward the door of a carefully closed hut, and crawling up to it on all-fours in most abject fashion, began whining to some one within.

"Ask what he is about, boy."

The lad asked the old cacique, who had accompanied them, and received for answer, that he was consulting the Daughter of the Sun.

"Here is our mare's nest at last," quoth Cary, as the Piache from whines rose to screams and gesticulations, and then to violent convulsions, foaming at the mouth, and rolling of the eyeballs, till he suddenly sank exhausted, and lay for dead.

"As good as a stage play."

"The devil has played his part," says Jack; "and now by the rules of all plays Vice should come on."

"And a very fair Vice it will be, I suspect; a right sweet Iniquity, my Jack! Listen."

And from the interior of the hut rose a low sweet song, at which all the simple Indians bowed their heads in reverence; and the English were hushed in astonishment; for the voice was not shrill or guttural, like that of an Indian, but round, clear, and rich, like a European's; and as it swelled and rose louder and louder, showed a compass and power which would have been extraordinary anywhere (and many a man of the party, as was usual in musical old England, was a good judge enough of such a matter, and could hold his part right well in glee, and catch, and roundelay, and psalm). And as it leaped, and ran, and sank again, and rose once more to fall once more, all but inarticulate, yet perfect in melody, like the voice of bird on bough, the wild wanderers were rapt in new delight, and did not wonder at the Indians as they bowed their heads, and welcomed the notes as messengers from some higher world. At last one triumphant burst, so shrill that all ears rang again, and then dead silence. The Piache, suddenly restored to life, jumped upright, and recommenced preaching at Amyas.

"Tell the howling villain to make short work of it, lad! His tune won't do after that last one."

The lad, grinning, informed Amyas that the Piache signified their acceptance as friends by the Daughter of the Sun; that her friends were theirs, and her foes theirs. Whereon the Indians set up a scream of delight, and Amyas, rolling another tobacco leaf up in another strip of plantain, answered,—

"Then let her give us some cassava," and lighted a fresh cigar.

Whereon the door of the hut opened, and the Indians prostrated themselves to the earth, as there came forth the same fair apparition which they had encountered upon the island, but decked now in feather-robes, and plumes of every imaginable hue.

Slowly and stately, as one accustomed to command, she walked up to Amyas, glancing proudly round on her prostrate adorers, and pointing with graceful arms to the trees, the gardens, and the huts, gave him to understand by signs (so expressive were her looks, that no words were needed) that all was at his service; after which, taking his hand, she lifted it gently to her forehead.

At that sign of submission a shout of rapture rose from the crowd; and as the mysterious maiden retired again to her hut, they pressed round the English, caressing and admiring, pointing with equal surprise to their swords, to their Indian bows and blow-guns, and to the trophies of wild beasts with which they were clothed; while women hastened off to bring fruit, and flowers, and cassava, and (to Amyas's great anxiety) calabashes of intoxicating drink; and, to make a long story short, the English sat down beneath the trees, and feasted merrily, while the drums and trumpets made hideous music, and lithe young girls and lads danced uncouth dances, which so scandalized both Brimblecombe and Yeo, that they persuaded Amyas to beat an early retreat. He was willing enough to get back to the island while the men were still sober; so there were many leave-takings and promises of return on the morrow, and the party paddled back to their island-fortress, racking their wits as to who or what the mysterious maid could be.

Amyas, however, had settled in his mind that she was one of the lost Inca race; perhaps a descendant of that very fair girl, wife of the Inca Manco, whom Pizarro, forty years before, had, merely to torture the fugitive king's heart, as his body was safe from the tyrant's reach, stripped, scourged, and shot to death with arrows, uncomplaining to the last.

They all assembled for the evening service (hardly a day had passed since they left England on which they had not done the same); and after it was over, they must needs sing a Psalm, and then a catch or two, ere they went to sleep; and till the moon was high in heaven, twenty mellow voices rang out above the roar of the cataract, in many a good old tune. Once or twice they thought they heard an echo to their song: but they took no note of it, till Cary, who had gone apart for a few minutes, returned, and whispered Amyas away.

"The sweet Iniquity is mimicking us, lad."

They went to the brink of the river; and there (for their ears were by this time dead to the noise of the torrent) they could hear plainly the same voice which had so surprised them in the hut, repeating, clear and true, snatches of the airs which they had sung. Strange and solemn enough was the effect of the men's deep voices on the island, answered out of the dark forest by those sweet treble notes; and the two young men stood a long while listening and looking out across the eddies, which swirled down golden in the moonlight: but they could see nothing beyond save the black wall of trees. After a while the voice ceased, and the two returned to dream of Incas and nightingales.

They visited the village again next day; and every day for a week or more: but the maiden appeared but rarely, and when she did, kept her distance as haughtily as a queen.

Amyas, of course, as soon as he could converse somewhat better with his new friends, was not long before he questioned the cacique about her. But the old man made an owl's face at her name, and intimated by mysterious shakes of the head, that she was a very strange personage, and the less said about her the better. She was "a child of the Sun," and that was enough.

"Tell him, boy," quoth Cary, "that we are the children of the Sun by his first wife; and have orders from him to inquire how the Indians have behaved to our step-sister, for he cannot see all their tricks down here, the trees are so thick. So let him tell us, or all the cassava plants shall be blighted."

"Will, Will, don't play with lying!" said Amyas: but the threat was enough for the cacique, and taking them in his canoe a full mile down the stream, as if in fear that the wonderful maiden should overhear him, he told them, in a sort of rhythmic chant, how, many moons ago (he could not tell how many), his tribe was a mighty nation, and dwelt in Papamene, till the Spaniards drove them forth. And how, as they wandered northward, far away upon the mountain spurs beneath the flaming cone of Cotopaxi, they had found this fair creature wandering in the forest, about the bigness of a seven years' child. Wondering at her white skin and her delicate beauty, the simple Indians worshipped her as a god, and led her home with them. And when they found that she was human like themselves, their wonder scarcely lessened. How could so tender a being have sustained life in those forests, and escaped the jaguar and the snake? She must be under some Divine protection: she must be a daughter of the Sun, one of that mighty Inca race, the news of whose fearful fall had reached even those lonely wildernesses; who had, many of them, haunted for years as exiles the eastern slopes of the Andes, about the Ucalayi and the Maranon; who would, as all Indians knew, rise again some day to power, when bearded white men should come across the seas to restore them to their ancient throne.

So, as the girl grew up among them, she was tended with royal honors, by command of the conjuror of the tribe, that so her forefather the Sun might be propitious to them, and the Incas might show favor to the poor ruined Omaguas, in the day of their coming glory. And as she grew, she had become, it seemed, somewhat of a prophetess among them, as well as an object of fetish-worship; for she was more prudent in council, valiant in war, and cunning in the chase, than all the elders of the tribe; and those strange and sweet songs of hers, which had so surprised the white men, were full of mysterious wisdom about the birds, and the animals, and the flowers, and the rivers, which the Sun and the Good Spirit taught her from above. So she had lived among them, unmarried still, not only because she despised the addresses of all Indian youths, but because the conjuror had declared it to be profane in them to mingle with the race of the Sun, and had assigned her a cabin near his own, where she was served in state, and gave some sort of oracular responses, as they had seen, to the questions which he put to her.

Such was the cacique's tale; on which Cary remarked, probably not unjustly, that he "dared to say the conjuror made a very good thing of it:" but Amyas was silent, full of dreams, if not about Manoa, still about the remnant of the Inca race. What if they were still to be found about the southern sources of the Amazon? He must have been very near them already, in that case. It was vexatious; but at least he might be sure that they had formed no great kingdom in that direction, or he should have heard of it long ago. Perhaps they had moved lately from thence eastward, to escape some fresh encroachment of the Spaniards; and this girl had been left behind in their flight. And then he recollected, with a sigh, how hopeless was any further search with his diminished band. At least, he might learn something of the truth from the maiden herself. It might be useful to him in some future attempt; for he had not yet given up Manoa. If he but got safe home, there was many a gallant gentleman (and Raleigh came at once into his mind) who would join him in a fresh search for the Golden City of Guiana; not by the upper waters, but by the mouth of the Orinoco.

So they paddled back, while the simple cacique entreated them to tell the Sun, in their daily prayers, how well the wild people had treated his descendant; and besought them not to take her away with them, lest the Sun should forget the poor Omaguas, and ripen their manioc and their fruit no more.

Amyas had no wish to stay where he was longer than was absolutely necessary to bring up the sick men from the Orinoco; but this, he well knew, would be a journey probably of some months, and attended with much danger.

Cary volunteered at once, however, to undertake the adventure, if half-a-dozen men would join him, and the Indians would send a few young men to help in working the canoe: but this latter item was not an easy one to obtain; for the tribe with whom they now were, stood in some fear of the fierce and brutal Guahibas, through whose country they must pass; and every Indian tribe, as Amyas knew well enough, looks on each tribe of different language to itself as natural enemies, hateful, and made only to be destroyed wherever met. This strange fact, too, Amyas and his party attributed to delusion of the devil, the divider and accuser; and I am of opinion that they were perfectly right: only let Amyas take care that while he is discovering the devil in the Indians, he does not give place to him in himself, and that in more ways than one. But of that more hereafter.

Whether, however, it was pride or shyness which kept the maiden aloof, she conquered it after a while; perhaps through mere woman's curiosity; and perhaps, too, from mere longing for amusement in a place so unspeakably stupid as the forest. She gave the English to understand, however, that though they all might be very important personages, none of them was to be her companion but Amyas. And ere a month was past, she was often hunting with him far and wide in the neighboring forest, with a train of chosen nymphs, whom she had persuaded to follow her example and spurn the dusky suitors around. This fashion, not uncommon, perhaps, among the Indian tribes, where women are continually escaping to the forest from the tyranny of the men, and often, perhaps, forming temporary communities, was to the English a plain proof that they were near the land of the famous Amazons, of whom they had heard so often from the Indians; while Amyas had no doubt that, as a descendant of the Incas, the maiden preserved the tradition of the Virgins of the Sun, and of the austere monastic rule of the Peruvian superstition. Had not that valiant German, George of Spires, and Jeronimo Ortal too, fifty years before, found convents of the Sun upon these very upper waters?

So a harmless friendship sprang up between Amyas and the girl, which soon turned to good account. For she no sooner heard that he needed a crew of Indians, than she consulted the Piache, assembled the tribe, and having retired to her hut, commenced a song, which (unless the Piache lied) was a command to furnish young men for Cary's expedition, under penalty of the sovereign displeasure of an evil spirit with an unpronounceable name—an argument which succeeded on the spot, and the canoe departed on its perilous errand.

John Brimblecombe had great doubts whether a venture thus started by direct help and patronage of the fiend would succeed; and Amyas himself, disliking the humbug, told Ayacanora that it would be better to have told the tribe that it was a good deed, and pleasing to the Good Spirit.

"Ah!" said she, naively enough, "they know better than that. The Good Spirit is big and lazy; and he smiles, and takes no trouble: but the little bad spirit, he is so busy—here, and there, and everywhere," and she waved her pretty hands up and down; "he is the useful one to have for a friend!" Which sentiment the Piache much approved, as became his occupation; and once told Brimblecombe pretty sharply, that he was a meddlesome fellow for telling the Indians that the

Good Spirit cared for them; "for," quoth he, "if they begin to ask the Good Spirit for what they want, who will bring me cassava and coca for keeping the bad spirit quiet?" This argument, however forcible the devil's priests in all ages have felt it to be, did not stop Jack's preaching (and very good and righteous preaching it was, moreover), and much less the morning and evening service in the island camp. This last, the Indians, attracted by the singing, attended in such numbers, that the Piache found his occupation gone, and vowed to put an end to Jack's Gospel with a poisoned arrow.

Which plan he (blinded by his master, Satan, so Jack phrased it) took into his head to impart to Ayacanora, as the partner of his tithes and offerings; and was exceedingly astonished to receive in answer a box on the ear, and a storm of abuse. After which, Ayacanora went to Amyas, and telling him all, proposed that the Piache should be thrown to the alligators, and Jack installed in his place; declaring that whatsoever the bearded men said must be true, and whosoever plotted against them should die the death.

Jack, however, magnanimously forgave his foe, and preached on, of course with fresh zeal; but not, alas! with much success. For the conjuror, though his main treasure was gone over to the camp of the enemy, had a reserve in a certain holy trumpet, which was hidden mysteriously in a cave on the neighboring hills, not to be looked on by woman under pain of death; and it was well known, and had been known for generations, that unless that trumpet, after fastings, flagellations, and other solemn rites, was blown by night throughout the woods, the palm-trees would bear no fruit; yea, so great was the fame of that trumpet, that neighboring tribes sent at the proper season to hire it and the blower thereof, by payment of much precious trumpery, that so they might be sharers in its fertilizing powers.

So the Piache announced one day in public, that in consequence of the impiety of the Omaguas, he should retire to a neighboring tribe, of more religious turn of mind; and taking with him the precious instrument, leave their palms to blight, and themselves to the evil spirit.

Dire was the wailing, and dire the wrath throughout the village. Jack's words were allowed to be good words; but what was the Gospel in comparison of the trumpet? The rascal saw his advantage, and began a fierce harangue against the heretic strangers. As he maddened, his hearers maddened; the savage nature, capricious as a child's, flashed out in wild suspicion. Women yelled, men scowled, and ran hastily to their huts for bows and blow-guns. The case was grown critical. There were not more than a dozen men with Amyas at the time, and they had only their swords, while the Indian men might muster nearly a hundred. Amyas forbade his men either to draw or to retreat; but poisoned arrows were weapons before which the boldest might well quail; and more than one cheek grew pale, which had seldom been pale before.

"It is God's quarrel, sirs all," said Jack Brimblecombe; "let Him defend the right."

As he spoke, from Ayacanora's hut arose her magic song, and quivered aloft among the green heights of the forest.

The mob stood spell-bound, still growling fiercely, but not daring to move. Another moment, and she had rushed out, like a very Diana, into the centre of the ring, bow in hand, and arrow on the string.

The fallen "children of wrath" had found their match in her; for her beautiful face was convulsed with fury. Almost foaming in her passion, she burst forth with bitter revilings; she pointed with admiration to the English, and then with fiercest contempt to the Indians; and at last, with fierce gestures, seemed to cast off the very dust of her feet against them, and springing to Amyas's side, placed herself in the forefront of the English battle.

The whole scene was so sudden, that Amyas had hardly discovered whether she came as friend or foe, before her bow was raised. He had just time to strike up her hand, when the arrow flew past the ear of the offending Piache, and stuck quivering in a tree.

"Let me kill the wretch!" said she, stamping with rage; but Amyas held her arm firmly.

"Fools!" cried she to the tribe, while tears of anger rolled down her cheeks. "Choose between me and your trumpet! I am a daughter of the Sun; I am white; I am a companion for Englishmen! But you! your mothers were Guahibas, and ate mud; and your fathers—they were howling apes! Let them sing to you! I shall go to the white men, and never sing you to sleep any more; and when the little evil spirit misses my voice, he will come and tumble you out of your hammocks, and make you dream of ghosts every night, till you grow as thin as blow-guns, and as stupid as aye-ayes!"*

This terrible counter-threat, in spite of the slight bathos involved, had its effect; for it appealed to that dread of the sleep world which is common to all savages: but the conjuror was ready to outbid the prophetess, and had begun a fresh oration, when Amyas turned the tide of war. Bursting into a huge laugh at the whole matter, he took the conjuror by his shoulders, sent him with one crafty kick half-a-dozen yards off upon his nose; and then, walking out of the ranks, shook hands round with all his Indian acquaintances.

Whereon, like grown-up babies, they all burst out laughing too, shook hands with all the English, and then with each other; being, after all, as glad as any bishops to prorogue the convocation, and let unpleasant questions stand over till the next session. The Piache relented, like a prudent man; Ayacanora returned to her hut to sulk; and Amyas to his island, to long for Cary's return, for he felt himself on dangerous ground.

At last Will returned, safe and sound, and as merry as ever, not having lost a man (though he had had a smart brush with the Guahibas). He brought back three of the wounded men, now pretty nigh cured; the other two, who had lost a leg apiece, had refused to come. They had Indian wives; more than they could eat; and tobacco without end: and if it were not for the gnats (of which Cary said that there were more mosquitoes than there was air), they should be the happiest men alive. Amyas could hardly blame the poor fellows; for the chance of their getting home through the forest with one leg each was very small, and, after all, they were making the best of a bad matter. And a very bad matter it seemed to him, to be left in a heathen land; and a still worse matter, when he overheard some of the men talking about their comrades' lonely fate, as if, after all, they were not so much to be pitied. He said nothing about it then, for he made a rule never to take notice of any facts which he got at by eavesdropping, however unintentional; but he longed that one of them would say as much to him, and he would "give them a piece of his mind." And a piece of his mind he had to give within the week; for while he was on a hunting party, two of his men were missing, and were not heard of for some days; at the end of which time the old cacique come to tell him that he believed they had taken to the forest, each with an Indian girl.

Amyas was very wroth at the news. First, because it had never happened before: he could say with honest pride, as Raleigh did afterwards when he returned from his Guiana voyage, that no Indian woman had ever been the worse for any man of his. He had preached on this point month after month, and practised what he preached; and now his pride was sorely hurt.

Moreover, he dreaded offence to the Indians themselves: but on this score the cacique soon comforted him, telling him that the girls, as far as he could find, had gone off of their own free will; intimating that he thought it somewhat an honor to the tribe that they had found favor in the eyes of the bearded men; and moreover, that late wars had so thinned the ranks of their men, that they were glad enough to find husbands for their maidens, and had been driven of late years to kill many of their female infants. This sad story, common perhaps to every American tribe, and one of the chief causes of their extermination, reassured Amyas somewhat: but he could not stomach either the loss of his men, or their breach of discipline; and look for them he would. Did any one know where they were? If the tribe knew, they did not care to tell: but Ayacanora, the moment she found out his wishes, vanished into the forest, and returned in two days, saying that she had found the fugitives; but she would not show him where they were, unless he promised not to kill them. He, of course, had no mind for so rigorous a method: he both needed the men, and he had no malice against them,—for the one, Ebsworthy, was a plain, honest, happy-go-lucky sailor, and as good a hand as there was in the crew; and the other was that same ne'er-do-weel Will Parracombe, his old schoolfellow, who had been tempted by the gipsy-Jesuit at Appledore, and resisting that bait, had made a very fair seaman.

So forth Amyas went, with Ayacanora as a guide, some five miles upward along the forest slopes, till the girl whispered, "There they are;" and Amyas, pushing himself gently through a thicket of bamboo, beheld a scene which, in spite of his wrath, kept him silent, and perhaps softened, for a minute.

On the farther side of a little lawn, the stream leapt through a chasm beneath overarching vines, sprinkling eternal freshness upon all around, and then sank foaming into a clear rock-basin, a bath for Dian's self. On its farther side, the crag rose some twenty feet in height, bank upon bank of feathered ferns and cushioned moss, over the rich green beds of which drooped a thousand orchids, scarlet, white, and orange, and made the still pool gorgeous with the reflection of their gorgeousness. At its more quiet outfall, it was half-hidden in huge fantastic leaves and tall flowering stems; but near the waterfall the grassy bank sloped down toward the stream, and there, on palm-leaves strewed upon the turf, beneath the shadow of the crags, lay the two men whom Amyas sought, and whom, now he had found them, he had hardly heart to wake from their delicious dream.

For what a nest it was which they had found! the air was heavy with the scent of flowers, and quivering with the murmur of the stream, the humming of the colibris and insects, the cheerful song of birds, the gentle cooing of a hundred doves; while now and then, from far away, the musical wail of the sloth, or the deep toll of the bell-bird, came softly to the ear. What was not there which eye or ear could need? And what which palate could need either? For on the rock above, some strange tree, leaning forward, dropped every now and then a luscious apple upon the grass below, and huge wild plantains bent beneath their load of fruit.

There, on the stream bank, lay the two renegades from civilized life. They had cast away their clothes, and painted themselves, like the Indians, with arnotto and indigo. One lay lazily picking up the fruit which fell close to his side; the other sat, his back against a cushion of soft moss, his hands folded languidly upon his lap, giving himself up to the soft influence of the narcotic coca-juice, with half-shut dreamy eyes fixed on the everlasting sparkle of the waterfall—

Somewhat apart crouched their two dusky brides, crowned with fragrant flowers, but working busily, like true women, for the lords whom they delighted to honor. One sat plaiting palm fibres into a basket; the other was boring the stem of a huge milk-tree, which rose like some mighty column on the right hand of the lawn, its broad canopy of leaves unseen through the dense underwood of laurel and bamboo, and betokened only by the rustle far aloft, and by the mellow shade in which it bathed the whole delicious scene.

Amyas stood silent for awhile, partly from noble shame at seeing two Christian men thus fallen of their own self-will; partly because—and he could not but confess that—a solemn calm brooded above that glorious place, to break through which seemed sacrilege even while he felt it a duty. Such, he thought, was Paradise of old; such our first parents' bridal bower! Ah! if man had not fallen, he too might have dwelt forever in such a home—with whom? He started, and shaking off the spell, advanced sword in hand.

The women saw him, and springing to their feet, caught up their long pocunas, and leapt like deer each in front of her beloved. There they stood, the deadly tubes pressed to their lips, eyeing him like tigresses who protect their young, while every slender limb quivered, not with terror, but with rage.

Amyas paused, half in admiration, half in prudence; for one rash step was death. But rushing through the canes, Ayacanora sprang to the front, and shrieked to them in Indian. At the sight of the prophetess the women wavered, and Amyas, putting on as gentle a face as he could, stepped forward, assuring them in his best Indian that he would harm no one.

"Ebsworthy! Parracombe! Are you grown such savages already, that you have forgotten your captain? Stand up, men, and salute!"

Ebsworthy sprang to his feet, obeyed mechanically, and then slipped behind his bride again, as if in shame. The dreamer turned his head languidly, raised his hand to his forehead, and then returned to his contemplation.

Amyas rested the point of his sword on the ground, and his hands upon the hilt, and looked sadly and solemnly upon the pair. Ebsworthy broke the silence, half reproachfully, half trying to bluster away the coming storm.

"Well, noble captain, so you've hunted out us poor fellows; and want to drag us back again in a halter, I suppose?"

"I came to look for Christians, and I find heathens; for men, and I find swine. I shall leave the heathens to their wilderness, and the swine to their trough. Parracombe!"

"He's too happy to answer you, sir. And why not? What do you want of us? Our two years vow is out, and we are free men now."

"Free to become like the beasts that perish? You are the queen's servants still, and in her name I charge you—"

"Free to be happy," interrupted the man. "With the best of wives, the best of food, a warmer bed than a duke's, and a finer garden than an emperor's. As for clothes, why the plague should a man wear them where he don't need them? As for gold, what's the use of it where Heaven sends everything ready-made to your hands? Hearken, Captain Leigh. You've been a good captain to me, and I'll repay you with a bit of sound advice. Give up your gold-hunting, and toiling and moiling after honor and glory, and copy us. Take that fair maid behind you there to wife; pitch here with us; and see if you are not happier in one day than ever you were in all your life before."

"You are drunk, sirrah! William Parracombe! Will you speak to me, or shall I heave you into the stream to sober you?"

"Who calls William Parracombe?" answered a sleepy voice.

"I, fool!—your captain."

"I am not William Parracombe. He is dead long ago of hunger, and labor, and heavy sorrow, and will never see Bideford town any more. He is turned into an Indian now; and he is to sleep, sleep, sleep for a hundred years, till he gets his strength again, poor fellow—"

"Awake, then, thou that sleepest, and arise from the dead, and Christ shall give thee light! A christened Englishman, and living thus the life of a beast?"

"Christ shall give thee light?" answered the same unnatural abstracted voice. "Yes; so the parsons say. And they say too, that He is Lord of heaven and earth. I should have thought His light was as near us here as anywhere, and nearer too, by the look of the place. Look round!" said he, waving a lazy hand, "and see the works of God, and the place of Paradise, whither poor weary souls go home and rest, after their masters in the wicked world have used them up, with labor and sorrow, and made them wade knee-deep in blood—I'm tired of blood, and tired of gold. I'll march no more; I'll fight no more; I'll hunger no more after vanity and vexation of spirit. What shall I get by it? Maybe I shall leave my bones in the wilderness. I can but do that here. Maybe I shall get home with a few pezos, to die an old cripple in some stinking hovel, that a monkey would scorn to lodge in here. You may go on; it'll pay you. You may be a rich man, and a knight, and live in a fine house, and drink good wine, and go to Court, and torment your soul with trying to get more, when you've got too much already; plotting and planning to scramble upon your neighbor's shoulders, as they all did—Sir Richard, and Mr. Raleigh, and Chichester, and poor dear old Sir Warham, and all of them that I used to watch when I lived before. They were no happier than I was then; I'll warrant they are no happier now. Go your ways, captain; climb to glory upon some other backs than ours, and leave us here in peace, alone with God and God's woods, and the good wives that God has given us, to play a little like school children. It's long since I've had play-hours; and now I'll be a little child once more, with the flowers, and the singing birds, and the silver fishes in the stream, that are at peace, and think no harm, and want neither clothes, nor money, nor knighthood, nor peerage, but just take what comes; and their heavenly Father feedeth them, and Solomon in all his glory was not arrayed like one of these—and will He not much more feed us, that are of more value than many sparrows?"

"And will you live here, shut out from all Christian ordinances?"

"Christian ordinances? Adam and Eve had no parsons in Paradise. The Lord was their priest, and the Lord was their shepherd, and He'll be ours too. But go your ways, sir, and send up Sir John Brimblecombe, and let him marry us here Church fashion (though we have sworn troth to each other before God already), and let him give us the Holy Sacrament once and for all, and then read the funeral service over us, and go his ways, and count us for dead, sir—for dead we are to the wicked worthless world we came out of three years ago. And when the Lord chooses to call us, the little birds will cover us with leaves, as they did the babies in the wood, and fresher flowers will grow out of our graves, sir, than out of yours in that bare Northam churchyard there beyond the weary, weary, weary sea."

His voice died away to a murmur, and his head sank on his breast.

Amyas stood spell-bound. The effect of the narcotic was all but miraculous in his eyes. The sustained eloquence, the novel richness of diction in one seemingly drowned in sensual sloth, were, in his eyes, the possession of some evil spirit. And yet he could not answer the Evil One. His English heart, full of the divine instinct of duty and public spirit, told him that it must be a lie: but how to prove it a lie? And he stood for full ten minutes searching for an answer, which seemed to fly farther and farther off the more he sought for it.

His eye glanced upon Ayacanora. The two girls were whispering to her smilingly. He saw one of them glance a look toward him, and then say something, which raised a beautiful blush in the maiden's face. With a playful blow at the speaker, she turned away. Amyas knew instinctively that they were giving her the same advice as Ebsworthy had given to him. Oh, how beautiful she was! Might not the renegades have some reason on their side after all.

He shuddered at the thought: but he could not shake it off. It glided in like some gaudy snake, and wreathed its coils round all his heart and brain. He drew back to the other side of the lawn, and thought and thought—

Should he ever get home? If he did, might he not get home a beggar? Beggar or rich, he would still have to face his mother, to go through that meeting, to tell that tale, perhaps, to hear those reproaches, the forecast of which had weighed on him like a dark thunder-cloud for two weary years; to wipe out which by some desperate deed of glory he had wandered the wilderness, and wandered in vain.

Could he not settle here? He need not be a savage, he and his might Christianize, civilize, teach equal law, mercy in war, chivalry to women; found a community which might be hereafter as strong a barrier against the encroachments of the Spaniard, as Manoa itself would have been. Who knew the wealth of the surrounding forests? Even if there were no gold, there were boundless vegetable treasures. What might he not export down the rivers? This might be the nucleus of a great commercial settlement—

And yet, was even that worth while? To settle here only to torment his soul with fresh schemes, fresh ambitions; not to rest, but only to change one labor for another? Was not your dreamer right? Did they not all need rest? What if they each sat down among the flowers, beside an Indian bride? They might live like Christians, while they lived like the birds of heaven.—

What a dead silence! He looked up and round; the birds had ceased to chirp; the parroquets were hiding behind the leaves; the monkeys were clustered motionless upon the highest twigs; only out of the far depths of the forest, the campanero gave its solemn toll, once, twice, thrice, like a great death-knell rolling down from far cathedral towers. Was it an omen? He looked up hastily at Ayacanora. She was watching him earnestly. Heavens! was she waiting for his decision? Both dropped their eyes. The decision was not to come from them.

A rustle! a roar! a shriek! and Amyas lifted his eyes in time to see a huge dark bar shoot from the crag above the dreamer's head, among the group of girls.

A dull crash, as the group flew asunder; and in the midst, upon the ground, the tawny limbs of one were writhing beneath the fangs of a black jaguar, the rarest and most terrible of the forest kings. Of one? But of which? Was it Ayacanora? And sword in hand, Amyas rushed madly forward; before he reached the spot those tortured limbs were still.

It was not Ayacanora, for with a shriek which rang through the woods, the wretched dreamer, wakened thus at last, sprang up and felt for his sword. Fool! he had left it in his hammock! Screaming the name of his dead bride, he rushed on the jaguar, as it crouched above its prey, and seizing its head with teeth and nails, worried it, in the ferocity of his madness, like a mastiff-dog.

The brute wrenched its head from his grasp, and raised its dreadful paw. Another moment and the husband's corpse would have lain by the wife's.

But high in air gleamed Amyas's blade; down with all the weight of his huge body and strong arm, fell that most trusty steel; the head of the jaguar dropped grinning on its victim's corpse;

"O Lord Jesus," said Amyas to himself, "Thou hast answered the devil for me! And this is the selfish rest for which I would have bartered the rest which comes by working where Thou hast put me!"

They bore away the lithe corpse into the forest, and buried it under soft moss and virgin mould; and so the fair clay was transfigured into fairer flowers, and the poor, gentle, untaught spirit returned to God who gave it.

And then Amyas went sadly and silently back again, and Parracombe walked after him, like one who walks in sleep.

Ebsworthy, sobered by the shock, entreated to come too: but Amyas forbade him gently,—

"No, lad, you are forgiven. God forbid that I should judge you or any man! Sir John shall come up and marry you; and then, if it still be your will to stay, the Lord forgive you, if you be wrong; in the meanwhile, we will leave with you all that we can spare. Stay here and pray to God to make you, and me too, wiser men."

And so Amyas departed. He had come out stern and proud; but he came back again like a little child.

Three days after Parracombe was dead. Once in camp he seemed unable to eat or move, and having received absolution and communion from good Sir John, faded away without disease or pain, "babbling of green fields," and murmuring the name of his lost Indian bride.

Amyas, too, sought ghostly council of Sir John, and told him all which had passed through his mind.

"It was indeed a temptation of Diabolus," said that simple sage; "for he is by his very name the divider who sets man against man, and tempts one to care only for oneself, and forget kin and country, and duty and queen. But you have resisted him, Captain Leigh, like a true-born Englishman, as you always are, and he has fled from you. But that is no reason why we should not flee from him too; and so I think the sooner we are out of this place, and at work again, the better for all our souls."

To which Amyas most devoutly said, "Amen!" If Ayacanora were the daughter of ten thousand Incas, he must get out of her way as soon as possible.

The next day he announced his intention to march once more, and to his delight found the men ready enough to move towards the Spanish settlements. One thing they needed: gunpowder for their muskets. But that they must make as they went along; that is, if they could get the materials. Charcoal they could procure, enough to set the world on fire; but nitre they had not yet seen; perhaps they should find it among the hills: while as for sulphur, any brave man could get that where there were volcanoes. Who had not heard how one of Cortez' Spaniards, in like need, was lowered in a basket down the smoking crater of Popocatepetl, till he had gathered sulphur enough to conquer an empire? And what a Spaniard could do an Englishman could do, or they would know the reason why. And if they found none—why clothyard arrows had done Englishmen's work many a time already, and they could do it again, not to mention those same blow-guns and their arrows of curare poison, which, though they might be useless against Spaniards' armor, were far more valuable than muskets for procuring food, from the simple fact of their silence.

One thing remained; to invite their Indian friends to join them. And that was done in due form the next day.

Ayacanora was consulted, of course, and by the Piache, too, who was glad enough to be rid of the rival preacher, and his unpleasantly good news that men need not worship the devil, because there was a good God above them. The maiden sang most melodious assent; the whole tribe echoed it; and all went smoothly enough till the old cacique observed that before starting a compact should be made between the allies as to their share of the booty.

Nothing could be more reasonable; and Amyas asked him to name his terms.

"You take the gold, and we will take the prisoners."

"And what will you do with them?" asked Amyas, who recollected poor John Oxenham's hapless compact made in like case.

"Eat them," quoth the cacique, innocently enough.

Amyas whistled.

"Humph!" said Cary. "The old proverb comes true—'the more the merrier: but the fewer the better fare.' I think we will do without our red friends for this time."

Ayacanora, who had been preaching war like a very Boadicea, was much vexed.

"Do you too want to dine off roast Spaniards?" asked Amyas.

She shook her head, and denied the imputation with much disgust.

Amyas was relieved; he had shrunk from joining the thought of so fair a creature, however degraded, with the horrors of cannibalism.

But the cacique was a man of business, and held out stanchly.

"Is it fair?" he asked. "The white man loves gold, and he gets it. The poor Indian, what use is gold to him? He only wants something to eat, and he must eat his enemies. What else will pay him for going so far through the forests hungry and thirsty? You will get all, and the Omaguas will get nothing."

The argument was unanswerable; and the next day they started without the Indians, while John Brimblecombe heaved many an honest sigh at leaving them to darkness, the devil, and the holy trumpet.

And Ayacanora?

When their departure was determined, she shut herself up in her hut, and appeared no more. Great was the weeping, howling, and leave-taking on the part of the simple Indians, and loud the entreaties to come again, bring them a message from Amalivaca's daughter beyond the seas, and help them to recover their lost land of Papamene; but Ayacanora took no part in them; and Amyas left her, wondering at her absence, but joyful and light-hearted at having escaped the rocks of the Sirens, and being at work once more.

CHAPTER XXV: HOW THEY TOOK THE GOLD-TRAIN

A fortnight or more has passed in severe toil, but not more severe than they have endured many a time before. Bidding farewell once and forever to the green ocean of the eastern plains, they have crossed the Cordillera; they have taken a longing glance at the city of Santa Fe, lying in the midst of rich gardens on its lofty mountain plateau, and have seen, as was to be expected, that it was far too large a place for any attempt of theirs. But they have not altogether thrown away their time. Their Indian lad has discovered that a gold-train is going down from Santa Fe toward the Magdalena; and they are waiting for it beside the miserable rut which serves for a road, encamped in a forest of oaks which would make them almost fancy themselves back again in Europe, were it not for the tree-ferns which form the undergrowth; and were it not, too, for the deep gorges opening at their very feet; in which, while their brows are swept by the cool breezes of a temperate zone, they can see far below, dim through their everlasting vapor-bath of rank hot steam, the mighty forms and gorgeous colors of the tropic forest.

They have pitched their camp among the tree-ferns, above a spot where the path winds along a steep hill-side, with a sheer cliff below of many a hundred feet. There was a road there once, perhaps, when Cundinamarca was a civilized and cultivated kingdom; but all which Spanish misrule has left of it are a few steps slipping from their places at the bottom of a narrow ditch of mud. It has gone the way of the aqueducts, and bridges, and post-houses, the gardens and the llama-flocks of that strange empire. In the mad search for gold, every art of civilization has fallen to decay, save architecture alone; and that survives only in the splendid cathedrals which have risen upon the ruins of the temples of the Sun, in honor of a milder Pantheon; if, indeed, that can be called a milder one which demands (as we have seen already) human sacrifices, unknown to the gentle nature-worship of the Incas.

And now, the rapid tropic vegetation has reclaimed its old domains, and Amyas and his crew are as utterly alone, within a few miles of an important Spanish settlement, as they would be in the solitudes of the Orinoco or the Amazon.

In the meanwhile, all their attempts to find sulphur and nitre have been unavailing; and they have been forced to depend after all (much to Yeo's disgust) upon their swords and arrows. Be it so: Drake took Nombre de Dios and the gold-train there with no better weapons; and they may do as much.

So, having blocked up the road above by felling a large tree across it, they sit there among the flowers chewing coca, in default of food and drink, and meditating among themselves the cause of a mysterious roar, which has been heard nightly in their wake ever since they left the banks of the Meta. Jaguar it is not, nor monkey: it is unlike any sound they know; and why should it follow them? However, they are in the land of wonders; and, moreover, the gold train is far more important than any noise.

At last, up from beneath there was a sharp crack and a loud cry. The crack was neither the snapping of a branch, nor the tapping of a woodpecker; the cry was neither the scream of the parrot, nor the howl of the monkey.

"That was a whip's crack," said Yeo, "and a woman's wail. They are close here, lads!"

"A woman's? Do they drive women in their gangs?" asked Amyas.

"Why not, the brutes? There they are, sir. Did you see their basnets glitter?"

"Men!" said Amyas, in a low voice, "I trust you all not to shoot till I do. Then give them one arrow, out swords, and at them! Pass the word along."

Up they came, slowly, and all hearts beat loud at their coming.

First, about twenty soldiers, only one-half of whom were on foot; the other half being borne, incredible as it may seem, each in a chair on the back of a single Indian, while those who marched had consigned their heaviest armor and their arquebuses into the hands of attendant slaves, who were each pricked on at will by the pike of the soldier behind them.

"The men are mad to let their ordnance out of their hands."

"Oh, sir, an Indian will pray to an arquebus not to shoot him; he sure their artillery is safe enough," said Yeo.

"Look at the proud villains," whispered another, "to make dumb beasts of human creatures like that!"

"Ten shot," counted the business-like Amyas, "and ten pikes; Will can tackle them up above."

Last of this troop came some inferior officer, also in his chair, who, as he went slowly up the hill, with his face turned toward the gang which followed, drew every other second the cigar from his lips, to inspirit them with those pious ejaculations to the various objects of his worship, divine, human, anatomic, wooden and textile, which earned for the pious Spaniards of the sixteenth century the uncharitable imputation of being at once the most fetish-ridden idolaters and the most abominable swearers of all Europeans.

"The blasphemous dog!" said Yeo, fumbling at his bow-string, as if he longed to send an arrow through him. But Amyas had hardly laid his finger on the impatient veteran's arm, when another procession followed, which made them forget all else.

A sad and hideous sight it was: yet one too common even then in those remoter districts, where the humane edicts were disregarded which the prayers of Dominican friars (to their everlasting honor be it spoken) had wrung from the Spanish sovereigns, and which the legislation of that most wise, virtuous, and heroic Inquisitor (paradoxical as the words may seem), Pedro de la Gasca, had carried into effect in Peru,—futile and tardy alleviations of cruelties and miseries unexampled in the history of Christendom, or perhaps on earth, save in the conquests of Sennacherib and Zingis Khan. But on the frontiers, where negroes were imported to endure the toil which was found fatal to the Indian, and all Indian tribes convicted (or suspected) of cannibalism were hunted down for the salvation of their souls and the enslavement of their bodies, such scenes as these were still too common; and, indeed, if we are to judge from Humboldt's impartial account, were not very much amended even at the close of the last century, in those much-boasted Jesuit missions in which (as many of them as existed anywhere but on paper) military tyranny was superadded to monastic, and the Gospel preached with fire and sword, almost as shamelessly as by the first Conquistadores.

A line of Indians, Negroes, and Zambos, naked, emaciated, scarred with whips and fetters, and chained together by their left wrists, toiled upwards, panting and perspiring under the burden of a basket held up by a strap which passed across their foreheads. Yeo's sneer was but too just; there were not only old men and youths among them, but women; slender young girls, mothers with children, running at their knee; and, at the sight, a low murmur of indignation rose from the ambushed Englishmen, worthy of the free and righteous hearts of those days, when Raleigh could appeal to man and God, on the ground of a common humanity, in behalf of the outraged heathens of the New World; when Englishmen still knew that man was man, and that the instinct of freedom was the righteous voice of God; ere the hapless seventeenth century had brutalized them also, by bestowing on them, amid a hundred other bad legacies, the fatal gift of negro-slaves.

But the first forty, so Amyas counted, bore on their backs a burden which made all, perhaps, but him and Yeo, forget even the wretches who bore it. Each basket contained a square package of carefully corded hide; the look whereof friend Amyas knew full well.

"What's in they, captain?"

"Gold!" And at that magic word all eyes were strained greedily forward, and such a rustle followed, that Amyas, in the very face of detection, had to whisper—

"Be men, be men, or you will spoil all yet!"

The last twenty, or so, of the Indians bore larger baskets, but more lightly freighted, seemingly with manioc, and maize-bread, and other food for the party; and after them came, with their bearers and attendants, just twenty soldiers more, followed by the officer in charge, who smiled away in his chair, and twirled two huge mustachios, thinking of nothing less than of the English arrows which were itching to be away and through his ribs. The ambush was complete; the only question how and when to begin?

Amyas had a shrinking, which all will understand, from drawing bow in cool blood on men so utterly unsuspicious and defenceless, even though in the very act of devilish cruelty—for devilish cruelty it was, as three or four drivers armed with whips lingered up and down the slowly staggering file of Indians, and avenged every moment's lagging, even every stumble, by a blow of the cruel manati-hide, which cracked like a pistol-shot against the naked limbs of the silent and uncomplaining victim.

Suddenly the casus belli, as usually happens, arose of its own accord.

The last but one of the chained line was an old gray-headed man, followed by a slender graceful girl of some eighteen years old, and Amyas's heart yearned over them as they came up. Just as they passed, the foremost of the file had rounded the corner above; there was a bustle, and a voice shouted, "Halt, senors! there is a tree across the path!"

"A tree across the path?" bellowed the officer, with a variety of passionate addresses to the Mother of Heaven, the fiends of hell, Saint Jago of Compostella, and various other personages; while the line of trembling Indians, told to halt above, and driven on by blows below, surged up and down upon the ruinous steps of the Indian road, until the poor old man fell grovelling on his face.

The officer leaped down, and hurried upward to see what had happened. Of course, he came across the old man.

"Sin peccado concebida! Grandfather of Beelzebub, is this a place to lie worshipping your fiends?" and he pricked the prostrate wretch with the point of his sword.

The old man tried to rise: but the weight on his head was too much for him; he fell again, and lay motionless.

The driver applied the manati-hide across his loins, once, twice, with fearful force; but even that specific was useless.

"Gastado, Senor Capitan," said he, with a shrug. "Used up. He has been failing these three months!"

"What does the intendant mean by sending me out with worn-out cattle like these? Forward there!" shouted he. "Clear away the tree, senors, and I'll soon clear the chain. Hold it up, Pedrillo!"

The driver held up the chain, which was fastened to the old man's wrist. The officer stepped back, and flourished round his head a Toledo blade, whose beauty made Amyas break the Tenth Commandment on the spot.

The man was a tall, handsome, broad-shouldered, high-bred man; and Amyas thought that he was going to display the strength of his arm, and the temper of his blade, in severing the chain at one stroke.

Even he was not prepared for the recondite fancies of a Spanish adventurer, worthy son or nephew of those first conquerors, who used to try the keenness of their swords upon the living bodies of Indians, and regale themselves at meals with the odor of roasting caciques.

The blade gleamed in the air, once, twice, and fell: not on the chain, but on the wrist which it fettered. There was a shriek—a crimson flash—and the chain and its prisoner were parted indeed.

One moment more, and Amyas's arrow would have been through the throat of the murderer, who paused, regarding his workmanship with a satisfied smile; but vengeance was not to come from him.

Quick and fierce as a tiger-cat, the girl sprang on the ruffian, and with the intense strength of passion, clasped him in her arms, and leaped with him from the narrow ledge into the abyss below.

There was a rush, a shout; all faces were bent over the precipice. The girl hung by her chained wrist: the officer was gone. There was a moment's awful silence; and then Amyas heard his body crashing through the tree-tops far below.

"Haul her up! Hew her in pieces! Burn the witch!" and the driver, seizing the chain, pulled at it with all his might, while all springing from their chairs, stooped over the brink.

Now was the time for Amyas! Heaven had delivered them into his hands. Swift and sure, at ten yards off, his arrow rushed through the body of the driver, and then, with a roar as of the leaping lion, he sprang like an avenging angel into the midst of the astonished ruffians.

His first thought was for the girl. In a moment, by sheer strength, he had jerked her safely up into the road; while the Spaniards recoiled right and left, fancying him for the moment some mountain giant or supernatural foe. His hurrah undeceived them in an instant, and a cry of "English! Lutheran dogs!" arose, but arose too late. The men of Devon had followed their captain's lead: a storm of arrows left five Spaniards dead, and a dozen more wounded, and down leapt Salvation Yeo, his white hair streaming behind him, with twenty good swords more, and the work of death began.

The Spaniards fought like lions; but they had no time to fix their arquebuses on the crutches; no room, in that narrow path, to use their pikes. The English had the wall of them; and to have the wall there, was to have the foe's life at their mercy. Five desperate minutes, and not a living Spaniard stood upon those steps; and certainly no living one lay in the green abyss below. Two only, who were behind the rest, happening to be in full armor, escaped without mortal wound, and fled down the hill again.

"After them! Michael Evans and Simon Heard; and catch them, if they run a league."

The two long and lean Clovelly men, active as deer from forest training, ran two feet for the Spaniard's one; and in ten minutes returned, having done their work; while Amyas and his men hurried past the Indians, to help Cary and the party forward, where shouts and musket shots announced a sharp affray.

Their arrival settled the matter. All the Spaniards fell but three or four, who scrambled down the crannies of the cliff.

"Let not one of them escape! Slay them as Israel slew Amalek!" cried Yeo, as he bent over; and ere the wretches could reach a place of shelter, an arrow was quivering in each body, as it rolled lifeless down the rocks.

"Now then! Loose the Indians!"

They found armorers tools on one of the dead bodies, and it was done.

"We are your friends," said Amyas. "All we ask is, that you shall help us to carry this gold down to the Magdalena, and then you are free."

Some few of the younger grovelled at his knees, and kissed his feet, hailing him as the child of the Sun: but the most part kept a stolid indifference, and when freed from their fetters, sat quietly down where they stood, staring into vacancy. The iron had entered too deeply into their soul. They seemed past hope, enjoyment, even understanding.

But the young girl, who was last of all in the line, as soon as she was loosed, sprang to her father's body, speaking no word, lifted it in her thin arms, laid it across her knees, kissed the fallen lips, stroked the furrowed cheeks, murmured inarticulate sounds like the cooing of a woodland dove, of which none knew the meaning but she, and he who heard not, for his soul had long since fled. Suddenly the truth flashed on her; silent as ever, she drew one long heaving breath, and rose erect, the body in her arms.

Another moment, and she had leaped into the abyss.

They watched her dark and slender limbs, twined closely round the old man's corpse, turn over, and over, and over, till a crash among the leaves, and a scream among the birds, told that she had reached the trees; and the green roof hid her from their view.

"Brave lass!" shouted a sailor.

"The Lord forgive her!" said Yeo. "But, your worship, we must have these rascals' ordnance."

"And their clothes too, Yeo, if we wish to get down the Magdalena unchallenged. Now listen, my masters all! We have won, by God's good grace, gold enough to serve us the rest of our lives, and that without losing a single man; and may yet win more, if we be wise, and He thinks good. But oh, my friends, remember Mr. Oxenham and his crew; and do not make God's gift our ruin, by faithlessness, or greediness, or any mutinous haste."

"You shall find none in us!" cried several men. "We know your worship. We can trust our general."

"Thank God!" said Amyas. "Now then, it will be no shame or sin to make the Indians carry it, saving the women, whom God forbid we should burden. But we must pass through the very heart of the Spanish settlements, and by the town of Saint Martha itself. So the clothes and weapons of these Spaniards we must have, let it cost us what labor it may. How many lie in the road?"

"Thirteen here, and about ten up above," said Cary.

"Then there are near twenty missing. Who will volunteer to go down over cliff, and bring up the spoil of them?"

"I, and I, and I;" and a dozen stepped out, as they did always when Amyas wanted anything done; for the simple reason, that they knew that he meant to help at the doing of it himself.

"Very well, then, follow me. Sir John, take the Indian lad for your interpreter, and try and comfort the souls of these poor heathens. Tell them that they shall all be free."

"Why, who is that comes up the road?"

All eyes were turned in the direction of which he spoke. And, wonder of wonders! up came none other than Ayacanora herself, blow-gun in hand, bow on back, and bedecked in all her feather garments, which last were rather the worse for a fortnight's woodland travel.

All stood mute with astonishment, as, seeing Amyas, she uttered a cry of joy, quickened her pace into a run, and at last fell panting and exhausted at his feet.

"I have found you!" she said; "you ran away from me, but you could not escape me!" And she fawned round Amyas, like a dog who has found his master, and then sat down on the bank, and burst into wild sobs.

"God help us!" said Amyas, clutching his hair, as he looked down upon the beautiful weeper. "What am I to do with her, over and above all these poor heathens?"

But there was no time to be lost, and over the cliff he scrambled; while the girl, seeing that the main body of the English remained, sat down on a point of rock to watch him.

After half-an-hour's hard work, the weapons, clothes, and armor of the fallen Spaniards were hauled up the cliff, and distributed in bundles among the men; the rest of the corpses were thrown over the precipice, and they started again upon their road toward the Magdalena, while Yeo snorted like a war-horse who smells the battle, at the delight of once more handling powder and ball.

"We can face the world now, sir! Why not go back and try Santa Fe, after all?"

But Amyas thought that enough was as good as a feast, and they held on downwards, while the slaves followed, without a sign of gratitude, but meekly obedient to their new masters, and testifying now and then by a sign or a grunt, their surprise at not being beaten, or made to carry their captors. Some, however, caught sight of the little calabashes of coca which the English carried. That woke them from their torpor, and they began coaxing abjectly (and not in vain) for a taste of that miraculous herb, which would not only make food unnecessary, and enable their panting lungs to endure that keen mountain air, but would rid them, for awhile at least, of the fallen Indian's most unpitying foe, the malady of thought.

As the cavalcade turned the corner of the mountain, they paused for one last look at the scene of that fearful triumph. Lines of vultures were already streaming out of infinite space, as if created suddenly for the occasion. A few hours and there would be no trace of that fierce fray, but a few white bones amid untrodden beds of flowers.

And now Amyas had time to ask Ayacanora the meaning of this her strange appearance. He wished her anywhere but where she was: but now that she was here, what heart could be so hard as not to take pity on the poor wild thing? And Amyas as he spoke to her had, perhaps, a tenderness in his tone, from very fear of hurting her, which he had never used before. Passionately she told him how she had followed on their track day and night, and had every evening made sounds, as loud as she dared, in hopes of their hearing her, and either waiting for her, or coming back to see what caused the noise.

Amyas now recollected the strange roaring which had followed them.

"Noises? What did you make them with?"

Ayacanora lifted her finger with an air of most self-satisfied mystery, and then drew cautiously from under her feather cloak an object at which Amyas had hard work to keep his countenance.

"Look!" whispered she, as if half afraid that the thing itself should hear her. "I have it—the holy trumpet!"

There it was verily, that mysterious bone of contention; a handsome earthen tube some two feet long, neatly glazed, and painted with quaint grecques and figures of animals; a relic evidently of some civilization now extinct.

Brimblecombe rubbed his little fat hands. "Brave maid! you have cheated Satan this time," quoth he; while Yeo advised that the "idolatrous relic" should be forthwith "hove over cliff."

"Let be," said Amyas. "What is the meaning of this, Ayacanora? And why have you followed us?"

She told a long story, from which Amyas picked up, as far as he could understand her, that that trumpet had been for years the torment of her life; the one thing in the tribe superior to her; the one thing which she was not allowed to see, because, forsooth, she was a woman. So she determined to show them that a woman was as good as a man; and hence her hatred of marriage, and her Amazonian exploits. But still the Piache would not show her that trumpet, or tell her where it was; and as for going to seek it, even she feared the superstitious wrath of the tribe at such a profanation. But the day after the English went, the Piache chose to express his joy at their departure; whereon, as was to be expected, a fresh explosion between master and pupil, which ended, she confessed, in her burning the old rogue's hut over his head, from which he escaped with loss of all his conjuring-tackle, and fled raging into the woods, vowing that he would carry off the trumpet to the neighboring tribe. Whereon, by a sudden impulse, the young lady took plenty of coca, her weapons, and her feathers, started on his trail, and ran him to earth just as he was unveiling the precious mystery. At which sight (she confessed) she was horribly afraid, and half inclined to run; but, gathering courage from the thought that the white men used to laugh at the whole matter, she rushed upon the hapless conjuror, and bore off her prize in triumph; and there it was!

"I hope you have not killed him?" said Amyas.

"I did beat him a little; but I thought you would not let me kill him."

Amyas was half amused with her confession of his authority over her; but she went on—

"And then I dare not go back to the Indians; so I was forced to come after you."

"And is that, then, your only reason for coming after us?" asked stupid Amyas.

He had touched some secret chord—though what it was he was too busy to inquire. The girl drew herself up proudly, blushing scarlet, and said:

"You never tell lies. Do you think that I would tell lies?"

On which she fell to the rear, and followed them steadfastly, speaking to no one, but evidently determined to follow them to the world's end.

They soon left the highroad; and for several days held on downwards, hewing their path slowly and painfully through the thick underwood. On the evening of the fourth day, they had reached the margin of a river, at a point where it seemed broad and still enough for navigation. For those three days they had not seen a trace of human beings, and the spot seemed lonely enough for them to encamp without fear of discovery, and begin the making of their canoes. They began to spread themselves along the stream, in search of the soft-wooded trees proper for their purpose; but hardly had their search begun, when, in the midst of a dense thicket, they came upon a sight which filled them with astonishment. Beneath a honeycombed cliff, which supported one enormous cotton-tree, was a spot of some thirty yards square sloping down to the stream, planted in rows with magnificent banana-plants, full twelve feet high, and bearing among their huge waxy leaves clusters of ripening fruit; while, under their mellow shade, yams and cassava plants were flourishing luxuriantly, the whole being surrounded by a hedge of orange and scarlet flowers. There it lay, streaked with long shadows from the setting sun, while a cool southern air rustled in the cotton-tree, and flapped to and fro the great banana-leaves; a tiny paradise of art and care. But where was its inhabitant?

Aroused by the noise of their approach, a figure issued from a cave in the rocks, and, after gazing at them for a moment, came down the garden towards them. He was a tall and stately old man, whose snow-white beard and hair covered his chest and shoulders, while his lower limbs were wrapt in Indian-web. Slowly and solemnly he approached, a staff in one hand, a string of beads in the other, the living likeness of some old Hebrew prophet, or anchorite of ancient legend. He bowed courteously to Amyas (who of course returned his salute), and was in act to speak, when his eye fell upon the Indians, who were laying down their burdens in a heap under the trees. His mild countenance assumed instantly an expression of the acutest sorrow and displeasure; and, striking his hands together, he spoke in Spanish:

"Alas! miserable me! Alas! unhappy senors! Do my old eyes deceive me, and is it one of those evil visions of the past which haunt my dreams by night; or has the accursed thirst of gold, the ruin of my race, penetrated even into this my solitude? Oh, senors, senors, know you not that you bear with you your own poison, your own familiar fiend, the root of every evil? And is it not enough for you, senors, to load yourselves with the wedge of Achan, and partake his doom, but you must make these hapless heathens the victims of your greed and cruelty, and forestall for them on earth those torments which may await their unbaptized souls hereafter?"

"We have preserved, and not enslaved these Indians, ancient senor," said Amyas, proudly; "and to-morrow will see them as free as the birds over our heads."

"Free? Then you cannot be countrymen of mine! But pardon an old man, my son, if he has spoken too hastily in the bitterness of his own experience. But who and whence are you? And why are you bringing into this lonely wilderness that gold—for I know too well the shape of those accursed packets, which would God that I had never seen!"

"What we are, reverend sir, matters little, as long as we behave to you as the young should to the old. As for our gold, it will be a curse or a blessing to us, I conceive, just as we use it well or ill; and so is a man's head, or his hand, or any other thing; but that is no reason for cutting off his limbs for fear of doing harm with them; neither is it for throwing away those packages, which, by your leave, we shall deposit in one of these caves. We must be your neighbors, I fear, for a day or two; but I can promise you, that your garden shall be respected, on condition that you do not inform any human soul of our being here."

"God forbid, senor, that I should try to increase the number of my visitors, much less to bring hither strife and blood, of which I have seen too much already. As you have come in peace, in peace depart. Leave me alone with God and my penitence, and may the Lord have mercy on you!"

And he was about to withdraw, when, recollecting himself, he turned suddenly to Amyas again—

"Pardon me, senor, if, after forty years of utter solitude, I shrink at first from the conversation of human beings, and forget, in the habitual shyness of a recluse, the duties of a hospitable gentleman of Spain. My garden, and all which it produces, is at your service. Only let me entreat that these poor Indians shall have their share; for heathens though they be, Christ died for them; and I cannot but cherish in my soul some secret hope that He did not die in vain."

"God forbid!" said Brimblecombe. "They are no worse than we, for aught I see, whatsoever their fathers may have been; and they have fared no worse than we since they have been with us, nor will, I promise you."

The good fellow did not tell that he had been starving himself for the last three days to cram the children with his own rations; and that the sailors, and even Amyas, had been going out of their way every five minutes, to get fruit for their new pets.

A camp was soon formed; and that evening the old hermit asked Amyas, Cary, and Brimblecombe to come up into his cavern.

They went; and after the accustomed compliments had passed, sat down on mats upon the ground, while the old man stood, leaning against a slab of stone surmounted by a rude wooden cross, which evidently served him as a place of prayer. He seemed restless and anxious, as if he waited for them to begin the conversation; while they, in their turn, waited for him. At last, when courtesy would not allow him to be silent any longer, he began with a faltering voice:

"You may be equally surprised, senors, at my presence in such a spot, and at my asking you to become my guests even for one evening, while I have no better hospitality to offer you."

"It is superfluous, senor, to offer us food in your own habitation when you have already put all that you possess at our command."

"True, senors: and my motive for inviting you was, perhaps, somewhat of a selfish one. I am possessed by a longing to unburthen my heart of a tale which I never yet told to man, and which I fear can give to you nothing but pain; and yet I will entreat you, of your courtesy, to hear of that which you cannot amend, simply in mercy to a man who feels that he must confess to some one, or die as miserable as he has lived. And I believe my confidence will not be misplaced, when it is bestowed upon you. I have been a cavalier, even as you are; and, strange as it may seem, that which I have to tell I would sooner impart to the ears of a soldier than of a priest; because it will then sink into souls which can at least sympathize, though they cannot absolve. And you, cavaliers, I perceive to be noble, from your very looks; to be valiant, by your mere presence in this hostile land; and to be gentle, courteous, and prudent, by your conduct this day to me and to your captives. Will you, then, hear an old man's tale? I am, as you see, full of words; for speech, from long disuse, is difficult to me, and I fear at every sentence lest my stiffened tongue should play the traitor to my worn-out brain: but if my request seems impertinent, you have only to bid me talk as a host should, of matters which concern his guests, and not himself."

The three young men, equally surprised and interested by this exordium, could only entreat their host to "use their ears as those of his slaves," on which, after fresh apologies, he began:

"Know, then, victorious cavaliers, that I, whom you now see here as a poor hermit, was formerly one of the foremost of that terrible band who went with Pizarro to the conquest of Peru. Eighty years old am I this day, unless the calendar which I have carved upon yonder tree deceives me; and twenty years old was I when I sailed with that fierce man from Panama, to do that deed with which all earth, and heaven, and hell itself, I fear, has rung. How we endured, suffered, and triumphed; how, mad with success, and glutted with blood, we turned our swords against each other, I need not tell to you. For what gentleman of Europe knows not our glory and our shame?"

His hearers bowed assent.

"Yes; you have heard of our prowess: for glorious we were awhile, in the sight of God and man. But I will not speak of our glory, for it is tarnished; nor of our wealth, for it was our poison; nor of the sins of my comrades, for they have expiated them; but of my own sins, senors, which are more in number than the hairs of my head, and a burden too great to bear. Miserere Domine!"

And smiting on his breast, the old warrior went on:

"As I said, we were mad with blood; and none more mad than I. Surely it is no fable that men are possessed, even in this latter age, by devils. Why else did I rejoice in slaying? Why else was I, the son of a noble and truthful cavalier of Castile, among the foremost to urge upon my general the murder of the Inca? Why did I rejoice over his dying agonies? Why, when Don Ferdinando de Soto returned, and upbraided us with our villainy, did I, instead of confessing the sin which that noble cavalier set before us, withstand him to his face, ay, and would have drawn the sword on him, but that he refused to fight a liar, as he said that I was?"

"Then Don de Soto was against the murder? So his own grandson told me. But I had heard of him only as a tyrant and a butcher."

"Senor, he was compact of good and evil, as are other men: he has paid dearly for his sin; let us hope that he has been paid in turn for his righteousness."

John Brimblecombe shook his head at this doctrine, but did not speak.

"So you know his grandson? I trust he is a noble cavalier?"

Amyas was silent; the old gentleman saw that he had touched some sore point, and continued:

"And why, again, senors, did I after that day give myself up to cruelty as to a sport; yea, thought that I did God service by destroying the creatures whom He had made; I who now dare not destroy a gnat, lest I harm a being more righteous than myself? Was I mad? If I was, how then was I all that while as prudent as I am this day? But I am not here to argue, senors, but to confess. In a word, there was no deed of blood done for the next few years in which I had not my share, if it were but within my reach. When Challcuchima was burned, I was consenting; when that fair girl, the wife of Inca Manco, was tortured to death, I smiled at the agonies at which she too smiled, and taunted on the soldiers, to try if I could wring one groan from her before she died. You know what followed, the pillage, the violence, the indignities offered to the virgins of the Sun. Senors, I will not pollute your chaste ears with what was done. But, senors, I had a brother."

And the old man paused awhile.

"A brother—whether better or worse than me, God knows, before whom he has appeared ere now. At least he did not, as I did, end as a rebel to his king! There was a maiden in one of those convents, senors, more beautiful than day: and (I blush to tell it) the two brothers of whom I spoke quarrelled for the possession of her. They struck each other, senors! Who struck first I know not; but swords were drawn, and—The cavaliers round parted them, crying shame. And one of those two brothers—the one who speaks to you now—crying, 'If I cannot have her, no man shall!' turned the sword which was aimed at his brother, against that hapless maiden—and—hear me out, senors, before you flee from my presence as from that of a monster!—stabbed her to the heart. And as she died—one moment more, senors, that I may confess all!—she looked up in my face with a smile as of heaven, and thanked me for having rid her once and for all from Christians and their villainy."

The old man paused.

"God forgive you, senor!" said Jack Brimblecombe, softly.

"You do not, then, turn from me, do not curse me? Then I will try you farther still, senors. I will know from human lips, whether man can do such deeds as I have done, and yet be pitied by his kind; that so I may have some hope, that where man has mercy, God may have mercy also. Do you think that I repented at those awful words? Nothing less, senors all. No more than I did when De Soto (on whose soul God have mercy) called me—me, a liar! I knew myself a sinner; and for that very reason I was determined to sin. I would go on, that I might prove myself right to myself, by showing that I could go on, and not be struck dead from heaven. Out of mere pride, senors, and self-will, I would fill up the cup of my iniquity; and I filled it.

"You know, doubtless, senors, how, after the death of old Almagro, his son's party conspired against Pizarro. Now my brother remained faithful to his old commander; and for that very reason, if you will believe it, did I join the opposite party, and gave myself up, body and soul, to do Almagro's work. It was enough for me, that the brother who had struck me thought a man right, for me to think that man a devil. What Almagro's work was, you know. He slew Pizarro, murdered him, senors, like a dog, or rather, like an old lion."

"He deserved his doom," said Amyas.

"Let God judge him, senor, not we; and least of all of us I, who drew the first blood, and perhaps the last, that day. I, senors, it was who treacherously stabbed Francisco de Chanes on the staircase, and so opened the door which else had foiled us all; and I—But I am speaking to men of honor, not to butchers. Suffice it that the old man died like a lion, and that we pulled him down, young as we were, like curs.

"Well, I followed Almagro's fortunes. I helped to slay Alvarado. Call that my third murder, if you will, for if he was traitor to a traitor, I was traitor to a true man. Then to the war; you know how Vaca de Castro was sent from Spain to bring order and justice where was naught but chaos, and the dance of all devils. We met him on the hills of Chupas. Peter of Candia, the Venetian villain, pointed our guns false, and Almagro stabbed him to the heart. We charged with our lances, man against man, horse against horse. All fights I ever fought" (and the old man's eyes flashed out the ancient fire) "were child's play to that day. Our lances shivered like reeds, and we fell on with battle-axe and mace. None asked for quarter, and none gave it; friend to friend, cousin to cousin—no, nor brother, O God! to brother. We were the better armed: but numbers were on their side. Fat Carbajal charged our cannon like an elephant, and took them; but Holguin was shot down. I was with Almagro, and we swept all before us, inch by inch, but surely, till the night fell. Then Vaca de Castro, the licentiate, the clerk, the schoolman, the man of books, came down on us with his reserve like a whirlwind. Oh! cavaliers, did not God fight against us, when He let us, the men of iron, us, the heroes of Cuzco and Vilcaconga, be foiled by a scholar in a black gown, with a pen behind his ear? We were beaten. Some ran; some did not run, senors; and I did not. Geronimo de Alvarado shouted to me, 'We slew Pizarro! We killed the tyrant!' and we rushed upon the conqueror's lances, to die like cavaliers. There was a gallant gentleman in front of me. His lance struck me in the crest, and bore me over my horse's croup: but mine, senors, struck him full in the vizor. We both went to the ground together, and the battle galloped over us.

"I know not how long I lay, for I was stunned: but after awhile I lifted myself. My lance was still clenched in my hand, broken but not parted. The point of it was in my foeman's brain. I crawled to him, weary and wounded, and saw that he was a noble cavalier. He lay on his back, his arms spread wide. I knew that he was dead: but there came over me the strangest longing to see that dead man's face. Perhaps I knew him. At least I could set my foot upon it, and say, 'Vanquished as I am, there lies a foe!' I caught hold of the rivets, and tore his helmet off. The moon shone bright, senors, as bright as she shines now—the glaring, ghastly, tell-tale moon, which shows man all the sins which he tries to hide; and by that moonlight, senors, I beheld the dead man's face. And it was the face of my brother!

"Did you ever guess, most noble cavaliers, what Cain's curse might be like? Look on me, and know!

"I tore off my armor and fled, as Cain fled—northward ever, till I should reach a land where the name of Spaniard, yea, and the name of Christian, which the Spaniard has caused to be blasphemed from east to west, should never come. I sank fainting, and waked beneath this rock, this tree, forty-four years ago, and I have never left them since, save once, to obtain seeds from Indians, who knew not that I was a Spanish Conquistador. And may God have mercy on my soul!"

The old man ceased; and his young hearers, deeply affected by his tale, sat silent for a few minutes. Then John Brimblecombe spoke:

"You are old, sir, and I am young; and perhaps it is not my place to counsel you. Moreover, sir, in spite of this strange dress of mine, I am neither more nor less than an English priest; and I suppose you will not be willing to listen to a heretic."

"I have seen Catholics, senor, commit too many abominations even with the name of God upon their lips, to shrink from a heretic if he speak wisely and well. At least, you are a man; and after all, my heart yearns more and more, the longer I sit among you, for the speech of beings of my own race. Say what you will, in God's name!"

"I hold, sir," said Jack, modestly, "according to holy Scripture, that whosoever repents from his heart, as God knows you seem to have done, is forgiven there and then; and though his sins be as scarlet, they shall be white as snow, for the sake of Him who died for all."

"Amen! Amen!" said the old man, looking lovingly at his little crucifix. "I hope and pray—His name is Love. I know it now; who better? But, sir, even if He have forgiven me, how can I forgive myself? In honor, sir, I must be just, and sternly just, to myself, even if God be indulgent; as He has been to me, who has left me here in peace for forty years, instead of giving me a prey to the first puma or jaguar which howls round me every night. He has given me time to work out my own salvation; but have I done it? That doubt maddens me at whiles. When I look upon that crucifix, I float on boundless hope: but if I take my eyes from it for a moment, faith fails, and all is blank, and dark, and dreadful, till the devil whispers me to plunge into yon stream, and once and for ever wake to certainty, even though it be in hell."

What was Jack to answer? He himself knew not at first. More was wanted than the mere repetition of free pardon.

"Heretic as I am, sir, you will not believe me when I tell you, as a priest, that God accepts your penitence."

"My heart tells me so already, at moments. But how know I that it does not lie?"

"Senor," said Jack, "the best way to punish oneself for doing ill, seems to me to go and do good; and the best way to find out whether God means you well, is to find out whether He will help you to do well. If you have wronged Indians in time past, see whether you cannot right them now. If you can, you are safe. For the Lord will not send the devil's servants to do His work."

The old man held down his head.

"Right the Indians? Alas! what is done, is done!"

"Not altogether, senor," said Amyas, "as long as an Indian remains alive in New Granada."

"Senor, shall I confess my weakness? A voice within me has bid me a hundred times go forth and labor, for those oppressed wretches, but I dare not obey. I dare not look them in the face. I should fancy that they knew my story; that the very birds upon the trees would reveal my crime, and bid them turn from me with horror."

"Senor," said Amyas, "these are but the sick fancies of a noble spirit, feeding on itself in solitude. You have but to try to conquer."

"And look now," said Jack, "if you dare not go forth to help the Indians, see now how God has brought the Indians to your own door. Oh, excellent sir—"

"Call me not excellent," said the old man, smiting his breast.

"I do, and shall, sir, while I see in you an excellent repentance, an excellent humility, and an excellent justice," said Jack. "But oh, sir, look upon these forty souls, whom we must leave behind, like sheep which have no shepherd. Could you not teach them to fear God and to love each other, to live like rational men, perhaps to die like Christians? They would obey you as a dog obeys his master. You might be their king, their father, yea, their pope, if you would."

"You do not speak like a Lutheran."

"I am not a Lutheran, but an Englishman: but, Protestant as I am, God knows, I had sooner see these poor souls of your creed, than of none."

"But I am no priest."

"When they are ready," said Jack, "the Lord will send a priest. If you begin the good work, you may trust to Him to finish it."

"God help me!" said the old warrior.

The talk lasted long into the night, but Amyas was up long before daybreak, felling the trees; and as he and Cary walked back to breakfast, the first thing which they saw was the old man in his garden with four or five Indian children round him, talking smilingly to them.

"The old man's heart is sound still," said Will. "No man is lost who still is fond of little children."

"Ah, senors!" said the hermit as they came up, "you see that I have begun already to act upon your advice."

"And you have begun at the right end," quoth Amyas; "if you win the children, you win the mothers."

"And if you win the mothers," quoth Will, "the poor fathers must needs obey their wives, and follow in the wake."

The old man only sighed. "The prattle of these little ones softens my hard heart, senors, with a new pleasure; but it saddens me, when I recollect that there may be children of mine now in the world—children who have never known a father's love—never known aught but a master's threats—"

"God has taken care of these little ones. Trust that He has taken care of yours."

That day Amyas assembled the Indians, and told them that they must obey the hermit as their king, and settle there as best they could: for if they broke up and wandered away, nothing was left for them but to fall one by one into the hands of the Spaniards. They heard him with their usual melancholy and stupid acquiescence, and went and came as they were bid, like animated machines; but the negroes were of a different temper; and four or five stout fellows gave Amyas to understand that they had been warriors in their own country, and that warriors they would be still; and nothing should keep them from Spaniard-hunting. Amyas saw that the presence of these desperadoes in the new colony would both endanger the authority of the hermit, and bring the Spaniards down upon it in a few weeks; so, making a virtue of necessity, he asked them whether they would go Spaniard-hunting with him.

This was just what the bold Coromantees wished for; they grinned and shouted their delight at serving under so great a warrior, and then set to work most gallantly, getting through more in the day than any ten Indians, and indeed than any two Englishmen.

So went on several days, during which the trees were felled, and the process of digging them out began; while Ayacanora, silent and moody, wandered into the woods all day with her blow-gun, and brought home at evening a load of parrots, monkeys, and curassows; two or three old hands were sent out to hunt likewise; so that, what with the game and the fish of the river, which seemed inexhaustible, and the fruit of the neighboring palm-trees, there was no lack of food in the camp. But what to do with Ayacanora weighed heavily on the mind of Amyas. He opened his heart on the matter to the old hermit, and asked him whether he would take charge of her. The latter smiled, and shook his head at the notion. "If your report of her be true, I may as well take in hand to tame a jaguar." However, he promised to try; and one evening, as they were all standing together before the mouth of the cave, Ayacanora came up smiling with the fruit of her day's sport; and Amyas, thinking this a fit opportunity, began a carefully prepared harangue to her, which he intended to be altogether soothing, and even pathetic,—to the effect that the maiden, having no parents, was to look upon this good old man as her father; that he would instruct her in the white man's religion (at which promise Yeo, as a good Protestant, winced a good deal), and teach her how to be happy and good, and so forth; and that, in fine, she was to remain there with the hermit.

She heard him quietly, her great dark eyes opening wider and wider, her bosom swelling, her stature seeming to grow taller every moment, as she clenched her weapons firmly in both her hands. Beautiful as she always was, she had never looked so beautiful before; and as Amyas spoke of parting with her, it was like throwing away a lovely toy; but it must be done, for her sake, for his, perhaps for that of all the crew.

The last words had hardly passed his lips, when, with a shriek of mingled scorn, rage, and fear, she dashed through the astonished group.

"Stop her!" were Amyas's first words; but his next were, "Let her go!" for, springing like a deer through the little garden and over the flower-fence, she turned, menacing with her blow-gun the sailors, who had already started in her pursuit.

"Let her alone, for Heaven's sake!" shouted Amyas, who, he scarce knew why, shrank from the thought of seeing those graceful limbs struggling in the seamen's grasp.

She turned again, and in another minute her gaudy plumes had vanished among the dark forest stems, as swiftly as if she had been a passing bird.

All stood thunderstruck at this unexpected end to the conference. At last Aymas spoke:

"There's no use in standing here idle, gentlemen. Staring after her won't bring her back. After all, I'm glad she's gone."

But the tone of his voice belied his words. Now he had lost her, he wanted her back; and perhaps every one present, except he, guessed why.

But Ayacanora did not return; and ten days more went on in continual toil at the canoes without any news of her from the hunters. Amyas, by the by, had strictly bidden these last not to follow the girl, not even to speak to her, if they came across her in their wanderings. He was shrewd enough to guess that the only way to cure her sulkiness was to outsulk her; but there was no sign of her presence in any direction; and the canoes being finished at last, the gold, and such provisions as they could collect, were placed on board, and one evening the party prepared for their fresh voyage. They determined to travel as much as possible by night, for fear of discovery, especially in the neighborhood of the few Spanish settlements which were then scattered along the banks of the main stream. These, however, the negroes knew, so that there was no fear of coming on them unawares; and as for falling asleep in their night journeys, "Nobody," the negroes said, "ever slept on the Magdalena; the mosquitoes took too good care of that." Which fact Amyas and his crew verified afterwards as thoroughly as wretched men could do.

The sun had sunk; the night had all but fallen; the men were all on board; Amyas in command of one canoe, Cary of the other. The Indians were grouped on the bank, watching the party with their listless stare, and with them the young guide, who preferred remaining among the Indians, and was made supremely happy by the present of Spanish sword and an English axe; while, in the midst, the old hermit, with tears in his eyes, prayed God's blessing on them.

"I owe to you, noble cavaliers, new peace, new labor, I may say, new life. May God be with you, and teach you to use your gold and your swords better than I used mine."

The adventurers waved their hands to him.

"Give way, men," cried Amyas; and as he spoke the paddles dashed into the water, to a right English hurrah! which sent the birds fluttering from their roosts, and was answered by the yell of a hundred monkeys, and the distant roar of the jaguar.

About twenty yards below, a wooded rock, some ten feet high, hung over the stream. The river was not there more than fifteen yards broad; deep near the rock, shallow on the farther side; and Amyas's canoe led the way, within ten feet of the stone.

As he passed, a dark figure leapt from the bushes on the edge, and plunged heavily into the water close to the boat. All started. A jaguar? No; he would not have missed so short a spring.

What, then? A human being?

A head rose panting to the surface, and with a few strong strokes the swimmer had clutched the gunwale. It was Ayacanora!

"Go back!" shouted Amyas. "Go back, girl!"

She uttered the same wild cry with which she had fled into the forest.

"I will die, then!" and she threw up her arms. Another moment, and she had sunk.

To see her perish before his eyes! who could bear that? Her hands alone were above the surface. Amyas caught convulsively at her in the darkness, and seized her wrist.

A yell rose from the negroes: a roar from the crew as from a cage of lions. There was a rush and a swirl along the surface of the stream; and "Caiman! caiman!" shouted twenty voices.

Now, or never, for the strong arm! "To larboard, men, or over we go!" cried Amyas, and with one huge heave he lifted the slender body upon the gunwale. Her lower limbs were still in the water, when, within arm's length, rose above the stream a huge muzzle. The lower jaw lay flat, the upper reached as high as Amyas's head. He could see the long fangs gleam white in the moonshine; he could see for one moment full down the monstrous depths of that great gape, which would have crushed a buffalo. Three inches, and no more, from that soft side, the snout surged up—

There was the gleam of an axe from above, a sharp ringing blow, and the jaws came together with a clash which rang from bank to bank. He had missed her! Swerving beneath the blow, his snout had passed beneath her body, and smashed up against the side of the canoe, as the striker, overbalanced, fell headlong overboard upon the monster's back.

"Who is it?"

"Yeo!" shouted a dozen.

Man and beast went down together, and where they sank, the moonlight shone on a great swirling eddy, while all held their breaths, and Ayacanora cowered down into the bottom of the canoe, her proud spirit utterly broken, for the first time, by the terror of that great need, and by a bitter loss. For in the struggle, the holy trumpet, companion of all her wanderings, had fallen from her bosom; and her fond hope of bringing magic prosperity to her English friends had sunk with it to the bottom of the stream.

None heeded her; not even Amyas, round whose knees she clung, fawning like a spaniel dog: for where was Yeo?

Another swirl; a shout from the canoe abreast of them, and Yeo rose, having dived clean under his own boat, and risen between the two.

"Safe as yet, lads! Heave me a line, or he'll have me after all."

But ere the brute reappeared, the old man was safe on board.

"The Lord has stood by me," panted he, as he shot the water from his ears. "We went down together: I knew the Indian trick, and being uppermost, had my thumbs in his eyes before he could turn: but he carried me down to the very mud. My breath was nigh gone, so I left go, and struck up: but my toes tingled as I rose again, I'll warrant. There the beggar is, looking for me, I declare!"

And, true enough, there was the huge brute swimming slowly round and round, in search of his lost victim. It was too dark to put an arrow into his eye; so they paddled on, while Ayacanora crouched silently at Amyas's feet.

"Yeo!" asked he, in a low voice, "what shall we do with her?"

"Why ask me, sir?" said the old man, as he had a very good right to ask.

"Because, when one don't know oneself, one had best inquire of one's elders. Besides, you saved her life at the risk of your own, and have a right to a voice in the matter, if any one has, old friend."

"Then, my dear young captain, if the Lord puts a precious soul under your care, don't you refuse to bear the burden He lays on you."

Amyas was silent awhile; while Ayacanora, who was evidently utterly exhausted by the night's adventure, and probably by long wanderings, watchings, and weepings which had gone before it, sank with her head against his knee, fell fast asleep, and breathed as gently as a child.

At last he rose in the canoe, and called Cary alongside.

"Listen to me, gentlemen, and sailors all. You know that we have a maiden on board here, by no choice of our own. Whether she will be a blessing to us, God alone can tell: but she may turn to the greatest curse which has befallen us ever since we came out over Bar three years ago. Promise me one thing, or I put her ashore the next beach, and that is, that you will treat her as if she were your own sister; and make an agreement here and now, that if the maid comes to harm among us, the man that is guilty shall hang for it by the neck till he's dead, even though he be I, Captain Leigh, who speak to you. I'll hang you, as I am a Christian; and I give you free leave to hang me."

"A very fair bargain," quoth Cary, "and I for one will see it kept to. Lads, we'll twine a double strong halter for the captain as we go down along."

"I am not jesting, Will."

"I know it, good old lad," said Cary, stretching out his own hand to him across the water through the darkness, and giving him a hearty shake. "I know it; and listen, men! So help me God! but I'll be the first to back the Captain in being as good as his word, as I trust he never will need to be."

"Amen!" said Brimblecombe. "Amen!" said Yeo; and many an honest voice joined in that honest compact, and kept it too, like men.

CHAPTER XXVI: HOW THEY TOOK THE GREAT GALLEON

One more glance at the golden tropic sea, and the golden tropic evenings, by the shore of New Granada, in the golden Spanish Main.

The bay of Santa Marta is rippling before the land-breeze one sheet of living flame. The mighty forests are sparkling with myriad fireflies. The lazy mist which lounges round the inner hills shines golden in the sunset rays; and, nineteen thousand feet aloft, the mighty peak of Horqueta cleaves the abyss of air, rose-red against the dark-blue vault of heaven. The rosy cone fades to a dull leaden hue; but only for awhile. The stars flash out one by one, and Venus, like another moon, tinges the eastern snows with gold, and sheds across the bay a long yellow line of rippling light. Everywhere is glory and richness. What wonder if the earth in that enchanted land be as rich to her inmost depths as she is upon the surface? The heaven, the hills, the sea, are one sparkling garland of jewels—what wonder if the soil be jewelled also? if every watercourse and bank of earth be spangled with emeralds and rubies, with grains of gold and feathered wreaths of native silver?

So thought, in a poetic mood, the Bishop of Cartagena, as he sat in the state cabin of that great galleon, The City of the True Cross, and looked pensively out of the window towards the shore. The good man was in a state of holy calm. His stout figure rested on one easy-chair, his stout ankles on another, beside a table spread with oranges and limes, guavas and pine-apples, and all the fruits of Ind.

An Indian girl, bedizened with scarfs and gold chains, kept off the flies with a fan of feathers; and by him, in a pail of ice from the Horqueta (the gift of some pious Spanish lady, who had "spent" an Indian or two in bringing down the precious offering), stood more than one flask of virtuous wine of Alicant. But he was not so selfish, good man, as to enjoy either ice or wine alone; Don Pedro, colonel of the soldiers on board, Don Alverez, intendant of his Catholic majesty's customs at Santa Marta, and Don Paul, captain of mariners in The City of the True Cross, had, by his especial request, come to his assistance that evening, and with two friars, who sat at the lower end of the table, were doing their best to prevent the good man from taking too bitterly to heart the present unsatisfactory state of his cathedral town, which had just been sacked and burnt by an old friend of ours, Sir Francis Drake.

"We have been great sufferers, senors,—ah, great sufferers," snuffled the bishop, quoting Scripture, after the fashion of the day, glibly enough, but often much too irreverently for me to repeat, so boldly were his texts travestied, and so freely interlarded by grumblings at Tita and the mosquitoes. "Great sufferers, truly; but there shall be a remnant,—ah, a remnant like the shaking of the olive tree and the gleaning grapes when the vintage is done.—Ah! Gold? Yes, I trust Our Lady's mercies are not shut up, nor her arms shortened.—Look, senors!"—and he pointed majestically out of the window. "It looks gold! it smells of gold, as I may say, by a poetical license. Yea, the very waves, as they ripple past us, sing of gold, gold, gold!"

"It is a great privilege," said the intendant, "to have comfort so gracefully administered at once by a churchman and a scholar."

"A poet, too," said Don Pedro. "You have no notion what sweet sonnets—"

"Hush, Don Pedro—hush! If I, a mateless bird, have spent an idle hour in teaching lovers how to sing, why, what of that? I am a churchman, senors; but I am a man and I can feel, senors; I can sympathize; I can palliate; I can excuse. Who knows better than I how much human nature lurks in us fallen sons of Adam? Tita!"

"Um?" said the trembling girl, with a true Indian grunt.

"Fill his excellency the intendant's glass. Does much more treasure come down, illustrious senor? May the poor of Mary hope for a few more crumbs from their Mistress's table?"

"Not a pezo, I fear. The big white cow up there"—and he pointed to the Horqueta—"has been milked dry for this year."

"Ah!" And he looked up at the magnificent snow peak. "Only good to cool wine with, eh? and as safe for the time being as Solomon's birds."

"Solomon's birds? Explain your recondite allusion, my lord."

"Enlighten us, your excellency, enlighten us."

"Ah! thereby hangs a tale. You know the holy birds who run up and down on the Prado at Seville among the ladies' pretty feet,—eh? with hooked noses and cinnamon crests? Of course. Hoopoes—Upupa, as the classics have it. Well, senors, once on a time, the story goes, these hoopoes all had golden crowns on their heads; and, senors, they took the consequences—eh? But it befell on a day that all the birds and beasts came to do homage at the court of his most Catholic majesty King Solomon, and among them came these same hoopoes; and they had a little request to make, the poor rogues. And what do you think it was? Why, that King Solomon would pray for them that they might wear any sort of crowns but these same golden ones; for—listen, Tita, and see the snare of riches—mankind so hunted, and shot, and trapped, and snared them, for the sake of these same golden crowns, that life was a burden to bear. So Solomon prayed, and instead of golden crowns, they all received crowns of feathers; and ever since, senors, they live as merrily as crickets in an oven, and also have the honor of bearing the name of his most Catholic majesty King Solomon. Tita! fill the senor commandant's glass. Fray Gerundio, what are you whispering about down there, sir?"

Fray Gerundio had merely commented to his brother on the bishop's story of Solomon's birds with an—

"O si sic omnia!—would that all gold would turn to feathers in like wise!"

"Then, friend," replied the other, a Dominican, like Gerundio, but of a darker and sterner complexion, "corrupt human nature would within a week discover some fresh bauble, for which to kill and be killed in vain."

"What is that, Fray Gerundio?" asked the bishop again.

"I merely remarked, that it were well for the world if all mankind were to put up the same prayer as the hoopoes."

"World, sir? What do you know about the world? Convert your Indians, sir, if you please, and leave affairs of state to your superiors. You will excuse him, senors" (turning to the Dons, and speaking in a lower tone). "A very worthy and pious man, but a poor peasant's son; and beside—

you understand. A little wrong here; too much fasting and watching, I fear, good man." And the bishop touched his forehead knowingly, to signify that Fray Gerundio's wits were in an unsatisfactory state.

The Fray heard and saw with a quiet smile. He was one of those excellent men whom the cruelties of his countrymen had stirred up (as the darkness, by mere contrast, makes the light more bright), as they did Las Casas, Gasca, and many another noble name which is written in the book of life, to deeds of love and pious daring worthy of any creed or age. True Protestants, they protested, even before kings, against the evil which lay nearest them, the sin which really beset them; true liberals, they did not disdain to call the dark-skinned heathen their brothers; and asserted in terms which astonish us, when we recollect the age in which they were spoken, the inherent freedom of every being who wore the flesh and blood which their Lord wore; true martyrs, they bore witness of Christ, and received too often the rewards of such, in slander and contempt. Such an one was Fray Gerundio; a poor, mean, clumsy-tongued peasant's son, who never could put three sentences together, save when he waxed eloquent, crucifix in hand, amid some group of Indians or negroes. He was accustomed to such rebuffs as the bishop's; he took them for what they were worth, and sipped his wine in silence; while the talk went on.

"They say," observed the commandant, "that a very small Plate-fleet will go to Spain this year."

"What else?" says the intendant. "What have we to send, in the name of all saints, since these accursed English Lutherans have swept us out clean?"

"And if we had anything to send," says the sea-captain, "what have we to send it in? That fiend incarnate, Drake—"

"Ah!" said his holiness; "spare my ears! Don Pedro, you will oblige my weakness by not mentioning that man;—his name is Tartarean, unfit for polite lips. Draco—a dragon—serpent—the emblem of Diabolus himself—ah! And the guardian of the golden apples of the West, who would fain devour our new Hercules, his most Catholic majesty. Deceived Eve, too, with one of those same apples—a very evil name, senors—a Tartarean name,—Tita!"

"Um!"

"Fill my glass."

"Nay," cried the colonel, with a great oath, "this English fellow is of another breed of serpent from that, I warrant."

"Your reason, senor; your reason?"

"Because this one would have seen Eve at the bottom of the sea, before he let her, or any one but himself, taste aught which looked like gold."

"Ah, ah!—very good! But—we laugh, valiant senors, while the Church weeps. Alas for my sheep!"

"And alas for their sheepfold! It will be four years before we can get Cartagena rebuilt again. And as for the blockhouse, when we shall get that rebuilt, Heaven only knows, while his majesty goes on draining the Indies for his English Armada. The town is as naked now as an Indian's back."

"Baptista Antonio, the surveyor, has sent home by me a relation to the king, setting forth our defenceless state. But to read a relation and to act on it are two cocks of very different hackles, bishop, as all statesmen know. Heaven grant we may have orders by the next fleet to fortify, or we shall be at the mercy of every English pirate!"

"Ah, that blockhouse!" sighed the bishop. "That was indeed a villainous trick. A hundred and ten thousand ducats for the ransom of the town! After having burned and plundered the one-half—and having made me dine with them too, ah! and sit between the—the serpent, and his lieutenant-general—and drunk my health in my own private wine—wine that I had from Xeres nine years ago, senors and offered, the shameless heretics, to take me to England, if I would turn Lutheran, and find me a wife, and make an honest man of me—ah! and then to demand fresh ransom for the priory and the fort—perfidious!"

"Well," said the colonel, "they had the law of us, the cunning rascals, for we forgot to mention anything but the town, in the agreement. Who would have dreamed of such a fetch as that?"

"So I told my good friend the prior, when he came to me to borrow the thousand crowns. It was Heaven's will. Unexpected like the thunderbolt, and to be borne as such. Every man must bear his own burden. How could I lend him aught?"

"Your holiness's money had been all carried off by them before," said the intendant, who knew, and none better, the exact contrary.

"Just so—all my scanty savings! desolate in my lone old age. Ah, senors, had we not had warning of the coming of these wretches from my dear friend the Marquess of Santa Cruz, whom I remember daily in my prayers, we had been like to them who go down quick into the pit. I too might have saved a trifle, had I been minded: but in thinking too much of others, I forgot myself, alas!"

"Warning or none, we had no right to be beaten by such a handful," said the sea-captain; "and a shame it is, and a shame it will be, for many a day to come."

"Do you mean to cast any slur, sir, upon the courage and conduct of his Catholic majesty's soldiers?" asked the colonel.

"I?—No; but we were foully beaten, and that behind our barricades too, and there's the plain truth."

"Beaten, sir! Do you apply such a term to the fortunes of war? What more could our governor have done? Had we not the ways filled with poisoned caltrops, guarded by Indian archers, barred with butts full of earth, raked with culverins and arquebuses? What familiar spirit had we, sir, to tell us that these villains would come along the sea-beach, and not by the high-road, like Christian men?"

"Ah!" said the bishop, "it was by intuition diabolic, I doubt not, that they took that way. Satanas must need help those who serve him; and for my part, I can only attribute (I would the captain here had piety enough to do so) the misfortune which occurred to art-magic. I believe these men to have been possessed by all fiends whatsoever."

"Well, your holiness," said the colonel, "there may have been devilry in it; how else would men have dared to run right into the mouths of our cannon, fire their shot against our very noses, and tumble harmless over those huge butts of earth?"

"Doubtless by force of the fiends which raged with them," interposed the bishop.

"And then, with their blasphemous cries, leap upon us with sword and pike? I myself saw that Lieutenant-General Carlisle hew down with one stroke that noble young gentleman the ensign-bearer, your excellency's sister's son's nephew, though he was armed cap-a-pie. Was not art-magic here? And that most furious and blaspheming Lutheran Captain Young, I saw how he caught our general by the head, after the illustrious Don Alonzo had given him a grievous wound, threw him to the earth, and so took him. Was not art-magic here?"

"Well, I say," said the captain, "if you are looking for art-magic, what say you to their marching through the flank fire of our galleys, with eleven pieces of ordnance, and two hundred shot playing on them, as if it had been a mosquito swarm? Some said my men fired too high: but that was the English rascals' doing, for they got down on the tide beach. But, senor commandant, though Satan may have taught them that trick, was it he that taught them to carry pikes a foot longer than yours?"

"Ah, well," said the bishop, "sacked are we; and San Domingo, as I hear, in worse case than we are; and St. Augustine in Florida likewise; and all that is left for a poor priest like me is to return to Spain, and see whether the pious clemency of his majesty, and of the universal Father, may not be willing to grant some small relief or bounty to the poor of Mary—perhaps—(for who knows?) to translate to a sphere of more peaceful labor one who is now old, senors, and weary with many toils—Tita! fill our glasses. I have saved somewhat—as you may have done, senors, from the general wreck; and for the flock, when I am no more, illustrious senors, Heaven's mercies are infinite; new cities will rise from the ashes of the old, new mines pour forth their treasures into the sanctified laps of the faithful, and new Indians flock toward the life-giving standard of the Cross, to put on the easy yoke and light burden of the Church, and—"

"And where shall I be then? Ah, where? Fain would I rest, and fain depart. Tita! sling my hammock. Senors, you will excuse age and infirmities. Fray Gerundio, go to bed!"

And the Dons rose to depart, while the bishop went on maundering,—

"Farewell! Life is short. Ah! we shall meet in heaven at last. And there are really no more pearls?"

"Not a frail; nor gold either," said the intendant.

"Ah, well! Better a dinner of herbs where love is, than—Tita!"

"My breviary—ah! Man's gratitude is short-lived, I had hoped—You have seen nothing of the Senora Bovadilla?"

"No."

"Ah! she promised:—but no matter—a little trifle as a keepsake—a gold cross, or an emerald ring, or what not—I forget. And what have I to do with worldly wealth!—Ah! Tita! bring me the casket."

And when his guests were gone, the old man began mumbling prayers out of his breviary, and fingering over jewels and gold, with the dull greedy eyes of covetous old age.

"Ah!—it may buy the red hat yet!—Omnia Romae venalia! Put it by, Tita, and do not look at it too much, child. Enter not into temptation. The love of money is the root of all evil; and Heaven, in love for the Indian, has made him poor in this world, that he may be rich in faith. Ah!—Ugh!—So!"

And the old miser clambered into his hammock. Tita drew the mosquito net over him, wrapt another round her own head, and slept, or seemed to sleep; for she coiled herself up upon the floor, and master and slave soon snored a merry bass to the treble of the mosquitoes.

It was long past midnight, and the moon was down. The sentinels, who had tramped and challenged overhead till they thought their officers were sound asleep, had slipped out of the unwholesome rays of the planet to seek that health and peace which they considered their right, and slept as soundly as the bishop's self.

Two long lines glided out from behind the isolated rocks of the Morro Grande, which bounded the bay some five hundred yards astern of the galleon. They were almost invisible on the glittering surface of the water, being perfectly white; and, had a sentinel been looking out, he could only have descried them by the phosphorescent flashes along their sides.

Now the bishop had awoke, and turned himself over uneasily; for the wine was dying out within him, and his shoulders had slipped down, and his heels up, and his head ached! so he sat upright in his hammock, looked out upon the bay, and called Tita.

"Put another pillow under my head, child! What is that? a fish?"

Tita looked. She did not think it was a fish: but she did not choose to say so; for it might have produced an argument, and she had her reasons for not keeping his holiness awake.

The bishop looked again; settled that it must be a white whale, or shark, or other monster of the deep; crossed himself, prayed for a safe voyage, and snored once more.

Presently the cabin-door opened gently, and the head of the senor intendant appeared.

Tita sat up; and then began crawling like a snake along the floor, among the chairs and tables, by the light of the cabin lamp.

"Is he asleep?"

"Yes: but the casket is under his head."

"Curse him! How shall we take it?"

"I brought him a fresh pillow half-an-hour ago; I hung his hammock wrong on purpose that he might want one. I thought to slip the box away as I did it; but the old ox nursed it in both hands all the while."

"What shall we do, in the name of all the fiends? She sails to-morrow morning, and then all is lost."

Tita showed her white teeth, and touched the dagger which hung by the intendant's side.

"I dare not!" said the rascal, with a shudder.

"I dare!" said she. "He whipt my mother, because she would not give me up to him to be taught in his schools, when she went to the mines. And she went to the mines, and died there in three months. I saw her go, with a chain round her neck; but she never came back again. Yes; I dare kill him! I will kill him! I will!"

The senor felt his mind much relieved. He had no wish, of course, to commit the murder himself; for he was a good Catholic, and feared the devil. But Tita was an Indian, and her being lost did not matter so much. Indians' souls were cheap, like their bodies. So he answered, "But we shall be discovered!"

"I will leap out of the window with the casket, and swim ashore. They will never suspect you, and they will fancy I am drowned."

"The sharks may seize you, Tita. You had better give me the casket."

Tita smiled. "You would not like to lose that, eh? though you care little about losing me. And yet you told me that you loved me!"

"And I do love you, Tita! light of my eyes! life of my heart! I swear, by all the saints, I love you. I will marry you, I swear I will—I will swear on the crucifix, if you like!"

"Swear, then, or I do not give you the casket," said she, holding out the little crucifix round her neck, and devouring him with the wild eyes of passionate unreasoning tropic love.

He swore, trembling, and deadly pale.

"Give me your dagger."

"No, not mine. It may be found. I shall be suspected. What if my sheath were seen to be empty?"

"Your knife will do. His throat is soft enough."

And she glided stealthily as a cat toward the hammock, while her cowardly companion stood shivering at the other end of the cabin, and turned his back to her, that he might not see the deed.

He stood waiting, one minute—two—five? Was it an hour, rather? A cold sweat bathed his limbs; the blood beat so fiercely within his temples, that his head rang again. Was that a death-bell tolling? No; it was the pulses of his brain. Impossible, surely, a death-bell. Whence could it come?

There was a struggle—ah! she was about it now; a stifled cry—Ah! he had dreaded that most of all, to hear the old man cry. Would there be much blood? He hoped not. Another struggle, and Tita's voice, apparently muffled, called for help.

"I cannot help you. Mother of Mercies! I dare not help you!" hissed he. "She-devil! you have begun it, and you must finish it yourself!"

A heavy arm from behind clasped his throat. The bishop had broken loose from her and seized him! Or was it his ghost? or a fiend come to drag him down to the pit? And forgetting all but mere wild terror, he opened his lips for a scream, which would have wakened every soul on board. But a handkerchief was thrust into his mouth and in another minute he found himself bound hand and foot, and laid upon the table by a gigantic enemy. The cabin was full of armed men, two of whom were lashing up the bishop in his hammock; two more had seized Tita; and more were clambering up into the stern-gallery beyond, wild figures, with bright blades and armor gleaming in the starlight.

"Now, Will," whispered the giant who had seized him, "forward and clap the fore-hatches on; and shout Fire! with all your might. Girl! murderess! your life is in my hands. Tell me where the commander sleeps, and I pardon you."

Tita looked up at the huge speaker, and obeyed in silence. The intendant heard him enter the colonel's cabin, and then a short scuffle, and silence for a moment.

But only for a moment; for already the alarm had been given, and mad confusion reigned through every deck. Amyas (for it was none other) had already gained the poop; the sentinels were gagged and bound; and every half-naked wretch who came trembling up on deck in his shirt by the main hatchway, calling one, "Fire!" another, "Wreck!" and another, "Treason!" was hurled into the scuppers, and there secured.

"Lower away that boat!" shouted Amyas in Spanish to his first batch of prisoners.

The men, unarmed and naked, could but obey.

"Now then, jump in. Here, hand them to the gangway as they come up."

It was done; and as each appeared he was kicked to the scuppers, and bundled down over the side.

"She's full. Cast loose now and off with you. If you try to board again we'll sink you."

"Fire! fire!" shouted Cary, forward. "Up the main hatchway for your lives!"

The ruse succeeded utterly; and before half-an-hour was over, all the ship's boats which could be lowered were filled with Spaniards in their shirts, getting ashore as best they could.

"Here is a new sort of camisado," quoth Cary. "The last Spanish one I saw was at the sortie from Smerwick: but this is somewhat more prosperous than that."

"Get the main and foresail up, Will!" said Amyas, "cut the cable; and we will plume the quarry as we fly."

"Spoken like a good falconer. Heaven grant that this big woodcock may carry a good trail inside!"

"I'll warrant her for that," said Jack Brimblecombe. "She floats so low."

"Much of your build, too, Jack. By the by, where is the commander?"

Alas! Don Pedro, forgotten in the bustle, had been lying on the deck in his shirt, helplessly bound, exhausting that part of his vocabulary which related to the unseen world. Which most discourteous act seemed at first likely to be somewhat heavily avenged on Amyas; for as he spoke, a couple of caliver-shots, fired from under the poop, passed "ping" "ping" by his ears, and Cary clapped his hand to his side.

"Hurt, Will?"

"A pinch, old lad—Look out, or we are 'allen verloren' after all, as the Flemings say."

And as he spoke, a rush forward on the poop drove two of their best men down the ladder into the waist, where Amyas stood.

"Killed?" asked he, as he picked one up, who had fallen head over heels.

"Sound as a bell, sir: but they Gentiles has got hold of the firearms, and set the captain free."

And rubbing the back of his head for a minute, he jumped up the ladder again, shouting—

"Have at ye, idolatrous pagans! Have at ye, Satan's spawn!"

Amyas jumped up after him, shouting to all hands to follow; for there was no time to be lost.

Out of the windows of the poop, which looked on the main-deck, a galling fire had been opened, and he could not afford to lose men; for, as far as he knew, the Spaniards left on board might still far outnumber the English; so up he sprang on the poop, followed by a dozen men, and there began a very heavy fight between two parties of valiant warriors, who easily knew each other apart by the peculiar fashion of their armor. For the Spaniards fought in their shirts, and in no other garments: but the English in all other manner of garments, tag, rag, and bobtail; and yet had never a shirt between them.

The rest of the English made a rush, of course, to get upon the poop, seeing that the Spaniards could not shoot them through the deck; but the fire from the windows was so hot, that although they dodged behind masts, spars, and every possible shelter, one or two dropped; and Jack Brimblecombe and Yeo took on themselves to call a retreat, and with about a dozen men, got back, and held a council of war.

What was to be done? Their arquebuses were of little use; for the Spaniards were behind a strong bulkhead. There were cannon: but where was powder or shot? The boats, encouraged by the clamor on deck, were paddling alongside again. Yeo rushed round and round, probing every gun with his sword.

"Here's a patararo loaded! Now for a match, lads."

Luckily one of the English had kept his match alight during the scuffle.

"Thanks be! Help me to unship the gun—the mast's in the way here."

The patararo, or brass swivel, was unshipped.

"Steady, lads, and keep it level, or you'll shake out the priming. Ship it here; turn out that one, and heave it into that boat, if they come alongside. Steady now—so! Rummage about, and find me a bolt or two, a marlin-spike, anything. Quick, or the captain will be over-mastered yet."

Missiles were found—odds and ends—and crammed into the swivel up to the muzzle: and, in another minute, its "cargo of notions" was crashing into the poop-windows, silencing the fire from thence effectually enough for the time.

"Now, then, a rush forward, and right in along the deck!" shouted Yeo; and the whole party charged through the cabin-doors, which their shot had burst open, and hewed their way from room to room.

In the meanwhile, the Spaniards above had fought fiercely: but, in spite of superior numbers, they had gradually given back before the "demoniacal possession of those blasphemous heretics, who fought, not like men, but like furies from the pit." And by the time that Brimblecombe and Yeo shouted from the stern-gallery below that the quarter-deck was won, few on either side but had their shrewd scratch to show.

"Yield, senor!" shouted Amyas to the commander, who had been fighting like a lion, back to back with the captain of mariners.

"Never! You have bound me, and insulted me! Your blood or mine must wipe out the stain!"

And he rushed on Amyas. There was a few moments' heavy fence between them; and then Amyas cut right at his head. But as he raised his arm, the Spaniard's blade slipped along his ribs, and snapped against the point of his shoulder-blade. An inch more to the left, and it would have been through his heart. The blow fell, nevertheless, and the commandant fell with it, stunned by the flat of the sword, but not wounded; for Amyas's hand had turned, as he winced from his wound. But the sea-captain, seeing Amyas stagger, sprang at him, and, seizing him by the wrist, ere he could raise his sword again, shortened his weapon to run him through. Amyas made a grasp at his wrist in return, but, between his faintness and the darkness, missed it.—Another moment, and all would have been over!

A bright blade flashed close past Amyas's ear; the sea-captain's grasp loosened, and he dropped a corpse; while over him, like an angry lioness above her prey, stood Ayacanora, her long hair floating in the wind, her dagger raised aloft, as she looked round, challenging all and every one to approach.

"Are you hurt?" panted she.

"A scratch, child.—What do you do here? Go back, go back."

Ayacanora slipped back like a scolded child, and vanished in the darkness.

The battle was over. The Spaniards, seeing their commanders fall, laid down their arms, and cried for quarter. It was given; the poor fellows were tied together, two and two, and seated in a row on the deck; the commandant, sorely bruised, yielded himself perforce; and the galleon was taken.

Amyas hurried forward to get the sails set. As he went down the poop-ladder, there was some one sitting on the lowest step.

"Who is here—wounded?"

"I am not wounded," said a woman's voice, low, and stifled with sobs.

It was Ayacanora. She rose, and let him pass. He saw that her face was bright with tears; but he hurried on, nevertheless.

"Perhaps I did speak a little hastily to her, considering she saved my life; but what a brimstone it is! Mary Ambree in a dark skin! Now then, lads! Get the Santa Fe gold up out of the canoes, and then we will put her head to the north-east, and away for Old England. Mr. Brimblecombe! don't say that Eastward-ho don't bring luck this time."

It was impossible, till morning dawned, either to get matters into any order, or to overhaul the prize they had taken; and many of the men were so much exhausted that they fell fast asleep on the deck ere the surgeon had time to dress their wounds. However, Amyas contrived, when once the ship was leaping merrily, close-hauled against a fresh land-breeze, to count his little flock, and found out of the forty-four but six seriously wounded, and none killed. However, their working numbers were now reduced to thirty-eight, beside the four negroes, a scanty crew enough to take home such a ship to England.

After awhile, up came Jack Brimblecombe on deck, a bottle in his hand.

"Lads, a prize!"

"Well, we know that already."

"Nay, but—look hither, and laid in ice, too, as I live, the luxurious dogs! But I had to fight for it, I had. For when I went down into the state cabin, after I had seen to the wounded; whom should I find loose but that Indian lass, who had just unbound the fellow you caught—"

"Ah! those two, I believe, were going to murder the old man in the hammock, if we had not come in the nick of time. What have you done with them?"

"Why, the Spaniard ran when he saw me, and got into a cabin; but the woman, instead of running, came at me with a knife, and chased me round the table like a very cat-a-mountain. So I ducked under the old man's hammock, and out into the gallery; and when I thought the coast was clear, back again I came, and stumbled over this. So I just picked it up, and ran on deck with my tail between my legs, for I expected verily to have the black woman's knife between my ribs out of some dark corner."

"Well done, Jack! Let's have the wine, nevertheless, and then down to set a guard on the cabin doors for fear of plundering."

"Better go down, and see that nothing is thrown overboard by Spaniards. As for plundering, I will settle that."

And Amyas walked forward among the men.

"Muster the men, boatswain, and count them."

"All here, sir, but the six poor fellows who are laid forward."

"Now, my men," said Amyas, "for three years you and I have wandered on the face of the earth, seeking our fortune, and we have found it at last, thanks be to God! Now, what was our promise and vow which we made to God beneath the tree of Guayra, if He should grant us good fortune, and bring us home again with a prize? Was it not, that the dead should share with the living; and that every man's portion, if he fell, should go to his widow or his orphans, or if he had none, to his parents?"

"It was, sir," said Yeo, "and I trust that the Lord will give these men grace to keep their vow. They have seen enough of His providences by this time to fear Him."

"I doubt them not; but I remind them of it. The Lord has put into our hands a rich prize; and what with the gold which we have already, we are well paid for all our labors. Let us thank Him with fervent hearts as soon as the sun rises; and in the meanwhile, remember all, that whosoever plunders on his private account, robs not the adventurers merely, but the orphan and the widow, which is to rob God; and makes himself partaker of Achan's curse, who hid the wedge of gold, and brought down God's anger on the whole army of Israel. For me, lest you should think me covetous, I could claim my brother's share; but I hereby give it up freely into the common stock, for the use of the whole ship's crew, who have stood by me through weal and woe, as men never stood before, as I believe, by any captain. So, now to prayers, lads, and then to eat our breakfast."

So, to the Spaniards' surprise (who most of them believed that the English were atheists), to prayers they went.

After which Brimblecombe contrived to inspire the black cook and the Portuguese steward with such energy that, by seven o'clock, the latter worthy appeared on deck, and, with profound reverences, announced to "The most excellent and heroical Senor Adelantado Captain Englishman," that breakfast was ready in the state-cabin.

"You will do us the honor of accompanying us as our guest, sir, or our host, if you prefer the title," said Amyas to the commandant, who stood by.

"Pardon, senor: but honor forbids me to eat with one who has offered to me the indelible insult of bonds."

"Oh!" said Amyas, taking off his hat, "then pray accept on the spot my humble apologies for all which has passed, and my assurances that the indignities which you have unfortunately endured, were owing altogether to the necessities of war, and not to any wish to hurt the feelings of so valiant a soldier and gentleman."

"It is enough, senor," said the commandant, bowing and shrugging his shoulders—for, indeed, he too was very hungry; while Cary whispered to Amyas—

"You will make a courtier, yet, old lad."

"I am not in jesting humor, Will: my mind sadly misgives me that we shall hear black news, and have, perhaps, to do a black deed yet, on board here. Senor, I follow you."

So they went down, and found the bishop, who was by this time unbound, seated in a corner of the cabin, his hands fallen on his knees, his eyes staring on vacancy, while the two priests stood as close against the wall as they could squeeze themselves, keeping up a ceaseless mutter of prayers.

"Your holiness will breakfast with us, of course; and these two frocked gentlemen likewise. I see no reason for refusing them all hospitality, as yet."

There was a marked emphasis on the last two words, which made both monks wince.

"Our chaplain will attend to you, gentlemen. His lordship the bishop will do me the honor of sitting next to me."

The bishop seemed to revive slowly as he snuffed the savory steam; and at last, rising mechanically, subsided into the chair which Amyas offered him on his left, while the commandant sat on his right.

"A little of this kid, my lord? No—ah—Friday, I recollect. Some of that turtle-fin, then. Will, serve his lordship; pass the cassava-bread up, Jack! Senor commandant! a glass of wine? You need it after your valiant toils. To the health of all brave soldiers—and a toast from your own Spanish proverb, 'To-day to me, tomorrow to thee!'"

"I drink it, brave senor. Your courtesy shows you the worthy countryman of General Drake, and his brave lieutenant."

"Drake! Did you know him, senor?" asked all the Englishmen at once.

"Too well, too well—" and he would have continued; but the bishop burst out—

"Ah, senor commandant! that name again! Have you no mercy? To sit between another pair of—, and my own wine, too! Ugh, ugh!"

The old gentleman, whose mouth had been full of turtle the whole time, burst into a violent fit of coughing, and was only saved from apoplexy by Cary's patting him on the back.

"Ugh, ugh! The tender mercies of the wicked are cruel, and their precious balms. Ah, senor lieutenant Englishman! May I ask you to pass those limes?—Ah! what is turtle without lime?—Even as a fat old man without money! Nudus intravi, nudus exeo—ah!"

"But what of Drake?"

"Do you not know, sir, that he and his fleet, only last year, swept the whole of this coast, and took, with shame I confess it, Cartagena, San Domingo, St. Augustine, and—I see you are too courteous, senors, to express before me what you have a right to feel. But whence come you, sir? From the skies, or the depth of the sea?"

"Art-magic, art-magic!" moaned the bishop.

"Your holiness! It is scarcely prudent to speak thus here," said the commandant, who was nevertheless much of the same opinion.

"Why, you said so yourself, last night, senor, about the taking of Cartagena."

The commandant blushed, and stammered out somewhat—"That it was excusable in him, if he had said, in jest, that so prodigious and curious a valor had not sprung from mortal source."

"No more it did, senor," said Jack Brimblecombe, stoutly: "but from Him who taught our 'hands to war, and our fingers to fight.'"

The commandant bowed stiffly. "You will excuse me, sir preacher: but I am a Catholic, and hold the cause of my king to be alone the cause of Heaven. But, senor captain, how came you thither, if I may ask? That you needed no art-magic after you came on board, I, alas! can testify but too well: but what spirit—whether good or evil, I ask not—brought you on board, and whence? Where is your ship? I thought that all Drake's squadron had left six months ago."

"Our ship, senor, has lain this three years rotting on the coast near Cape Codera."

"Ah! we heard of that bold adventure—but we thought you all lost in the interior."

"You did? Can you tell me, then, where the senor governor of La Guayra may be now?"

"The Senor Don Guzman de Soto," said the commandant, in a somewhat constrained tone, "is said to be at present in Spain, having thrown up his office in consequence of domestic matters, of which I have not the honor of knowing anything."

Amyas longed to ask more: but he knew that the well-bred Spaniard would tell him nothing which concerned another man's wife; and went on.

"What befell us after, I tell you frankly."

And Amyas told his story, from the landing at Guayra to the passage down the Magdalena. The commandant lifted up his hands.

"Were it not forbidden to me, as a Catholic, most invincible senor, I should say that the Divine protection has indeed—"

"Ah," said one of the friars, "that you could be brought, senors, to render thanks for your miraculous preservation to her to whom alone it is due, Mary, the fount of mercies!"

"We have done well enough without her as yet," said Amyas, bluntly.

"The Lord raised up Nebuchadnezzar of old to punish the sins of the Jewish Church; and He has raised up these men to punish ours!" said Fray Gerundio.

"But Nebuchadnezzar fell, and so may they," growled the other to himself. Jack overheard him.

"I say, my lord bishop," called he from the other end of the table. "It is our English custom to let our guests be as rude as they like; but perhaps your lordship will hint to these two friars, that if they wish to keep whole skins, they will keep civil tongues."

"Be silent, asses! mules!" shouted the bishop, whose spirits were improving over the wine, "who are you, that you cannot eat dirt as well as your betters?"

"Well spoken, my lord. Here's the health of our saintly and venerable guest," said Cary: while the commandant whispered to Amyas, "Fat old tyrant! I hope you have found his money—for I am sure he has some on board, and I should be loath that you lost the advantage of it."

"I shall have to say a few words to you about that money this morning, commandant: by the by, they had better be said now. My lord bishop, do you know that had we not taken this ship when we did, you had lost not merely money, as you have now, but life itself?"

"Money? I had none to lose! Life?—what do you mean?" asked the bishop, turning very pale.

"This, sir. That it ill befits one to lie, whose throat has been saved from the assassin's knife but four hours since. When we entered the stern-gallery, we found two persons, now on board this ship, in the very act, sir, and article, of cutting your sinful throat, that they might rob you of the casket which lay beneath your pillow. A moment more, and you were dead. We seized and bound them, and so saved your life. Is that plain, sir?"

The bishop looked steadfastly and stupidly into Amyas's face, heaved a deep sigh, and gradually sank back in his chair, dropping the glass from his hand.

"He is in a fit! Call in the surgeon! Run!" and up jumped kind-hearted Jack, and brought in the surgeon of the galleon.

"Is this possible, senor?" asked the commandant.

"It is true. Door, there! Evans! go and bring in that rascal whom we left bound in his cabin!"

Evans went, and the commandant continued—

"But the stern-gallery? How, in the name of all witches and miracles, came your valor thither?"

"Simply enough, and owing neither to witch nor miracle. The night before last we passed the mouth of the bay in our two canoes, which we had lashed together after the fashion I had seen in the Moluccas, to keep them afloat in the surf. We had scraped the canoes bright the day before, and rubbed them with white clay, that they might be invisible at night; and so we got safely to the Morro Grande, passing within half a mile of your ship."

"Oh! my scoundrels of sentinels!"

"We landed at the back of the Morro, and lay there all day, being purposed to do that which, with your pardon, we have done. We took our sails of Indian cloth, whitened them likewise with clay which we had brought with us from the river (expecting to find a Spanish ship as we went along the coast, and determined to attempt her, or die with honor), and laid them over us on the canoes, paddling from underneath them. So that, had your sentinels been awake, they would have hardly made us out, till we were close on board. We had provided ourselves, instead of ladders, with bamboos rigged with cross-pieces, and a hook of strong wood at the top of each; they hang at your stern-gallery now. And the rest of the tale I need not tell you."

The commandant rose in his courtly Spanish way,—

"Your admirable story, senor, proves to me how truly your nation, while it has yet, and I trust will ever have, to dispute the palm of valor with our own, is famed throughout the world for ingenuity, and for daring beyond that of mortal man. You have succeeded, valiant captain, because you have deserved to succeed; and it is no shame to me to succumb to enemies who have united the cunning of the serpent with the valor of the lion. Senor, I feel as proud of becoming your guest as I should have been proud, under a happier star, of becoming your host."

"You are, like your nation, only too generous, senor. But what noise is that outside? Cary, go and see."

But ere Cary could reach the door, it was opened; and Evans presented himself with a terrified face.

"Here's villainy, sir! The Don's murdered, and cold; the Indian lass fled; and as we searched the ship for her, we found an Englishwoman, as I'm a sinful man!—and a shocking sight she is to see!"

"An Englishwoman?" cried all three, springing forward.

"Bring her in!" said Amyas, turning very pale; and as he spoke, Yeo and another led into the cabin a figure scarcely human.

An elderly woman, dressed in the yellow "San Benito" of the Inquisition, with ragged gray locks hanging about a countenance distorted by suffering and shrunk by famine. Painfully, as one unaccustomed to the light, she peered and blinked round her. Her fallen lip gave her a half-idiotic expression; and yet there was an uneasy twinkle in the eye, as of boundless terror and suspicion. She lifted up her fettered wrist to shade her face; and as she did so, disclosed a line of fearful scars upon her skinny arm.

"Look there, sirs!" said Yeo, pointing to them with a stern smile. "Here's some of these Popish gentry's handiwork. I know well enough how those marks came;" and he pointed to the similar scars on his own wrist.

The commandant, as well as the Englishmen, recoiled with horror.

"Holy Virgin! what wretch is this on board my ship? Bishop, is this the prisoner whom you sent on board?"

The bishop, who had been slowly recovering his senses, looked at her a moment; and then thrusting his chair back, crossed himself, and almost screamed, "Malefica! Malefica! Who brought her here? Turn her away, gentlemen; turn her eye away; she will bewitch, fascinate"—and he began muttering prayers.

Amyas seized him by the shoulder, and shook him on to his legs.

"Swine! who is this? Wake up, coward, and tell me, or I will cut you piecemeal!"

But ere the bishop could answer, the woman uttered a wild shriek, and pointing to the taller of the two monks, cowered behind Yeo.

"He here?" cried she, in broken Spanish. "Take me away! I will tell you no more. I have told you all, and lies enough beside. Oh! why is he come again? Did they not say that I should have no more torments?"

The monk turned pale: but like a wild beast at bay, glared firmly round on the whole company; and then, fixing his dark eyes full on the woman, he bade her be silent so sternly, that she shrank down like a beaten hound.

"Silence, dog!" said Will Cary, whose blood was up, and followed his words with a blow on the monk's mouth, which silenced him effectually.

"Don't be afraid, good woman, but speak English. We are all English here, and Protestants too. Tell us what they have done for you."

"Another trap! another trap!" cried she, in a strong Devonshire accent. "You be no English! You want to make me lie again, and then torment me. Oh! wretched, wretched that I am!" cried she, bursting into tears. "Whom should I trust? Not myself: no, nor God; for I have denied Him! O Lord! O Lord!"

Amyas stood silent with fear and horror; some instinct told him that he was on the point of hearing news for which he feared to ask. But Jack spoke—

"My dear soul! my dear soul! don't you be afraid; and the Lord will stand by you, if you will but tell the truth. We are all Englishmen, and men of Devon, as you seem to be by your speech; and this ship is ours; and the pope himself sha'n't touch you."

"Devon?" she said doubtingly; "Devon! Whence, then?"

"Bideford men. This is Mr. Will Cary, to Clovelly. If you are a Devon woman, you've heard tell of the Carys, to be sure."

The woman made a rush forward, and threw her fettered arms round Will's neck,—

"Oh, Mr. Cary, my dear life! Mr. Cary! and so you be! Oh, dear soul alive! but you're burnt so brown, and I be 'most blind with misery. Oh, who ever sent you here, my dear Mr. Will, then, to save a poor wretch from the pit?"

"Who on earth are you?"

"Lucy Passmore, the white witch to Welcombe. Don't you mind Lucy Passmore, as charmed your warts for you when you was a boy?"

"Lucy Passmore!" almost shrieked all three friends. "She that went off with—"

"Yes! she that sold her own soul, and persuaded that dear saint to sell hers; she that did the devil's work, and has taken the devil's wages;—after this fashion!" and she held up her scarred wrists wildly.

"Where is Dona de—Rose Salterne?" shouted Will and Jack.

"Where is my brother Frank?" shouted Amyas.

"Dead, dead, dead!"

"I knew it," said Amyas, sitting down again calmly.

"How did she die?"

"The Inquisition—he!" pointing to the monk. "Ask him—he betrayed her to her death. And ask him!" pointing to the bishop; "he sat by her and saw her die."

"Woman, you rave!" said the bishop, getting up with a terrified air, and moving as far as possible from Amyas.

"How did my brother die, Lucy?" asked Amyas, still calmly.

"Who be you, sir?"

A gleam of hope flashed across Amyas—she had not answered his question.

"I am Amyas Leigh of Burrough. Do you know aught of my brother Frank, who was lost at La Guayra?"

"Mr. Amyas! Heaven forgive me that I did not know the bigness of you. Your brother, sir, died like a gentleman as he was."

"But how?" gasped Amyas.

"Burned with her, sir!"

"Is this true, sir?" said Amyas, turning to the bishop, with a very quiet voice.

"I, sir?" stammered he, in panting haste. "I had nothing to do—I was compelled in my office of bishop to be an unwilling spectator—the secular arm, sir; I could not interfere with that—any more than I can with the Holy Office. I do not belong to it—ask that gentleman—sir! Saints and angels, sir! what are you going to do?" shrieked he, as Amyas laid a heavy hand upon his shoulder, and began to lead him towards the door.

"Hang you!" said Amyas. "If I had been a Spaniard and a priest like yourself, I should have burnt you alive."

"Hang me?" shrieked the wretched old Balaam; and burst into abject howls for mercy.

"Take the dark monk, Yeo, and hang him too. Lucy Passmore, do you know that fellow also?"

"No, sir," said Lucy.

"Lucky for you, Fray Gerundio," said Will Cary; while the good friar hid his face in his hands, and burst into tears. Lucky it was for him, indeed; for he had been a pitying spectator of the tragedy. "Ah!" thought he, "if life in this mad and sinful world be a reward, perhaps this escape is vouchsafed to me for having pleaded the cause of the poor Indian!"

But the bishop shrieked on.

"Oh! not yet. An hour, only an hour! I am not fit to die."

"That is no concern of mine," said Amyas. "I only know that you are not fit to live."

"Let us at least make our peace with God," said the dark monk.

"Hound! if your saints can really smuggle you up the back-stairs to heaven, they will do it without five minutes' more coaxing and flattering."

Fray Gerundio and the condemned man alike stopped their ears at the blasphemy.

"Oh, Fray Gerundio!" screamed the bishop, "pray for me. I have treated you like a beast. Oh, Fray, Fray!"

"Oh, my lord! my lord!" said the good man, as with tears streaming down his face he followed his shrieking and struggling diocesan up the stairs, "who am I? Ask no pardon of me. Ask pardon of God for all your sins against the poor innocent savages, when you saw your harmless sheep butchered year after year, and yet never lifted up your voice to save the flock which God had committed to you. Oh, confess that, my lord! confess it ere it be too late!"

"I will confess all about the Indians, and the gold, and Tita too, Fray; peccavi, peccavi—only five minutes, senors, five little minutes' grace, while I confess to the good Fray!"—and he grovelled on the deck.

"I will have no such mummery where I command," said Amyas, sternly. "I will be no accomplice in cheating Satan of his due."

"If you will confess," said Brimblecombe, whose heart was melting fast, "confess to the Lord, and He will forgive you. Even at the last moment mercy is open. Is it not, Fray Gerundio?"

"It is, senor; it is, my lord," said Gerundio; but the bishop only clasped his hands over his head.

"Then I am undone! All my money is stolen! Not a farthing left to buy masses for my poor soul! And no absolution, no viaticum, nor anything! I die like a dog and am damned!"

"Clear away that running rigging!" said Amyas, while the dark Dominican stood perfectly collected, with something of a smile of pity at the miserable bishop. A man accustomed to cruelty, and firm in his fanaticism, he was as ready to endure suffering as to inflict it; repeating to himself the necessary prayers, he called Fray Gerundio to witness that he died, however unworthy, a martyr, in charity with all men, and in the communion of the Holy Catholic Church; and then, as he fitted the cord to his own neck, gave Fray Gerundio various petty commissions about his sister and her children, and a little vineyard far away upon the sunny slopes of Castile; and so died, with a "Domine, in manus tuas," like a valiant man of Spain.

Amyas stood long in solemn silence, watching the two corpses dangling above his head. At last he drew a long breath, as if a load was taken off his heart.

Suddenly he looked round to his men, who were watching eagerly to know what he would have done next.

"Hearken to me, my masters all, and may God hearken too, and do so to me, and more also, if, as long as I have eyes to see a Spaniard, and hands to hew him down, I do any other thing than hunt down that accursed nation day and night, and avenge all the innocent blood which has been shed by them since the day in which King Ferdinand drove out the Moors!"

"Amen!" said Salvation Yeo. "I need not to swear that oath, for I have sworn it long ago, and kept it. Will your honor have us kill the rest of the idolaters?"

"God forbid!" said Cary. "You would not do that, Amyas?"

"No; we will spare them. God has shown us a great mercy this day, and we must be merciful in it. We will land them at Cabo Velo. But henceforth till I die no quarter to a Spaniard."

"Amen!" said Yeo.

Amyas's whole countenance had changed in the last half-hour. He seemed to have grown years older. His brow was wrinkled, his lip compressed, his eyes full of a terrible stony calm, as of one who had formed a great and dreadful purpose, and yet for that very reason could afford to be quiet under the burden of it, even cheerful; and when he returned to the cabin he bowed courteously to the commandant, begged pardon of him for having played the host so ill, and entreated him to finish his breakfast.

"But, senor—is it possible? Is his holiness dead?"

"He is hanged and dead, senor. I would have hanged, could I have caught them, every living thing which was present at my brother's death, even to the very flies upon the wall. No more words, senor; your conscience tells you that I am just."

"Senor," said the commandant—"one word—I trust there are no listeners—none of my crew, I mean; but I must exculpate myself in your eyes."

"Walk out, then, into the gallery with me."

"To tell you the truth, senor—I trust in Heaven no one overhears.—You are just. This Inquisition is the curse of us, the weight which is crushing out the very life of Spain. No man dares speak. No man dares trust his neighbor, no, not his child, or the wife of his bosom. It avails nothing to be a good Catholic, as I trust I am," and he crossed himself, "when any villain whom you may offend, any unnatural son or wife who wishes to be rid of you, has but to hint heresy against you, and you vanish into the Holy Office—and then God have mercy on you, for man has none. Noble ladies of my family, sir, have vanished thither, carried off by night, we know not why; we dare not ask why. To expostulate, even to inquire, would have been to share their fate. There is one now, senor—Heaven alone knows whether she is alive or dead!—It was nine years since, and we have never heard; and we shall never hear."

And the commandant's face worked frightfully.

"She was my sister, senor!"

"Heavens! sir, and have you not avenged her?"

"On churchmen, senor, and I a Catholic? To be burned at the stake in this life, and after that to all eternity beside? Even a Spaniard dare not face that. Beside, sir, the mob like this Inquisition, and an Auto-da-fe is even better sport to them than a bull-fight. They would be the first to tear a man in pieces who dare touch an Inquisitor. Sir, may all the saints in heaven obtain me forgiveness for my blasphemy, but when I saw you just now fearing those churchmen no more than you feared me, I longed, sinner that I am, to be a heretic like you."

"It will not take long to make a brave and wise gentleman who has suffered such things as you have, a heretic, as you call it—a free Christian man, as we call it."

"Tempt me not, sir!" said the poor man, crossing himself fervently. "Let us say no more. Obedience is my duty; and for the rest the Church must decide, according to her infallible authority—for I am a good Catholic, senor, the best of Catholics, though a great sinner.—I trust no one has overheard us!"

Amyas left him with a smile of pity, and went to look for Lucy Passmore, whom the sailors were nursing and feeding, while Ayacanora watched them with a puzzled face.

"I will talk to you when you are better, Lucy," said he, taking her hand. "Now you must eat and drink, and forget all among us lads of Devon."

"Oh, dear blessed sir, and you will send Sir John to pray with me? For I turned, sir, I turned: but I could not help it—I could not abear the torments: but she bore them, sweet angel—and more than I did. Oh, dear me!"

"Lucy, I am not fit now to hear more. You shall tell me all to-morrow;" and he turned away.

"Why do you take her hand?" said Ayacanora, half-scornfully. "She is old, and ugly, and dirty."

"She is an Englishwoman, child, and a martyr, poor thing; and I would nurse her as I would my own mother."

"Why don't you make me an Englishwoman, and a martyr? I could learn how to do anything that that old hag could do!"

"Instead of calling her names, go and tend her; that would be much fitter work for a woman than fighting among men."

Ayacanora darted from him, thrust the sailors aside, and took possession of Lucy Passmore.

"Where shall I put her?" asked she of Amyas, without looking up.

"In the best cabin; and let her be served like a queen, lads."

"No one shall touch her but me;" and taking up the withered frame in her arms, as if it were a doll, Ayacanora walked off with her in triumph, telling the men to go and mind the ship.

"The girl is mad," said one.

"Mad or not, she has an eye to our captain," said another.

"And where's the man that would behave to the poor wild thing as he does?"

"Sir Francis Drake would, from whom he got his lesson. Do you mind his putting the negro lass ashore after he found out about—"

"Hush! Bygones be bygones, and those that did it are in their graves long ago. But it was too hard of him on the poor thing."

"If he had not got rid of her, there would have been more throats than one cut about the lass, that's all I know," said another; "and so there would have been about this one before now, if the captain wasn't a born angel out of heaven, and the lieutenant no less."

"Well, I suppose we may get a whet by now. I wonder if these Dons have any beer aboard."

"Naught but grape vinegar, which fools call wine, I'll warrant."

"There was better than vinegar on the table in there just now."

"Ah," said one grumbler of true English breed, "but that's not for poor fellows like we."

"Don't lie, Tom Evans; you never were given that way yet, and I don't think the trade will suit a good fellow like you."

The whole party stared; for the speaker of these words was none other than Amyas himself, who had rejoined them, a bottle in each hand.

"No, Tom Evans. It has been share and share alike for three years, and bravely you have all held up, and share alike it shall be now, and here's the handsel of it. We'll serve out the good wine fairly all round as long as it lasts, and then take to the bad: but mind you don't get drunk, my sons, for we are much too short of hands to have any stout fellows lying about the scuppers."

But what was the story of the intendant's being murdered? Brimblecombe had seen him run into a neighboring cabin; and when the door of it was opened, there was the culprit, but dead and cold, with a deep knife-wound in his side. Who could have done the deed? It must have been Tita, whom Brimblecombe had seen loose, and trying to free her lover.

The ship was searched from stem to stern: but no Tita. The mystery was never explained. That she had leapt overboard, and tried to swim ashore, none doubted: but whether she had reached it, who could tell? One thing was strange; that not only had she carried off no treasure with her, but that the gold ornaments which she had worn the night before, lay together in a heap on the table, close by the murdered man. Had she wished to rid herself of everything which had belonged to her tyrants?

The commandant heard the whole story thoughtfully.

"Wretched man!" said he, "and he has a wife and children in Seville."

"A wife and children?" said Amyas; "and I heard him promise marriage to the Indian girl."

That was the only hint which gave a reason for his death. What if, in the terror of discovery and capture, the scoundrel had dropped any self-condemning words about his marriage, any prayer for those whom he had left behind, and the Indian had overheard them? It might be so; at least sin had brought its own punishment.

And so that wild night and day subsided. The prisoners were kindly used enough; for the Englishman, free from any petty love of tormenting, knows no mean between killing a foe outright, and treating him as a brother; and when, two days afterwards, they were sent ashore in the canoes off Cabo Velo, captives and captors shook hands all round; and Amyas, after returning the commandant his sword, and presenting him with a case of the bishop's wine, bowed him courteously over the side.

"I trust that you will pay us another visit, valiant senor capitan," said the Spaniard, bowing and smiling.

"I should most gladly accept your invitation, illustrious senor commandant; but as I have vowed henceforth, whenever I shall meet a Spaniard, neither to give nor take quarter, I trust that our paths to glory may lie in different directions."

The commandant shrugged his shoulders; the ship was put again before the wind, and as the shores of the Main faded lower and dimmer behind her, a mighty cheer broke from all on board; and for once the cry from every mouth was Eastward-ho!

Scrap by scrap, as weakness and confusion of intellect permitted her, Lucy Passmore told her story. It was a simple one after all, and Amyas might almost have guessed it for himself. Rose had not yielded to the Spaniard without a struggle. He had visited her two or three times at Lucy's house (how he found out Lucy's existence she herself could never tell, unless from the Jesuits) before she agreed to go with him. He had gained Lucy to his side by huge promises of Indian gold; and, in fine, they had gone to Lundy, where the lovers were married by a priest, who was none other, Lucy would swear, than the shorter and stouter of the two who had carried off her husband and his boat—in a word, Father Parsons.

Amyas gnashed his teeth at the thought that he had had Parsons in his power at Brenttor down, and let him go. It was a fresh proof to him that Heaven's vengeance was upon him for letting one of its enemies escape. Though what good to Rose or Frank the hanging of Parsons would have been, I, for my part, cannot see.

But when had Eustace been at Lundy? Lucy could throw no light on that matter. It was evidently some by-thread in the huge spider's web of Jesuit intrigue, which was, perhaps, not worth knowing after all.

They sailed from Lundy in a Portugal ship, were at Lisbon a few days (during which Rose and Lucy remained on board), and then away for the West Indies; while all went merry as a marriage bell. "Sir, he would have kissed the dust off her dear feet, till that evil eye of Mr. Eustace's came, no one knew how or whence." And, from that time, all went wrong. Eustace got power over Don Guzman, whether by threatening that the marriage should be dissolved, whether by working on his superstitious scruples about leaving his wife still a heretic, or whether (and this last Lucy much suspected) by insinuations that her heart was still at home in England, and that she was longing for Amyas and his ship to come and take her home again; the house soon became a den of misery, and Eustace the presiding evil genius. Don Guzman had even commanded him to leave it—and he went; but, somehow, within a week he was there again, in greater favor than ever. Then came preparations to meet the English, and high words about it between Don Guzman and Rose; till a few days before Amyas's arrival, the Don had dashed out of the house in a fury, saying openly that she preferred these Lutheran dogs to him, and that he would have their hearts' blood first, and hers after.

The rest was soon told. Amyas knew but too much of it already. The very morning after he had gone up to the villa, Lucy and her mistress were taken (they knew not by whom) down to the quay, in the name of the Holy Office, and shipped off to Cartagena.

There they were examined, and confronted on a charge of witchcraft, which the wretched Lucy could not well deny. She was tortured to make her inculpate Rose; and what she said, or did not say, under the torture, the poor wretch could never tell. She recanted, and became a Romanist; Rose remained firm. Three weeks afterwards, they were brought out to an Auto-da-fe; and there, for the first time, Lucy saw Frank walking, dressed in a San Benito, in that ghastly procession. Lucy was adjudged to receive publicly two hundred stripes, and to be sent to "The Holy House" at Seville to perpetual prison. Frank and Rose, with a renegade Jew, and a negro who had been convicted of practising "Obi," were sentenced to death as impenitent, and delivered over to the secular arm, with prayers that there might be no shedding of blood. In compliance with which request, the Jew and the negro were burnt at one stake, Frank and Rose at another. She thought they did not feel it more than twenty minutes. They were both very bold and steadfast, and held each other's hand (that she would swear to) to the very last.

And so ended Lucy Passmore's story. And if Amyas Leigh, after he had heard it, vowed afresh to give no quarter to Spaniards wherever he should find them, who can wonder, even if they blame?

CHAPTER XXVII: HOW SALVATION YEO FOUND HIS LITTLE MAID AGAIN

And so Ayacanora took up her abode in Lucy's cabin, as a regularly accredited member of the crew.

But a most troublesome member; for now began in her that perilous crisis which seems to endanger the bodies and souls of all savages and savage tribes, when they first mingle with the white man; that crisis which, a few years afterwards, began to hasten the extermination of the North American tribes; and had it not been for the admirable good sense and constancy of Amyas, Ayacanora might have ended even more miserably than did the far-famed Pocahontas, daughter of the Virginian king; who, after having been received at Court by the old pedant James the First, with the honors of a sister sovereign, and having become the reputed ancestress of more than one ancient Virginian family, ended her days in wretchedness in some Wapping garret.

For the mind of the savage, crushed by the sight of the white man's superior skill, and wealth, and wisdom, loses at first its self-respect; while his body, pampered with easily obtained luxuries, instead of having to win the necessaries of life by heavy toil, loses its self-helpfulness; and with self-respect and self-help vanish all the savage virtues, few and flimsy as they are, and the downward road toward begging and stealing, sottishness and idleness, is easy, if not sure.

And down that road, it really seemed at first, that poor Ayacanora was walking fast. For the warrior-prophetess of the Omaguas soon became, to all appearance, nothing but a very naughty child; and the Diana of the Meta, after she had satisfied her simple wonder at the great floating house by rambling from deck to deck, and peeping into every cupboard and cranny, manifested a great propensity to steal and hide (she was too proud or too shy to ask for) every trumpery which smit her fancy; and when Amyas forbade her to take anything without leave, threatened to drown herself, and went off and sulked all day in her cabin. Nevertheless, she obeyed him, except in the matter of sweet things. Perhaps she craved naturally for the vegetable food of her native forests; at all events the bishop's stores of fruit and sweetmeats diminished rapidly; and what was worse, so did the sweet Spanish wine which Amyas had set apart for poor Lucy's daily cordial. Whereon another severe lecture, in which Amyas told her how mean it was to rob poor sick Lucy; whereat she, as usual, threatened to drown herself; and was running upon deck to do it, when Amyas caught her and forgave her. On which a violent fit of crying, and great penitence and promises; and a week after, Amyas found that she had cheated Satan and her own conscience by tormenting the Portuguese steward into giving her some other wine instead: but luckily for her, she found Amyas's warnings about wine making her mad so far fulfilled, that she did several foolish things one evening, and had a bad headache next morning; so the murder was out, and Amyas ordered the steward up for a sound flogging; but Ayacanora, honorably enough, not only begged him off, but offered to be whipped instead of him, confessing that the poor fellow spoke truly when he swore that she had threatened to kill him, and that he had given her the wine in bodily fear for his life.

However, her own headache and Amyas's cold looks were lesson enough, and after another attempt to drown herself, the wilful beauty settled down for awhile; and what was better, could hardly be persuaded, thenceforth to her dying day, to touch fermented liquors.

But, in the meanwhile, poor Amyas had many a brains-beating as to how he was to tame a lady who, on the least provocation, took refuge in suicide. Punish her he dared not, even if he had the heart. And as for putting her ashore, he had an instinct, and surely not a superstitious one, that her strange affection for the English was not unsent by Heaven, and that God had committed her into his charge, and that He would require an account at his hands of the soul of that fair lost lamb.

So, almost at his wits' end, he prayed to God, good simple fellow, and that many a time, to show him what he should do with her before she killed either herself, or what was just as likely, one of the crew; and it seemed best to him to make Parson Jack teach her the rudiments of Christianity, that she might be baptized in due time when they got home to England.

But here arose a fresh trouble—for she roundly refused to learn of Jack, or of any one but Amyas himself; while he had many a good reason for refusing the office of schoolmaster; so, for a week or two more, Ayacanora remained untaught, save in the English tongue, which she picked up with marvellous rapidity.

And next, as if troubles would never end, she took a violent dislike, not only to John Brimblecombe, whose gait and voice she openly mimicked for the edification of the men; but also to Will Cary, whom she never allowed to speak to her or approach her. Perhaps she was jealous of his intimacy with Amyas; or perhaps, with the subtle instinct of a woman, she knew that he was the only other man on board who might dare to make love to her (though Will, to do him justice, was as guiltless of any such intention as Amyas himself). But when she was remonstrated with, her only answer was that Cary was a cacique as well as Amyas, and that there ought not to be two caciques; and one day she actually proposed to Amyas to kill his supposed rival, and take the ship all to himself; and sulked for several days at hearing Amyas, amid shouts of laughter, retail her precious advice to its intended victim.

Moreover, the negroes came in for their share, being regarded all along by her with an unspeakable repugnance, which showed itself at first in hiding from them whenever she could, and, afterwards, in throwing at them everything she could lay hands on, till the poor Quashies, in danger of their lives, complained to Amyas, and got rest for awhile.

Over the rest of the sailors she lorded it like a very princess, calling them from their work to run on her errands and make toys for her, enforcing her commands now and then by a shrewd box on the ears; while the good fellows, especially old Yeo, like true sailors, petted her, obeyed her, even jested with her, much as they might have done with a tame leopard, whose claws might be unsheathed and about their ears at any moment. But she amused them, and amused Amyas too. They must of course have a pet; and what prettier one could they have? And as for Amyas, the constant interest of her presence, even the constant anxiety of her wilfulness, kept his mind busy, and drove out many a sad foreboding about that meeting with his mother, and the tragedy which he had to tell her, which would otherwise, so heavily did they weigh on him, have crushed his spirit with melancholy, and made all his worldly success and marvellous deliverance worthless in his eyes.

At last the matter, as most things luckily do, came to a climax; and it came in this way.

The ship had been slipping along now for many a day, slowly but steadily before a favorable breeze. She had passed the ring of the West India islands, and was now crawling, safe from all pursuit, through the vast weed-beds of the Sargasso Sea. There, for the first time, it was thought safe to relax the discipline which had been hitherto kept up, and to "rummage" (as was the word in those days) their noble prize. What they found, of gold and silver, jewels, and merchandise, will interest no readers. Suffice it to say, that there was enough there, with the other treasure, to make Amyas rich for life, after all claims of Cary's and the crew, not forgetting Mr. Salterne's third, as owner of the ship, had been paid off. But in the captain's cabin were found two chests, one full of gorgeous Mexican feather dresses, and the other of Spanish and East Indian finery, which, having come by way of Havana and Cartagena, was going on, it seemed, to some senora or other at the Caracas. Which two chests were, at Cary's proposal, voted amid the acclamations of the crew to Ayacanora, as her due and fit share of the pillage, in consideration of her Amazonian prowess and valuable services.

So the poor child took greedy possession of the trumpery, had them carried into Lucy's cabin, and there knelt gloating over them many an hour. The Mexican work she chose to despise as savage; but the Spanish dresses were a treasure; and for two or three days she appeared on the quarter-deck, sunning herself like a peacock before the eyes of Amyas in Seville mantillas, Madrid hats, Indian brocade farthingales, and I know not how many other gewgaws, and dare not say how put on.

The crew tittered: Amyas felt much more inclined to cry. There is nothing so pathetic as a child's vanity, saving a grown person aping a child's vanity; and saving, too, a child's agony of disappointment when it finds that it has been laughed at instead of being admired. Amyas would have spoken, but he was afraid: however, the evil brought its own cure. The pageant went on, as its actor thought, most successfully for three days or so; but at last the dupe, unable to contain herself longer, appealed to Amyas,—"Ayacanora quite English girl now; is she not?"—heard a titter behind her, looked round, saw a dozen honest faces in broad grin, comprehended all in a moment, darted down the companion-ladder, and vanished.

Amyas, fully expecting her to jump overboard, followed as fast as he could. But she had locked herself in with Lucy, and he could hear her violent sobs, and Lucy's faint voice entreating to know what was the matter.

In vain he knocked. She refused to come out all day, and at even they were forced to break the door open, to prevent Lucy being starved.

There sat Ayacanora, her finery half torn off, and scattered about the floor in spite, crying still as if her heart would break; while poor Lucy cried too, half from fright and hunger, and half for company.

Amyas tried to comfort the poor child, assured her that the men should never laugh at her again; "But then," added he, "you must not be so—so—" What to say he hardly knew.

"So what?" asked she, crying more bitterly than ever.

"So like a wild girl, Ayacanora."

Her hands dropped on her knees: a strong spasm ran through her throat and bosom, and she fell on her knees before him, and looked up imploringly in his face.

"Yes; wild girl—poor, bad wild girl. . . . But I will be English girl now!"

"Fine clothes will never make you English, my child," said Amyas.

"No! not English clothes—English heart! Good heart, like yours! Yes, I will be good, and Sir John shall teach me!"

"There's my good maid," said Amyas. "Sir John shall begin and teach you to-morrow."

"No! Now! now! Ayacanora cannot wait. She will drown herself if she is bad another day! Come, now!"

And she made him fetch Brimblecombe, heard the honest fellow patiently for an hour or more, and told Lucy that very night all that he had said. And from that day, whenever Jack went in to read and pray with the poor sufferer, Ayacanora, instead of escaping on deck as before, stood patiently trying to make it all out, and knelt when he knelt, and tried to pray too—that she might have an English heart; and doubtless her prayers, dumb as they were, were not unheard.

So went on a few days more, hopefully enough, without any outbreak, till one morning, just after they had passed the Sargasso-beds. The ship was taking care of herself; the men were all on deck under the awning, tinkering, and cobbling, and chatting; Brimblecombe was catechising his fair pupil in the cabin; Amyas and Cary, cigar in mouth, were chatting about all heaven and earth, and, above all, of the best way of getting up a fresh adventure against the Spaniards as soon as they returned; while Amyas was pouring out to Will that dark hatred of the whole nation, that dark purpose of revenge for his brother and for Rose, which had settled down like a murky cloud into every cranny of his heart and mind. Suddenly there was a noise below; a scuffle and a shout, which made them both leap to their feet; and up on deck rushed Jack Brimblecombe, holding his head on with both his hands.

"Save me! save me from that she-fiend! She is possessed with a legion! She has broken my nose—torn out half my hair!—and I'm sure I have none to spare! Here she comes! Stand by me, gentlemen both! Satanas, I defy thee!" And Jack ensconced himself behind the pair, as Ayacanora whirled upon deck like a very Maenad, and, seeing Amyas, stopped short.

"If you had defied Satan down below there," said Cary, with a laugh, "I suspect he wouldn't have broken out on you so boldly, Master Jack."

"I am innocent—innocent as the babe unborn! Oh! Mr. Cary! this is too bad of you, sir!" quoth Jack indignantly, while Amyas asked what was the matter.

"He looked at me," said she, sturdily.

"Well, a cat may look at a king."

"But he sha'n't look at Ayacanora. Nobody shall but you, or I'll kill him!"

In vain Jack protested his innocence of having even looked at her. The fancy (and I verily believe it was nothing more) had taken possession of her. She refused to return below to her lesson. Jack went off grumbling, minus his hair, and wore a black eye for a week after.

"At all events," quoth Cary, re-lighting his cigar, "it's a fault on the right side."

"God give me grace, or it may be one on the wrong side for me."

"He will, old heart-of-oak!" said Cary, laying his arm around Amyas's neck, to the evident disgust of Ayacanora, who went off to the side, got a fishing-line, and began amusing herself therewith, while the ship slipped on quietly and silently as ever, save when Ayacanora laughed and clapped her hands at the flying-fish scudding from the bonitos. At last, tired of doing nothing, she went forward to the poop-rail to listen to John Squire the armorer, who sat tinkering a headpiece, and humming a song, mutato nomine, concerning his native place—

"'Tis Sunderland, John Squire, to the song, and not Bidevor," said his mate.

"Well, Bidevor's so good as Sunderland any day, for all there's no say-coals there blacking a place about; and makes just so good harmonies, Tommy Hamblyn—

Here Yeo broke in—

"Aren't you ashamed, John Squire, to your years, singing such carnal vanities, after all the providences you have seen? Let the songs of Zion be in your mouth, man, if you must needs keep a caterwauling all day like that."

"You sing 'em yourself then, gunner."

"Well," says Yeo, "and why not?" And out he pulled his psalm-book, and began a scrap of the grand old psalm—

"Humph!" said John Squire. "Very good and godly: but still I du like a merry catch now and then, I du. Wouldn't you let a body sing 'Rumbelow'—even when he's heaving of the anchor?"

"Well, I don't know," said Yeo; "but the Lord's people had better praise the Lord then too, and pray for a good voyage, instead of howling about—

"Is that fit talk for immortal souls? How does that child's-trade sound beside the Psalms, John Squire?"

Now it befell that Salvation Yeo, for the very purpose of holding up to ridicule that time-honored melody, had put into it the true nasal twang, and rung it out as merrily as he had done perhaps twelve years before, when he got up John Oxenham's anchor in Plymouth Sound. And it befell also that Ayacanora, as she stood by Amyas's side, watching the men, and trying to make out their chat, heard it, and started; and then, half to herself, took up the strain, and sang it over again, word for word, in the very same tune and tone.

Salvation Yeo started in his turn, and turned deadly pale.

"Who sung that?" he asked quickly.

"The little maid here. She's coming on nicely in her English," said Amyas.

"The little maid?" said Yeo, turning paler still. "Why do you go about to scare an old servant, by talking of little maids, Captain Amyas? Well," he said aloud to himself, "as I am a sinful saint, if I hadn't seen where the voice came from, I could have sworn it was her; just as we taught her to sing it by the river there, I and William Penberthy of Marazion, my good comrade. The Lord have mercy on me!"

All were silent as the grave whenever Yeo made any allusion to that lost child. Ayacanora only, pleased with Amyas's commendation, went humming on to herself—

Yeo started up from the gun where he sat.

"I can't abear it! As I live, I can't! You, Indian maiden, where did you learn to sing that there?"

Ayacanora looked up at him, half frightened by his vehemence, then at Amyas, to see if she had been doing anything wrong; and then turned saucily away, looked over the side, and hummed on.

"Ask her, for mercy's sake—ask her, Captain Leigh!"

"My child," said Amyas, speaking in Indian, "how is it you sing that so much better than any other English? Did you ever hear it before?"

Ayacanora looked up at him puzzled, and shook her head; and then—

"If you tell Indian to Ayacanora, she dumb. She must be English girl now, like poor Lucy."

"Well then," said Amyas, "do you recollect, Ayacanora—do you recollect—what shall I say? anything that happened when you were a little girl?"

She paused awhile; and then moving her hands overhead—

"Trees—great trees like the Magdalena—always nothing but trees—wild and bad everything. Ayacanora won't talk about that."

"Do you mind anything that grew on those trees?" asked Yeo, eagerly.

She laughed. "Silly! Flowers and fruit, and nuts—grow on all trees, and monkey-cups too. Ayacanora climbed up after them—when she was wild. I won't tell any more."

"But who taught you to call them monkey-cups?" asked Yeo, trembling with excitement.

"Monkey's drink; mono drink."

"Mono?" said Yeo, foiled on one cast, and now trying another. "How did you know the beasts were called monos?"

"She might have heard it coming down with us," said Cary, who had joined the group.

"Ay, monos," said she, in a self-justifying tone. "Faces like little men, and tails. And one very dirty black one, with a beard, say Amen in a tree to all the other monkeys, just like Sir John on Sunday."

This allusion to Brimblecombe and the preaching apes upset all but old Yeo.

"But don't you recollect any Christians?—white people?"

She was silent.

"Don't you mind a white lady?"

"Um?"

"A woman, a very pretty woman, with hair like his?" pointing to Amyas.

"No."

"What do you mind, then, beside those Indians?" added Yeo, in despair.

She turned her back on him peevishly, as if tired with the efforts of her memory.

"Do try to remember," said Amyas; and she set to work again at once.

"Ayacanora mind great monkeys—black, oh, so high," and she held up her hand above her head, and made a violent gesture of disgust.

"Monkeys? what, with tails?"

"No, like man. Ah! yes—just like Cooky there—dirty Cooky!"

And that hapless son of Ham, who happened to be just crossing the main-deck, heard a marlingspike, which by ill luck was lying at hand, flying past his ears.

"Ayacanora, if you heave any more things at Cooky, I must have you whipped," said Amyas, without, of course, any such intention.

"I'll kill you, then," answered she, in the most matter-of-fact tone.

"She must mean negurs," said Yeo; "I wonder where she saw them, now. What if it were they Cimaroons?"

"But why should any one who had seen whites forget them, and yet remember negroes?" asked Cary.

"Let us try again. Do you mind no great monkeys but those black ones?" asked Amyas.

"Yes," she said, after a while,—"devil."

"Devil?" asked all three, who, of course, were by no means free from the belief that the fiend did actually appear to the Indian conjurors, such as had brought up the girl.

"Ay, him Sir John tell about on Sundays."

"Save and help us!" said Yeo; "and what was he like unto?"

She made various signs to intimate that he had a monkey's face, and a gray beard like Yeo's. So far so good: but now came a series of manipulations about her pretty little neck, which set all their fancies at fault.

"I know," said Cary, at last, bursting into a great laugh. "Sir Urian had a ruff on, as I live! Trunk-hose too, my fair dame? Stop—I'll make sure. Was his neck like the senor commandant's, the Spaniard?"

Ayacanora clapped her hands at finding herself understood, and the questioning went on.

"The 'devil' appeared like a monkey, with a gray beard, in a ruff;—humph!—"

"Ay!" said she in good enough Spanish, "Mono de Panama; viejo diablo de Panama."

Yeo threw up his hands with a shriek—"Oh Lord of all mercies! Those were the last words of Mr. John Oxenham! Ay—and the devil is surely none other than the devil Don Francisco Xararte! Oh dear! oh dear! oh dear! my sweet young lady! my pretty little maid! and don't you know me? Don't you know Salvation Yeo, that carried you over the mountains, and used to climb for the monkey-cups for you, my dear young lady? And William Penberthy too, that used to get you flowers; and your poor dear father, that was just like Mr. Cary there, only he had a black beard, and black curls, and swore terribly in his speech, like a Spaniard, my dear young lady?"

And the honest fellow, falling on his knees, covered Ayacanora's hands with kisses; while all the crew, fancying him gone suddenly mad, crowded aft.

"Steady, men, and don't vex him!" said Amyas. "He thinks that he has found his little maid at last."

"And so do I, Amyas, as I live," said Cary.

"Steady, steady, my masters all! If this turn out a wrong scent after all, his wits will crack. Mr. Yeo, can't you think of any other token?"

Yeo stamped impatiently. "What need then? it's her, I tell ye, and that's enough! What a beauty she's grown! Oh dear! where were my eyes all this time, to behold her, and not to see her! 'Tis her very mortal self, it is! And don't you mind me, my dear, now? Don't you mind Salvation Yeo, that taught you to sing 'Heave my mariners all, O!' a-sitting on a log by the boat upon the sand, and there was a sight of red lilies grew on it in the moss, dear, now, wasn't there? and we made posies of them to put in your hair, now?"—And the poor old man ran on in a supplicating, suggestive tone, as if he could persuade the girl into becoming the person whom he sought.

Ayacanora had watched him, first angry, then amused, then attentive, and at last with the most intense earnestness. Suddenly she grew crimson, and snatching her hands from the old man's, hid her face in them, and stood.

"Do you remember anything of all this, my child?" asked Amyas, gently.

She lifted up her eyes suddenly to his, with a look of imploring agony, as if beseeching him to spare her. The death of a whole old life, the birth of a whole new life, was struggling in that beautiful face, choking in that magnificent throat, as she threw back her small head, and drew in her breath, and dashed her locks back from her temples, as if seeking for fresh air. She shuddered, reeled, then fell weeping on the bosom, not of Salvation Yeo, but of Amyas Leigh.

He stood still a minute or two, bearing that fair burden, ere he could recollect himself. Then,—

"Ayacanora, you are not yet mistress of yourself, my child. You were better to go down, and see after poor Lucy, and we will talk about it all to-morrow."

She gathered herself up instantly, and with eyes fixed on the deck slid through the group, and disappeared below.

"Ah!" said Yeo, with a tone of exquisite sadness; "the young to the young! Over land and sea, in the forests and in the galleys, in battle and prison, I have sought her! And now!—"

"My good friend," said Amyas, "neither are you master of yourself yet. When she comes round again, whom will she love and thank but you?"

"You, sir! She owes all to you; and so do I. Let me go below, sir. My old wits are shaky. Bless you, sir, and thank you for ever and ever!"

And Yeo grasped Amyas's hand, and went down to his cabin, from which he did not reappear for many hours.

From that day Ayacanora was a new creature. The thought that she was an Englishwoman; that she, the wild Indian, was really one of the great white people whom she had learned to worship, carried in it some regenerating change: she regained all her former stateliness, and with it a self-restraint, a temperance, a softness which she had never shown before. Her dislike to Cary and Jack vanished. Modest and distant as ever, she now took delight in learning from them about England and English people; and her knowledge of our customs gained much from the somewhat fantastic behaviour which Amyas thought good, for reasons of his own, to assume toward her. He assigned her a handsome cabin to herself, always addressed her as madam, and told Cary, Brimblecombe, and the whole crew that as she was a lady and a Christian, he expected them to behave to her as such. So there was as much bowing and scraping on the poop as if it had been a prince's court: and Ayacanora, though sorely puzzled and chagrined at Amyas's new solemnity, contrived to imitate it pretty well (taking for granted that it was the right thing); and having tolerable masters in the art of manners (for both Amyas and Cary were thoroughly well-bred men), profited much in all things, except in intimacy with Amyas, who had, cunning fellow, hit on this parade of good manners, as a fresh means of increasing the distance between him and her. The crew, of course, though they were a little vexed at losing their pet, consoled themselves with the thought that she was a "real born lady," and Mr. Oxenham's daughter, too; and there was not a man on board who did not prick up his ears for a message if she approached him, or one who would not have, I verily believe, jumped overboard to do her a pleasure.

Only Yeo kept sorrowfully apart. He never looked at her, spoke to her, met her even, if he could. His dream had vanished. He had found her! and after all, she did not care for him? Why should she?

But it was hard to have hunted a bubble for years, and have it break in his hand at last. "Set not your affections on things on the earth," murmured Yeo to himself, as he pored over his Bible, in the vain hope of forgetting his little maid.

But why did Amyas wish to increase the distance between himself and Ayacanora? Many reasons might be given: I deny none of them. But the main one, fantastic as it may seem, was simply, that while she had discovered herself to be an Englishwoman, he had discovered her to be a Spaniard. If her father were seven times John Oxenham (and even that the perverse fellow was inclined to doubt), her mother was a Spaniard—Pah! one of the accursed race; kinswoman—perhaps, to his brother's murderers! His jaundiced eyes could see nothing but the Spanish element in her; or, indeed, in anything else. As Cary said to him once, using a cant phrase of Sidney's, which he had picked up from Frank, all heaven and earth were "spaniolated," to him. He seemed to recollect nothing but that Heaven had "made Spaniards to be killed, and him to kill them." If he had not been the most sensible of John Bulls, he would certainly have forestalled the monomania of that young Frenchman of rank, who, some eighty years after him, so maddened his brain by reading of the Spanish cruelties, that he threw up all his prospects and turned captain of filibusters in the West Indies, for the express purpose of ridding them of their tyrants; and when a Spanish ship was taken, used to relinquish the whole booty to his crew, and reserve for himself only the pleasure of witnessing his victims' dying agonies.

But what had become of that bird-like song of Ayacanora's which had astonished them on the banks of the Meta, and cheered them many a time in their anxious voyage down the Magdalena? From the moment that she found out her English parentage, it stopped. She refused utterly to sing anything but the songs and psalms which she picked up from the English. Whether it was that she despised it as a relic of her barbarism, or whether it was too maddening for one whose heart grew heavier and humbler day by day, the nightingale notes were heard no more.

So homeward they ran, before a favoring southwest breeze: but long ere they were within sight of land, Lucy Passmore was gone to her rest beneath the Atlantic waves.

CHAPTER XXVIII: HOW AMYAS CAME HOME THE THIRD TIME

It is the evening of the 15th of February, 1587, and Mrs. Leigh (for we must return now to old scenes and old faces) is pacing slowly up and down the terrace-walk at Burrough, looking out over the winding river, and the hazy sand-hills, and the wide western sea, as she has done every evening, be it fair weather or foul, for three weary years. Three years and more are past and gone, and yet no news of Frank and Amyas, and the gallant ship and all the gallant souls therein; and loving eyes in Bideford and Appledore, Clovelly and Ilfracombe, have grown hollow with watching and with weeping for those who have sailed away into the West, as John Oxenham sailed before them, and have vanished like a dream, as he did, into the infinite unknown. Three weary years, and yet no word. Once there was a flush of hope, and good Sir Richard (without Mrs. Leigh's knowledge), had sent a horseman posting across to Plymouth, when the news arrived that Drake, Frobisher, and Carlisle had returned with their squadron from the Spanish Main. Alas! he brought back great news, glorious news; news of the sacking of Cartagena, San Domingo, Saint Augustine; of the relief of Raleigh's Virginian Colony: but no news of the Rose, and of those who had sailed in her. And Mrs. Leigh bowed her head, and worshipped, and said, "The Lord gave, and the Lord hath taken away; blessed be the name of the Lord!"

Her hair was now grown gray; her cheeks were wan; her step was feeble. She seldom went from home, save to the church, and to the neighboring cottages. She never mentioned her sons' names; never allowed a word to pass her lips, which might betoken that she thought of them; but every day, when the tide was high, and red flag on the sandhills showed that there was water over the bar, she paced the terrace-walk, and devoured with greedy eyes the sea beyond in search of the sail which never came. The stately ships went in and out as of yore; and white sails hung off the bar for many an hour, day after day, month after month, year after year: but an instinct within told her that none of them were the sails she sought. She knew that ship, every line of her, the cut of every cloth; she could have picked it out miles away, among a whole fleet, but it never came, and Mrs. Leigh bowed her head and worshipped, and went to and fro among the poor, who looked on her as an awful being, and one whom God had brought very near to Himself, in that mysterious heaven of sorrow which they too knew full well. And lone women and bed-ridden men looked in her steadfast eyes, and loved them, and drank in strength from them; for they knew (though she never spoke of her own grief) that she had gone down into the fiercest depths of the fiery furnace, and was walking there unhurt by the side of One whose form was as of the Son of God. And all the while she was blaming herself for her "earthly" longings, and confessing nightly to Heaven that weakness which she could not shake off, which drew her feet at each high tide to the terrace-walk beneath the row of wind-clipt trees.

But this evening Northam is in a stir. The pebble ridge is thundering far below, as it thundered years ago: but Northam is noisy enough without the rolling of the surge. The tower is rocking with the pealing bells: the people are all in the streets shouting and singing round bonfires. They are burning the pope in effigy, drinking to the queen's health, and "So perish all her enemies!" The hills are red with bonfires in every village; and far away, the bells of Bideford are answering the bells of Northam, as they answered them seven years ago, when Amyas returned from sailing round the world. For this day has come the news that Mary Queen of Scots is beheaded in Fotheringay; and all England, like a dreamer who shakes off some hideous nightmare, has leapt up in one tremendous shout of jubilation, as the terror and the danger of seventeen anxious years is lifted from its heart for ever.

Yes, she is gone, to answer at a higher tribunal than that of the Estates of England, for all the noble English blood which has been poured out for her; for all the noble English hearts whom she has tempted into treachery, rebellion, and murder. Elizabeth's own words have been fulfilled at last, after years of long-suffering,—

And now she can do evil no more. Murder and adultery, the heart which knew no forgiveness, the tongue which could not speak truth even for its own interest, have past and are perhaps atoned for; and her fair face hangs a pitiful dream in the memory even of those who knew that either she, or England, must perish.

And Mrs. Leigh, Protestant as she is, breathes a prayer, that the Lord may have mercy on that soul, as "clear as diamond, and as hard," as she said of herself. That last scene, too, before the fatal block—it could not be altogether acting. Mrs. Leigh had learned many a priceless lesson in the last seven years; might not Mary Stuart have learned something in seventeen? And Mrs. Leigh had been a courtier, and knew, as far as a chaste Englishwoman could know (which even in those coarser days was not very much), of that godless style of French court profligacy in which poor Mary had had her youthful training, amid the Medicis, and the Guises, and Cardinal Lorraine; and she shuddered, and sighed to herself"—To whom little is given, of them shall little be required!" But still the bells pealed on and would not cease.

What was that which answered them from afar out of the fast darkening twilight? A flash, and then the thunder of a gun at sea.

Mrs. Leigh stopped. The flash was right outside the bar. A ship in distress it could not be. The wind was light and westerly. It was a high spring-tide, as evening floods are always there. What could it be? Another flash, another gun. The noisy folks of Northam were hushed at once, and all hurried into the churchyard which looks down on the broad flats and the river.

There was a gallant ship outside the bar. She was running in, too, with all sails set. A large ship; nearly a thousand tons she might be; but not of English rig. What was the meaning of it? A Spanish cruiser about to make reprisals for Drake's raid along the Cadiz shore! Not that, surely. The Don had no fancy for such unscientific and dare-devil warfare. If he came, he would come with admiral, rear-admiral, and vice-admiral, transports, and avisos, according to the best-approved methods, articles, and science of war. What could she be?

Easily, on the flowing tide and fair western wind, she has slipped up the channel between the two lines of sandhill. She is almost off Appledore now. She is no enemy; and if she be a foreigner, she is a daring one, for she has never veiled her topsails,—and that, all know, every foreign ship must do within sight of an English port, or stand the chance of war; as the Spanish admiral found, who many a year since was sent in time of peace to fetch home from Flanders Anne of Austria, Philip the Second's last wife.

For in his pride he sailed into Plymouth Sound without veiling topsails, or lowering the flag of Spain. Whereon, like lion from his den, out rushed John Hawkins the port admiral, in his famous Jesus of Lubec (afterwards lost in the San Juan d'Ulloa fight), and without argument or parley, sent a shot between the admiral's masts; which not producing the desired effect, alongside ran bold Captain John, and with his next shot, so says his son, an eye-witness, "lackt the admiral through and through;" whereon down came the offending flag; and due apologies were made, but not accepted for a long time by the stout guardian of her majesty's honor. And if John Hawkins did as much for a Spanish fleet in time of peace, there is more than one old sea-dog in Appledore who will do as much for a single ship in time of war, if he can find even an iron pot to burn powder withal.

The strange sail passed out of sight behind the hill of Appledore; and then there rose into the quiet evening air a cheer, as from a hundred throats. Mrs. Leigh stood still, and listened. Another gun thundered among the hills; and then another cheer.

It might have been twenty minutes before the vessel hove in sight again round the dark rocks of the Hubbastone, as she turned up the Bideford river. Mrs. Leigh had stood that whole time perfectly motionless, a pale and scarcely breathing statue, her eyes fixed upon the Viking's rock.

Round the Hubbastone she came at last. There was music on board, drums and fifes, shawms and trumpets, which wakened ringing echoes from every knoll of wood and slab of slate. And as she opened full on Burrough House, another cheer burst from her crew, and rolled up to the hills from off the silver waters far below, full a mile away.

Mrs. Leigh walked quickly toward the house, and called her maid,—

"Grace, bring me my hood. Master Amyas is come home!"

"No, surely? O joyful sound! Praised and blessed be the Lord, then; praised and blessed be the Lord! But, madam, however did you know that?"

"I heard his voice on the river; but I did not hear Mr. Frank's with him, Grace!"

"Oh, be sure, madam, where the one is the other is. They'd never part company. Both come home or neither, I'll warrant. Here's your hood, madam."

And Mrs. Leigh, with Grace behind her, started with rapid steps towards Bideford.

Was it true? Was it a dream? Had the divine instinct of the mother enabled her to recognize her child's voice among all the rest, and at that enormous distance; or was her brain turning with the long effort of her supernatural calm?

Grace asked herself, in her own way, that same question many a time between Burrough and Bideford. When they arrived on the quay the question answered itself.

As they came down Bridgeland Street (where afterwards the tobacco warehouses for the Virginia trade used to stand, but which then was but a row of rope-walks and sailmakers' shops), they could see the strange ship already at anchor in the river. They had just reached the lower end of the street, when round the corner swept a great mob, sailors, women, 'prentices, hurrahing, questioning, weeping, laughing: Mrs. Leigh stopped; and behold, they stopped also.

"Here she is!" shouted some one; "here's his mother!"

"His mother? Not their mother!" said Mrs. Leigh to herself, and turned very pale; but that heart was long past breaking.

The next moment the giant head and shoulders of Amyas, far above the crowd, swept round the corner.

"Make a way! Make room for Madam Leigh!"—And Amyas fell on his knees at her feet.

She threw her arms round his neck, and bent her fair head over his, while sailors, 'prentices, and coarse harbor-women were hushed into holy silence, and made a ring round the mother and the son.

Mrs. Leigh asked no question. She saw that Amyas was alone.

At last he whispered, "I would have died to save him, mother, if I could."

"You need not tell me that, Amyas Leigh, my son."

Another silence.

"How did he die?" whispered Mrs. Leigh.

"He is a martyr. He died in the———"

Amyas could say no more.

"The Inquisition?"

"Yes."

A strong shudder passed through Mrs. Leigh's frame, and then she lifted up her head.

"Come home, Amyas. I little expected such an honor—such an honor—ha! ha! and such a fair young martyr, too; a very St. Stephen! God, have mercy on me; and let me not go mad before these folk, when I ought to be thanking Thee for Thy great mercies! Amyas, who is that?"

And she pointed to Ayacanora, who stood close behind Amyas, watching with keen eyes the whole.

"She is a poor wild Indian girl—my daughter, I call her. I will tell you her story hereafter."

"Your daughter? My grand-daughter, then. Come hither, maiden, and be my grand-daughter."

Ayacanora came obedient, and knelt down, because she had seen Amyas kneel.

"God forbid, child! kneel not to me. Come home, and let me know whether I am sane or mazed, alive or dead."

And drawing her hood over her face, she turned to go back, holding Amyas tight by one hand, and Ayacanora by the other.

The crowd let them depart some twenty yards in respectful silence, and then burst into a cheer which made the old town ring.

Mrs. Leigh stopped suddenly.

"I had forgotten, Amyas. You must not let me stand in the way of your duty. Where are your men?"

"Kissed to death by this time; all of them, that is, who are left."

"Left?"

"We went out a hundred, mother, and we came home forty-four—if we are at home. Is it a dream, mother? Is this you? and this old Bridgeland Street again? As I live, there stands Evans the smith, at his door, tankard in hand, as he did when I was a boy!"

The brawny smith came across the street to them; but stopped when he saw Amyas, but no

Frank.

"Better one than neither, madam!" said he, trying a rough comfort. Amyas shook his hand as he passed him; but Mrs. Leigh neither heard nor saw him nor any one.

"Mother," said Amyas, when they were now past the causeway, "we are rich for life."

"Yes; a martyr's death was the fittest for him."

"I have brought home treasure untold."

"What, my boy?"

"Treasure untold. Cary has promised to see to it to-night."

"Very well. I would that he had slept at our house. He was a kindly lad, and loved Frank. When did he?"—

"Three years ago, and more. Within two months of our sailing."

"Ah! Yes, he told me so."

"Told you so?"

"Yes; the dear lad has often come to see me in my sleep; but you never came. I guessed how it was—as it should be."

"But I loved you none the less, mother!"

"I know that, too: but you were busy with the men, you know, sweet; so your spirit could not come roving home like his, which was free. Yes—all as it should be. My maid, and do you not find it cold here in England, after those hot regions?"

"Ayacanora's heart is warm; she does not think about cold."

"Warm? perhaps you will warm my heart for me, then."

"Would God I could do it, mother!" said Amyas, half reproachfully.

Mrs. Leigh looked up in his face, and burst into a violent flood of tears.

"Sinful! sinful that I am!"

"Blessed creature!" cried Amyas, "if you speak so I shall go mad. Mother, mother, I have been dreading this meeting for months. It has been a nightmare hanging over me like a horrible black thunder-cloud; a great cliff miles high, with its top hid in the clouds, which I had to climb, and dare not. I have longed to leap overboard, and flee from it like a coward into the depths of the sea.—The thought that you might ask me whether I was not my brother's keeper—that you might require his blood at my hands—and now, now! when it comes! to find you all love, and trust, and patience—mother, mother, it's more than I can bear!" and he wept violently.

Mrs. Leigh knew enough of Amyas to know that any burst of this kind, from his quiet nature, betokened some very fearful struggle; and the loving creature forgot everything instantly, in the one desire to soothe him.

And soothe him she did; and home the two went, arm in arm together, while Ayacanora held fast, like a child, by the skirt of Mrs. Leigh's cloak. The self-help and daring of the forest nymph had given place to the trembling modesty of the young girl, suddenly cast on shore in a new world, among strange faces, strange hopes, and strange fears also.

"Will your mother love me?" whispered she to Amyas, as she went in.

"Yes; but you must do what she tells you."

Ayacanora pouted.

"She will laugh at me, because I am wild."

"She never laughs at any one."

"Humph!" said Ayacanora. "Well, I shall not be afraid of her. I thought she would have been tall like you; but she is not even as big as me."

This hardly sounded hopeful for the prospect of Ayacanora's obedience; but ere twenty-four hours had passed, Mrs. Leigh had won her over utterly; and she explained her own speech by saying that she thought so great a man ought to have a great mother. She had expected, poor thing, in her simplicity, some awful princess with a frown like Juno's own, and found instead a healing angel.

Her story was soon told to Mrs. Leigh, who of course, woman-like, would not allow a doubt as to her identity. And the sweet mother never imprinted a prouder or fonder kiss upon her son's forehead, than that with which she repaid his simple declaration, that he had kept unspotted, like a gentleman and a Christian, the soul which God had put into his charge.

"Then you have forgiven me, mother?"

"Years ago I said in this same room, what should I render to the Lord for having given me two such sons? And in this room I say it once again. Tell me all about my other son, that I may honor him as I honor you."

And then, with the iron nerve which good women have, she made him give her every detail of Lucy Passmore's story and of all which had happened from the day of their sailing to that luckless night at Guayra. And when it was done, she led Ayacanora out, and began busying herself about the girl's comforts, as calmly as if Frank and Amyas had been sleeping in their cribs in the next room.

But she had hardly gone upstairs, when a loud knock at the door was followed by its opening hastily; and into the hall burst, regardless of etiquette, the tall and stately figure of Sir Richard Grenville.

Amyas dropped on his knees instinctively. The stern warrior was quite unmanned; and as he bent over his godson, a tear dropped from that iron cheek, upon the iron cheek of Amyas Leigh.

"My lad! my glorious lad! and where have you been? Get up, and tell me all. The sailors told me a little, but I must hear every word. I knew you would do something grand. I told your mother you were too good a workman for God to throw away. Now, let me have the whole story. Why, I am out of breath! To tell truth, I ran three-parts of the way hither."

And down the two sat, and Amyas talked long into the night; while Sir Richard, his usual stateliness recovered, smiled stern approval at each deed of daring; and when all was ended, answered with something like a sigh:

"Would God that I had been with you every step! Would God, at least, that I could show as good a three-years' log-book, Amyas, my lad!"

"You can show a better one, I doubt not."

"Humph! With the exception of one paltry Spanish prize, I don't know that the queen is the better, or her enemies the worse, for me, since we parted last in Dublin city."

"You are too modest, sir."

"Would that I were; but I got on in Ireland, I found, no better than my neighbors; and so came home again, to find that while I had been wasting my time in that land of misrule, Raleigh had done a deed to which I can see no end. For, lad, he has found (or rather his two captains, Amadas and Barlow, have found for him) between Florida and Newfoundland, a country, the like of which, I believe, there is not on the earth for climate and fertility. Whether there be gold there, I know not, and it matters little; for there is all else on earth that man can want; furs, timber, rivers, game, sugar-canes, corn, fruit, and every commodity which France, Spain, or Italy can yield, wild in abundance; the savages civil enough for savages, and, in a word, all which goes to the making of as noble a jewel as her majesty's crown can wear. The people call it Wingandacoa; but we, after her majesty, Virginia."

"You have been there, then?"

"The year before last, lad; and left there Ralf Lane, Amadas, and some twenty gentlemen, and ninety men, and, moreover, some money of my own, and some of old Will Salterne's, which neither of us will ever see again. For the colony, I know not how, quarrelled with the Indians (I fear I too was over-sharp with some of them for stealing—if I was, God forgive me!), and could not, forsooth, keep themselves alive for twelve months; so that Drake, coming back from his last West Indian voyage, after giving them all the help he could, had to bring the whole party home. And if you will believe it, the faint-hearted fellows had not been gone a fortnight, before I was back again with three ships and all that they could want. And never was I more wroth in my life, when all I found was the ruins of their huts, which (so rich is the growth there) were already full of great melons, and wild deer feeding thereon—a pretty sight enough, but not what I wanted just then. So back I came; and being in no overgood temper, vented my humors on the Portugals at the Azores, and had hard fights and small booty. So there the matter stands, but not for long; for shame it were if such a paradise, once found by Britons, should fall into the hands of any but her majesty; and we will try again this spring, if men and money can be found. Eh, lad?"

"But the prize?"

"Ah! that was no small make-weight to our disasters, after all. I sighted her for six days' sail from the American coast: but ere we could lay her aboard it fell dead calm. Never a boat had I on board—they were all lost in a gale of wind—and the other ships were becalmed two leagues astern of me. There was no use lying there and pounding her till she sank; so I called the carpenter, got up all the old chests, and with them and some spars we floated ourselves alongside, and only just in time. For the last of us had hardly scrambled up into the chains, when our crazy Noah's ark went all aboard, and sank at the side, so that if we had been minded to run away, Amyas, we could not; whereon, judging valor to be the better part of discretion (as I usually do), we fell to with our swords and had her in five minutes, and fifty thousand pounds' worth in her, which set up my purse again, and Raleigh's too, though I fear it has run out again since as fast as it ran in."

And so ended Sir Richard's story.

Amyas went the next day to Salterne, and told his tale. The old man had heard the outlines of it already: but he calmly bade him sit down, and listened to all, his chin upon his hand, his elbows on his knees. His cheek never blanched, his lips never quivered throughout. Only when Amyas came to Rose's marriage, he heaved a long breath, as if a weight was taken off his heart.

"Say that again, sir!"

Amyas said it again, and then went on; faltering, he hinted at the manner of her death.

"Go on, sir! Why are you afraid? There is nothing to be ashamed of there, is there?"

Amyas told the whole with downcast eyes, and then stole a look at his hearer's face. There was no sign of emotion: only somewhat of a proud smile curled the corners of that iron mouth.

"And her husband?" asked he, after a pause.

"I am ashamed to have to tell you, sir, that the man still lives."

"Still lives, sir?"

"Too true, as far as I know. That it was not my fault, my story bears me witness."

"Sir, I never doubted your will to kill him. Still lives, you say? Well, so do rats and adders. And now, I suppose, Captain Leigh, your worship is minded to recruit yourself on shore a while with the fair lass whom you have brought home (as I hear) before having another dash at the devil and his kin!"

"Do not mention that young lady's name with mine, sir; she is no more to me than she is to you; for she has Spanish blood in her veins."

Salterne smiled grimly.

"But I am minded at least to do one thing, Mr. Salterne, and that is, to kill Spaniards, in fair fight, by land and sea, wheresoever I shall meet them. And, therefore, I stay not long here, whithersoever I may be bound next."

"Well, sir, when you start, come to me for a ship, and the best I have is at your service; and, if she do not suit, command her to be fitted as you like best; and I, William Salterne, will pay for all which you shall command to be done."

"My good sir, I have accounts to square with you after a very different fashion. As part-adventurer in the Rose, I have to deliver to you your share of the treasure which I have brought home."

"My share, sir? If I understood you, my ship was lost off the coast of the Caracas three years agone, and this treasure was all won since?"

"True; but you, as an adventurer in the expedition, have a just claim for your share, and will receive it."

"Captain Leigh, you are, I see, as your father was before you, a just and upright Christian man: but, sir, this money is none of mine, for it was won in no ship of mine.—Hear me, sir! And if it had been, and that ship"—(he could not speak her name)—"lay safe and sound now by Bideford quay, do you think, sir, that William Salterne is the man to make money out of his daughter's sin and sorrow, and to handle the price of blood? No, sir! You went like a gentleman to seek her, and like a gentleman, as all the world knows, you have done your best, and I thank you: but our account ends there. The treasure is yours, sir; I have enough, and more than enough, and none, God help me, to leave it to, but greedy and needy kin, who will be rather the worse than the better for it. And if I have a claim in law for aught—which I know not, neither shall ever ask—why, if you are not too proud, accept that claim as a plain burgher's thank-offering to you, sir, for a great and a noble love which you and your brother have shown to one who, though I say it, to my shame, was not worthy thereof."

"She was worthy of that and more, sir. For if she sinned like a woman, she died like a saint."

"Yes, sir!" answered the old man, with a proud smile; "she had the right English blood in her, I doubt not; and showed it at the last. But now, sir, no more of this. When you need a ship, mine is at your service; till then, sir, farewell, and God be with you."

And the old man rose, and with an unmoved countenance, bowed Amyas to the door. Amyas went back and told Cary, bidding him take half of Salterne's gift: but Cary swore a great oath that he would have none of it.

"Heir of Clovelly, Amyas, and want to rob you? I who have lost nothing,—you who have lost a brother! God forbid that I should ever touch a farthing beyond my original share!"

That evening a messenger from Bideford came running breathlessly up to Burrough Court. The authorities wanted Amyas's immediate attendance, for he was one of the last, it seemed, who had seen Mr. Salterne alive.

Salterne had gone over, as soon as Amyas departed, to an old acquaintance; signed and sealed his will in their presence with a firm and cheerful countenance, refusing all condolence; and then gone home, and locked himself into Rose's room. Supper-time came, and he did not appear. The apprentices could not make him answer, and at last called in the neighbors, and forced the door. Salterne was kneeling by his daughter's bed; his head was upon the coverlet; his Prayer-book was open before him at the Burial Service; his hands were clasped in supplication; but he was dead and cold.

His will lay by him. He had left all his property among his poor relations, saving and excepting all money, etc., due to him as owner and part-adventurer of the ship Rose, and his new bark of three hundred tons burden, now lying East-the-water; all which was bequeathed to Captain Amyas Leigh, on condition that he should re-christen that bark the Vengeance,—fit her out with part of the treasure, and with her sail once more against the Spaniard, before three years were past.

And this was the end of William Salterne, merchant.

CHAPTER XXIX: HOW THE VIRGINIA FLEET WAS STOPPED BY THE QUEEN'S COMMAND

And now Amyas is settled quietly at home again; and for the next twelve months little passes worthy of record in these pages. Yeo has installed himself as major domo, with no very definite functions, save those of walking about everywhere at Amyas's heels like a lank gray wolf-hound, and spending his evenings at the fireside, as a true old sailor does, with his Bible on his knee, and his hands busy in manufacturing numberless nicknacks, useful and useless, for every member of the family, and above all for Ayacanora, whom he insults every week by humbly offering some toy only fit for a child; at which she pouts, and is reproved by Mrs. Leigh, and then takes the gift, and puts it away never to look at it again. For her whole soul is set upon being an English maid; and she runs about all day long after Mrs. Leigh, insisting upon learning the mysteries of the kitchen and the still-room, and, above all, the art of making clothes for herself, and at last for everybody in Northam. For first, she will be a good housewife, like Mrs. Leigh; and next a new idea has dawned on her: that of helping others. To the boundless hospitality of the savage she has been of course accustomed: but to give to those who can give nothing in return, is a new thought. She sees Mrs. Leigh spending every spare hour in working for the poor, and visiting them in their cottages. She sees Amyas, after public thanks in church for his safe return, giving away money, food, what not, in Northam, Appledore, and Bideford; buying cottages and making them almshouses for worn-out mariners; and she is told that this is his thank-offering to God. She is puzzled; her notion of a thank-offering was rather that of the Indians, and indeed of the Spaniards,—sacrifices of human victims, and the bedizenment of the Great Spirit's sanctuary with their skulls and bones. Not that Amyas, as a plain old-fashioned churchman, was unmindful of the good old instinctive rule, that something should be given to the Church itself; for the vicar of Northam was soon resplendent with a new surplice, and what was more, the altar with a splendid flagon and salver of plate (lost, I suppose, in the civil wars) which had been taken in the great galleon. Ayacanora could understand that: but the almsgiving she could not, till Mrs. Leigh told her, in her simple way, that whosoever gave to the poor, gave to the Great Spirit; for the Great Spirit was in them, and in Ayacanora too, if she would be quiet and listen to him, instead of pouting, and stamping, and doing nothing but what she liked. And the poor child took in that new thought like a child, and worked her fingers to the bone for all the old dames in Northam, and went about with Mrs. Leigh, lovely and beloved, and looked now and then out from under her long black eyelashes to see if she was winning a smile from Amyas. And on the day on which she won one, she was good all day; and on the day on which she did not, she was thoroughly naughty, and would have worn out the patience of any soul less chastened than Mrs. Leigh's. But as for the pomp and glory of her dress, there was no keeping it within bounds; and she swept into church each Sunday bedizened in Spanish finery, with such a blaze and rustle, that the good vicar had to remonstrate humbly with Mrs. Leigh on the disturbance which she caused to the eyes and thoughts of all his congregation. To which Ayacanora answered, that she was not thinking about them, and they need not think about her; and that if the Piache (in plain English, the conjuror), as she supposed, wanted a present, he might have all her Mexican feather-dresses; she would not wear them—they were wild Indian things, and she was an English maid—but they would just do for a Piache; and so darted upstairs, brought them down, and insisted so stoutly on arraying the vicar therein, that the good man beat a swift retreat. But he carried off with him, nevertheless, one of the handsomest mantles, which, instead of selling it, he converted cleverly enough into an altar-cloth; and for several years afterwards, the communion at Northam was celebrated upon a blaze of emerald, azure, and crimson, which had once adorned the sinful body of some Aztec prince.

So Ayacanora flaunted on; while Amyas watched her, half amused, half in simple pride of her beauty; and looked around at all gazers, as much as to say, "See what a fine bird I have brought home!"

Another great trouble which she gave Mrs. Leigh was her conduct to the ladies of the neighborhood. They came, of course, one and all, not only to congratulate Mrs. Leigh, but to get a peep at the fair savage; but the fair savage snubbed them all round, from the vicar's wife to Lady Grenville herself, so effectually, that few attempted a second visit.

Mrs. Leigh remonstrated, and was answered by floods of tears. "They only come to stare at a poor wild Indian girl, and she would not be made a show of. She was like a queen once, and every one obeyed her; but here every one looked down upon her." But when Mrs. Leigh asked her, whether she would sooner go back to the forests, the poor girl clung to her like a baby, and entreated not to be sent away, "She would sooner be a slave in the kitchen here, than go back to the bad people."

And so on, month after month of foolish storm and foolish sunshine; but she was under the shadow of one in whom was neither storm nor sunshine, but a perpetual genial calm of soft gray weather, which tempered down to its own peacefulness all who entered its charmed influence; and the outbursts grew more and more rare, and Ayacanora more and more rational, though no more happy, day by day.

And one by one small hints came out which made her identity certain, at least in the eyes of Mrs. Leigh and Yeo. After she had become familiar with the sight of houses, she gave them to understand that she had seen such things before. The red cattle, too, seemed not unknown to her; the sheep puzzled her for some time, and at last she gave Mrs. Leigh to understand that they were too small.

"Ah, madam," quoth Yeo, who caught at every straw, "it is because she has been accustomed to those great camel sheep (llamas they call them) in Peru."

But Ayacanora's delight was a horse. The use of tame animals at all was a daily wonder to her; but that a horse could be ridden was the crowning miracle of all; and a horse she would ride, and after plaguing Amyas for one in vain (for he did not want to break her pretty neck), she proposed confidentially to Yeo to steal one, and foiled in that, went to the vicar and offered to barter all her finery for his broken-kneed pony. But the vicar was too honest to drive so good a bargain, and the matter ended, in Amyas buying her a jennet, which she learned in a fortnight to ride like a very Gaucho.

And now awoke another curious slumbering reminiscence. For one day, at Lady Grenville's invitation, the whole family went over to Stow; Mrs. Leigh soberly on a pillion behind the groom, Ayacanora cantering round and round upon the moors like a hound let loose, and trying to make Amyas ride races with her. But that night, sleeping in the same room with Mrs. Leigh, she awoke shrieking, and sobbed out a long story how the "Old ape of Panama," her especial abomination, had come to her bedside and dragged her forth into the courtyard, and how she had mounted a horse and ridden with an Indian over great moors and high mountains down into a dark wood, and there the Indian and the horses vanished, and she found herself suddenly changed once more into a little savage child. So strong was the impression, that she could not be persuaded that the thing had not happened, if not that night, at least some night or other. So Mrs. Leigh at last believed the same, and told the company next morning in her pious way how the Lord had revealed in a vision to the poor child who she was, and how she had been exposed in the forests by her jealous step-father, and neither Sir Richard nor his wife could doubt but that hers was the true solution. It was probable that Don Xararte, though his home was Panama, had been often at Quito, for Yeo had seen him come on board the Lima ship at Guayaquil, one of the nearest ports. This would explain her having been found by the Indians beyond Cotopaxi, the nearest peak of the Eastern Andes, if, as was but too likely, the old man, believing her to be Oxenham's child, had conceived the fearful vengeance of exposing her in the forests.

Other little facts came to light one by one. They were all connected (as was natural in a savage) with some animal or other natural object. Whatever impressions her morals or affections had received, had been erased by the long spiritual death of that forest sojourn; and Mrs. Leigh could not elicit from her a trace of feeling about her mother, or recollection of any early religious teaching. This link, however, was supplied at last, and in this way.

Sir Richard had brought home an Indian with him from Virginia. Of his original name I am not sure, but he was probably the "Wanchese" whose name occurs with that of "Manteo."

This man was to be baptized in the church at Bideford by the name of Raleigh, his sponsors being most probably Raleigh himself, who may have been there on Virginian business, and Sir Richard Grenville. All the notabilities of Bideford came, of course, to see the baptism of the first "Red man" whose foot had ever trodden British soil, and the mayor and corporation-men appeared in full robes, with maces and tipstaffs, to do honor to that first-fruits of the Gospel in the West.

Mrs. Leigh went, as a matter of course, and Ayacanora would needs go too. She was very anxious to know what they were going to do with the "Carib."

"To make him a Christian."

"Why did they not make her one?"

Because she was one already. They were sure that she had been christened as soon as she was born. But she was not sure, and pouted a good deal at the chance of an "ugly red Carib" being better off than she was. However, all assembled duly; the stately son of the forest, now transformed into a footman of Sir Richard's, was standing at the font; the service was half performed when a heavy sigh, or rather groan, made all eyes turn, and Ayacanora sank fainting upon Mrs. Leigh's bosom.

She was carried out, and to a neighboring house; and when she came to herself, told a strange story. How, as she was standing there trying to recollect whether she too had ever been baptized, the church seemed to grow larger, the priest's dress richer; the walls were covered with pictures, and above the altar, in jewelled robes, stood a lady, and in her arms a babe. Soft music sounded in her ears; the air was full (on that she insisted much) of fragrant odor which filled the church like mist; and through it she saw not one, but many Indians, standing by the font; and a lady held her by the hand, and she was a little girl again.

And after, many questionings, so accurate was her recollection, not only of the scene, but of the building, that Yeo pronounced:

"A christened woman she is, madam, if Popish christening is worth calling such, and has seen Indians christened too in the Cathedral Church at Quito, the inside whereof I know well enough, and too well, for I sat there three mortal hours in a San Benito, to hear a friar preach his false doctrines, not knowing whether I was to be burnt or not next day."

So Ayacanora went home to Burrough, and Raleigh the Indian to Sir Richard's house. The entry of his baptism still stands, crooked-lettered, in the old parchment register of the Bideford baptisms for 1587-3:

His name occurs once more, a year and a month after:

But it is not this time among the baptisms. The free forest wanderer has pined in vain for his old deer-hunts amid the fragrant cedar woods, and lazy paddlings through the still lagoons, where water-lilies sleep beneath the shade of great magnolias, wreathed with clustered vines; and now he is away to "happier hunting-grounds," and all that is left of him below sleeps in the narrow town churchyard, blocked in with dingy houses, whose tenants will never waste a sigh upon the Indian's grave. There the two entries stand, unto this day; and most pathetic they have seemed to me; a sort of emblem and first-fruits of the sad fate of that worn-out Red race, to whom civilization came too late to save, but not too late to hasten their decay.

But though Amyas lay idle, England did not. That spring saw another and a larger colony sent out by Raleigh to Virginia, under the charge of one John White. Raleigh had written more than once, entreating Amyas to take the command, which if he had done, perhaps the United States had begun to exist twenty years sooner than they actually did. But his mother had bound him by a solemn promise (and who can wonder at her for asking, or at him for giving it?) to wait at home with her twelve months at least. So, instead of himself, he sent five hundred pounds, which I suppose are in Virginia (virtually at least) until this day; for they never came back again to him.

But soon came a sharper trial of Amyas's promise to his mother; and one which made him, for the first time in his life, moody, peevish, and restless, at the thought that others were fighting Spaniards, while he was sitting idle at home. For his whole soul was filling fast with sullen malice against Don Guzman. He was losing the "single eye," and his whole body was no longer full of light. He had entered into the darkness in which every man walks who hates his brother; and it lay upon him like a black shadow day and night. No company, too, could be more fit to darken that shadow than Salvation Yeo's. The old man grew more stern in his fanaticism day by day, and found a too willing listener in his master; and Mrs. Leigh was (perhaps for the first and last time in her life) seriously angry, when she heard the two coolly debating whether they had not committed a grievous sin in not killing the Spanish prisoners on board the galleon.

It must be said, however (as the plain facts set down in this book testify), that if such was the temper of Englishmen at that day, the Spaniards had done a good deal to provoke it; and were just then attempting to do still more.

For now we are approaching the year 1588, "which an astronomer of Konigsberg, above a hundred years before, foretold would be an admirable year, and the German chronologers presaged would be the climacterical year of the world."

The prophecies may stand for what they are worth; but they were at least fulfilled. That year was, indeed, the climacterical year of the world; and decided once and for all the fortunes of the European nations, and of the whole continent of America.

No wonder, then, if (as has happened in each great crisis of the human race) some awful instinct that The Day of the Lord was at hand, some dim feeling that there was war in heaven, and that the fiends of darkness and the angels of light were arrayed against each other in some mighty struggle for the possession of the souls of men, should have tried to express itself in astrologic dreams, and, as was the fashion then, attributed to the "rulers of the planetary houses" some sympathy with the coming world-tragedy.

But, for the wise, there needed no conjunction of planets to tell them that the day was near at hand, when the long desultory duel between Spain and England would end, once and for all, in some great death-grapple. The war, as yet, had been confined to the Netherlands, to the West Indies, and the coasts and isles of Africa; to the quarters, in fact, where Spain was held either to have no rights, or to have forfeited them by tyranny. But Spain itself had been respected by England, as England had by Spain; and trade to Spanish ports went on as usual, till, in the year 1585, the Spaniard, without warning, laid an embargo on all English ships coming to his European shores. They were to be seized, it seemed, to form part of an enormous armament, which was to attack and crush, once and for all—whom? The rebellious Netherlanders, said the Spaniards: but the queen, the ministry, and, when it was just not too late, the people of England, thought otherwise. England was the destined victim; so, instead of negotiating, in order to avoid fighting, they fought in order to produce negotiation. Drake, Frobisher, and Carlisle, as we have seen, swept the Spanish Main with fire and sword, stopping the Indian supplies; while Walsingham (craftiest, and yet most honest of mortals) prevented, by some mysterious financial operation, the Venetian merchants from repairing the Spaniards' loss by a loan; and no Armada came that year.

In the meanwhile, the Jesuits, here and abroad, made no secret, among their own dupes, of the real objects of the Spanish armament. The impious heretics,—the Drakes and Raleighs, Grenvilles and Cavendishes, Hawkinses and Frobishers, who had dared to violate that hidden sanctuary of just half the globe, which the pope had bestowed on the defender of the true faith,— a shameful ruin, a terrible death awaited them, when their sacrilegious barks should sink beneath the thunder of Spanish cannon, blessed by the pope, and sanctified with holy water and prayer to the service of "God and his Mother." Yes, they would fall, and England with them. The proud islanders, who had dared to rebel against St. Peter, and to cast off the worship of "Mary," should bow their necks once more under the yoke of the Gospel. Their so-called queen, illegitimate, excommunicate, contumacious, the abettor of free-trade, the defender of the Netherlands, the pillar of false doctrine throughout Europe, should be sent in chains across the Alps, to sue for her life at the feet of the injured and long-suffering father of mankind, while his nominee took her place upon the throne which she had long since forfeited by her heresy.

"What nobler work? How could the Church of God be more gloriously propagated? How could higher merit be obtained by faithful Catholics? It must succeed. Spain was invincible in valor, inexhaustible in wealth. Heaven itself offered them an opportunity. They had nothing now to fear from the Turk, for they had concluded a truce with him; nothing from the French, for they were embroiled in civil war. The heavens themselves had called upon Spain to fulfil her heavenly mission, and restore to the Church's crown this brightest and richest of her lost jewels. The heavens themselves called to a new crusade. The saints, whose altars the English had rifled and profaned, called them to a new crusade. The Virgin Queen of Heaven, whose boundless stores of grace the English spurned, called them to a new crusade. Justly incensed at her own wrongs and indignities, that 'ever-gracious Virgin, refuge of sinners, and mother of fair love, and holy hope,' adjured by their knightly honor all valiant cavaliers to do battle in her cause against the impious harlot who assumed her titles, received from her idolatrous flatterers the homage due to Mary alone, and even (for Father Parsons had asserted it, therefore it must be true) had caused her name to be substituted for that of Mary in the Litanies of the Church. Let all who wore within a manly heart, without a manly sword, look on the woes of 'Mary,'—her shame, her tears, her blushes, her heart pierced through with daily wounds, from heretic tongues, and choose between her and Elizabeth!"

So said Parsons, Allen, and dozens more; and said more than this, too, and much which one had rather not repeat; and were somewhat surprised and mortified to find that their hearers, though they granted the premises, were too dull or carnal to arrive at the same conclusion. The English lay Romanists, almost to a man, had hearts sounder than their heads, and, howsoever illogically, could not help holding to the strange superstition that, being Englishmen, they were bound to fight for England. So the hapless Jesuits, who had been boasting for years past that the persecuted faithful throughout the island would rise as one man to fight under the blessed banner of the pope and Spain, found that the faithful, like Demas of old, forsook them and "went after this present world;" having no objection, of course, to the restoration of Popery: but preferring some more comfortable method than an invasion which would inevitably rob them of their ancestral lands and would seat needy and greedy Castilians in their old country houses, to treat their tenants as they had treated the Indians of Hispaniola, and them as they had treated the caciques.

But though the hearts of men in that ungodly age were too hard to melt at the supposed woes of the Mary who reigned above, and too dull to turn rebels and traitors for the sake of those thrones and principalities in supra-lunar spheres which might be in her gift: yet there was a Mary who reigned (or ought to reign) below, whose woes (like her gifts) were somewhat more palpable to the carnal sense. A Mary who, having every comfort and luxury (including hounds and horses) found for her by the English Government, at an expense which would be now equal to some twenty thousand a year, could afford to employ the whole of her jointure as Queen Dowager of France (probably equal to fifty thousand a year more), in plotting the destruction of the said government, and the murder of its queen; a Mary who, if she prospered as she ought, might have dukedoms, and earldoms, fair lands and castles to bestow on her faithful servants; a Mary, finally, who contrived by means of an angel face, a serpent tongue, and a heart (as she said herself) as hard as a diamond, to make every weak man fall in love with her, and, what was worse, fancy more or less that she was in love with him.

Of her the Jesuits were not unmindful; and found it convenient, indeed, to forget awhile the sorrows of the Queen of Heaven in those of the Queen of Scots. Not that they cared much for those sorrows; but they were an excellent stock-in-trade. She was a Romanist; she was "beautiful and unfortunate," a virtue which, like charity, hides the multitude of sins; and therefore she was a convenient card to play in the great game of Rome against the Queen and people of England; and played the poor card was, till it got torn up by over-using. Into her merits or demerits I do not enter deeply here. Let her rest in peace.

To all which the people of England made a most practical and terrible answer. From the highest noble to the lowest peasant, arose one simultaneous plebiscitum: "We are tired of these seventeen years of chicanery and terror. This woman must die: or the commonweal of England perish!" We all know which of the two alternatives was chosen.

All Europe stood aghast: but rather with astonishment at English audacity, than with horror at English wickedness. Mary's own French kinsfolk had openly given her up as too bad to be excused, much less assisted. Her own son blustered a little to the English ambassador; for the majesty of kings was invaded: whereon Walsingham said in open council, that "the queen should send him a couple of hounds, and that would set all right." Which sage advice (being acted on, and some deer sent over and above) was so successful that the pious mourner, having run off (Randolph says, like a baby to see the deer in their cart), returned for answer that he would "thereafter depend wholly upon her majesty, and serve her fortune against all the world; and that he only wanted now two of her majesty's yeoman prickers, and a couple of her grooms of the deer." The Spaniard was not sorry on the whole for the catastrophe; for all that had kept him from conquering England long ago was the fear lest, after it was done, he might have had to put the crown thereof on Mary's head, instead of his own. But Mary's death was as convenient a stalking-horse to him as to the pope; and now the Armada was coming in earnest.

Elizabeth began negotiating; but fancy not that she does nothing more, as the following letter testifies, written about midsummer, 1587.

"F. Drake to Captain Amyas Leigh. This with haste.

"DEAR LAD,

"As I said to her most glorious majesty, I say to you now. There are two ways of facing an enemy. The one to stand off, and cry, 'Try that again, and I'll strike thee'; the other to strike him first, and then, 'Try that at all, and I'll strike thee again.' Of which latter counsel her majesty so far approves, that I go forthwith (tell it not in Gath) down the coast, to singe the king of Spain's beard (so I termed it to her majesty, she laughing), in which if I leave so much as a fishing-boat afloat from the Groyne unto Cadiz, it will not be with my good will, who intend that if he come this year, he shall come by swimming and not by sailing. So if you are still the man I have known you, bring a good ship round to Plymouth within the month, and away with me for hard blows and hard money, the feel of both of which you know pretty well by now.

"Thine lovingly,

"F. Drake."

Amyas clutched his locks over this letter, and smoked more tobacco the day he got it than had ever before been consumed at once in England. But he kept true to his promise; and this was his reply:—

"Amyas Leigh to the Worshipful Sir F. Drake, Admiral of her Majesty's Fleet in Plymouth.

"MOST HONORED SIR,

"A magician keeps me here, in bilboes for which you have no picklock; namely, a mother who forbids. The loss is mine: but Antichrist I can fight any year (for he will not die this bout, nor the next), while my mother—but I will not trouble your patience more than to ask from you to get me news, if you can, from any prisoners of one Don Guzman Maria Magdalena Sotomayor de Soto; whether he is in Spain or in the Indies; and what the villain does, and where he is to be found. This only I entreat of you, and so remain behind with a heavy heart.

"Yours to command in all else, and I would to Heaven, in this also,

"AMYAS LEIGH."

I am sorry to have to say, that after having thus obeyed his mother, Master Amyas, as men are too apt to do, revenged himself on her by being more and more cross and disagreeable. But his temper amended much, when, a few months after, Drake returned triumphant, having destroyed a hundred sail in Cadiz alone, taken three great galleons with immense wealth on board, burnt the small craft all along the shore, and offered battle to Santa Cruz at the mouth of the Tagus. After which it is unnecessary to say, that the Armada was put off for yet another year.

This news, indeed, gave Amyas little comfort; for he merely observed, grumbling, that Drake had gone and spoiled everybody else's sport: but what cheered him was news from Drake that Don Guzman had been heard of from the captain of one of the galleons; that he was high in favor in Spain, and commandant of soldiers on board one of the largest of the marquis's ships.

And when Amyas heard that, a terrible joy took possession of him. When the Armada came, as come it would, he should meet his enemy at last! He could wait now patiently: if—and he shuddered at himself, as he found himself in the very act of breathing a prayer that Don Guzman might not die before that meeting.

In the meanwhile, rumor flew thousand-tongued through the length and breadth of the land; of vast preparations going on in Spain and Italy; of timber felled long before for some such purpose, brought down to the sea, and sawn out for shipbuilding; of casting of cannon, and drilling of soldiers; of ships in hundreds collecting at Lisbon; of a crusade preached by Pope

Sixtus the Fifth, who had bestowed the kingdom of England on the Spaniard, to be enjoyed by him as vassal tributary to Rome; of a million of gold to be paid by the pope, one-half down at once, the other half when London was taken; of Cardinal Allen writing and printing busily in the Netherlands, calling on all good Englishmen to carry out, by rebelling against Elizabeth, the bull of Sixtus the Fifth, said (I blush to repeat it) to have been dictated by the Holy Ghost; of Inquisitors getting ready fetters and devil's engines of all sorts; of princes and noblemen, flocking from all quarters, gentlemen selling their private estates to fit out ships; how the Prince of Melito, the Marquess of Burgrave, Vespasian Gonzaga, John Medicis, Amadas of Savoy, in short, the illegitimate sons of all the southern princes, having no lands of their own, were coming to find that necessary of life in this pleasant little wheat-garden. Nay, the Duke of Medina Sidonia had already engaged Mount-Edgecombe for himself, as the fairest jewel of the south; which when good old Sir Richard Edgecombe heard, he observed quietly, that in 1555 he had the pleasure of receiving at his table at one time the admirals of England, Spain, and the Netherlands, and therefore had experience in entertaining Dons; and made preparations for the visit by filling his cellars with gunpowder, with a view to a house-warming and feu-de-joie on the occasion. But as old Fuller says, "The bear was not yet killed, and Medina Sidonia might have catched a great cold, had he no other clothes to wear than the skin thereof."

So flew rumor, false and true, till poor John Bull's wits were well-nigh turned: but to the very last, after his lazy fashion, he persuaded himself that it would all come right somehow; that it was too great news to be true; that if it was true, the expedition was only meant for the Netherlands; and, in short, sat quietly over his beef and beer for many a day after the French king had sent him fair warning, and the queen, the ministry, and the admirals had been assuring him again and again that he, and not the Dutchman, was the destined prey of this great flight of ravenous birds.

At last the Spaniard, in order that there should be no mistake about the matter, kindly printed a complete bill of the play, to be seen still in Van Meteran, for the comfort of all true Catholics, and confusion of all pestilent heretics; which document, of course, the seminary priests used to enforce the duty of helping the invaders, and the certainty of their success; and from their hands it soon passed into those of the devout ladies, who were not very likely to keep it to themselves; till John Bull himself found his daughters buzzing over it with very pale faces (as young ladies well might who had no wish to follow the fate of the damsels of Antwerp), and condescending to run his eye through it, discovered, what all the rest of Europe had known for months past, that he was in a very great scrape.

Well it was for England, then, that her Tudor sovereigns had compelled every man (though they kept up no standing army) to be a trained soldier. Well it was that Elizabeth, even in those dangerous days of intrigue and rebellion, had trusted her people enough, not only to leave them their weapons, but (what we, forsooth, in these more "free" and "liberal" days dare not do) to teach them how to use them. Well it was, that by careful legislation for the comfort and employment of "the masses" (term then, thank God, unknown), she had both won their hearts, and kept their bodies in fighting order. Well it was that, acting as fully as Napoleon did on "la carriere ouverte aux talens," she had raised to the highest posts in her councils, her army, and her navy, men of business, who had not been ashamed to buy and sell as merchants and adventurers. Well for England, in a word, that Elizabeth had pursued for thirty years a very different course from that which we have been pursuing for the last thirty, with one exception, namely, the leaving as much as possible to private enterprise.

There we have copied her: would to Heaven that we had in some other matters! It is the fashion now to call her a despot: but unless every monarch is to be branded with that epithet whose power is not as circumscribed as Queen Victoria's is now, we ought rather to call her the most popular sovereign, obeyed of their own free will by the freest subjects which England has ever seen; confess the Armada fight to have been as great a moral triumph as it was a political one; and (now that our late boasting is a little silenced by Crimean disasters) inquire whether we have not something to learn from those old Tudor times, as to how to choose officials, how to train a people, and how to defend a country.

To return to the thread of my story.

January, 1587-8, had well-nigh run through, before Sir Richard Grenville made his appearance on the streets of Bideford. He had been appointed in November one of the council of war for providing for the safety of the nation, and the West Country had seen nothing of him since. But one morning, just before Christmas, his stately figure darkened the old bay-window at Burrough, and Amyas rushed out to meet him, and bring him in, and ask what news from Court.

"All good news, dear lad, and dearer madam. The queen shows the spirit of a very Boadicea or Semiramis; ay, a very Scythian Tomyris, and if she had the Spaniard before her now, would verily, for aught I know, feast him as the Scythian queen did Cyrus, with 'Satia te sanguine, quod sitisti.'"

"I trust her most merciful spirit is not so changed already," said Mrs. Leigh.

"Well, if she would not do it, I would, and ask pardon afterwards, as Raleigh did about the rascals at Smerwick, whom Amyas knows of. Mrs. Leigh, these are times in which mercy is cruelty. Not England alone, but the world, the Bible, the Gospel itself, is at stake; and we must do terrible things, lest we suffer more terrible ones."

"God will take care of world and Bible better than any cruelty of ours, dear Sir Richard."

"Nay, but, Mrs. Leigh, we must help Him to take care of them! If those Smerwick Spaniards had not been—"

"The Spaniard would not have been exasperated into invading us."

"And we should not have had this chance of crushing him once and for all; but the quarrel is of older standing, madam, eh, Amyas? Amyas, has Raleigh written to you of late?"

"Not a word, and I wonder why."

"Well; no wonder at that, if you knew how he has been laboring. The wonder is, whence he got the knowledge wherewith to labor; for he never saw sea-work to my remembrance."

"Never saw a shot fired by sea, except ours at Smerwick, and that brush with the Spaniards in 1579, when he sailed for Virginia with Sir Humphrey; and he was a mere crack then."

"So you consider him as your pupil, eh? But he learnt enough in the Netherland wars, and in

Ireland too, if not of the strength of ships, yet still of the weakness of land forces; and would you believe it, the man has twisted the whole council round his finger, and made them give up the land defences to the naval ones."

"Quite right he, and wooden walls against stone ones for ever! But as for twisting, he would persuade Satan, if he got him alone for half an hour."

"I wish he would sail for Spain then, just now, and try the powers of his tongue," said Mrs. Leigh.

"But are we to have the honor, really?"

"We are, lad. There were many in the council who were for disputing the landing on shore, and said—which I do not deny—that the 'prentice boys of London could face the bluest blood in Spain. But Raleigh argued (following my Lord Burleigh in that) that we differed from the Low Countries, and all other lands, in that we had not a castle or town throughout, which would stand a ten days' siege, and that our ramparts, as he well said, were, after all, only a body of men. So, he argued, as long as the enemy has power to land where he will, prevention, rather than cure, is our only hope; and that belongs to the office, not of an army, but of a fleet. So the fleet was agreed on, and a fleet we shall have."

"Then here is his health, the health of a true friend to all bold mariners, and myself in particular! But where is he now?"

"Coming here to-morrow, as I hope—for he left London with me, and so down by us into Cornwall, to drill the train-bands, as he is bound to do, being Seneschal of the Duchies and Lieutenant-General of the county."

"Besides Lord Warden of the Stanneries! How the man thrives!" said Mrs. Leigh.

"How the man deserves to thrive!" said Amyas; "but what are we to do?"

"That is the rub. I would fain stay and fight the Spaniards."

"So would I; and will."

"But he has other plans in his head for us."

"We can make our own plans without his help."

"Heyday, Amyas! How long? When did he ask you to do a thing yet and you refuse him?"

"Not often, certainly; but Spaniards I must fight."

"Well, so must I, boy: but I have given a sort of promise to him, nevertheless."

"Not for me too, I hope?"

"No: he will extract that himself when he comes; you must come and sup to-morrow, and talk it over."

"Be talked over, rather. What chestnut does the cat want us monkeys to pull out of the fire for him now, I wonder?"

"Sir Richard Grenville is hardly accustomed to be called a monkey," said Mrs. Leigh.

"I meant no harm; and his worship knows it, none better: but where is Raleigh going to send us, with a murrain?"

"To Virginia. The settlers must have help: and, as I trust in God, we shall be back again long before this armament can bestir itself."

So Raleigh came, saw, and conquered. Mrs. Leigh consented to Amyas's going (for his twelve-month would be over ere the fleet could start) upon so peaceful and useful an errand; and the next five months were spent in continual labor on the part of Amyas and Grenville, till seven ships were all but ready in Bideford river, the admiral whereof was Amyas Leigh.

But that fleet was not destined ever to see the shores of the New World: it had nobler work to do (if Americans will forgive the speech) than even settling the United States.

It was in the long June evenings, in the year 1588; Mrs. Leigh sat in the open window, busy at her needle-work; Ayacanora sat opposite to her, on the seat of the bay, trying diligently to read "The History of the Nine Worthies," and stealing a glance every now and then towards the garden, where Amyas stalked up and down as he had used to do in happier days gone by. But his brow was contracted now, his eyes fixed on the ground, as he plodded backwards and forwards, his hands behind his back, and a huge cigar in his mouth, the wonder of the little boys of Northam, who peeped in stealthily as they passed the iron-work gates, to see the back of the famous fire-breathing captain who had sailed round the world and been in the country of headless men and flying dragons, and then popped back their heads suddenly, as he turned toward them in his walk. And Ayacanora looked, and looked, with no less admiration than the urchins at the gate: but she got no more of an answering look from Amyas than they did; for his head was full of calculations of tonnage and stowage, of salt pork and ale-barrels, and the packing of tools and seeds; for he had promised Raleigh to do his best for the new colony, and he was doing it with all his might; so Ayacanora looked back again to her book, and heaved a deep sigh. It was answered by one from Mrs. Leigh.

"We are a melancholy pair, sweet chuck," said the fair widow. "What is my maid sighing about, there?"

"Because I cannot make out the long words," said Ayacanora, telling a very white fib.

"Is that all? Come to me, and I will tell you."

Ayacanora moved over to her, and sat down at her feet.

"H—e, he, r—o, ro, i—c—a—l, heroical," said Mrs. Leigh.

"But what does that mean?"

"Grand, good, and brave, like—"

Mrs. Leigh was about to have said the name of one who was lost to her on earth. His fair angelic face hung opposite upon the wall. She paused unable to pronounce his name; and lifted up her eyes, and gazed on the portrait, and breathed a prayer between closed lips, and drooped her head again.

Her pupil caught at the pause, and filled it up for herself—

"Like him?" and she turned her head quickly toward the window.

"Yes, like him, too," said Mrs. Leigh, with a half-smile at the gesture. "Now, mind your book. Maidens must not look out of the window in school hours."

"Shall I ever be an English girl?" asked Ayacanora.

"You are one now, sweet; your father was an English gentleman."

Amyas looked in, and saw the two sitting together.

"You seem quite merry there," said he.

"Come in, then, and be merry with us."

He entered, and sat down; while Ayacanora fixed her eyes most steadfastly on her book.

"Well, how goes on the reading?" said he; and then, without waiting for an answer—"We shall be ready to clear out this day week, mother, I do believe; that is, if the hatchets are made in time to pack them."

"I hope they will be better than the last," said Mrs. Leigh. "It seems to me a shameful sin to palm off on poor ignorant savages goods which we should consider worthless for ourselves."

"Well, it's not over fair: but still, they are a sight better than they ever had before. An old hoop is better than a deer's bone, as Ayacanora knows,—eh?"

"I don't know anything about it," said she, who was always nettled at the least allusion to her past wild life. "I am an English girl now, and all that is gone—I forget it."

"Forget it?" said he, teasing her for want of something better to do. "Should not you like to sail with us, now, and see the Indians in the forests once again?"

"Sail with you?" and she looked up eagerly.

"There! I knew it! She would not be four-and-twenty hours ashore, but she would be off into the woods again, bow in hand, like any runaway nymph, and we should never see her more."

"It is false, bad man!" and she burst into violent tears, and hid her face in Mrs. Leigh's lap.

"Amyas, Amyas, why do you tease the poor fatherless thing?"

"I was only jesting, I'm sure," said Amyas, like a repentant schoolboy. "Don't cry now, don't cry, my child, see here," and he began fumbling in his pockets; "see what I bought of a chapman in town to-day, for you, my maid, indeed, I did."

And out he pulled some smart kerchief or other, which had taken his sailor's fancy.

"Look at it now, blue, and crimson, and green, like any parrot!" and he held it out.

She looked round sharply, snatched it out of his hand, and tore it to shreds.

"I hate it, and I hate you!" and she sprang up and darted out of the room.

"Oh, boy, boy!" said Mrs. Leigh, "will you kill that poor child? It matters little for an old heart like mine, which has but one or two chords left whole, how soon it be broken altogether; but a young heart is one of God's precious treasures, Amyas, and suffers many a long pang in the breaking; and woe to them who despise Christ's little ones!"

"Break your heart, mother?"

"Never mind my heart, dear son; yet how can you break it more surely than by tormenting one whom I love, because she loves you?"

"Tut! play, mother, and maids' tempers. But how can I break your heart? What have I done? Have I not given up going again to the West Indies for your sake? Have I not given up going to Virginia, and now again settled to go after all, just because you commanded? Was it not your will? Have I not obeyed you, mother, mother? I will stay at home now, if you will. I would rather rust here on land, I vow I would, than grieve you—" and he threw himself at his mother's knees.

"Have I asked you not to go to Virginia? No, dear boy, though every thought of a fresh parting seems to crack some new fibre within me, you must go! It is your calling. Yes; you were not sent into the world to amuse me, but to work. I have had pleasure enough of you, my darling, for many a year, and too much, perhaps; till I shrank from lending you to the Lord. But He must have you. . . . It is enough for the poor old widow to know that her boy is what he is, and to forget all her anguish day by day, for joy that a man is born into the world. But, Amyas, Amyas, are you so blind as not to see that Ayacanora—"

"Don't talk about her, poor child. Talk about yourself."

"How long have I been worth talking about? No, Amyas, you must see it; and if you will not see it now, you will see it one day in some sad and fearful prodigy; for she is not one to die tamely. She loves you, Amyas, as a woman only can love."

"Loves me? Well, of course. I found her, and brought her home; and I don't deny she may think that she owes me somewhat—though it was no more than a Christian man's duty. But as for her caring much for me, mother, you measure every one else's tenderness by your own."

"Think that she owes you somewhat? Silly boy, this is not gratitude, but a deeper affection, which may be more heavenly than gratitude, as it may, too, become a horrible cause of ruin. It rests with you, Amyas, which of the two it will be."

"You are in earnest?"

"Have I the heart or the time to jest?"

"No, no, of course not; but, mother, I thought it was not comely for women to fall in love with men?"

"Not comely, at least, to confess their love to men. But she has never done that, Amyas; not even by a look or a tone of voice, though I have watched her for months."

"To be sure, she is as demure as any cat when I am in the way. I only wonder how you found it out."

"Ah," said she, smiling sadly, "even in the saddest woman's soul there linger snatches of old music, odors of flowers long dead and turned to dust—pleasant ghosts, which still keep her mind attuned to that which may be in others, though in her never more; till she can hear her own wedding-hymn re-echoed in the tones of every girl who loves, and sees her own wedding-torch re-lighted in the eyes of every bride."

"You would not have me marry her?" asked blunt, practical Amyas.

"God knows what I would have—I know not; I see neither your path nor my own—no, not after weeks and months of prayer. All things beyond are wrapped in mist; and what will be, I know not, save that whatever else is wrong, mercy at least is right."

"I'd sail to-morrow, if I could. As for marrying her, mother—her birth, mind me—"

"Ah, boy, boy! Are you God, to visit the sins of the parents upon the children?"

"Not that. I don't mean that; but I mean this, that she is half a Spaniard, mother; and I cannot!—Her blood may be as blue as King Philip's own, but it is Spanish still! I cannot bear the thought that my children should have in their veins one drop of that poison."

"Amyas! Amyas!" interrupted she, "is this not, too, visiting the parents' sins on the children?"

"Not a whit; it is common sense,—she must have the taint of their bloodthirsty humor. She has it—I have seen it in her again and again. I have told you, have I not? Can I forget the look of her eyes as she stood over that galleon's captain, with the smoking knife in her hand.—Ugh! And she is not tamed yet, as you can see, and never will be:—not that I care, except for her own sake, poor thing!"

"Cruel boy! to impute as a blame to the poor child, not only the errors of her training, but the very madness of her love!"

"Of her love?"

"Of what else, blind buzzard? From the moment that you told me the story of that captain's death, I knew what was in her heart—and thus it is that you requite her for having saved your life!"

"Umph! that is one word too much, mother. If you don't want to send me crazy, don't put the thing on the score of gratitude or duty. As it is, I can hardly speak civilly to her (God forgive me!) when I recollect that she belongs to the crew who murdered him"—and he pointed to the picture, and Mrs. Leigh shuddered as he did so.

"You feel it! You know you feel it, tender-hearted, forgiving angel as you are; and what do you think I must feel?"

"Oh, my son, my son!" cried she, wringing her hands, "if I be wretch enough to give place to the devil for a moment, does that give you a right to entertain and cherish him thus day by day?"

"I should cherish him with a vengeance, if I brought up a crew of children who could boast of a pedigree of idolaters and tyrants, hunters of Indians, and torturers of women! How pleasant to hear her telling Master Jack, 'Your illustrious grand-uncle the pope's legate, was the man who burned Rose Salterne at Cartagena;' or Miss Grace, 'Your great-grandfather of sixteen quarterings, the Marquis of this, son of the Grand-equerry that, and husband of the Princess t'other, used to feed his bloodhounds, when beef was scarce, with Indians' babies!' Eh, mother? These things are true, and if you can forget them, I cannot. Is it not enough to have made me forego for awhile my purpose, my business, the one thing I live for, and that is, hunting down the Spaniards as I would adders or foxes, but you must ask me over and above to take one to my bosom?"

"Oh, my son, my son! I have not asked you to do that; I have only commanded you, in God's name, to be merciful, if you wish to obtain mercy. Oh, if you will not pity this poor maiden, pity yourself; for God knows you stand in more need of it than she does!"

Amyas was silent for a minute or two; and then,—

"If it were not for you, mother, would God that the Armada would come!"

"What, and ruin England?"

"No! Curse them! Not a foot will they ever set on English soil, such a welcome would we give them. If I were but in the midst of that fleet, fighting like a man—to forget it all, with a galleon on board of me to larboard, and another to starboard—and then to put a linstock in the magazine, and go aloft in good company—I don't care how soon it comes, mother, if it were not for you."

"If I am in your way, Amyas, do not fear that I shall trouble you long."

"Oh, mother, mother, do not talk in that way! I am half-mad, I think, already, and don't know what I say. Yes, I am mad; mad at heart, though not at head. There's a fire burning me up, night and day, and nothing but Spanish blood will put it out."

"Or the grace of God, my poor wilful child! Who comes to the door?—so quickly, too?"

There was a loud hurried knocking, and in another minute a serving-man hurried in with a letter.

"This to Captain Amyas Leigh with haste, haste!"

It was Sir Richard's hand. Amyas tore it open; and "a loud laugh laughed he."

"The Armada is coming! My wish has come true, mother!"

"God help us, it has! Show me the letter."

It was a hurried scrawl.

"DR. GODSON,—Walsingham sends word that the Ada. sailed from Lisbon to the Groyne the 18. of May. We know no more, but have commandment to stay the ships. Come down, dear lad, and give us counsel; and may the Lord help His Church in this great strait.

"Your loving godfather,

"R. G."

"Forgive me, mother, mother, once for all!" cried Amyas, throwing his arms round her neck.

"I have nothing to forgive, my son, my son! And shall I lose thee, also?"

"If I be killed, you will have two martyrs of your blood, mother!—"

Mrs. Leigh bowed her head, and was silent. Amyas caught up his hat and sword, and darted forth toward Bideford.

Amyas literally danced into Sir Richard's hall, where he stood talking earnestly with various merchants and captains.

"Gloria, gloria! gentles all! The devil is broke loose at last; and now we know where to have him on the hip!"

"Why so merry, Captain Leigh, when all else are sad?" said a gentle voice by his side.

"Because I have been sad a long time, while all else were merry, dear lady. Is the hawk doleful when his hood is pulled off, and he sees the heron flapping right ahead of him?"

"You seem to forget the danger and the woe of us weak women, sir?"

"I don't forget the danger and the woe of one weak woman, madam, and she the daughter of a man who once stood in this room," said Amyas, suddenly collecting himself, in a low stern voice. "And I don't forget the danger and the woe of one who was worth a thousand even of her. I don't forget anything, madam."

"Nor forgive either, it seems."

"It will be time to talk of forgiveness after the offender has repented and amended; and does the sailing of the Armada look like that?"

"Alas, no! God help us!"

"He will help us, madam," said Amyas.

"Admiral Leigh," said Sir Richard, "we need you now, if ever. Here are the queen's orders to furnish as many ships as we can; though from these gentlemen's spirit, I should say the orders were well-nigh needless."

"Not a doubt, sir; for my part, I will fit my ship at my own charges, and fight her too, as long as

I have a leg or an arm left."

"Or a tongue to say, never surrender, I'll warrant!" said an old merchant. "You put life into us old fellows, Admiral Leigh: but it will be a heavy matter for those poor fellows in Virginia, and for my daughter too, Madam Dare, with her young babe, as I hear, just born."

"And a very heavy matter," said some one else, "for those who have ventured their money in these cargoes, which must lie idle, you see, now for a year maybe—and then all the cost of unlading again—"

"My good sir," said Grenville, "what have private interests to do with this day? Let us thank God if He only please to leave us the bare fee-simple of this English soil, the honor of our wives and daughters, and bodies safe from rack and fagot, to wield the swords of freemen in defence of a free land, even though every town and homestead in England were wasted with fire, and we left to rebuild over again all which our ancestors have wrought for us in now six hundred years."

"Right, sir!" said Amyas. "For my part, let my Virginian goods rot on the quay, if the worst comes to the worst. I begin unloading the Vengeance to-morrow; and to sea as soon as I can fill up my crew to a good fighting number."

And so the talk ran on; and ere two days were past, most of the neighboring gentlemen, summoned by Sir Richard, had come in, and great was the bidding against each other as to who should do most. Cary and Brimblecombe, with thirty tall Clovelly men, came across the bay, and without even asking leave of Amyas, took up their berths as a matter of course on board the Vengeance. In the meanwhile, the matter was taken up by families. The Fortescues (a numberless clan) offered to furnish a ship; the Chichesters another, the Stukelys a third; while the merchantmen were not backward. The Bucks, the Stranges, the Heards, joyfully unloaded their Virginian goods, and replaced them with powder and shot; and in a week's time the whole seven were ready once more for sea, and dropped down into Appledore pool, with Amyas as their admiral for the time being (for Sir Richard had gone by land to Plymouth to join the deliberations there), and waited for the first favorable wind to start for the rendezvous in the Sound.

At last, upon the twenty-first of June, the clank of the capstans rang merrily across the flats, and amid prayers and blessings, forth sailed that gallant squadron over the bar, to play their part in Britain's Salamis; while Mrs. Leigh stood watching as she stood once before, beside the churchyard wall: but not alone this time; for Ayacanora stood by her side, and gazed and gazed, till her eyes seemed ready to burst from their sockets. At last she turned away with a sob,—

"And he never bade me good-bye, mother!"

"God forgive him! Come home and pray, my child; there is no other rest on earth than prayer for woman's heart!"

They were calling each other mother and daughter then? Yes. The sacred fire of sorrow was fast burning out all Ayacanora's fallen savageness; and, like a Phoenix, the true woman was rising from those ashes, fair, noble, and all-enduring, as God had made her.

CHAPTER XXX: HOW THE ADMIRAL JOHN HAWKINS TESTIFIED AGAINST CROAKERS

What if the spectators who last summer gazed with just pride upon the noble port of Plymouth, its vast breakwater spanning the Sound, its arsenals and docks, its two estuaries filled with gallant ships, and watched the great screw-liners turning within their own length by force invisible, or threading the crowded fleets with the ease of the tiniest boat,—what if, by some magic turn, the nineteenth century, and all the magnificence of its wealth and science, had vanished—as it may vanish hereafter—and they had found themselves thrown back three hundred years into the pleasant summer days of 1588?

Mount Edgecombe is still there, beautiful as ever: but where are the docks, and where is Devonport? No vast dry-dock roofs rise at the water's edge. Drake's island carries but a paltry battery, just raised by the man whose name it bears; Mount Wise is a lone gentleman's house among fields; the citadel is a pop-gun fort, which a third-class steamer would shell into rubble for an afternoon's amusement. And the shipping, where are they? The floating castles of the Hamoaze have dwindled to a few crawling lime-hoys; and the Catwater is packed, not as now, with merchant craft, but with the ships who will to-morrow begin the greatest sea-fight which the world has ever seen.

There they lie, a paltry squadron enough in modern eyes; the largest of them not equal in size to a six-and-thirty-gun frigate, carrying less weight of metal than one of our new gun-boats, and able to employ even that at not more than a quarter of our modern range. Would our modern spectators, just come down by rail for a few hours, to see the cavalry embark, and return tomorrow in time for dinner, have looked down upon that petty port, and petty fleet, with a contemptuous smile, and begun some flippant speech about the progress of intellect, and the triumphs of science, and our benighted ancestors? They would have done so, doubt it not, if they belonged to the many who gaze on those very triumphs as on a raree-show to feed their silly wonder, or use and enjoy them without thankfulness or understanding, as the ox eats the clover thrust into his rack, without knowing or caring how it grew. But if any of them were of the class by whom those very triumphs have been achieved; the thinkers and the workers, who, instead of entering lazily into other men's labors, as the mob does, labor themselves; who know by hard experience the struggles, the self-restraints, the disappointments, the slow and staggering steps, by which the discoverer reaches to his prize; then the smile of those men would not have been one of pity, but rather of filial love. For they would have seen in those outwardly paltry armaments the potential germ of that mightier one which now loads the Black Sea waves; they would have been aware, that to produce it, with such materials and knowledge as then existed, demanded an intellect, an energy, a spirit of progress and invention, equal, if not superior, to those of which we now so loudly boast.

But if, again, he had been a student of men rather than of machinery, he would have found few nobler companies on whom to exercise his discernment, than he might have seen in the little terrace bowling-green behind the Pelican Inn, on the afternoon of the nineteenth of July. Chatting in groups, or lounging over the low wall which commanded a view of the Sound and the shipping far below, were gathered almost every notable man of the Plymouth fleet, the whole posse comitatus of "England's forgotten worthies." The Armada has been scattered by a storm. Lord Howard has been out to look for it, as far as the Spanish coast; but the wind has shifted to the south, and fearing lest the Dons should pass him, he has returned to Plymouth, uncertain whether the Armada will come after all or not. Slip on for a while, like Prince Hal, the drawer's apron; come in through the rose-clad door which opens from the tavern, with a tray of long-necked Dutch glasses, and a silver tankard of wine, and look round you at the gallant captains, who are waiting for the Spanish Armada, as lions in their lair might wait for the passing herd of deer.

    See those five talking earnestly, in the centre of a ring, which longs to overhear, and yet is too respectful to approach close. Those soft long eyes and pointed chin you recognize already; they are Walter Raleigh's. The fair young man in the flame-colored doublet, whose arm is round Raleigh's neck, is Lord Sheffield; opposite them stands, by the side of Sir Richard Grenville, a man as stately even as he, Lord Sheffield's uncle, the Lord Charles Howard of Effingham, lord high admiral of England; next to him is his son-in-law, Sir Robert Southwell, captain of the Elizabeth Jonas: but who is that short, sturdy, plainly dressed man, who stands with legs a little apart, and hands behind his back, looking up, with keen gray eyes, into the face of each speaker? His cap is in his hands, so you can see the bullet head of crisp brown hair and the wrinkled forehead, as well as the high cheek bones, the short square face, the broad temples, the thick lips, which are yet firm as granite. A coarse plebeian stamp of man: yet the whole figure and attitude are that of boundless determination, self-possession, energy; and when at last he speaks a few blunt words, all eyes are turned respectfully upon him;—for his name is Francis Drake.

    A burly, grizzled elder, in greasy sea-stained garments, contrasting oddly with the huge gold chain about his neck, waddles up, as if he had been born, and had lived ever since, in a gale of wind at sea. The upper half of his sharp dogged visage seems of brick-red leather, the lower of badger's fur; and as he claps Drake on the back, and, with a broad Devon twang, shouts, "be you a coming to drink your wine, Francis Drake, or be you not?—saving your presence, my lord;" the lord high admiral only laughs, and bids Drake go and drink his wine; for John Hawkins, admiral of the port, is the patriarch of Plymouth seamen, if Drake be their hero, and says and does pretty much what he likes in any company on earth; not to mention that to-day's prospect of an Armageddon fight has shaken him altogether out of his usual crabbed reserve, and made him overflow with loquacious good-humor, even to his rival Drake.

    So they push through the crowd, wherein is many another man whom one would gladly have spoken with face to face on earth. Martin Frobisher and John Davis are sitting on that bench, smoking tobacco from long silver pipes; and by them are Fenton and Withrington, who have both tried to follow Drake's path round the world, and failed, though by no fault of their own. The man who pledges them better luck next time, is George Fenner, known to "the seven Portugals," Leicester's pet, and captain of the galleon which Elizabeth bought of him. That short prim man in the huge yellow ruff, with sharp chin, minute imperial, and self-satisfied smile, is

Richard Hawkins, the Complete Seaman, Admiral John's hereafter famous and hapless son. The elder who is talking with him is his good uncle William, whose monument still stands, or should stand, in Deptford Church; for Admiral John set it up there but one year after this time; and on it record how he was, "A worshipper of the true religion, an especial benefactor of poor sailors, a most just arbiter in most difficult causes, and of a singular faith, piety, and prudence." That, and the fact that he got creditably through some sharp work at Porto Rico, is all I know of William Hawkins: but if you or I, reader, can have as much or half as much said of us when we have to follow him, we shall have no reason to complain.

There is John Drake, Sir Francis' brother, ancestor of the present stock of Drakes; and there is George, his nephew, a man not overwise, who has been round the world with Amyas; and there is Amyas himself, talking to one who answers him with fierce curt sentences, Captain Barker of Bristol, brother of the hapless Andrew Barker who found John Oxenham's guns, and, owing to a mutiny among his men, perished by the Spaniards in Honduras, twelve years ago. Barker is now captain of the Victory, one of the queen's best ships; and he has his accounts to settle with the Dons, as Amyas has; so they are both growling together in a corner, while all the rest are as merry as the flies upon the vine above their heads.

But who is the aged man who sits upon a bench, against the sunny south wall of the tavern, his long white beard flowing almost to his waist, his hands upon his knees, his palsied head moving slowly from side to side, to catch the scraps of discourse of the passing captains? His great-grandchild, a little maid of six, has laid her curly head upon his knees, and his grand-daughter, a buxom black-eyed dame of thirty, stands by him and tends him, half as nurse, and half, too, as showman, for he seems an object of curiosity to all the captains, and his fair nurse has to entreat again and again, "Bless you, sir, please now, don't give him no liquor, poor old soul, the doctor says." It is old Martin Cockrem, father of the ancient host, aged himself beyond the years of man, who can recollect the bells of Plymouth ringing for the coronation of Henry the Eighth, and who was the first Englishman, perhaps, who ever set foot on the soil of the New World. There he sits, like an old Druid Tor of primeval granite amid the tall wheat and rich clover crops of a modern farm. He has seen the death of old Europe and the birth-throes of the new. Go to him, and question him; for his senses are quick as ever; and just now the old man seems uneasy. He is peering with rheumy eyes through the groups, and seems listening for a well-known voice.

"There 'a be again! Why don't 'a come, then?"

"Quiet, gramfer, and don't trouble his worship."

"Here an hour, and never speak to poor old Martin! I say, sir"—and the old man feebly plucks Amyas's cloak as he passes. "I say, captain, do 'e tell young master old Martin's looking for him."

"Marcy, gramfer, where's your manners? Don't be vexed, sir, he'm a'most a babe, and tejous at times, mortal."

"Young master who?" says Amyas, bending down to the old man, and smiling to the dame to let him have his way.

"Master Hawkins; he'm never been a-near me all day."

Off goes Amyas; and, of course, lays hold of the sleeve of young Richard Hawkins; but as he is in act to speak, the dame lays hold of his, laughing and blushing.

"No, sir, not Mr. Richard, sir; Admiral John, sir, his father; he always calls him young master, poor old soul!" and she points to the grizzled beard and the face scarred and tanned with fifty years of fight and storm.

Amyas goes to the Admiral, and gives his message.

"Mercy on me! Where be my wits? Iss, I'm a-coming," says the old hero in his broadest Devon, waddles off to the old man, and begins lugging at a pocket. "Here, Martin, I've got mun, I've got mun, man alive; but his Lordship keept me so. Lookee here, then! Why, I do get so lusty of late, Martin, I can't get to my pockets!"

And out struggle a piece of tarred string, a bundle of papers, a thimble, a piece of pudding-tobacco, and last of all, a little paper of Muscovado sugar—then as great a delicacy as any French bonbons would be now—which he thrusts into the old man's eager and trembling hand.

Old Martin begins dipping his finger into it, and rubbing it on his toothless gums, smiling and nodding thanks to his young master; while the little maid at his knee, unrebuked, takes her share also.

"There, Admiral Leigh; both ends meet—gramfers and babies! You and I shall be like to that one day, young Samson!"

"We shall have slain a good many Philistines first, I hope."

"Amen! so be it; but look to mun! so fine a sailor as ever drank liquor; and now greedy after a hit of sweet trade! 'tis piteous like; but I bring mun a hit whenever I come, and he looks for it. He's one of my own flesh like, is old Martin. He sailed with my father Captain Will, when they was both two little cracks aboard of a trawler; and my father went up, and here I am—he didn't, and there he is. We'm up now, we Hawkinses. We may be down again some day."

"Never, I trust," said Amyas.

"'Tain't no use trusting, young man: you go and do. I do hear too much of that there from my lad. Let they ministers preach till they'm black in the face, works is the trade!" with a nudge in Amyas's ribs. "Faith can't save, nor charity nether. There, you tell with him, while I go play bowls with Drake. He'll tell you a sight of stories. You ask him about good King Hal, now, just—"

And off waddled the Port Admiral.

"You have seen good King Henry, then, father?" said Amyas, interested.

The old man's eyes lighted at once, and he stopped mumbling his sugar.

"Seed mun? Iss, I reckon. I was with Captain Will when he went to meet the Frenchman there to Calais—at the Field, the Field—"

"The Field of the Cloth of Gold, gramfer," suggested the dame.

"That's it. Seed mun? Iss, fegs. Oh, he was a king! The face o' mun like a rising sun, and the back o' mun so broad as that there" (and he held out his palsied arms), "and the voice of mun! Oh, to hear mun swear if he was merry, oh, 'tas royal!—Seed mun? Iss, fegs! And I've seed mun do what few has; I've seed mun christle like any child."

"What—cry?" said Amyas. "I shouldn't have thought there was much cry in him."

"You think what you like—"

"Gramfer, gramfer, don't you be rude, now—

"Let him go on," said Amyas.

"I seed mun christle; and, oh dear, how he did put hands on mun's face; and 'Oh, my gentlemen,' says he, 'my gentlemen! Oh, my gallant men!' Them was his very words."

"But when?"

"Why, Captain Will had just come to the Hard—that's to Portsmouth—to speak with mun, and the barge Royal lay again the Hard—so; and our boot alongside—so; and the king he standth as it might be there, above my head, on the quay edge, and she come in near abreast of us, looking most royal to behold, poor dear! and went to cast about. And Captain Will, saith he, 'Them lower ports is cruel near the water;' for she had not more than a sixteen inches to spare in the nether overloop, as I heard after. And saith he, 'That won't do for going to windward in a say, Martin.' And as the words came out of mun's mouth, your worship, there was a bit of a flaw from the westward, sharp like, and overboard goeth my cap, and hitth against the wall, and as I stooped to pick it up, I heard a cry, and it was all over!"

"He is telling of the Mary Rose, sir."

"I guessed so."

"All over: and the cry of mun, and the screech of mun! Oh, sir, up to the very heavens! And the king he screeched right out like any maid, 'Oh my gentlemen, oh my gallant men!' and as she lay on her beam-ends, sir, and just a-settling, the very last souls I seen was that man's father, and that man's. I knowed mun by their armor."

And he pointed to Sir George Carew and Sir Richard Grenville.

"Iss! Iss! Drowned like rattens. Drowned like rattens!"

"Now; you mustn't trouble his worship any more."

"Trouble? Let him tell till midnight, I shall be well pleased," said Amyas, sitting down on the bench by him. "Drawer! ale—and a parcel of tobacco."

And Amyas settled himself to listen, while the old man purred to himself—

"Iss. They likes to hear old Martin. All the captains look upon old Martin."

"Hillo, Amyas!" said Cary, "who's your friend? Here's a man been telling me wonders about the River Plate. We should go thither for luck there next time."

"River Plate?" said old Martin. "It's I knows about the River Plate; none so well. Who'd ever been there, nor heard of it nether, before Captain Will and me went, and I lived among the savages a whole year; and audacious civil I found 'em if they'd had but shirts to their backs; and so was the prince o' mun, that Captain Will brought home to King Henry; leastwise he died on the voyage; but the wild folk took it cruel well, for you see, we was always as civil with them as Christians, and if we hadn't been, I should not have been here now."

"What year was that?"

"In the fifteen thirty: but I was there afore, and learnt the speech o' mun; and that's why Captain Will left me to a hostage, when he tuked their prince."

"Before that?" said Cary; "why, the country was hardly known before that."

The old man's eyes flashed up in triumph.

"Knowed? Iss, and you may well say that! Look ye here! Look to mun!" and he waved his hand round—"There's captains! and I'm the father of 'em all now, now poor Captain Will's in gloory; I, Martin Cockrem! . . . Iss, I've seen a change. I mind when Tavistock Abbey was so full o' friars, and goolden idols, and sich noxious trade, as ever was a wheat-rick of rats. I mind the fight off Brest in the French wars—Oh, that was a fight, surely!—when the Regent and the French Carack were burnt side by side, being fast grappled, you see, because of Sir Thomas Knivet; and Captain Will gave him warning as he ran a-past us, saying, says he—"

"But," said Amyas, seeing that the old man was wandering away, "what do you mind about America?"

"America? I should think so! But I was a-going to tell you of the Regent—and seven hundred Englishmen burnt and drowned in her, and nine hundred French in the Brest ship, besides what we picked up. Oh dear! But about America."

"Yes, about America. How are you the father of all the captains?"

"How? you ask my young master! Why, before the fifteen thirty, I was up the Plate with Cabot (and a cruel fractious ontrustful fellow he was, like all they Portingals), and bid there a year and more, and up the Paraguaio with him, diskivering no end; whereby, gentles, I was the first Englishman, I hold, that ever sot a foot on the New World, I was!"

"Then here's your health, and long life, sir!" said Amyas and Cary.

"Long life? Iss, fegs, I reckon, long enough a'ready! Why, I mind the beginning of it all, I do. I mind when there wasn't a master mariner to Plymouth, that thought there was aught west of the Land's End except herrings. Why, they held them, pure watches, that if you sailed right west away far enough, you'd surely come to the edge, and fall over cleve. Iss—'Twas dark parts round here, till Captain Will arose; and the first of it I mind was inside the bar of San Lucar, and he and I were boys about a ten year old, aboord of a Dartmouth ship, and went for wine, and there come in over the bar he that was the beginning of it all."

"Columbus?"

"Iss, fegs, he did, not a pistol-shot from us; and I saw mun stand on the poop, so plain as I see you; no great shakes of a man to look to nether; there's a sight better here, to plase me, and we was disappointed, we lads, for we surely expected to see mun with a goolden crown on, and a sceptre to a's hand, we did, and the ship o' mun all over like Solomon's temple for gloory. And I mind that same year, too, seeing Vasco da Gama, as was going out over the bar, when he found the Bona Speranza, and sailed round it to the Indies. Ah, that was the making of they rascally Portingals, it was! . . . And our crew told what they seen and heerd: but nobody minded sich things. 'Twas dark parts, and Popish, then; and nobody knowed nothing, nor got no schooling, nor cared for nothing, but scrattling up and down alongshore like to prawns in a pule. Iss, sitting in darkness, we was, and the shadow of death, till the day-spring from on high arose, and shined upon us poor out-o'-the-way folk—The Lord be praised! And now, look to mun!" and he waved his hand all round—"Look to mun! Look to the works of the Lord! Look to the captains! Oh blessed sight! And one's been to the Brazils, and one to the Indies, and the Spanish Main, and the

North-West, and the Rooshias, and the Chinas, and up the Straits, and round the Cape, and round the world of God, too, bless His holy name; and I seed the beginning of it; and I'll see the end of it too, I will! I was born into the old times: but I'll see the wondrous works of the new, yet, I will! I'll see they bloody Spaniards swept off the seas before I die, if my old eyes can reach so far as outside the Sound. I shall, I knows it. I says my prayers for it every night; don't I, Mary? You'll bate mun, sure as Judgment, you'll bate mun! The Lord'll fight for ye. Nothing'll stand against ye. I've seed it all along—ever since I was with young master to the Honduras. They can't bide the push of us! You'll bate mun off the face of the seas, and be masters of the round world, and all that therein is. And then, I'll just turn my old face to the wall, and depart in peace, according to his word.

"Deary me, now, while I've been telling with you, here've this little maid been and ate up all my sugar!"

"I'll bring you some more," said Amyas; whom the childish bathos of the last sentence moved rather to sighs than laughter.

"Will ye, then? There's a good soul, and come and tell with old Martin. He likes to see the brave young gentlemen, a-going to and fro in their ships, like Leviathan, and taking of their pastime therein. We had no such ships to our days. Ah, 'tis grand times, beautiful times surely—and you'll bring me a bit sugar?"

"You were up the Plate with Cabot?" said Cary, after a pause. "Do you mind the fair lady Miranda, Sebastian de Hurtado's wife?"

"What! her that was burnt by the Indians? Mind her? Do you mind the sun in heaven? Oh, the beauty! Oh, the ways of her! Oh, the speech of her! Never was, nor never will be! And she to die by they villains; and all for the goodness of her! Mind her? I minded naught else when she was on deck."

"Who was she?" asked Amyas of Cary.

"A Spanish angel, Amyas."

"Humph!" said Amyas. "So much the worse for her, to be born into a nation of devils."

"They'em not all so bad as that, yer honor. Her husband was a proper gallant gentleman, and kind as a maid, too, and couldn't abide that De Solis's murderous doings."

"His wife must have taught it him, then," said Amyas, rising. "Where did you hear of these black swans, Cary?"

"I have heard of them, and that's enough," answered he, unwilling to stir sad recollections.

"And little enough," said Amyas. "Will, don't talk to me. The devil is not grown white because he has trod in a lime-heap."

"Or an angel black because she came down a chimney," said Cary; and so the talk ended, or rather was cut short; for the talk of all the groups was interrupted by an explosion from old John Hawkins.

"Fail? Fail? What a murrain do you here, to talk of failing? Who made you a prophet, you scurvy, hang-in-the-wind, croaking, white-livered son of a corby-crow?"

"Heaven help us, Admiral Hawkins, who has put fire to your culverins in this fashion?" said

Lord Howard.

"Who? my lord! Croakers! my lord! Here's a fellow calls himself the captain of a ship, and her majesty's servant, and talks about failing, as if he were a Barbican loose-kirtle trying to keep her apple-squire ashore! Blurt for him, sneak-up! say I."

"Admiral John Hawkins," quoth the offender, "you shall answer this language with your sword."

"I'll answer it with my foot; and buy me a pair of horn-tips to my shoes, like a wraxling man. Fight a croaker? Fight a frog, an owl! I fight those that dare fight, sir!"

"Sir, sir, moderate yourself. I am sure this gentleman will show himself as brave as any, when it comes to blows: but who can blame mortal man for trembling before so fearful a chance as this?"

"Let mortal man keep his tremblings to himself, then, my lord, and not be like Solomon's madmen, casting abroad fire and death, and saying, it is only in sport. There is more than one of his kidney, your lordship, who have not been ashamed to play Mother Shipton before their own sailors, and damp the poor fellows' hearts with crying before they're hurt, and this is one of them. I've heard him at it afore, and I'll present him, with a vengeance, though I'm no church-warden."

"If this is really so, Admiral Hawkins—"

"It is so, my lord! I heard only last night, down in a tavern below, such unbelieving talk as made me mad, my lord; and if it had not been after supper, and my hand was not oversteady, I would have let out a pottle of Alicant from some of their hoopings, and sent them to Dick Surgeon, to wrap them in swaddling-clouts, like whining babies as they are. Marry come up, what says Scripture? 'He that is fearful and faint-hearted among you, let him go and'—what? son Dick there? Thou'rt pious, and read'st thy Bible. What's that text? A mortal fine one it is, too."

"'He that is fearful and faint-hearted among you, let him go back,'" quoth the Complete Seaman. "Captain Merryweather, as my father's command, as well as his years, forbid his answering your challenge, I shall repute it an honor to entertain his quarrel myself—place, time, and weapons being at your choice."

"Well spoken, son Dick!—and like a true courtier, too! Ah! thou hast the palabras, and the knee, and the cap, and the quip, and the innuendo, and the true town fashion of it all—no old tarry-breeks of a sea-dog, like thy dad! My lord, you'll let them fight?"

"The Spaniard, sir; but no one else. But, captains and gentlemen, consider well my friend the Port Admiral's advice; and if any man's heart misgives him, let him, for the sake of his country and his queen, have so much government of his tongue to hide his fears in his own bosom, and leave open complaining to ribalds and women. For if the sailor be not cheered by his commander's cheerfulness, how will the ignorant man find comfort in himself? And without faith and hope, how can he fight worthily?"

"There is no croaking aboard of us, we will warrant," said twenty voices, "and shall be none, as long as we command on board our own ships."

Hawkins, having blown off his steam, went back to Drake and the bowls.

"Fill my pipe, Drawer—that croaking fellow's made me let it out, of course! Spoil-sports! The father of all manner of troubles on earth, be they noxious trade of croakers! 'Better to meet a bear robbed of her whelps,' Francis Drake, as Solomon saith, than a fule who can't keep his mouth shut. What brought Mr. Andrew Barker to his death but croakers? What stopped Fenton's China voyage in the '82, and lost your nephew John, and my brother Will, glory and hard cash too, but croakers? What sent back my Lord Cumberland's armada in the '86, and that after they'd proved their strength, too, sixty o' mun against six hundred Portugals and Indians; and yet wern't ashamed to turn round and come home empty-handed, after all my lord's expenses that he had been at? What but these same beggarly croakers, that be only fit to be turned into yellow-hammers up to Dartymoor, and sit on a tor all day, and cry 'Very little bit of bread, and no chee-e-ese!' Marry, sneak-up! say I again."

"And what," said Drake, "would have kept me, if I'd let 'em, from ever sailing round the world, but these same croakers? I hanged my best friend for croaking, John Hawkins, may God forgive me if I was wrong, and I threatened a week after to hang thirty more; and I'd have done it, too, if they hadn't clapped tompions into their muzzles pretty fast."

"You'm right, Frank. My old father always told me—and old King Hal (bless his memory!) would take his counsel among a thousand;—'And, my son,' says he to me, 'whatever you do, never you stand no croaking; but hang mun, son Jack, hang mun up for an ensign. There's Scripture for it,' says he (he was a mighty man to his Bible, after bloody Mary's days, leastwise), 'and 'tis written,' says he, 'It's expedient that one man die for the crew, and that the whole crew perish not; so show you no mercy, son Jack, or you'll find none, least-wise in they manner of cattle; for if you fail, they stamps on you, and if you succeeds, they takes the credit of it to themselves, and goes to heaven in your shoes.' Those were his words, and I've found mun true.— Who com'th here now?"

"Captain Fleming, as I'm a sinner."

"Fleming? Is he tired of life, that he com'th here to look for a halter? I've a warrant out against mun, for robbing of two Flushingers on the high seas, now this very last year. Is the fellow mazed or drunk, then? or has he seen a ghost? Look to mun!"

"I think so, truly," said Drake. "His eyes are near out of his head."

The man was a rough-bearded old sea-dog, who had just burst in from the tavern through the low hatch, upsetting a drawer with all his glasses, and now came panting and blowing straight up to the high admiral,—

"My lord, my lord! They'm coming! I saw them off the Lizard last night!"

"Who? my good sir, who seem to have left your manners behind you."

"The Armada, your worship—the Spaniard; but as for my manners, 'tis no fault of mine, for I never had none to leave behind me."

"If he has not left his manners behind," quoth Hawkins, "look out for your purses, gentlemen all! He's manners enough, and very bad ones they be, when he com'th across a quiet Flushinger."

"If I stole Flushingers' wines, I never stole negurs' souls, Jack Hawkins; so there's your answer. My lord, hang me if you will; life's short and death's easy 'specially to seamen; but if I didn't see the Spanish fleet last sun-down, coming along half-moon wise, and full seven mile from wing to wing, within a four mile of me, I'm a sinner."

"Sirrah," said Lord Howard, "is this no fetch, to cheat us out of your pardon for these piracies of yours?"

"You'll find out for yourself before nightfall, my lord high admiral. All Jack Fleming says is, that this is a poor sort of an answer to a man who has put his own neck into the halter for the sake of his country."

"Perhaps it is," said Lord Howard. "And after all, gentlemen, what can this man gain by a lie, which must be discovered ere a day is over, except a more certain hanging?"

"Very true, your lordship," said Hawkins, mollified. "Come here, Jack Fleming—what wilt drain, man? Hippocras or Alicant, Sack or John Barleycorn, and a pledge to thy repentance and amendment of life."

"Admiral Hawkins, Admiral Hawkins, this is no time for drinking."

"Why not, then, my lord? Good news should be welcomed with good wine. Frank, send down to the sexton, and set the bells a-ringing to cheer up all honest hearts. Why, my lord, if it were not for the gravity of my office, I could dance a galliard for joy!"

"Well, you may dance, port admiral: but I must go and plan, but God give to all captains such a heart as yours this day!"

"And God give all generals such a head as yours! Come, Frank Drake, we'll play the game out before we move. It will be two good days before we shall be fit to tackle them, so an odd half-hour don't matter."

"I must command the help of your counsel, vice-admiral," said Lord Charles, turning to Drake.

"And it's this, my good lord," said Drake, looking up, as he aimed his bowl. "They'll come soon enough for us to show them sport, and yet slow enough for us to be ready; so let no man hurry himself. And as example is better than precept, here goes."

Lord Howard shrugged his shoulders, and departed, knowing two things: first, that to move Drake was to move mountains; and next, that when the self-taught hero did bestir himself, he would do more work in an hour than any one else in a day. So he departed, followed hastily by most of the captains; and Drake said in a low voice to Hawkins:

"Does he think we are going to knock about on a lee-shore all the afternoon and run our noses at night—and dead up-wind, too—into the Dons' mouths? No, Jack, my friend. Let Orlando-Furioso-punctilio-fire- eaters go and get their knuckles rapped. The following game is the game, and not the meeting one. The dog goes after the sheep, and not afore them, lad. Let them go by, and go by, and stick to them well to windward, and pick up stragglers, and pickings, too, Jack—the prizes, Jack!"

"Trust my old eyes for not being over-quick at seeing signals, if I be hanging in the skirts of a fat-looking Don. We'm the eagles, Drake; and where the carcase is, is our place, eh?"

And so the two old sea-dogs chatted on, while their companions dropped off one by one, and only Amyas remained.

"Eh, Captain Leigh, where's my boy Dick?"

"Gone off with his lordship, Sir John."

"On his punctilios too, I suppose, the young slashed-breeks. He's half a Don, that fellow, with his fine scholarship, and his fine manners, and his fine clothes. He'll get a taking down before he dies, unless he mends. Why ain't you gone too, sir?"

"I follow my leader," said Amyas, filling his pipe.

"Well said, my big man," quoth Drake. "If I could lead you round the world, I can lead you up Channel, can't I?—Eh? my little bantam-cock of the Orinoco? Drink, lad! You're over-sad to-day."

"Not a whit," said Amyas. "Only I can't help wondering whether I shall find him after all."

"Whom? That Don? We'll find him for you, if he's in the fleet. We'll squeeze it out of our prisoners somehow. Eh, Hawkins? I thought all the captains had promised to send you news if they heard of him."

"Ay, but it's ill looking for a needle in a haystack. But I shall find him. I am a coward to doubt it," said Amyas, setting his teeth.

"There, vice-admiral, you're beaten, and that's the rubber. Pay up three dollars, old high-flyer, and go and earn more, like an honest adventurer."

"Well," said Drake, as he pulled out his purse, "we'll walk down now, and see about these young hot-heads. As I live, they are setting to tow the ships out already! Breaking the men's backs over-night, to make them fight the lustier in the morning! Well, well, they haven't sailed round the world, Jack Hawkins."

"Or had to run home from San Juan d'Ulloa with half a crew."

"Well, if we haven't to run out with half crews. I saw a sight of our lads drunk about this morning."

"The more reason for waiting till they be sober. Besides, if everybody's caranting about to once each after his own men, nobody'll find nothing in such a scrimmage as that. Bye, bye, Uncle Martin. We'm going to blow the Dons up now in earnest."

CHAPTER XXXI: THE GREAT ARMADA

And now began that great sea-fight which was to determine whether Popery and despotism, or Protestantism and freedom, were the law which God had appointed for the half of Europe, and the whole of future America. It is a twelve days' epic, worthy, as I said in the beginning of this book, not of dull prose, but of the thunder-roll of Homer's verse: but having to tell it, I must do my best, rather using, where I can, the words of contemporary authors than my own.

"The Lord High Admirall of England, sending a pinnace before, called the Defiance, denounced war by discharging her ordnance; and presently approaching with in musket-shot, with much thundering out of his own ship, called the Arkroyall (alias the Triumph), first set upon the admirall's, as he thought, of the Spaniards (but it was Alfonso de Leon's ship). Soon after, Drake, Hawkins, and Frobisher played stoutly with their ordnance on the hindmost squadron, which was commanded by Recalde." The Spaniards soon discover the superior "nimbleness of the English ships;" and Recalde's squadron, finding that they are getting more than they give, in spite of his endeavors, hurry forward to join the rest of the fleet. Medina the Admiral, finding his ships scattering fast, gathers them into a half-moon; and the Armada tries to keep solemn way forward, like a stately herd of buffaloes, who march on across the prairie, disdaining to notice the wolves which snarl around their track. But in vain. These are no wolves, but cunning hunters, swiftly horsed, and keenly armed, and who will "shamefully shuffle" (to use Drake's own expression) that vast herd from the Lizard to Portland, from Portland to Calais Roads; and who, even in this short two hours' fight, have made many a Spaniard question the boasted invincibleness of this Armada.

One of the four great galliasses is already riddled with shot, to the great disarrangement of her "pulpits, chapels," and friars therein assistant. The fleet has to close round her, or Drake and Hawkins will sink her; in effecting which manoeuvre, the "principal galleon of Seville," in which are Pedro de Valdez and a host of blue-blooded Dons, runs foul of her neighbor, carries away her foremast, and is, in spite of Spanish chivalry, left to her fate. This does not look like victory, certainly. But courage! though Valdez be left behind, "our Lady," and the saints, and the bull Caena Domini (dictated by one whom I dare not name here), are with them still, and it were blasphemous to doubt. But in the meanwhile, if they have fared no better than this against a third of the Plymouth fleet, how will they fare when those forty belated ships, which are already whitening the blue between them and the Mewstone, enter the scene to play their part?

So ends the first day; not an English ship, hardly a man, is hurt. It has destroyed for ever, in English minds, the prestige of boastful Spain. It has justified utterly the policy which the good Lord Howard had adopted by Raleigh's and Drake's advice, of keeping up a running fight, instead of "clapping ships together without consideration," in which case, says Raleigh, "he had been lost, if he had not been better advised than a great many malignant fools were, who found fault with his demeanor."

Be that as it may, so ends the first day, in which Amyas and the other Bideford ships have been right busy for two hours, knocking holes in a huge galleon, which carries on her poop a maiden with a wheel, and bears the name of Sta. Catharina. She had a coat of arms on the flag at her sprit, probably those of the commandant of soldiers; but they were shot away early in the fight, so Amyas cannot tell whether they were De Soto's or not. Nevertheless, there is plenty of time for private revenge; and Amyas, called off at last by the admiral's signal, goes to bed and sleeps soundly.

But ere he has been in his hammock an hour, he is awakened by Cary's coming down to ask for orders.

"We were to follow Drake's lantern, Amyas; but where it is, I can't see, unless he has been taken up aloft there among the stars for a new Drakium Sidus."

Amyas turns out grumbling: but no lantern is to be seen; only a sudden explosion and a great fire on board some Spaniard, which is gradually got under, while they have to lie-to the whole night long, with nearly the whole fleet.

The next morning finds them off Torbay; and Amyas is hailed by a pinnace, bringing a letter from Drake, which (saving the spelling, which was somewhat arbitrary, like most men's in those days) ran somewhat thus:—

"DEAR LAD,—I have been wool-gathering all night after five great hulks, which the Pixies transfigured overnight into galleons, and this morning again into German merchantmen. I let them go with my blessing; and coming back, fell in (God be thanked!) with Valdez' great galleon; and in it good booty, which the Dons his fellows had left behind, like faithful and valiant comrades, and the Lord Howard had let slip past him, thinking her deserted by her crew. I have sent to Dartmouth a sight of noblemen and gentlemen, maybe a half-hundred; and Valdez himself, who when I sent my pinnace aboard must needs stand on his punctilios, and propound conditions. I answered him, I had no time to tell with him; if he would needs die, then I was the very man for him; if he would live, then, buena querra. He sends again, boasting that he was Don Pedro Valdez, and that it stood not with his honor, and that of the Dons in his company. I replied, that for my part, I was Francis Drake, and my matches burning. Whereon he finds in my name salve for the wounds of his own, and comes aboard, kissing my fist, with Spanish lies of holding himself fortunate that he had fallen into the hands of fortunate Drake, and much more, which he might have kept to cool his porridge. But I have much news from him (for he is a leaky tub); and among others, this, that your Don Guzman is aboard of the Sta. Catharina, commandant of her soldiery, and has his arms flying at her sprit, beside Sta. Catharina at the poop, which is a maiden with a wheel, and is a lofty built ship of 3 tier of ordnance, from which God preserve you, and send you like luck with.

"Your deare Friend and Admirall,

"F. Drake.

"She sails in this squadron of Recalde. The Armada was minded to smoke us out of Plymouth; and God's grace it was they tried not: but their orders from home are too strait, and so the slaves fight like a bull in a tether, no farther than their rope, finding thus the devil a hard master, as do most in the end. They cannot compass our quick handling and tacking, and take us for very witches. So far so good, and better to come. You and I know the length of their foot of old. Time and light will kill any hare, and they will find it a long way from Start to Dunkirk."

"The admiral is in a gracious humor, Leigh, to have vouchsafed you so long a letter."

"St. Catherine! why, that was the galleon we hammered all yesterday!" said Amyas, stamping on the deck.

"Of course it was. Well, we shall find her again, doubt not. That cunning old Drake! how he has contrived to line his own pockets, even though he had to keep the whole fleet waiting for him."

"He has given the lord high admiral the dor, at all events."

"Lord Howard is too high-hearted to stop and plunder, Papist though he is, Amyas."

Amyas answered by a growl, for he worshipped Drake, and was not too just to Papists.

The fleet did not find Lord Howard till nightfall; he and Lord Sheffield had been holding on steadfastly the whole night after the Spanish lanterns, with two ships only. At least there was no doubt now of the loyalty of English Roman Catholics, and indeed, throughout the fight, the Howards showed (as if to wipe out the slurs which had been cast on their loyalty by fanatics) a desperate courage, which might have thrust less prudent men into destruction, but led them only to victory. Soon a large Spaniard drifts by, deserted and partly burnt. Some of the men are for leaving their place to board her; but Amyas stoutly refuses. He has "come out to fight, and not to plunder; so let the nearest ship to her have her luck without grudging." They pass on, and the men pull long faces when they see the galleon snapped up by their next neighbor, and towed off to Weymouth, where she proves to be the ship of Miguel d'Oquenda, the vice-admiral, which they saw last night, all but blown up by some desperate Netherland gunner, who, being "misused," was minded to pay off old scores on his tyrants.

And so ends the second day; while the Portland rises higher and clearer every hour. The next morning finds them off the island. Will they try Portsmouth, though they have spared Plymouth? The wind has shifted to the north, and blows clear and cool off the white-walled downs of Weymouth Bay. The Spaniards turn and face the English. They must mean to stand off and on until the wind shall change, and then to try for the Needles. At least, they shall have some work to do before they round Purbeck Isle.

The English go to the westward again: but it is only to return on the opposite tack; and now begin a series of manoeuvres, each fleet trying to get the wind of the other; but the struggle does not last long, and ere noon the English fleet have slipped close-hauled between the Armada and the land, and are coming down upon them right before the wind.

And now begins a fight most fierce and fell. "And fight they did confusedly, and with variable fortunes; while, on the one hand, the English manfully rescued the ships of London, which were hemmed in by the Spaniards; and, on the other side, the Spaniards as stoutly delivered Recalde being in danger." "Never was heard such thundering of ordnance on both sides, which notwithstanding from the Spaniards flew for the most part over the English without harm. Only Cock, an Englishman" (whom Prince claims, I hope rightfully, as a worthy of Devon), "died with honor in the midst of the enemies in a small ship of his. For the English ships, being far the lesser, charged the enemy with marvellous agility; and having discharged their broadsides, flew forth presently into the deep, and levelled their shot directly, without missing, at those great and unwieldy Spanish ships." "This was the most furious and bloody skirmish of all" (though ending only, it seems, in the capture of a great Venetian and some small craft), "in which the lord admiral fighting amidst his enemies' fleet, and seeing one of his captains afar off (Fenner by name, he who fought the seven Portugals at the Azores), cried, 'O George, what doest thou? Wilt thou now frustrate my hope and opinion conceived of thee? Wilt thou forsake me now?' With which words he being enflamed, approached, and did the part of a most valiant captain;" as, indeed, did all the rest.

Night falls upon the floating volcano; and morning finds them far past Purbeck, with the white peak of Freshwater ahead; and pouring out past the Needles, ship after ship, to join the gallant chase. For now from all havens, in vessels fitted out at their own expense, flock the chivalry of England; the Lords Oxford, Northumberland, and Cumberland, Pallavicin, Brooke, Carew, Raleigh, and Blunt, and many another honorable name, "as to a set field, where immortal fame and honor was to be attained." Spain has staked her chivalry in that mighty cast; not a noble house of Arragon or Castile but has lent a brother or a son—and shall mourn the loss of one: and England's gentlemen will measure their strength once for all against the Cavaliers of Spain. Lord Howard has sent forward light craft into Portsmouth for ammunition: but they will scarce return to-night, for the wind falls dead, and all the evening the two fleets drift helpless with the tide, and shout idle defiance at each other with trumpet, fife, and drum.

The sun goes down upon a glassy sea, and rises on a glassy sea again. But what day is this? The twenty-fifth, St. James's-day, sacred to the patron saint of Spain. Shall nothing be attempted in his honor by those whose forefathers have so often seen him with their bodily eyes, charging in their van upon his snow-white steed, and scattering Paynims with celestial lance? He might have sent them, certainly, a favoring breeze; perhaps, he only means to try their faith; at least the galleys shall attack; and in their van three of the great galliasses (the fourth lies half-crippled among the fleet) thrash the sea to foam with three hundred oars apiece; and see, not St. James leading them to victory, but Lord Howard's Triumph, his brother's Lion, Southwell's Elizabeth Jonas, Lord Sheffield's Bear, Barker's Victory, and George Fenner's Leicester, towed stoutly out, to meet them with such salvoes of chain-shot, smashing oars, and cutting rigging, that had not the wind sprung up again toward noon, and the Spanish fleet come up to rescue them, they had shared the fate of Valdez and the Biscayan. And now the fight becomes general. Frobisher beats down the Spanish admiral's mainmast; and, attacked himself by Mexia and Recalde, is rescued by Lord Howard; who, himself endangered in his turn, is rescued in his turn; "while after that day" (so sickened were they of the English gunnery) "no galliasse would adventure to fight."

And so, with variable fortune, the fight thunders on the livelong afternoon, beneath the virgin cliffs of Freshwater; while myriad sea-fowl rise screaming up from every ledge, and spot with their black wings the snow-white wall of chalk; and the lone shepherd hurries down the slopes above to peer over the dizzy edge, and forgets the wheatear fluttering in his snare, while he gazes trembling upon glimpses of tall masts and gorgeous flags, piercing at times the league-broad veil of sulphur-smoke which welters far below.

So fares St. James's-day, as Baal's did on Carmel in old time, "Either he is talking, or he is pursuing, or he is on a journey; or peradventure he sleepeth, and must be awaked." At least, the only fire by which he has answered his votaries, has been that of English cannon: and the Armada, "gathering itself into a roundel," will fight no more, but make the best of its way to Calais, where perhaps the Guises' faction may have a French force ready to assist them, and then to Dunkirk, to join with Parma and the great flotilla of the Netherlands.

So on, before "a fair Etesian gale," which follows clear and bright out of the south-southwest, glide forward the two great fleets, past Brighton Cliffs and Beachy Head, Hastings and Dungeness. Is it a battle or a triumph? For by sea Lord Howard, instead of fighting is rewarding; and after Lord Thomas Howard, Lord Sheffield, Townsend, and Frobisher have received at his hands that knighthood, which was then more honorable than a peerage, old Admiral Hawkins kneels and rises up Sir John, and shaking his shoulders after the accolade, observes to the representative of majesty, that his "old woman will hardly know herself again, when folks call her My Lady."

And meanwhile the cliffs are lined with pike-men and musketeers, and by every countryman and groom who can bear arms, led by their squires and sheriffs, marching eastward as fast as their weapons let them, towards the Dover shore. And not with them alone. From many a mile inland come down women and children, and aged folk in wagons, to join their feeble shouts, and prayers which are not feeble, to that great cry of mingled faith and fear which ascends to the throne of God from the spectators of Britain's Salamis.

Let them pray on. The danger is not over yet, though Lord Howard has had news from Newhaven that the Guises will not stir against England, and Seymour and Winter have left their post of observation on the Flemish shores, to make up the number of the fleet to an hundred and forty sail—larger, slightly, than that of the Spanish fleet, but of not more than half the tonnage, or one third the number of men. The Spaniards are dispirited and battered, but unbroken still; and as they slide to their anchorage in Calais Roads on the Saturday evening of that most memorable week, all prudent men know well that England's hour is come, and that the bells which will call all Christendom to church upon the morrow morn, will be either the death-knell or the triumphal peal of the Reformed faith throughout the world.

A solemn day that Sabbath must have been in country and in town. And many a light-hearted coward, doubtless, who had scoffed (as many did) at the notion of the Armada's coming, because he dare not face the thought, gave himself up to abject fear, "as he now plainly saw and heard that of which before he would not be persuaded." And many a brave man, too, as he knelt beside his wife and daughters, felt his heart sink to the very pavement, at the thought of what those beloved ones might be enduring a few short days hence, from a profligate and fanatical soldiery, or from the more deliberate fiendishness of the Inquisition. The massacre of St. Bartholomew, the fires of Smithfield, the immolation of the Moors, the extermination of the West Indians, the fantastic horrors of the Piedmontese persecution, which make unreadable the too truthful pages of Morland,—these were the spectres, which, not as now, dim and distant through the mist of centuries, but recent, bleeding from still gaping wounds, flitted before the eyes of every

Englishman, and filled his brain and heart with fire.

He knew full well the fate in store for him and his. One false step, and the unspeakable doom which, not two generations afterwards, befell the Lutherans of Magdeburg, would have befallen every town from London to Carlisle. All knew the hazard, as they prayed that day, and many a day before and after, throughout England and the Netherlands. And none knew it better than she who was the guiding spirit of that devoted land, and the especial mark of the invaders' fury; and who, by some Divine inspiration (as men then not unwisely held), devised herself the daring stroke which was to anticipate the coming blow.

But where is Amyas Leigh all this while? Day after day he has been seeking the Sta. Catharina in the thickest of the press, and cannot come at her, cannot even hear of her: one moment he dreads that she has sunk by night, and balked him of his prey; the next, that she has repaired her damages, and will escape him after all. He is moody, discontented, restless, even (for the first time in his life) peevish with his men. He can talk of nothing but Don Guzman; he can find no better employment, at every spare moment, than taking his sword out of the sheath, and handling it, fondling it, talking to it even, bidding it not to fail him in the day of vengeance. At last, he has sent to Squire, the armorer, for a whetstone, and, half-ashamed of his own folly, whets and polishes it in bye-corners, muttering to himself. That one fixed thought of selfish vengeance has possessed his whole mind; he forgets England's present need, her past triumph, his own safety, everything but his brother's blood. And yet this is the day for which he has been longing ever since he brought home that magic horn as a fifteen years boy; the day when he should find himself face to face with an invader, and that invader Antichrist himself. He has believed for years with Drake, Hawkins, Grenville, and Raleigh, that he was called and sent into the world only to fight the Spaniard: and he is fighting him now, in such a cause, for such a stake, within such battle-lists, as he will never see again: and yet he is not content, and while throughout that gallant fleet, whole crews are receiving the Communion side by side, and rising with cheerful faces to shake hands, and to rejoice that they are sharers in Britain's Salamis, Amyas turns away from the holy elements.

"I cannot communicate, Sir John. Charity with all men? I hate, if ever man hated on earth."

"You hate the Lord's foes only, Captain Leigh."

"No, Jack, I hate my own as well."

"But no one in the fleet, sir?"

"Don't try to put me off with the same Jesuit's quibble which that false knave Parson Fletcher invented for one of Doughty's men, to drug his conscience withal when he was plotting against his own admiral. No, Jack, I hate one of whom you know; and somehow that hatred of him keeps me from loving any human being. I am in love and charity with no man, Sir John Brimblecombe—not even with you! Go your ways in God's name, sir! and leave me and the devil alone together, or you'll find my words are true."

Jack departed with a sigh, and while the crew were receiving the Communion on deck, Amyas sate below in the cabin sharpening his sword, and after it, called for a boat and went on board Drake's ship to ask news of the Sta. Catharina, and listened scowling to the loud chants and tinkling bells, which came across the water from the Spanish fleet. At last, Drake was summoned by the lord admiral, and returned with a secret commission, which ought to bear fruit that night; and Amyas, who had gone with him, helped him till nightfall, and then returned to his own ship as Sir Amyas Leigh, Knight, to the joy and glory of every soul on board, except his moody self.

So there, the livelong summer Sabbath-day, before the little high-walled town and the long range of yellow sandhills, lie those two mighty armaments, scowling at each other, hardly out of gunshot. Messenger after messenger is hurrying towards Bruges to the Duke of Parma, for light craft which can follow these nimble English somewhat better than their own floating castles; and, above all, entreating him to put to sea at once with all his force. The duke is not with his forces at Dunkirk, but on the future field of Waterloo, paying his devotions to St. Mary of Halle in Hainault, in order to make all sure in his Pantheon, and already sees in visions of the night that gentle-souled and pure-lipped saint, Cardinal Allen, placing the crown of England on his head. He returns for answer, first, that his victual is not ready; next, that his Dutch sailors, who have been kept at their post for many a week at the sword's point, have run away like water; and thirdly, that over and above all, he cannot come, so "strangely provided" of great ordnance and musketeers are those five-and-thirty Dutch ships, in which round-sterned and stubborn-hearted heretics watch, like terriers at a rat's hole, the entrance of Nieuwport and Dunkirk. Having ensured the private patronage of St. Mary of Halle, he will return to-morrow to make experience of its effects: but only hear across the flats of Dixmude the thunder of the fleets, and at Dunkirk the open curses of his officers. For while he has been praying and nothing more, the English have been praying, and something more; and all that is left for the Prince of Parma is, to hang a few purveyors, as peace offerings to his sulking army, and then "chafe," as Drake says of him, "like a bear robbed of her whelps."

For Lord Henry Seymour has brought Lord Howard a letter of command from Elizabeth's self; and Drake has been carrying it out so busily all that Sunday long, that by two o'clock on the Monday morning, eight fire-ships "besmeared with wild-fire, brimstone, pitch, and resin, and all their ordnance charged with bullets and with stones," are stealing down the wind straight for the Spanish fleet, guided by two valiant men of Devon, Young and Prowse. (Let their names live long in the land!) The ships are fired, the men of Devon steal back, and in a moment more, the heaven is red with glare from Dover Cliffs to Gravelines Tower; and weary-hearted Belgian boors far away inland, plundered and dragooned for many a hideous year, leap from their beds, and fancy (and not so far wrongly either) that the day of judgment is come at last, to end their woes, and hurl down vengeance on their tyrants.

And then breaks forth one of those disgraceful panics, which so often follow overweening presumption; and shrieks, oaths, prayers, and reproaches, make night hideous. There are those too on board who recollect well enough Jenebelli's fire-ships at Antwerp three years before, and the wreck which they made of Parma's bridge across the Scheldt. If these should be like them! And cutting all cables, hoisting any sails, the Invincible Armada goes lumbering wildly out to sea, every ship foul of her neighbor.

The largest of the four galliasses loses her rudder, and drifts helpless to and fro, hindering and confusing. The duke, having (so the Spaniards say) weighed his anchor deliberately instead of leaving it behind him, runs in again after awhile, and fires a signal for return: but his truant sheep are deaf to the shepherd's pipe, and swearing and praying by turns, he runs up Channel towards Gravelines picking up stragglers on his way, who are struggling as they best can among the flats and shallows: but Drake and Fenner have arrived as soon as he. When Monday's sun rises on the quaint old castle and muddy dykes of Gravelines town, the thunder of the cannon recommences, and is not hushed till night. Drake can hang coolly enough in the rear to plunder when he thinks fit; but when the battle needs it, none can fight more fiercely, among the foremost; and there is need now, if ever. That Armada must never be allowed to re-form. If it does, its left wing may yet keep the English at bay, while its right drives off the blockading Hollanders from Dunkirk port, and sets Parma and his flotilla free to join them, and to sail in doubled strength across to the mouth of Thames.

So Drake has weighed anchor, and away up Channel with all his squadron, the moment that he saw the Spanish fleet come up; and with him Fenner burning to redeem the honor which, indeed, he had never lost; and ere Fenton, Beeston, Crosse, Ryman, and Lord Southwell can join them, the Devon ships have been worrying the Spaniards for two full hours into confusion worse confounded.

But what is that heavy firing behind them? Alas for the great galliasse! She lies, like a huge stranded whale, upon the sands where now stands Calais pier; and Amyas Preston, the future hero of La Guayra, is pounding her into submission, while a fleet of hoys and drumblers look on and help, as jackals might the lion.

Soon, on the south-west horizon, loom up larger and larger two mighty ships, and behind them sail on sail. As they near a shout greets the Triumph and the Bear; and on and in the lord high admiral glides stately into the thickest of the fight.

True, we have still but some three-and-twenty ships which can cope at all with some ninety of the Spaniards: but we have dash, and daring, and the inspiration of utter need. Now, or never, must the mighty struggle be ended. We worried them off Portland; we must rend them in pieces now; and in rushes ship after ship, to smash her broadsides through and through the wooden castles, "sometimes not a pike's length asunder," and then out again to re-load, and give place meanwhile to another. The smaller are fighting with all sails set; the few larger, who, once in, are careless about coming out again, fight with top-sails loose, and their main and foreyards close down on deck, to prevent being boarded. The duke, Oquenda, and Recalde, having with much ado got clear of the shallows, bear the brunt of the fight to seaward; but in vain. The day goes against them more and more, as it runs on. Seymour and Winter have battered the great San Philip into a wreck; her masts are gone by the board; Pimentelli in the San Matthew comes up to take the mastiffs off the fainting bull, and finds them fasten on him instead; but the Evangelist, though smaller, is stouter than the Deacon, and of all the shot poured into him, not twenty "lackt him thorough." His masts are tottering; but sink or strike he will not.

"Go ahead, and pound his tough hide, Leigh," roars Drake off the poop of his ship, while he hammers away at one of the great galliasses. "What right has he to keep us all waiting?"

Amyas slips in as best he can between Drake and Winter; as he passes he shouts to his ancient enemy,—

"We are with you, sir; all friends to-day!" and slipping round Winter's bows, he pours his broadside into those of the San Matthew, and then glides on to re-load; but not to return. For not a pistol shot to leeward, worried by three or four small craft, lies an immense galleon; and on her poop—can he believe his eyes for joy?—the maiden and the wheel which he has sought so long!

"There he is!" shouts Amyas, springing to the starboard side of the ship. The men, too, have already caught sight of that hated sign; a cheer of fury bursts from every throat.

"Steady, men!" says Amyas, in a suppressed voice. "Not a shot! Re-load, and be ready; I must speak with him first;" and silent as the grave, amid the infernal din, the Vengeance glides up to the Spaniard's quarter.

"Don Guzman Maria Magdalena Sotomayor de Soto!" shouts Amyas from the mizzen rigging, loud and clear amid the roar.

He has not called in vain. Fearless and graceful as ever, the tall, mail-clad figure of his foe leaps up upon the poop-railing, twenty feet above Amyas's head, and shouts through his vizor,—

"At your service, sir whosoever you may be."

A dozen muskets and arrows are levelled at him; but Amyas frowns them down. "No man strikes him but I. Spare him, if you kill every other soul on board. Don Guzman! I am Captain Sir Amyas Leigh; I proclaim you a traitor and a ravisher, and challenge you once more to single combat, when and where you will."

"You are welcome to come on board me, sir," answers the Spaniard, in a clear, quiet tone; "bringing with you this answer, that you lie in your throat;" and lingering a moment out of bravado, to arrange his scarf, he steps slowly down again behind the bulwarks.

"Coward!" shouts Amyas at the top of his voice.

The Spaniard re-appears instantly. "Why that name, senor, of all others?" asks he in a cool, stern voice.

"Because we call men cowards in England, who leave their wives to be burnt alive by priests."

The moment the words had passed Amyas's lips, he felt that they were cruel and unjust. But it was too late to recall them. The Spaniard started, clutched his sword-hilt, and then hissed back through his closed vizor,—

"For that word, sirrah, you hang at my yardarm, if Saint Mary gives me grace."

"See that your halter be a silken one, then," laughed Amyas, "for I am just dubbed knight." And he stepped down as a storm of bullets rang through the rigging round his head; the Spaniards are not as punctilious as he.

"Fire!" His ordnance crash through the stern-works of the Spaniard; and then he sails onward, while her balls go humming harmlessly through his rigging.

Half-an-hour has passed of wild noise and fury; three times has the Vengeance, as a dolphin might, sailed clean round and round the Sta. Catharina, pouring in broadside after broadside, till the guns are leaping to the deck-beams with their own heat, and the Spaniard's sides are slit and spotted in a hundred places. And yet, so high has been his fire in return, and so strong the deck defences of the Vengeance, that a few spars broken, and two or three men wounded by musketry, are all her loss. But still the Spaniard endures, magnificent as ever; it is the battle of the thresher and the whale; the end is certain, but the work is long.

"Can I help you, Captain Leigh?" asked Lord Henry Seymour, as he passes within oar's length of him, to attack a ship ahead. "The San Matthew has had his dinner, and is gone on to Medina to ask for a digestive to it."

"I thank your lordship: but this is my private quarrel, of which I spoke. But if your lordship could lend me powder—"

"Would that I could! But so, I fear, says every other gentleman in the fleet."

A puff of wind clears away the sulphurous veil for a moment; the sea is clear of ships towards the land; the Spanish fleet are moving again up Channel, Medina bringing up the rear; only some two miles to their right hand, the vast hull of the San Philip is drifting up the shore with the tide, and somewhat nearer the San Matthew is hard at work at her pumps. They can see the white stream of water pouring down her side.

"Go in, my lord, and have the pair," shouts Amyas.

"No, sir! Forward is a Seymour's cry. We will leave them to pay the Flushingers' expenses." And on went Lord Henry, and on shore went the San Philip at Ostend, to be plundered by the Flushingers; while the San Matthew, whose captain, "on a hault courage," had refused to save himself and his gentlemen on board Medina's ship, went blundering miserably into the hungry mouths of Captain Peter Vanderduess and four other valiant Dutchmen, who, like prudent men of Holland, contrived to keep the galleon afloat till they had emptied her, and then "hung up her banner in the great church of Leyden, being of such a length, that being fastened to the roof, it reached unto the very ground."

But in the meanwhile, long ere the sun had set, comes down the darkness of the thunderstorm, attracted, as to a volcano's mouth, to that vast mass of sulphur-smoke which cloaks the sea for many a mile; and heaven's artillery above makes answer to man's below. But still, through smoke and rain, Amyas clings to his prey. She too has seen the northward movement of the Spanish fleet, and sets her topsails; Amyas calls to the men to fire high, and cripple her rigging: but in vain: for three or four belated galleys, having forced their way at last over the shallows, come flashing and sputtering up to the combatants, and take his fire off the galleon. Amyas grinds his teeth, and would fain hustle into the thick of the press once more, in spite of the galleys' beaks.

"Most heroical captain," says cary, pulling a long face, "if we do, we are stove and sunk in five minutes; not to mention that Yeo says he has not twenty rounds of great cartridge left."

So, surely and silent, the Vengeance sheers off, but keeps as near as she can to the little squadron, all through the night of rain and thunder which follows. Next morning the sun rises on a clear sky, with a strong west-north-west breeze, and all hearts are asking what the day will bring forth.

They are long past Dunkirk now; the German Ocean is opening before them. The Spaniards, sorely battered, and lessened in numbers, have, during the night, regained some sort of order. The English hang on their skirts a mile or two behind. They have no ammunition, and must wait for more. To Amyas's great disgust, the Sta. Catharina has rejoined her fellows during the night.

"Never mind," says Cary; "she can neither dive nor fly, and as long as she is above water, we— What is the admiral about?"

He is signalling Lord Henry Seymour and his squadron. Soon they tack, and come down the wind for the coast of Flanders. Parma must be blockaded still; and the Hollanders are likely to be too busy with their plunder to do it effectually. Suddenly there is a stir in the Spanish fleet. Medina and the rearmost ships turn upon the English. What can it mean? Will they offer battle once more? If so, it were best to get out of their way, for we have nothing wherewith to fight them. So the English lie close to the wind. They will let them pass, and return to their old tactic of following and harassing.

"Good-bye to Seymour," says Cary, "if he is caught between them and Parma's flotilla. They are going to Dunkirk."

"Impossible! They will not have water enough to reach his light craft. Here comes a big ship right upon us! Give him all you have left, lads; and if he will fight us, lay him alongside, and die boarding."

They gave him what they had, and hulled him with every shot; but his huge side stood silent as the grave. He had not wherewithal to return the compliment.

"As I live, he is cutting loose the foot of his mainsail! the villain means to run."

"There go the rest of them! Victoria!" shouted Cary, as one after another, every Spaniard set all the sail he could.

There was silence for a few minutes throughout the English fleet; and then cheer upon cheer of triumph rent the skies. It was over. The Spaniard had refused battle, and thinking only of safety, was pressing downward toward the Straits again. The Invincible Armada had cast away its name, and England was saved.

"But he will never get there, sir," said old Yeo, who had come upon deck to murmur his Nunc Domine, and gaze upon that sight beyond all human faith or hope: "Never, never will he weather the Flanders shore, against such a breeze as is coming up. Look to the eye of the wind, sir, and see how the Lord is fighting for His people!"

Yes, down it came, fresher and stiffer every minute out of the gray north-west, as it does so often after a thunder-storm; and the sea began to rise high and white under the "Claro Aquilone," till the Spaniards were fain to take in all spare canvas, and lie-to as best they could; while the English fleet, lying-to also, awaited an event which was in God's hands and not in theirs.

"They will be all ashore on Zealand before the afternoon," murmured Amyas; "and I have lost my labor! Oh, for powder, powder, powder! to go in and finish it at once!"

"Oh, sir," said Yeo, "don't murmur against the Lord in the very day of His mercies. It is hard, to be sure; but His will be done."

"Could we not borrow powder from Drake there?"

"Look at the sea, sir!"

And, indeed, the sea was far too rough for any such attempt. The Spaniards neared and neared the fatal dunes, which fringed the shore for many a dreary mile; and Amyas had to wait weary hours, growling like a dog who has had the bone snatched out of his mouth, till the day wore on; when, behold, the wind began to fall as rapidly as it had risen. A savage joy rose in Amyas's heart.

"They are safe! safe for us! Who will go and beg us powder? A cartridge here and a cartridge there?—anything to set to work again!"

Cary volunteered, and returned in a couple of hours with some quantity: but he was on board again only just in time, for the south-wester had recovered the mastery of the skies, and Spaniards and English were moving away; but this time northward. Whither now? To Scotland? Amyas knew not, and cared not, provided he was in the company of Don Guzman de Soto.

The Armada was defeated, and England saved. But such great undertakings seldom end in one grand melodramatic explosion of fireworks, through which the devil arises in full roar to drag Dr. Faustus forever into the flaming pit. On the contrary, the devil stands by his servants to the last, and tries to bring off his shattered forces with drums beating and colors flying; and, if possible, to lull his enemies into supposing that the fight is ended, long before it really is half over. All which the good Lord Howard of Effingham knew well, and knew, too, that Medina had one last card to play, and that was the filial affection of that dutiful and chivalrous son, James of Scotland. True, he had promised faith to Elizabeth: but that was no reason why he should keep it. He had been hankering and dabbling after Spain for years past, for its absolution was dear to his inmost soul; and Queen Elizabeth had had to warn him, scold him, call him a liar, for so doing; so the Armada might still find shelter and provision in the Firth of Forth. But whether Lord Howard knew or not, Medina did not know, that Elizabeth had played her card cunningly, in the shape of one of those appeals to the purse, which, to James's dying day, overweighed all others save appeals to his vanity. "The title of a dukedom in England, a yearly pension of 5000 pounds, a guard at the queen's charge, and other matters" (probably more hounds and deer), had steeled the heart of the King of Scots, and sealed the Firth of Forth. Nevertheless, as I say, Lord Howard, like the rest of Elizabeth's heroes, trusted James just as much as James trusted others; and therefore thought good to escort the Armada until it was safely past the domains of that most chivalrous and truthful Solomon. But on the 4th of August, his fears, such as they were, were laid to rest. The Spaniards left the Scottish coast and sailed away for Norway; and the game was played out, and the end was come, as the end of such matters generally comes, by gradual decay, petty disaster, and mistake; till the snow-mountain, instead of being blown tragically and heroically to atoms, melts helplessly and pitiably away.

CHAPTER XXXII: HOW AMYAS THREW HIS SWORD INTO THE SEA

Yes, it is over; and the great Armada is vanquished. It is lulled for awhile, the everlasting war which is in heaven, the battle of Iran and Turan, of the children of light and of darkness, of Michael and his angels against Satan and his fiends; the battle which slowly and seldom, once in the course of many centuries, culminates and ripens into a day of judgment, and becomes palpable and incarnate; no longer a mere spiritual fight, but one of flesh and blood, wherein simple men may choose their sides without mistake, and help God's cause not merely with prayer and pen, but with sharp shot and cold steel. A day of judgment has come, which has divided the light from the darkness, and the sheep from the goats, and tried each man's work by the fire; and, behold, the devil's work, like its maker, is proved to have been, as always, a lie and a sham, and a windy boast, a bladder which collapses at the merest pinprick. Byzantine empires, Spanish Armadas, triple-crowned papacies, Russian despotisms, this is the way of them, and will be to the end of the world. One brave blow at the big bullying phantom, and it vanishes in sulphur-stench; while the children of Israel, as of old, see the Egyptians dead on the sea-shore,—they scarce know how, save that God has done it, and sing the song of Moses and of the Lamb.

And now, from England and the Netherlands, from Germany and Geneva, and those poor Vaudois shepherd-saints, whose bones for generations past

to be, indeed, the seed of the Church, and a germ of new life, liberty, and civilization, even in these very days returning good for evil to that Piedmont which has hunted them down like the partridges on the mountains;—from all of Europe, from all of mankind, I had almost said, in which lay the seed of future virtue and greatness, of the destinies of the new-discovered world, and the triumphs of the coming age of science, arose a shout of holy joy, such as the world had not heard for many a weary and bloody century; a shout which was the prophetic birth-paean of North America, Australia, New Zealand, the Pacific Islands, of free commerce and free colonization over the whole earth.

"There was in England, by the commandment of her majesty," says Van Meteran, "and likewise in the United Provinces, by the direction of the States, a solemn festival day publicly appointed, wherein all persons were solemnly enjoined to resort unto ye Church, and there to render thanks and praises unto God, and ye preachers were commanded to exhort ye people thereunto. The aforesaid solemnity was observed upon the 29th of November: which day was wholly spent in fasting, prayer, and giving of thanks.

"Likewise the Queen's Majesty herself, imitating ye ancient Romans, rode into London in triumph, in regard of her own and her subjects' glorious deliverance. For being attended upon very solemnly by all ye principal Estates and officers of her Realm, she was carried through her said City of London in a triumphant Chariot, and in robes of triumph, from her Palace unto ye said Cathedral Church of St. Paul, out of ye which ye Ensigns and Colours of ye vanquished Spaniards hung displayed. And all ye Citizens of London, in their liveries, stood on either side ye street, by their several Companies, with their ensigns and banners, and the streets were hanged on both sides with blue Cloth, which, together with ye foresaid banners, yielded a very stately and gallant prospect. Her Majestie being entered into ye Church together with her Clergy and Nobles, gave thanks unto God, and caused a public Sermon to be preached before her at Paul's Cross; wherein none other argument was handled, but that praise, honour, and glory might be rendered unto God, and that God's Name might be extolled by thanksgiving. And with her own princely voice she most Christianly exhorted ye people to do ye same; whereunto ye people, with a loud acclamation, wished her a most long and happy life to ye confusion of her foes."

Yes, as the medals struck on the occasion said, "It came, it saw, and it fled!" And whither? Away and northward, like a herd of frightened deer, past the Orkneys and Shetlands, catching up a few hapless fishermen as guides; past the coast of Norway, there, too, refused water and food by the brave descendants of the Vikings; and on northward ever towards the lonely Faroes, and the everlasting dawn which heralds round the Pole the midnight sun.

Their water is failing; the cattle must go overboard; and the wild northern sea echoes to the shrieks of drowning horses. They must homeward at least, somehow, each as best he can. Let them meet again at Cape Finisterre, if indeed they ever meet. Medina Sidonia, with some five-and twenty of the soundest and best victualled ships, will lead the way, and leave the rest to their fate. He is soon out of sight; and forty more, the only remnant of that mighty host, come wandering wearily behind, hoping to make the south-west coast of Ireland, and have help, or, at least, fresh water there, from their fellow Romanists. Alas for them!—

For now comes up from the Atlantic, gale on gale; and few of that hapless remnant reached the shores of Spain.

And where are Amyas and the Vengeance all this while?

At the fifty-seventh degree of latitude, the English fleet, finding themselves growing short of provision, and having been long since out of powder and ball, turn southward toward home, "thinking it best to leave the Spaniard to those uncouth and boisterous northern seas." A few pinnaces are still sent onward to watch their course: and the English fleet, caught in the same storms which scattered the Spaniards, "with great danger and industry reached Harwich port, and there provide themselves of victuals and ammunition," in case the Spaniards should return; but there is no need for that caution. Parma, indeed, who cannot believe that the idol at Halle, after all his compliments to it, will play him so scurvy a trick, will watch for weeks on Dunkirk dunes, hoping against hope for the Armada's return, casting anchors, and spinning rigging to repair their losses.

The Armada is away on the other side of Scotland, and Amyas is following in its wake.

For when the lord high admiral determined to return, Amyas asked leave to follow the Spaniard; and asked, too, of Sir John Hawkins, who happened to be at hand, such ammunition and provision as could be afforded him, promising to repay the same like an honest man, out of his plunder if he lived, out of his estate if he died; lodging for that purpose bills in the hands of Sir John, who, as a man of business, took them, and put them in his pocket among the thimbles, string, and tobacco; after which Amyas, calling his men together, reminded them once more of the story of the Rose of Torridge and Don Guzman de Soto, and then asked:

"Men of Bideford, will you follow me? There will be plunder for those who love plunder;

revenge for those who love revenge; and for all of us (for we all love honor) the honor of having never left the chase as long as there was a Spanish flag in English seas."

And every soul on board replied, that they would follow Sir Amyas Leigh around the world.

There is no need for me to detail every incident of that long and weary chase; how they found the Sta. Catharina, attacked her, and had to sheer off, she being rescued by the rest; how when Medina's squadron left the crippled ships behind, they were all but taken or sunk, by thrusting into the midst of the Spanish fleet to prevent her escaping with Medina; how they crippled her, so that she could not beat to windward out into the ocean, but was fain to run south, past the Orkneys, and down through the Minch, between Cape Wrath and Lewis; how the younger hands were ready to mutiny, because Amyas, in his stubborn haste, ran past two or three noble prizes which were all but disabled, among others one of the great galliasses, and the two great Venetians, La Ratta and La Belanzara—which were afterwards, with more than thirty other vessels, wrecked on the west coast of Ireland; how he got fresh water, in spite of certain "Hebridean Scots" of Skye, who, after reviling him in an unknown tongue, fought with him awhile, and then embraced him and his men with howls of affection, and were not much more decently clad, nor more civilized, than his old friends of California; how he pacified his men by letting them pick the bones of a great Venetian which was going on shore upon Islay (by which they got booty enough to repay them for the whole voyage), and offended them again by refusing to land and plunder two great Spanish wrecks on the Mull of Cantire (whose crews, by the by, James tried to smuggle off secretly into Spain in ships of his own, wishing to play, as usual, both sides of the game at once; but the Spaniards were stopped at Yarmouth till the council's pleasure was known—which was, of course, to let the poor wretches go on their way, and be hanged elsewhere); how they passed a strange island, half black, half white, which the wild people called Raghary, but Cary christened it "the drowned magpie;" how the Sta. Catharina was near lost on the Isle of Man, and then put into Castleton (where the Manx-men slew a whole boat's-crew with their arrows), and then put out again, when Amyas fought with her a whole day, and shot away her mainyard; how the Spaniard blundered down the coast of Wales, not knowing whither he went; how they were both nearly lost on Holyhead, and again on Bardsey Island; how they got on a lee shore in Cardigan Bay, before a heavy westerly gale, and the Sta. Catharina ran aground on Sarn David, one of those strange subaqueous pebble-dykes which are said to be the remnants of the lost land of Gwalior, destroyed by the carelessness of Prince Seithenin the drunkard, at whose name each loyal Welshman spits; how she got off again at the rising of the tide, and fought with Amyas a fourth time; how the wind changed, and she got round St. David's Head;—these, and many more moving incidents of this eventful voyage, I must pass over without details, and go on to the end; for it is time that the end should come.

It was now the sixteenth day of the chase. They had seen, the evening before, St. David's Head, and then the Welsh coast round Milford Haven, looming out black and sharp before the blaze of the inland thunder-storm; and it had lightened all round them during the fore part of the night, upon a light south-western breeze.

In vain they had strained their eyes through the darkness, to catch, by the fitful glare of the flashes, the tall masts of the Spaniard. Of one thing at least they were certain, that with the wind as it was, she could not have gone far to the westward; and to attempt to pass them again, and go northward, was more than she dare do. She was probably lying-to ahead of them, perhaps between them and the land; and when, a little after midnight, the wind chopped up to the west, and blew stiffly till day break, they felt sure that, unless she had attempted the desperate expedient of running past them, they had her safe in the mouth of the Bristol Channel. Slowly and wearily broke the dawn, on such a day as often follows heavy thunder; a sunless, drizzly day, roofed with low dingy cloud, barred and netted, and festooned with black, a sign that the storm is only taking breath awhile before it bursts again; while all the narrow horizon is dim and spongy with vapor drifting before a chilly breeze. As the day went on, the breeze died down, and the sea fell to a long glassy foam-flecked roll, while overhead brooded the inky sky, and round them the leaden mist shut out alike the shore and the chase.

Amyas paced the sloppy deck fretfully and fiercely. He knew that the Spaniard could not escape; but he cursed every moment which lingered between him and that one great revenge which blackened all his soul. The men sate sulkily about the deck, and whistled for a wind; the sails flapped idly against the masts; and the ship rolled in the long troughs of the sea, till her yard-arms almost dipped right and left.

"Take care of those guns. You will have something loose next," growled Amyas.

"We will take care of the guns, if the Lord will take care of the wind," said Yeo.

"We shall have plenty before night," said Cary, "and thunder too."

"So much the better," said Amyas. "It may roar till it splits the heavens, if it does but let me get my work done."

"He's not far off, I warrant," said Cary. "One lift of the cloud, and we should see him."

"To windward of us, as likely as not," said Amyas. "The devil fights for him, I believe. To have been on his heels sixteen days, and not sent this through him yet!" And he shook his sword impatiently.

So the morning wore away, without a sign of living thing, not even a passing gull; and the black melancholy of the heaven reflected itself in the black melancholy of Amyas. Was he to lose his prey after all? The thought made him shudder with rage and disappointment. It was intolerable. Anything but that.

"No, God!" he cried, "let me but once feel this in his accursed heart, and then—strike me dead, if Thou wilt!"

"The Lord have mercy on us," cried John Brimblecombe. "What have you said?"

"What is that to you, sir? There, they are piping to dinner. Go down. I shall not come."

And Jack went down, and talked in a half-terrified whisper of Amyas's ominous words.

All thought that they portended some bad luck, except old Yeo.

"Well, Sir John," said he, "and why not? What better can the Lord do for a man, than take him home when he has done his work? Our captain is wilful and spiteful, and must needs kill his man himself; while for me, I don't care how the Don goes, provided he does go. I owe him no grudge, nor any man. May the Lord give him repentance, and forgive him all his sins: but if I could but see him once safe ashore, as he may be ere nightfall, on the Mortestone or the back of Lundy, I would say, 'Lord, now lettest Thou Thy servant depart in peace,' even if it were the lightning which was sent to fetch me."

"But, master Yeo, a sudden death?"

"And why not a sudden death, Sir John? Even fools long for a short life and a merry one, and shall not the Lord's people pray for a short death and a merry one? Let it come as it will to old Yeo. Hark! there's the captain's voice!"

"Here she is!" thundered Amyas from the deck; and in an instant all were scrambling up the hatchway as fast as the frantic rolling of the ship would let them.

Yes. There she was. The cloud had lifted suddenly, and to the south a ragged bore of blue sky let a long stream of sunshine down on her tall masts and stately hull, as she lay rolling some four or five miles to the eastward: but as for land, none was to be seen.

"There she is; and here we are," said Cary; "but where is here? and where is there? How is the tide, master?"

"Running up Channel by this time, sir."

"What matters the tide?" said Amyas, devouring the ship with terrible and cold blue eyes. "Can't we get at her?"

"Not unless some one jumps out and shoves behind," said Cary. "I shall down again and finish that mackerel, if this roll has not chucked it to the cockroaches under the table."

"Don't jest, Will! I can't stand it," said Amyas, in a voice which quivered so much that Cary looked at him. His whole frame was trembling like an aspen. Cary took his arm, and drew him aside.

"Dear old lad," said he, as they leaned over the bulwarks, "what is this? You are not yourself, and have not been these four days."

"No. I am not Amyas Leigh. I am my brother's avenger. Do not reason with me, Will: when it is over I shall be merry old Amyas again," and he passed his hand over his brow.

"Do you believe," said he, after a moment, "that men can be possessed by devils?"

"The Bible says so."

"If my cause were not a just one, I should fancy I had a devil in me. My throat and heart are as hot as the pit. Would to God it were done, for done it must be! Now go."

Cary went away with a shudder. As he passed down the hatchway he looked back. Amyas had got the hone out of his pocket, and was whetting away again at his sword-edge, as if there was some dreadful doom on him, to whet, and whet forever.

The weary day wore on. The strip of blue sky was curtained over again, and all was dismal as before, though it grew sultrier every moment; and now and then a distant mutter shook the air to westward. Nothing could be done to lessen the distance between the ships, for the Vengeance had had all her boats carried away but one, and that was much too small to tow her: and while the men went down again to finish dinner, Amyas worked on at his sword, looking up every now and then suddenly at the Spaniard, as if to satisfy himself that it was not a vision which had vanished.

About two Yeo came up to him.

"He is ours safely now, sir. The tide has been running to the eastward for this two hours."

"Safe as a fox in a trap. Satan himself cannot take him from us!"

"But God may," said Brimblecombe, simply.

"Who spoke to you, sir? If I thought that He—There comes the thunder at last!"

And as he spoke an angry growl from the westward heavens seemed to answer his wild words, and rolled and loudened nearer and nearer, till right over their heads it crashed against some cloud-cliff far above, and all was still.

Each man looked in the other's face: but Amyas was unmoved.

"The storm is coming," said he, "and the wind in it. It will be Eastward-ho now, for once, my merry men all!"

"Eastward-ho never brought us luck," said Jack in an undertone to Cary. But by this time all eyes were turned to the north-west, where a black line along the horizon began to define the boundary of sea and air, till now all dim in mist.

"There comes the breeze."

"And there the storm, too."

And with that strangely accelerating pace which some storms seem to possess, the thunder, which had been growling slow and seldom far away, now rang peal on peal along the cloudy floor above their heads.

"Here comes the breeze. Round with the yards, or we shall be taken aback."

The yards creaked round; the sea grew crisp around them; the hot air swept their cheeks, tightened every rope, filled every sail, bent her over. A cheer burst from the men as the helm went up, and they staggered away before the wind, right down upon the Spaniard, who lay still becalmed.

"There is more behind, Amyas," said Cary. "Shall we not shorten sail a little?"

"No. Hold on every stitch," said Amyas. "Give me the helm, man. Boatswain, pipe away to clear for fight."

It was done, and in ten minutes the men were all at quarters, while the thunder rolled louder and louder overhead, and the breeze freshened fast.

"The dog has it now. There he goes!" said Cary.

"Right before the wind. He has no liking to face us."

"He is running into the jaws of destruction," said Yeo. "An hour more will send him either right up the Channel, or smack on shore somewhere."

"There! he has put his helm down. I wonder if he sees land?"

"He is like a March hare beat out of his country," said Cary, "and don't know whither to run next."

Cary was right. In ten minutes more the Spaniard fell off again, and went away dead down wind, while the Vengeance gained on him fast. After two hours more, the four miles had diminished to one, while the lightning flashed nearer and nearer as the storm came up; and from the vast mouth of a black cloud-arch poured so fierce a breeze that Amyas yielded unwillingly to hints which were growing into open murmurs, and bade shorten sail.

On they rushed with scarcely lessened speed, the black arch following fast, curtained by the flat gray sheet of pouring rain, before which the water was boiling in a long white line; while every moment behind the watery veil, a keen blue spark leapt down into the sea, or darted zigzag through the rain.

"We shall have it now, and with a vengeance; this will try your tackle, master," said Cary.

The functionary answered with a shrug, and turned up the collar of his rough frock, as the first drops flew stinging round his ears. Another minute and the squall burst full upon them, in rain, which cut like hail—hail which lashed the sea into froth, and wind which whirled off the heads of the surges, and swept the waters into one white seething waste. And above them, and behind them and before them, the lightning leapt and ran, dazzling and blinding, while the deep roar of the thunder was changed to sharp ear-piercing cracks.

"Get the arms and ammunition under cover, and then below with you all," shouted Amyas from the helm.

"And heat the pokers in the galley fire," said Yeo, "to be ready if the rain puts our linstocks out. I hope you'll let me stay on deck, sir, in case—"

"I must have some one, and who better than you? Can you see the chase?"

No; she was wrapped in the gray whirlwind. She might be within half a mile of them, for aught they could have seen of her.

And now Amyas and his old liegeman were alone. Neither spoke; each knew the other's thoughts, and knew that they were his own. The squall blew fiercer and fiercer, the rain poured heavier and heavier. Where was the Spaniard?

"If he has laid-to, we may overshoot him, sir!"

"If he has tried to lay-to, he will not have a sail left in the bolt-ropes, or perhaps a mast on deck. I know the stiff-neckedness of those Spanish tubs. Hurrah! there he is, right on our larboard bow!"

There she was indeed, two musket-shots' off, staggering away with canvas split and flying.

"He has been trying to hull, sir, and caught a buffet," said Yeo, rubbing his hands. "What shall we do now?"

"Range alongside, if it blow live imps and witches, and try our luck once more. Pah! how this lightning dazzles!"

On they swept, gaining fast on the Spaniard. "Call the men up, and to quarters; the rain will be over in ten minutes."

Yeo ran forward to the gangway; and sprang back again, with a face white and wild—

"Land right ahead! Port your helm, sir! For the love of God, port your helm!"

Amyas, with the strength of a bull, jammed the helm down, while Yeo shouted to the men below.

She swung round. The masts bent like whips; crack went the fore-sail like a cannon. What matter? Within two hundred yards of them was the Spaniard; in front of her, and above her, a huge dark bank rose through the dense hail, and mingled with the clouds; and at its foot, plainer every moment, pillars and spouts of leaping foam.

"What is it, Morte? Hartland?"

It might be anything for thirty miles.

"Lundy!" said Yeo. "The south end! I see the head of the Shutter in the breakers! Hard a-port yet, and get her close-hauled as you can, and the Lord may have mercy on us still! Look at the Spaniard!"

Yes, look at the Spaniard!

On their left hand, as they broached-to, the wall of granite sloped down from the clouds toward an isolated peak of rock, some two hundred feet in height. Then a hundred yards of roaring breaker upon a sunken shelf, across which the race of the tide poured like a cataract; then, amid a column of salt smoke, the Shutter, like a huge black fang, rose waiting for its prey; and between the Shutter and the land, the great galleon loomed dimly through the storm.

He, too, had seen his danger, and tried to broach-to. But his clumsy mass refused to obey the helm; he struggled a moment, half hid in foam; fell away again, and rushed upon his doom.

"Lost! lost! lost!" cried Amyas madly, and throwing up his hands, let go the tiller. Yeo caught it just in time.

"Sir! sir! What are you at? We shall clear the rock yet."

"Yes!" shouted Amyas, in his frenzy; "but he will not!"

Another minute. The galleon gave a sudden jar, and stopped. Then one long heave and bound, as if to free herself. And then her bows lighted clean upon the Shutter.

An awful silence fell on every English soul. They heard not the roaring of wind and surge; they saw not the blinding flashes of the lightning; but they heard one long ear-piercing wail to every saint in heaven rise from five hundred human throats; they saw the mighty ship heel over from the wind, and sweep headlong down the cataract of the race, plunging her yards into the foam, and showing her whole black side even to her keel, till she rolled clean over, and vanished for ever and ever.

"Shame!" cried Amyas, hurling his sword far into the sea, "to lose my right, my right! when it was in my very grasp! Unmerciful!"

A crack which rent the sky, and made the granite ring and quiver; a bright world of flame, and then a blank of utter darkness, against which stood out, glowing red-hot every mast, and sail, and rock, and Salvation Yeo as he stood just in front of Amyas, the tiller in his hand. All red-hot, transfigured into fire; and behind, the black, black night.

A whisper, a rustling close beside him, and Brimblecombe's voice said softly:

"Give him more wine, Will; his eyes are opening."

"Hey day?" said Amyas, faintly, "not past the Shutter yet! How long she hangs in the wind!"

"We are long past the Shutter, Sir Amyas," said Brimblecombe.

"Are you mad? Cannot I trust my own eyes?"

There was no answer for awhile.

"We are past the Shutter, indeed," said Cary, very gently, "and lying in the cove at Lundy."

"Will you tell me that that is not the Shutter, and that the Devil's-limekiln, and that the cliff—

that villain Spaniard only gone—and that Yeo is not standing here by me, and Cary there forward, and—why, by the by, where are you, Jack Brimblecombe, who were talking to me this minute?"

"Oh, Sir Amyas Leigh, dear Sir Amyas Leigh," blubbered poor Jack, "put out your hand, and feel where you are, and pray the Lord to forgive you for your wilfulness!"

A great trembling fell upon Amyas Leigh; half fearfully he put out his hand; he felt that he was in his hammock, with the deck beams close above his head. The vision which had been left upon his eye-balls vanished like a dream.

"What is this? I must be asleep? What has happened? Where am I?"

"In your cabin, Amyas," said Cary.

"What? And where is Yeo?"

"Yeo is gone where he longed to go, and as he longed to go. The same flash which struck you down, struck him dead."

"Dead? Lightning? Any more hurt? I must go and see. Why, what is this?" and Amyas passed his hand across his eyes. "It is all dark—dark, as I live!" And he passed his hand over his eyes again.

There was another dead silence. Amyas broke it.

"Oh, God!" shrieked the great proud sea-captain, "Oh, God, I am blind! blind! blind!" And writhing in his great horror, he called to Cary to kill him and put him out of his misery, and then wailed for his mother to come and help him, as if he had been a boy once more; while Brimblecombe and Cary, and the sailors who crowded round the cabin-door, wept as if they too had been boys once more.

Soon his fit of frenzy passed off, and he sank back exhausted.

They lifted him into their remaining boat, rowed him ashore, carried him painfully up the hill to the old castle, and made a bed for him on the floor, in the very room in which Don Guzman and Rose Salterne had plighted their troth to each other, five wild years before.

Three miserable days were passed within that lonely tower. Amyas, utterly unnerved by the horror of his misfortune, and by the over-excitement of the last few weeks, was incessantly delirious; while Cary, and Brimblecombe, and the men nursed him by turns, as sailors and wives only can nurse; and listened with awe to his piteous self-reproaches and entreaties to Heaven to remove that woe, which, as he shrieked again and again, was a just judgment on him for his wilfulness and ferocity. The surgeon talked, of course, learnedly about melancholic humors, and his liver's being "adust by the over-pungency of the animal spirits," and then fell back on the universal panacea of blood-letting, which he effected with fear and trembling during a short interval of prostration; encouraged by which he attempted to administer a large bolus of aloes, was knocked down for his pains, and then thought it better to leave Nature to her own work. In the meanwhile, Cary had sent off one of the island skiffs to Clovelly, with letters to his father, and to Mrs. Leigh, entreating the latter to come off to the island: but the heavy westerly winds made that as impossible as it was to move Amyas on board, and the men had to do their best, and did it well enough.

On the fourth day his raving ceased: but he was still too weak to be moved. Toward noon, however, he called for food, ate a little, and seemed revived.

"Will," he said, after awhile, "this room is as stifling as it is dark. I feel as if I should be a sound man once more if I could but get one snuff of the sea-breeze."

The surgeon shook his head at the notion of moving him: but Amyas was peremptory.

"I am captain still, Tom Surgeon, and will sail for the Indies, if I choose. Will Cary, Jack Brimblecombe, will you obey a blind general?"

"What you will in reason," said they both at once.

"Then lead me out, my masters, and over the down to the south end. To the point at the south end I must go; there is no other place will suit."

And he rose firmly to his feet, and held out his hands for theirs.

"Let him have his humor," whispered Cary. "It may be the working off of his madness."

"This sudden strength is a note of fresh fever, Mr. Lieutenant," said the surgeon, "and the rules of the art prescribe rather a fresh blood-letting."

Amyas overheard the last word, and broke out:

"Thou pig-sticking Philistine, wilt thou make sport with blind Samson? Come near me to let blood from my arm, and see if I do not let blood from thy coxcomb. Catch him, Will, and bring him me here!"

The surgeon vanished as the blind giant made a step forward; and they set forth, Amyas walking slowly, but firmly, between his two friends.

"Whither?" asked Cary.

"To the south end. The crag above the Devil's-limekiln. No other place will suit."

Jack gave a murmur, and half-stopped, as a frightful suspicion crossed him.

"That is a dangerous place!"

"What of that?" said Amyas, who caught his meaning in his tone. "Dost think I am going to leap over cliff? I have not heart enough for that. On, lads, and set me safe among the rocks."

So slowly, and painfully, they went on, while Amyas murmured to himself:

"No, no other place will suit; I can see all thence."

So on they went to the point, where the cyclopean wall of granite cliff which forms the western side of Lundy, ends sheer in a precipice of some three hundred feet, topped by a pile of snow-white rock, bespangled with golden lichens. As they approached, a raven, who sat upon the topmost stone, black against the bright blue sky, flapped lazily away, and sank down the abysses of the cliff, as if he scented the corpses underneath the surge. Below them from the Gull-rock rose a thousand birds, and filled the air with sound; the choughs cackled, the hacklets wailed, the great blackbacks laughed querulous defiance at the intruders, and a single falcon, with an angry bark, dashed out from beneath their feet, and hung poised high aloft, watching the sea-fowl which swung slowly round and round below.

It was a glorious sight upon a glorious day. To the northward the glens rushed down toward the cliff, crowned with gray crags, and carpeted with purple heather and green fern; and from their feet stretched away to the westward the sapphire rollers of the vast Atlantic, crowned with a thousand crests of flying foam. On their left hand, some ten miles to the south, stood out against the sky the purple wall of Hartland cliffs, sinking lower and lower as they trended away to the southward along the lonely ironbound shores of Cornwall, until they faded, dim and blue, into the blue horizon forty miles away.

The sky was flecked with clouds, which rushed toward them fast upon the roaring south-west wind; and the warm ocean-breeze swept up the cliffs, and whistled through the heather-bells, and howled in cranny and in crag,

while Amyas, a proud smile upon his lips, stood breasting that genial stream of airy wine with swelling nostrils and fast-heaving chest, and seemed to drink in life from every gust. All three were silent for awhile; and Jack and Cary, gazing downward with delight upon the glory and the grandeur of the sight, forgot for awhile that their companion saw it not. Yet when they started sadly, and looked into his face, did he not see it? So wide and eager were his eyes, so bright and calm his face, that they fancied for an instant that he was once more even as they.

A deep sigh undeceived them. "I know it is all here—the dear old sea, where I would live and die. And my eyes feel for it; feel for it—and cannot find it; never, never will find it again forever! God's will be done!"

"Do you say that?" asked Brimblecombe, eagerly.

"Why should I not? Why have I been raving in hell-fire for I know not how many days, but to find out that, John Brimblecombe, thou better man than I?"

"Not that last: but Amen! Amen! and the Lord has indeed had mercy upon thee!" said Jack, through his honest tears.

"Amen!" said Amyas. "Now set me where I can rest among the rocks without fear of falling—for life is sweet still, even without eyes, friends—and leave me to myself awhile."

It was no easy matter to find a safe place; for from the foot of the crag the heathery turf slopes down all but upright, on one side to a cliff which overhangs a shoreless cove of deep dark sea, and on the other to an abyss even more hideous, where the solid rock has sunk away, and opened inland in the hillside a smooth-walled pit, some sixty feet square and some hundred and fifty in depth, aptly known then as now, as the Devil's-limekiln; the mouth of which, as old wives say, was once closed by the Shutter-rock itself, till the fiend in malice hurled it into the sea, to be a pest to mariners. A narrow and untrodden cavern at the bottom connects it with the outer sea; they could even then hear the mysterious thunder and gurgle of the surge in the subterranean adit, as it rolled huge boulders to and fro in darkness, and forced before it gusts of pent-up air. It was a spot to curdle weak blood, and to make weak heads reel: but all the fitter on that account for Amyas and his fancy.

"You can sit here as in an arm-chair," said Cary, helping him down to one of those square natural seats so common in the granite tors.

"Good; now turn my face to the Shutter. Be sure and exact. So. Do I face it full?"

"Full," said Cary.

"Then I need no eyes wherewith to see what is before me," said he, with a sad smile. "I know every stone and every headland, and every wave too, I may say, far beyond aught that eye can reach. Now go, and leave me alone with God and with the dead!"

They retired a little space and watched him. He never stirred for many minutes; then leaned his elbows on his knees, and his head upon his hands, and so was still again. He remained so long thus, that the pair became anxious, and went towards him. He was asleep, and breathing quick and heavily.

"He will take a fever," said Brimblecombe, "if he sleeps much longer with his head down in the sunshine."

"We must wake him gently if we wake him at all." And Cary moved forward to him.

As he did so, Amyas lifted his head, and turning it to right and left, felt round him with his sightless eyes.

"You have been asleep, Amyas."

"Have I? I have not slept back my eyes, then. Take up this great useless carcase of mine, and lead me home. I shall buy me a dog when I get to Burrough, I think, and make him tow me in a string, eh? So! Give me your hand. Now march!"

His guides heard with surprise this new cheerfulness.

"Thank God, sir, that your heart is so light already," said good Jack; "it makes me feel quite upraised myself, like."

"I have reason to be cheerful, Sir John; I have left a heavy load behind me. I have been wilful, and proud, and a blasphemer, and swollen with cruelty and pride; and God has brought me low for it, and cut me off from my evil delight. No more Spaniard-hunting for me now, my masters. God will send no such fools as I upon His errands."

"You do not repent of fighting the Spaniards."

"Not I: but of hating even the worst of them. Listen to me, Will and Jack. If that man wronged me, I wronged him likewise. I have been a fiend when I thought myself the grandest of men, yea, a very avenging angel out of heaven. But God has shown me my sin, and we have made up our quarrel forever."

"Made it up?"

"Made it up, thank God. But I am weary. Set me down awhile, and I will tell you how it befell."

Wondering, they set him down upon the heather, while the bees hummed round them in the sun; and Amyas felt for a hand of each, and clasped it in his own hand, and began:

"When you left me there upon the rock, lads, I looked away and out to sea, to get one last snuff of the merry sea-breeze, which will never sail me again. And as I looked, I tell you truth, I could see the water and the sky; as plain as ever I saw them, till I thought my sight was come again. But soon I knew it was not so; for I saw more than man could see; right over the ocean, as I live, and away to the Spanish Main. And I saw Barbados, and Grenada, and all the isles that we ever sailed by; and La Guayra in Caracas, and the Silla, and the house beneath it where she lived. And I saw him walking with her on the barbecue, and he loved her then. I saw what I saw; and he loved her; and I say he loves her still.

"Then I saw the cliffs beneath me, and the Gull-rock, and the Shutter, and the Ledge; I saw them, William Cary, and the weeds beneath the merry blue sea. And I saw the grand old galleon, Will; she has righted with the sweeping of the tide. She lies in fifteen fathoms, at the edge of the rocks, upon the sand; and her men are all lying around her, asleep until the judgment-day."

Cary and Jack looked at him, and then at each other. His eyes were clear, and bright, and full of meaning; and yet they knew that he was blind. His voice was shaping itself into a song. Was he inspired? Insane? What was it? And they listened with awe-struck faces, as the giant pointed down into the blue depths far below, and went on.

"And I saw him sitting in his cabin, like a valiant gentleman of Spain; and his officers were sitting round him, with their swords upon the table at the wine. And the prawns and the crayfish and the rockling, they swam in and out above their heads: but Don Guzman he never heeded, but sat still, and drank his wine. Then he took a locket from his bosom; and I heard him speak, Will, and he said: 'Here's the picture of my fair and true lady; drink to her, senors all.' Then he spoke to me, Will, and called me, right up through the oar-weed and the sea: 'We have had a fair quarrel, senor; it is time to be friends once more. My wife and your brother have forgiven me; so your honor takes no stain.' And I answered, 'We are friends, Don Guzman; God has judged our quarrel and not we.' Then he said, 'I sinned, and I am punished.' And I said, 'And, senor, so am I.' Then he held out his hand to me, Cary; and I stooped to take it, and awoke."

He ceased: and they looked in his face again. It was exhausted, but clear and gentle, like the face of a new-born babe. Gradually his head dropped upon his breast again; he was either swooning or sleeping, and they had much ado to get him home. There he lay for eight-and-forty hours, in a quiet doze; then arose suddenly, called for food, ate heartily, and seemed, saving his eyesight, as whole and sound as ever. The surgeon bade them get him home to Northam as soon as possible, and he was willing enough to go. So the next day the Vengeance sailed, leaving behind a dozen men to seize and keep in the queen's name any goods which should be washed up from the wreck.

CHAPTER XXXIII: HOW AMYAS LET THE APPLE FALL

It was the first of October. The morning was bright and still; the skies were dappled modestly from east to west with soft gray autumn cloud, as if all heaven and earth were resting after those fearful summer months of battle and of storm. Silently, as if ashamed and sad, the Vengeance slid over the bar, and passed the sleeping sand-hills and dropped her anchor off Appledore, with her flag floating half-mast high; for the corpse of Salvation Yeo was on board.

A boat pulled off from the ship, and away to the western end of the strand; and Cary and Brimblecombe helped out Amyas Leigh, and led him slowly up the hill toward his home.

The crowd clustered round him, with cheers and blessings, and sobs of pity from kind-hearted women; for all in Appledore and Bideford knew well by this time what had befallen him.

"Spare me, my good friends," said Amyas, "I have landed here that I might go quietly home, without passing through the town, and being made a gazing-stock. Think not of me, good folks, nor talk of me; but come behind me decently, as Christian men, and follow to the grave the body of a better man than I."

And, as he spoke, another boat came off, and in it, covered with the flag of England, the body of Salvation Yeo.

The people took Amyas at his word; and a man was sent on to Burrough, to tell Mrs. Leigh that her son was coming. When the coffin was landed and lifted, Amyas and his friends took their places behind it as chief mourners, and the crew followed in order, while the crowd fell in behind them, and gathered every moment; till ere they were halfway to Northam town, the funeral train might number full five hundred souls.

They had sent over by a fishing-skiff the day before to bid the sexton dig the grave; and when they came into the churchyard, the parson stood ready waiting at the gate.

Mrs. Leigh stayed quietly at home; for she had no heart to face the crowd; and though her heart yearned for her son, yet she was well content (when was she not content?) that he should do honor to his ancient and faithful servant; so she sat down in the bay-window, with Ayacanora by her side; and when the tolling of the bell ceased, she opened her Prayer-book, and began to read the Burial-service.

"Ayacanora," she said, "they are burying old Master Yeo, who loved you, and sought you over the wide, wide world, and saved you from the teeth of the crocodile. Are you not sorry for him, child, that you look so gay to-day?"

Ayacanora blushed, and hung down her head; she was thinking of nothing, poor child, but Amyas.

The Burial-service was done; the blessing said; the parson drew back: but the people lingered and crowded round to look at the coffin, while Amyas stood still at the head of the grave. It had been dug by his command, at the west end of the church, near by the foot of the tall gray windswept tower, which watches for a beacon far and wide over land and sea. Perhaps the old man might like to look at the sea, and see the ships come out and in across the bar, and hear the wind, on winter nights, roar through the belfry far above his head. Why not? It was but a fancy:

and yet Amyas felt that he too should like to be buried in such a place; so Yeo might like it also.

Still the crowd lingered; and looked first at the grave and then at the blind giant who stood over it, as if they felt, by instinct, that something more ought to come. And something more did come. Amyas drew himself up to his full height, and waved his hand majestically, as one about to speak; while the eyes of all men were fastened on him.

Twice he essayed to begin; and twice the words were choked upon his lips; and then,—

"Good people all, and seamen, among whom I was bred, and to whom I come home blind this day, to dwell with you till death—Here lieth the flower and pattern of all bold mariners; the truest of friends, and the most terrible of foes; unchangeable of purpose, crafty of council, and swift of execution; in triumph most sober, in failure (as God knows I have found full many a day) of endurance beyond mortal man. Who first of all Britons helped to humble the pride of the Spaniard at Rio de la Hacha and Nombre, and first of all sailed upon those South Seas, which shall be hereafter, by God's grace, as free to English keels as is the bay outside. Who having afterwards been purged from his youthful sins by strange afflictions and torments unspeakable, suffered at the hands of the Popish enemy, learned therefrom, my masters, to fear God, and to fear naught else; and having acquitted himself worthily in his place and calling as a righteous scourge of the Spaniard, and a faithful soldier of the Lord Jesus Christ, is now exalted to his reward, as Elijah was of old, in a chariot of fire unto heaven: letting fall, I trust and pray, upon you who are left behind the mantle of his valor and his godliness, that so these shores may never be without brave and pious mariners, who will count their lives as worthless in the cause of their Country, their Bible, and their Queen. Amen."

And feeling for his companions' hands he walked slowly from the churchyard, and across the village street, and up the lane to Burrough gates; while the crowd made way for him in solemn silence, as for an awful being, shut up alone with all his strength, valor, and fame, in the dark prison-house of his mysterious doom.

He seemed to know perfectly when they had reached the gates, opened the lock with his own hands, and went boldly forward along the gravel path, while Cary and Brimblecombe followed him trembling; for they expected some violent burst of emotion, either from him or his mother, and the two good fellows' tender hearts were fluttering like a girl's. Up to the door he went, as if he had seen it; felt for the entrance, stood therein, and called quietly, "Mother!"

In a moment his mother was on his bosom.

Neither spoke for awhile. She sobbing inwardly, with tearless eyes, he standing firm and cheerful, with his great arms clasped around her.

"Mother!" he said at last, "I am come home, you see, because I needs must come. Will you take me in, and look after this useless carcase? I shall not be so very troublesome, mother,—shall I?" and he looked down, and smiled upon her, and kissed her brow.

She answered not a word, but passed her arm gently round his waist, and led him in.

"Take care of your head, dear child, the doors are low." And they went in together.

"Will! Jack!" called Amyas, turning round: but the two good fellows had walked briskly off.

"I'm glad we are away," said Cary; "I should have made a baby of myself in another minute, watching that angel of a woman. How her face worked and how she kept it in!"

"Ah, well!" said Jack, "there goes a brave servant of the queen's cut off before his work was a quarter done. Heigho! I must home now, and see my old father, and then—"

"And then home with me," said Cary. "You and I never part again! We have pulled in the same boat too long, Jack; and you must not go spending your prize-money in riotous living. I must see after you, old Jack ashore, or we shall have you treating half the town in taverns for a week to come."

"Oh, Mr. Cary!" said Jack, scandalized.

"Come home with me, and we'll poison the parson, and my father shall give you the rectory."

"Oh, Mr. Cary!" said Jack.

So the two went off to Clovelly together that very day.

And Amyas was sitting all alone. His mother had gone out for a few minutes to speak to the seamen who had brought up Amyas's luggage, and set them down to eat and drink; and Amyas sat in the old bay-window, where he had sat when he was a little tiny boy, and read "King Arthur," and "Fox's Martyrs," and "The Cruelties of the Spaniards." He put out his hand and felt for them; there they lay side by side, just as they had lain twenty years before. The window was open; and a cool air brought in as of old the scents of the four-season roses, and rosemary, and autumn gilliflowers. And there was a dish of apples on the table: he knew it by their smell; the very same old apples which he used to gather when he was a boy. He put out his hand, and took them, and felt them over, and played with them, just as if the twenty years had never been: and as he fingered them, the whole of his past life rose up before him, as in that strange dream which is said to flash across the imagination of a drowning man; and he saw all the places which he had ever seen, and heard all the words which had ever been spoken to him—till he came to that fairy island on the Meta; and he heard the roar of the cataract once more, and saw the green tops of the palm-trees sleeping in the sunlight far above the spray, and stept amid the smooth palm-trunks across the flower-fringed boulders, and leaped down to the gravel beach beside the pool: and then again rose from the fern-grown rocks the beautiful vision of Ayacanora—Where was she? He had not thought of her till now. How he had wronged her! Let be; he had been punished, and the account was squared. Perhaps she did not care for him any longer. Who would care for a great blind ox like him, who must be fed and tended like a baby for the rest of his lazy life? Tut! How long his mother was away! And he began playing again with his apples, and thought about nothing but them, and his climbs with Frank in the orchard years ago.

At last one of them slipt through his fingers, and fell on the floor. He stooped and felt for it: but he could not find it. Vexatious! He turned hastily to search in another direction, and struck his head sharply against the table.

Was it the pain, or the little disappointment? or was it the sense of his blindness brought home to him in that ludicrous commonplace way, and for that very reason all the more humiliating? or was it the sudden revulsion of overstrained nerves, produced by that slight shock? Or had he become indeed a child once more? I know not; but so it was, that he stamped on the floor with pettishness, and then checking himself, burst into a violent flood of tears.

A quick rustle passed him; the apple was replaced in his hand, and Ayacanora's voice sobbed out:

"There! there it is! Do not weep! Oh, do not weep! I cannot bear it! I will get you all you want! Only let me fetch and carry for you, tend you, feed you, lead you, like your slave, your dog! Say that I may be your slave!" and falling on her knees at his feet, she seized both his hands, and covered them with kisses.

"Yes!" she cried, "I will be your slave! I must be! You cannot help it! You cannot escape from me now! You cannot go to sea! You cannot turn your back upon wretched me. I have you safe now! Safe!" and she clutched his hands triumphantly. "Ah! and what a wretch I am, to rejoice in that! to taunt him with his blindness! Oh, forgive me! I am but a poor wild girl—a wild Indian savage, you know: but—but—" and she burst into tears.

A great spasm shook the body and soul of Amyas Leigh; he sat quite silent for a minute, and then said solemnly:

"And is this still possible? Then God have mercy upon me a sinner!"

Ayacanora looked up in his face inquiringly: but before she could speak again, he had bent down, and lifting her as the lion lifts the lamb, pressed her to his bosom, and covered her face with kisses.

The door opened. There was the rustle of a gown; Ayacanora sprang from him with a little cry, and stood, half-trembling, half-defiant, as if to say, "He is mine now; no one dare part him from me!"

"Who is it?" asked Amyas.

"Your mother."

"You see that I am bringing forth fruits meet for repentance, mother," said he, with a smile.

He heard her approach. Then a kiss and a sob passed between the women; and he felt Ayacanora sink once more upon his bosom.

"Amyas, my son," said the silver voice of Mrs. Leigh, low, dreamy, like the far-off chimes of angels' bells from out the highest heaven, "fear not to take her to your heart again; for it is your mother who has laid her there."

"It is true, after all," said Amyas to himself. "What God has joined together, man cannot put asunder."

From that hour Ayacanora's power of song returned to her; and day by day, year after year, her voice rose up within that happy home, and soared, as on a skylark's wings, into the highest heaven, bearing with it the peaceful thoughts of the blind giant back to the Paradises of the West, in the wake of the heroes who from that time forth sailed out to colonize another and a vaster England, to the heaven-prospered cry of Westward-Ho!

Printed in Poland
by Amazon Fulfillment
Poland Sp. z o.o., Wrocław